Lucas Hawkins, Jordan Cross and Griff Cabot
had devoted their lives to the CIA's elite
External Security Team

And now?

They were three men with secret identities
and hidden agendas—sworn to protect the world
from terrorism...and tamed by a woman's love

Relive the romance

by Request®

Three complete novels
by one of your favorite authors

Dear Reader,

I can't tell you how delighted I am that Harlequin is reprinting the first three MEN OF MYSTERY novels. Through the years I've done several different series for Intrigue and Historicals, but this is the one that seems to have resonated most strongly with readers. Now, after the events of September 11, the heroes of this CIA antiterrorist unit seem even more heroic to me—as I hope they will to you.

The MEN OF MYSTERY books began with a request from the editors of Intrigue to create a series about a group of men who had had their identities destroyed. I came up with the idea of an elite group of CIA operatives, an antiterrorist team that was being disbanded by the agency. The stories of these agents, which now number seven novels and one novella, began with the three connected tales in this volume.

The first of them, *The Bride's Protector,* won the RITA® Award for Best Romantic Suspense of 1999. *The Stranger She Knew* won the Dorothy Parker Award as the Outstanding Series Romance of 1999. The final story in this volume, *Her Baby, His Secret,* was a *Romantic Times* Top Pick. I hope you enjoy them all! And if you do, please watch for the next installment of MEN OF MYSTERY, *Rafe Sinclair's Revenge,* which will be out in November 2002.

Thank you so much for reading!

Love,

Gayle Wilson

GAYLE WILSON

Men of Mystery

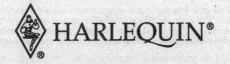

HARLEQUIN®

TORONTO • NEW YORK • LONDON
AMSTERDAM • PARIS • SYDNEY • HAMBURG
STOCKHOLM • ATHENS • TOKYO • MILAN • MADRID
PRAGUE • WARSAW • BUDAPEST • AUCKLAND

HARLEQUIN BOOKS

by Request—MEN OF MYSTERY

Copyright © 2002 by Harlequin Books S.A.

ISBN 0-373-18506-5

The publisher acknowledges the copyright holder of the individual works as follows:
THE BRIDE'S PROTECTOR
Copyright © 1999 by Mona Gay Thomas
THE STRANGER SHE KNEW
Copyright © 1999 by Mona Gay Thomas
HER BABY, HIS SECRET
Copyright © 1999 by Mona Gay Thomas

This edition published by arrangement with Harlequin Books S.A.

Visit us at www.eHarlequin.com

Printed in U.S.A.

CONTENTS

THE BRIDE'S PROTECTOR

Prologue

This was, of course, what he did. He was the unquestioned master of a skill the CIA believed there was no longer any need for. A skill…

The man he was watching moved, and without any conscious thought, his brain directed his body to adjust the rifle the fraction of a millimeter that would again place his target in its crosshairs. He supposed that at one time he had had to think about making that alignment. But no longer.

Just as there was no longer any adrenaline rush to overcome. No tremor of hand or glint of perspiration on the motionless finger that held on the trigger. After that infinitesimal, automatic adjustment, his entire body was again absolutely motionless. And it could remain that way for endless minutes.

No nerves. No compunction concerning what he was about to do. He had made his peace with that a long time ago. And of course, in this case…

He eased in a breath, aware that the line of thinking he had begun to pursue was not an indulgence he could afford. This was simply another job. Another target. Another slow squeeze of the trigger. Danger passed. Threat resolved. Lives saved.

Just another job, he told himself again, forcing the rhythm of his breathing back into the familiar calm of duty. Away from the images of what had been done to his friend.

It had taken him months to reach this place. To find this man. This time. This moment. *Just another job.*

His entire world was focused now on his rifle sight, sharp, clear and utterly unmoving. His finger completed the slow pull it had begun. The remarkable brain that functioned behind the ice-blue eyes, locked now on their target, was once more in complete and total control of every emotion.

The shot was true. He knew that without even watching the result. Instead, as soon as he released the trigger, his hands began the familiar tasks of picking up the casing and disassembling the custom-made, lightweight rifle. Those actions, too, were automatic and unthinking.

It was finished in a matter of seconds, less than a minute, certainly. He could hear, on some level at least, the commotion from the street below, just as he had probably unconsciously heard the shot.

He didn't think about either. Picking up the rattan case that now contained the silencer and the strapped-down, high-powered rifle with which he had just killed a man, the operative known only as Hawk descended the curving staircase that led downward from the roof where he had waited for his victim. He didn't appear to hurry. There was, after all, no need for haste.

When he reached the street, he put the case on top of his left shoulder, holding it in place with the long, brown fingers of his left hand. Dressed in the traditional headdress, which covered his dark blond hair, and a white robe, both totally unremarkable in this locale, he moved with utter and unhurried confidence through the throng that crowded the narrow streets of Baghdad. His skin was tanned darkly enough to allow him to pass for a native—at least to the casual observer.

There was nothing about his appearance that might cause anyone to give him a second glance. Nothing to cause comment. Nothing out of the ordinary. Nothing that would betray the fact that he didn't fit into this society. Just as he had never fit into any other.

It was not until he turned into the shadowed arches of an ancient building, blocks away from the roof from which he had fired the fatal shot, that he paused. He made a pretense of adjusting the case he carried, and the hard line of his mouth moved only enough to whisper the phrase he had waited months to say.

"Rest in peace, Griff," the man called Hawk said softly. "Rest in peace, my friend. The debt is paid."

Chapter One

"I knew you'd be the most beautiful bride in the world," Amir al-Ahmad said softly. His deep voice, with its slight British accent, was filled with satisfaction and a hint of possession, something Tyler Stewart had certainly noticed before.

"Turn around, my darling, so we can see every inch of you," he ordered. His full lips tilted upward beneath the dark mustache, a smile intended to soften the effect of what had been—almost—a command.

"I think *you've* seen more than enough," Tyler objected with a laugh. "The groom's not supposed to even glimpse the bride on their wedding day, and you're demanding the full runway show."

"And why should I not see the woman who will become my wife in…" Amir paused, consulting the gold Rolex he wore before he looked up at her, smiling again "…in a little more than an hour? Besides, that is *not* a custom in my country, I assure you," he said, unmoved by her objection.

Tyler knew, of course, she shouldn't be surprised. After all, her fiancé had listened to none of the objections she had tried to make throughout the course of their whirlwind courtship. Why should she think that would change now?

"Please, darling," he urged again, the false patience of his tone clearly expressing his impatience, "we are all waiting."

Fighting a frisson of resentment, Tyler smiled at him instead of arguing. Her smile was forced, perhaps, but she was determined not to let anything spoil this day. Not Amir's tendency to ride roughshod over anyone else's suggestions. Not even the building anxiety she had felt during the last week.

Despite her repeated mental lectures, that sense of foreboding had been present the whole time her bridesmaids had clustered around her, laughing and chattering, helping her dress. Making all the old prenuptial, off-color jokes.

Just prewedding jitters, Tyler had told herself over and over. *Just nerves. Stress. All perfectly normal.*

She took a deep breath, striving for serenity. After all, Amir's request was simple enough. And he was right. Why should he be expected to observe traditions he didn't understand?

Just as she didn't understand the ones that had shaped his personality. The ones that would soon govern her life. That was probably part of her apprehension, she acknowledged. She knew so little about the culture from which he came, despite hours spent at the library trying to remedy that ignorance. And sometimes it seemed she knew even less about her fiancé himself.

Obediently, however, she made the slow pirouette he'd requested, showing off the designer gown that Amir had chosen. And paid for, of course. The yards of silk organza that made up its bell-shaped skirt and short train swung gracefully as she circled. The elegant Manhattan hotel suite, one of the two floors of rooms Amir had rented for the wedding entourage, certainly provided an appropriate background.

"Breathtaking," he said. "But I always knew you would be."

Always. The word reverberated in her mind. This was really for always.

"Thank you," she said softly. "The dress is wonderful, Amir. Thank you for that, too."

"I don't want your gratitude, Tyler. You're to be my wife. I am looking forward to having the right to take care of you," he said softly. "The privilege."

She could see the approving smiles on the faces of the watching women, but for some reason, the romantic words jarred. Maybe because that sounded like something Paul might have said. The part about taking care of her. And Paul...

Was something else she wasn't going to think about, she decided, pushing the pain of that away. It had nothing to do with today, she told herself, and shouldn't be allowed to spoil what was supposed to be a joyous occasion. The most wonderful day in a woman's life.

Deliberately, she smiled at her fiancé again, the movement less forced this time. She held his eyes, trying, as she had so many times before, to read past their opaque blackness and into the soul of the man. Maybe that was also part of the problem. She never seemed to know what he was thinking. Or feeling.

Educated at Eton and Cambridge, Amir al-Ahmad seemed almost British, even to the Saville Row suits and school ties he favored. He was handsome, in a darkly exotic way, and probably more sophisticated than anyone she had ever known. And, of course, he was also immensely wealthy. Riches beyond anything she could imagine, produced by the seemingly endless supply of oil that lay beneath the forbidding surface of his country.

According to everyone she knew, he was, therefore, everything a reasonable woman could possibly want in a husband. And apparently he had fallen head over heels in love with Tyler Stewart the first time he had seen her.

She couldn't imagine why. She had finally been forced, however, to accept that it must have happened. Which *did* make her the luckiest woman in the world, she supposed. At least that was the other thing everyone told her. And she had the evidence of her own experiences with Amir. All as charmingly romantic as the statement he had just made.

"Well, aren't you even going to look at yourself?" Cammie Torrence asked in exasperation. Her maid of honor's suggestion destroyed the awkward silence that had fallen when Tyler failed to respond to Amir's claim. Cammie took her shoulders and turned her to face the hotel suite's floor-length, gilt-framed mirror.

For the first time Tyler surveyed the finished product of this morning's efforts. At what she saw reflected there, she took another breath, this one deep enough that the white veil, gossamer sheer and touched delicately with seed pearls, lifted like a cloud around her bare shoulders.

The exquisite lace that comprised the bodice of the gown she wore was cut so that it ran straight across her chest and upper arms. The line of the material lay just above the beginning swell of her breasts. The bodice narrowed to show off the twenty-three-inch waist she worked so hard to maintain, and then spread out into those billowing yards of silk organza.

It was strange, but Tyler couldn't remember ever having been a bride before. Surely she had been. Surely at some time in the last twenty years she had been photographed for a bridal magazine, these familiar features topped by a spill of veil and a small, artfully arranged spray of flowers.

If I was, she thought, still studying her reflection with a detached and professional appraisal, *I hope I looked happier. Younger. More at peace.*

Her lips tightened against the surge of anxiety, and she watched in the mirror as the creases formed at the corners of her mouth. And she could clearly see, as she had been able to for the last few years, the fine lines etched by time into the delicate skin around those famous violet eyes.

She turned her head, unconsciously examining the still-taut line of her jaw, looking for the smallest sag and thankfully not finding it. *Not bad,* she thought. *Not too bad for an old broad.*

"What do you think?" Cammie asked softly, interrupting that unconscious assessment.

Tyler smiled at her maid of honor, catching her eyes in the glass and holding on to the friendship in them. "I think…" she began, and then her gaze shifted to the figure standing behind Cammie. Amir al-Ahmad. To whom she would be married in a little more than an hour. "I think I look like a bride," she finished.

They all laughed. Even Amir smiled, his dark eyes moving away from hers to study her reflection in the mirror. In them was again possession, which was not, she realized, the emotion she had always dreamed she would see in her bridegroom's eyes.

"Will your father approve of this?" she asked, denying that small disappointment, burying it with all the other anxieties that had been growing in her heart as this day approached. "I'm sure this is not anything like what the women in your country—"

"My father will adore you," Amir interrupted, sweeping that particular worry away with his accustomed surety.

He walked across the short span of carpet that separated them and put his hands on her upper arms, almost exactly as Cammie had done. His long brown fingers, however, closed tightly over the off-the-shoulder sleeves of the wedding gown, the rich ivory lost under their covering darkness.

"There is absolutely nothing for you to worry about. As for what is expected of the women of my country, that's really of no concern to you. Do you think I shall require that you put on *hijab?* We are not so old-fashioned as you seem to imagine."

He smiled at her again, his expression almost paternalistic. "Nothing will change about your life, Tyler. Except, after today, I shall finally have the right to make you mine."

He paused, and Tyler wondered if the others had been aware of that slight emphasis. *Finally the right to make you mine.* Which she hadn't been.

Another tradition of his country? Or, as he had hinted, an aspect of his religion? She hadn't asked. She had been grateful for his lack of sexual pressure, especially considering all the other pressures he had imposed. That had been, for some reason, the one reassuring element in the breakneck speed at which this relationship had developed.

"And," he added, "finally I shall have the right to take care of you."

Again their eyes met in the glass. Tyler wanted to say that she had been taking care of herself just fine for the last thirty-eight years, thank you very much. That she certainly didn't need anyone's help in that department. And she might have said exactly that three months ago. But now...

Now, she conceded, her confidence was shaken. She was scared. Almost as frightened as when she had shown up in Paul Tarrant's office more than two decades ago, a skinny seventeen-year-old refugee from a little hick town in Mississippi.

This was almost the same feeling. Except twenty years ago she had fervently believed that, with a little luck and a whole lot of perseverance, she would succeed. She had had stars in her eyes, incredible dreams in her heart and almost two hundred carefully hoarded dollars in her vinyl pocketbook. The difference between then and now was that she no longer had any of those things. Not even the two hundred dollars.

"I know," she said softly. "I know you will."

She pulled her gaze from his, finding her reflection again in the glass. Was that woman someone who had made a bargain with the devil for her bruised and battered soul? Or was she really, as they all told her, the luckiest woman alive?

That was a question she had wrestled with since Amir had proposed the first time, three days after they met. Laughing, she had turned him down, of course, but her refusal hadn't made a dent in his supreme self-confidence. He'd acted exactly as if she had agreed, lavishing her with expensive gifts that she had honestly tried to refuse. She had even sent them back, but Amir had had them delivered to her again, accompanied by his secretary this time, a very charming Englishman, who had also made most of the arrangements for this wedding.

"Really, my dear," Malcolm Truett had assured her, *"it is much easier to let him have his way. He will in the end, you know. Simply because he always has. And, after all, he is very much in love with you."*

Tyler had held on to those words like a talisman during the bouts of doubt and uncertainty about this marriage, to which she had finally agreed. She needed desperately to believe it was true, and she didn't really know why she found that so hard.

Maybe it had something to do with the fine lines and creases the morning sun was so clearly illuminating in her face. Or the knowledge that there were so many other, far more beautiful women in this city. Woman who were educated. Smarter. Wittier. More at ease in social occasions. And far younger.

Why in the world would Amir al-Ahmad, who could have almost any woman in the world, have chosen a fading model as the object of his affections? Despite her very prolonged "fifteen minutes of fame," Tyler found it hard to believe she would qualify any longer as a trophy wife. At least not for someone like Amir, whose father was reputed to be one of the richest men in the world.

Why, then, would Amir have chosen her? Other than for the reason he claimed—that he was in love with her and wanted to take care of her. That was the only conclusion she had come up with, despite endless hours she had spent worrying over that question in the short weeks since she'd accepted his proposal.

"And now, my darling," Amir said, "I am going back to my suite to dress. Then I'm going downstairs to await my father's arrival. I hope you understand the honor he pays us in attending today. I want to show him how grateful we are for his kindness."

"Of course," Tyler said. She was beginning to feel like a marionette. Amir pulled the strings, and she agreed with whatever he said. But thinking that was ungrateful, of course. And petty. She hoped she was neither.

He was naturally delighted his father was coming to the ceremony. There had been some doubt about that even as late as yesterday, but Amir was his father's oldest as well as his favorite son. Tyler understood that Sheikh Rashad al-Ahmad had made a tremendous concession in leaving his country. For security reasons that was something he seldom did. But he had come to New York to be present at this wedding, despite the fact that today would be only a civil ceremony.

Although Tyler hadn't really understood the reasons for this formality, Amir insisted it was important to protect her legal rights before they traveled to his country for the religious ceremony. Besides, he said, it would give her friends a chance to attend the wedding, and it would give him a chance to show her off to the assembled international media, something that wouldn't be allowed at the other ceremony.

He would take care of everything, he had promised. Every detail. She wouldn't have to worry about a thing. Once again, she had found herself steamrollered into agreeing.

"It's much simpler to let him have his way. He will in the end, you know." Malcolm Truett had been right. The truth of that was something she had discovered more and more frequently as the weeks wound down to the wedding day.

"I'll send someone to escort you downstairs to the ballroom when it's time for the ceremony. From today, you'll have to be far more conscious of security. The price of the politics in our part of the world, I'm afraid. And the money," he added, his tone humorously self-deprecating. "I hope you understand."

She nodded, not even bothering to voice her agreement this time. How had she gotten herself into all this? she wondered.

Her eyes flicked back to the image in the glass. She didn't look much different from the confident woman who had appeared on all those magazine covers through the years. Not spineless. Or as if she had been run over by a steamroller. Or defeated.

The word appeared in her brain, and, interested in where the concept had come from, she examined it. Defeated enough by what Paul had done that she'd decided to roll over and play dead? Or defeated enough that she would let Amir's suave determination sweep her along with whatever he wanted her to do?

In the mirror, she watched him stride across the room behind her. The door was opened by one of the ever-present, eternally silent bodyguards, who followed him through it and into the hall, white robes billowing behind. She knew that that kind of security, and the restrictions it imposed, would now become part of her own life.

Never again to be able to decide the course of her day according to mood or whim... To get into a car and take off for a weekend. To go shopping on the spur of the moment. Call a girlfriend to meet for lunch. Never again to be completely alone. Completely unguarded...

"I think," she said, turning around to escape the image in the glass as much as those frightening mental pictures, "if you all don't mind, I think I'd like a few minutes alone. Just a little solitude. To settle my nerves, I guess."

"Alone?" Susan Brooker questioned. "Are you sure that—"

"I'm sure," Tyler assured her. "I just need a minute to unwind. Time to get my act together before we do this."

"Are you all right?" Cammie asked softly, her voice touched with real concern.

"I'm fine," Tyler promised, reaching out to put her hand reassuringly on her maid of honor's forearm. "I just need...a little peace and quiet."

"You aren't nervous, are you?" Cammie teased, sounding relieved. "Every woman in New York is wishing she was in your shoes, and you're shaking like a leaf."

Cammie had put her own fingers over hers, which Tyler

realized *were* trembling as they rested on her friend's arm. Cammie tightened her hand reassuringly over those cold fingers.

"That man's crazy about you," she said. "It's obvious in everything he says and does. And his daddy owns a *country*. A whole country. I don't know what more you could ask for."

Cammie was almost ten years younger than she, although according to Tyler's biography the difference in their ages was not as great. Paul had kept adjusting her age downward through the years, just as he'd told all those silly stories about her background. But still, Cammie had been a model long enough to know how this business worked and to understand the insecurities inherent in it. The not-unjustified insecurities.

Marrying Amir had seemed an answer to everything. He had appeared like a godsend at the darkest moment of Tyler's life. He had been a miracle she hadn't even had strength enough to pray for. So she didn't know why, suddenly, she was overwhelmed with doubts about what she was doing.

"It's going to be all right," Cammie said more softly, squeezing her fingers again. "I promise it will be."

Tyler smiled, grasping at those reassuring, kind words just as she had held on to Malcolm Truett's through these last stressful weeks. "I know," she said. "This is just the jitters. Every bride has them. I don't know why I should be an exception."

"Maybe because you, of all people, have no reason for them. You've got the world by the tail. All you have to do is hang on. This is a *really* good thing," Cammie said, her voice full of sincerity. "*He* is."

Their eyes met. Unlike Amir's, Cammie's were clear and open and filled with understanding. She knew exactly what Tyler had faced in the last three months—the double blow of Paul's death and the revelations that had followed it. She would understand why those had been enough to destroy

Tyler's confidence. In her judgment about people. And in her future.

"A good thing?" Tyler asked, smiling. "You promise me that, oh wise Martha-clone?"

"I promise," Cammie said solemnly, her voice made strong with confidence, as if she could convince Tyler by her own conviction. Her tone lightened when she continued. "Now I'm going to run all these yakking women out and let you get ready to charm the assembled masses and your new daddy-in-law," Cammie said, broadening the last words with her natural Southern accent.

That was something that she, like Tyler, had worked for years to erase, but sometimes when they were together, they fell back into the comforting rhythm, to words drawn out to too many elongated syllables, and dropped *g*'s.

"You gotta charm the pants off that old man, honey," Cammie ordered. "He might even give you your own oil field. That's real job security."

Tyler laughed, feeling better than she had all morning. Cammie was right. Amir *was* a good thing. Especially the way her life had been going. He loved her. And she...

She hesitated, thinking for the first time about what those words really meant, before she forced herself to finish the thought. And she loved him.

Of course she did, she decided, wondering why her mind had faltered over the phrase. She must. She would never have agreed to marry him otherwise. Not for the money. Not even for the security he seemed so eager to provide. That wasn't the way she had been brought up. That wasn't what marriage was all about.

She watched in gratitude as Cammie efficiently ushered everyone out of the room. After the door had closed behind them, Tyler turned back, facing her image in the full-length glass again. Despite the famous bone structure, the gleaming blue-black hair and the wide violet eyes, reassuringly the same, the woman reflected there seemed almost a stranger.

Prewedding jitters? she thought. Was that really what this was all about? Or was it something much deeper? Scarlett O'Hara holding up that turnip and shouting into the night, *"As God is my witness, I'll never be hungry again"*?

Tyler's mouth inched upward, amused by the probably too accurate comparison. Some uptown psychiatrist would have had a field day with her life, she thought. She'd never given any of them a chance, of course. That, too, wasn't the way she had been raised. Instead, she had poured all the emotions from her painful past into her determination to succeed. To leave everything else behind her. Back in Covington, Mississippi.

Up until a couple of months ago she'd really believed she had done that. But then, for more than twenty years, she had also believed in Paul Tarrant. She had trusted that he would always be there to look after her interests. He had become the caring father she had never had, the guiding hand in her long success and her most trusted friend.

Suddenly, so quickly it seemed impossible to comprehend, he was dead, the victim of a massive coronary, and she had been alone. And devastated. Just when she needed him the most, Paul was gone, and she had been left to face a career that was going nowhere. Was nowhere, she amended honestly. The woman reflected in this glass was no longer in demand. Wrong look, wrong decade, wrong something. And suddenly it had all been over.

Paul's death, coming almost at the same time she had had that realization, had been a terrible blow, but the one that followed had been infinitely worse. She had never begrudged Paul his agent's commission, taken out of every check she received. After all, he had kept her working through the vagaries of one of the most fickle professions in the world.

She had thought from the beginning that her time in this business would be short. Only as long as her particular "look" was in demand. That's all any model could expect—except for the very privileged few who somehow hung on through trends and fads. With Paul's direction, for almost twenty years Tyler Stewart had been one of those few.

But she had never forgotten that five-room house in Covington, featured in none of the colorful biographies Paul had fabricated. That dilapidated little house where a girl named Tommie Sue Prator had once lived. And Tyler knew there was still a lot of Tommie Sue left in her. Most of it in the form of scar tissue.

Her mother had scrimped and saved to provide them the most basic necessities after her daddy had run off. Sometimes it had been a struggle just to get enough to eat. Tommie Sue had always done without things other kids took for granted, even in a place like Covington, where nobody had much. Those memories you never forgot. Deprivations your soul never recovered from.

As a result, Tyler Stewart had never taken anything for granted, especially not success. Every job she got, she had asked Paul to invest most of the money she made. That growing nest egg would provide security when this dream ended.

She thought he had done it. Thought he knew people who would know the right things to do with that money. The safe things. He had assured her over and over that it was in good hands. That he was taking care of her. Taking care of her future.

Maybe he'd tried. It had taken her a month or so after his death before she could come to that more charitable assessment. At first the realization that there was nothing left of all that money had left her numb. Then angry. And finally just bitter.

It seemed the only thing Paul Tarrant had been good at was peddling the unique bone structure and incredible violet eyes that had transformed Tommie Sue Prator into the woman in the glass. A woman called Tyler Stewart.

She hadn't worried when the contracts had gotten fewer and fewer. She had known that was inevitable as the years took their toll, and as other girls, younger, with a fresher look, moved up to claim their rightful places at the top of the heap.

Tyler had had a great ride on that merry-go-round. She had grabbed the brass ring, and she had been more than ready to retire. Ready to do something with her life that had meaning. More meaning than smiling into a camera.

Smile, Tyler. The familiar words echoed inside her head. All those smiles. Provided willingly even when she didn't feel like smiling. Just smiling anyway to protect that future.

Just as they expected her to do today. Just as Amir would probably instruct her to do if he thought about it. After all, that was what she had done for years. Surely she could do it a little longer, and then, if she did…

Again her brain hesitated over the painful thought. But this was the reality that had brought her to this day. *If she did exactly what Amir wanted her to do, then she'd be safe again.*

Her future with him wouldn't be snatched away from her as the one she had worked so hard to provide for herself had been. The prenuptial contracts they had signed would assure that, no matter what happened, she would always be taken care of.

All she had to do was to say "I do." Simple enough. Just a couple of whispered words, and the pain of Paul's betrayal would be over and her fears about the years ahead would be ended. Erased. Then maybe the memory of her mother's short, sad life would finally stop haunting her.

Tyler closed her eyes, feeling the burn of tears behind her lids. Why was this so hard? Everyone she knew thought this marriage was wonderful. That Amir adored her. That she was the luckiest woman in the world. And all she could think was…*there's something wrong.* Wrong about all of this. About today. *It wouldn't feel this way if I were doing the right thing.* That was it, of course. No matter what anyone else said, she shouldn't *feel* like something was wrong, if what she was doing was right.

She took another deep breath, watching the veil float

around her shoulders. It was one thing, however, to acknowledge that wrongness here. To confess her doubts. Alone. In her room. Away from Amir's self-confidence, which had belittled every doubt and disclaimer she made, making her feel…

Like Tommie Sue. The realization was startling, and then she knew it shouldn't have been. That was exactly how Amir treated her. Just as Paul had. *"Just smile at them, sweetheart,"* Paul would say with a laugh, *"but don't open your mouth."*

For years she had done just that. Hiding who she was beneath the way she looked. Hiding everything, because she had felt that if they ever found out, it would all be over. The dream. The security.

Paul had always made her feel that way—inadequate. Not very bright. In need of his guidance. Maybe she *had* once been all those things, but she'd thought she had outgrown those feelings. She had made herself over in her own image. Ironically, it was the same image Paul had created for her.

She wouldn't go back, she decided fiercely. Not back to being Tommie Sue. Not to feeling as if she had no right to an opinion. No right to say no. To make a decision. She couldn't marry Amir if that's what he expected.

And it's just a little late to have arrived at this conclusion, she realized in panic. About four weeks too late.

Maybe if she told him how she felt… Surely they could talk about this. Surely it wasn't too late for that. There was still time.

Tyler turned away from the mirror and hurried across the vast, empty suite. She didn't know what she could say to Amir that might make a difference, but she knew, no matter what happened today, for her own self-preservation she had to make an effort to say something.

THE MAN CALLED HAWK stared at his reflection in the wide, well-lit bathroom mirror, its edges still hazed with the fog from his shower. He had been in the process of wiping off the middle section of the glass with one of the huge towels the hotel provided, when he'd caught a glimpse of his face.

For some reason the infinitely familiar landscape of his rugged features stopped him, making him pause in his preparations for shaving the two-day growth of beard. He leaned forward, studying the harsh contours of his own face, as if the man in the mirror were a stranger.

He leaned closer, his hands resting flat on the expensive marble of the countertop, one on either side of the shell-shaped sink. The hotels Hawk normally frequented were not equipped like this. He was unaccustomed to, and a little uncomfortable with, the luxury that surrounded him.

But then this wasn't exactly a "normal" situation. Nothing about this one-night stopover in New York was normal. He was not here on an assignment. There was no mandate to carry out. No job which he would do, unquestioning, because he trusted the man who had assigned it.

That man, Griffon Cabot, was dead—killed months ago in a terrorist attack in front of the gates of CIA headquarters at Langley. With his death, the team Cabot had slowly and painstakingly built during the last fifteen years would be dismantled by the same government that had suggested its creation.

The External Security Team would be cut out of the intelligence community, as swiftly and efficiently destroyed as a malignancy under a surgeon's scalpel. That was exactly what the current government saw the team to be—a dangerous cancer that must be eradicated.

And that destruction would start, Hawk knew, with him. He had given them the perfect opportunity, of course, with his last mission. The assassination in Baghdad had not been sanctioned, and that made him a rogue. A very dangerous loose cannon, at least in the agency's eyes.

Not that he gave a damn. He knew that kill he had carried out would only be the excuse they used for their actions. Which he had known all along were inevitable. As soon as he learned Griff Cabot had been one of the victims of that massacre, Hawk had known it was over. For all of them. All the men who had worked for Griff through the years were finished with service, with love of country, with duty.

All over but the shouting, Hawk thought cynically. He suspected he was in for more than his share of that. His lips flattened, and the pale blue eyes narrowed.

Hawk, however, was no longer conscious of the image in the glass, no longer aware that it mirrored his movements. He was thinking instead, just as he had been since he'd arrived in the States last night. Thinking about what came next.

He had known this day was also inevitable, and he couldn't explain why he hadn't been better prepared for it. Maybe *not* contemplating the future was simply part of his personality—the product of that same cold control that allowed him to put everything out of his head and focus solely on a job. The same control that allowed him to be the consummate weapon his government had forged him into.

Because Hawk had been owned, trained and used by the United States government since he'd turned seventeen. That's when, as an alternative to going to prison, a belligerent teenager named Lucas Hawkins had been offered an "opportunity" to join the military. He had been given that chance—one last chance—by a hard-assed Texas judge. Seeing the truth of that warning in the judge's cold eyes, Hawk had accepted the invitation, smart enough even then to know the old bastard was right.

It was in the Corps that he had found the family he'd never known. Found a real job. A sense of accomplishment. And the infinitely precious knowledge that he could do something of value. Something that could make him a person of worth.

Eventually, somebody had recognized the potential of the shrewd and pragmatic mind that lay beneath his unpolished exterior. He had been moved into military intelligence, and then, finally, the identity of a soldier named Lucas Hawkins had merged into that of a CIA operative known only as Hawk.

Now the government that had created him would cut him loose. With a pension for those years of service, if he was lucky. With the skills they had taught him. And with the other skills he had taught himself, he thought, thin lips twisting into the semblance of a smile. And none of those peculiar talents would translate well to the civilian world. Not unless he wanted to move to the other side of the equation, to cohabitate for a change with the bad guys. Where he could probably make a hell of a lot more money than he was making now, or ever had made, he conceded, his lips tilting fractionally at the corners again.

But what he did had never been about money. At least not after he'd met Griff Cabot and become a member of his team. By that time Hawk knew all about the lure of esprit de corps and had believed himself sophisticated enough to avoid its entrapment. He had been wrong. Proven wrong by the caliber of man Cabot was. A man whose careful and considered offer of friendship had drawn the man who would be called Hawk like a hearth fire's warmth on a long winter's night.

Now that friendship was over, and he was going to have to find something to do with the *next* forty years of his life. And for some inexplicable reason, all that was why he had ended up spending last night here. In Griff Cabot's favorite New York hotel, where they put fresh flowers and exotic fruit in your room and chocolate on the pillow of your bed when they thoughtfully turned it down.

A place he could definitely afford and a place where he just as definitely knew he didn't belong. The problem was that Hawk hadn't figured out yet exactly where he *did* belong.

Chapter Two

"My dear!" Malcolm Truett exclaimed. The Englishman's pleasant voice, normally controlled, held a note of shock. He had stepped around the corner just as Tyler got off the elevator. His widened eyes took in her full bridal regalia before he asked, "Whatever are you doing *here?*"

"Here" was another of those cultural differences, Tyler realized belatedly. Amir had rented two floors of this stately Manhattan hotel to house the members of the wedding party. The women occupied rooms on the floor above, including the suite where they had helped her dress this morning. The men of the party, including Amir, were housed on this one.

In her hurry to talk to her fiancé before he went downstairs, Tyler hadn't even thought about those restrictions. Or the reasons behind them. The implication was plain, however, in Truett's eyes and in his voice. She shouldn't be on this floor. It was off-limits. But those restrictions were part of the reason she had come.

"I need to talk to Amir," she said, smiling at his secretary, who had always been kind. "I want to catch him before he goes downstairs to meet his father. It's very important."

Truett's eyes studied her face. Their irises were almost exactly the same shade as his gray brows, now arched in surprise. His lips pursed slightly, as if in thought, before he spoke.

"Then I'm very sorry, my dear. You've just missed him,

I'm afraid. I saw him leave his room not two minutes ago and get into the lift.'' His gaze darted toward the door of what she assumed to be Amir's suite, almost directly across the hall, and then came back to her.

Tyler hadn't thought Amir would have had time to change. It had been less than fifteen minutes since he'd left her upstairs. Maybe his father had arrived early or maybe something had come up concerning the arrangements in the hotel's grand ballroom, which was to be used for the cere-mony. Whatever had happened, Tyler was bitterly disap-pointed to have missed him. She had steeled herself, deter-mined to make her fiancé listen. And instead...

''Are you sure?'' she asked, hearing the elevator doors begin to close behind her. She glanced over her shoulder to check that the train of her gown wasn't in their way. But that had been a foolish question, she realized, when her gaze returned to Malcolm Truett's face. Amir's secretary always knew everything. If he said he had seen Amir go downstairs, then she could be certain he had.

''Oh, quite sure,'' he said emphatically. ''We even spoke. There were a few things Amir wanted me to take care of. Not two minutes ago, I promise you. And then he went downstairs.''

He reached past her and punched the Down button for the elevator, apparently in response to the urgency of his errands. His eyes came back to her, again assessing her fea-tures.

''If there is something *I* may do, Ms. Stewart, I should be delighted to be of assistance. If this is an emergency...'' Discreetly, the Englishman let the question trail.

An emergency? Was it enough of an emergency to inter-rupt Amir's reunion with his father? Or was it simply a resurgence of the anxiety she had lived with for weeks? The anxiety that everyone, including Amir, had assured her would disappear from her life forever as soon as she whis-pered those vows. Which she was supposed to do in less than an hour.

"It's not an emergency," she admitted.

"Then may I suggest you really *must* return to your suite? The sheikh will be arriving at any moment. He may come up with Amir, since there is some time before the ceremony. I'm sure you don't want to chance having to meet him for the first time in this hallway. That might be somewhat awkward, I should think."

Truett's eyes held hers, willing her to agree. Just as Amir's always did. "However," he added, apparently not finding the expected acquiescence there, "I shall be sure to tell Amir that you wish to speak to him. In private, of course. Will that do?"

He had already made his diagnosis. The same one she had considered. *Prewedding jitters.* His prescription seemed to be simply keep the bride calm until Amir could work his magic. And get her out of the middle of the hall before the sheikh saw her.

Maybe he was right. Perhaps that would be best. When Malcolm gave him that message, Amir would come to her room. They would have some privacy, and she could pour out all the concerns and questions he hadn't listened to before. And demand some answers. Before it was too late. Because otherwise…

The thought was shocking. It was not the one that had sent her here. And at this stage, it was almost unthinkable. *Almost,* she repeated mentally. But was it more unthinkable than the other?

"Maybe that *would* be best," she agreed softly, still coming to terms with the realization that in less than an hour her choices would be far more limited than they were right now.

"I'm sure it will be," Truett said kindly. He reached behind her and this time impatiently punched both the elevator direction indicators. One for her, to go back up to her room, and apparently the other for him, to attend to Amir's errands.

"I think I should take the stairs," she suggested, "rather than wait here."

That would make an accidental meeting with Amir and his father, which Truett had implied might be imminent, less likely. As much as she needed to talk to her fiancé, this wasn't where she wanted to do it. Nor did she want to embarrass him by being where she wasn't supposed to be. That might make Amir too angry to listen to anything she had to say.

"Quite right, my dear," Truett said, his relief almost palpable. "And very wise, I might add. I can have someone escort you to your room. I'm very much afraid that I must be engaged elsewhere, but I'm sure there's someone here who…"

Truett's voice faded as he glanced back at the row of doors that stretched along the hall. There had been no traffic in the hallway since their conversation had begun. The whole floor seemed remarkably quiet. Almost empty.

But then, Tyler realized, it might very well be empty. She had no idea how many people Amir had brought with him. Most of these rooms could *be* unoccupied, as they were on the floor above.

"That won't be necessary," she said. "I'm perfectly capable of finding my way upstairs." There must have been more of a bite in the words than she was aware of—an unintended backlash of her frustration over missing Amir—because Truett apologized at once.

"Of course you are, my dear. My offer was simply a matter of courtesy, I assure you." He reached out and stabbed the buttons once more. Apparently he was dealing with his own set of frustrations.

"Well, I'm sure you have more important things to attend to," she said.

"More important than the bride herself? I think not," he said gallantly, "but Amir was, I'm afraid, very insistent that I handle these matters myself. But you're right about the stairs. Everyone seems to have chosen this moment to engage the lifts."

Even the al-Ahmads weren't rich or powerful enough to commandeer all the elevators, as much as they might have liked to, Tyler thought, as she started down the hall toward the exit sign. It was not until she was halfway there that she realized she couldn't get back into her own room. Not unless she wanted to go downstairs to the lobby for a key. In her agitation, she hadn't remembered to pick hers up before she left her room.

She turned and saw that Truett was almost under the exit sign at the opposite end of the corridor. She hurried down the long hall, calling his name. He turned as soon as he heard her, but when she reached him, she read annoyance in his features.

"I don't have my key," she explained, a little out of breath. "If you're on your way to the lobby, could you have them send someone up to let me into my room?"

Again there was a fraction of a second's hesitation, and the muscles in the face of Amir's secretary seemed to tighten. *He's probably thinking that he doesn't have time for this,* Tyler thought. No time to deal with whatever feminine nonsense had sent her down here—where she wasn't supposed to be. After all, Truett had *important* things to take care of. Things Amir had asked him to handle.

"Well, I wasn't *going* to the lobby," he said.

This time his tone was almost petulant. She was interfering with whatever duties he was supposed to be carrying out, and it was annoying the hell out of him.

"Wherever you *are* going," she said patiently, "could you possibly call the desk when you get there and ask them to send someone to let me into my room? I'll meet them there."

The gray eyes assessed her again. Then his fingers, thin and white, fished into the pocket of his formal striped vest and retrieved a plastic key. "This is a passkey," he said, explaining as if she were a child. "You may give it to whomever Amir sends to bring you downstairs for the ceremony. And now, if you'll excuse me, Ms. Stewart, I am afraid I really must go."

"Of course," she said, taking the key. Malcolm was the one who had made the arrangements with the hotel, for all these rooms, empty or otherwise. She supposed it shouldn't be surprising the hotel would have provided him with a passkey, which probably only worked for the rooms on these two floors.

Without waiting for her response, Amir's secretary turned and continued his journey to the stairs. He didn't look back at her, not even when he opened the door and disappeared through it.

Tyler shook her head. She was no closer to a resolution of her situation than she had been before. Coming down here had been a wild-goose chase, she thought angrily, beginning to retrace her steps to the opposite end of the hall, deliberately rejecting the exit Malcolm had taken. Considering Truett's attitude, she wondered if he would even give Amir her message.

Prewedding jitters. Even she had bought into that explanation, but now she knew that what was troubling her was something more. This encounter with Amir's secretary had reinforced what she had known, deep inside, since the beginning of this. Maybe her sense of foreboding had been a remnant of those survival skills she had learned years ago.

Skills Tommie Sue had learned, she amended, which had served her well. Except with Paul, whom she had trusted. Lesson number one, she thought. The dangers of trusting someone else to look out for her best interests.

As she walked by it, she glanced up at the door Truett's eyes had indicated was Amir's suite. And then her steps slowed until she came to a complete stop a few feet beyond it. She looked at the passkey in her hand, her mind racing.

She might not have another chance. Truett might not give Amir her message. Or her fiancé might not come in response, even if he received it. Then there wouldn't *be* a

moment alone with him to sort through these growing fears
and to ask her questions. Not before it was too late. Not
before they came for her, to take her down to the ballroom.

Before they came for her? she thought. Why had those
words rung so strongly in her head? They sounded as if she
were a prisoner of some kind. Which she certainly didn't
intend to be.

She turned back to the door of Amir's suite. Without
giving herself time to think about all the reasons why waiting in his room to confront her fiancé might not be a good
idea, including his and his father's displeasure, she pushed
the passkey into the slot and watched the light blink accom-
modatingly. She pressed down the handle and pushed the
door inward.

As it opened, her eyes seemed to focus like a camera lens
on the unexpected scene before her. There were three men
in the huge room she had expected to find empty, two of
them dressed in the traditional *thoabs* Amir's bodyguards
wore. They were standing just outside the open doors that
led out onto the room's narrow terrace, which overlooked
the street below.

Security, she thought, already in place for the sheikh's
arrival. She didn't even realize why she had made that assumption until she heard the crack of a rifle. The sound was
strangely muffled, but still she knew what it was. After all,
she also had the evidence of her eyes.

She must have made some response. The robed men
turned, their eyes tracking in surprise to the opening door.
And then, having watched long enough to be satisfied with
the effects of the shot he had just fired, the one in Western
dress, the one with the rifle, finally turned toward her as
well, their eyes meeting across the vastness of the suite.

Everyone seemed frozen in place for the two or three
seconds it took for the heavy door to begin to close. Tyler
had time to see one of the robed men start across the room.
And to see the rifle the stranger held tracking away from

whatever its target had been below and toward her before the door banged shut, separating her from the scene.

Since the rifle had begun to swing toward her, the primitive part of her brain had been directing Tyler to get away from the door. At the same time, it had been supplying to her bloodstream the flood of adrenaline that would make escape possible. Just as she moved, instinctive survival skills taking control, she heard the elevator bell behind her.

One of the cars Malcolm Truett had called for while they'd been talking had finally arrived. Gathering the organza skirt up in both hands, despite the passkey still clutched unthinkingly in her right, Tyler ran toward the possibility that bell represented. When she rounded the corner, the doors of an elevator, thankfully the one nearest the hall, were standing open.

Without slowing down, she slipped through the suddenly narrowing space between them. Frantically she pressed the sides of her gown down with both hands. Trying desperately not to let the bell-shaped skirt touch anything that would make those doors glide open again and begin that mindless mechanical wait for a nonexistent passenger.

She made it, except for the tail of her train, which was caught between the doors. She turned, jerking the fabric free, just as the elevator jolted, thankfully beginning its descent.

Down, she realized, looking up at the numbers above her head. Judging by the speed, the elevator was heading all the way to the lobby. Where everyone would be gathered, waiting for the ceremony to begin. The press. Members of the wedding party. Arriving guests. The sheikh and his entourage...

The sheikh? The image of that rifle focused on something in the street below was back in her head. Along with Amir's comment about the dangers of the politics of his region. The dangers of all that money.

Had someone attacked the sheikh as he arrived? Were those men in Amir's room protecting Sheikh al-Ahmad or was something else going on? Something far more sinister? The memory of the rifle tracking away from the street toward her seemed to indicate that it was. And suddenly Malcolm Truett's words echoed in her head. *"You've just missed him, I'm afraid. I saw him leave his room not two minutes ago and get on the lift."*

Her hand reached out, almost without her conscious direction, to slap frantically at the buttons. Her eyes were still watching the numbers at the top. *Ten, nine, eight.* Had she waited too late to stop the car's descent? Surely, as slow as the damn thing had been in arriving...

The elevator slowed, again jolting slightly, and Tyler closed her eyes, her relief so strong it was almost as paralyzing as her fear. The bell chimed; the doors glided open. There was no one in the hall. She was safe. At least for the moment.

She stepped out, hesitating until the doors began closing behind her, reminding her that they would be able to tell that this particular car had stopped on the sixth floor. One of many cars, she reassured herself. All of them coming and going. Hard to trace one, especially if you weren't sure which one you needed to be tracking. Still, she knew she had to get out of here, just in case the men from Amir's room had reached the elevators before the indicator light had blinked off.

She ran to the end of the short hall that housed the elevators and stood a second looking both ways, up and down the sixth-floor hallway. Far to her left, at the end, was an exit sign. She gathered up her skirts again and ran. There was no one in the hall. No people who could be questioned about what they had seen. No one, then, who could give them any information about where she had gone.

She ran toward the promise of the stairwell, a half-formed plan in her head to try to get out of the building through the basement or service entrance. Just to get away from the hotel and this nightmare, away from whatever the hell was going on.

Gripping the organza skirt, bunched in both hands as if it were dirty laundry, she ran helter-skelter as she had when she was a child, totally focused on the promise of the exit sign ahead. And then, behind her, she heard the soft chime of the elevator bell. Her heart rate accelerated, sudden terror causing another rush of adrenaline. The exit was too far away, she realized in that split second. In this straight, empty hall she would be visible to anyone peering around that corner as she had done. And if they'd brought the rifle with them…

She realized suddenly that she still held the passkey in her right hand, its plastic clinging to her damp palm. She had wondered if it would work only on rooms on the floors Amir had rented. She couldn't even think about that possibility now.

She turned to her right, responding again to instinct and not intellect, and slid the passkey into the slot of a door. Frantically, she pushed down the handle and felt it give. She almost fell inside as the door opened.

She turned around, slamming it behind her. Fingers trembling, she twisted the night latch and pushed the safety bolt into place. Then she collapsed against the door, heart pounding wildly, heated cheek pressed against the cold, reassuringly solid barrier she'd put between herself and whoever was out there.

Even if they had heard the sound of the closing door, she prayed they wouldn't be able to tell which one of all those on this long empty hall it had been. Hopefully they hadn't rounded the corner during the seconds it had taken her to reach her decision. Hopefully they hadn't seen her disappear into this room.

All she needed was a little luck, she thought, which she hadn't had yet. Just some luck, please God. She finally turned to examine the room she'd entered, praying it was empty. Or at least that there would be no men in *dishdashas*.

There weren't. There was only one man, and he certainly

wasn't wearing one of those voluminous robes. As a matter of fact, he seemed to be wearing...nothing at all.

Almost nothing, she amended, her eyes dropping from bronzed shoulders and chest to the hotel towel that was twisted into place around his midsection, the damp terry cloth riding low on narrow hips. He didn't have a rifle. Instead, he held a very big handgun, which was pointed straight at her heart.

"Come right in," he invited, his voice almost as menacing as the gun. Cold blue eyes pierced her, their threat holding her like an insect pinned on a board, her back against his door. "Don't bother to knock. After all," he asked reasonably, "what's a little breaking and entering between friends?"

HAWK DIDN'T KNOW what the hell was going on, but he hadn't been born yesterday. More like a hundred years ago in terms of experience, and in his business, the unexpected was almost always the deadly. He didn't like surprises, not of any kind. Not even if they came wrapped in what seemed to be a pretty enticing package. He had already decided the packaging on this one was going to be interesting, even before she turned around.

Warned by the noise, he'd made it out of the bathroom, gun in hand, in time to watch her lock and bolt his door and fall against it in relief. Which meant she was running from someone. Or at least that's what he was *supposed* to think she was doing.

When she turned around, the situation had suddenly gotten a whole lot more interesting. Hawk might be aware of all the old truths about beauty being only skin-deep and the dangers of judging a book by its cover, but clear-eyed knowledge of the undeniable veracity of those didn't prevent his body's quick physical response.

"You don't understand," she said, eyes widening at the sight of the 9 mm Browning he held trained on the center of her chest.

It was a gun intended to intimidate, and apparently it was having the desired effect. The flush of color—from fear or exertion—that had been in her cheeks drained away just as soon as the violet eyes located and recognized the significance of the semiautomatic he held. Shocked, they jumped from the gun back up to his, stretching wide.

They really were violet, he thought. At least the part of the iris that remained visible after the dark pupil's dilation was a deep purplish blue.

"Then why don't you make me understand," he suggested calmly, and watched her take a long, shuddering breath.

She moistened her lips with her tongue, leaving it visible a moment before her top teeth, which were very white and even, replaced it, fastening nervously over her bottom lip. Her eyes studied his, looking for some clue that would help her know what to tell him.

Whoever she was, whatever the hell she was here for, she was good, Hawk conceded. It looked real. Even the physiological reactions—neck flush, pupil expansion, the visibly throbbing pulse in her temple—were right on target. And those things were extremely difficult to fake.

"I was running away...." she began, and then she stopped, her teeth gnawing once more on her bottom lip.

Not bad at all, Hawk complimented mentally. That indecision had been a nice touch. He said nothing in response, however. He didn't prod, letting her decide what she wanted to tell him. After she had, he'd make his own interpretation.

"I decided not to go through with it—with the wedding, I mean. And so...I ran away."

And left some poor bastard standing at the altar, Hawk thought, fighting an inclination to laugh. The sense of threat was beginning to evaporate. With its disappearance, this encounter became even more interesting. For another reason entirely.

Hawk was familiar with menace. He had a long and intimate acquaintance with death and danger. But it had been a hell of a long time since he'd been with a woman, especially one who looked like this.

Since before Griff's death, he realized, surprised by that fact now that he bothered to think about it. That had been months ago. In the meantime, determined to find the terrorist who had given the order for that attack at headquarters, he had been living like a monk. So it was no wonder he was reacting like an adolescent to a woman's presence in his room. She had an intriguing face, he admitted. And an enticing body, if a little emaciated for his tastes. Her story even made sense, considering what she was wearing.

"And they're looking for you?" he asked, deciding to prompt her, now that he had come to the conclusion she wasn't dangerous.

"I...I think so," she said, seeming to consider the question. "They were coming toward the door. I know they saw me. They must have known I'd seen them."

That sequence didn't make a whole hell of a lot of sense to Hawk, but he wasn't listening only to her words. He was reading tone. Level of stress. Evaluating, just as he had been taught. What he came up with was fear. She was scared to death. And her fear was nothing that made his well-developed instincts react with any sort of flight-or-fight impulse.

They heard the noises at the same time. Her gaze flew upward to meet his again, away from its fascinated appraisal of the Browning, and they listened together, unspeaking, to what was happening down the hall.

Someone had begun pounding on doors. Sometimes there was a pause between knocks. Sometimes there was conversation, distant and indistinct, in response to that knocking. But the one thing that became unmistakably clear as they listened was that those sounds were moving down the hallway. Coming ever closer to the door at the woman's back. The door to this room.

"Please don't let them in," she begged, her voice a whisper. "Don't let them find me. Please, please help me."

Her tongue appeared again, touched her bottom lip with a gleam of moisture and was then replaced once more by those even white teeth. Her eyes held his, the plea in them as clear as the one she had expressed.

Hawk had no intention of letting anyone into his room, of course, and that had nothing to do with her. Whoever was out there, whatever this was all about, whatever the truth behind the story she had told him, he knew they were both a lot safer with that door between them and whoever was knocking on all the others. He had no intention of opening his.

His eyes checked the safety bolt she had thrown, the one he had neglected to put on. He wondered at that aberration in his routine. But then, no one had known he was here. They couldn't have. No one could even have known he was back in the States.

Apparently the luxury of this place, unusual in his life, had overcome his habitual cautions. Or maybe that had been some end-of-mission ennui. The knowledge that all that was over, probably forever.

His normal paranoia had seemed unnecessary and even a little weird, out of place in this setting. After all, this impromptu visit to New York wasn't professional. Not an assignment. It was just a private stop, a memorial of sorts, that absolutely no one could have known about.

He had locked all the safety locks last night, of course. When he'd opened the door this morning to retrieve the copy of the *Times* he'd ordered along with his breakfast, however, he had failed to retake those extra security measures. He had expected no one but the maids to be interested in this room and its occupant.

There was no way anyone could have traced his movements during the last few weeks. He was far too careful to allow that. He was a professional at this game. He had been for a very long time. And he was also a man without an identity. Without a name. Certainly not the one he had put down in the hotel register when he'd checked in last night, the one that matched the false identification he'd handed the clerk.

So whoever was outside in the hall, knocking on doors, wasn't looking for Hawk. That didn't mean, however, that he was going to let them in. He wondered, strictly as a matter of idle curiosity, just how much of that decision was based on the color of the woman's eyes. On the entreaty in them.

"Step away from the door," he ordered softly.

The momentary indecision in those eyes seemed to indicate she was still trying to decide if she could trust him. As the knocking came closer, however, she obeyed, slipping past him and moving farther into his room. He kept the Browning trained on her. The skirt of the gown she wore brushed against his bare calves as she went by, a sensation that didn't help the uncomfortable tightness in Hawk's groin.

Neither did the subtle scent of her body, drifting to him as she moved. It had been a long time since he'd been close enough to a woman to be aware of her perfume. And women in the countries where he'd spent the last few months didn't smell anything like this, he acknowledged ruefully.

Instead of heading across the room, as he had expected her to, the woman disappeared into the bathroom where he'd just finished shaving, closing and then locking the door behind her. The firm line of Hawk's mouth tilted again into an almost forgotten alignment, amused at her expectation that the flimsy bathroom door would offer any protection. If this one and the Browning didn't keep whoever was out there out there, then the bathroom door wouldn't do her any good at all.

He wondered if she was really this afraid. And if so, then why the hell she had agreed to marry the guy in the first place. Of course, he'd seen people do all sorts of unfathomable things in the name of love. Even intelligent, reasonable people. People like Griff. But love was something about which Hawk readily acknowledged he understood very little.

Whoever was knocking was next door now, he realized, getting back to the business at hand, about which he understood a great deal. Hawk put his ear against the door, hoping to overhear the questions they were asking. This time, however, there were none. Apparently there was no one in that room. Which meant...

The knock he'd been expecting pounded suddenly against the outside of the door he was leaning against. He waited a few seconds—timing the pause—before he responded. "Who is it?"

"Hotel security," an accented voice outside the door avowed.

Hawk wondered briefly if that could be true, and then he decided, even if it were, it didn't change anything. There was no reason to let security into his room, and a couple of very good ones that argued for keeping them out. One of those reasons was hiding in his bathroom. The other was the fact that the fewer people who saw his face, the better Hawk liked it.

"What do you want?" he asked.

"We'd like to ask you some questions."

"Ask away," Hawk invited.

"May we come in?" A different voice. Same accent, not quite so heavy, and a lighter tone.

"I don't see any point," Hawk advised. "I haven't done anything that security might be interested in."

There was a hesitation. They were probably silently communicating about the situation, thinking over what they could say to convince him to let them make a search of this room.

"We're looking for a woman," the same voice said finally.

"Aren't we all?" Hawk asked, deliberately coloring his comment with humor. Letting them hear it. There was no response. No chuckle. No acknowledgment.

"What's she done?" he asked into the void.

Another hesitation.

"We need to ask her some questions."

"Then you're wasting your time. There's no woman in this room, gentlemen, and I was about to step into the shower. So if you'll excuse me..."

"Wait a minute," the first voice said, now with a hint of aggression.

Obligingly, Hawk waited, imagining the scene outside. They were obviously still trying to decide what to do since he was being obstinate, something that apparently hadn't happened with any of the other guests on this hall. Hawk didn't like things that made him different, that made him stand out from the crowd, but he knew that in this instance, being a little conspicuous was a better option than opening the door and letting them inside. For those same two very good reasons.

"We need to check out your room, sir. We believe the woman we're looking for may be dangerous."

"They all are, son," Hawk agreed, again letting his amusement show. "And I have to tell you, I'm beginning to lose patience with you guys. I'm not hiding a woman in here, I promise you. And I don't think one's going to break into my room, so why don't you two just get on with your search and let me get back to my shower." When he suggested the last, his voice was carefully wiped clean of that hint of humor.

There was no answer, but Hawk waited patiently through the long silence. Waited until he heard the knocking begin on the next door down the hallway. At least one of the men had moved on. Maybe both. There really wasn't a whole hell of a lot they could do about his refusal to open his door.

Despite what they claimed, he didn't believe they were hotel security. The tone hadn't been right. Or the questions. Whoever they were, they had apparently realized that if they pushed him too hard, he might put in a call to the management, which would put a swift end to their ability to search. For some reason they weren't willing to risk that.

However, after the conversation he'd just had, Hawk didn't believe either of them was a jilted bridegroom, which meant, he supposed...

The blue eyes shifted to the bathroom door, which was still closed. He had answered their questions—or at least he'd made a response to their demands. *Now,* he thought, *it's time to answer mine.*

He walked across the thick carpet, his bare feet making no sound, deliberately giving her no warning. He raised his right leg, drawing the knee back with a practiced motion, and with the bottom of his bare foot, kicked open the bathroom door, breaking the lock she had turned to keep him out.

Chapter Three

When the door came slamming into the room, Tyler stumbled backward, trying to get out of its way, and almost fell into the shower stall. Her back and shoulders banged against the glass enclosure, rattling the doors, which thankfully held.

She threw her hand up to maintain her balance, and her flailing fingers dislodged the wedding dress she had hung over the top of the stall. She caught it with her knee, trying to prevent the designer gown from dropping to the floor.

It was only as she stood there, balanced on one leg, the other raised and bent at the knee, the wedding dress draped over it, that she realized how little she was wearing. She became aware of it only when the man's eyes reminded her.

It was the first time she had seen any sort of emotion in their blue depths. Anything other than cold threat. What she saw in them now wasn't cold. She quickly lowered her leg, grabbing the dress as it began to fall.

She had locked the door. What the hell kind of person would…? Then she answered her own question. The kind who had kept those men from finding her. The kind who carried a very big gun and who looked as if he knew how to use it. And the kind who wasn't even bothering to pretend his eyes weren't examining her body.

Her shaking hands lifted the bridal gown to her breasts in an attempt to cover some of that exposed skin. Her underwear, designed to fit under the low-cut neckline of the dress, apparently wasn't doing much of that.

His eyes openly examined the strapless, skin-colored lace corselette before they moved down the length of sheer silk stockings to the white peau de soie heels. Even considering how long her legs were, that examination seemed to take forever.

Tyler had paraded down a lot of runways wearing less than she had on right now, but somehow that was very different from the one-on-one, up-close-and-very-personal assessment this man was making. Her eyes lifted longingly to the broken door, hanging a little drunkenly on its hinges.

There was a dark brown terry-cloth robe hanging on the back of it. That's what she had intended to put on when she started taking off the bridal gown. Only he hadn't given her enough time. Or the privacy a locked door would seem to demand from any civilized person.

Civilized. The possibility that he really wasn't was frightening. Between them they weren't wearing enough clothing to start a small fire. Not that she had wanted to start anything. She just wanted to get into something less conspicuous than what she'd been wearing and then she wanted to get out of here. Out of the hotel. Out of the insane situation she'd somehow gotten herself into by agreeing to marry Amir.

The man's gaze finally came back to her face, and meeting his eyes, Tyler felt her fear explode again, almost as strongly as it had been when she'd opened Amir's door. She wondered suddenly why she had believed she could trust this man. He looked as dangerous now as the men who had been standing on that narrow terrace, one of them pointing a rifle into the street.

She stood motionless, trying to read the face of this stranger to whom she had appealed for help. Trying to decide if he meant to hurt her. After all, he had kicked in the door she'd locked, and he had slowly examined her exposed body, neither of which seemed to bode well for his intentions.

"Now why don't you tell me what's *really* going on," he said.

His voice was very calm, and she realized that whatever had been in his eyes a moment ago, that smoldering blue heat, was gone. Snuffed out as easily as someone might pinch out the flame on one of those tiny candles on a child's birthday cake.

She felt a little of her tension ease, but she didn't know what to tell him. She wasn't sure what she had seen—a security operation or an assassination. And even if it were the latter, she didn't know if Amir was involved. Or who was.

She really knew nothing other than the fact that she'd seen someone in Western attire fire a shot off the terrace of Amir's suite as two of his bodyguards watched. She had no way of knowing what, if anything, that meant.

"I needed to get out of this dress," she said, trying to think what she *could* tell him. What would be safe. And true. After all, the only thing that was important now was getting out of here. The Tommie Sue part of her had been screaming that warning since before the door upstairs banged closed, separating her from the man with the rifle.

"It's too conspicuous," she added, lifting the wedding gown she still held in her left hand a fraction of an inch.

"Who were the men outside?" he asked, ignoring the gesture. Ignoring what she'd said.

"Hotel security," she suggested, remembering their claim.

"I don't think so," he retorted, but his voice was still calm. "And I don't think they were the groomsmen of any wedding party. So why don't you just tell me what's really going on before I lose patience with whatever game you're playing."

She hesitated again, still not sure what to do. She had witnessed something she knew instinctively she wasn't supposed to see. From their reaction, she believed no one was supposed to see what those men had done. She just wasn't sure telling *this* man about it was the smartest thing she could do. She didn't know who *he* was, either. What he was, she amended. Because he was obviously something outside her experience.

"I was supposed to get married," Tyler said again, deciding, even as she talked, how much of the truth to tell him and how much she should hide. As certain as she was that she had to get out of this hotel, out of the wedding, she didn't feel she could make accusations against Amir when she had no proof that he, or anybody else, had done anything wrong.

There was probably a perfectly harmless explanation of what she had seen. After all, her feelings were colored by the realization that she had made a serious mistake in agreeing to this marriage. Amir's was not a world she could enter, but that didn't mean he was guilty of—

"And?" the blue-eyed man prodded.

"And...I decided at the last minute I didn't want to go through with it. I ran away and some people, some of the wedding party, came looking for me."

She paused, assessing her audience. His eyes had not left her face after their initial, unhurried scrutiny of her body. But they revealed nothing of what he might be thinking. No clue to that and therefore no help in shaping her narrative.

"I just don't want them to find me," she finished, deciding finally that the less said about what she'd seen the better.

Maybe this man *could* help her. That's what she had thought at first. That had been her instinctive reaction to him. But now something about him bothered her—almost the same sense of wrongness that the men with the rifle had caused.

In his case, however, it wasn't the gun he held. It was something about his eyes. Their coldness. Their... emptiness. She shivered at the unexpected descriptive her brain had suggested. *Empty,* she thought. That's exactly what they were.

"You think they would call in security to help them look?" he asked.

"Maybe," she agreed, trying to think why they might. When an explanation occurred to her, she hesitated about voicing it. After all, he didn't look very gullible. "If they thought something had happened to me," she continued. "My fiancé's very wealthy, so if they didn't know I'd run away…"

She realized suddenly that she shouldn't have told him about Amir's money. Probably not a smart move, considering the situation, but it seemed too late to back out of the story now.

"They might call in security if they thought someone might have…" She paused, wondering if she was simply giving him ideas. Out of the frying pan and into the fire?

"Abducted you?" he supplied smoothly when she hesitated.

His tone had changed again, but she still couldn't read it. Damn it, she couldn't figure him out. Not enough to know whether she could afford to tell him the truth. Whether she dared to do that and then appeal for his help. "Maybe," she agreed.

"Why would they say you're dangerous?" he asked.

"Is that what they told you?"

He nodded, his mouth shifting at the corners. Not quite a smile, but something. A change of expression, she thought. *Almost* an expression, at least, and not that cold mask.

"I'm not dangerous," she promised softly.

The subtle expression she had noticed before flickered again. Obviously he thought her claim was amusing. And she knew why. *Because he's the one with the great big gun. And because he really is dangerous.*

"Okay," he agreed, seeming to accept what she had said, although his eyes were still amused. "So what now?"

Which, unbelievably, seemed to imply he was willing to

help her. Tyler took a breath, trying to think what to do. Anything but let those men find her, she decided. "Could I stay here?" she suggested. "Stay in your room?" *Into the fire.*

"You could...but I'm leaving," he said, blue eyes guileless. "I have a plane to catch."

Maybe he'd take her out of the hotel with him, she thought, grasping at possibilities. If she were wearing different clothing, with something over her head to hide her hair and part of her face... Hope began to grow. They would be looking for a bride—a bride alone—and she would have become someone else.

"I could go with you," she said.

The corners of his lips lifted minutely. "But I don't have another ticket," he said.

There was a suggestive undercurrent in his refusal, and only when she heard it did she realize how her request might have been interpreted.

"I didn't mean on the plane. Just...away from the hotel. They'll be looking for a bride. For a woman alone..."

The words trailed away because even in her mind the plan was unfinished. But surely he'd be willing to do that. It wasn't much to ask. Men were supposed to respond to women in distress. Some kind of code of chivalry.

Yeah, right, her mind jeered. *And how many men do you know who follow such a code? Especially if it puts them in danger?*

But maybe, she thought, looking into his considering eyes, maybe *he* would. Especially since he *didn't* know that the men looking for her also had guns. She wondered again if she should tell him what they'd been doing. Tell him about the rifle.

Not telling him was unfair, but there was no one else she could turn to. And there was always the possibility that she had been wrong. That she'd put the wrong interpretation on what she'd seen. That it didn't mean anything. Nothing sinister.

This man had a gun, and he looked as if he knew how to use it. If she had to pull *someone* into this, and she didn't see any other way to get out of the hotel, then surely it would be better to choose a person who seemed capable of dealing with the risk. And he did, she realized. That, too, was in his eyes.

"All right," he said unexpectedly. "Out of the hotel and into a cab. I'll drop you wherever you say. Within reason."

She nodded, willing to agree to anything. His offer was the best she was likely to get. If he would get her out of the hotel, she'd worry then about what came next.

"There's a robe behind the door," she said. "Would you hand it to me?"

Surprise flickered briefly in his eyes and was controlled. He caught the broken door with his free hand, pulling it toward him. Without releasing her gaze or his gun, he reached behind it with that same hand and took down the robe she'd asked for. He tossed it to her, and she caught it awkwardly.

She waited a moment, hoping he'd have the decency to go into the other room. Finally she hung the wedding dress across the top of shower enclosure again. Then she turned her back and slipped her arms into the sleeves of the robe. She didn't turn around until she was knotting the sash around her waist.

His eyes had lightened, and she realized he was laughing at her. Not *laughing,* she amended. She wondered if he even knew how to laugh, but there was no doubt he was amused. And she didn't understand why she had turned her back. She was comfortable with her body, at ease with showing it off. That had been an integral part of her profession, so her reaction to this one man looking at her was hard to explain.

"You planning on wearing that?" he asked. His eyes remained on hers. They didn't examine the bathrobe, even though he was obviously referring to it. "Because if so, I have to tell you that it will attract as much attention as the wedding thing.''

"I thought maybe I could borrow something of yours," she suggested.

His eyes moved up and down her body, appraising, but doing it quickly this time. Asexually. Then he stepped out of the bathroom and walked over to the double closet. He pulled a small black nylon bag, duffel shaped, off the shelf and pitched it unceremoniously onto the bed.

"There's not much there," he said, "but you're welcome to anything you think might fit."

She hesitated only a second before she walked across to the foot of the king-size bed and bent to pull the bag toward her. As she did, she glanced up and found his eyes on the shadowed cleavage the corselette had been designed to create, emphasized now by her leaning position. She straightened quickly, the bag in her hand, and his eyes came up to meet hers. This time there was nothing in them but amusement.

Her mouth tightened. For some reason, despite the seriousness of her situation, Tyler was a little annoyed that amusement seemed to be the only emotion she had the ability to evoke in this man. She hadn't intended to be provocative. She had simply been reaching for the bag, but still...

Not quite sure why she was angry, she unzipped the duffel with more force than was necessary and began rummaging through its contents. He had certainly told the truth. There wasn't much here. A couple of changes of underwear—briefs and T-shirts rolled neatly together to conserve space. Two pairs of worn jeans, also rolled and not folded. A knit golf shirt. And another shirt—this one a long-sleeved white button-down. A pair of cotton knit athletic shorts. Several pairs of socks. Loafers and some well-used running shoes.

She glanced up, assessing him, wondering if the jeans would be worth trying. He was only an inch or so taller than she. Narrow hipped and flat bellied enough that they might be possible. Out of the pile she'd created on the unmade bed, she picked a pair of jeans and the white button-down, along with the running shoes and a couple of pairs of thick athletic socks.

She didn't look at him again until she had chosen the items and was ready to make the trip back into the bathroom to try them on. When she did, his eyes were uncommunicative, neither disagreeing with nor commending her choices.

"Are these okay?" she asked. "Okay to borrow? I can mail them back to you. You'll just have to give me your address."

"Throw them away."

"But the shoes are—"

"I don't want them back," he said. "Not any of it."

"You don't want to give me an address," she concluded.

"Would you give me yours?" he asked.

She wouldn't, of course. She was a woman, and he was a stranger. And besides, after what she had seen, she didn't want anyone associated with this hotel to be able to find her.

"No," she said truthfully.

He nodded. They stood a moment without speaking, eyes holding. His seemed open and honest for the first time. But they weren't, she knew in her gut. That was only for show. He had forgotten how to be open. That cold control was habitual, and she wondered what was behind it. And then decided that wasn't any of her business. That was something she didn't need to know—what had made this man so hard.

She took the items she'd picked out and retreated into the bathroom. There was no way to lock the door this time, but then he'd already demonstrated how inadequate that would be in keeping out someone who was determined to get in. If he wanted to, there was nothing she could do to prevent him.

But as she began to dress, she realized she was no longer afraid that he might assault her. She felt a lot of emotions about the man she had appealed to for help, but fear was not one of them. Not any longer.

There had been only one brief glimpse of the man beneath the controlled facade—that moment when he'd broken down the door, demanding answers. She hadn't given him any. She still hadn't told him the truth, and he probably was aware of that, but it seemed he was willing to help her anyway.

And maybe, she thought, it was safer if he *didn't* know what she'd seen. Safer for him. Still, the urge to tell him had been almost overpowering. For some strange reason, she had really wanted to tell the man with the cold blue eyes all about it.

WHEN SHE CAME OUT of the bathroom, he was standing just beside the bed, almost where he had been before. Now, however, he was dressed in the other pair of jeans and the knit shirt, the pale blue of its faded cotton a contrast to his darkly tanned skin. The towel he had wrapped around his waist had been thrown on the bed, but the clothing she had rummaged through was no longer there. She assumed he had stuffed it back into the bag.

His hair was completely dry, and it was lighter than she'd realized at first, sun streaked and very short. On him, however, the length looked good. Almost military. He wasn't handsome. His features were too strong for that, too harsh, but he was striking. *You'd probably give him a second look,* Tyler thought. Most women would.

"What do you think?" she asked, clearing those assessments from her head. It didn't matter how he looked, as long as he was willing to help her get out of here. And after that, she would never see him again.

His eyes examined her again, but this time she had given him permission. She had used one of her stockings as a belt, threading the silk through the loops of the jeans to hold them up. She had tied the tails of the shirt in front and turned up the cuffs a couple of times. The double layer of thick socks insured that the running shoes would probably stay on her feet long enough for her to walk to a cab. She hadn't been able to do anything about her hair, except to take it down and comb it out.

"Here," he said, reaching into the closet and tossing a black baseball-style cap on the foot of the bed. A pair of mirrored sunglasses was already lying there. "Stuff your hair inside. Maybe with the glasses…" He shrugged.

She nodded, grateful for the elements he had added to her disguise, neither of which would be out of place with her outfit. Actually, what she was wearing hadn't looked all that ridiculous when she'd surveyed the finished product in the bathroom mirror.

"I don't know what to do with these," she said, holding up the bridal garments.

"Leave them," he suggested.

She almost smiled at his casual disposal of several thousand dollars worth of designer clothing. And she had thought about that, but if the wedding gown were found in his room, she would have tied him to her. Maybe put him in danger. Because then whoever was looking for her could find out his name.

"I can't," she said, again trying to think of a reason he might believe. "They're not mine," she said finally.

"Not yours?" he questioned, the hint of suspicion clear.

"They belong to a friend."

"You borrowed a wedding dress?"

Which was not all that unusual, she knew, but apparently he'd never heard of the practice. "Not exactly. It belongs to a designer friend. I wore it—" She almost said "as a favor," which would be too revealing. Indicative of the fact that she was someone whose wedding would attract a lot of media attention.

"To save money," she amended.

He nodded. Apparently that was something he understood.

"And I promised to return it," she added. "So I have to."

He seemed to be considering what to do about that, although they both knew the dress wouldn't fit into the black bag, which seemed to be all the luggage he had with him. Finally he walked over to the closet and pulled out the plastic laundry sack the hotel provided, holding it out to her. She'd have to crush the dress to make it fit, but that was better than the alternative.

She dropped the shoes into the bottom and, folding the veil, stuffed it in on top of them. The dress was a harder proposition, but by folding and pushing, she managed to get it in. She looked up when she'd finished, and he held out his hand for the sack.

"You carry the duffel," he suggested.

He was probably right. It would be obvious that the black bag didn't hold a wedding gown. Obvious to anyone who might be looking for one.

She picked up the cap and stuffed her hair into it. Then she slipped on the sunglasses he'd thrown on the foot of the bed, hiding her eyes. Finally she slung the strap of the black bag across her left shoulder, positioning it comfortably on her back.

There was nothing about her appearance that would attract attention. This kind of attire was almost a uniform for a certain segment of the urban young, and with her figure she could still pass for twenty-something. More importantly, she now looked as if she belonged with him. He was a man who would probably be attracted to a woman who would dress in this very casual way, even in the environs of this old and elegant downtown hotel.

He also looked like a man who would be attractive to such a woman. Probably attractive to any woman, she admitted. He looked dangerous. Exciting. And undeniably sexy. Tyler was a little surprised by her own admission.

"Ready?" he asked.

"As ready as I'll ever be," she agreed reluctantly, and watched him open the door.

After he checked out the hall, he signaled for her to join him. The short walk to the elevator and the ride down were thankfully uneventful. Tyler kept her face turned down, the bill of the baseball cap he'd given her shadowing her features.

Her nervousness didn't seem to have rubbed off on her companion. He acted as if what they were doing was routine. There was nothing furtive about his manner, and no one who got on the elevator gave either of them a second glance.

When the doors opened on the lobby, Tyler was aware from the volume of the noise that something was going on. For one thing, it was almost wall-to-wall people. She reached out and grabbed her escort's arm, keeping her head bent and her eyes lowered. She intended to let him lead her past anyone who might be looking for her. However, they could barely push their way off the car. The way across the lobby was blocked by the crowd.

There seemed to be a lot of noise coming from outside, too. The thrump of a helicopter circling overhead. Sirens. Tyler realized only now that she had heard those upstairs, but they were such a familiar background noise in this city that she hadn't paid much attention to the distant wail. Only, the wails weren't distant anymore. They were loud, really loud, because they all seemed to be converging on this building.

"Something's happened outside," her companion said under his breath. Tyler raised her eyes and found he was looking toward the row of glass doors under the striped awnings at the front of the lobby. When she turned, she realized he was right.

The sidewalk was crowded with people, including a lot of men in Middle Eastern garb and members of the media. There were also cops, uniformed and not. To someone who had lived in New York City as long as Tyler had, however, they were as obviously cops as if they'd been sporting badges.

"What is it?" she asked, shaken by her growing realization of what had happened, still hoping somehow she was wrong.

"Something out on the street," he said. "But it seems connected with the hotel. They're not letting anyone leave."

Her heart plummeted. Her fingers tightened convulsively on his arm, and he glanced down. She met his eyes, glad that the fear in hers would be hidden by the dark lenses. Glad that he wouldn't be able to read what else was almost certain to be in them—knowledge of exactly what was going on outside and an immediate, sharp increase in her terror, which had begun to ease with his steady confidence.

"What do we do?" she asked, desperate now to get out of here. She couldn't change what had occurred. All she could do was try to protect herself.

"See anybody you know?" her companion asked, his own eyes scanning the lobby.

The men in Amir's room? she wondered. And then her brain began to function. He meant the wedding party. Her gaze also circled the waiting throng, searching. He was right, she realized. No one was being allowed to leave the hotel.

As a result the lobby was filled with angry people, suitcases beside them as they waited for permission to leave. Permission to catch their trains or planes. She wondered if anyone had taken time to explain to them what was going on.

"By the far doors," she said, recognizing a familiar figure in the sea of strangers. It was Susan Brooker, conspicuous because of the bridesmaid's dress she wore. Susan's attention was on whatever drama was unfolding outside the glass doors.

Tyler also discovered that there were several of Amir's men in the lobby, dark eyes searching the milling crowd. And she knew who *they* were looking for. "Can't we go out the back?'' she asked, trying to keep her voice steady, to control the surging panic.

''I don't think they're letting anyone out. Not from any entrance. If they were, this mob would already be gone.''

Of course they weren't. She knew, even if he didn't, what the cops were looking for. They were looking for an assassin. Searching for a murderer. Murderers, she amended. Murderers whose faces she had seen. For one split second, at least.

And those men might be here in the lobby. Looking for someone who was the right height. The right build. The right—

''Come on,'' her companion ordered softly.

He turned, pulling her with him since her fingers were still fastened in a death grip around his arm. He plowed politely, but with purpose, through the angry crowd. They had fought their way across the lobby before Tyler realized where he was headed.

''Wait a minute,'' she protested when he finally stopped at the door of the Grill Room, the most casual of the hotel's five restaurants. Even if he thought they couldn't get out, she wasn't going to sit down and eat.

''I'm not going in there,'' she said.

''You want out of the hotel, don't you?'' he asked.

''Yes,'' she agreed, wondering what he was planning.

''Then come on,'' he said.

''What are you going to do?'' she asked.

''Get us out,'' he said simply.

It sounded as if he thought he knew exactly how to do that. The calm surety was in his voice again, and because she didn't know what else to do, Tyler followed him.

The dark pub-style restaurant didn't seem as affected by the commotion out front as the rest of the hotel. The waiters were still moving about, and there were a few people sitting at the tables, finishing brunch or talking over coffee.

''Something in the back,'' Tyler's companion requested

of the hostess. "And give us a few minutes alone before you send a waiter," he added softly.

The woman's eyes assessed what she could see of Tyler's face, hidden by the cap and dark glasses, and then came back to his. She smiled in understanding. "Right this way."

The table she led them to was about as far away from the hubbub out front as they could hope for, in a dark corner not far from swinging doors that apparently led to the kitchen. Tyler slipped into the chair that faced them, her back to the rest of the room. She slid the black bag off her shoulder as the hostess put down menus and left them alone. Tyler glanced up to find the blue-eyed man, watching her from across the table. His eyes, shadowed in the dimness, seemed cold again.

"Anything you want to tell me?" he said, his voice too low for anyone else to hear.

"Like what?" she asked.

He had realized her need to get out of the hotel had something to do with what was going on out front. From there, it wasn't too great a leap to arrive at the possibility that she might know something about what that was. But that was the key he was missing. He didn't know what had happened to cause the excitement, so he couldn't begin to guess what she'd seen.

"That's a hell of a lot of commotion for a runaway bride."

"That doesn't have anything to do with me," she denied.

She hated to lie to him. She wasn't good at lying, but it probably didn't matter. He hadn't believed anything she'd said from the beginning, and yet he'd still agreed to help her.

His eyes were still trained on her face. "Eventually you'll have to trust someone," he warned softly.

"I thought you were going to get us out of here," she reminded him, ignoring the invitation to confide. But God, it was tempting. So damn tempting she had to lock her teeth into her tongue to keep the story in. He nodded, still studying her face, but thankfully he didn't push it.

"Distraction," he said. "I'll provide it and then you go. Your best shot is through that door."

He gestured to his left with a tilt of his head, not even looking in that direction. Apparently he had already checked everything out. Tyler turned to see what he meant. There was a set of double glass doors that led to a side street. Outside them, his back to the restaurant, stood a uniformed policeman.

"There's only one guy out there, and a lot of confusion," her companion stated. "He's not going to be able to handle everyone. And they'll concentrate on the front."

"What are you going to do?" Nothing he was saying made much sense, although he acted as if it did.

He ignored the question. "Don't hesitate," he ordered. "Just go. The first couple of minutes are crucial. When you get outside, mingle with the crowds. Go in whatever direction the most people seem to be headed. Get in the middle of the pack, and whatever you do, don't look back. Just walk. Your normal stride. Head up. None of that eyes-on-the-ground crap you pulled in the lobby. When you're a few blocks away, grab a cab or get on the subway."

"Where are you going?" she asked. She had thought they would go out together. He'd get a cab and drop her on his way to the airport. That had been the plan upstairs.

"I'll be heading in the opposite direction," he said. The corners of his mouth lifted slightly, just as they had before.

"I don't have any money," she said.

He stood, reaching into the front pocket of his jeans, and laid a few folded bills on the table beside her. She picked them up without looking at them and pushed them into the breast pocket of the shirt she was wearing.

"You understand what you're going to do?" he asked.

She nodded, and then, compelled by what he was doing for her, she offered an explanation he couldn't possibly understand, and probably didn't really want to hear. "I didn't have anything to do with what happened," she whispered. "I told you the truth. I want you to know that. But...I saw them."

Despite her previous intention not to involve him any more than was necessary in her danger, she hadn't been able to resist adding the last. It was an opening if he wanted to take it. Not exactly a request for his help, but an admission that there was more to this than she'd told him. *You'll have to trust somebody,* he had said. Apparently she had chosen to trust him, and she waited for his reaction.

The blue eyes rested on her face a moment, but he made no verbal response. Finally he stepped across the space that separated them and put the plastic laundry sack stuffed with the wedding dress beside her chair.

Without straightening, he gripped the arms of the chair she was sitting in, and then he leaned down—slowly, his eyes still examining her face. Tyler realized she was closer to him than she had ever been before, close enough that she could smell the hotel's soap and shampoo, the same subtle scents that had dominated the steamy bathroom upstairs.

There was something totally different, however, about the current effect of those aromas. Because now they were emanating from a strongly masculine body in very close proximity to hers.

She honestly had no idea what he intended, but she was fascinated enough that she didn't move, didn't even think about protesting his unexpected nearness. Maybe, she thought, there were some last-minute instructions he didn't want to chance anyone else overhearing.

His head began to lower. She watched, almost mesmerized, as his mouth opened, tilting to align itself to fit over hers. Only then did she realize what was about to happen.

His lips were warm. Despite the fact that they appeared hard and thin, they were unbelievably soft, lingering a heartbeat over hers before they applied pressure. When they did, the sensation was incredibly sensuous.

It created an anticipation she hadn't felt in too many

years. The feelings that suddenly flooded her body had almost been forgotten—the same expectation she had felt before all the firsts in her life, so intense this time it was frightening. She had never felt anything like this when Amir kissed her. Or anyone else, she acknowledged, surprised by that realization.

After only a few seconds, his tongue pushed into her mouth, seeking contact with hers. Later she would wonder if, in that small hesitation, he had deliberately given her an opportunity to deny him. And when she didn't take it... couldn't take it...

His kiss was expert. And thorough. She had been kissed by a lot of men, but never by one who was so ruthlessly in control of what was happening. Or so sensually dominant. His hands never left the arms of her chair. His body was not making contact with hers, but his mouth ravaged until there was nothing left for her to do but respond. Respond with all the emotions that were surging through her. That was automatic. Unthinking. It was as if she had been unconsciously considering the possibility of this man kissing her the entire time she'd known him. Preparing for it.

And she wasn't ready for the kiss to be over when his head finally lifted away, the dampness his mouth had left on hers causing her lips to cling to his a second, as if they, too, were reluctant for this to be over.

In unspoken protest of his desertion, she put the fingers of her left hand against his cheek, almost desperate to hold on to him in some way. His skin was freshly shaved, but still rough under her fingertips. Completely and obviously masculine.

The blue eyes looking down into hers were unfathomable—not cold and yet not filled with the same searing heat of desire she had briefly been allowed to see before. They seemed almost questioning. As if he were as disconcerted by what had just happened between them as she was?

Slowly her thumb traced across his bottom lip, touching the gleam of moisture her tongue had left. She wanted his mouth over hers again. She was hoping his head would lower as it had before. Hoping…

Instead, abruptly breaking the spell he'd created, he straightened his elbows, lifting his body away from hers in one smooth progression and releasing the arms of her chair. Almost in the same motion, he turned and picked up the duffel bag at her side.

He slung it over his shoulder, and then, without looking at her again, he walked unhurriedly toward the doors that led to the kitchen. He pushed through them as if he had the right.

She watched him disappear, still disoriented by the unexpected kiss. By the depth of the feelings it had aroused. Need. Loneliness. Desire. And a hunger she hadn't even been aware existed until he had tantalizingly answered it.

Gradually, she began to think again, to wonder what would happen next. He hadn't told her what to expect. She had no idea what—

Even considering what he *had* told her, she hadn't been expecting the noise that erupted, and it took a second for her brain to register its meaning. But if she hadn't, the people rushing out of the kitchen would have given her all the information she needed.

From the first shout of "Fire," people in the restaurant began to respond. That warning, along with the alarm, was too much to ignore. Or else the shouted word broke the paralysis that the unexpected volume of the fire alarm had caused.

Tyler picked up the plastic bag, remembering her instructions. The first minutes would be crucial, he'd said. Because this was unexpected, of course. Even for the cops. There weren't that many people in the restaurant to begin with, but panicked, they made quite a crowd trying to push their way out that side entrance. Too many for the single cop to restrain, even if he'd had the presence of mind to try.

Despite everything that had happened, Tyler almost smiled as she moved out into the mob in the street. The same thing must be happening with the people in the lobby. They, too, it seemed, were flooding out of the hotel, their determination overpowering the flustered cops.

It had all been as easy as the blue-eyed man had promised. Everything had gone exactly as he had said it would. She resisted the impulse to look for him, keeping her head up and her eyes straight ahead, exactly as he'd told her. There was no challenge. No rifle shot. There was nothing except the normal flow of traffic and the crowds.

It took her only minutes to walk the six blocks she had decided on. Only an additional minute to hail a cab. When she was safely inside, she couldn't resist the urge to look back.

She didn't know what she had been looking for, but whatever it was, she didn't find it. There was no one following her. Not the men she had seen. No one from the wedding party. Certainly not the man with the cold blue eyes.

Chapter Four

Although Hawk had been conscious of a bone-deep fatigue throughout the short flight from New York to Virginia, he had refused to think about it. Or the reasons behind it. There was, after all, one more thing he had to do—one last step on this journey he had willingly begun more than six months ago. Then and only then would it be over.

He had concentrated so long on his quest for revenge, blocking everything else from his mind, that it was difficult to give himself permission to remember the other. To focus on Griff's life, rather than on the senseless brutality of his death. And as he walked across the tree-shaded tranquillity of the vast cemetery, its quietness crosshatched by miles and miles of simple markers, Hawk thought that maybe, in some strange way, this would be the proper place to finally do that.

Griff Cabot had known all the dark and dirty secrets the powerful of the world hide. A cold-war warrior, he had been left behind on the empty battlefield of a war that supposedly had already been won.

"We seem to be the only ones left who understand the world is still a dangerous place for freedom," Griff would say, smiling a little to lessen the reality of all he asked of the team through the years. *"Think of what you're doing as sentry duty. Standing guard over the things you love."*

Standing guard. And now, for Hawk, and for the rest of them as well, that duty, that sacred responsibility, was over.

He topped the slight rise that looked down on the area of the cemetery he sought. From where he stood, he could see a figure standing beside the small granite stone that marked Griff Cabot's grave. A woman, slender and blond, wearing a sleeveless black dress. Her hair had been gathered in a chignon low on the back of her neck, but the breeze whipped strands of it free. As he watched, she raised her hand and, turning her head, pushed an errant tendril away. Turning enough that he could see her face.

Claire Heywood, Hawk realized. Although he had never met her, there was no doubt in his mind of the identification. And no doubt that her being here was the last thing Griff would have wanted. Cabot had taken a lot of precautions to insure that there was nothing about his relationship with Claire that was open or known, nothing that could possibly expose her to his enemies.

Hawk stopped beside one of the massive trees that shaded the rise, still far enough away that he could be sure she would remain unaware of his presence. He didn't want to intrude on her grief. His own could wait. It had waited, his emotions carefully controlled, for over six months. Another few minutes wouldn't make any difference in what he had come here to do.

He watched as the woman Griff Cabot had loved reached out to touch the top of the granite marker. Using it for balance, she stooped down beside the grave and placed something on the grass. Then her hand lifted to the stone, fingers slowly tracing over the letters that had been cut into it.

Touching Griff's name, Hawk realized. His throat closed suddenly, painfully hard and tight. His lips flattened, fighting the emotional pull. He didn't want to be a witness to this. Griff Cabot had been his friend. He and the team had been the only family Hawk had ever known, sharing a bond of brotherhood stronger than that of blood, perhaps because it had been forged in secrecy and death. In their dependence on one another.

The woman at the grave bowed her head, fingers still touching the stone marker. *At least,* Hawk thought, watching her, *at least I don't have to live with regret.*

Claire Heywood had chosen to break all ties with Cabot only a few months before his death. No one on the team had talked much about it, of course, especially not Griff, but Hawk imagined most of them had come to their own conclusion about what had happened. Hawk had. He believed that two people with very differing views of the world had fallen deeply in love. And because of those differences, the relationship had been impossible.

Finally Claire's hand fell away from the face of the stone, and then she stood, looking down a long moment on the grave. She turned away and began to walk toward Hawk, another mourner in a place that had, through the years, seen millions come and go. She did not look back at the grave of the man who was, here at least, only another soldier, fallen in his country's wars.

Her eyes met Hawk's as she climbed the slope. She nodded slightly as she passed by, but they didn't speak. After all, they were strangers, and she could have no idea that he was here for the same reasons that had drawn her to this place.

Hawk waited a long time before he finally walked down to the grave. As he approached, he realized there was a blotch of what appeared to be blood on the smooth green lawn. When he reached the marker, however, Hawk saw that the spot of crimson was a rose, widely opened in the oppressive heat of the Virginia summer. A few of the petals had dropped and scattered, maybe as Claire Heywood placed it on the ground.

Hawk's lips tilted. No one would have been more amused by the romantic absurdity than Griff, he thought. And then Hawk's smile faded because he knew that wasn't true. Not true simply because the rose had been left by the woman Griff loved.

Hawk looked down at the wilted flower, again fighting the release of emotions he had so long controlled. Losing that battle, he finally allowed his blurring eyes to move upward to the letters Claire Heywood had traced in the face of the stone. Brutally new. Too sharp. Like his grief.

Below Griff's name, engraved in Latin, was a single sentence: *Dulce et decorum est pro patria mori.* A strange inscription for someone as coldly rational as Cabot. *Sweet and proper to die for your country?* Again his lips tilted as Hawk remembered Griff's hardheaded pragmatism.

He wondered who had chosen that epitaph. Someone at the agency? It sounded like them. Of course, it didn't matter what they put on the stone. Griff Cabot's memorial had been written in the lives he had touched. Including Hawk's. And in the continued strength of the country he had loved and protected.

Standing guard, Hawk thought again. And then the long brown fingers that had closed unerringly around the trigger of that rifle in Baghdad closed again over what *he* had brought to lay on Griff's grave. He bent, placing the casing of the bullet with which he had taken revenge for Cabot's murder beside the wilting rose. The pairing was as incongruous maybe as Claire and Griff's had been. But even so, they belonged together. Here, at least.

"Rest in peace, my friend," Hawk said, the same words he had whispered in Baghdad. And finally, it was truly over.

QUITE A CONTRAST to where he'd spent last night, Hawk thought, pitching the black bag onto the narrow bed. It bounced a little as it hit the sagging mattress, and his mind flashed back to the scene in the hotel room this morning. To the image of this same bag on another bed. To a woman reaching for it, the lapels of the robe she wore falling open, exposing the beginning swell of ivory breasts and the shadowed valley between.

The tightening in his groin caused Hawk to destroy the image, to wipe it out of his mind with that practiced control. Despite the length of his sexual abstinence, he still wasn't sure why he had reacted so strongly to that woman. The same way he was reacting now, simply to the memory of her.

He wasn't an adolescent. He had gone for longer periods without sex, his mind too absorbed by a mission to think about his physical needs. And after all, she was nothing like his normal taste in women. Nothing like any woman he'd ever known, he admitted. Out of his realm of experience, which, he acknowledged without any pride or arrogance, was extensive.

Hawk's mouth tightened, remembering the way she had reacted to his insultingly prolonged appraisal of her body. Remembering his own reaction, that powerful surge of sexual hunger. And remembering the kiss.

That had been intended to exorcise the demons she'd created. The decision to kiss her had probably been as insulting as his deliberate examination of her body. But it had become something else. Maybe because her response had been totally unexpected.

He could still feel her fingers resting against his cheek, expressing a tenderness that was light-years away from his usual encounters with women. About as far as this dingy apartment was removed from the luxury of the hotel where he had slept last night, he thought, taking a deep breath.

This was his reality. And it was past time for him to get back to it, he decided, pushing the memory of the woman out of his head. He punched the button on his answering machine to play the single message left during the long weeks he'd been gone.

Hawk didn't have the kind of friends who left messages. It was a pastime too dangerous in their line of work. The one on the machine was short and impersonal.

"This is Mike down at Ken's Electronics. Just calling to tell you your VCR's ready." That was followed by a phone number, and then the computer voice of Hawk's answering machine gave a date and time. The message had been left a couple of days before. About the same time he had been boarding a plane in Athens to fly back to the States, Hawk realized.

He hadn't left a VCR for repair, of course, although there was a Ken's Electronics in this small Virginia town. And if anyone bothered to check, the repair shop would probably even have a VCR, held in the same name Hawk had used to rent this apartment. *If* anyone bothered to check.

He took another breath, trying to think. He was aware again of his fatigue—too extreme to be explained by his activities the last few days. Despite jet lag, he had even slept last night, thanks to the help of half a bottle of pretty good bourbon. That wasn't his normal remedy for insomnia, but at the time it had seemed an appropriate ending to the success of the mission he'd undertaken. Celebrating alone, in a place Griff had loved.

At least the whiskey had kept him from having to think about what came next, and eventually it had let him sleep, so he shouldn't be feeling this exhaustion. This...mental lethargy. This letdown. However, the only plan he'd been able to formulate on the flight home was to report in, take a long, hot shower and then sleep for a couple of days.

He needed the shower. It seemed years since this morning's, and a lot had happened in the meantime. His mind had insisted on replaying all of it during the plane ride. He still didn't know what had occurred to cause the excitement at the hotel. There hadn't been enough time for the papers at the airport to have gotten the story out. Besides, Hawk hadn't really cared, not beyond an idle curiosity.

The woman he had helped wasn't his responsibility. The fact that he had taken the trouble to get her out of the situation was still surprising to him, because he was not by nature given to playing Good Samaritan. The hard lips tilted at that thought. Very few people would classify Hawk as a Good Samaritan. At least not those who knew him professionally. And there weren't any who knew him any other way. The man called Hawk was a loner, by inclination and preference.

The image of the woman's face reappeared in his mind's eye, her voice sincere, almost apologetic, violet eyes pleading. *"I didn't have anything to do with what happened out there,"* she had said. *"I want you to know that. But...I saw them."*

Well, good for you, Hawk thought cynically, denying the pull of that appeal, just as he had when she'd made it. *Whatever you saw sure as hell is nothing to me. Nothing to do with me. You just keep running, sweetheart, and maybe if you're lucky, you'll even get away.*

Hawk turned from the answering machine, denying the strength of those memories: the length of long, shapely legs, the shadowed cleavage between the high breasts, even the remembrance of the way her lips had felt moving against his. There was no room in his life for those. Someone had left him a message, left it in such a way that he understood it meant trouble. Probably official trouble for him. That was nothing he hadn't been expecting.

Reluctantly Hawk left the stifling apartment where, during his brief stay, he hadn't even bothered to turn on the air-conditioning, and walked a few blocks. He picked the middle phone booth out of a row that stood on an isolated corner.

There wasn't much traffic, but his blue eyes continued to scan both it and the streets around him as he punched in a number. He wondered briefly who would answer, which of them would have gone to the trouble to call.

Not Griff, he thought, his throat tightening. Never again would Griff Cabot issue an order or debrief him after a mission. Compliment him on a job well done. Talk to him as a friend. Or issue a warning, he thought, listening to the distant ringing.

"Hawk," he said as soon as he heard someone pick up. His eyes were still searching the street around him.

"Don't even think about coming in."

Hawk recognized the deep voice. He supposed he should have known who it would be. "What's going on?" he asked.

"They know about Baghdad," Jordan Cross said.

There had been no doubt in Hawk's mind they would figure that out. His skill was its own signature, and given the target, they wouldn't have needed much help to finger him as the shooter.

"Okay," he said simply. He would have to take that heat. It had been an unsanctioned hit. Diplomatically, his target had been off-limits, and the State Department would be in an uproar.

Hawk had never even hesitated over the possible repercussions—political or personal. Not once he had been certain in his own mind that his victim had been responsible for Griff's death. And for the deaths of the others who had died in that senseless massacre. Secretaries and clerks. People who had nothing to do with the clandestine work of the CIA. A lot of innocent people who had died so those bastards could make some kind of political statement.

If it came down to it, Hawk could prove that the man he had taken out had been responsible for those deaths. He had made sure he had that proof. He thought it might buy him a little forgiveness, despite the current climate in the government about the team and its mission.

"And they've tied you to what happened at the hotel in New York this morning," Jordan continued. "Maybe just their way of justifying the knives that were already out."

There was a question implied by the last, but Hawk said nothing in response, thinking instead about the import of that. *"What happened at the hotel in New York this morning."* He still didn't know, and up to this point he hadn't cared.

His decision to help the woman had been quixotic and unplanned. He had the skills, so he had used them. But if he were going to get the blame for something, he figured he ought to take the trouble to find out exactly what it was he was supposed to have done.

"You do that one?" Cross asked.

A friend's voice, Hawk reminded himself. *A friend's question. No blame involved. Simply a request for the truth.*

"It wasn't me," he said. He knew, of course, what "that one" implied, so the situation he hadn't cared enough to find out about suddenly became a little clearer.

"They're putting you in the hotel. Right in the middle of the thing. They even have pictures. Watch yourself. They're dead serious about this."

"Thanks for the warning." Hawk acknowledged his debt, while ignoring the unintended irony of the adjective Jordan had used.

"We owe you," the disembodied voice responded.

"Nobody owes me anything," Hawk declared harshly. "It was personal. Just for Griff," he added softly, trying to modify the unintended sharpness of his voice.

That was true. He probably couldn't explain to anyone what Griff Cabot's friendship had meant to him. Maybe he didn't have to, he thought. Not to this man, at least.

"I just thought you should know you're not alone. You can call in a lot of favors for what you did. If you need them."

Hawk had been a loner too long to believe he would ever need anyone's help. The corners of his lips inched upward fractionally, but his voice when he spoke reflected none of that amusement. "I'll keep that in mind," he said. Then, without saying goodbye, he placed the receiver back on the hook.

They've tied you to what happened in New York this morning. He still didn't have any idea to what—or rather to *whom*—they had tied him. Obviously something they believed they could use to get rid of him, without having to admit he had been justified in what he'd done in Iraq.

The blue eyes searched the area around the phones. Then the man called Hawk stepped away from the one he had chosen and crossed the street to the neighborhood newsstand. Once there, it wasn't hard to figure out what they had fingered him for. All the afternoon editions carried the story, even the locals.

The man called Hawk didn't make many mistakes. In his line of work, one was usually the total allotment. That first mistake was very often the last an operative got a chance to make. And he had made his, Hawk thought in disgust, scanning the long columns of text. A hell of one, apparently.

Sheer fluke? Accident? A simple case of being in the wrong place at the wrong time? Except Hawk didn't believe much in coincidences. Not even violet-eyed ones who begged for his help. Maybe especially not that kind.

He had been so damn sure no one could know he was in New York, absolutely certain no one could have traced his movements from Baghdad. And maybe they hadn't. It was always possible someone had recognized him when he checked in and decided to make the most of the opportunity. He couldn't be sure at this point how it had come about, but someone had played him for a fool.

Hawk had known she was good, had acknowledged it from the first, but still he had gone along for the ride. Not many people through the years had succeeded in taking advantage of him. Not many had had guts enough to try.

They probably had him on video, he realized. That's what Cross meant about pictures. The hotel's security cameras. A grainy black-and-white image of one of the government's top covert operatives—a highly specialized black ops agent—walking through the lobby of the hotel where this morning's assassination had been carried out.

Whoever the hell that woman was, she had gotten him. Despite his initial instinct that she hadn't been telling the truth. She had set him up, exactly as she'd been sent to do. And because of that aberration in his normally careful behavior, they were going to pin this assassination on him.

I must be getting old, Hawk thought, shaking his head in disbelief. But despite his participation in his own destruction, he thought somebody owed him an explanation. And he might as well start looking for one from the person who had suckered him in. The woman with the violet eyes.

TYLER PUT HER PURSE and the battered bag on the bed. The suitcase she'd picked out at the pawnshop where she'd hocked the wedding gown and her engagement ring looked right at home. But the Louis Vuitton purse she'd gone by her apartment to retrieve when she left the hotel looked totally out of place.

She had taken a dangerous chance, she knew, remembering the pounding at the front door as she'd climbed out the window and hurried, knees shaking, down the fire escape. It had been a long way down, especially carrying the laundry bag and the purse. But she had known she'd need some ID to show the airlines, and the purse also contained her credit cards. She had transferred the essentials to the new purse Amir had bought for the honeymoon. She hadn't thought she'd need her social security card or her credit cards, so thankfully they were still in this one.

She pushed her fingers into the mattress of the bed, feeling it sag, hearing the reminiscent, metallic creak of the springs. She had spent the first seventeen years of her life in this room. And not much had changed about it, she thought.

But change always came slowly to Covington. Despite the proliferation of fast-food places and discount stores, she had had no trouble finding her way from the interstate exit to the front door. The tree-shaded dwellings she passed on the way had seemed exactly the same, except for the colors of their paint or the variety of flowers wilting in their beds.

Even the thick humidity was exactly as she remembered. Lying in this bed, night after night, trying to sleep despite the heat. The double windows would be open to let in any stirring of the heavy air, and the tree frogs would be almost loud enough to drown out the sound of her parents' fighting. Almost loud enough.

She took a breath, pushing those memories away. She interlocked the fingers of her hands at the base of her skull, slipping them under her hair and lifting it off her neck. She could feel the perspiration underneath the heavy mass of curls. She pulled her elbows forward and then pushed them back to stretch out the tiredness that had settled between her shoulders.

As tired as she was, however, she wondered if she'd be able to sleep in the heat. Despite the money Tyler had sent home through the years, there was still no air-conditioning. Of course, Aunt Martha hadn't been much inclined to change, either. No more than the rest of Covington.

When her great-aunt had died in her sleep, at age ninety, Tyler had come home to make arrangements for the funeral. Instead of staying at the house, however, she had checked into one of the motels on the interstate. Before she returned to New York, she'd made arrangements for someone to clean the house, but she still hadn't gotten around to putting it on the market.

She didn't really understand why she hesitated. Leaving this place twenty years ago had been no less an escape than the one she had made from New York this morning. Not just an escape from Aunt Martha and her eternal predictions of hellfire and damnation, but an escape from almost everything that had happened while she lived in this room.

Her mother and father had married because she was already on the way, and they had both, at one time or another, expressed regret over their union. As a child, she had blamed herself for the unhappiness that permeated the very walls of this house. It had echoed in the darkness as she lay in this bed, night after night, trying to ignore their angry voices. Their endless quarreling.

Her father had left for good when she was five. The shouting recriminations had disappeared, replaced by a grinding poverty, of body and soul, that her mother had never escaped. That's when Aunt Martha had come to live with them. To help out, she used to tell people. To take care of the child.

Tyler took another breath, realizing she had allowed herself to be drawn again into the past. Back to the sermons and restrictions and endless punishments. To the constant reiteration that she was simply a cross her great-aunt had shouldered because it was her Christian duty. Again, it had been made abundantly clear to Tyler that she was an unwanted burden. When her mother died, she had felt she'd lost the only person who had really ever loved her. She had taken what was left in the bank account and run. As fast and as far as she could.

And yet today, when she had stood at the reservation desk at the airport, trying to think where she could go, where she'd be safe, she'd been drawn back here by the sense of sanctuary this house always seemed to provide.

When she was a little girl, playing in someone else's yard, she would often lose track of the time. Then, as shadows lengthened with the quick fall of summer night, she would run across lawns rich with the scent of mown grass, and over the rough warmth of sidewalks. Familiar textures under her bare feet.

In the distance she would hear her mother calling, and she would fly toward the sound of that beloved voice, ignoring the lights that reached from the open windows of the houses she passed. And as soon as she climbed the steps of the front porch, she would know she was safe. Safe from the shadows. From the imagined terrors of the night. Safe from everything.

Tyler had felt something of that same relief when she drove the rental car into the yard at twilight and parked it in the graveled driveway, right under the oak tree, which had once held a rope swing. Her swing. Her yard. Her mother's house.

She realized that she was still standing beside the narrow bed, and the room was in almost total darkness now. She reached out and clicked on the bedside lamp, welcoming its glow as another escape from shadows, those of memory this time.

The base of the lamp was in the shape of a ballerina, arms reaching upward toward the bulb and pointed toes arching on the tarnished brass stand. The deep rose of its shade softened the ugliness of the room, just as it always had.

Tyler ran the tips of her fingers slowly down the porcelain of the dancer's body. There had never been enough money for lessons, of course, but that hadn't kept her from dancing. Moving in a awkward parody of ballet around this crowded room. Pretending she was the ballerina on the lamp.

Despite the poverty of her existence, nothing had ever stopped Tyler from pretending. She had had so many dreams, and most of them had been born in this room. She would lie in this bed, listening to the bitter voices, and gradually block them out with the glittering, impossible visions in her imagination.

Images of what she would be when she was grown. Of where she would travel. Exotic places, always so far from this town, this house. Images of when she would finally be *somebody*. Little-girl dreams.

Which had almost all come true, she thought with a sense of wonder. Perhaps desperation *was* the mother of ambition. *Lives of quiet desperation.* She couldn't remember who had said that, but it fit the ones that had been lived in this house.

What a useless and maudlin journey into the past, she thought, shaking her head. She walked over to the windows and pushed them open, hoping for a breeze. Instead, the familiar scent of honeysuckle whispered into the stifling room.

How long had it had been since she had tasted the single drop of sweetness at the end of a honeysuckle stamen? That had been another childhood game, one that required no expenditure of her mother's hard-earned money. Tyler had been good at those. Imagination was free, and hers had been her savior.

A trill of childish laughter floated in, the distant sound traveling clearly through the soft twilight shadows. This rural Mississippi night didn't seem any different from those of twenty years ago. The child she had once been had come home. Running from shadows. From the darkness. From her own fears and terrors.

But this time those were not imagined. She had bought an afternoon paper at the airport, almost furtive about the ordinary purchase when she had seen the headline. The assassination of Sheikh Rashad al-Ahmad had been front page news.

And only now, locked inside this house, so far from that hotel in New York, was she beginning to feel safe again. She had taken all the precautions she could think of to keep anyone from finding her. She had paid cash for the plane ticket, and it had been issued in her real name. She had used her social security card, which had never been changed, as identification.

She hadn't been Tommie Sue Prator in over twenty years, and thankfully none of the silly stories Paul had told made reference to the realities of this life. So she should be safe, she told herself. At least for tonight, and tomorrow she'd be able to think about what she should do.

She would have to go to the authorities, she had finally realized, as she read the paper on the plane. They were equipped to sort out guilt and innocence. She didn't have to accuse, but she *did* have to tell them what she'd seen.

She was standing in front of the open window, her arms crossed over her breasts, running her palms slowly up and down her upper arms as if she were cold. As if the breath of air that brought the scent of the honeysuckle into the room had been the least bit cooling.

Until she had returned to this reality, to being Tommie Sue again, she hadn't realized that the life she had been living was like some fantastic dream. Amir. The limitless wealth. His whirlwind courtship and the hurried arrangements for the wedding. His father's assassination.

Those things were from a world so far away it had no relation to the dingy wallpaper and the sagging mattresses of this one. Almost no relation to her. Certainly no relation to who she really was. They seemed literally from another universe. An alternate reality. And that realization was comforting. It added a little to the sense of sanctuary she had found.

Despite the heat, she shivered, thinking about those men on the terrace. Seeing the rifle swing away from the man who had just been killed and toward her. Determined not to give in to her fears, however, she turned away from the open windows and the outside darkness. As she did, she caught a glimpse of motion in the mirror of her great-grandmother's dresser, and it stopped her.

The face that had graced dozens of magazine covers, its paleness highlighted by the shadows behind, stared back at her from the age-clouded glass. The famous violet eyes were wide and dark, of no discernible color in the gloom.

No reason at all to be afraid here, she assured herself again, fighting another involuntary shiver. *No reason at all.*

IT HADN'T TAKEN HAWK LONG to find his mystery woman. He had some advantages, of course. Computers made this kind of search easy and fast. As always, he was surprised at the amount of information available about the lives of ordinary people. And at how simple it was to find it. He had started with the story she had told him about running away from her wedding. He had assumed it was a lie and there would be nothing in it worth pursuing. What he found was something very different.

There *had* been a wedding scheduled to take place at the hotel today, and that wedding was the reason Sheikh Rashad al-Ahmad had come to New York. To attend a civil ceremony between his oldest son and heir, Amir, and a woman named Tyler Stewart.

The slowly materializing images on the screen, appearing in answer to his requests, confirmed that Tyler Stewart was indeed the woman who had entered his hotel room. Some of the pictures were prewedding publicity shots, but most came from the covers of magazines or ad campaigns in which she'd appeared. In those she was tastefully, and yet somehow almost always provocatively posed, showing off the body he'd examined today.

Her attitude in these pictures was quite a contrast to the modesty she'd displayed when he'd broken down the door. An act? he wondered. If so, she was a damn fine actress. But he had already figured out that much, Hawk acknowledged ruefully.

As he continued to read, he realized that at least another one of his initial impressions had also been correct. Tyler Stewart was totally outside his previous experiences with women. Successful, with a long international career, she was probably very well off in her own right. Not in comparison to her bridegroom, Hawk thought, but certainly in comparison to him.

And her wedding had lured al-Ahmad the father out of his desert stronghold and right into the sights of an assassin. His son was already blaming extremists. The sheikh had been the target of coups in the past, including a couple of assassination attempts. If the hastily arranged wedding had been set up simply to provide the opportunity for another...

Then someone was working in league with the fundamentalists. Nothing Hawk read about playboy Amir al-Ahmad indicated that he was interested in pursuing *Sharia,* the Moslem equivalent of the straight and narrow. And after all, if a fundamentalist revolution succeeded in his country, as it had in Iran, no one would have more to lose than Amir. Which brought Hawk back to the other party in this wedding. Right back to Tyler Stewart.

Since no one had yet thought to cancel his clearances, Hawk had access to databases that would have been difficult for the average searcher to utilize, but he still couldn't find anything to tie Stewart to the extremists. However, information about her background before she began modeling was vague and contradictory. Apparently she had told a variety of stories about her past.

And according to the papers, no one had seen her since the assassination. The reporters who had broached the subject to Amir al-Ahmad had gotten some story about her being overcome by shock and sorrow. Which might be true.

But maybe, Hawk thought, she had done just exactly what she'd told him she was going to—get out of the hotel and away. Just exactly what she had conned him into helping her do. At the same time putting him on the hotel security tapes.

When he checked, however, there was no Tyler Stewart listed as a passenger on any of the flights out of the New York area this afternoon. He did run across a name on one of the lists that triggered a memory. Something he'd seen when he was researching her background. And when Hawk backtracked, he found it. Just what he had been looking for.

When he left the university computer center, Hawk went straight to the bus station in Alexandria, where he retrieved his emergency kit from the locker he'd rented. The small nylon gym bag contained money and everything else Hawk would need to create a new identity.

He used part of the cash to purchase a change of clothes and some toiletries, which he stuffed into the bag. And the other thing Hawk bought with the money was a plane ticket to Mississippi. A ticket that would take him to the same city into which a woman named Tommie Sue Prator had flown this afternoon.

Chapter Five

When Tyler awoke, coming out of sleep too quickly, she had been dreaming about something she knew she should remember. Something she *wanted* to remember. She lay for a long time in the darkness, trying to reenter the fabric of her dream, before she finally admitted it was gone. Irreparably destroyed.

She wondered if that dream could have had anything to do with the man who had kissed her yesterday. She remembered, almost against her will, how his lips had felt. And his tongue, demanding, making slow, heated contact with hers, its movement as controlled and assured as the man himself.

That same heat flooded her body now, stirred by memory. Tyler stretched languidly, savoring the unaccustomed feeling. Still trying to remember if she had been dreaming about him. It had been pleasant, she knew, so she wondered why she had been drawn away. Usually when she awakened like this, jerked from sleep, it was because of a nightmare, something from which her subconscious needed to escape.

She glanced at the clock beside the bed. It was a little after four. Not yet dawn, but the lesser darkness that was its herald. She closed her eyes, but they wouldn't stay closed. The hint of disquietude she had felt on awakening was still here, hiding in the once-familiar shadows of the bedroom.

She rolled onto her side, pushing the limp feather pillow into a more comfortable position, attempting to find a cool spot on its cotton case against which to rest her cheek. She closed her eyes, thinking how easily she had once been able to block out all the unpleasantness of her life.

Now that old magic was gone, swallowed up by the darkness. By the events of yesterday. Or by the fact that the dreams she had once had no longer offered any promise for the future. They represented the past, and she had not been able yet to formulate others for the years that lay ahead.

All she had come up with was her agreement to marry Amir. She was still amazed by the depth of that self-deception. Why had it taken her so long to realize her own motives? And to know how wrong they were? She had been afraid, she admitted. Afraid of whatever came next. Of facing it alone. So she had convinced herself, or let others convince her, that marrying Amir would be smart. Safe. And even moral. Now she knew it would have been none of those things.

She pushed the sheet off her legs and sat up on the edge of the bed. She put her bare feet on the smoothness of the hardwood floor, the only cool surface in the room. With both hands, she lifted her hair off the back of her neck.

It was too hot to sleep. Too hot to get comfortable. Maybe that's why she had awakened. Maybe it was just the heat. Warm milk had been Aunt Martha's standard cure for insomnia. Although the thought was unappealing in the stifling humidity, Tyler decided it was a better solution than worry.

When she entered the dark kitchen, she walked over to the sink and opened the cabinet above it. The glasses were still there, standing upside down in the same sentinel-like rows her aunt had always placed them in. It was not until she picked one up and turned toward the refrigerator that her sleep-dazed brain remembered. All the perishables would have been thrown out.

She went back to the sink, turning on the faucet and letting the water run a few seconds before she put the glass under its stream. When she lifted the water to her lips, the first sip was as familiar as the kitchen, the taste faintly metallic. She turned around, leaning back against the edge of the counter. She lifted the glass again, her eyes drifting across the kitchen.

There were two men standing in the doorway that led onto the back porch. Watching her. Even in the darkness, she could see the gleam of the white robes they wore, although their faces were dark and featureless.

This is the nightmare, she thought. It had to be. They were totally out of place in her mother's kitchen. Out of place in this life. *Nightmare,* she thought again.

Yet some more rational part of her knew it wasn't. They were undeniably real. She could see the two shapes building out of the darkness, robes billowing slightly as they walked.

Coming toward her, she realized. She seemed paralyzed by her fear, caught in that same icy terror in which one waits for the horror of one's own nightmare to become reality.

Then, suddenly, that paralysis released. She raised her hand and threw the glass at them. In the same motion she turned, running toward the door that led to the hallway and the open windows of the bedroom. She knew she didn't have a prayer of reaching those windows before they could get to her, but she also knew she had to try.

She heard the glass shatter half a heartbeat before the first shot sounded. That bullet struck the frame of the door in front of her. She felt flecks of broken wood, which had splintered under its impact, strike her face. She threw up her arm to protect her eyes, the action only a reflex.

She seemed to be moving in slow motion, a journey through a nightmare. Two more shots followed the first, so rapidly one seemed an echo of the other. Then, finally, she was through the door and into the hall. She must have hit her arm on something. She felt it as she skidded around the corner, but despite her awareness of the blow, there was little pain. Just an aftermath of tingling nerve endings.

The bedroom doorway loomed suddenly before her, dark and inviting. A minute more of safety. She slid into it, bare feet seeking traction on the smooth wood of the ancient floor. A hand grabbed at her as she came through the opening, and she fought against its grip.

The hard fingers, closing tight as a vise over her wrist, didn't loosen even as she twisted her arm, prying at them with her other hand. It did no good. Instead, she was pulled to the side and slammed against the wall, her captor's body pressed against hers, holding her prisoner.

At least she'd tried, she thought, trapped behind the solid strength of the man who had caught her. She should have known there would be more of them. That they wouldn't let her get away this time. They had let that happen once, at the hotel. They wouldn't make that mistake again.

Her head hurt from where he had slammed her against the wall. And the arm she had hit coming through the kitchen door was beginning to burn like someone was holding a blowtorch to the back of it. The man leaning against her was too close, deliberately pushing his body into hers so she couldn't move, couldn't breathe. The hard muscles of his back ground into the softness of her breasts.

She eased a shallow inhalation into her starving lungs. Despite her fear, the automatic physiological functions hadn't stopped. Precious air. Maybe one of the last breaths she would draw. Precious, life-sustaining air that smelled like…

She opened her eyes and frantically pushed her head up a fraction of an inch, forcing it up against the back of his muscled shoulder, trying desperately to see. Trying not to hope, not even to imagine…

The man whose body was glued to the front of hers didn't make any verbal response, but suddenly, unbelievingly, there was more pressure. He was pushing her more firmly into the wall, but she had already managed to lift her head far enough that she could see his arm. Outstretched. And in his hand...

She took another breath, this one savoring. Because she had been right. The fragrance she had recognized was the faint scent of the hotel's soap and underlying that... She had to snatch another breath before she could even complete the thought. Underlying that was the very masculine, somehow familiar scent of his body. Closer even than it had been yesterday when he bent to kiss her.

She could feel against her cheek the slight coarseness of the knit shirt he wore. Could see the pale blue of its sleeve. And at the end of that, a corded arm and a hand whose long brown fingers were wrapped around a very big gun.

And that outstretched arm was as steady as it had been yesterday morning, waiting now for those men to follow her through that doorway. With his other hand, the man with the cold blue eyes reached behind him and found her arm, the one she had hit on the frame. He gripped it, right above the elbow, and squeezed gently.

She wasn't sure if that was supposed to be reassurance or a question. But she nodded, head moving against the back of his shoulder, able to move only slightly because of the pressure he was exerting to keep her there. Behind his body. Safe.

He squeezed her arm again. Silent communication. For the first time since she had seen the robed men in the kitchen, hope flooded her heart. Her almost mindless terror eased. She didn't know why he was here, a miracle as inexplicable as finding him in the hotel had been, but somehow she knew he'd keep her safe.

He had his whole concentration fixed on the doorway that led to the hall. Still waiting for someone to come through it. Suddenly he moved. His left arm came around to the front, its hand fastening under the right, which held the big gun, helping to cradle and support its weight. Then she heard what he had heard. Footsteps. Coming toward them down the hall.

She watched as he eased away from the wall, his movements soundless. Unlike whoever had been in the kitchen. But then, they didn't know they had anything to fear. They thought only she was here. Only a woman, hiding in the darkness.

When they came through the doorway, it was worse than anything she could have imagined. The size of the room magnified the sound, and the flashes from the muzzles of the guns, spitting into the darkness like lightning, terrified her. She slid down the wall, putting her hands over her ears.

It seemed to go on a long time, but she knew it lasted only seconds. When it was over, she waited, the total and complete silence left behind almost as frightening as the noise.

Nothing moved in the dark room. There was no sound except her heart, beating in her throat so loudly that it seemed if anyone were left alive after that barrage of gunfire, they would be able to hear it. Finally, she couldn't stand not knowing. She lowered her hands and slowly raised her head.

The man with the blue eyes was still there, standing just where he had been before it all started. The gun he had held was still supported by both hands. His knees were slightly bent, his attention focused on the doorway leading out of the bedroom.

There were no more footsteps there. And she found herself hoping, more fiercely than she had ever hoped for the fulfillment of any of those impossible dreams she had had when she used to sleep in this small dark room. Hoping that the men who had come into her mother's kitchen were dead.

She didn't know how she became aware of movement at the window. She was still looking at his back, the light shirt that stretched across his broad shoulders palely visible in the darkness. Suddenly she saw, peripherally and almost subliminally, that something was at the window. She turned her head, eyes wide, straining against the outside darkness. The flash of motion was white, and so she shouted a warning her brain didn't formulate, her outcry primitive. Instinctive.

"Behind you."

She must have pointed before she screamed. She must have made some betraying movement, because the bullets that sprayed the wall above her head seemed to come almost before her warning. She dropped to the floor, curled into a fetal position, hands attempting to protect her head as pieces of the wall and ceiling rained around her.

The deep cough that answered that assault was familiar now. She had heard it during the earlier exchange, firing steadily, the crack of its echo reverberating in the enclosed space. *His gun,* she thought. Tyler made herself open her eyes. She could still see the pale blue shirt. He had pivoted to face the new threat, squeezing off shots as evenly as he had before.

Two or three. Maybe four. She lost count. But the last one put an end to everything. Whoever had been outside fell into the open window, his body draped limply over the sill, half in and half out, the trailing *gutra* touching the hardwood floor.

Again the silence that fell after all the noise was too profound. She watched the blue-eyed man turn, focusing the gun on the hall again and then swinging it back to the windows. There was no more movement. No footsteps in the hall. No sound in the silence except their breathing. His and hers.

Finally he walked toward her, footsteps crunching over the debris the automatic weapon had cut from the wall and blown across the room. She watched him, long legs in worn jeans materializing out of the darkness. Slowly her gaze climbed upward to his face. His pale blue eyes seemed luminous in the predawn shadows. Her own, pupils wide, were finally able to see him clearly. Same harsh features. Slightly crooked nose.

"I thought the South was famous for hospitality," he

said. His tone was prosaic, infinitely calm and touched with amusement.

Hot moisture stung her eyes. Whoever he was, he had saved her life. Again. And he acted as if what had just occurred was a minor inconvenience in what was supposed to have been a visit to a sleepy little Southern town.

She blinked back the tears, ashamed to cry in the face of his nonchalance. His acceptance of the violence that had exploded around them. Of the deaths he had caused. But then, he was used to this, she thought, shivering. Accustomed to death? He must be, to do what he had just done.

He *was* dangerous. She had known that yesterday. And he was fully capable of dealing with all this. With these people. She was not. Nothing in her life had prepared her for what had happened to her the last two days.

"Are you sure that's all of them?" she asked, holding on to the calmness in his eyes. Wanting his reassurance that this was over. She wanted it *all* to be over, but she knew it wasn't, of course. At least he was here. And as long as he was… As long as he was here, she thought again, she would be safe.

"The two of them who came in the back and the driver," he said. "He was the one at the windows. He just got here a little quicker than I anticipated."

Slowly she realized the unmistakable implications of that. "You watched them?" she asked. "You watched those men come into my house?" If he had seen them come into the house, why hadn't he done something about it before they had started shooting? Why hadn't he—

"I wasn't sure why they were here," he said. "After that garbage you told me yesterday, I figured they might have just come to woo you back for another attempt at a wedding."

His tone was mocking. She had lied to him yesterday, and he knew it. She had told him she had nothing to do with what had happened in front of the hotel. That hadn't been true, of course. And now…

"I think you and I should talk," he said softly, almost as if he had read her thoughts. "And I think this time you should tell me the truth."

"About what happened yesterday?" she asked.

"For starters," he agreed.

"I saw them," she whispered. She had told him that before, but only at the end. And she had lied about all the other, at least lied by omission. "I saw the assassins," she continued, making her voice stronger, determined now to tell him all of it. "They were standing on the balcony looking down into the street in front of the hotel. I heard the shot. Then they turned around and…they saw me. I let the door close, and I ran."

"Who are *they?*" he asked.

"Two of them… I think they were bodyguards of my fiancé. There were so many of them that I never learned all their faces, but I had seen these two before. I didn't know the other man at all. He was…I think he was a Westerner. At least, he wasn't wearing a robe. He's the one who had the rifle."

Her rescuer nodded. The approaching dawn touched his fair hair with a shimmer of light. "Who sent you to get me?" he asked.

"Sent me?" she repeated. "Nobody sent me. I was… terrified because I'd seen them. I was trying to get away."

"Just an accident that it was *my* room you entered?"

"Yes," she whispered.

She knew as she said it that he didn't believe her. That was in his tone; mocking again. And even she thought it was strange that she would have chosen the room of this man. A man who had his own gun and knew how to use it. A man who knew how to get her out of a hotel that was surrounded by a million cops.

"Nothing like that *ever* happens by chance," he said. "Not to me."

But going into his room had, Tyler thought. His had been

the nearest door. She'd had a passkey. And she'd been terrified. It had been…happenstance. Random choice. Chance.

"First you just walk in on the assassins, and then you come straight to me?" he said, his voice full of sarcasm and disbelief. "You're going to have to do better than that. Like explaining where you got a passkey."

From the beginning, she thought. Maybe if she told him all of it… "I was supposed to get married," she said, her voice trembling with the need to get it out. "To Shcikh al-Ahmad's son. But…I realized I had agreed because I was afraid. I'd just let Amir talk me into it. And suddenly I realized that everything about my life would be so…"

The hesitant explanation faded because she knew he wouldn't understand what had driven her to Amir's room yesterday. *She* hadn't understood all her reasons. She had just known, almost instinctively, that what she was about to do was wrong. But that part wasn't important to him. It wasn't the truth he had demanded.

"I realized I couldn't go through with it without talking to Amir. Without making him promise…" She shook her head, knowing that wasn't relevant, either. "I knew his father was due to arrive, but I needed to see Amir before the ceremony. So I went down to the men's floor, and Malcolm Truett, Amir's secretary, said I'd just missed him. That Amir had already gone down to meet his father. He implied I shouldn't be there. That the sheikh wouldn't like it if they came back upstairs and found me on that floor."

She took a breath, thinking about what had happened next. "But I hadn't brought the key to my room with me, and Malcolm was in a hurry to run some errand Amir had sent him on.…"

She paused again, remembering that chain of events. If Malcolm had known what was going on, surely he would not have given her that passkey. It would have been too dangerous. So he couldn't have known, she realized.

"And…" the blue-eyed man prodded.

"He gave me a passkey," she said softly, still trying to make sense out of what had happened.

"Why would *he* have a passkey?"

"He arranged the hotel reservations. He was in charge of the rooms. I don't know why they would give him a key, other than convenience. Or security, maybe."

"And instead of going upstairs and using the key to get back into your own room..." her rescuer suggested, apparently having followed her disjointed narrative.

"I opened Amir's door." She hesitated, realizing that she had only assumed it was his, because Truett's eyes had moved to it when he'd told her Amir had gone downstairs. "The one Malcolm indicated was Amir's door," she corrected. "And I saw them on the terrace. I saw what they were doing."

"And they saw you?" There was no inflection in his voice.

"They saw me," she agreed softly. "I let the door close, and as it did, I heard the elevator. Malcolm had punched both buttons while we were talking. I didn't know which elevator had arrived, but I got on and when it started down, I realized I couldn't go to the lobby. I didn't know who they had shot, or even, at that point, if they had shot *anybody*. I thought it might be some kind of security thing. Protection for the sheikh. I didn't know, but by then, I had realized I couldn't do it. I couldn't marry Amir, I mean. I couldn't live like that."

The spate of words stopped again. He wouldn't care about that. About her reasons. He just wanted to know why she had pulled him into what had happened.

"So you got off the elevator..." he said.

"I slapped at the buttons, hoping it would stop. Hoping I was in time. When it did, I don't think I even knew what floor I was on. I ran toward the exit at the end of the hall. But then I heard the elevator again. The bell. I heard it behind me. I thought they were coming, so I used the passkey. I slid it into the nearest door, and…that was your room.''

He said nothing. Although the room had lightened, she couldn't read his face well enough to know whether he believed her. ''I wanted to tell you what I'd seen,'' she said. ''I tried to tell you in the restaurant.'' *And instead of answering, you kissed me.* Somehow the remembrance of that kiss seemed even more intimate, here in the darkness of her bedroom, than it had then.

''I didn't want to get you involved,'' she said. ''I didn't want to pull someone else into that, but you seemed to know what you were doing. You seemed so capable. So…''

Dangerous. The word echoed in her brain. It was what he had seemed tonight. He had saved her life again. She didn't know why. Or why he had followed her here. But she did know he had dealt with the situation tonight with the same cool competence he had used to get her out of the hotel. Despite Amir's men and all those cops.

Cops. As soon as she thought the word, the explanation for all those things occurred to her. And it made sense. Suddenly *something* made sense out of his presence here tonight. Of the fact that he had come all the way to Mississippi to find her. It even made sense of what he had done. It explained everything that had been so puzzling about this man from the beginning.

''*That's* why you're here,'' she said. He was some kind of cop, of course. It was obvious, now that she put the clues together. ''I told you in the restaurant that I saw them, and when you found out what had happened, what they had done, you came here to find out exactly what I saw.''

Her voice had risen with her growing excitement. That would explain everything. Why he carried a gun. His certainty about what would happen when the alarms went off. About how the cop on the street would react.

''You're…'' She hesitated, thinking about who they would send. FBI? CIA? She wasn't sure, but it didn't really matter who he worked for. ''You're some kind of federal agent," she said. "You're trying to find out who killed Amir's father."

She should have gone straight to the police when she left the hotel. She would have, if she hadn't been so terrified. But all she had been able to think about was getting away. Away from Amir, even if he had had nothing to do with his father's death. But now, of course...

"I'll tell them what I saw," she said. "I'll tell it to whoever you want me to." She expected some reaction, but his eyes were considering. And still cold.

His response, when it finally came, wasn't what she had expected. Again it was prosaic, in strong contrast to her sudden sense of euphoria. "You should pack a few things," he suggested.

"All right," she agreed, a little let down by his tone. But obviously he was going to take her with him. Back to New York?

"Not much. One small bag."

Those directions were as precise as the ones he had given her about getting away from the hotel yesterday. And she was more than willing to do what he told her. After all, he was one of the good guys. She'd be safe with him. Far safer than she would be here alone. Tonight had proved the fallacy of that.

"And get dressed," he said, holding his hand out. "You won't want to travel in what you're wearing."

The blue eyes, however, didn't examine the sheer nightgown. They focused instead on her face, and in the growing light of dawn, she could find nothing in them like the flare of desire she had seen yesterday.

She put her fingers into his. Hers were cold against the warmth of his hand. Soft against its callused strength. He pulled her up, but as soon as she was upright, the room began to swim. She closed her eyes, swaying toward him. He took a step nearer, pushing his body against hers. Supporting.

"You're okay. Just shock," he said. The breath from his

words, as warm as his fingers, stirred against her temple. The soft words seemed to give permission, and without having the strength to resist their invitation, she accepted, leaning into his body. Resting her forehead against his cheek.

His arms didn't enclose her. He didn't touch her in any other way, and after a moment even his fingers let go of her hand. He stepped back, but he waited a moment before he turned away, maybe to make sure that she wasn't going to faint.

That would be nice, she thought, watching him walk across the room. If she fainted, maybe her head would stop hurting and her arm wouldn't feel like it was on fire.

He disappeared into the hallway, and she closed her eyes, leaning back against the wall. Unconsciously, she rubbed at the back of her arm, wincing as she touched the area that hurt the worst. An area that was wet, she realized. She glanced down and was surprised to find that the fingers of her hand had come away covered with blood. Which was also dripping off her left elbow, a small pool of it forming on the wooden floor.

Seeing that made her light-headed again, so she closed her eyes and leaned back against the wall, wondering why her arm was bleeding, wondering what she could have hit it on to do that much damage. She didn't open her eyes until she heard him come back into the room, shoes crunching on the debris.

She watched him walk over to the man hanging over the windowsill. He reached under the headdress to check for a pulse. Apparently he didn't find one, because he gripped the back of the man's robe and pulled, jerking him up off the sill and into the room. The body crumpled bonelessly to the floor, hitting headfirst. She closed her eyes at the sickening noise, but then, curious about what he was doing, she forced them open. He was bent down beside the corpse, methodically searching it.

"Is he dead?" she asked.

"Very," he said succinctly. "They all are."

Three dead men in her mother's house. Bleeding all over Aunt Martha's spotless floors.

"What are you going to do with them?" she asked.

"Leave them." He didn't look at her.

"Maybe we should call the sheriff," she suggested hesitantly. They had to do something. You didn't just leave bodies lying around. Not in Covington, Mississippi, you didn't.

"You never know in a situation like this who you can trust."

"But why would you think that the sheriff—"

"I don't," he said. "I just don't trust many people. That's how I've managed to stay alive this long. Since that's worked well in the past, I think we'll keep playing by my rules."

The blue eyes finally lifted to her face. They were cold again, commanding obedience. And they were still full of certainty. Still absolutely sure of what he was doing.

Maybe because they were so sure, she nodded. She didn't have any choice but to play by his rules, she thought. After all, he was the one who knew what he was doing.

At her agreement, he went back to the task he'd undertaken. She wondered what he was looking for. Identification, she supposed. And she wondered suddenly if she would recognize the dead man. Could he be one of Amir's numerous bodyguards? One of the men who had been in that room yesterday?

Thinking for the first time about that possibility, Tyler pushed away from the wall, moving carefully because she didn't want to make a fool of herself by fainting. Holding her left arm against her body, the palm of her right hand cupped around the elbow, she walked over to the fallen man. There was enough light in the room now that there was no doubt.

"He's not one of them," she said. "Not one of the ones at the hotel." She had been afraid, since she had seen them so briefly, that she wouldn't be able to identify them. But there was no doubt in her mind that this man hadn't been there.

He didn't look much like a conspirator. Or a killer. He looked as if he were sleeping. Too much at peace to have died so violently. But it might just as easily have been her lying in that pool of blood, she thought. Or the man with the blue eyes.

"I don't even know your name," she said.

His eyes came up suddenly, locking with hers. They held a moment, assessing. She understood his hesitation. His caution was habitual, not personal. He was just doing his job.

"Call me Hawk," he said finally.

Not his real name. She understood that also.

"Hawk," she repeated.

"For now," he agreed, eyes holding hers.

She nodded, although she wasn't sure exactly what that meant. She had bent forward a little, arms crossed over her stomach and her shoulders hunched, giving in to the searing pain that continued to burn across the back of her arm.

"What's wrong?" Hawk asked.

Without waiting for an answer, he stood up, rising in one fluid motion, and closed the distance that separated them. Unaccountably, at his nearness she found herself thinking about yesterday, about when he'd leaned down to kiss her. About the warmth of his lips moving against hers.

"I hurt my arm," she said, looking up into his face. Remembering.

Hawk, however, apparently wasn't bothered by those same thoughts. He stuck the pistol into the waistband of his jeans, took her left arm in both hands and turned it.

Finally she looked down, pulling her gaze away from those compelling features. He was holding her upper arm toward the thin light coming in through the windows. In that position she could see the bloody slash across the back of it.

"What in the world?" she whispered.

"Looks like somebody shot you," Hawk said.

"Shot me?" The blow she had felt stumbling through the kitchen door? Could that have been—

"Or you got hit by a ricochet, maybe even one of mine. I don't suppose it makes all that much difference *how* it happened."

She looked up again at his face. His eyes were very blue, focused on hers. There was something different about them. They were not like they had ever been before. Not cold. And not heated by the sexual desire she had seen so briefly. They were full, instead, of something else.

Even as she looked at him, trying to decipher whatever was hidden in the blue depths, the control that seemed so much a part of him reasserted itself. His gaze fell, returning to the gash a bullet had plowed across the outside of her bare arm. The light, thick lashes screened his eyes. But his lips tightened, a small muscle jumping beside his mouth.

"It doesn't hurt that much. I know..." She hesitated, unsure how to phrase what she thought she should say. "I know if you did it, you didn't mean to."

Hawk's mouth relaxed slightly, his lips moving, maybe even into the beginnings of a smile, but he kept his eyes on the wound, stretching the skin around it to judge the depth. She gasped at the sudden pain and then caught her bottom lip with her teeth, determined to prevent any other reaction. He released her arm immediately.

He turned and walked back into the hall. She thought about telling him he wouldn't find anything to bandage it with, if that's what he was looking for. She wasn't sure, however, whether the people who had been hired to clean the house would have thrown away any first-aid supplies. Before she could decide, Hawk reappeared, carrying a folded dish towel. He handed it to her, but he didn't offer to look at the injury again.

"Press it against the cut until the bleeding stops. You should wash it out with some kind of antiseptic," he advised.

She nodded, obediently pressing the soft cloth against the

wound. He didn't seem too concerned. If he'd had *any* experience at all with bullet wounds, it was more than she had had, so she hoped he knew what he was talking about. And maybe there were still some aspirin in the medicine chest.

"Can you manage to pack a suitcase?" he asked.

"Of course," she said.

"Then you better get dressed and do it. I parked the rental about half a mile away. I'll go get it. You be ready when I get back." The blue eyes were cold again, once more commanding her obedience. But they were still full of certainty. Still absolutely sure of what he was doing.

Still playing by his rules, she thought. But it didn't seem she really had any other choice.

BUYING INTO THE IDEA that what had happened yesterday had been a coincidence still bothered him, Hawk thought, as he jogged to where he had parked the car. For one thing, it went against all his previous experience. And against his natural cynicism.

But Hawk had also learned a long time ago to trust his instincts about people, and they were telling him now that Tyler Stewart had told him the truth. She had dragged him into the middle of that assassination by chance. A coincidence, but one that, given his past, no one else was likely to believe in.

The one time in my life I decide to play the white knight, Hawk thought, almost amused at the realization, *and where does it get me? Into a whole hell of a lot of trouble.*

The agency believed he'd made yesterday's hit. Not a totally unreasonable assumption, considering that he'd made the one in Baghdad without their approval. Maybe they thought Griff's death had driven him over the edge. Or maybe they believed he'd taken out al-Ahmad because the sheikh had ties to the terrorist Hawk had targeted.

He couldn't know what they thought or what assumptions they were acting under. But he had been warned by a man working on the inside, with access to solid information. A man he knew he could trust.

The other thing he now knew was something he should have realized all along. Instead, he had only belatedly recognized the possibilities it presented as he had listened to the halting story she told him.

What he had finally figured out was that Tyler Stewart was the one person who could prove he had had nothing to do with that assassination. If she hadn't been involved in setting him up, then she was exactly what she had claimed—an innocent bystander. And she was all that stood between him and a death sentence. Which wouldn't, of course, be the kind they handed out in any court of law.

Hawk had already had his day in court. A long time ago. "Last chance," that old Texas judge had warned him. Luckily, Hawk had believed him. He had taken the chance he'd been offered, and it had changed his life.

This time, he knew, there would be no warning. Not any beyond the one he'd already received from Jordan Cross. *Dead serious.*

Chapter Six

"Where are we going?"

It was the first question she'd asked since they'd left the house, and Hawk had been surprised by her restraint. He had been expecting her to ask a whole lot more of them.

But she trusted him, he remembered. She thought he was some fearless federal agent who had been sent to rescue her from the assassins. Sent out to bring her in so she could give the authorities a description. It was a pleasant scenario, he supposed, and if it kept her compliant and cooperative, then far be it from him to disillusion her.

"Somewhere safe," he said.

He had been trying to think where the hell that might be. There weren't many places that were "safe" when you had the full force of the United States government on your tail. And when you were traveling with a woman who apparently had half the extremists in the Middle East trying to kill her.

"By the way," Tyler Stewart said, "I want to thank you."

"Thank me for what?" he asked. He concentrated on the road a moment, and then, when she didn't answer, he glanced at her. The violet-blue eyes, wide and sincere, surrounded by that sweep of long dark lashes, were focused on his face.

"I know I should have said it all before," she said. "Yesterday when you helped me get out of the hotel. For coming to find me. Certainly for what happened back at the house. For saving my life.'' She paused, the litany of his good deeds apparently finished.

At least I hope it is, Hawk thought. *I hope to hell that's all she's got to say.*

"I should have already told you how grateful I am, but…I guess this has thrown me. I've never been involved with anything like this before,'' she added unnecessarily.

He closed his lips, clamping them shut over the denial he wanted to make. *I came to find you because I thought you had set me up. And because I intended to force the truth about what happened yesterday out of you, any way I could.*

"If you hadn't come for me,'' she continued, her voice low, unconsciously intimate in the close confines of the car, "I know what would have happened back there. Even *with* you there…''

They had almost succeeded. She didn't say it, but that was certainly the truth. Hawk had almost let them get to her because he had been acting on the assumption that she had been in on the deal yesterday. They had almost succeeded, he thought again, remembering the gash the bullet had cut across the back of her arm. He didn't want her thanks. He sure as hell didn't deserve them. Because he hadn't come to save her. And because he was using her. He sure didn't want to listen to her gratitude over what he was supposedly doing *for* her.

"I thought I was safe back there,'' she said. "I thought they wouldn't be able to track me down.''

He said nothing, keeping his eyes resolutely on the road ahead. She had been wrong about that, of course. It hadn't taken them any longer to find her than it had taken him. Even without access to the government databases he had used. At least now she seemed to understand that part of her situation.

"So I just wanted to say thank you for taking the trouble to come for me. And for what you did back there.''

He hadn't lied to her, he reminded himself. She had come

up with the idea that he was investigating the assassination. He just hadn't corrected it. After all, he *was* a federal agent. Not the kind she was imagining him to be, of course. Not anything at all like the kind of agent she was imagining.

"It's my job," he said. Despite his cynicism, the falseness of that lie was bitter on his tongue.

She's my ace in the hole, Hawk told himself, fighting the unfamiliar surge of guilt. *My sleeve card. The only person in the world who can prove I had nothing to do with that hit. I need you, Tyler Stewart. Not the other way around.*

"Maybe so," she said, "but…forgive me if knowing that doesn't prevent me from being grateful. They would have killed me if you hadn't been there."

A real white knight, Hawk thought, mocking himself. *Just riding in for the rescue.* He wondered why he was feeling so damn guilty about this. After all, whoever had killed the sheikh really couldn't afford to have her running around telling everyone what she'd seen. Telling *anyone,* he amended.

And it hadn't taken them long to track her down. *The bad guys,* he thought, mocking her simplistic view of the world—everything in black and white. But she was right. They would have killed her. He had a brief mental picture of her body lying on the hardwood floor of that little house, blood pooling and then slowly congealing under it.

It was as simple as that, just as black and white. The lips that had been so warm yesterday when he had put his mouth—

He cleared the memory from his head, knowing he couldn't afford to think about that. Couldn't afford to think about her in that way. It had been a mistake to allow himself to touch her, as big a mistake as playing Good Samaritan, but Hawk had believed he'd never see her again. The stolen kiss had seemed a harmless, pleasant diversion for a man who hadn't had any lately.

And it had been pleasant, he acknowledged. Too pleasant, and maybe not so harmless, because it might already have affected his judgment. Hawk couldn't afford that. He didn't have time for diversions or distractions. So he had told himself that the kiss hadn't had anything to do with bringing her with him. That his decision had nothing to do with the sexuality that had flared, so strong and unexpected, between them.

His reasons had been strictly self-interest. Self-preservation. *Just covering my ass,* he reiterated, arguing against his inherent honesty. *Nothing else.* If there was the remotest possibility he could use her to clear himself with the agency, then he couldn't let some nutcases take her out.

Nutcases. The word rang sourly through his guilt, a strange choice for someone like him. Ninety-five percent of the population of this country would probably think that term applied pretty well to Hawk himself.

The good citizens of this country didn't want to acknowledge that occasionally their government needed to eliminate someone whose potential for human destruction, or whose developing taste for it, negated his right to coexist on the planet among sane people. They wouldn't want to admit that such eliminations had been carried out in the past or to think about the possibility that, human nature being what it was, there might be a need for something like that to be done again in the future.

That wouldn't be up to Hawk, of course. Deciding when such a scenario had occurred was the job of men like Griff Cabot. Had been Griff's job, Hawk amended. Past tense.

"Apparently it isn't easy for you to accept thanks for what you do," Tyler said, interrupting that introspection.

He realized he hadn't answered her. She had taken his prolonged silence for modesty, and her voice was touched with amusement.

"Sorry if I embarrassed you," she continued, "but…without you, I would have been in a whole lot of trouble back there."

Hawk fought the urge to look at her again, keeping his eyes on the road, as if its few curves and rises demanded his full attention. She was still in a lot of trouble. They both were. More trouble than she could probably imagine.

However, if being with him gave her comfort, some sense of safety, then he wasn't about to destroy that pleasant little fantasy. She *was* better off with him. Because he was better off with her alive, so he'd try very hard to keep her that way.

That's all it was, he told himself. Just a matter of practicality. Just good old cold-blooded pragmatism. Even if Tyler Stewart had looked like somebody's grandmother, he'd have taken her with him.

Of course, he admitted, if she'd looked like somebody's grandmother, they wouldn't be here. She wouldn't have been able to get away with wearing his clothes yesterday. Somehow, the remembrance of the way his jeans had looked, worn denim stretched over her slim derriere and down that incredible length of leg, sneaked back into his head. Sneaked in right past the need to think about where they were going to hole up.

"We're still in a lot of trouble," he warned.

That was the truth, and it was only fair she understand it. They might get into another situation where she needed to do exactly what she was told and do it quickly. She needed to understand that he was in charge. And he supposed she needed to keep believing his primary objective in all this was to keep her safe until she could make an identification of the assassins.

Ace in the hole, he thought. That's all she was. No more Good Samaritan. That was a lesson he had learned, and Hawk never allowed himself to forget any of the lessons life taught him.

"So where are we going?" she asked again.

"Somewhere nice and quiet where I can think," Hawk said.

"Not back to New York?"

"Not yet," he said, trying to think of a reason she'd buy. "I need to be sure it's safe to bring you in. And since there are foreign nationals involved, we may need to wait a couple of days to see what shakes out. We'll hole up somewhere.''

Hawk needed to know whether his picture was being splashed across the front pages. It wouldn't be the photo from his security file. They wouldn't use that one, of course. If any pictures had been released, they would have been the grainy shots from the hotel security cameras Jordan had told him about.

And if those pictures *were* in the papers, then Hawk would know that the manhunt was on. And he understood too well what kind of hunt it would be. After all, they couldn't afford to let him come to trial. He knew too many things they wouldn't want anyone to know. Hawk would never be allowed on any witness stand.

If they went public with the search for him, then it would mean a shoot-to-kill had been issued. One of those ''suspect is armed and dangerous'' deals. In his case, he acknowledged grimly, they'd be right.

Hawk had been more than willing to take his punishment for the unauthorized kill he'd made in Iraq. For taking down Griff's murderer. He had thought he knew what that punishment would involve. But forced retirement and a lot of unpleasantness was a long way from being the scapegoat for someone else's assassination. He remembered the pictures of Oswald being gunned down in Dallas. Those were black and whites also. Just as the grainy shots the hotel cameras produced would be.

Hawk didn't intend to be this generation's Lee Harvey Oswald. Not if he could help it, he decided. Not if there was anything at all he could do to protect himself. And in order to do that, he knew, he also had to protect the woman beside him.

''WHERE ARE WE?'' Tyler asked.

Hawk glanced at her, again feeling the impact of those remarkable eyes, despite the fact that they now reflected all she had been through the last two days. The midnight black hair was disordered, the smooth skin of her cheeks nearly devoid of color, and she was still incredibly beautiful.

At least she was awake, Hawk thought, and asking questions. Far more normal than just accepting his decisions, more normal than that implicit trust in him she'd exhibited so far.

She had slept during a lot of the long drive, and Hawk had been surprised to find himself worrying about her. In the course of the day, she had made a couple of offers to share the driving, but despite his fatigue and lack of sleep, Hawk had refused.

After what had happened in Mississippi, that unexpected barrage of gunfire in the quiet dawn, he had been expecting a state trooper to appear in his rearview mirror at any moment. He had been expecting *somebody* to show up behind them through the half-dozen states they had crossed in the course of the long day.

Hawk didn't understand why he was so edgy. It wasn't like him. He knew, at least intellectually, that there was no way they could have traced him through the ID he'd used to rent this car. Griff had supplied those identification papers, part of the kit Hawk had picked up in Alexandria. There would be no record of them with any government agency, no way in hell to trace the name on them back to the man called Hawk.

The emergency kits were something no one on the team had ever expected to have to use, but Griff had insisted they each have one. *Just in case,* Cabot had said, with that enigmatic half smile. In case of something like this, Hawk guessed.

He knew the agency would pick up his trail eventually, but it would take them a while. And the fact that no one had shown the least interest in the rental car so far was reassuring.

The last time they stopped for gas, Hawk had bought all the newspapers available at the small convenience store. He had tossed them into the back seat without taking time to read them, nothing beyond a quick scan of the headlines.

Yesterday's assassination was no longer front page headlines, not in the locals. There would be information about it inside, however, and he wanted to read everything carefully. That could wait a little longer, he had decided, knowing how close they were to the destination they had just reached.

"We're at a friend's house," Hawk explained, bringing the car to a stop at the end of the familiar road. No explanation beyond that. After all, there wasn't much more to say.

The roughness of the ride down the private road had probably awakened her. At the best of times, this was little better than a trail. Now it was potholed with washouts from the spring rains. This year, of course, no one had issued the orders for the needed repairs.

"It doesn't look as if anyone's home," she said.

Her eyes were examining the house that loomed above them. There was exhaustion in her voice. Maybe disappointment. She must have been expecting to be somewhere sanctioned and official by now. And she probably felt almost as wasted as he did, Hawk realized, in spite of the fact that she'd had some sleep. After all, she'd been shot, she had finally had to come to grips with the fact that someone was trying to kill her, and she had watched three men die. Then she'd been dragged halfway across the country by a total stranger.

By a stalwart federal agent hot on the trail of the assassins. By a hero who was supposed to be taking her somewhere she'd be safe. Where she would help him catch the bad guys. *White knight,* Hawk thought. Again the image rankled.

She turned to face him, probably because he had been simply watching her instead of answering her question. The fragile skin around her eyes was slightly discolored, yellowed like old bruises. The eyes themselves, however, were clear and bright.

And maybe a little too bright. Fever? Hawk wondered. Not this soon, he reasoned, reassuring himself. It might not happen at all, if she'd done what he'd told her and cleaned the wound with antiseptic. Even if she hadn't, it probably wouldn't make much difference. After all, the furrow the bullet had cut in her arm was little more than a deep scratch.

"No one's home," he acknowledged.

His reluctance to answer had nothing to do with her question. It was just a reality he preferred not to think about. Now, he realized, he would be forced to. He hadn't been planning on coming here when they left Mississippi. He had simply headed east, homing instinct. But when he had remembered Griff's place a few hours ago, it seemed perfect. An answer to their every need. For a few days, anyway.

This old house was what people like the Cabots called a summer home. Its irregular collection of towers and jutting roof lines perched above an isolated stretch of rock-strewn Virginia beach, looking as if it might tumble into the green churn of the Atlantic below with the first storm. It hadn't, of course. Not in the hundred years or so since it had been built.

Hawk had come here occasionally with Griff. Once or twice with the others—the members of the team. They had come to plan. Or to debrief. To celebrate.

Once Griff had brought him here after a mission that had gone wrong. Brought him here to recuperate. That time was something else Hawk didn't want to remember, so with the ease of long practice, he pushed the thought out of his head, closing and locking mental doors that shouldn't have been opened.

The house had a modern security system, of course, the best money could buy, but Hawk knew all the codes. He was good with numbers, good at remembering them. So unless someone had taken the trouble to change things, he could get them in. And once inside, they'd be safe. It would be the perfect hideout, at least until Hawk could get a handle on what was going down.

"Come on," he ordered softly.

Without waiting for her to obey, he opened the door and climbed out of the car, legs stiff from long hours behind the wheel. He opened the back door and retrieved the suitcase she'd brought and then led the way up the steep path to the steps.

He was conscious that she was climbing slowly, lagging behind him, but he didn't look back. While she slept during the drive, Hawk had acknowledged something pretty damn disturbing. He liked looking at Tyler Stewart. Liked it a lot. And that was dangerous. Just like the kiss that never should have happened, his attraction to this woman had no place in what was going on.

This was no different than a mission. He had never allowed himself to indulge physical appetites while on assignment. That was simply another form of discipline, and Hawk understood all about discipline. It was something else, like death and danger, with which he had a long and intimate acquaintance. Abstinence was simply another aspect of that.

When he reached the top of the steps, Hawk walked across the wooden veranda and punched the code into the incongruous security pad by the front door. The doorknob turned under his hand, and relieved, he pushed it inward. Apparently the house hadn't been sold. At least nobody had changed the codes.

The interior was dark, the air inside hinting at mildew and coastal dampness. The prospect it offered wasn't inviting, but then he hadn't expected a welcoming committee. Griff Cabot was dead. No one else was in residence. Which was exactly why they were here.

"Are you sure this is okay?" Tyler asked, her question mirroring his hesitation. She was standing on the porch behind him, looking into the house through the open door.

Hawk realized that he had hesitated on the threshold because he was dreading this confrontation. He was putting off facing his ghosts, he supposed. And she had taken her cue from his reluctance.

"You have a better idea?" he asked sharply, his voice tight and hard with the unexpected force of those emotions. Without waiting for her answer, he stepped inside. The house was exactly as he remembered, except the familiar pieces of furniture were now covered with white cotton holland covers, their massive, indistinct shapes ghostly in the dimness.

Griff's house. It would be full of reminders. Of him. Of the close-knit team he'd built. Memories of what they had accomplished together. Of friendships. Some of those already destroyed, perhaps, by what Hawk had been accused of. Not the Iraqi assassination, but the other. Going rogue. Operating outside the careful limits Cabot had set.

But worrying about that was something else he didn't have time for, Hawk told himself. The battle that was coming would demand control and a cold, clear-eyed logic. Not emotion. Not of any kind.

"Your friend's not been here in a while, I would guess," Tyler said from behind him.

Again, Hawk explained nothing and offered no information. "I'm going to pull the car into the garage. You can go on upstairs. Pick out a bedroom. I'll bring your suitcase up when I finish."

She nodded, her gaze moving slowly around the entry hall and the formal parlor that lay through the opened doors on the right. "You think your friend might have some aspirin?" she asked.

"Probably," he said. "Headache?"

She turned her head, her eyes meeting his and holding them a moment. She nodded and then looked away again, pretending to examine the shadowed furnishings.

"Your arm?" he said.

She had been holding her left elbow in the palm of her right hand again, so that her arms were crossed over her stomach. She released her hold at his question, but she didn't straighten the injured arm. "It's a little sore," she admitted.

There was pain medication here, he knew. He had been given some the last time he'd come. That time he didn't want to remember. "There's probably some kind of pain-killer around," he said. "I'll find you something when I've hidden the car."

"Thank you," she said.

She started toward the staircase, its rosewood banisters curving gracefully toward the shadows of the second floor. As she walked, she again cupped her elbow, holding the arm against her body. When she reached the foot of the stairs, she released it to put her right hand on the railing, and began to climb.

Too slowly, Hawk thought. Again he felt that same touch of unease as when she had been sleeping in the car. Especially when he contrasted those careful movements to the way she had moved yesterday. There were all kinds of logical explanations for the anxiety that was stirring unpleasantly in his gut, beginning with the fact that Tyler Stewart was the one person who could clear him of al-Ahmad's assassination, and the knowledge that the assassins didn't intend for her to tell anyone what she had seen.

Those were reasons enough to be worried about the effects of her injury. Reasons enough even if he were unwilling to acknowledge the true cause of his apprehension. Hawk had buried that, too. Buried it with the feelings that being back in this house had evoked.

He realized suddenly that she had stopped on the first landing. She was looking down at him. Probably wondering what the hell he was doing standing here watching her. Just watching her, as he had in the car. That was becoming a habit, Hawk thought, angry at himself. At his lack of control.

As he had told her, there were things he needed to do. Priorities, he reminded himself. First things first. Hawk turned away, retracing his steps through the front door.

He brought the newspapers and his bag into the house this time. He spent a few minutes making sure the security system was rearmed, and checking everything out downstairs before he picked them up again, along with Tyler's suitcase, which was still sitting by the front door, and climbed the stairs to the second floor.

He called her name when he reached the top. The only answer was the slight echo the solid wood walls threw back at him. Finally he started opening doors. He put the papers and his bag in the same suite he'd occupied during those long weeks of convalescence. And he found the pain medication he'd left behind, still in the drawer of the table by the bed. There were at least a half dozen of the big white capsules left.

Taking them with him, he continued to open doors. He found her in the fourth suite. Its bedroom was large and pleasant, decorated in shades of rose. An old-fashioned mahogany four-poster dominated the center of the room.

Tyler was lying across it. She was stretched out on her right side, eyes closed. She hadn't undressed or turned back the coverlet, and she didn't move when he opened the door. Hawk walked over the faded Oriental rug and set her suitcase down at the foot of the bed. The rug was thick enough that she might not have heard him, but again Hawk felt an unaccustomed flare of anxiety. She looked exhausted. Sick. Too damn vulnerable.

"Tyler," he said softly. Slowly, in response to her name, her eyes opened.

"Did you find some aspirin?" she asked. Her tone was calm and rational, completely normal.

Hawk took a breath in relief. He didn't know why he had been so concerned. Maybe because he didn't have much experience with illness or injury. Other than his own infrequent ones—and those he usually ignored.

"Something better," he said, holding the brown plastic prescription bottle up to show her. "Pain pills."

She pushed up, propping herself on the elbow of her uninjured arm, but her movements were careful. There had been enough time, Hawk knew, for swelling and soreness to set in. Any movement probably hurt like hell.

He walked to the side of the bed, opening the bottle and rolling two of the big capsules into his hand. He held them out to her. She looked up at his face, eyes searching it quickly before they fell to the medicine.

She didn't reach for the capsules for a moment, and when she did, she used her left hand. Her fingers trembled slightly when she picked them off his outstretched palm, but he was relieved to see her use the arm at all.

"Could I have some water, please?" she asked softly.

He nodded and headed to the bathroom. He remembered swallowing the pills dry, as large as they were. Reaching for them in the middle of the night, hand trembling as hers had done, when the pain had gotten too bad to endure.

By the time he got back with the water, she had managed to sit up, shoulders propped against the pillows she'd stacked together against the headboard. However, her head was back and her eyes were again closed.

In the low light from the bedside lamp, Hawk could see the tracery of blue veins in the thin, nearly transparent skin of her eyelids, and even the small network of lines around them. He had never noticed those before, and they, too, made her seem vulnerable. More…real, somehow. No longer like the images he'd seen on the computer screen, but just a woman, like any other woman he'd ever known.

"Tyler," he said, offering the glass.

Her eyes opened immediately. She had been holding the capsules in her right hand, and she put them into her mouth before she reached for the water. She drank all of it, drank it as if she had been really thirsty.

Fever? Hawk wondered again, resisting the urge to put his fingers against her forehead to find out. That was another temptation it would be better to avoid.

"Thank you," she said, finally looking up at him.

"I brought your suitcase up," he said, without acknowledging her thanks. Belatedly, he was wondering if he should have given her two of the capsules. That was the prescribed dosage for him, for his weight. Not for her thin fragility.

These pills had been pretty potent, he remembered. He had spent a lot of time sleeping during the weeks he'd been forced to take them. Of course, that sleep might simply have been another form of escape, and not so much the result of the medication.

"Thanks," she said again, her eyes were still on his face.

She seemed to be waiting for whatever else he intended to say. Only, Hawk couldn't think of anything else. All he could think of was how fragile she seemed. How damned vulnerable.

"I should probably look at your arm," he suggested.

Her eyes widened slightly, again searching his. That had surprised her. And it made him examine his own motives. He had a vested interest in her health, he reminded himself. And since there was no one else around to take care of her...

"You need some help getting your clothes off?" he asked.

She was still watching his face. Slowly her lips tilted, and the surprise that had been in her eyes was replaced by amusement.

"I think I'd be worried if that offer had come from anyone else," she said. "Other than you," she added softly. "Thanks, but I can still manage my own clothes." She had cleared the amusement from her voice, but it lingered in her eyes. "But before you go, you could put my suitcase on the bed for me?"

Hawk hadn't thought about how his offer might be interpreted. He had been surprised by the quiet humor that had infused her response. Or by its implication. For a second, he had been at a loss about how to respond. But her request for the case seemed to make a response unnecessary. And it gave him an excuse to move. Away from her. Away from the charged atmosphere.

Or maybe that was only in his head, he thought, as he

walked to the foot of the bed and picked up the bag. Maybe there had been no other connotation in her words, and when he repeated them mentally, he couldn't really find anything sexual. But he had felt it. It had been in her eyes.

Still thinking about exactly what he had seen there, he set the suitcase down on the bed beside her. He unzipped it before he looked up. Her eyes were impassive now. Calm and ordinary.

''Thank you,'' she said again, smiling at him. There was no provocation in this smile. When he didn't return it, after a moment her eyes fell and, one-handed, she began going through the clothing in the bag. She didn't look up at him again.

Hawk watched a few seconds longer, and then, realizing that he was doing it again, he turned and left the bedroom, closing the door behind him to give her some privacy.

Chapter Seven

When Hawk knocked on that same door almost thirty minutes later, he had managed a hot shower and had finally changed out of the clothes he'd been wearing for the last two days. Despite the cumulative effects of the lack of sleep, he felt better, more like himself. And more in control.

Tyler gave him permission to enter, and when he did, he was relieved to find she was sitting up in the bed. The pillows were still stacked behind her, but this time she had folded the comforter down across the foot of the bed. The sheet had been pulled up to her waist.

She was wearing a sleeveless nightgown, not, of course, the same one she'd been wearing this morning. That had been blue. He remembered he'd had a hell of a time keeping his eyes off the low neckline that edged just below the beginning swell of her breasts. This one was white, and the fabric seemed a little more substantial. At least he couldn't see either the shape or the rose-tinged darkness of her nipples through it.

When he realized what he'd been thinking, Hawk pulled his attention back to her face. Too damn pale. And she was cradling the injured arm again, the elbow resting once more in the steadying palm of her right hand.

"Ready for me to take a look at that?" Hawk asked, gesturing toward her body with a lift of his chin. He could see that the wound was covered by a thick gauze pad, heavily stained with blood. It was dark, however, and not fresh. Which meant this was probably the same pad she had put over it before they left Mississippi this morning.

She nodded, shifting her weight to make a place for him to sit on the bed beside her. That wasn't what he'd intended, but he supposed it was natural in this situation. It would allow him to get close enough to examine the injury without making her move any more than was necessary. It would also put him close enough to examine a lot of other things, he thought. Too close for comfort. Finally, however, he eased down on the bed beside her.

She raised her eyes to his, still trusting. Depending on him to take care of her. To take care of everything. Almost annoyed by that unquestioning trust, Hawk deliberately broke the contact by looking down at her arm.

"It's going to hurt like hell when I take this off," he warned. He was touching the corner of the gauze pad, and his fingers looked very dark in contrast to its whiteness.

"I know," she said.

"You want it quick or slow?" he asked.

His mother used to ask him that when he was a kid. Back when she'd still been taking care of him and not the other way around. She had always asked that same question before she pulled off a bandage. Hawk always chose quick, but he was that kind. The "do what you have to do and I'll deal with it" kind.

He looked up from the stained gauze to find Tyler's lips tilting again, their upward alignment subtle, almost a smile. And what he found in her eyes was what he had seen there before.

Despite the harshness of his features, there was apparently something about him that women found intriguing. Hawk had seen this same unspoken invitation in a lot of eyes through the years. Had seen it too many times to be mistaken about what it meant.

"Either way," she said softly. "I don't have a preference. Whichever way you want to do it is fine with me."

He wondered if that was supposed to be the double entendre his brain was suggesting. Even if it were, however, he had already made his decision about that. Not the time or the place. Not the woman. Definitely not the situation.

He grasped the gauze he had touched so lightly before and jerked it off. The cloth ripped from the gash with a sound that was audible. As was her gasp of pain. When he looked up, she had locked those even white teeth into her bottom lip, and her eyes were brimming with tears.

"Sorry," Hawk said, disgusted with himself. He had done that deliberately, and it had been nothing less than an act of cruelty, like kicking a kitten. He even knew *why* he had done it. Because he needed to destroy whatever image seemed to be building up in her mind about who and what he was.

He was no Good Samaritan. Nobody's white knight. She needed to figure that out, and maybe, he thought, she needed a little help doing it. When she had, there would be no more of the kind of invitation he had just read in her eyes.

"It's okay," she said softly. "Quick is better, I guess."

There was no anger in her voice. She didn't seem to be blaming him for the pain he'd just inflicted. Maybe she hadn't realized he was bastard enough to want to hurt her because he believed she was attracted to him. Or maybe, he thought, inherently honest, he had hurt her because she was a temptation he was having a hard time denying.

Angry with himself even if she wasn't, Hawk looked down at the wound. His lips flattened at what he saw. Because he'd ripped off the bandage, the slash was oozing blood again.

The area around it was red and swollen. He put his fingers, gently this time, next to the damaged skin. They looked as out of place against the cream of her arm as they had touching the white gauze. He could feel the heat of infection beneath the smooth surface.

"Did you wash this out with antiseptic?" he asked. He

didn't add, *like I told you to,* but it was implied. And she would know it.

"I couldn't find anything. I tried to clean it with soap and water, but apparently…"

He didn't look up. Instead, he pressed the swollen areas around the gash, using her breathing to gauge how sore it was. Her soft inhalations were uneven, sometimes sharply drawn, but none as obvious as the first gasp had been.

"I brought some salve," he said finally. The wound wasn't too badly infected, he decided. More painful than dangerous. "That should help it heal. Maybe even help with the soreness."

Hawk opened the first-aid kit and took the antibiotic ointment out. He slipped his left hand under her arm, lifting and turning it toward him. Her skin was still cool, incredibly soft against the hardness of his fingers. He ignored the sensation and squeezed a thick thread of salve along the track the bullet had made. Then, with his right forefinger, he rubbed the ointment into the torn flesh. He became aware that she was holding her breath as he worked. It took him a couple of seconds to realize he'd been doing the same thing.

"Almost through," he said in reassurance, as he recapped the tube of salve and laid it back in the kit. Using his teeth, he tore the top off one of the cellophane envelopes that held sterile dressings and awkwardly removed a new piece of gauze. He laid the dressing over the gash, pressing it into the salve to make sure it would stay. Finally, he put a strip of adhesive tape across the top and bottom.

"We'll see how it looks in the morning." He replaced the tape in the kit and turned back to find that she was looking down at his handiwork.

"Boy Scouts?" she asked, her eyes lifting from the neat bandage to his. That same smile played around her lips again.

"I was *never* a Boy Scout," he said, holding her eyes. Another warning, if she was smart enough to take it.

"Military?" she suggested, apparently undaunted by his tone. Her eyes held, waiting for an answer. Almost demanding one.

"The less you know about me, the better."

"You could tell me, but then you'd have to kill me. I saw that movie." Her voice was rich with amusement, and the smile had widened.

Playing games, Hawk thought, inexplicably angered by the fact that she could smile. Could still think this was all some big adventure. Despite the fact that she had a bullet wound in her arm. Despite the fact that some very ruthless people were trying to kill her so she wouldn't be able to identify them. Despite the fact that she was being used by a government assassin trying to clear himself of a murder charge.

She couldn't know that, of course. She didn't know anything about him, about who he was, and that was exactly the way Hawk intended to keep it.

"I guess I owe you another thank-you," she said. "The list of things I owe you for is getting pretty long."

"You don't owe me anything," he said. He closed the lid to the first-aid kit with a snap and stood up. The quicker he got out of here and let her get some rest, the better. The better for both of them. Of course, he still had a few things to take care of before he could allow himself to make up any lost sleep.

"Why is that so hard for you?" she asked softly. His eyes, when he looked up, must have reflected his question because she added, clarifying, "Why is it so hard for you to accept thanks for what you do?"

Because whatever I do is strictly motivated by self-interest. Hawk wondered what she would say if he told her that. "You better get some sleep," he said instead. "The pain pills should help."

She held his eyes so that he was again forced to break the contact. He turned and walked back across the faded carpet to the door. She didn't speak again until his hand was on the knob.

"Marines?"

He turned, slanting a look at her over his shoulder. From this distance, the effects of the last thirty-six hours weren't that evident. She looked a lot like the bride who'd invaded his hotel suite. Almost too beautiful to be real.

"A few good men," she said. "I think that would probably appeal to you. I think it certainly fits."

There had been the slightest slur to her words. Apparently, the capsules he'd given her were taking effect. He'd check on her when he came back upstairs—before he chose one of the beds up here and passed out on it. She'd be asleep by then. That would be safer. A whole lot safer for both of them, he decided.

A few good men. For some reason the phrase kept repeating in his consciousness as he went down the stairs, taking them two at a time despite his tiredness. But that was not something that applied to him, Hawk thought. He was not in that category. And he never had been.

HAWK HAD CONSIDERED the wisdom of making this call a long time before he finally dialed the number. But an offer of help had been extended. At the time, Hawk had believed he'd never have to take advantage of it. He didn't like being obligated to anybody. However, he needed information the newspapers hadn't provided. He had read them all, sitting in Griff's study as the summer darkness finally closed in.

And there was really no reason not to call, he'd finally decided. The phone line from the summer house would be secure, and he knew that whatever line Jordan Cross was using would be secure as well. He would never have given him this number if it weren't, Hawk thought, listening to the distant ringing.

As soon as Cross answered, Hawk asked, without identifying himself, "Your offer still good?" He had decided on no preliminaries. He needed a couple of favors, and if

Jordan had developed any qualms in the last twenty-four hours, Hawk wanted to know about them. He thought he'd be able to tell by Jordan's first unguarded reaction. What Hawk heard, however, was only silence. It went on long enough to make him uncomfortable. Just before he decided to break the connection, Jordan spoke.

"Of course," he said. "Whatever you need. You know that."

This time the silence was on Hawk's end as he tried to decide how sincere that agreement had been. But he really didn't have all that many options, he told himself. There was no room in this situation for his stubborn pride, because his was not the only life at stake. If it had been, he acknowledged, he'd never have made this call. And, he admitted, that was another effect on this situation that Tyler had had. Because of her, Hawk could no longer afford to be a loner.

"Just information," he said finally.

"Shoot."

"How'd you hear they had fingered me for New York?"

"There was talk here. It appeared to be solid."

Here would mean within the CIA. "Someone on the team mention it?" he asked.

"As a matter of fact…" Jordan hesitated, maybe trying to remember. "A couple of people. There was speculation that it had something to do with what you'd done in Iraq."

"Who knew about Iraq?"

"It didn't take much to figure that out. I knew it had to be you as soon as the news broke. Most of the team would know. Most of the company would probably suspect we had something to do with the hit, given Griff's death and the guy's reputation."

"And the one in New York?"

"You showed up on the security tapes."

"Why would the company review those tapes?"

"I don't know. Maybe they didn't. Maybe that came from outside. Whoever made you, it didn't take long for the fact you had been in that hotel that morning to get around."

Any leaks within the agency—the "company" to insiders—were deliberate, just as they were in the rest of the government.

"We figured that *if* you did it, al-Ahmad must have been involved in the Langley massacre. Maybe financial backing or something."

"He wasn't involved," Hawk said, his voice full of surety. He had gotten the man responsible for that. The one in Baghdad. The one who had given the orders. As far as he had been able to discover, there had been no one else in on the deal in any way.

"Then maybe they just plan to use what happened in New York to bring you down. Then they won't have to admit they were going to let Griff's killer get away with it and were even going to punish the man who had decided he wasn't."

Hawk had known that's how the agency would react and had accepted it. But coming after him personally, as Jordan had warned him they were after New York, was something he hadn't counted on and didn't understand.

"They haven't released the pictures from the hotel cameras," Hawk said. Those pictures had been one thing he'd been looking for when he'd bought the newspapers. And he hadn't found them.

"It's coming," Jordan said softly, probably knowing this was the worst news Hawk could receive. "Somehow Amir al-Ahmad found out that the hotel has pictures of whoever set off the fire alarms. He wants them made public. He's demanding we go all out to find that man."

"So why haven't they?" Hawk asked.

"The company's making sure no one can possibly trace the man in those pictures back to the agency. If anyone does, there are bound to be accusations of a CIA plot. Given the volatility of the region, there's no telling what reaction that might set off."

"They really think I hit the sheikh?"

"Maybe," Jordan said. "They know it was you in Baghdad."

Still, in spite of whatever pressure Amir al-Ahmad was exerting, there seemed to be no reason the CIA would go public with a hunt for one of its own agents—and a lot of reasons not to. Especially given the things Hawk knew.

"Any other rumors about New York?" he asked. "About who might really have been involved?"

"You're the only rumor circulating here on that one, my friend," Cross told him. His voice was slightly amused. "The sheikh's son is claiming the assassination was an attempted coup. The fundamentalists hit the sheikh. The son's out of the country. Perfect opportunity for them to take over. He may be right. We don't have any reports of anything happening in his country, but al-Ahmad had for years been resisting attempts by the extremists to loosen his control. And there *have* been two previous attempts on his life."

The stakes in that struggle were very high, Hawk knew. The income from the oil produced ran into the billions of dollars annually, most of that becoming the personal property of the al-Ahmad family. Although the standard of living in their country was fairly high, there was no doubt the royal family benefitted far more than the people from that valuable natural resource. The extremists wanted to change that situation.

In the last year or so, al-Ahmad had lived as almost a prisoner to his wealth. And the strategy had apparently worked. Until he had agreed to come to the States to attend his son's wedding. A serious error in judgment.

"I need some background," Hawk said, remembering what Tyler had told him. "What do you know about Amir al-Ahmad?"

"That he lives well," Jordan said. "His tastes run to expensive toys and beautiful women. The model for a bachelor playboy. Most people were surprised he was planning to settle down. Everybody figured there must have been pressure from the old man, but the bride didn't seem to be someone the sheikh would have picked out. Wrong religion. Wrong nationality.''

''His father was coming to the wedding,'' Hawk said.

''To everyone's surprise. However, he and the son were close. Amir was being groomed to take over, but not for a while. The sheikh was a vigorous man in his late fifties. He could have lived another thirty years or so.''

With Amir waiting in the wings, Hawk thought. ''The son have any ties to the extremists?'' Hawk asked.

''Not except as a target,'' Jordan said. Then, because he was smart, the point of that question hit him. ''You think he had something to do with his father's death?''

''I don't know,'' Hawk said.

''Maybe the company does,'' Jordan suggested.

''Maybe,'' Hawk said, thinking about the possibilities. ''Could you put together a file for me? Everything that's public on both Ahmads. And everything the company's got that's not.''

Again there was the smallest hesitation. Hawk felt that prickling of unease until he heard Cross's suggestion.

''I can ask Jake Holt. I don't have to tell him who it's for.'' Jake was another of Cabot's team, and the kind of search Hawk had just requested was his specialty. By the time Holt got through, there wouldn't be a shred of information in any file on the al-Ahmads he hadn't dug out.

''Okay,'' Hawk agreed.

''Anything else?'' Jordan asked.

Hawk hesitated, knowing in his gut there was too much about this whole thing that didn't add up.

''There was a witness,'' he said.

The pause was longer this time, but the implications were obvious. ''A witness to the assassination?'' Jordan said.

''Someone who saw three men in one of the rooms Amir al-Ahmad had rented. She saw one of them fire a rifle off that balcony. A witness who isn't mentioned in any of the papers, although someone was searching the hotel for her within minutes.''

"Can she identify the men she saw?"

"It's possible," Hawk said, wishing that he'd taken more care with his pronouns.

"It may not matter," Jordan warned. "Not as far as the company's concerned."

Hawk understood the warning. They intended to rein Hawk in, one way or another.

"It might matter to them if I go public," Hawk suggested.

There was silence at the other end. Hawk could imagine what Jordan Cross was thinking.

"You don't mean that," Jordan said finally.

"I don't owe anybody any loyalty," Hawk said, remembering the years Cabot had worked to put this team in place, and how quickly after his death they had decided to dismantle it. "Not anymore. They're setting me up to take the heat for something they know I didn't do."

"Maybe they don't know," Cross said.

"Then there's too much they don't know," Hawk said bitterly. "About me. About what we did."

"Get out," Jordan suggested. "Just get out of the country and stay out. Disappear. You can do that."

"And have them send somebody like you after me?" Hawk asked, his voice mocking, but unamused.

"It won't be me. I can promise you that."

The corners of Hawk's lips lifted a little at the quiet assurance. "But it *will* be somebody," he said. "I know how that works. And in the meantime…" For some reason Hawk hesitated, reluctant to mention that he had the witness with him, although he had trusted this man with his life on more than one occasion. "I'll check back with you in a day or two," he said.

"Ask for a meeting."

"They'd never go for it," Hawk said, thinking for the first time about the possibility.

"They might. If you can really produce a witness who saw someone else pull the trigger…" Jordan paused, letting the suggestion sink in.

It was risky, but it might work. They wouldn't want Hawk talking. He was one of the people who really knew too much. Too much about things the government didn't want the public to find out about. Things the press would love to get hold of. As a matter of fact, Hawk realized, the media might be a valuable ally, if it came down to that kind of battle.

"I'll think about it," Hawk promised, knowing now that it had been suggested, he really would. Going public about the secrets he'd willingly kept all these years went against every principle he had lived by. And besides, a meeting with the agency would solve both his problems. It would provide a forum where Tyler could clear him of al-Ahmad's assassination, and then... Then the agency could provide some real protection for her from the assassins. Whoever they were.

Hawk knew it would be tricky to arrange a face-to-face without putting himself in a position where he no longer had any control. He wasn't sure of the agency's agenda where he was concerned. Still, it was an idea worth considering. Especially when he realized that right now he didn't have another one.

"By the way," Hawk said, "I need an ID on some bodies."

"Bodies?" Jordan repeated. "Plural?"

"I left three of them in a vacant house in a little town called Covington. That's in Mississippi. Maybe somebody's discovered them by now. If not, give the locals an anonymous tip that they should be looking. Then see if you can find out who they worked for."

"Connected to the assassination?"

"I think so," Hawk said. He would be willing to bet that the three worked for Amir al-Ahmad, considering that two of his bodyguards had apparently been in on the hit against the sheikh, and it had been made from one of Amir's rooms. That was according to Tyler. But none of that had been in any of the papers, either.

"You *think* so?"

"That's why I need an ID," Hawk said.

"You kill 'em?"

"Only because they were trying real hard to kill me," Hawk said innocently, and listened to another brief silence.

"How do I reach you when I have something?" Cross asked.

"I'll call you."

"Give me twenty-four hours."

"I owe you," Hawk said softly, knowing how true that was.

"You don't owe me anything," Jordan said. "I told you. You can call in a lot of favors. Count this as one of them."

Hawk thought about expressing his gratitude, not just for what Cross was doing, but for the fact that he still believed in him. In spite of what the agency was suggesting.

Instead of giving in to that impulse, Hawk put the phone gently back in its cradle and sat a moment, thinking about the conversation. At least he had put something into motion. And for tonight, this seemed to be all he could do. His brain dull with fatigue, he couldn't think of anything else.

His gaze moved over the surface of Griff's desk. It was as neat and ordered as the man himself. Hawk's eyes circled the room: to an overstuffed sofa, invitingly placed in front of the fireplace; floor-to-ceiling bookshelves crammed with leather-bound volumes; carefully chosen paintings. All of it tasteful. Reflecting the Cabot wealth. But there was almost nothing personal, Hawk realized. Nothing really of Griff.

There was one silver-framed photo on the desk. It was a color snapshot of a child. A little girl, a blue-eyed blonde, who looked about six years old. Her age was pretty easy to determine because the broad grin revealed two missing front teeth.

Not Griff's child, Hawk knew. Cabot had never married, despite the fact that he had been in love with Claire Heywood for years. A man in Griff's position made a lot of enemies. Some of them ruthless enough to use a loved one. For blackmail. Or as a target for retaliation.

That was one reason most of the members of the team didn't have dependents. Or, like Cabot, took care to see that any emotional ties they formed remained hidden, the people they cared about safe. Maybe that explained why there was nothing of Claire in this room. Or maybe, Hawk realized, that was simply because Griff didn't want any reminders of what had happened between them.

The ending of their relationship had been Claire's decision, Hawk knew. It would never have been Cabot's. Not unless he thought that who he was might endanger her in some way. But Griff had been very careful to see that didn't happen.

Hawk picked up the picture of the child, studying the face a moment before he realized what he was looking at. He had believed that there were no pictures here of the woman Griff Cabot had loved. He'd been wrong. But few people would ever associate this snaggle-toothed little girl with Claire Heywood today, Hawk thought, as he put the photo back on the desk. That this picture was still here, despite the severing of their relationship, was a gesture as enigmatic as Cabot himself had been. Cool, pragmatic, infinitely careful, and yet…

Romantic, Hawk's brain supplied. It was not a word he would ever before have applied to his friend. He had thought they were cut from the same cloth. Cynical. Realistic about the world they lived in. It was surprising to realize Hawk hadn't understood all the facets of the man he had worked with so closely. The only man he had ever considered a friend.

BEFORE HE WENT UPSTAIRS, Hawk made a final check of the house. As he did, he acknowledged that he couldn't remember ever being this tired, this burned out. It was not just lack of sleep, he knew, although the effects of the few hours he'd grabbed on the flight from Virginia had long ago worn off. Hawk had been shortchanged on sleep a lot of times, and he knew what that felt like. This was deeper. As much mental as physical.

Part of it was letdown from the end of his months-long quest to find Cabot's murderer. That desire had been a white-hot flame that flared so brightly it had kept him going, almost without having to think. Now he was, and none of the things he was thinking about were pleasant.

Like the realization that the agency he worked for was ready to betray him. To sic the dogs on him. Despite what he had done for them through the years, they were playing with Hawk's life, because he had disobeyed an order.

An order that hadn't made any sense in the first place, he thought, turning off the light when he reached the top of the staircase and plunging the house into darkness. All except for the faint glow coming from down the hall. From the bedroom Tyler Stewart had chosen.

He needed to check on her before he crashed, he remembered. He had promised himself he would. She'd be asleep by now. He'd take one last look. Check for fever. Then he'd turn off the lamp beside her bed and leave her alone.

One last job to perform. Then he would relax his vigilance, shut off the analytical mind, which insisted on going over and over the events of the last two days, and sleep. One final duty.

HER HEAD WAS TURNED slightly to the side on the pillow. She was still holding the elbow of the injured left arm protectively in the palm of her other hand. And she was so beautiful.

Nobody who had been through what she had the last two days should look like this. That was exactly what he had been thinking in the car today. Her mouth should fall open as she slept, the muscles in her face lax and unattractive. There should even be the occasional soft snore. A trickle of saliva.

There damn well should be something that made her as

human as the rest of us, Hawk thought. And there wasn't. His lips tightened, remembering how she'd looked when he'd stolen those forbidden glances at the passenger seat. Just like she did now. Like some damn sleeping beauty. Fairy-tale princess. *A model,* he thought in disbelief. Just my luck to get my ass caught in a crack with a woman like this.

Except, surprisingly, he had found she had a brain. And guts. He would have to give her that, he admitted. She might not have managed on her own to escape this morning, but she'd given them a run for their money. She hadn't rolled over and played dead. She hadn't done that at the hotel, either. And for somebody whose life was as far removed from all this as hers must have been, that was something.

Despite his tiredness, Hawk hesitated a few minutes longer, standing just inside the door of the bedroom. The soft light from the lamp highlighted the high cheekbone turned toward him, emphasizing the intriguing hollow underneath. It exposed the shadows of exhaustion around her eyes, her long lashes resting against them like a fan.

The light also played over the delicate curve of her jaw. It gleamed in the blue-black hair, which was spread like a skein of tangled silk over the pillows. Even against their whiteness, her skin looked like alabaster. Almost translucent.

He thought about closing the door and leaving. Safest thing, he told himself again, but he had come here to check on her. To make sure she was all right. And it was all just a matter of discipline. Another job. One last duty before he could sleep, he reiterated. He crossed the thick carpet toward the bed, his footsteps soundless.

The sleeper didn't stir. The fan of lashes didn't quiver, and her breathing was deep and regular, moving the small, perfect breasts slowly up and down under the fabric of her gown.

When he reached the bed, Hawk stood for another moment looking down at her. From here, he could see again the subtle signs of maturity revealed in her face. The telltale effects of the years. She must be at least in her late thirties, he thought, judging by those lines and creases.

Not as young as he'd imagined in the beginning. He had thought she was a girl when he'd first seen her. She wasn't, of course. She was a woman. The only problem was Hawk liked women. Preferred them, in fact. He always had.

Almost without thinking, he put the back of his bent fingers against her cheek. And was relieved to find the skin was cool. Incredibly smooth. Despite his touch, she didn't awaken. The capsules he'd given her had done their job. Between their effects, her exhaustion and the injury, she was out like a light. Good for the duration.

Hawk removed his fingers and stood beside the bed, his hands hanging loosely at his side. Controlled. Then, his eyes never leaving the face of the woman, he bent forward and turned off the lamp on the table, plunging this room, too, into darkness. He took a step backward, away from the bed. Away from the temptation she represented.

But he didn't leave. After a few seconds, his eyes had adjusted to the lack of light in the room. The first thing they picked out of the gloom was the pale perfection of her profile, framed by that black-as-midnight hair. Then the slender column of her throat. Exposed. Vulnerable. And finally, almost naturally somehow, they found again the regular rise and fall of her breasts.

Unaware of the passage of time, Hawk didn't know how long he stood watching her sleep. Thinking about things he couldn't afford to think about. Things he knew he had no right to think about. Imagining things that could never happen.

And feeling the growing response of his body to those images. A hard, aching surge of longing. Desire. Need.

He needed a woman. Any woman would do. Any woman's body would ease the physical need, put an end to this painful ache, too-long denied. *Any woman would do.*

But he wanted *this* one. *This* woman. He had wanted her

from the beginning. And now, finally, standing in the darkness watching her sleep, he acknowledged that.

The man called Hawk had, however, learned a lot of lessons through the years about controlling both need and want. He would control this. And as soon as he could, he would get her into the hands of someone who would offer her more protection from the people who were hunting her than he could.

Nobody's white knight, he thought again. He never had been, and no matter what she believed about him, Hawk knew the truth. All the truths about the man he really was.

One of those truths was that right now Tyler Stewart needed protection from him as much as she did from the assassins. And the sooner he got her off his hands, the better it would be for both of them.

Chapter Eight

"I think we should try for a meeting," Hawk said into the phone. The morning sun washed the desk he was sitting behind in light, reflecting off the glass that covered the image in the small silver frame.

"What changed your mind?" Jordan Cross asked.

Hawk knew the answer, of course, but it was something he would never confess. Not considering the things that were likely to result from the meeting he'd just suggested.

"It seems the smartest thing to do," he said, instead of explaining. "Once they put my picture out, any chance of making a deal is over. And the witness needs protection. The real kind. The kind they can provide."

That was a decision he had reached last night, after hours spent tossing and turning. The vision of Tyler Stewart, the thought of her vulnerability, kept intruding between him and the sleep he needed.

If Amir al-Ahmad had been involved in his father's death, then he now had the means to send out an army of assassins to find his fiancée, a woman whose face was too well-known to allow her to simply disappear. So damn beautiful and because of that, so vulnerable. Hawk would willingly give his life to keep Tyler safe, but with those odds, he had finally been forced to the conclusion that, despite his experience at this kind of game, that might not be enough.

He also knew that eventually the government would find

him, no matter how skillfully he played hide-and-seek. Especially if they chose to go public with the search by releasing the pictures from the hotel cameras. Hawk understood what that would mean. Every law enforcement officer in the country would be after him.

Using his own psychological profile against him, the agency would eventually find a pattern of behavior he wasn't aware of. They would use everything in the bag of tricks they had access to and all their experts to figure out what Hawk would do next. Where he would go. And there was always the possibility that when they found him, if she were still with him, Tyler might get hurt. That was a chance Hawk wasn't willing to take.

"You want me to set it up?"

A friend's offer, of course, but if Jordan tried to act as a go-between, the agency would know they had been in contact. No matter what story the two of them came up with, the company would suspect Cross's loyalty lay more with the team than with them. And Hawk would no longer have access to the information Jordan was providing.

"I don't want you tied to me," Hawk said.

"They're going to deep-six the team. We both know that. My name's bound to be high on their list of people they can do without." Jordan was too smart never to have crossed the boundary between playing by the rules and questioning them. That was one reason Griff had valued him so highly.

"Yeah, but keep your nose clean and you may still get that sweet government pension," Hawk said.

The laughter on the other end indicated Jordan's appreciation of the sarcasm, as well as his knowledge of the exact size of that pension.

"Besides," Hawk added, "you're my inside line. I don't want to risk that. I may need you later. More than I need you as negotiator now."

"So who did you have in mind?"

"It's got to be somebody with no connections to the team," he answered. "But somebody who's very familiar with how things work. Someone they can't bully. Maybe even…someone they're afraid of. Someone we can trust.''

"You don't want much, do you?" Jordan said, his voice filled with amusement at Hawk's list.

"I just want a slightly more equal playing field," Hawk replied softly, thinking about the truth of that.

"They aren't afraid of many people," Cross said, his voice serious again. That was another reality they were both aware of. "A lawyer, maybe?" he suggested. "Somebody with a lot of clout. Ex-congressman who's gone into private practice, but still has influence on the Hill."

"Maybe," Hawk conceded, considering those possibilities. Unconsciously, his gaze lifted, looking right into the blue eyes of the child in the silver-framed photograph.

"You have somebody in mind?" the voice on the other end of the line asked. "Somebody who's going to make the company think twice about whatever action they take where you're concerned?"

He had had this same thought before, Hawk realized. Just a general idea then. Not personalized. He had already realized there was only one possible ally the agency feared who might also be interested in fighting this one-sided battle.

"Claire Heywood," Hawk said softly.

He wasn't sure he had intended to voice that name aloud, but it was too late to take it back. The quiet on the other end of the phone line stretched across several slow heartbeats. And with Jordan's silence Hawk realized how impossible the suggestion was. *Griff will kill me if I involve her in this,* he thought.

Then, suddenly, overpoweringly, Hawk was again aware of that sense of loss. Griff Cabot would never know what he had done. But *he* would know. And he would never forgive himself if anything went wrong. "Bad idea," Hawk said.

"No," Jordan Cross replied, finally responding to a name he had obviously never expected. "Actually…" He hesitated before he went on. "Actually, it's a very good idea. But she's out of the country. She has been…since Griff's death, I think.''

"She's back," Hawk said softly. "I saw her at the grave."

The silence was almost as prolonged as before. "She's just not…'' Cross paused again, probably thinking about the difficulties inherent in that choice. "Not someone I would ever have come up with," he said finally.

"Forget it. She won't agree," Hawk said flatly, sorry now he had allowed it to go this far, even one person beyond himself. Pulling Claire Heywood into his situation was not something he could ever allow to happen.

Maybe Hawk had not fully understood the reasons behind the lengths Cabot went to in order to keep his relationship with the woman he loved separate from his professional life. Now he did. But he also knew he couldn't sacrifice Claire Heywood, not even to protect Tyler.

"I think she might," Jordan said. "If the approach is right. She's perfect, damn it, and you know it."

There was a trace of excitement in Cross's voice. And Heywood *was* perfect. She had the right tools and impeccable credentials, just as Hawk had laid them out before he had even thought of her in conjunction with this.

The only child of the union between one of the most respected journalists in the capital and a wealthy Washington socialite, who just happened to be the daughter of a former head of the CIA, Claire Heywood was also a highly regarded lawyer. She was often called in as a consultant by the networks to comment on any story they were running that had both legal and political overtones.

Perhaps at first that had been because she was her father's daughter, but her insider's understanding of Washington was undisputed. And Claire was not only popular with the public, her insight, intelligence and honesty were also respected by the elite of both parties.

And since half the power brokers in the capital had also jiggled her as an infant on their knees, she had unquestioned access to the conclaves of influence, including those within the tight-knit intelligence community. Which was where she had met Griff Cabot. Where they had begun a relationship that had ended only when she had broken it off, more than a year ago.

"No," Hawk said softly, remembering that relationship.

Claire Heywood might be a perfect go-between, but she was also off-limits. Griff had placed her off-limits; therefore, she still was. Hawk's lips flattened, and he pulled his eyes away from the photograph, denying the temptation.

Tyler Stewart was standing in the door of Griff's study, watching him. She had found a robe somewhere. It was a dark navy velour, obviously a man's garment. She had belted it tightly around her slim waist, and it almost touched the top of her feet, which were slender and bare.

Her black hair was loose, its natural curl unrestrained. The color of her eyes was intensified by the dark blue of the robe. Still slightly shadowed, they were focused on him now and smiling.

"May I come in?" she asked politely.

Hawk felt his body respond, his arousal incredibly quick and powerful. He nodded permission before he spoke again into the phone he was holding. "I'll talk to you later," he said to Cross. "Something's just come up."

He saw Tyler's smile widen and then dissolve into laughter at the unintended sexual connotation. He couldn't remember having seen her laugh before, and he couldn't take his eyes off her face. He hadn't been able to, not since he'd looked up and found her in the doorway.

"Maybe I'll have something definite for you by then," Jordan said. "I'll try."

Hawk put the receiver down, almost before the sound of the last word had faded, no longer thinking about what they'd been discussing. After his nod of permission, Tyler had walked over to the desk. She stood before him, looking down at the stack of newspapers he'd read before he went upstairs last night.

She had just showered. He could smell the soap. Now that

she was this close, he could tell that her hair was damp, the moisture adding highlights to the midnight strands. She was wearing no makeup, and she was so beautiful he wanted to pull the too-large, too-masculine robe off her body, which he suspected might be nude underneath, and make love to her.

Here. On the top of Griff's big desk. Or on the softness of the Oriental rug. It didn't matter. He just wanted to push into her, to feel her body move under his. Responding to him. Answering every demand. More than answering. Matching them. Exceeding them.

"Good morning," she said softly, her eyes on his face.

Hawk realized he had simply been watching her, imagining the same things he had forbidden himself to think about last night as he had stood by her bed. Things he couldn't afford to think about.

"Did you sleep?" he asked. Safe topic for conversation.

"Like the dead," she said, and then suddenly her smile widened. "Not such a good analogy, I guess. Not after yesterday."

He held her gaze, not wanting to make small talk. Thinking, against his will, about exactly what he did want.

"Those are some pretty powerful pills you gave me," she said after a moment.

"How's the arm?" he asked.

She touched the back of her left arm lightly with her fingers, running them up and down against the softness of the velour. "Sore," she admitted.

"Want me to take another look at it?" he asked.

Whatever had been there yesterday was suddenly back in her eyes, and after a few seconds, she shook her head, making him wonder if he'd been right about what she was wearing under that robe. Not wearing, he amended.

"Maybe later," she offered. "We probably should change the dressing eventually. Put on some more salve."

"Okay," he said.

They were both remembering. He knew he was. Touching her skin, his fingers on the soft silken underside of her arm.

Sitting beside her on a bed. The conjunction of Tyler Stewart and bed in his mind was not a safe one, but despite his vaunted self-discipline, he was having a hard time denying the appeal of that combination.

Maybe that appeal was in his eyes because suddenly hers fell, the fan of dark lashes shielding whatever she had been thinking. "Did I make the papers?" she asked, turning the top one on the stack toward her.

He knew she didn't care about whatever was in the papers. It had simply been something to say. And that had nothing to do with what was happening between them. Except, of course, it did. A lot to do with why there could be nothing between them.

At his continued silence, her eyes lifted again. "Hawk?" she questioned softly, examining his face. "Is something wrong?"

Everything you believe about me, he thought, but instead of telling her that, he shook his head. No explanations. He had already decided that. And no confession. If he succeeded in setting up the meeting he'd asked Jordan to work on, she'd know all of it soon enough.

She waited a moment, eyes still on his, but Hawk's face gave nothing away, the control too ingrained to be destroyed by his dread of what she would feel when she found out who and what he was. And why he had really come to find her.

Finally her eyes went back to the paper, and he watched her begin to read. He didn't bother to wonder which one she'd chosen. They all carried essentially the same story.

"So I'm in seclusion. Grief stricken over the sheikh's death," she said, her eyes still scanning the columns of text. "How long does Amir think he can get away with that?"

"Just until they find you," Hawk said.

Her eyes came up, no longer smiling. The remembrance of what had happened in Mississippi was in them.

"He was in on it," Tyler said. "He had to have been. My God, he *was* involved in his own father's death."

SHE SUPPOSED she had to have known all along that Amir was involved. Malcolm had told her he had just left the room. The same room where the assassins had been waiting.

"They know the shot came from the hotel," she said. "I thought they could trace the path of a bullet. They should be able to figure out it came from Amir's room."

"In those circumstances, from that height and at that angle, it would be hard to prove exactly where a bullet came from. It must have gone nearly straight down. Besides, even tracing it to a floor wouldn't prove Amir had anything to do with the assassination. He's blaming it on the religious extremists in his country who had targeted the sheikh before. And they *could* have infiltrated Amir's entourage. Bought somebody off."

"But you don't believe that?" she asked.

"Not really. If he had just left that room, then he had to have known what was going on."

She nodded. That was the same conclusion she had come to, as incredible as it seemed. "Why would he kill his own father?"

She realized, even as she asked, how ridiculous that question was. People killed members of their families every day. Mothers killed their own children. And for far less reason than the billions of dollars and the almost unlimited power that were involved here.

"Dumb question," she said, without giving Hawk time to answer. "It was all about the money. I guess he just didn't have enough." Her tone was bitter, thinking of what she had seen Amir spend in the last six weeks. A lot of it had been lavished on her, on the wedding. Now she knew why, of course.

She laughed, shaking her head at her gullibility. "I always wondered why he picked me," she said. "But I guess I just didn't..." She hesitated, embarrassed to admit that she hadn't wanted to question his proposal. That she had wanted so much to believe that he loved her. That he wanted to take care of her.

"Why would you wonder?" Hawk asked.

Apparently Hawk hadn't figured this part out yet. But then he wasn't the one who had all along felt that sense of wrongness. Those feelings she had tried so hard to ignore. Sadly, she had succeeded in blocking them from her mind. At least up to the final morning. The morning of the wedding.

"Out of all the women he could have chosen, I always wondered why he would want me," she said. "Now I know." At last she understood what had really been going on with Amir's determined courtship. She supposed it *was* better to know, even if the knowledge was painful. "He needed someone who would agree to marry him quickly and without asking too many inconvenient questions about the arrangements. Someone…"

She paused again, recognizing finally that she had been absolutely perfect for Amir's plan. She didn't know exactly how much Amir had known about her situation when he met her. But obviously, it had been enough to realize she would be a potential target. And eventually she had shared everything that had gone on in her life. Paul's betrayal. The loss of her career and her savings.

So Amir would have realized how vulnerable she would be to his flattery. How worried about the future. Insecure about her ability to make a living. *"Just smile at them, sweetheart, but don't open your mouth."*

"Almost any woman would have jumped at the chance," Hawk said softly. "You had no reason to doubt his motives."

"A few," she said bitterly. "If I'd stopped to think it all out." But there was no doubt Amir's rush to get her to the altar had been balm to her battered self-esteem. *God,* she thought, *I was such easy prey.*

"I wonder what he would have done about the wedding if his father hadn't agreed to come to New York," she said.

She knew now that had been the whole point of that civil ceremony. All Amir's talk about showing her off was to cover his real motive. Which was getting his father out of his protected stronghold so he could be killed. Putting his father in a situation where *he* was vulnerable.

"If his father *hadn't* agreed to come, what story do you suppose he would have given to the press about why the ceremony had to be cancelled?" she asked. It was rhetorical, of course. Because none of it mattered now.

"Maybe it wouldn't have been called off," Hawk said. "He had nothing to lose."

"Marrying a woman he didn't love?" she asked. Amir hadn't loved her, of course. That was something else she had felt all along. Felt and ignored. Denied as much as she'd denied her own lack of feeling for him.

"A civil marriage wouldn't have been binding on him. It would have given you no rights. He could divorce you at any time."

"And all the prenuptial contracts we signed were to have gone into force when the religious ceremony took place," Tyler admitted. "It never would have. He would never have gone through with that, would he?"

"Probably not," Hawk agreed softly.

"I made it so easy for him," Tyler said bitterly. "I thought he wanted to take care of me. All he really wanted..." *Was to use me.* The words were in her head, but it was painful to admit that she had let herself be used again. First by Paul and then by Amir.

"Anyone who has the capacity to trust can be taken advantage of," Hawk said.

"The capacity to trust?" she repeated. "I guess that's one way of putting it."

She remembered what Hawk had said the first day. The day at the hotel. *You have to trust somebody.* In this situation she knew she did. And she would rather put her trust in Hawk than in anyone else right now. After all, he was the one who had come to find her. The one who had saved her life. Twice.

"As soon as I'm sure it's safe," he said, "I'll take you in and you can tell them what you saw. When you've done that, it should take some of the pressure off. Ahmad will realize he has nothing to gain by...hunting you down."

"What I saw doesn't prove Amir was involved," she said.

"Maybe not. If you're thinking of the kind of proof that can be taken to a court of law. You should realize, however, that even if you could prove he was involved, he'll probably never be charged."

"Why not?"

"Ahmad's head of state now. Diplomatically, he's off-limits. And he'll deny it, of course. He'll blame the assassination on the extremists. Or on a CIA plot," Hawk said, his lips twisting. "The agency's always a convenient scapegoat for the odd assassination or two."

"He'll get away with murder? The murder of his own father?"

"Probably," Hawk agreed.

"Then why do I have to testify?" she asked. She should have known this was the way the world worked. For people like Amir, anyway. People with that much money.

"You need to tell what you saw to prove to him that you can't hurt him. Not officially, anyway."

"And unofficially?" she asked.

"Maybe. Maybe some people will continue to believe he was involved. Most won't give a damn. It will be just a little added celebrity. Make him more interesting. After all, he has enough money to buy forgiveness for almost anything."

"Even for murder?" she asked.

"Far more than enough for murder," Hawk said, his eyes again cold and hard.

The capacity to trust, she thought. This man had lost that long ago. He knew how the world really worked, and that made him more cynical than she would ever be, despite the betrayals in her life. But still, she thought, finding comfort in the realization, Hawk believed some things were worth fighting for. Justice. The law. He must, or he wouldn't be who and what he was.

"All you have to do is tell them what you saw," he said

again. "Tell them about the man who pulled the trigger and about the others in the room. Then they'll put you somewhere safe until it's over."

"*They'll* put me somewhere safe?" she repeated. *Not Hawk. Not any longer.* She would no longer be his responsibility, and she supposed he would be glad.

"Something like witness protection," he explained.

"And I won't see you again?" she asked.

"Probably not," he said. There was no regret in his eyes or in his face. It was a simple statement of fact.

Hawk had a job to do. And he was doing it to the best of his ability. As he would for anyone in her situation. At least he had no ulterior motives where she was concerned. Not of any kind, apparently. Not even the ones she had found herself thinking more and more about, the longer she was around him.

But Hawk's disinterest had been pretty obvious. Despite the feelings that had been building up in her head about him. More self-delusion, she supposed. Or a very one-sided dream. A fantasy. And it was about time she grew out of those, too.

"THIS IS NOT MY AREA of expertise," Claire Heywood stated, after she'd listened to her caller's explanation. "Perhaps if you'd told my secretary what this was about—"

"He's innocent." The deep voice on the other end of the line interrupted her polite rejection. "He's being targeted by some powerful people to take the blame for something he didn't do. I think *that's* within your area of expertise, isn't it?"

Claire lay down the pen with which she'd been making a series of meaningless doodles as she listened. This man had insisted on talking to her personally, refusing to provide any information to her secretary. Normally, Jane would have gotten rid of him, simply on the basis of his reluctance to reveal who he was or what he wanted to talk about.

However, he had made his request so persuasively, in such an impassioned manner, that the usually immovable Jane had given in. Maybe he had managed that miracle through the undeniably appealing quality of his voice.

Claire had known almost from the beginning of his spiel that she wasn't going to touch this case, but for some reason she had listened anyway. *Just a sucker for an attractive male voice,* she thought, her lips tilting a little. She had listened this long because it had been a while since she'd really enjoyed hearing a man's voice. Since before Griff's death.

Suddenly, thinking about him, her sense of loss and anger, all the regret she had felt over the things she had said, surged upward from where she'd enclosed them. Escaping from that tight little box where she had determinedly buried her feelings about Griffon Cabot.

She remembered the jolt of excitement she'd felt the first time *he* called her. Her body had reacted as soon as she recognized his voice, which had been as deep and pleasant as this one. It, too, had been touched with this same hint of Southern accent, the kind that spelled old money and good schools.

"Or doesn't that mean anything in this town anymore?" the man on the phone asked.

"Everyone's entitled to a presumption of innocence," Claire said. Somehow her fingers had found the damn pen again. This time she had drawn a box on the pad in front of her, and then placed a smaller one inside it. She recognized the symbolism.

"Except nobody seems willing to make that presumption in this case," he said.

"I'm sorry. Really I am, but I can't help your friend. I can give you a list of names, some very fine lawyers who would be much more—"

"They're going to release his picture," the voice on the phone said. "Which will start a manhunt. Despite the fact that they probably know he had nothing to do with this assassination."

With this *assassination.* The middle word in that phrase

had been emphasized, and it triggered the association he had obviously been trying for.

"*This* assassination?" Claire questioned. Her voice was very low, but she couldn't have prevented herself from asking if her life depended on it. He was probably counting on that.

"He's a friend of mine. And our circle of friends is…limited. We've always looked out for one another's interests. I think maybe you understand what I'm talking about."

The words beat at Claire's consciousness, making her think about things she didn't want to think about. *Griff's team?* she wondered. *Can that possibly be what this is about?*

She had wondered when she'd heard about the earlier assassination. The one in Baghdad. She had considered the possibility that Griff's people had been involved. Because, of course, it had been rumored in the intelligence community that the terrorist in Iraq was the man who had been responsible for the attack in which Griff had been killed. And now this man seemed to be implying…

"I'm not the lawyer your friend needs," she said truthfully. "However much I might *like* to help him…" She hesitated deliberately, hoping he would understand why she couldn't do what he'd asked. "You want the best representation for your friend, I'm sure."

"I'm not talking about *legal* representation," he said.

That threw her. She had thought that's where this was leading. What else could they possibly want from her?

"Then…I'm afraid I don't understand," she said.

"Why don't we meet somewhere, and I can explain it to you," he suggested.

"I don't think—"

"Somewhere public." He broke into her refusal. "Wherever you say. You can trust me, Ms. Heywood. After all, we had a mutual friend. A very good friend."

Had a mutual friend. Past tense. The quiet words echoed as the others had. She hadn't been mistaken. This *was* about Griff. About a member of his team.

That had been something Griff had eventually told her about. Eventually and not immediately, of course, because he must have known she wouldn't approve. Griff believed the kinds of things they did were necessary for national security, but Claire had never bought into his reasoning.

It was an argument they had had time and time again, with Griff reasonably, logically and calmly defending his decisions. Acknowledging that he would make the same kinds of decisions in the future if the nation's security demanded them. And always she had argued in favor of other actions, other options.

And yet when she had heard about the death of the man in Iraq, there had been no regret in her heart. No outrage that someone had killed him. She had felt only gratitude to whichever of those men had taken revenge for Griff's death. For the death of a good man. *A very good friend.*

"The Lincoln Memorial," she said softly, her agreement surprising her as much as it probably would him. As it would have surprised anyone who knew her. "The foot of the statue. Three o'clock."

She put down the phone without waiting for his confirmation. She was still holding the pen, she realized. Because her fingers were trembling, she laid it down on the pad, beside the series of boxes she had drawn as she listened, each one smaller and more tightly enclosed than the last.

She put her head in her hands and closed her eyes, fighting the sting of tears. She had sworn she wouldn't cry. No tears for Griff. Or for her. Or for anyone else. Because she knew that her tears wouldn't change anything.

Nothing would change. She didn't believe in an eye for an eye. Since childhood she had been taught that was wrong. Still, when she had heard someone had killed that bastard in Baghdad, there had been a surge of exaltation so strong it had almost frightened her. An age-old, primitive desire for revenge. And she had recognized at that moment that she might even have done it had she had the expertise or the opportunity.

But there was no one to whom she could ever have made that admission. Like her attendance at this meeting she'd just arranged, no one who knew her would believe the thought of tracking down Griff's murderer had even crossed her mind.

But whoever he was, the man who had pulled that trigger in Baghdad, she knew exactly how he felt. And if the man they were accusing of the sheikh's death was the same one, and if, as her caller suggested, he *was* being set up in retaliation for what he'd done for Griff…

She sat for a few minutes staring out the window of her office, situated in the heart of the most powerful nation in the world. A strength protected, Griff had insisted, by men such as these.

They weren't interested in her legal expertise. They were smart enough to know that would be worthless in this case. So that meant they wanted something else. They wanted what she *could* give them. An insider's knowledge? She knew people who would know what was really going on. She thought of her grandfather. After all, as they said in Washington, there was no one as well connected as an old spook.

And her father. Of course, her connection there might be important to them also, she realized. The press was an incredibly potent force, especially in this world dominated by politics and intrigue. Even the Griff Cabots of this world recognized that. Now all she had to decide was whether she was willing to use those connections on behalf of Griff's friend.

Chapter Nine

"There's a witness who will testify that she saw the real assassins," Jordan Cross said. "A witness who can identify those men, none of whom were my friend."

It was the same voice, Claire thought, but somehow it was even more compelling in person. And the man was as intriguing as his voice. He was tall and dark, almost as handsome as Griff. His eyes, dead-of-winter gray, should have been cold as sleet. They were passionate instead, full of intelligence and purpose. Intent on making her believe that she should help them.

"Then he needs to turn himself in to the authorities and let her do just that. As soon as he can," Claire suggested calmly, fighting his power.

They were standing in the shadowed memorial, right at Mr. Lincoln's feet. The place was crawling with tourists, cranky kids in tow, snapping endless photographs, most of them across the breathtaking vista of the reflecting pool.

No one seemed to be paying them the slightest attention. Except, Claire had noticed, for the occasional feminine glance that touched on her companion and then came back, lingering a few seconds longer than was absolutely necessary on his face. She didn't blame them. Jordan Cross was as good to look at as he was to listen to. That was the name he had used when he'd introduced himself, but she couldn't know if it was his real one.

"There are a couple of problems with doing that," Jordan said softly. The gray eyes circled the crowd around them and then returned to hers. "For one thing, they don't intend to give him a chance to talk. Not even to prove his innocence."

"Why not?" Claire asked.

His well-shaped lips tightened as he continued to hold her gaze, considering, perhaps, what to tell her. "They ordered him to stay out of Iraq. He didn't. Someone had killed a friend of his. Maybe the only friend Hawk ever had."

He obviously thought that what the man he called Hawk had done was honorable. Therefore, he was willing to use any weapon he had to protect him, even Claire's feelings for Griff.

"He'll come in and take the heat for what he did in Baghdad," Cross continued. "But he wants to bring in the witness to al-Ahmad's assassination. She testifies to Hawk's innocence, and then they put her in witness protection."

"He must realize that…" Claire took a breath, trying to think how to phrase what had to be said.

"He's prepared to accept punishment that's appropriate."

"Prison?" she asked.

"Why should he go to prison? He executed a murderer. The agency knows that. Their hands haven't always been so clean."

"Maybe they're turning over a new leaf," she suggested.

"But you don't change the rules in the middle of the game. Especially if someone's been playing that game as long as Hawk."

"I think they can change the rules whenever they want to," she reminded him softly. "It's their game. Who's going to stop them?"

"That's where you come in," he said, smiling at her.

His smile was undeniably powerful. And suddenly Claire found herself wondering exactly what kinds of jobs Jordan Cross himself had done for Griff.

"I don't understand what you think I can do," she said.

"Hawk knows a lot of things the agency wouldn't be eager to have become public."

"So we threaten that he'll make them public? The same kinds of things this man Hawk did in Baghdad?" Her feelings about those were probably revealed in her tone, because he reacted.

"You really have no idea, Ms. Heywood, about the *kinds* of things Hawk has done for this country."

"I'm sorry, Mr. Cross, but my ideas about national policy differed from Griff's. They differed a great deal. So don't expect me to feel gratitude for Hawk's contributions."

"Is that why you broke with Griff? Because you didn't approve of what we did?" There was a thread of anger in Jordan's voice. For the first time the gray eyes were as cold as she had imagined they could be.

"Whatever was between Griff Cabot and me is none of your business."

Angered by his criticism, the same one she had made of herself often enough after Griff's death, she started across the floor of the memorial toward the steps. His hand on her elbow stopped her. His grip wasn't hard enough to bruise, but she was surprised he would touch her like that. She couldn't ever remember being forcibly detained. Not in her entire life.

"We're not playing games, Ms. Heywood," he said, his voice very low, his mouth close to her ear so no one around them could hear what he said. "A man's life is at stake. A good man, whether you want to believe that or not. A man whose neck is in this noose because he went after Griff's killer. And you should remember that Cabot and the others were just that terrorist's latest victims. They wouldn't have been his last, I can promise you. Whatever your politics, however deeply you feel about them, you can't possibly believe that preventing that murderer from killing again wasn't justified."

Claire had stopped because she didn't have a choice. But what he said was compelling. Especially given his obvious conviction. And especially for someone who prided herself on dealing with the truths that lay hidden under all the convoluted rationales of national politics.

"What do you want from me?" she asked, held now not by the grip of his hand, but by his sincerity. She wondered again in what capacity Jordan Cross had functioned for Griff's team.

"We want you to act as a go-between. Set up a forum where Hawk can make his case. Get them to promise two things—protection for the witness and to let Hawk walk out when the meeting's over. In exchange, he gives them his oath to keep quiet about what he knows."

"Would he go public?" she asked. Keeping that trust was the essence of the relationship the team shared. Even she knew enough about Griff's work to understand that.

"I'd bet my life he wouldn't," Jordan said, his lips relaxing suddenly into a smile. "But they won't know that. And with Hawk's background...I don't think, even with all they know about each of us, they can be completely sure he won't."

"If this works, I want to be there," Claire said. "At the meeting." From the quickly concealed reaction in his eyes she realized she had surprised him. Probably because he thought there was an element of danger involved. She didn't care. She wanted to meet the man who had killed the terrorist in Iraq. She wanted to make her own judgment.

Jordan nodded slowly, only after he'd considered his options. "That might not be a bad idea. It offers Hawk more protection. It might even make our witness feel more comfortable to have another woman there."

"A woman?"

"Hawk tracked her down just in time to keep the real assassins from killing her. She's been with him since."

"With him where?"

"I don't know," Cross said. "He hasn't told me."

"Doesn't he trust you?" she asked, challenging.

"I didn't need to know," Jordan Cross said, smiling.

"The only thing I do need to know is if you are willing to help him."

"I'm not exactly willing," she stated.

"I know," he said, holding her eyes.

"But…I'll see what I can do," she said softly.

There was a long silence, and finally Jordan broke it. "I don't know if it's important to you, but Griff wasn't often wrong about people. He wasn't wrong about Hawk. And I knew he hadn't made a mistake when he chose you."

She wasn't exactly sure what that meant, but she could tell from his tone and from what was in his eyes that it was supposed to be a compliment. "Thank you," she said finally, her voice as low as his had been.

"How long will it take you to contact them?" he asked.

"One phone call," she said.

She had surprised him again. Maybe he hadn't thought she'd know who to call. She had her grandfather to thank for that information. And her grandfather's name would be a powerful introduction to the person she would need to contact to set up this meeting.

"Then I'll call you tonight," Cross said.

He released her arm and turned, striding across the floor of the memorial. His figure was almost immediately swallowed up in the crowd of tourists coming up the stairs. Claire watched until he had disappeared, his words echoing in her head. *"I knew he hadn't made a mistake when he chose you."*

It had been almost flattering to be included in that circle. The people Griff Cabot had chosen. And of them all, only she, apparently, had ever failed to live up to Griff's expectations. Now, it seemed, she was going to be given a second chance.

"SHE WANTS TO BE IN on the meeting," Jordan said.

"Too risky."

"That's the only way she'll do it."

"Then we don't do it," Hawk said, more than willing to

let this whole plan drop. He hadn't dreamed Cross would go to Claire Heywood. He had thought Jordan understood that she was off-limits, that Hawk had changed his mind. He had found out only when he called Jordan tonight that he'd been wrong.

"You want your witness in protection?" Jordan asked.

"Yes," Hawk said.

"Then this is how we do it."

Jordan was waiting for him to respond, he knew, but Hawk didn't like either of the choices. They had had no right to involve Claire Heywood in this, although it seemed she was willing to be involved. And if she *did* manage to set this up, then Tyler would be protected.

"By the way," Jordan said into his silence, "they found no bodies in that house in Mississippi. Apparently when your assailants didn't report back, somebody came out and collected the corpses. They even cleaned up the mess."

"Efficient bastards, aren't they?" Hawk said.

"They've got lots of money. And lots of willing helpers. Speaking of helpers, NYPD's officially releasing the shots from the security videos tomorrow. You know what that means."

Hawk did, of course. All of it. He had gone over and over the options. There hadn't been that many to begin with. A nationwide manhunt would restrict his movements more than they were restricted now. Eventually, he knew, someone at the agency would remember this place. Maybe even remember that he had been brought here to recuperate after that botched mission. And when they did, someone would come out to check.

Or some of Amir al-Ahmad's money would buy that information. Just as they probably already had his picture. Maybe even his name. If you're willing to throw enough money at something, you can always shake loose someone who is willing to talk, Hawk thought.

If those bodies in Mississippi had been retrieved, then they knew Tyler Stewart was no longer alone and defenseless. Someone in al-Ahmad's group had probably already put two and two together and figured out who was with her. Track Hawk down, and they'd find her. And when the law put out those bulletins tomorrow…

He and Tyler needed to get out of here, he realized again, but he knew there was really no place to go. And in less than twenty-four hours his face would be almost as familiar to the public as Tyler Stewart's was now.

"Tell her to do it," he said softly.

"Claire's office," Jordan said. "Noon tomorrow. There's a parking garage below and a basement entry." He gave the address and the codes for entering the garage. "Park in spot 121 and take the elevator to the sixth floor. They'll be in her office."

"How did she arrange that?" Hawk asked, amused at the thought of them coming to her.

"I didn't ask," Jordan said. "I wasn't sure I wanted to know." The deep voice was filled with amusement. And admiration.

Griff would kill me, Hawk thought again, but this time the thought of Griff's displeasure had nothing to do with the possibility of involving Claire Heywood with his enemies.

HAWK WASN'T SURE how he had ended up here, standing again at midnight outside the door of the room where Tyler was sleeping. Maybe it had been Jordan's phone call. The realization that it was all winding down. Very soon looking after Tyler Stewart would be someone else's responsibility. Hawk knew, because he was aware of how those things worked, that when it was, he'd never see her again.

So maybe that's why he was here. Because right now she was still his. His to protect. *Standing guard over the things you love.* Griff's words, which had once meant something entirely different to him, echoed in his head.

But they were as true now as they had been when his total loyalty had been to a friend. To his country. Hawk had never failed either of them. Never failed in doing his duty. He wouldn't fail here.

He reminded himself that nothing had happened last night. He had stood beside her bed, watching her sleep, and then he had left. Tonight would be the same. He would check to make sure she was all right and he'd leave. It was all a matter of discipline, he told himself as he opened the door.

The lamp beside the bed was on again. Tyler had fallen asleep tonight while reading, her shoulders propped on the pile of pillows she had stacked against the headboard. The newspapers she had brought up from Griff's study were spread out on the bed around her. There was a glass half-full of water on the bedside table, beside the opened bottle of the pain medication he'd left here yesterday.

Hawk's eyes came back to the sleeping woman. Her right hand again cupped the elbow of her left arm. Still sore. Painful enough that she had taken more of the capsules. And if she slept sitting up like this all night, he thought, that wouldn't be the only discomfort. She would probably sleep a lot better if—

Bad idea, he told himself harshly, fighting the image that had appeared in his head. *Leave her the hell alone,* he ordered. If she wasn't comfortable, there was nothing he could do about it. Nothing he should do. What he *should* do was leave. Back out of this room and close the door between them. He couldn't afford another mistake. He had made enough of them already where she was concerned.

He should never have played Good Samaritan. Never have kissed her. Never allowed himself to even think about doing it again. Or about any of the other things he had imagined last night as he stood in this same dark room, watching her sleep.

But she would sleep more comfortably if he gathered up the scattered papers. Maybe removed one of those pillows from behind her shoulders. He could do that without waking her, especially with the pills she'd taken. Then he'd leave.

That's all, he told himself, taking a step forward. And then another, his eyes never leaving her face. Slow, silent footsteps, until at last he was standing beside her bed. Exactly where he had been last night. Fighting the same battle he had fought then.

Slowly he reached out and picked up one of the papers. She didn't stir, despite the soft rustle of the pages. He gathered the rest of them off the counterpane, not bothering to stack or refold. When he had them all, he bent and put them down beside the bed. When he straightened, he realized that, despite the noise, she was still sleeping as soundly as she had been when he entered the room. As soundly as last night.

Then he reached out again, big fingers moving with deliberate slowness, highly disciplined, and switched off the bedside lamp. He waited in the darkness until his eyes adjusted, her face floating up out of the shadows. Infinitely beautiful. Peaceful.

One last task, he thought, stepping nearer the bed. He bent toward her. She wouldn't wake up, not with the effect of the capsules. She would never know he'd been here. She hadn't known last night.

Hawk slipped his right arm under her shoulders, lifting them. At the same time he pulled the top pillow out with his left hand. Removed it with infinite care and patience.

Suddenly her breathing changed. Her lips parted. Her tongue appeared between them, easing out to touch the top one with moisture. She turned her head, her hair brushing against his neck.

With her first movement, Hawk froze, his arm still behind her back. Her eyes didn't open, however. And after an endless wait, he took a breath in relief. She had settled back into sleep, her cheek resting now against his shoulder. She didn't move again, other than the measured regularity of her breathing.

She hadn't awakened, only stirred in her sleep. But now, he realized, if he removed his arm, her head would be against the headboard. He needed to move her a little farther down the bed.

He pulled back the sheet with his left hand and slipped his left arm under the crook of her knees. He lifted, right arm under her back, surprised at how little she weighed. She was so thin she was almost…fragile.

Hawk laid her back on the bed, her dark head settled on a single pillow. *Better,* he thought, carefully sliding his left arm from beneath her knees. Remembering to take another breath.

He glanced to his left, his eyes searching in the darkness for the sheet he'd pulled away. She'd get a better night's sleep this way, he thought again, congratulating himself on his success. Preparing to ease his other arm from behind her back.

Instead, her right arm lifted and her hand found the back of Hawk's neck. The movement was slow, almost languid. Sleepy. But her fingers touched his hair, and then they opened, sliding upward, widened to cup the back of his head.

Hawk froze, not daring to breathe. He was still bending over her, one arm beneath her shoulders. When he looked back toward the head of the bed, almost dreading what he'd find, her eyes were open. Focused on his face. There was no surprise in them. No dismay at finding him here. No shock that he was bending over her in the inviting darkness of her bedroom. Her lips moved again. This time their corners edged upward. Tilted. She was smiling at him, he realized.

The fingers that were at the back of his head shifted, no longer drifting through the short, thick hair, but applying pressure. Downward pressure. Her face moved slightly, chin lifting toward his. Her mouth opened. Inviting also. Promising. Both beautiful and vulnerable.

Hawk's head lowered in response. There was no conscious decision involved. There were no cautions left in his brain. Because Hawk was no longer thinking. He was feeling. Needing and wanting. Responding to an enticement that he knew was probably drug induced. It didn't matter. It was far too late to withdraw. His mouth found hers, and the contact between them was as powerful as it had been before, that first time he'd foolishly allowed himself to kiss her.

Heat and movement. Incredible hunger. His. And hers. There was nothing one-sided about what was happening. Hawk was aware of that. If he hadn't been, he might have found the strength to stop. He didn't, because it was obvious she didn't want him to stop.

Instead, her desire matched his. Her tongue explored, challenged, taunted. Her lips released, more tempting in their small denial, and then as quickly found his mouth again, renewing the contact between them with the same hot surge of need he had felt before, simply standing beside the bed watching her sleep.

She wanted this. There was no doubt about that. Wanted his mouth over hers. Wanted him... *Wanted him?* Sanity reared its ugly head. Only two days ago, she was supposed to marry someone else. Maybe, dazed by sleep, she thought...

Infuriated at the possibility that she might not know who he was, Hawk raised his head, pushing strongly against the slender fingers threaded through his hair. Her eyes opened again. What was in them now was clearly shock. Her lips were parted, and he fought the urge to cover them with his.

What the hell does it matter who she thinks *she's kissing?* he wondered savagely. The reality was she was kissing *him.* He was the one who was here in the darkness. Her small breasts were rising and falling against *his* chest, her fingers locked in *his* hair. What kind of stupid bastard would question that reality?

This kind. The kind of bastard *he* was, Hawk thought, watching her eyes widen at the anger in his face. Seeing the tip of her tongue ease between the trembling lips. Wanting it moving again under his.

"I'm not Ahmad," he said, his voice harsh with need.

He wanted to see that knowledge in the depths of her eyes. To read it in her face. The words were only a whisper, but they seemed to echo in the darkness, filling the small loneliness of space he had created between his mouth and her lips.

"I know," she said. "I know you're not Amir."

Her hand slipped from behind his head to cup his cheek. Her thumb caressed the tightness of the muscle beside his mouth. Even under that gentle pressure, it didn't relax. The tension didn't ease. None of the tension between them.

"I don't want there to be any mistake," Hawk said, his voice cold. Her eyes searched his face, and even in the darkness he could see the pain in them.

"Hawk," she whispered.

He wasn't sure if his name was protest or affirmation. Confirmation that what he had just accused her of was untrue, or proof that she knew exactly who he was. Not the fiancé she had almost certainly been sleeping with only a couple of days ago.

That realization hit him hard, nausea stirring at the thought of someone else making love to her. Of her responding to another man as she had been responding to him. Inviting someone else—

"What's wrong?" she asked, just as she had today. Her fingers moved against his cheek, nails scoring lightly over his skin as they traced downward. "What's wrong?" she repeated more softly, pressing her thumb again into the tension at the corner of his mouth.

"Did you love him?" he asked.

Her hand fell away from his face. It curled against her throat. The knob of bone in her wrist was very prominent. Thin. Like a child's bone. Fragile and vulnerable.

"No," she whispered. Her eyes didn't avoid his.

"You agreed to marry him." That had been in the back of Hawk's mind all along, almost from the moment she had entered his room, begging for his help.

"It wasn't for the money."

"Then why?" he asked. Other than the fact that he had that much money, why would she agree to marry a man she didn't love?

"Because I was afraid."

The words were only a breath, but he was so close that he heard them. Too close. He could smell the fragrance of her body, released by the warmth of the bed or by the heat of the kiss they had shared.

"Afraid of what?"

He wasn't really thinking anymore about what she was saying. He had accepted her denial because he wanted to believe it. Needed to believe. Because he wanted to touch her. To put his fingers around that childlike wrist. To put his lips against her throat, exactly where her hand lay, fingers curved inward and relaxed. Trusting. He wanted to bury his face in the shadowed softness between the rise and fall of her small breasts.

He wanted her. His body ached with how much he wanted to bury himself within her. Deep and hard and tight. And as wet as only he could make her. He could. He knew that. Had never doubted it.

I know you're not Amir, she had said. And then his name. The only name she knew. Hawk. The single syllable had slipped out of her mouth as smoothly as he wanted to push into her body.

"Afraid of what came next, I guess," she whispered finally. "Afraid of the rest of my life. Of what it was going to be. Afraid of being alone. Afraid...there were no more dreams."

Hawk didn't have any idea what she was talking about. There *were* no more dreams. He had known that for a long time. Since before his mother died. No more dreams. Not in this world. Not in Hawk's life, at least.

"Dreams?" he asked. He had intended the word to be mocking, but it sounded only questioning, his voice almost as soft as hers.

"Dreams," she repeated. "I thought there were no more

dreams left to come true. But...I guess maybe I was wrong.''

Her hand moved, fingers touching his face again. The tips of them slid over his cheek, then lightly traced the outline of his lips. She was watching him, watching her hand move against his mouth. Then her thumb found his eyelid, and she brushed it across the short thick lashes.

He turned his head, avoiding her touch. Avoiding the tenderness it communicated more clearly than words.

''Make love to me,'' she whispered.

This wasn't the way it was supposed to be, Hawk thought. This was something that should never have been allowed to happen between the two of them.

No more dreams... That had reverberated in his head, echoing all that he already knew. All that life had taught a man called Hawk.

But maybe, just maybe, she *was* wrong, he thought, his mouth lowering slowly to destroy the emptiness between them. Maybe they both were.

Chapter Ten

When her eyelids finally drifted upward again, Hawk was watching her, blue eyes luminous in the darkness. She had seen them like that once before, she remembered. The night he had come to her mother's house in Mississippi. Had come to find her and to keep her safe.

Now he was lying beside her in the bed where they had just made love. Where she had begged him to make love to her. Two days ago he had been a stranger, and she had been about to marry another man. And now...

His features were set, his expression unreadable. But his gaze traveled slowly over her face, almost as if he'd never seen her before. Maybe he was as disconcerted by what had just happened between them as she was.

Two strangers. Who had met by chance. In circumstances that had nothing to do with love. That had far more to do with death and dying. His world and not hers. And he was still almost a stranger. A man she knew only as Hawk.

"Your arm hurt?" he asked.

Only with his question did she realize that it did, and that she was holding it. Like a reprimanded child, she removed her fingers from the gauze he had put over the gash.

"It's a little sore," she admitted.

"I guess this didn't help."

"Not my arm," she said softly, finally smiling at him.

"You didn't take the pain capsules," he said.

"I took one when I lay down to read the papers. Two had knocked me out last night. I decided I didn't want to be that drugged. Just...pleasantly unaware that anything hurt."

"Is that what this was all about?" he asked.

It took her a minute to put it together.

"You think I asked you to make love to me because I took a pain pill?" she asked, her voice climbing at the end of the question. She found it incredible that he didn't understand.

"Did you?"

"No," she said quickly, because that hadn't been the reason, of course. However, with his question, she did wonder if she would have been so open about what she felt if she hadn't taken that capsule. "Maybe it made it easier," she acknowledged.

"Easier?"

"Easier for me to admit what I wanted," she said. "But... I think I've wanted you to make love to me almost since the beginning. At least since you kissed me."

His eyes came up, locking suddenly with hers. She didn't flinch from their assessment. What she had told him was the truth. And she wasn't ashamed of it.

That was something she hadn't admitted then, not even to herself, or maybe she hadn't known, given everything else that had been going on. But she had been attracted to him in the hotel that day. She had wondered then what this would be like—Hawk's lovemaking—and now she knew.

And she wanted him still. Wanted him again, she amended. As much, or maybe more, she realized, than before he had taken her. *Taken her.* The words echoed in her consciousness. Out of place. So foreign to what she had always thought should happen between a man and a woman. She didn't think she had ever used the term in connection with making love. Now, however, she knew exactly what it meant.

Hawk had taken her. He hadn't talked to her, hadn't whispered words of seduction. And he hadn't pretended that he was doing anything other than what he had done. He had consumed her. Invaded and conquered, just as his kiss had taken the first day she'd met him. *Taken,* she repeated mentally, acknowledging the truth of what had happened between them.

But at the same time, she knew that he had taken nothing she hadn't willingly given. Nothing she didn't intend for him to have. Eventually. It was just that the way he had made love to her was so different. Powerful and unrestrained.

He was different from any other man she had ever known, of course. Harder. More cynical. Maybe even smarter—except apparently about knowing what she felt.

"Maybe we should try for slow," she suggested, her voice low and husky from thinking about the possibility. This was the image she had gotten when he had asked that question: *Do you want it quick or slow?* The thought of making love to him had been in her brain, triggered by those words, although she had known that wasn't what he meant.

Quick or slow? A choice between the almost primitive force his lovemaking had just been or the tantalizing tenderness she believed he could be capable of. She had no reason to think that, and she wondered why she did. He was not a gentle man. She had known it all along, and nothing that had happened between them had contradicted her initial judgment.

"It's...been a long time," he said. "I didn't mean to be rough."

The confession surprised her. Hawk would have no trouble finding a woman, of course, so his abstinence would have been by choice. And it seemed a strange choice for a man like him.

"I didn't mean that," she said. "I want you to make love to me again. And just...give me a little more time to enjoy it," she added, the soft suggestion teasing. She smiled at him, but the line of his mouth didn't move, the blue eyes still searching her face. Apparently whatever he found there was reassuring.

"You didn't enjoy that?" he asked, his voice suddenly more relaxed than she'd ever heard it, its timbre totally changed by the undeniable thread of amusement. "Are you trying to tell me that wasn't satisfactory?"

He would know better. Her responses had left no doubt about how much she had enjoyed his lovemaking. "I'm going to assume that's a rhetorical question," she said.

He held her eyes a few seconds longer, and then, without answering, he rolled onto his back. He put his hands, fingers interlocked, behind his head. His gaze seemed to be examining the ceiling as intently as it had her face.

She turned on her right side, propping herself on her elbow, high enough above him that she could see most of his body. The same broad shoulders and chest she had seen at the hotel, long, smooth muscles lying under tanned skin. Flat stomach.

Her eyes moved downward, examining what the towel had covered that day. Nothing was hidden now. There was nothing about his body she hadn't been made aware of. Nothing about hers he didn't know intimately.

Her fingers lifted, touching the mat of coarse hair on his chest. They moved almost as if asking permission. After what had happened between them, she shouldn't have to ask. Permission had definitely been granted, she decided. Reciprocal permission.

He turned his head in response to the small caress. She smiled at him again, moving her hand slowly, enjoying the texture of the dark, hair-roughened skin. The muscled firmness underneath. The feel of his nipples, hardening under her fingers. She liked touching him, savored the realization that she had the right to do that now.

"So how about slow?" she said again, her voice deliberately teasing. She didn't understand his hesitation in responding to her invitation.

"What did you mean before about dreams?" he asked.

But that conversation seemed to have happened a long time ago, and it was hard to remember exactly what she had been thinking. As a matter of fact, it had been pretty damned difficult to think at all just then.

He had asked about Amir. Why she had agreed to marry him. And foolishly, she had tried to explain. There was no *real* explanation of what she had done, of course. She had already admitted that. And this—what had happened tonight—was more proof of how wrong she had been.

It was almost ironic. Just as she had decided this particular dream was the one that would never come true, out of all the other seemingly impossible ones that already had, she had stumbled across this man.

This man, she thought. A man called Hawk. About whom she knew nothing. From whom she would learn nothing. Nothing he didn't want her to know. Nothing about who he really was.

All she knew was that he matched those long-ago dreams. Those cherished girlhood fantasies she had never openly confessed to anyone. Dreams of finding someone this strong. This *good.*

Her lips tilted when she realized the unintended sexual connotation of that word. That was certainly true, as she had reason to know, but it wasn't what she meant.

Just *good,* she thought. Old-fashioned, one-of-the-good-guys kind of goodness. White hat. Hero. She wondered what Hawk would say if she called him that. Her smile widened as she thought about his probable reaction.

"There's something funny about those dreams?" he asked.

She realized he was still watching her. Waiting for her answer. And lost in memory, she had almost forgotten his question. "I was beginning to believe I'd never meet someone like you," she said softly. "Not in this lifetime."

Again there was a silence, but his eyes were still focused intently on hers. "Someone like me?" he repeated finally. "What the hell is that supposed to mean?"

His voice was harsh, and she knew she couldn't explain to him what she'd been thinking. She couldn't imagine being foolish enough to confess to the romantic nonsense that had been running through her mind. Or to confess the dreams she had once had.

"As strong as you," she offered. *As good,* her heart added.

His lips moved, pursing a little as if he were thinking about that, and then, in amazement, she watched them lift, moving upward at the corners. Almost a smile.

"But then you've been hanging around guys like Amir," he suggested.

Who probably wasn't good. Or strong. Not any of the things she had once dreamed the man she would fall in love with would be.

"Would you quit bringing Amir up?" she said. Once again she deliberately made her voice teasing. She didn't want to think about Amir. About what a fool he had made of her. She didn't want those feelings to spoil what was happening here.

"Did *you?*" Hawk asked. The smile had disappeared, and his voice had changed. Hardened. It was cold once more, no hint of amusement in this question.

It took a second to figure out what he was asking, and when she did her own smile faded as well. There was nothing she could say about her relationship with Amir that Hawk would believe. Probably no one would believe the truth. It *was* pretty unbelievable, and that also made her feel like a fool. To realize how easily *she* had accepted Amir's explanations.

"Does it matter?" she asked instead.

Hawk's mouth tightened. "It shouldn't," he admitted.

"But it does?"

"Forget it," he said. "Forget I asked."

He turned his head, eyes focused upward again.

"You wouldn't understand," she said. An evasion. And it sounded whining and childish.

"Try me," he suggested, eyes still on the ceiling.

Men weren't supposed to care about the *whys* of stuff like that. It was surprising to her that he wanted to know. Even a little flattering, that whether or not she had made love to Amir seemed to matter to him.

"We didn't have that kind of relationship," she said.

"Why not?" he asked.

They had been engaged, if only for a few weeks. And most people would expect that would lead to some intimacy.

"He implied it was because of his religion." Even as she said it, she felt stupid. Used. Gullible.

"And you believed him."

She could read nothing in Hawk's tone. No skepticism. No mockery. But he was very good at hiding what he thought.

"Because I wanted to believe him, I guess. Because..."

"Because?" he prodded when she stopped.

"Because I didn't feel that way about him."

"You were going to marry him," Hawk said.

Almost an accusation. At least it felt like one. *Because I was alone. Scared. Betrayed. Numb with grief and fear.* And none of those were reasons she wanted to take out and examine. Or expose to someone else's examination. Not even to defend herself from what Hawk seemed to be suggesting.

"It's pretty complicated," she offered instead. Another evasion.

"I'm not going anywhere. Not tonight."

She took a breath. The darkness helped, and the fact that he wasn't looking at her.

"My agent had just died. Someone I trusted. A...mentor, I suppose. And when he died, I found out he hadn't done some of the things he'd promised to do. Some investments he was supposed to make with the money I'd earned hadn't been made. The money was gone, and at the same time, I realized my career was going nowhere. There was nothing else I knew how to do. I never had anything but this," she said softly.

She touched her cheek with the tips of her fingers, but Hawk wasn't looking at her, so he didn't see the gesture. And he said nothing in response to what she'd told him, his eyes still on the ceiling.

"When Amir showed up," she continued, "marrying him seemed like a good idea. Everyone told me it was. Something safe. Somewhere to go." She hesitated, waiting for some response, some reaction to what she had said, but there was none. "I guess none of that makes much sense to you, does it?"

Hawk would always know where he was going. That incredible surety would never falter. And he had probably never depended on another person in his entire life.

"Maybe," he said.

Comforted a little by the soft agreement, even as grudging as it sounded, she went on, trying to make sense of what had happened, maybe as much for herself as for him. "And then the morning of the wedding, I realized that...what I was doing was wrong. Wrong for me. For him. All of it was wrong. For the wrong reasons. I wasn't in love with him."

The last she added almost as an afterthought. Just in case Hawk hadn't understood the wrongness she had discovered. Finally, after a long time, he turned his head. His eyes moved over her face, again searching. But she had nothing to hide. What she had told him was the truth.

"You want another one of those pills?" he asked.

The question seemed out of context. She hadn't even been thinking about the dull ache in her arm. It was an unimportant background element to the things that had been going on between the two of them.

"I'm..." she began, intending to deny the pain he seemed concerned about. Then she realized that his eyes had lightened and the tightness around his lips had eased. "Why?" she asked instead, suspicious of that relaxation.

"Slow," he said. "I just thought you might want a little something to make this time *easier,* too."

The inflection of the word was mocking. But it was also gently teasing. Inviting her to participate in that subtle mockery. Inviting her—

"But if not, I guess we'll just have to employ some of that old tried and true," he said.

"What's that?" she asked, anticipation stirring.

"You know," he whispered.

He turned his body toward hers, propping himself on his elbow just as she was. They were lying face-to-face. Body-to-body. Hardly three inches between them.

"No," she said, her mouth suddenly almost too dry to get the words out, her heartbeat accelerating. "No, I don't know."

He leaned toward her. She thought at first he intended to kiss her. She couldn't remember that he had kissed her when they'd made love.

He didn't now. Instead, his mouth lowered to the square of gauze he'd placed over her injury. He brushed it with his lips, the gesture tender, especially for a man like Hawk. Then he leaned back a fraction of an inch. His mouth was almost touching the front of her shoulder now.

"Foreplay," he said softly.

The single word was moist and hot against her skin. She waited, wondering if he would put his lips where his breath had touched. Wondering if he'd kiss her there. Wanting him to.

There had been nothing like what he was suggesting in the explosion that had occurred between them before. That had been hard and fast and exciting. Without preliminaries. And very definitely out of the narrow range of her experience.

"You know what that is?" he asked, his mouth closer than before. Warm breath moved against her collarbone now. Tantalizingly near.

She closed her eyes, anticipation so strong it was almost culmination. She nodded, and then, afraid he couldn't see, she whispered, "Yes."

His hand found her breast, thumb moving back and forth over the pearled bud of its nipple. His fingers were a little rough, their hard masculinity incredibly sensuous.

His palm enclosed, squeezing the soft globe. The pressure was exquisite, pain and pleasure inextricably mixed. The breath she took in response was a soft hint of sound, broken, automatic.

He reacted by easing his body against her, pushing her down to her back, in the most vulnerable position a woman can assume. Open. Unprotected. Unquestioning.

He put his leg over both of hers. The contrast between the hair-roughened skin of his thigh and the smoothness of hers was also sensuous. She expected him to lift his body over hers, as he had done before.

Suddenly, despite her teasing request for slow, she wanted him to do that. To do it quickly. Wanted him to push into her again, hard and incredibly strong. So sure of what he was doing. In control.

That wasn't what he did, however. He eased closer, the front of his body leaning against the side of hers, his erection pressed into her hipbone. His hand cupped her breast, pulling it toward his descending mouth. His lips fastened over the nipple he'd teased, and he began suckling like an infant, the pull of his mouth hard and strong.

The words reverberated in her head. He was exactly that. So hard. So incredibly strong. Exactly as she wanted him to be.

It seemed she could feel the movement of his mouth deep within her body. Moving low inside. The sudden flood of moisture that resulted from that pressure was hot, rich, more profuse than it had ever been before. Readying her trembling body for what she knew was to come.

The glide of his tongue replaced the demanding caress of his lips. It circled, leaving a trail of moisture over all the sensitive nerve endings. Then the warmth of his breath touched where his tongue had been, evaporating the trace of wetness into shivering sensation.

Enough, she wanted to tell him. *More than enough. Now. Do it now. Make love to me before I die of wanting you.*

She said nothing, of course, and his teeth nibbled the hard nub his tongue had created. He wasn't gentle. Again she realized that the feelings he created verged on the edge of pain. Walking that thin, erotic line between agony and ecstasy.

She put her hand on his cheek. Protest or caress? Even she wasn't sure. It didn't matter because it had no effect on what he was doing. And she had known that it wouldn't.

She realized finally that his hand no longer cupped the breast his teeth and lips were tormenting. It was moving instead. Tracing over the bones in her rib cage. Finding with his fingertips the small protrusion of her hipbone. Sliding across the softness of her belly. His thumb dipped into her navel and circled. Slow. Infinitely patient.

Two distinctly different sensations. Almost too much for her mind to hold on to at one time. Too much for her body to bear. His mouth, teasing painfully against her breast. And the slow downward glide of his fingers. Moving so tenderly, so incredibly slowly, over her skin.

She knew what he intended. Again anticipation surged. She was already savoring the first knowing movement of his fingers. And there was no doubt now that they *would* be knowing.

Do you know what that is? he had asked. Foreplay. Now she knew, if she had not before. He had taught her, a lesson she had begged him for.

The fingers that had been tenderly examining every inch of her skin suddenly invaded. They were long, hard and demanding—as demanding as his body had been before. Only with their touch did she realize she was sore. The pleasantly satisfying soreness that follows hard lovemaking.

It had been a long time, he'd told her. An apology, she thought. But it had been a long time for her, too. A long emptiness, and she wanted him to fill it. To fill her, just as he had before.

His fingers moved in and out as the back of his thumb began to caress the center of her need. All her needs. She knew he could satisfy every one. Satisfy her, more than she had ever dreamed anyone could. She arched upward, trying to increase the pressure. To quicken the tempo of what he was doing.

His mouth suddenly fastened over hers, his tongue's invasion matching the unrelenting movement of his fingers. Waves of sensation roared through her body, touching nerves and muscles in their path with sweet heat. Powerful. Demanding more than she could give.

Too many sensations, she thought again, her brain shattering under their impact, the ability to think spiraling away in the darkness. It was too much. More than she could bear.

The waves of sensation converged into one, lifting her, and she was powerless against its flood. Was drowning in it. Drowning in feelings. Heat. Fire.

Her body arched again and again, fighting it, and then, finally, because she had no choice, simply riding the crest like a spent swimmer. He wouldn't release her. He wouldn't let her go. Again and again he demanded. And every time, her body answered, responding to his touch.

Only when she truly believed she would shatter, as her mind had done, under the repeated ecstasy, did he relent. His head lifted, his lips hovering an inch above hers. His fingers stilled, allowing her body to slowly descend from the mountain of sensations he had built. Her breathing eased, and finally she found the strength to open her eyes. To look into his.

"Too much," she whispered. It was the last rational thought she had in the maelstrom of feelings he'd created.

"No," he said softly, shifting his body. "Not nearly enough." He pushed into her, the size and strength of his erection almost frightening. Almost.

His hips began to move above her in the darkness, the dampness of his chest clinging to the softness of her breasts and stomach. And she was aware of the other wetness. *Too much,* she thought again. *Too wet.*

His movements were controlled, powerfully driven by the muscles in his thighs and buttocks. Deep enough to take her to the edge of pain. And then the long, slow withdrawal. So slow. Anticipation building again. Waiting for the next downward thrust. Bone against bone. Hard and hot and deep. So deep.

Although she would not have believed it to be possible, the same sensations that had destroyed her intellect were building again. Swelling from the inside outward. Clawing this time for release, a release that was nowhere near. Too wet. Too slow.

Now, she thought. Her demand, and unspoken. *Now.* She lifted trembling legs, unsure her exhausted muscles would obey the command of her brain. She wrapped them as tightly as she could around his waist, drawing him to her. Into her. With his next thrust, so deep she knew he had touched the walls of her soul, she cried out.

Still he didn't give in. His control. His decision. Slow withdrawal. A small seep of cold air between the hot slickness of their skins.

Desertion. Just like everyone else always had, he was leaving her. *Don't go,* she thought. *Don't leave me.*

"No," she begged, turning her head against the dampness of his shoulder to gasp out the plea. "No," she whispered again. "Don't go." Her nails dug into the strong, broad back that strained above her. She felt him flinch at the unexpected pain.

He punished her for it, driving into her body until she cried out again at the unrelenting force of what he was doing. Finally, just when she thought she could stand no more, his voice joined hers, at first guttural, hoarse with need, and then triumphant.

The crest of the wave that had carried her alone found them both. And it was strong enough to carry them together this time, their bodies still entwined in the concealing darkness.

Chapter Eleven

The razor was drawn downward again, revealing a path of brown skin in the middle of the white foam. Hawk's eyes were fixed resolutely on the image in the mirror, watching the movement of his hand, following each stroke. As if this familiar ritual, something he must have done almost every morning of his adult life, demanded his full attention.

"Did you know?" Tyler asked him again. "Had you already set this meeting up?" *Before you came to my room? Before you made love to me through those endless hours? Did you know that today this would be over, and I'd never see you again?*

She didn't understand why she didn't pose all those questions aloud. Why she didn't demand answers she was certainly entitled to. Old lessons, maybe. Never forgotten. *Just smile at them, sweetheart, but don't open your mouth.*

"I knew," Hawk said.

Another stroke, pulling the blade downward over the golden whiskers that had brushed erotically against her skin last night. His hand was as steady as it had always been. As steady as when he had held the gun on her that first day. As unwavering as when he'd shot those men in her mother's house in Mississippi.

"Then why?" she whispered.

Not demanding, not even now, she realized. Her soft question had been almost plaintive instead. Begging him to make her understand why last night had happened. Why he had allowed that to happen if he already knew...

If he already knew she would never see him again. The words echoed painfully in her head, as they had been since he'd told her. To be fair, something she wasn't in the mood to do, he *had* warned her. Only yesterday, she realized, although it seemed an eternity ago. He had told her that after she gave her description of the assassins to the authorities, someone else would provide protection for her. That it wouldn't be him. Couldn't be him.

He had even told her that would happen soon. But still, she hadn't believed it would be like this. This...unexpected. This painful. Especially after last night.

Hawk turned his head, no longer focusing on the mirror, no longer pretending he needed to watch the long, brown fingers direct the razor. The half-finished shave should have made him look ridiculous, but it didn't.

One lean, tanned cheek was completely exposed. The once-broken nose. His lips, which she had thought were thin and hard, and which she had learned last night were not. She remembered the feel of them moving over her skin. Moving under hers. Suckling her breast.

She pulled her gaze away from them. Away from the knot of tension at their corner. And looked into his eyes instead. They were cold. As empty as they had seemed the day she'd met him. Almost as frightening. She had thought, after last night, that she would never see them like this again. Without feeling. Without emotion.

"I didn't mean for that to happen," he said softly.

She was surprised he bothered to explain that much, given what was in his eyes. Given the kind of man she knew him to be. And what he had said was probably even true, she thought, because he had never lied to her before. He had told her all the unpleasant truths her situation demanded. But still...

"You came to my room," she said, hoping for something more. More than this coldness. This *truth*.

"To make sure you were all right."

She shook her head. That was his self-deception. "You didn't have to—"

"I came the night before," he interrupted. "To see if you had a fever. I touched you. You didn't wake up. You didn't even move. Last night I thought you'd taken the pain capsules again. There was a glass of water on the table. The cap was off the bottle. I had no reason to think you hadn't."

Everything he said was logical. He hadn't come to her room with the intention of making love to her. And he wouldn't have if she hadn't invited him to. At least that's what he was suggesting. Maybe it was true. Except, even if it were, she didn't think it changed what had happened between them. To them.

"So what do we do?" she asked.

And waited, hoping that his eyes would soften as they had last night. Lighten with amusement as she had seen them do then. Or darken with passion as they had when he breathed that single, tantalizing word against her bare shoulder. *Foreplay.*

"We go to this meeting. You tell them exactly what you saw. *That's* what we do," he said, his voice low and hard. And then he added, almost spoiling the effect he had tried for; "Because there's nothing else we can do."

"I can think of a couple of things," she said.

She wasn't going to make this easy for him. Despite her inability to rail at him for what he'd done, she hadn't achieved all she had the last twenty years without stubbornness. Without the determination not to let anything defeat her dreams. After all, this was the only one that was left, and she didn't intend to lose it.

Despite the fact that he had said almost nothing to her last night, had made no promises and suggested no future for them together, she didn't believe that what had happened had been only physical. *The last of the dreamers,* she supposed, mocking her naiveté, but for some reason she believed that for Hawk as well, last night had been about more than two bodies in the darkness. About more than satisfying needs.

"Nothing else that will work," Hawk said.

He was still holding the razor, but at least he wasn't using it. At least he was still looking at her. But nothing had changed in the cold blue depths of his eyes.

"I trust you more than I trust them," she said. She didn't want to go into witness protection. She didn't want her life, even with her current problems, to change, to disappear, to be destroyed. And now that she'd found him, she didn't want to lose Hawk.

"I can't keep you safe," he said. "They can. It's as simple as that."

His tone said "end of argument." And she knew she was supposed to shut up and do what she was told. That seemed to be what he expected. What everyone always expected of her. Only this was too important. Too important not to fight for.

"Then I guess I won't be safe. Because…I'd still rather be with you."

He said nothing for a long time. His eyes didn't flinch at the offer she had made. An obvious and unapologetic offer. Made without any explanation to soften the proposal that lay at its heart. Demanding nothing in return. Nothing except to be allowed to stay with him.

"It's no good," he said finally. "It won't work."

His eyes told her nothing, their lightness seeming suddenly as opaque as Amir's had always been, as good at hiding his motives. And she had to wonder about those. Why Hawk was so eager to get rid of her. In such a damned hurry to get her off his hands.

"I'm not asking you for anything," she said softly. "You do understand that? Nothing but to stay with you."

"That's your problem. You *should* be asking," he said.

"What does that mean?" she asked, stung by his rejection. Humiliated by the criticism it implied.

"You were willing to go along with whatever Amir

wanted because it was easier than standing on your own two feet. You want to stay with me because it's easier than doing the right thing. Easier than telling the truth about what happened and dealing with the consequences."

"That's not true. And it's not fair," she said hotly.

It wasn't. She had made her own way since she was seventeen. And she hadn't done too badly. Except in trusting Paul. And it was because of his betrayal, she now knew, that she had gone along with what Amir had wanted.

But she had really thought Amir loved her. She had thought maybe that would be enough, as close to the heart of that old, almost-forgotten dream as she was likely to get. She hadn't been able to figure out any other reason for Amir's whirlwind courtship. And she had really tried. But of course, she could never have imagined, not in a million years, that he was simply using her to set up his father. Using her.

"Nothing is ever *fair*," Hawk said softly. "Life isn't. You don't need me. Or Amir. You don't need anybody."

A tough old broad, she thought. Maybe he even meant to be flattering, but this wasn't a matter of need. Maybe she *didn't* need him. But she wanted him. She would always want him.

"One more question," she said softly.

He didn't nod or give her permission, but his eyes didn't release hers. They held on, and so she asked the only question that mattered now. And hoped he'd tell her the truth about this, too.

"If it were different…" she said, wondering if he'd understand. "If they weren't looking for me," she continued. "If we had met some other time, some other way. If all this weren't going on, then…"

She paused, not even sure now what she wanted to ask. He had made no promises last night. Given no commitment. Said nothing besides what his hands and body had told her. And maybe she had been wrong about what she thought they were saying.

"If everything about this was different…" Her voice faded, but she was still watching his eyes. Still hoping for something.

"If we were different people," he said softly.

Not a question, maybe, but she nodded. "Yes," she whispered.

"Then I guess the outcome might be…different, too."

Not exactly all she had wanted. But something. Maybe even as much as a man called Hawk could give. As much as he was capable of giving. That and last night.

And those were, of course, far more than she had had before.

HE HADN'T PARTICULARLY liked this setup from the beginning, Hawk thought, as he pulled the rental car into the underground garage. Despite the fact that it was a little before noon, it was almost dark in this concrete hole, dug to provide below-the-street parking for the tenants of this exclusive office building.

Maybe he hadn't liked the arrangements, but he trusted Jordan Cross. After all, as he had told Tyler at the beginning of all this, eventually you had to trust someone. And if Claire Heywood was willing to help, then he supposed it would have to be on her terms. Despite the premonition that stalked along the nerve endings at the back of his neck. Despite the fact that he knew there were too many factors in this situation he wouldn't be able to control.

Hell, he couldn't even control himself, Hawk thought in disgust. He glanced to his right, toward the passenger seat, and found that Tyler was looking at him, wide violet-blue eyes locked on his face.

What kind of bastard would do what he had done? he wondered again, as he had been all morning. What kind of son of a bitch makes love to a woman he's never going to see again? A woman he knows he's going to hand over to someone else's control in less than twenty-four hours? What kind of man lacks the discipline to deny himself that long?

"Now what?" she asked, seeing his eyes on her. Despite the question, her voice was almost disinterested. Certainly it was without the emotion that had colored the others she had asked this morning.

"We wait here until it's time to go up," he said.

She nodded, turning her head to look out the window on the passenger side of the car. The view in that direction was not all that interesting—an indistinct row of parked cars stretching off into the darkness. A concrete wall.

"Is this where we say goodbye?" she asked, her gaze still directed outside.

Hawk didn't answer. There really wasn't much point in discussing goodbyes. He had never been good at them. And he understood, even if she didn't, that in a few minutes everything she thought she knew about him, all those fantasies she'd dreamed up about why he had come to find her and exactly what he was bringing her here to do, would be exposed for what they were. Myths. Fantasies. Lies.

He could tell himself from now to eternity that they weren't his lies. That he hadn't been the one who had thought them up. But that didn't really matter. She believed them. Believed he was someone—something—very different from what he really was. And considering how al-Ahmad had used her, finding that out would probably have been devastating, whenever and however she discovered the truth. But after what he had done last night…

Hawk took a breath, his chest tight with self-loathing. Just a little discipline, he thought, just some damn self-control, and none of that would have happened. She would have walked away from him today—maybe with regret. With anger that he hadn't told her the truth. But certainly not with what she would inevitably feel after today's revelations.

"Hawk," she said softly.

His eyes were examining his hand, the right one, the one that was still, for some reason, gripping the wheel. At the sound of his name, the only name she knew and would probably ever know, he watched his fingers tighten, brown skin stretching taut around the muscles and sinews and bones that had never before failed him. That had never trembled or faltered in carrying out a mission.

His hand was trembling now. Trembling with need. Trembling because he wanted to touch her. To put his fingers against the softness of her cheek. To touch her breasts. To pull her to him and explain. To tell her that for him last night had been...

Something that had never happened before. Totally out of the range of his experience. With women. With relationships. Not that anything he had ever had with another woman could be called a relationship. There had been nothing remotely like this. Nothing that had ever involved his feelings. His emotions. His mind.

But if he told her that, he knew, it would simply make what was about to happen worse. If it could possibly get any worse.

Another betrayal. Because she had trusted him. With her life. Trusted him to protect her and to keep her safe. Trusted him with her body. Trusted him to love her.

And in the end, Hawk had been no more worthy of that trust than her fiancé had. Or the agent she had told him about. Like them, he, too, had used her.

Sleeve card. Ace in the hole. Those motives, which he had readily admitted to at the beginning of this, were not, of course, what he felt now. But telling her that wouldn't make what he had to do any easier. Or what she had to do. After this meeting, she had to walk away from him. To walk away and never look back. For her sake. To keep her safe. And learning how he felt, knowing what last night had meant to him, would make none of that easier.

"Hawk," she said again, and finally he lifted his eyes from the contemplation of his hand. "It doesn't have to be like this," she said. "It doesn't have to end this way. You said that once I'd testified, it would take the pressure off. That Amir would know I couldn't really hurt him. After that's over, why can't we—"

The knock on the glass of the window beside him interrupted her. Hawk turned his head to find Jordan Cross bending down to peer into the interior of the car. The sickening rush of fear in the pit of Hawk's stomach eased with the sight of the familiar face.

But it could have been anybody knocking on that window—al-Ahmad's men, the company's. Hawk hadn't even been aware that someone was approaching the car, he'd been focused so intently on whatever she had been saying. Like an amateur, he realized.

And that was why, of course, there had never been room in his life for a relationship like this. Because he couldn't afford the distraction. Not in his line of work.

He rolled down the window.

"It's time," Cross said. He had already straightened again, no longer looking inside the car.

Hawk knew that his eyes would be searching their surroundings, examining them for anything out of the ordinary. Anything suspicious. Just as Hawk *should* have been doing.

"What are you doing here?" Hawk asked.

"My operation," Jordan said. "I don't plan on making an appearance upstairs, but I wanted to make sure there was nobody waiting down here for you."

"Risky," Hawk said. They had agreed Jordan shouldn't be connected to him because of repercussions within the agency. Hawk still thought that was the best way to do this.

"Somebody tell you that you were supposed to have all the fun?" Cross asked. And then he cleared the amusement from his deep voice. "Our esteemed colleagues aren't down here. They came in the front. That's what Heywood told them to do."

"How much does she know?"

"I thought she should know it all. Makes it easier to play the hand if you've seen the cards. You ready?"

As ready as I'll ever be, Hawk thought. He rolled up the window and then put his hand on the door handle. He was aware that Jordan had already stepped away from the car, allowing him room to open the door and climb out. He was also aware that Tyler was still watching him.

This would be his last chance to say something to her, alone and without anyone else listening. Last chance to explain. Last chance to tell her how he felt.

Instead of taking it, the man called Hawk opened the door of the car he had rented at an airport in Mississippi and stepped out into the heat and darkness of a private parking garage in Washington, D.C. The end of a journey.

And his last chance, he thought again, standing up and closing the door behind him. This time he didn't take it. At least, he thought, as he put his hand into the one Jordan Cross extended, he still had enough self-discipline left to accomplish that.

"WE UNDERSTOOD YOU WANTED to talk to my client."

As she made the opening gambit, Claire Heywood's voice was controlled and professional, sounding exactly like the high-priced attorney she was.

"Your client?" the assistant deputy director of operations questioned.

"For these purposes," Claire said smoothly.

Her long blond hair was arranged again in a neat chignon. Today there were no disordered strands floating around the pale oval of her face. No tears. No black dress. She was wearing a simple red suit that shouted money and power, but it was a nicely discreet shout, appropriate for the elegant office they were in. And her eyes were as dispassionate as her voice.

They hadn't been. Hawk knew from their reaction that she had recognized him from the cemetery. Her pupils had widened slightly when her secretary escorted them into the room. Claire Heywood's gaze had met his, acknowledgment of that recognition in it, maybe acknowledgment of what he had done for Griff as well. Maybe even…gratitude? he thought, questioning the emotions he saw there. However, she had said nothing, gesturing them toward the two leather chairs that were aligned on her side of the wide conference table.

The representatives of the government were already seated on the other side. There were three of them, but Hawk recognized only one man. The others were new or had been pulled in from some other division. It was even possible they were State Department and not CIA.

That was probably the case, Hawk decided, considering the way their eyes examined him, as if he was something that disturbed their bureaucratic smugness. Or frightened them. Like he was some viper that had just come slithering out from under a rock and into their civilized little meeting.

But it really didn't matter what they thought about him. Hawk knew that the man in the middle was the one who counted. The one he would have to convince. The one Tyler would have to convince, he amended, if this was going to work.

Hawk planned to offer no defense of what he had done in Baghdad. As far was he was concerned, that act didn't need defending. He was prepared to offer them proof of the terrorist's guilt, to make threats about going public if he had to, but he was not prepared to beg for their understanding. Not even Carl Steiner's.

Steiner had been a friend of Griff's, and Hawk supposed he had been the logical one to take over the unit after the massacre. Hawk had no way of knowing how Steiner felt about the team or even whether he was the one who had insisted on its dissolution. He supposed he'd find out in the course of this meeting exactly where Steiner stood about a lot of things.

"I think Mr. Hawkins is probably well aware of what we want to talk to him about," Steiner said.

"Why don't we make certain of that?" Claire suggested. "We understand you believe Mr. Hawkins has some connection to the assassination of Sheikh Rashad al-Ahmad."

"*Some* connection?" Steiner questioned, his tone amused.

"Maybe you'd like to characterize exactly what you believe Mr. Hawkins' association to be," Claire suggested.

Hawk didn't look at Tyler. He didn't know if enough had already been said to make her start thinking. To make her start wondering why they were talking about him, instead of about what she believed they were here to discuss.

"I saw the men who killed the sheikh," Tyler said into the small silence that had fallen after Claire's suggestion. "I believe I can identify them."

Steiner's eyes moved to study her face for the first time, and then they flicked back to Hawk's, questioning, before they returned to focus on the woman who had just spoken.

"Ms. Stewart, I believe," he said. "Sheikh Amir al-Ahmad's fiancée?"

"I was," Tyler said.

"I'm sure Amir al-Ahmad would be very interested in learning what you saw," Steiner suggested. "He's trying very hard to track down the extremists who were involved in his father's death, some of whom, he now believes, had infiltrated his own entourage. He is also, I'm told, interested in making public the pictures of the man who set off the fire alarms that day. A man whose actions were captured by the hotel security cameras. He wants those pictures made available to the nation's law enforcement agencies as quickly as possible." As Steiner uttered the last sentence, his eyes moved back to Hawk's.

And you will, you son of a bitch, Hawk thought, *just as soon as you're sure no one can trace the man in those pictures back to the company.*

"Amir is interested in finding out who pulled the fire alarm?" Tyler asked, obviously puzzled.

However, her voice seemed as steady as Claire's had been. As calm and unintimidated. *Maybe,* Hawk thought, *because she still doesn't understand what's going on.*

"As he will certainly be interested in what you saw. I'm surprised you haven't already communicated that information to him. Forgive me, Ms. Stewart, but I understood you were with al-Ahmad's party. In seclusion, I believe, the sheikh said.''

Hawk was aware that Tyler had turned to look at him. For direction, maybe, but he didn't meet her eyes. He didn't want to watch what would happen in them when she finally understood.

"The man who pulled the fire alarm," Tyler said, "had nothing to do with the assassination. That was…something else entirely."

"You seem certain of that," Steiner said, his eyes finally leaving their contemplation of Hawk's set face to find hers again. "But then, that is, of course, why Hawkins brought you here, isn't it. To tell us what he *didn't* do."

There was a pause before Tyler answered. "I came here to identify the assassins," she said, her voice low. There was something in her tone that hadn't been there before, however. Some hint of unease. She was disturbed, perhaps, by the direction this was taking.

"Or to assure us that Lucas Hawkins wasn't one of them?" Steiner suggested.

The silence stretched again. Longer this time. The blinds were pulled against the glare outside, and the stripes of sunshine that escaped between them, thin, white and dazzling in the pleasant dimness, fell like bars across the mahogany table.

"Hawk had nothing to do with Sheikh al-Ahmad's death."

"Forgive me, Ms. Stewart, but I'm afraid given Hawkins' past, and his rather remarkable credentials for doing exactly that, not many people are going to believe you. Even we found Hawkins' presence in the hotel that day a little too…coincidental."

"Coincidental?" Tyler repeated.

"A highly skilled…marksman just happened to be in the same hotel when an assassination occurs. A marksman who had that very day returned from the Middle East, where he had killed another man, in much the same manner in which

Sheikh Rashad al-Ahmad was murdered. An assassin who was captured on video pulling hotel fire alarms, the effect of which was to empty that hotel of suspects, despite the fact that at the time it had been surrounded by police and FBI agents. Of course your fiancé is interested in this man. Especially considering, I suppose, that you are now traveling in his company.''

There was complete silence around the table. It seemed that no one breathed.

''Hawk?'' Tyler Stewart said softly. Almost the same way she had whispered his name last night. Except then...

''Would you like to deny for Ms. Stewart the validity of the things I've just said?'' Steiner said. ''If so, Hawkins, I assure you we'd all be interested in hearing those denials. I'm sure Ms. Stewart would be. Considering her situation.''

Hawk had known this moment would come, but as he did with everything that didn't bear thinking about, he had put it out of his mind. Like Griff's death. The end of the team. Losing Tyler.

That was almost a physical pain—the thought of turning her over to someone like Steiner. But Steiner, he reminded himself, was someone who could protect her, someone who could keep her safe.

''I don't deny them,'' Hawk said quietly, his eyes resolutely on his locked hands, which rested, unmoving, on the mahogany table. ''I don't deny that I did any of those things.''

Chapter Twelve

"But I had nothing to do with Rashad al-Ahmad's assassination, and you know it," Hawk added softly.

They did know it. Steiner's eyes left no doubt about what he knew. *And*, Hawk realized, *they don't care about the sheikh's death. That isn't why they're here. That isn't why they agreed to this meeting*. He supposed he had known that all along.

"How would we know that, Mr. Hawkins? Apparently you've become a man who chooses his own targets. Based solely on his own judgment. How could we know you weren't responsible for the sheikh's death?"

"Because you know me," Hawk said. He kept his voice low, but the bitterness was there. "You have more than twenty years worth of knowing exactly who and what I am."

Steiner pulled a file, which had been lying on the table beside him since the beginning of the meeting, toward him and opened it. Hawk recognized its type. He had seen others like it on Griff's desk. He supposed all of them had dossiers like this.

Most of the time they would be locked away, accessible only to those with a "need to know" about the aspect of national security Griff's team had dealt with. Now Steiner was one of those with an official need to know.

"Lucas Hawkins," Steiner read aloud, his voice without

inflection or emotion. "Code name: Hawk. Father: unknown. Mother: Lucille Hawkins. Mother's occupation: prostitute." The black eyes lifted to Hawk's, as if for confirmation of those simple facts. "I believe she died of a heroin overdose when you were seven."

Hawk said nothing, his eyes still meeting Steiner's, his features set. But in his mind's eye was his mother's thin, wasted face, her skin without color except for the brown stain in the sunken sockets around her eyes, which were open, glazed and staring. Just the way she had looked the day he'd come home from school and found her body.

But Hawk wasn't going to give this son of a bitch the satisfaction of knowing he remembered that. Or remembered any of what had come after her death. That long, dark nightmare of abuse and neglect at the hands of the state.

After a moment the assistant deputy director's eyes returned to the page before him, and he began to read again.

"For the next ten years, Lucas Hawkins passed through a succession of over thirty foster homes and various juvenile detention facilities. His longest stay in any one of those was for seven months, when he was nine. He was eleven when he was arrested the first time. Not the last time he was arrested, of course," Steiner added, glancing at the faces of the people aligned across the massive table from him.

Hawk remembered that incident, too. He had run away again, not traveling very fast because his drunken foster father's last beating had broken his arm and a couple of ribs. He had gotten caught stealing something to eat from a convenience store.

The cops had fed him, he remembered, and were amazed at what he managed to shovel down. They kept buying, and he kept eating, trying to make up for the meals he'd missed. They had been kind in a rough way, but Hawk had put up such a fight when they'd tried to take him home that they had no choice but to turn him over to juvenile services. That was the first time he'd ended up in detention. But it hadn't been the last.

"Each criminal offense more serious than the one before," Steiner intoned solemnly, like a master of ceremonies at some macabre awards dinner.

Although his gaze hadn't faltered from its contemplation of the assistant deputy director's face, Hawk hadn't realized Steiner's eyes had returned to the record in front of him until he began to read aloud again. Hawk's mind had been drifting instead, back to those events of almost thirty years ago.

Whatever this bastard wants to tell them doesn't matter, he assured himself. It was ancient history. Unimportant. What he had done for the last twenty years was his life. The important part of it, anyway. Griff had convinced him of that.

"The last of those arrests occurred when Hawkins was seventeen. I won't bore you with the details. It's sufficient to say that the incident involved the infliction of, and I'm quoting the arresting officer here, "grave bodily harm on another minor." I believe all of this is correct so far, Hawkins," Steiner said. He looked up from the file, his brows lifting, but again Hawk made no response.

"Is this necessary?" Claire Heywood asked, her voice tight, revealing emotion for the first time. "I don't think Mr. Hawkins' personal history is relevant to our purposes."

"I had supposed Hawkins intended to make his history relevant. I thought that was the purpose behind this meeting."

"The *purpose* of this meeting is to clear Mr. Hawkins of any suspicion of the sheikh's death. Surely the misfortunes he suffered as a child—"

"I see," Steiner interrupted. "Then you are more interested in current material, I suppose. Of course, the current material *is* the crux of this matter, isn't it, Ms. Heywood. The *real* reason we're all here."

"The reason we're here is because you're trying to set me up for something I didn't do," Hawk interjected, tired of listening to Steiner's crap.

None of this had anything to do with getting Tyler into protective custody. Apparently, however, Steiner was determined they were going to deal with the accusations against Hawk before they could move on to the other.

"I didn't have anything to do with Rashad al-Ahmad's death," Hawk said very distinctly. "And I'm warning you. I don't intend to go down for that."

"So you've brought us your personal witness to prove your innocence," Steiner said, his voice amused.

"Ms. Stewart can verify I had nothing to do with that assassination."

"And that is, of course, why you brought her here. All the way from…Mississippi, I believe. To clear you of that charge."

Another silence, Hawk's this time. He didn't waste much time wondering how they knew about Mississippi. It never did any good to question their sources. And he supposed at this point there was no reason not to admit the truth. By now Tyler would have figured out what was going on. Now she knew why he had intervened that night. And exactly why he had brought her here.

"It's one of the reasons," he agreed. It had been the only one at the beginning, but it was far less important now than the other.

"Then she's very valuable to you," Steiner said. "*If* she can indeed verify that you had nothing to do with that murder." His eyes shifted from Hawk's face to Tyler's. "Are you prepared to do that, Ms. Stewart? Is that why you're here? To clear Lucas Hawkins of that charge?"

Hawk wanted to look at her, to turn his head and find out what was in her eyes, but he didn't. He had done that in the car, and it had been a mistake. It had weakened him. He couldn't afford to be weak now. He watched Steiner's face instead.

"Hawk had nothing to do with the assassination of Sheikh al-Ahmad," Tyler said softly. Just on cue, Hawk thought. "I saw the men who did. I believe two of them were Amir al-Ahmad's personal bodyguards. And there was a man in Western dress. Not Hawk," she clarified quickly. "That man was the one who had the rifle. The one who fired the shot."

"And Hawkins had nothing to do with the assassination?"

"He couldn't have. I saw them all. I heard the gun go off. Hawk wasn't there. He wasn't involved."

"Then why did he set off the fire alarms?" Steiner asked.

"Because I asked him to help me get out of the hotel."

"And why did *you* need to get out of the hotel? That was, I believe, to be the location of your wedding."

"I didn't know who was involved in the assassination. The shots were fired from the balcony of my fiancé's room. I had gone there to speak to him, and when I opened the door, I saw them. Because it *was* his room..." Tyler hesitated, apparently hesitant to accuse Amir without more proof than that.

"I indicated that Sheikh Amir al-Ahmad now suspects some of his own people might have been involved in this," Steiner said.

Tyler said nothing for a moment. Hawk again fought the urge to look at her.

"But it's possible, isn't it," she suggested finally, "that Amir himself was involved?"

"In his own father's death?" Steiner questioned.

He sounds as if that's unthinkable, Hawk thought, but it was an act, of course. Nothing was truly unthinkable. Especially to someone like Steiner.

"Ten billion dollars a year is a lot of incentive," Hawk said. "There are people in this town who would kill you for your pocket change."

"We have no reason to suspect Amir al-Ahmad of having any role in his father's death," the assistant deputy director said. "The extremists had long ago targeted their country for a takeover. And they had made at least two previous attempts on the sheikh's life. Perhaps Ms. Stewart would be willing to make herself available to the new sheikh in order to identify which members of his staff she saw on that balcony."

"Ms. Stewart will make herself available to *you*," Hawk said. "Not to Amir."

"But I'm afraid we are no longer involved in the investigation of the al-Ahmad assassination," Steiner replied. "Not in any...enforcement capacity."

"What the hell does that mean?" Hawk asked, his eyes narrowing.

"We believe that the action taken against the sheikh represented an attempt to carry out an internal coup. A national matter, probably religious in nature. It is in the best interests of the United States not to interfere in any way with the ongoing investigation of the sheikh's death. An investigation being very competently carried out by his own countrymen and their appointed agents."

"They killed a man on a New York City street," Hawk said. "They blew away a visiting head of state right in the heart of our largest city. Are you saying that's none of our business?"

"Visiting is, I believe, the operative word here," Carl Steiner said, his voice expressing disinterest. "A *private* visit. Which was not State Department sponsored. Or sanctioned. Perhaps if they had requested security..." He shrugged, letting the suggestion trail, his dark eyes meeting Hawk's.

They were triumphant, Hawk realized. The nausea that had formed in Hawk's throat when Steiner suggested Tyler make herself available to Amir for questioning was joined now by a prickle of ice skating along his spine.

"However, there are other matters which we, as representatives of the United States, are still very much interested in resolving," Steiner continued. "Matters having to do with this government's authority. With...obeying orders," he said almost delicately, his black eyes still locked on Hawk's.

"The assassination in Iraq," Hawk said, laying out the accusation Steiner was dancing around, probably because of Claire Heywood's presence. They had wanted Hawk for that all along. They were determined to rein him in. Maybe even to punish him for going against orders.

"Unless, of course, Ms. Stewart is prepared to provide an alibi for that murder also," the assistant deputy director said.

"You know why I went to Baghdad," Hawk said.

"I know you had been told *not* to go. And told that your target there was off-limits."

"My target there," Hawk repeated mockingly, "killed Griffon Cabot and five others in a senseless massacre of innocent people who were on their way to work. I knew who ordered that attack. You knew who ordered it. An international terrorist with enough blood on his hands to float a couple of battleships."

"Someone who was off-limits," Steiner said again.

"Is he right?" Claire Heywood asked softly.

Steiner's eyes shifted to her, and in them was surprise. "Right about what?"

"About the man in Baghdad being responsible for the Langley incident?"

"We have no proof of that," Steiner said.

"I have proof." Hawk's voice was calm and emotionless again. He had himself under control. He could do that as long as he didn't think about Tyler. He had to convince Steiner to put her into protection, and if the price of that was to let them have him for what he had done in Baghdad, then so be it. "Do you really want proof?"

"You may present it. It will have to be analyzed, of course," Steiner said.

Hawk laughed, the short sound devoid of humor. "*Everything* has to be analyzed," he said. "To see who we might offend. To determine if our so-called allies will approve. Whatever happened to right and wrong? Whatever happened to doing the right thing, the right thing for *this* country, and letting the chips fall where they may?''

''And you intend to determine what is right?'' Steiner asked. ''You and you alone will make that decision? The world is more complicated, Mr. Hawkins, than your narrow vision of it.''

''Only to you,'' Hawk said. ''Only to bastards like you and your pious bureaucratic brotherhood.''

No one said anything for a moment. Steiner's eyes were angry, but still confident. And why the hell shouldn't they be? Hawk thought bitterly. Steiner held the winning hand. He had apparently known that since the beginning. Because he really did know all about Hawk. All the psychological babble that they had collected on him for years. Somehow they had put that together with the fact that he had taken Tyler Stewart with him from Mississippi and kept her with him. And this time, by putting two and two together, they had somehow arrived at the correct conclusion.

''What do you want?'' Hawk said finally. It was time to give in to the inevitable and make the deal.

''We want you to agree to answer some questions about what happened in Iraq.''

''And where does this questioning take place?'' Hawk asked, simply as a matter of form.

''At one of our secured facilities. You will be well treated. I think you know that.''

Fed and clothed and housed, Hawk thought, at the expense of the state. Not much different from getting the little pension he'd lost. ''And what do *I* get in exchange for my cooperation?''

''We're not offering you a deal.''

''You better be,'' Hawk warned softly.

''Certain terms were set when you agreed to this meeting,'' Claire reminded Steiner.

''The situation has changed,'' he said.

''You son of a bitch,'' Hawk said, his voice filled with

cold hatred. The men on either side of Steiner shifted uncomfortably, but he seemed unaffected.

"What do you want?" Steiner asked, his voice amused again.

It was almost as if he were making a concession. One that they all would know he wasn't compelled to make. As if the agency was no longer worried about whatever threat Hawk might represent to them, but was willing to give a little out of the goodness of its heart, a concept Hawk knew to be a joke. Or as one might concede some advantage to an outmatched opponent, simply to be sporting.

Even as he was thinking that, Hawk was amending his demands. After all, there was only one that mattered. And there was no reason why Steiner shouldn't grant it, especially if Hawk gave them what they wanted. It would be no skin off his nose, and he would leave with what the company had sent him here to get.

"Ms. Stewart tells her story about what she saw to the proper authorities. Ours, not theirs," Hawk said. "Then they take it from there. The agency sees to it that the assassins can't possibly find her. You keep her hidden for as long as it takes to track them down."

"Witness protection?"

"Whatever you want to call it," Hawk agreed. *Whatever will keep her safe.* "But she doesn't tell that story to al-Ahmad. She tells it to our people. And then she disappears until you catch the assassins."

"Of course," Steiner agreed softly. His eyes fell, the dark lashes hiding the sudden gleam of satisfaction that had clearly been in them.

And why the hell shouldn't he be satisfied? Hawk thought. He had what he had come for. He had Hawk.

Hawk didn't know what the outcome of this agreement would be for him. It didn't really matter. It wasn't as if he had had a whole lot of other plans for the future.

"And we want the tapes from the security cameras. All copies of them, and those pictures are not to be made public," Claire Heywood said, her voice clear and decisive again. In charge. "And whatever material that file contains."

Steiner looked at her, almost for the first time since she had opened the meeting. His lips twisted, a small mocking expression of amusement. He closed the file and pushed it toward her across the expanse of the table.

"That's the last of it, you know," he said.

"The last of what?" Claire asked, pulling the file to her.

"The last records of a man called Hawk. As far as the government is concerned—as far as the world is concerned—" he amended, "Lucas Hawkins does not now and never has existed."

They had erased everything, Hawk realized, chilled. He had known they would doctor the records so that there would be no connection between him and the agency. But this...

He supposed he should have known. When they released those pictures from the hotel cameras, they would want to be absolutely certain that nothing could possibly be traced back to them. No matter who was doing the tracing.

"You can't do that," Claire said.

Hawk wondered if she really believed what she had just said. Because, of course, they could do anything they wanted. He'd thought she knew how things worked here. He did. They could do any damn thing they wanted. To him. To his life.

"We already have," Steiner said. "What you hold is all that remains of Lucas Hawkins." His eyes came back to Hawk's. "Talk and be damned," he challenged softly. "There is nothing left, not one line of print, not one computer reference, not one pay voucher, not one record in any file anywhere that can be used to verify your existence. Much less anything you *claim* to have done during the last ten years. The only thing that going public about those things will garner you is a hell of a lot of enemies. People have long memories when it comes to murder."

"I never *murdered* anyone," Hawk said.

"That's a matter of semantics, isn't it," Steiner said. "Or maybe a matter of your politics." He stood up. Surprised by the abruptness of the movement, the men on either side of him hurriedly rose also.

"Do we have a deal?" Hawk asked.

"You walk out that door with us, and we do."

"Those aren't the terms we agreed to," Claire said angrily.

"Conditions have changed. You no longer have anything to bargain with. No one will believe whatever stories you tell."

"They may believe the story I tell," Claire said.

"Let it go," Hawk said softly. "It's over."

He wouldn't allow Claire Heywood to sacrifice herself in a crusade she couldn't win. None of them would win in that case. He put his hand on the edge of the table, preparing to push out of the plush softness of the big leather chair. The sense of fatigue that had haunted him after Baghdad was overwhelming again.

Tyler's fingers were suddenly on top of his. They were cold, but not trembling. He almost pulled his hand away. Almost stood, ignoring the entreaty her gesture represented. Something prevented him. Maybe his fatigue. Or the knowledge that this was the last time he would see her. Or maybe, once again, as in that dark bedroom last night, his self-control had broken. He turned his head slowly and met her eyes. In his was nothing that he didn't intend to be there. And in hers…

"Is what he said true?" she asked.

What part of it? Hawk wondered. *Calling what happened in Iraq a murder? Saying I no longer exist? All of those things he read out of my file? What he implied about my reasons for bringing you here today?* But of course, there was some element of truth in all of those. Enough that he supposed it didn't matter anymore about the parts that weren't true.

"Yes," he said simply.

She slowly removed her hand from his, putting it in her lap with the other. He could still feel the imprint of her fingers, however, burning against his skin. *Last time,* he thought. *Last touch. Last chance.*

Then the man who had been called Hawk stood and followed Carl Steiner out of the room. He didn't look back.

"WHAT DO I DO NOW?" Tyler asked finally into the silence they left behind. "I thought…" She hesitated, unsure of all her conclusions. Confused by the abrupt ending to this. For one thing, no one had taken down a word she had said about the assassination. They hadn't seemed even remotely interested in the story she had come here to tell.

She thought she had been following the conversation, despite the references to people and events she had no knowledge of. The man who was in charge had agreed to put her in Witness Protection. Which was exactly what Hawk had told her would happen. Nothing else, however, had been anything at all like what she had been led to expect.

"They'll send someone for you," the blond woman beside her said softly. "Until they do, we just stay here. I'm Claire Heywood, by the way," she added, holding out her hand.

The handshake was awkward because of their positions. They were still sitting on the same side of the conference table, the chair Hawk had occupied during the meeting between them.

"You're Hawk's lawyer?" Tyler asked hesitantly. There had been no introductions. She had assumed that everyone else in the room knew one another.

"Not really," Claire said. "Just…a friend, I suppose. A friend of a friend's," she added after a moment.

"Then you knew what that was all about," Tyler suggested.

"Some of it," Claire agreed.

"Hawk killed a man in Baghdad."

"Yes," Claire said. Her voice was softer than it had been before, almost reluctant.

"But why?" Tyler asked, shaking her head. "That's not...I mean, I know that he's..." She almost said "dangerous." He was. She had recognized that from the beginning, but she had thought that was because of his job. Because of being an agent. Now she wasn't sure exactly what he was.

It had gradually become obvious that Hawk hadn't been sent to Mississippi to rescue her. He hadn't come to protect her from the people who were hunting her. Or even to bring her here so she could identify them. That identification had been made only because she had pushed it into the conversation, and no one had seemed really interested.

According to the man in the middle, Hawk had brought her here to clear *him* of the assassination of the sheikh. But he had never indicated to her that he was a suspect. He had saved her life, but apparently even that had been done for his own purposes. Not because he was acting under orders or investigating the assassination, but because she was the one person who could prove Hawk hadn't done it. Which meant, she supposed...

That he had been using her, she acknowledged. And it also meant that nothing of what she thought she knew about Hawk was true. At least not his motives for doing what he had done. And one of those involved what had happened between them last night.

"Who is he?" Tyler asked, pulling away from the pain of that. She was trying to understand what Hawk had done and why. And trying not to judge until she knew everything.

Claire didn't answer for a moment, her eyes filled with sympathy. And when she did, it really wasn't the explanation Tyler had asked for.

"He's a man who believes that in order to keep this country safe, sometimes someone has to do things..." She hesitated before she went on. "Things the rest of us don't always approve of. Or understand. Things that may, on the surface…'' She paused again, her eyes full of some emotion Tyler didn't understand. Maybe some of the same confusion she was feeling.

''But he *is* a government agent?'' Tyler asked softly.

''Yes,'' Claire agreed.

At least she hadn't been wrong about that, Tyler thought. At least he was one of the good guys.

''A very specialized agent,'' Claire said.

''He kills people,'' Tyler said simply. ''Officially kills people, I mean.''

Claire's eyes reflected a touch of shock at her bluntness, but that gave way almost immediately to amusement. ''You don't find that…repugnant?'' she asked, accurately reading her tone.

''I've known a couple of people the world would probably be better off without, and my circle of acquaintance isn't all that large,'' Tyler said.

She was finally beginning to put some of this into perspective. Hawk was a government assassin. That's why he had been an immediate suspect in the sheikh's death. That's why just his appearance on the hotel security tapes had made them think he had something to with it. And that's why he had come to find her. Because she was the one person who could prove he didn't.

He hadn't told her the complete truth about who he was. And there was really no reason why he should have. She didn't imagine he just went around announcing something like that. As Claire Heywood suggested, there were plenty of people who would find that to be repugnant.

''If you consider all that goes on in the world,'' Tyler said, ''all the crazy people like Hitler who get into power and then decide they can do anything they want to… I guess it isn't too hard to understand why the government would feel that some of them have to be stopped.''

''And that makes sense to you?'' Claire asked softly. ''It makes sense for Hawk to be the one to do that?''

''It makes sense to me that *someone* has to do it.''

Claire held her eyes, searching them.

"You think...what Hawk does is wrong?" Tyler asked.

"I don't know," Claire said. "I thought I did. There are certainly laws against it. Strongly stated national policies. But...I had a friend who believed as you do. That occasionally *someone* has to do it."

"Hawk's friend? The friend of a friend?"

Claire nodded again. "Hawk's friend."

"I don't think he has many," Tyler said.

He had always seemed so alone to her. Maybe that had even been part of his appeal. His aloneness. His emptiness. Always before she had seemed to gravitate to someone who would take care of her. He had accused her of that. And yet in Hawk...

She realized suddenly what she had been thinking. And the incredible flaws in her reasoning. Hawk didn't need *her* to take care of *him*. Hawk didn't need anyone. He never would. He had made that abundantly clear.

He believed in standing on his own two feet. Just as he had told her she had to do. It hadn't been a fair criticism of her life, but he didn't really know her life. What it had been. Why she had done the things she had. Trusting Paul. Agreeing to marry Amir. Loving Hawk.

Loving Hawk. Suddenly her vision blurred, Claire Heywood's classic features disappearing behind a mist of tears. Tyler had never told him that, and she wondered now if it would have made a difference. Wondered if he really hadn't known.

Considering the things in the file Claire Heywood was holding, it was possible he hadn't understood. Possible that he hadn't known he could be loved. She understood that feeling all too well—wondering how someone could find you worthy to love. She had wondered that about Amir. Had wondered why in the world, out of all the women out there, he would love someone like her.

"Do you think that, while we're waiting, I could read that?" Tyler asked. She reached across the space and touched the manila file with the tips of her fingers. "If it's not…classified or something?"

Claire hesitated a moment, and then she pushed the folder along the table. "It probably is," she said, smiling, "but I don't think that matters much now."

Tyler thought about what she already knew. About the things this file contained. The things that had been read aloud today. Bare bones of a story she could certainly put flesh to. A history of pain and deprivation that made her own life seem privileged and protected. At least someone had loved her. At least there had always been a home to run to. A sanctuary.

And for Hawk… With trembling fingers, Tyler Stewart opened the file they had been given. They were still shaking as they fanned the stack of papers the folder contained.

And her eyes, when she raised them to Claire Heywood's, were again touched with moisture. "There's nothing here," she said softly. There hadn't been. Not one written word. Every page of the final file on Lucas Hawkins was totally blank.

Chapter Thirteen

Three weeks later

"So you can see that there really is no reason for you to remain here any longer," Carl Steiner said. "And I'm sure you'd rather be somewhere else," he added, smiling at her.

"Are you saying that Truett actually confessed to planning the sheikh's assassination?" Tyler asked, trying to make sense of something that seemed unbelievable. After all, she *knew* Malcolm Truett. Maybe the CIA could believe it, but she found the scenario Steiner had just outlined to be incredible.

"He'd been working for the extremists long before he became Amir al-Ahmad's personal secretary."

"But why would he become so involved in the internal affairs of a place halfway around the world? In a religious struggle that didn't even involve his own religion?"

"He believed the Ahmads were raping resources that belonged to the people of their country, and that those people were getting far too little in return. There are those, Ms. Stewart, who are altruistic enough to go to a great deal of trouble to attempt to right the perceived wrongs of the world. The English have a reputation for idealism."

"But he must have known that Amir would step into his father's place. That nothing would change."

"He was hoping for something more. An uprising, encouraged by the fundamentalists, as soon as news of the sheikh's death reached his homeland. With Amir out of the country for the wedding, it was the perfect opportunity for them to act.''

"But they didn't?"

"Apparently not. Not that we're aware of. Maybe Truett's plans weren't that extreme. Maybe he simply believed he could influence the son as he couldn't the father. Perhaps the new sheikh *will* be more progressive regarding his people's needs.''

"I didn't think the extremists were interested in progress,'' she suggested quietly.

"I'm not sure exactly what they're most interested in. Maybe Truett saw his involvement with the extremists as a means to an end. We may never know what his real motives were.''

"What will happen to him?" Tyler asked. Despite the Westernization of Amir's country, the penalties for treason there were harsh. And primitive. That was one of the things that had stuck in her mind from her reading—how traitors were punished.

"Mr. Truett has already chosen his own punishment.''

"I don't understand.''

"He committed suicide shortly after he signed his confession. The sheikh wasn't prepared for such an act of desperation and hadn't taken any measures to prevent it.''

Maybe Truett's suicide wasn't surprising, considering what he could expect at the hands of Amir's courts. The unbelievable thing to Tyler was the whole idea of Truett's guilt. The concept that he had been responsible for the sheikh's death. Amir had warned her, however, that politics in the region were often deadly. So she supposed anything *could* be possible.

"Then who were the men I saw? The ones on the terrace of Amir's room?"

"You were right about that. Two of them were members of Amir al-Ahmad's personal guard. Fortunately, through

Truett's confession, they've been identified and sent home to stand trial. All but the shooter himself. He hasn't been found. Some professional they hired. Totally apolitical.''

"Someone who kills for money?" Tyler asked.

"Not as unusual as you'd imagine," Steiner said. "In any case," he concluded, standing up, "I think you are safe to assume your life can go back to normal. Back to what it was before you opened that door and saw the men on the balcony that day."

Back to normal, Tyler thought. *Back to what it was before you opened that door...* She took a deep breath, thinking about her life. So many things had changed there was almost no life to go back to. At least nothing she wanted to go back to.

"Is there anything else?" Steiner asked kindly.

He hadn't had to come out to the safe house where she was being kept, and explain the situation to her. They had all been kind, the men who had guarded her these last weeks, but they hadn't talked to her about the assassination. No one had questioned what she had seen or asked her to identify anyone.

However, neither had Steiner again suggested she tell Amir what she saw. He had abided by the agreement made in Claire Heywood's office. And now that agreement was ended. The assassins had been caught, and so Tyler had nothing to fear.

"How can you be certain that Amir had nothing to do with his father's death?" she asked.

"We did our own investigation, of course. According to the terms of our agreement."

The agreement with Hawk, she thought. The deal he had made with them for her safety. Apparently Steiner had stuck to the terms they'd hammered out.

"We found nothing to tie al-Ahmad to the plot against his father," he continued. "Instead, everything we discovered pointed to an attempted fundamentalist coup."

"But you can't be absolutely sure?" she asked.

"If I *weren't* sure, Ms. Stewart, I wouldn't be suggesting this," he said, smiling at her.

"It doesn't feel right," she said softly. "Not Malcolm."

"It's hard to judge the depths of someone's political beliefs and commitments from a social acquaintance. Would it make you feel better to see the material we have tying him to the extremists? Those connections are fairly well documented. And besides..." Steiner hesitated a moment before he went on. "It's over. As far as the world community is concerned, the assassins have been caught. Amir al-Ahmad is going back to his country to make sure things stay calm there."

"So...it doesn't really matter any longer what I might say," she suggested. "Is that what you're telling me?"

"It no longer matters to anyone what you saw that day," he agreed, "or what you say about it. You have no reason to be afraid."

Which was essentially what Hawk had told her. Even if Amir were guilty, once he realized she couldn't hurt him there would be no reason for him to have any further interest in her.

"However," Steiner added, perhaps reading the doubt in her eyes, "if you're uncomfortable with the situation, we can provide a more...permanent arrangement. A change of identity or relocation, at least. Most people in your situation would resist something that drastic, which is why I didn't propose it to begin with. And I really don't think it's necessary, Ms. Stewart. If I thought you were in any danger, I'd never have suggested this."

She nodded. What he said made sense. It made sense even if Amir had been involved, and with Steiner's repeated assurances, she was beginning to question her feelings about that. After all, it was entirely possible that when she had realized marrying Amir was a mistake, she'd transferred her sense of wrongness about that to the other situation. To the assassination.

Maybe Malcolm had even been trying to foster that belief

by what he had said to her that day. Maybe he had been so desperate to get her away from the area that he had given her the passkey to get rid of her, afraid that she might see or hear something that would make her suspicious.

And as for Amir's claim that she was grief stricken and in seclusion, which had seemed to be even more proof of his guilt, maybe that was nothing more than his overweening pride. He would never admit that his bride had simply run away on the day of their wedding. It was entirely possible it had all happened exactly as Steiner indicated.

"Is there anything else?" Steiner asked again.

"I don't suppose there is," she said reluctantly, trying to think what came next.

"Someone will drive you to the airport when you're ready," he said. "We'll provide a ticket for wherever you want to go. It's the least we can do in exchange for your cooperation."

Although she couldn't quite figure out what cooperation they wanted to compensate her for, she couldn't afford to turn his offer down. Her options were pretty limited. She could go back to New York, she supposed, but she didn't have enough money to pay last month's rent, much less this one's.

She needed to sell her furniture and sublet the apartment. The furniture should bring in enough to pay off some of the bills. And there was the house in Mississippi, of course. Selling it wouldn't realize much, but enough to pay off the rest of what she owed on her credit cards. And enough to keep her afloat until she could figure out what to do with the rest of her life.

Suddenly an image of that sagging front porch intruded into her thoughts, along with the remembrance of the spreading oak that shaded it and the old-fashioned swing. The scent of honeysuckle drifting in with the evening breeze. Her mother's voice, calling her home from the darkness.

"Covington," she said softly.

"I beg your pardon?" Carl Steiner said.

She looked up, surprised to find he was still there. Surprised she had spoken the word out loud. "Covington, Mississippi," she said. "I think that's where I start."

"Start?" Steiner repeated.

"The rest of my life," she said, smiling at him.

"YOU'RE NOT SUPPOSED to be here," Hawk said.

He hadn't moved, other than to lift his head from the pillow to see who had come into the room. Fingers interlocked behind his head, he was stretched out on the bed, staring at the ceiling. He had done a lot of that during the weeks they had held him here. A lot of thinking. Remembering. And none of it had been easy.

The muscles in his stomach had tightened, however, as soon as he recognized his visitor. He didn't want to hear whatever Jordan Cross had come to say. He could tell that by what was in the gray eyes.

"Jake pulled this location out of the computers. I told the guys outside that Steiner sent me to question you, but they're probably busy verifying that right now, so we don't have long."

"And when they find out he didn't send you?" Hawk asked.

No one had questioned him about anything. They weren't interested in why Hawk had gone to Baghdad. He had known that all along. They were holding him as an act of discipline. And he supposed he was lucky they were doing it in a safe house rather than a prison. When Steiner had said a "secured facility," that's what Hawk had been expecting.

"By then we'll be gone," Jordan said.

"I made a deal. I can't *be* gone."

"He let her go," Jordan said.

Hawk's body came off the bed in one fluid motion. "What the hell do you mean, he let her go?"

"Amir al-Ahmad's secretary confessed to planning the

assassination. Right before he conveniently committed suicide."

"His secretary," Hawk said disbelievingly.

"Male type. English. Supposedly the mastermind of an extremist coup."

"Supposedly?"

"Jake says the background on that is manufactured, created after the fact. Probably by al-Ahmad."

"And Steiner didn't bother to check it out?"

"All I know is he considers the case closed. *And* the assassins duly caught. So…"

"That stupid son of a bitch," Hawk said softly.

Jordan's eyes hadn't changed, and Hawk still didn't like what he was seeing in them. "Where is she?" he asked.

"Jake says she took a flight to Mississippi. This morning. The agency paid for the ticket."

"I hope you brought some money," Hawk said, starting toward the door, "because I doubt they're going to pay for mine."

"There are four of them out there," Jordan warned. "You want some help?"

Hawk turned, his blue eyes resting briefly on Jordan Cross's face. "Only if you want to give it," he said softly.

"I didn't come out here for the scenery," Jordan said, and realized this was the first time he'd ever seen Hawk laugh.

SOMEONE HAD CLEANED UP the mess. They hadn't repaired the damaged wall or replaced the bullet-scarred door frame, but the debris on the floor had been cleaned up. And the blood.

Standing now in the afternoon sunshine that was painting patterns of light on the old wooden floors, Tyler realized that it all seemed like some long-ago nightmare. Like a bad dream. As unreal, in a very different way, of course, as the few days that had followed it. The days she had spent with Hawk.

She put her suitcase down on the sagging mattress. It was the same battered case she had bought in the New York pawnshop that day. She'd been carrying it around since, with the same items of clothing she'd bought at the airport stuffed inside.

She walked over to the windows and pushed them up. It seemed hotter inside than out, and the bank clock she'd passed on the way had read 97 degrees. With the house closed up, that probably meant the temperature in this room was pushing 100, despite the shade the oak provided.

Which meant she'd spend another night tossing and turning in the heat. When Cammie sent her the money from the sale of her furniture—if there was anything left after she paid Tyler's rent and the utilities—the first thing she was going to buy was a window unit for this room. Then at least she'd be able to sleep.

She walked back to the kitchen. She had set the groceries she'd picked up on her way home on the wooden table. There was only one sack because her cash was running low, and she didn't want to put anything else on her credit cards unless she absolutely had to. As it was, she had two rental cars sitting out in the gravel driveway. She'd have to figure out a way to get those turned in. And think about getting some kind of secondhand car of her own for transportation to and from work.

Thinking about that, she took the local paper out of the grocery sack and laid it on the table before she put the few things she'd bought into the refrigerator. There had to be some job she could do listed in the want ads, even if the position was only temporary. Until she could find something better.

And there was a junior college less than fifteen miles away. She might be the oldest freshman on campus, but she liked the idea of going to school. Of picking out classes. Of studying for them. She had always wanted to go to college, but there had never been time. Now there was time for a lot of things.

She had already invited Cammie for a visit. Which meant, she supposed, that she needed to do something about making this place a little more inviting. Guest worthy. An update was definitely in order, she thought, looking around the kitchen.

Fresh paint would help. Some inexpensive fabric she could make into curtains, using Aunt Martha's old pedal machine. They'd be pretty simple, given her level of skill, but they would be bright and clean. And a coat of wax on the floors would cost her nothing but elbow grease. Maybe a wallpaper border at the top of the freshly painted walls. *Yellow for in here,* she thought, *and for the bedrooms…*

Her eyes dropped from the border she was envisioning just below the old-fashioned acoustic tiles and found a man standing in the door that led into the house from the porch. Just where the robed men had stood the night Hawk had rescued her.

This one wasn't wearing a robe. He had on a business suit and white shirt, but he was one of Amir's bodyguards. One of the two who had been in the hotel room that day. One of the two who had, according to Steiner, been sent home to stand trial for the assassination. She recognized him immediately, and in his dark eyes was a mocking acknowledgment that he had known she would.

He was holding an automatic weapon, holding it loosely and with a great deal of confidence. She thought it was the same kind that had cut the wall above her head to ribbons that night. She watched it swing away from her as he turned, allowing Amir to brush past him and walk into the kitchen.

"You have certainly proven to be a *most* unsatisfactory fiancée, my darling," he said. "An enormous amount of trouble."

There were several men behind him, Tyler realized. More of his omnipresent bodyguards. However, they were all in Western dress today, which would be much less noticeable here than the *dishdashas*. With them was the other guard she had seen in Amir's suite that day. The day his father had been murdered.

"They told me you were going home. That it was all over," she said.

Amir's dark head tilted, questioning. "Over?" he repeated.

"The CIA told me about Malcolm."

"They bought into the idea of Malcolm as the mastermind?" he asked, his voice amused. "That's rather entertaining, isn't it?"

She had been right all along. She had known in her heart it was Amir. But Steiner had seemed so sure, and now it was too late, she thought, a layer of ice forming around her heart, seeping outward to chill the blood in her veins.

"You, on the other hand, didn't buy into that, did you?" Amir suggested, still smiling. "That's all right, my beloved. It really doesn't matter what you believe. Or what you say. It never mattered, I suppose, but it might have been a bit awkward—at least socially—to have my fiancée suggesting I had killed my own father. I really don't like things that are awkward or unpleasant. You know me that well, I think."

"I won't say anything," she promised, her voice soft with fear. She hoped he could read her sincerity. She had done the right thing. She had gone to the authorities and had told them what she'd seen. Even what she suspected. No one had been interested in listening to her.

"Oh, I'm sure you mean that. Just as I'm sure Malcolm meant well when he stupidly gave you that passkey. But you see, that wasn't what I had told him to do. And I also don't like people who don't do what they're told. Exactly what they're told. You, however, always did. So you have one last job to perform, Tyler, and then…" Amir paused, his smile widening beneath the soft dark mustache "…then, my darling, it really will be all over."

"What do you want?" she asked, wondering what that phrase implied. Afraid that she knew. She could feel the paralyzing force of her fear, but she fought it, trying to think.

She had run from them that night. There had seemed to be a chance then that she might be able to get away in the concealing darkness. But now, in the daylight, running seemed pointless. And she remembered the bullets hitting the frame of the door, the pain in her arm and a gun, such as the ones they now held, totally destroying the wall above her head. She had survived that night only because of Hawk's intervention. And now there was no Hawk to help her. There was no one to help her.

"A final appearance," Amir said. "It will be just another performance for the cameras, Tyler. You've done a lot of those. And all you have to do this time, my darling, is smile."

WHEN THEY REACHED IT, the little house was empty. The door was unlocked, and Tyler's suitcase was on the bed in the bedroom. There was some food in the refrigerator and the local paper was spread out on the kitchen table. The windows in the bedroom were open, the heated air filled with the scent of honeysuckle that climbed, wild and unrestrained, over a hedge just outside.

"Maybe she's at a neighbor's," Jordan said. "Out to eat. Something harmless."

Hawk knew what had prompted that remark. It seemed too peaceful for anything to be really wrong. There was nothing here but the distant sounds of children playing. The scent of honeysuckle drifting in at the open windows. Age-yellowed lace curtains occasionally moving in the heavy air. An old house set under the shade of a big oak. Peaceful. As long as you didn't notice the scars that pocked the bedroom wall.

"Call Jake," Hawk ordered. "Tell him we need to know *exactly* where al-Ahmad is right now. And we need his itinerary."

IT HAD FELT STRANGE to be dressed again in these clothes. They were some of the things Amir had chose for her trousseau. Tyler was aware of that as they put them on her, but the whole time it felt as if they were dressing a mannequin.

They had even brought someone in to fix her hair and her makeup. The hairdresser had tried to talk to her, but what they had given her was so strong she hadn't been able to formulate any answers. After a while he had simply done what he had been instructed to do and had left. She was still sitting in the chair where they had placed her, looking into the mirror. Looking at someone who was a stranger.

Since they had given her the shot everything seemed to be happening to someone else. It was as if she were in someone else's body, watching these things being done. She closed her eyes, fighting the nausea she had experienced ever since Amir's physician had plunged that needle into her arm. She had fought them, as long as she was able, but it hadn't done any good, of course. She hadn't been strong enough to win.

Hawk could have. He would have fought them for her. But Hawk wasn't here, she remembered. He had left, like everyone else, and she would never see him again. The sense of his loss was strong enough to push into her consciousness, past the effects of the drug.

Amir was saying something, she realized. His voice came from a long way away, distant and hollow, echoing in her head like the voices in dreams. He wasn't speaking English, she finally realized, so surely he didn't expect her to answer.

Then someone else responded. Someone nearby. The doctor, she recognized, turning her head toward the sound of his voice. He was standing at her elbow, shaking his head. Amir gestured, and the doctor helped her stand.

When she was upright, her head swam, and she swallowed hard, denying the building nausea. She swayed a little and one of the bodyguards put his hand under her other arm. Amir crossed the distance between them and caught her chin in his fingers, turning her head to make her look into his eyes.

"You will smile," he said loudly, his tone menacing, despite the fact that he sounded as if he were talking to a not-very-bright child, "when and if I tell you to."

She tried to make her eyes defiant, but the sickness pushed into her throat and her knees were so weak. She was cold and spasms of shivers racked her body. If he turned her loose, she was sure she'd fall.

"Do you understand me?" he demanded, still speaking too loudly, his voice echoing in her head. She should say no, but she couldn't remember why. And it was so much easier to agree. Then maybe he would leave her alone and stop shouting at her.

The doctor said something else, the unfamiliar words fluttering at the edge of her fogged mind. Amir answered him with an expletive from his own language that she had heard him use before. Then he leaned close to her face, close enough that she could see the pores in his skin, the individual hairs in his black mustache. He spoke very distinctly.

"You will smile and wave when I tell you. Do you understand me, Tyler? Because, my darling, if you don't, the doctor will give you another shot, which he says might stop your heart. And you don't want that to happen, do you?"

She shook her head slowly, moving it against the hard pressure his fingers were exerting on her chin. She didn't want her heart to stop. She didn't want to die. *Hawk,* she thought again, and felt the burn of tears.

The fingers holding her chin tightened painfully. "You will not cry. I do not want them to see tears. I want them to see a very happy woman, smiling and waving as she departs for what will be her new country. Do you understand me, Tyler?"

Smile, Tyler. She had known all along that's what Amir would tell her. *Smile at them, but don't open your mouth. Just smile, and it will all be over. If you smile at them, everything will be all right.* It always had been.

And after all, she thought, she knew how to smile. For the cameras. For everyone who was watching. *Smile and it will all be over.* Slowly, watching his cold black eyes for approval, Tyler nodded.

Chapter Fourteen

The metal steps to the private jet seemed miles away from the limousine, but she had realized when they helped her from the hotel and into the car that her depth perception was distorted by whatever they had given her.

She closed her eyes against the late afternoon glare and swallowed, trying to produce some moisture in her dry mouth. At least the nausea was a little better, and she wondered if that meant the drug was wearing off.

She knew what Amir wanted her to do. He had explained it several times during the ride over from the hotel. They would go up the steps to the jet together, turn at the top and wave and smile for the assembled media. *"Smile, Tyler"* drifted through her head again, seeming so familiar. And... distasteful.

Someone opened the door on her side of the car, and Amir was there, holding out his hand. She wondered what would happen if she refused to get out. If she refused to walk with him up those steps. Refused to get on the plane.

Almost as if he had read her mind, Amir said, his voice low and angry, "I'll have you carried on board if I have to. I'll tell them some story about stress and exhaustion. But if you force me to do that, Tyler, you'll be very sorry. Do you understand me? I promise you'll be *very* sorry," he warned.

She believed him. His eyes, as cold and as black as she knew his heart to be, *told* her to believe him. She wondered why she had thought Hawk's eyes were cold. They weren't, not compared to these, but she obeyed Amir because she knew she had no choice. She put out her hand, and he pulled her from the car.

She swayed against him, fighting vertigo, nausea, an inability to move or to think. He put his arm around her, his left hand cupping her left elbow.

"Walk," he ordered. "And smile, damn you. Smile, my darling, or I promise you you'll be sorry you were ever born. Very sorry you ever stuck your nose into things you don't understand. Things that don't concern you."

She wanted to argue. Wanted to deny that she had done anything wrong, but the words wouldn't form. It was all she could do to concentrate on putting one foot in front of the other, even with his supportive arm around her waist.

The journey to the foot of the metal steps was endless. He had given her sunglasses in the car, to cover the too-wide dilation of her pupils. To hide the effects of whatever they had injected. But still the glare and the heat reflecting off the tarmac were making her sick.

"I can't," she whispered, looking up from the foot of the stairs to the open door of the plane. She couldn't climb those steps, no matter what Amir did to her or threatened to do. And she was beginning to realize that once she was on board the jet, he could do anything he wanted to her. No one would ever know what had happened. No one would ever see her again. She would simply disappear into that unfamiliar world she had feared from the beginning. The world where Amir's word was literally the law.

"I can't," she said again, trying desperately to think what she could do.

Amir turned around to face the crowd, carrying her with him, almost lifting her and propelling her at the same time with his grip on her arm. She could see the muscle jumping in his jaw as it clenched. He was furious, but she knew she couldn't get on that plane.

They were facing the assembled throng of reporters, too

many for this location normally. He must have arranged for some of them to be here in this small Mississippi city. Arranged for them to come out on a hot afternoon to see this performance.

"Smile, damn you," he demanded, the words hissed under his breath. His own smile was broad and obviously false. Obvious at least to her. His right hand, the one that was not gripping her arm hard enough to bruise, lifted to wave at the crowd.

That gesture provoked a flurry of flashes from the cameras. Their lights seemed to explode in Tyler's eyes, blinding her, even with the protection of the glasses. It was all too much for her sensitized senses to deal with. The heat and glare. The noise. The smell of jet fuel. All of it too much.

The pressure on her arm increased. She whimpered with the pain, but the sound was lost in the roar of the jet engines behind her. No one heard her. No one would hear her if she cried out for help. He had planned it this way, of course.

So it was up to her. She had to get away from him. Break his grip on her arm and run toward the crowd. Surely he wouldn't shoot her in front of all these people.

After all, Amir was safe. He had nothing to fear from her. Someone had told her that. Nothing to fear. But if he shot her, then they would know what he had done. On some level she realized that the effects of the drug were wearing off. She could think again. Form words. Take some action. And she had to. It was her only chance.

She struggled, trying to pull her arm from his hold, but she seemed to be powerless against that relentless grip. Her struggle had no effect, except to cause Amir to pull her body closer to his, holding her tightly against his side. To the watching reporters, it must have appeared to be a spontaneous and loving embrace, because he continued to wave at them with his other hand and the cameras continued to flash.

He said something. Not to her, she knew, because it wasn't in English. She didn't understand until the doctor moved into her field of vision, the sun glinting off his wire-frame glasses. He carried his bag in one hand, and even as she watched, he reached inside with his other hand. His back to the crowd as he walked, he took a syringe from his case. It was full of the colorless liquid with which they had injected her before.

For a moment her heart stopped, just as Amir had promised, but then she realized that was only her fear. He hadn't touched her. The doctor was walking toward them from the limousine, and Amir was still crushing her against his side, waving to the crowd. The noise of the engines was deafening. And the glare of the sun blinded her.

What was happening seemed to be occurring in slow motion. Like a nightmare, she thought. The final one. Because when he reached her, Amir's doctor would put that needle into her arm, using his body to shield what he was doing from the cameras. Then somehow, probably with the doctor's help, Amir would get her on that plane. And it would be over. Everything, all the dreams, would finally be over.

Hawk, she thought. All the dreams, including that one. But Hawk had left her, just like everyone else in her life had left her. Because she wouldn't stand on her own two feet. Because she went along with what everyone told her. Because he thought she wasn't strong. And now she would never get the chance to prove to him that he was wrong.

Last chance, she thought. *My last chance.*

Maybe because she had stopped struggling or maybe because the doctor was so close, Amir's grip on her body loosened minutely. She looked up at him, eyes narrowed against the sun. He was looking out into the crowd, still waving. Still pretending this was what he wanted them to believe it was—a gloriously happy couple on their way to begin a new life together.

She turned away from his false smile and realized the doctor was almost there, the syringe he held concealed in the palm of his hand. Amir's men were standing by the limousine, their white robes billowing in the hot air, blown by the jet engines. And there was another guard, she knew, waiting at the top of the stairs. That was always the way they did it. He would have a weapon hidden in the plane beside him, ready to protect Amir in case of trouble.

She remembered the heat and fire of the bullet that had hit her arm and the devastation on the bedroom wall, but she blocked those fears from her mind. *Last chance* echoed in her head, and gathering every ounce of resistance in her drugged body, she shifted her weight to her left leg and kicked Amir as hard as she could in the shin with her right foot.

The blow seemed without force to her, but he reacted with surprise, just as she'd prayed he would. His hold on her body slackened even more. She twisted free and staggered past the doctor, who grabbed at her. She managed to side-step him, but she stumbled as she did. She somehow regained her precarious balance and began to run toward the cameras. *Smile, Tyler* floated through her head, but she wasn't smiling, of course. She was running for her life.

Her legs kept refusing to obey the commands of her brain. She staggered drunkenly across the tarmac, the crowd wavering in and out of her vision. They looked distorted, their mouths opening and closing like beached fish, but she ran toward them, fighting to stay upright. Fighting to stay alive. Fighting to stay on her own two feet.

She didn't make it. Her right leg folded under her suddenly, and unable to regain her equilibrium, she pitched forward to the ground. She got her hands out to break her fall, but she was down. And despite how much she wanted to live, she knew she wasn't going to be able to get up again. Not in time to keep them from reaching her.

She was still looking toward the crowd, and from where she lay on the ground, she stretched one imploring arm out to them. Appealing for someone to help her. Surely someone would see what was happening. Surely now they knew what Amir was doing.

Instead they began to run away from her, scattering in a

panicked flurry, like doves in the middle of a hunt. Running from something. She turned her head to see what was happening behind her. Both Amir and the doctor had been coming toward her, just as she had known they would.

But for some reason their forward motion had checked. Amir shouted something, and the doctor started forward again. As he did, a spray of fragments kicked up from the tarmac in front of his feet. He had stopped again, jumping backward, before Tyler heard the crack of the rifle.

Rifle, she thought, her dazed brain beginning to understand why everyone was running. *Rifle,* she thought again, turning her head, eyes searching the roofs of the terminal and the towers. Someone was shooting at Amir and his men. Someone…

ANOTHER JOB, Hawk thought, the crosshairs of his sight holding a second on the doctor before they lifted to Amir. Al-Ahmad's handsome face was suffused with color. He was clearly furious. Hawk watched as he gestured to someone behind him.

"The one on the steps of the plane," Jordan warned. "He's got a weapon."

Obediently Hawk lifted the scope, finding the figure in the doorway of the plane. He was pointing a Uzi toward the woman on the ground, hesitating to fire only because Amir and the doctor were in his way. And as soon as they realized that, Hawk knew, the man at the top of the stairs would spray the runway.

That man was shouting something now. Through the scope, Hawk watched his mouth moving, opening and closing on the words. Telling the others to get out of the way? Surely Amir wouldn't be stupid enough to order them to kill Tyler in front of all these people.

But maybe he thought he could get away with that. After all, he had gotten away with killing his own father. All he had to do was shoot her and get on that plane and fly away.

He could worry about a story to explain it all later. Tie her to the plot somehow. Only this time, Hawk thought…

The man he was watching brought the gun into firing position, and in response Hawk squeezed the trigger. Same slow squeeze as always. He was surprised that his hand wasn't trembling. It had trembled that day in the parking garage, but now it was as steady as it had always been.

Another job. Another target. Danger passed. Threat resolved. Lives saved. Or in this case, Hawk thought, life saved. One solitary life. That of the woman he loved.

He watched as the man he had shot tumbled off the metal platform that had been rolled up to the door of the plane. Hawk took his eye off the scope and looked down on the scene unfolding below, the characters in the drama slightly distorted by the heat waves shimmering up from the tarmac.

The Uzi bounced down the steps as the robed figure rolled bonelessly behind it. Hawk's gaze moved back to Tyler, struggling to get up. *Someone will come to help her,* he thought. *Someone out of that crowd will realize what's wrong.* He had, simply by watching her walk beside Amir from the limousine to the foot of the steps.

They had drugged her to make her carry out this farce. A performance for the press. For whoever Amir believed might still care about his role in his father's death. He apparently hadn't realized that no one cared. Just as no one cared enough to come to the aid of the woman who had finally managed to push herself up to her hands and knees.

There was movement to Tyler's left, and Hawk pulled his eyes away from her figure. He couldn't think about her as a person. Not about what she was feeling. Not about going down to her. His job was here. The important job. At least for now.

What he had seen peripherally was Amir, bending to pick up the Uzi that had fallen almost at his feet. He had stooped, lifting the weapon and then turning toward the barriers that had been created to keep the media at a distance.

Hawk put his eye again on the scope, lining up his target

in the crosshairs. Even as he did it, he couldn't conceive that Amir would be foolish enough to shoot. He had nothing to gain by this and everything to lose. Nothing to gain…

Apparently Amir al-Ahmad didn't realize that. Or he no longer cared. In Hawk's sights, the sheikh's face was a distorted mask of fury as he aimed the weapon. Aimed it right at the fallen woman. A woman who had defied him by running away from him in front of all those people. Spoiling the picture he had wanted to create for the media.

Hawk's finger tightened against the trigger, steady and unhurried, and suddenly a small, dark circle appeared in the forehead of the man in the crosshairs. The Uzi continued to fire as Amir fell forward, squeezing the trigger in a reflex motion as he died. Bullets hit the tarmac, sending up sprays of dust and debris wherever they struck.

Hawk forgot to breathe as he watched them, praying to a God he didn't know for a miracle he didn't deserve. Still praying when he pulled back from the scope, and his eyes, unaided by artificial magnification, found the woman they had sought.

On her feet. Moving again in a slow stagger toward the terminal. Still alive.

"Give me that," Jordan said, taking the rifle from Hawk's hands.

Now they were trembling, Hawk realized, shaking with fear. Shaking with the need to touch her. To hold her. To verify what his eyes were telling him.

"I'll take it from here," Cross said.

Hawk turned to look at his friend, and watched the gray eyes lighten and the well-shaped lips curve into a smile at what was in his face.

"You know what will happen if you do this," Hawk said.

"I'll tell them Steiner sent me," Jordan said, his smile widening. "Go on. Get her out of here. I'll handle the rest."

"I can't let you," Hawk said. He knew what it would do to Jordan's career. They had already destroyed *his* life, but so far he had managed to keep Cross almost in the clear.

"I told you. It just speeds up the inevitable," Jordan said. "Besides, Griff was my friend, too."

He was looking down at the runway, rifle held at the ready. Perhaps his aim wasn't as deadly as Hawk's, but then no one else on the tarmac below was attempting to move toward the weapon lying beside Amir's body. And if they somehow found the guts to try, a bullet in the ground nearby would probably put an end to that bravado.

After all, the sheikh was dead. There was no one to give them further orders. Without Amir to urge them on, neither the doctor nor the bodyguards by the huge black car seemed particularly eager to challenge the skill of the unseen shooter.

"Go on," Jordan said again, his voice soft. "And Hawk?"

Hawk had already begun to move, but he stopped, his eyes shifting to the man who had been beside him almost all the way.

"Godspeed, my friend. And good luck," Jordan added.

The man called Hawk nodded, the movement small. Contained. Both acknowledgment and thanks. Unspoken. As always.

Then Jordan Cross's gaze fell again to the runway. Crouching low, Hawk began to move, across the rooftop and toward the door that would lead to the service stairs they had climbed to this vantage point. There were debts to be paid, he thought, no matter what Jordan said. Debts to Cross for taking the blame for this. To Jake for tracking down the flight plans Amir's pilot had been required to file. Hawk wouldn't forget what he owed to either of them. He never forgot those things.

Hawk heard feet pounding across the roof behind him. Airport security had finally arrived. He also heard Jordan's shout of identification. "Jordan Cross. This is a CIA operation." Jordan was CIA, of course, and more importantly, he could still prove it. Hawk couldn't have. Not anymore. That was why Cross had taken the rifle from him.

Imagining Steiner's reaction to the uproar this shoot-out would cause, a small satisfied smile flickered at the corners of Hawk's lips as he began to descend the concrete stairs.

EVERY TIME SHE OPENED her eyes, he was there. Watching her. Or holding her. Through the bouts of nausea, she held on to what was in his eyes. To something he had never allowed her to see in them before. And he cared for her through the long dark hours with the same tenderness with which he had once made love to her. The slow time. She smiled, remembering.

"What's so funny?" he asked, his voice soft and intimate.

That shouldn't be surprising, she supposed, since he was lying beside her on the bed. They were in a motel, she guessed, allowing her gaze to move around the room. She remembered the beige-tiled bathroom. Typical motel. He had carried her there a few times. Literally carried her. And she supposed she should be embarrassed to have him take care of her in those very intimate ways. But she wasn't. She wanted him here. She wanted Hawk beside her. Whatever the situation.

"Not very much," she said softly, cupping his cheek with her hand. His skin was unshaven, and she liked the brush of the golden whiskers against her fingers. Evocative of that night.

"How do you feel?" he asked.

He was lying on his side, one arm under his head. She had to turn her own head to see him, but at least she could do that now without setting off the nausea.

"Like a couple of Mac trucks ran over me, and then rolled back and forth over the dying body a few times."

He reached out and touched her bare arm. She flinched a little. That was one of the bruises she'd gotten fighting Amir's guards, she supposed, looking down at the place his fingers had found. She was wearing only her underwear, she realized, but she couldn't remember undressing. Or remember Hawk undressing her. She thought she might like to be able to remember that.

Of course, she didn't remember much of anything after the injection. And all of what she could remember was hazy, like something that had happened a long time ago. Or had happened to someone else.

But she remembered Hawk finding her, appearing out of the crowd at the airport like a miracle. She remembered him picking her up and carrying her in his arms through the terminal building and outside. He had told someone he was a doctor. Since they couldn't possibly believe what he *really* was, that was probably as good a lie as any.

She didn't remember much of anything else until she woke up in this room, and Hawk was taking care of her. Caring for her as her mother might have long ago. His hands, long, dark and so strong, had been as gentle as hers.

"Thank you," Tyler said softly, fighting tears that she recognized, due to the lingering effects of the drug, were too close to the surface.

"For what?" he asked, his voice amused.

"For everything," she whispered. "For coming to my rescue again. For this. For…being here."

"Go back to sleep," he said, dismissing her gratitude.

"You'll still be here when I wake up?" she asked, her eyes searching his. He had never lied to her. He hadn't told her everything, but what he *had* told her had always been the truth.

"I'm not going anywhere," he promised. "Not without you."

The tears threatened again, but they were different tears. Happy crying, her mother used to say.

"I'll be here when you wake up," Hawk said softly. "I'll be right here beside you until you tell me to go away."

She smiled at that, but she didn't tell him why. She'd tell him later, she decided, holding the blue eyes until her heavy lids drifted downward. Once or twice she forced them up again, just to be sure he was still there. To be sure he wasn't a dream. And she would find that same surety in the steady blue gaze. Finally, trusting in what he had promised, she slept.

"I WAS PLANNING to make new curtains for in here," Tyler said, watching Hawk's face. He seemed so out of place here. Alien to this rural peacefulness. To this little house. His life had been so different.

Of course, she admitted, for the last twenty years, so had hers. But this would always be home to her, and so she felt as if she belonged. She had wondered, even when she suggested they come here, if it would ever feel like that to Hawk. Like home.

"And I want to paint the walls," she added, when he didn't respond. "And the ones in the bedrooms, too."

She knew she was talking about things that couldn't possibly mean anything to a man like Hawk. Domestic trivia. They hadn't even discussed what came next, if anything, but still she couldn't seem to do anything about the hope that had been growing in her heart. A hope that Hawk would want to stay, now that it was over.

"It is over, isn't it?" she asked, needing his reassurance. "I mean…Steiner won't expect you to go back? He won't try to make you, will he?"

"We had a deal. Which I honored until Steiner broke it. He's got to know from what happened at the airport yesterday that he didn't fulfill his part. I don't think they'll come after me, but…if they want to, Tyler, they can find me anywhere I go. I don't intend to run from them. Or to hide."

"But you *think* Steiner will leave you alone."

"I think even Steiner should have trouble sleeping at night when he thinks about what he almost let Amir do to you," he said, his voice bitter.

She nodded, remembering what had happened. And thinking about what *would* have happened if it hadn't been for Hawk. She thought about expressing her gratitude again, but he wouldn't want to hear that.

She took a breath, her eyes finding the mark the bullet had made on the door frame. She wanted every bit of evidence of the nightmare they had lived erased. Even the scars, if possible.

"And I want to do something about the damage to the wall in the bedroom," she said.

"Are you expecting me to offer to fix that?" Hawk asked, his lips touched with the small smile she had seen there too seldom.

Exactly what *had* she been expecting, she wondered, when she suggested they come here? "Do you know how to fix it?" she asked, smiling back at him.

"I don't know anything about taking care of a house. About paint. *Or* fixing walls."

She nodded, but she didn't say anything. This was up to him. His decision. His choice. And whatever he decided, she would learn to live with it. On her own two feet.

"If there's a hardware store in town," he said, his eyes still on her face, "maybe somebody there could tell me what to do."

She nodded again. "Probably," she agreed.

The silence stretched.

"You haven't even asked about the other," he said finally.

"The other what?"

"Why I didn't tell you the truth," he said.

"I guess you had a good reason. And...I didn't tell you the truth, either. Not at the beginning."

"I was afraid you'd think I was like him."

"Like Amir?" she asked, her voice puzzled. "Why would I think you were like Amir?"

Hawk hesitated, and his lips tightened a little before he answered. "I thought you'd think I'd just been using you."

"Were you?" she asked.

"At first."

She nodded again. "Well, at first I was using you, too. That's how you got involved in all this. I guess I can't blame you for doing that. I got you into it, and I was the only one who could get you out. It just made sense that I do that."

He said nothing for a long time, so long that she wondered if she'd said something wrong.

"And the other?" he asked softly.

"The other?"

"Making love to you."

"Were you just…using me then?"

"No," he said. "That was never what that was about."

"What *was* it about?" she asked, and held her breath.

"What I said, I guess. Making love to you."

"No ulterior motives," she said, remembering to breathe.

"A couple, but not any you need to worry about."

She laughed, and watched his eyes lighten. The corners of his hard mouth moved. Fractionally.

"And I want a wallpaper border," she said. "They probably have those at the hardware store, too."

"With instructions?" he asked.

"I don't know. But it can't be too hard. If everybody else can figure it out, surely the two of us together…" She hesitated, wondering if she had overstepped some invisible boundary. No commitments had been made. Not about anything. Not even about wallpaper.

"I think the two of us together can probably handle most things," he said. "Even wallpaper. If you want to try."

"If *I* want to try?" she asked.

"You heard what Steiner said. I don't have a lot of experience at…families. Or homes. I guess I'm not…a very good risk at any of those."

She nodded again, her throat closing at his unemotional dismissal of all that pain. She conquered the tears he wouldn't want to see. Hawk wouldn't want her to cry for him, ever. But for a man like Hawk to make a commitment of this kind, a commitment to build a home—and a family—together, would take an enormous amount of courage.

"Are you saying you *want* to have a home? And a family?" she asked. She needed to be sure she understood before the dream got totally out of control.

"I'm saying I want *you*," he said. "No ulterior motives. But…no restrictions either, I guess. I figured you'd want both of those."

"Yes," she said softly. "I want it all. All of the above. And I think we probably better hurry about at least one of them."

His eyes changed, darkening a little, and his head tilted. "The wallpaper?" he asked innocently.

"No," she said.

"I didn't think so."

"But…I guess we could take a look at that wall before you go to the store."

"The one in the bedroom?" Hawk asked.

"That's the one," she acknowledged. "Ulterior motives," she added softly. "I guess I should warn you. Mine may fall into the category of…using you."

He nodded this time. "You still have that wedding thing?"

"The bridal gown?"

"That's the one," he said, deliberately mimicking her comment about the wall.

"I hocked it," she said.

He laughed, and she decided she really liked hearing that.

"The last of the romantics," he suggested.

"The last of the dreamers," she corrected. "Why did you ask about the dress?"

"I thought the hardware store might know about churches, too," he said. "And about preachers."

"Are you proposing to me, Lucas Hawkins?"

"I think that's exactly what I'm doing," Hawk said.

"Then do it right," she demanded. "I want it done right."

He laughed again and closed the space between them. He took her in his arms and kissed her on the mouth. Not particularly passionate or possessive, but just…right, she thought. Just exactly right.

"Tommy Sue Prator," he said, his mouth moving against her cheek, "will you marry me?"

"Just as soon as you fix that wall," she whispered.

"Then I guess we better go take a look at it," Hawk said. He bent, slipping his right arm under her knees. He carried her through the door with the bullet-scarred frame and into the bedroom. Just, of course, to look at the wall.

Epilogue

"You do know what this means?" Carl Steiner asked, his finger tapping the grainy black-and-white photograph at the top of the stack of newspapers on his desk.

Jordan Cross glanced down at the picture, then wondered why he had bothered. It wasn't any different from the others he would find in that stack. Jordan was in almost all of them, of course. Along with scenes of the carnage at the airport.

What had happened there was the most exciting thing the locals had seen in a long time. Amir had deliberately gathered as much of the media as he could round up on such short notice, so there were a lot of cameras in that crowd. Apparently they were all snapping when Jordan and airport security stepped through the door to the staircase that led down from the roof.

At least none of them had gotten a good shot of Hawk, Jordan thought philosophically. He was sorry that hadn't been the case with him, but he had known exactly what he was doing when he had taken that rifle out of Hawk's hands. And he hadn't hesitated.

Griff Cabot had been his friend. Hawk had taken the heat for what they *all* had wanted to do to that bastard in Iraq. And Jordan was more than willing to take the blame for what Hawk had done yesterday.

"I suppose this means my services here are no longer

needed," Jordan said, lifting his eyes from the photograph to meet Steiner's.

"I'm afraid that's the least of it," Steiner replied, leaning back in his chair and tenting his fingers.

"The *least* of it?"

Maybe Steiner really didn't understand what the team had meant to them. If that was true, it was pretty damned ironic that he was the one who was now in charge.

Missing Griff had eaten at Jordan's gut the last six months, of course, but that had been more about personal friendship than any kind of professional anxiety. They had all known things would change with Griff's death, but for someone like Steiner to come in here—

"I'm afraid that as a result of what you did yesterday you've acquired a whole lot of enemies," Steiner said, interrupting that train of thought. "All of Hawk's. Al-Ahmad's followers. And the agency's enemies, as well. You've become our...public face, so to speak, and you'll probably spend the rest of your life looking over your shoulder to see which of those is after you."

Steiner lifted his hands, tapping the tips of his steepled fingers in front of his mouth as if he were thinking. Jordan waited, not sure where he was headed with this. Other than to try to frighten him.

If that was what the assistant deputy director was attempting, it wasn't having much effect. Nothing Steiner was saying was news to Jordan. He had recognized all these things yesterday. *Before* he'd made his offer to Hawk.

"Of course, there *is* a way to keep you safe," Steiner said. "Something we've certainly done before."

"And what is that?" Jordan asked, interested to hear what his new boss was proposing.

"A new face," Steiner said, looking down again at the stack of papers. "A new identity to go with it."

"I'm not sure I'm all that tired of the old one," Jordan said carefully, controlling his inclination to laugh.

They'd gotten rid of the problem Hawk represented by

destroying his identity. Apparently, they intended to do the same thing to Jordan. Give him a new face, a new ID. And a new life to go with it. All *outside* the agency.

There wasn't much doubt now where Steiner was heading. Of course, they had all understood that the team, as they knew it, was doomed. But this…

"And *I'm* not sure you really have much choice," Steiner said softly. "After yesterday, you'll be a marked man, Cross. Hunted for the rest of your life. I'm simply offering you an out. My best advice is to take it. With the skills you've learned here, you won't have any trouble starting over."

Starting over. That was an opportunity a lot of people would love to have, he supposed. Jordan Cross wasn't sure he was one of them. But from the look in Steiner's eyes, he also wasn't sure he had much option. They would cut him loose with all the enemies Steiner had warned him about on his tail, or they'd do exactly what they'd offered. Give him a new face and a new name.

With all that had taken place recently within the agency, so much had changed already about his life. Griff's death. The dissolution of the team. Hawk's "disappearance."

Jordan wasn't sure what there was left here to hold on to. Except an identity that would be, he knew, just as dangerous as Steiner had promised. At least what they were offering gave him a chance.

"Okay," he said softly.

"I don't think you'll ever be sorry," Steiner said.

And of course, Steiner would be wrong about that, as well.

THE STRANGER SHE KNEW

Prologue

"By the way, your brother-in-law stopped in today."

The comment impacted like a sledgehammer to the gut, but Kathleen Sorrel, long accustomed to hiding her feelings, didn't react—at least not outwardly. Instead, her hands, which had been guiding her son's arm into the sleeve of his jacket, completed that task and moved on to the next, competently fitting the two halves of the plastic zipper together.

No one watching could possibly have guessed that the safe, secure world she thought she had built in this tiny Southern community had just exploded. Struggling to maintain her composure, Kathleen didn't try to formulate an answer. She didn't even raise her eyes to the day care worker's face, afraid they'd reveal her shock.

Miss Judy, she thought, dredging up the woman's name from the orientation visit she'd made here six months ago. Not Jamie's or Meg's teacher, but a helper, she remembered. Right now Miss Judy seemed to be in charge of overseeing the late-afternoon rush of departing children.

Kathleen's mind had seized on solving the identification problem because it had been too frozen to deal with the other. Numb with anger that they would come into the center. Sick with fear—a fear she had almost managed to forget in the quiet tranquillity of these last few months.

Finally she succeeded in making the ends of the zipper connect and, pulling the tab upward, she closed the green corduroy jacket over Jamie's tummy and chest. The coat was a hand-me-down from Meg, still a little too big, but Jamie would grow into it over the winter. Kathleen had learned to buy things that were unisex, so both children got the benefit of wearing them.

"Sorry," Miss Judy said. "I guess that should be your *ex*-brother-in-law."

The woman's voice was softer. Far less cheerful than when she'd made her initial announcement about the unexpected visitor. Kathleen gave her credit for reading body language, which probably meant Miss Judy was also good with the kids. And that was nice, of course, but her own children wouldn't be around long enough to benefit from her skill.

Kathleen finally raised her eyes to the woman's face. On their way up, they brushed over the wind-chapped cheeks of her two-year-old. Maybe checking to be sure that he was unaffected by what had just happened. A mother's glance for reassurance.

Jamie reached for the pin Kathleen had put on this morning, a small silver cat that curled against the collar of her navy blouse. It was almost hidden by her coat, but Jamie loved the pin, and his fingers stretched toward it just as they had when she had put him into his car seat at the beginning of this day.

Which seemed to have been a hundred years ago. A lifetime ago, at least. Someone else's lifetime.

"And exactly what did my brother-in-law want?" Kathleen asked.

She congratulated herself on the calmness of her voice, and on the lack of sarcasm when she repeated the lie he had told them. *Brother-in-law.* But after all, she was holding Jamie, and she could see Meg, her red jacket and long black hair a distinctive combination in the sea of children.

Her daughter's head was bent forward, the top of it almost touching the silver-blond bangs of her best friend. Apparently, they were sharing little-girl secrets. *Safe,* Kathleen told herself. Both the children were safe. That was all that mattered. At least for the moment.

"Nothing really. Just…" Miss Judy paused, shrugging slim shoulders. "He was looking us over. Checking things out for your husband, he said. Ex-husband," she corrected, a slight flush of color beginning to seep into her cheeks. "Just making sure that we were…a good facility, I guess. He didn't ask to see the kids. We would have called you if there had been anything like that. But…I mean, people come to see the *school* all the time, Mrs. Pearson. Parents. Grandparents. Prospective customers. We don't keep those kinds of people out."

Those kinds of people. The ordinary words echoed in Kathleen's head. *You really don't have any idea about the "kind of people" you let in here today,* she thought, but she said nothing, her copper-penny eyes meeting the apologetic blue ones of the worker throughout her flustered explanation. Finally the woman seemed to run down.

"I'm sorry if you're upset," Miss Judy added after a moment of strained silence.

"I'm not upset," Kathleen lied.

She picked Jamie up, settling him on her hip with the ease of long practice. He was certainly capable of walking to the car on his own, but she wanted out of here. Wanted to get *them* out of here. Right now, the sooner the better.

"Meg," she called.

Her daughter turned at once, waving goodbye to her friend before she skipped over to join them. Meg was generally obedient, because she wanted everyone to be pleased with her. She didn't like anger or disagreements. Just like her mother, Rob used to say. Maybe too much so, Kathleen thought.

"Mrs. Pearson?"

Kathleen had reached the door, its frame festooned with taped-up pumpkins the children had made, their bright green leaves and stems glued on, not always in exactly the right place. Escape had been so close she could almost taste the bite of the outside air, could almost feel its cold comfort against the heat building in her cheeks, but obediently, she turned back in response to the worker's call.

"He didn't do anything," Miss Judy said. "He just took a look around. Honest."

Just took a look around, Kathleen repeated mentally. Just an innocent visit to a small, private day care center.

"He seemed like a really nice guy," the woman added, her voice sincere. She was still trying to make everything all right again.

Kathleen nodded, fighting the nausea that was pushing into her throat, because she understood, even if this woman didn't, that her world would never really be "all right" again. She opened the outside door and, her hand on Meg's shoulder, she guided her daughter through it and out into the twilight, carrying the pleasantly heavy weight of her son on her hip.

Her eyes scanned the graveled lot in front of the old Victorian house, which had been transformed several years ago into the Wee Folks Play School. She found nothing out of the ordinary, just normal sights and sounds. Children's laughter coming from inside, the noise they made loud enough to reach out into the twilight.

Another mother had just gotten out of her car, slamming its door in her hurry to get into the warmth of the building. From the fenced-off playground, Kathleen could hear the creak of wooden swings pushed by the wind. Gusts rippled the black puddles of rainwater that stood in the shallow depressions the children's feet had made.

Nothing out of the ordinary, she thought again. Nothing that was any different from any other fall afternoon when she had picked her children up here. Nothing to be afraid of.

But by the time she deposited Jamie in his car seat, Kathleen's hands were shaking. There was no one to see, so the discipline she had practiced in the building began to splinter.

To disintegrate into a thousand and one pieces, each sharp, jagged and terrifying.

"Mommy?" Meg questioned softly.

Kathleen fought off the tears that had begun to burn behind her lids. There was no sense in frightening the children. No sense in letting them see how upset she was. No sense in disrupting their lives any more than she knew she would have to.

Kathleen was their security. She understood that. She was the absolute center of their world, and she was determined that no matter what Rob had done, no matter what she felt about its effect on their lives, she would never let the two of them know how shaky that center could sometimes be.

So when she lifted her gaze to her daughter's face, her smile was back in place. Uneasiness was still in the wide gray eyes looking up at her. Little-girl eyes that sometimes seemed far too adult for their age.

"Are you crying?" Meg asked, her voice full of concern and a touch of shock. She had never seen her mother cry. Or rage. Or do any of the things Kathleen had wanted to do during the last thirty-four months.

"Something in my eye," Kathleen said. "The wind."

Meg nodded, but her eyes clung to her mother's face, doubtful. Seeking assurance that all was indeed still right in her five-year-old world.

"How about Mickey D's for supper?" Kathleen asked, keeping her strained smile in place through sheer willpower.

"Hamburgers?" Meg said, her voice skeptical.

"You and I haven't shared an order of fries in a while. And I thought maybe a milk shake," she offered, sweetening the deal.

"Chocolate?" Meg questioned, apparently hardly able to believe her luck, but willing to take advantage of any weakness her mother displayed.

"I think that can be arranged. Are you buckled up?"

"Yes, ma'am," Meg said, patting the shoulder strap.

"Good girl," Kathleen said automatically.

She closed the back door, her eyes circling the area around the car again. There was not one single thing that shouldn't be here. Nothing out of the ordinary. An ordinary little Arkansas town on an ordinary fall evening.

She opened the driver's side door and slid in behind the wheel. Her eyes moved up to the image reflected in the rearview mirror. Jamie's head had already begun to droop, long, doll-like lashes drifting downward over his cheeks. He'd be asleep before she got out of the lot, and she knew from experience that he'd sleep all the way home.

Meg was looking out the window, examining the gathering darkness. As Kathleen watched, her daughter blew on the glass, using her breath to fog it. With one small finger, she drew a pumpkin, lopsided and asymmetrical, but obviously a pumpkin, especially when she added the stem.

"Happy Halloween, Mommy," she said, her eyes turning to meet Kathleen's in the mirror. "I forgot to tell you."

"Happy Halloween to you, too, sweetheart," Kathleen said, her heart squeezing with how much she loved them. They were her whole world, and she would do anything to keep them safe. *Anything,* she promised silently.

"When we get home, will it be time for trick or treat?" Meg asked.

Trick or treat. Kathleen supposed it was appropriate this had happened today. There seemed to have been few treats in the last three years. A lot of tricks, however, just like this one.

That's really all it was, her logical side argued. With its reemergence, she was beginning to get control of her terror. This had simply been their way of reminding her they were still out there. That they knew where she was. That they were watching. And waiting.

This time, she thought with a tinge of satisfaction, it had taken them over six months to find her. She was getting better. One day she would succeed, and then, she prayed, it would finally be over. And as long as Rob stayed away from them, she could keep Meg and Jamie safe. She *would* keep them safe, she vowed.

"Mommy?" Meg's voice came from the back seat, questioning her delay in starting the engine or her lack of response to the question about trick-or-treating.

"We'll see," she said, trying to decide if that childhood pleasure would be possible now. She hated to disappoint her daughter, but she couldn't be sure that they were through with this particular trick.

Kathleen didn't want to give them an opportunity to frighten the children again. She didn't intend for Jamie and Meg to grow up in fear. She had ample cause to know exactly how stressful that was. And if they missed trick-or-treating, she'd think of something that would make up for it. She was good at that—at compensating for all they were missing.

But at least they were safe, she reminded herself. Just as long as Rob stayed away from them. Surely he must understand that. No matter what else her husband had done, no matter how disillusioned she was with the person he had become, Kathleen couldn't believe the man she had once loved, the man she had married, would do anything to endanger his own children.

But of course, he already had, she thought, rage at his greed and stupidity boiling up unexpectedly within her. She resolutely tamped it down, because dwelling on that was worse than useless. It was something she couldn't change, no matter how much she wanted to.

What she had to concentrate on was keeping the children safe and staying one step ahead of the people who were looking for Rob. Just one step, she vowed. That's all that was necessary, and then eventually… Eventually it would all be over. One way or another, she thought, it would be over.

"Ready to roll?" she asked, relaxing the death grip she'd taken on the steering wheel. Her moment of anger had helped. Buoyed by her renewed determination to worry about nothing but protecting her children, Kathleen found her hands were no longer trembling when she put the key into the ignition and started the car.

IT WASN'T A BAD FACE. It was, Jordan Cross acknowledged, even an interesting one. The problem was it wasn't *his* face. Only now, he supposed, it really was. So he'd better start getting used to it.

Jordan took a deep breath, watching the man reflected in the mirror do the same. The inhalation lifted wide shoulders and expanded a muscled chest covered by a faded navy sweatshirt. His body, at least, was the same. As was the blue-black hair. And his eyes, slate-gray and calm, staring out at him from that stranger's face. Remarkably calm, considering.

"What do you think?" the plastic surgeon asked. His question was neutral, but his tone was definitely self-congratulatory.

Jordan supposed that the surgeon had a right to the smugness he seemed to feel. He had done exactly what he had been told to do—subtly restructure a face that had suddenly, and dangerously, become too well-known. Too familiar to the enemy.

Enemies, Cross amended. He had certainly made a few of those in his years with the CIA, especially during the last decade, when he'd been a member of Griff Cabot's External Security Team. But the enemies who had necessitated this transformation he'd made recently, in his last unofficial and unsanctioned mission, during which he had willingly risked both his life and his career for a friend.

Actually, he acknowledged, for two friends—one living and one dead. Griff Cabot's senseless murder had set off the chain of events that had led to this transformation.

Griff's death had changed them all, of course. All the members of his team. They had been closer than brothers, a bond forged in shared danger, in having to depend on one another, sometimes for their very lives. And their respect for Cabot had kept that bond strong.

Griff's had been the intellect that created the whole concept of the team and its simple mandate. The External Security Team's job was to seek out and destroy the madmen whose mania for global domination or terrorism threatened the free world.

Standing guard over those we love. That was their mission, Griff had always told them, and it was a goal worthy of its cost.

Only Griff really knew the individual price each of them had paid for belonging to the team, perhaps because he knew them so well. And Griff, too, had paid a steep, personal price, Jordan thought, remembering Cabot's loss of Claire Heywood.

When one of those madmen had targeted Griff for assassination, the team had taken its revenge. Lucas Hawkins, who had been best suited for the task, had pulled the trigger that brought down Griff's murderer. But the act had been done on behalf of the team. For all they owed Griff. Something he, personally, couldn't begin to repay, Jordan acknowledged.

And that's why, only a few days later, as the flashbulbs exploded around him, Jordan had been holding a rifle on the rooftop of an airport building in Mississippi, announcing to the world that he was a CIA operative.

In that one operation he had acquired a lot more enemies—not all of them his. And due to the publicity resulting from that utterly reckless piece of derring-do, those enemies had all learned exactly what Jordan Cross looked like.

Or what he *had* looked like. Up until the agency determined that this was the best way—the safest way—for Cross to deal with having had his cover blown.

At the thought, a small, ironic smile lifted the corners of the alien mouth in the mirror. He hadn't *had* his cover blown, of course. He had done that himself. His choice, and one he had made willingly. To help a friend. To pay a debt.

Whatever the virtue of those motives, the results had been the same. His face, the real one, had ended up plastered under a few thousand newspaper banners. His name had been tied to events he'd had little or no part in, and his identity had been inextricably mixed up with the deeds of a CIA assassin code-named Hawk. The friend for whom he had taken the heat that had led to the creation of the man reflected now in the mirror.

"I think there's not much left of *me*," Jordan said softly.

"I thought that was the whole idea," the surgeon responded, smiling. "I *did* warn you."

"I know. But still…it's a little disconcerting."

"To face a stranger in the mirror?"

Cross nodded. That was exactly it. To find a stranger's face looking back at him. And to know that for the rest of his life that would be the case.

"You'll get used to it," the doctor promised, his voice still touched with amusement. "Soon that will be the face you expect to see when you look in a mirror."

Jordan nodded, still studying his reflection. The differences were subtle because they had tried to keep it as simple as possible. The surgeries had been spaced out over a ten-week period. And finally, today, the doctor had removed the bandages from the last of them. There was still some swelling and bruising, but the basic likeness that had emerged from under the bandages was fairly clear.

There had been changes in the bone structure, but those had deliberately been kept to a minimum. The nose, of course. And the shape of his chin. His hairline had been permanently changed. The cheekbones seemed more prominent, but that might simply be because of what they had done with the skin that covered them. Because of these procedures, Jordan now looked younger than his thirty-nine years.

That, too, had been part of the plan. The papers they'd provided to go with this new face gave his age as thirty-four. That fit with the relative smoothness of the skin around his eyes and with the lessening of the slight creases age and experience had cut into the lean cheeks.

A stranger's face. If, as they said, a man's face revealed his character, then Jordan Cross was no longer here. This face seemed virtually unmarked. Not the face of a man who had had his particular experiences. But perhaps those were something else better forgotten. Or, Jordan admitted, at least hidden.

He supposed, however, that the doctor was right. He would get used to it. To the face. To the fact that he didn't work for the agency any longer. To the dissolution of the elite External Security Team he had been a member of the last ten years. Eventually he'd get used to it all.

A new life. An opportunity to start over. To make different choices and to head in a totally different direction. All at the government's expense.

The small smile again touched the corners of the stranger's mouth. *His* mouth, he thought, commanding his senses to make the mental adjustment the surgeons had physically created. *His* face. His life—new, unfettered by the past. A chance to do it all again. There weren't many people who were given that opportunity, he acknowledged. And there were probably a lot who would give everything they owned to have it. Jordan Cross, however, hadn't been one of them.

"Am I free to go?" he asked, turning away from the mirror. He had seen enough for one day. Had enough to deal with.

"Whenever you want," the surgeon said.

"Thanks," Cross said. He held out his hand. The doctor's felt smooth and soft against his own callused palm.

"Do you know yet where that will be?" the surgeon asked.

To tell the doctor anything about his intentions would be a breach of security. His own security. That's what this metamorphosis was all about—to allow Jordan Cross to disappear. To melt into another man's body. Another identity.

One with no connection to his own. And, of course, he didn't owe the doctor any explanation.

"I don't have a clue," Jordan said, and watched the surgeon's smile widen.

He was probably imagining that answer to be an evasion, Jordan thought. The logical one that his situation certainly called for. It wasn't. It was simply the truth. Because Jordan really didn't have any clue at all about what would come next.

"BUT I DON'T WANT to leave," Meg said, her soft voice plaintive, verging on tearful.

"I know," Kathleen agreed, folding another of the garments she had taken from the dresser drawer in the bedroom the children shared. "But we have to. So..." She hesitated over the meaningless platitude she was about to offer.

She understood what Meg was feeling. She, too, had loved this town. Her secretarial job was the best she'd had in any of the scattered locations they'd lived in. She liked her boss, a young attorney with a small, but growing practice. He had been especially understanding of Kathleen's situation because he had children of his own, and a working wife.

And the rental house Kathleen had found, though tiny and old, was well maintained. It even had a fenced-in yard and a swing set. It had all been perfect.

Maybe that was why she had relaxed her guard, why today had shaken her so much. Kathleen had wanted so much to believe things could work out that she had begun imagining this situation would be permanent—at least as permanent as anything they were likely to find in the nomadic existence Rob had forced upon them.

"Why, Mommy?" Meg begged. "I like it here. I like my school. I have lots of friends. Please let's don't move again."

Kathleen hesitated, then laid Jamie's T-shirt on top of the stack in the suitcase. This had been easier when Meg was younger. Now she was almost six. She understood more about what packing these battered suitcases meant. More about loss.

"We don't have a choice, Meggie," Kathleen said softly. "I'm so sorry, baby, but we have to leave. We'll find another school. One you'll like just as well, I promise."

"I was going to be a Pilgrim," Meg said, her chin quivering and the gray eyes finally filling with tears. "In the pageant."

Thanksgiving, Kathleen thought. A role in a school play. Something every child was entitled to. Like enjoying Halloween. Although Meg had tried to be brave, the milk shakes hadn't made up for missing trick or treat. Kathleen understood that.

But no matter what she told herself, she hadn't been able to take the children out into the darkness. Not even to visit the few houses on their quiet street. They had had a party instead, dressing up in their discount-store costumes while they ate supper. She'd filled their plastic pumpkins with most of the Halloween candy she'd bought, and Meg had been allowed to drop treats in the baskets of the few children who came to their door.

It hadn't been the same, of course. Nothing had been the same since Rob had walked away from their home in New Orleans, taking their security with him. Destroying their childhood, Kathleen thought bitterly.

She took a breath, trying to quell that surge of resentment. It wouldn't do any good. It was simply turning her into something she didn't want to be. At thirty-one she felt like a bitter old woman, struggling to survive in a world she didn't understand, one that was not of her making.

"Maybe the new school will have a pageant," Kathleen said, forcing enthusiasm into her voice.

"But all the parts will already be given out."

"I'll ask them to find a part for you. I promise, Meggie. I promise I'll ask."

Slowly her daughter nodded, swallowing against the lump

the threatening tears had caused in her throat, the small movement strong enough to be visible.

"Good girl," Kathleen said, complimenting her bravery. "You are such a good girl. It'll be all right. You'll see," she promised.

Again Meg nodded. Kathleen smiled at her, and then turned to look at Jamie, who was sleeping, his bottom sticking up in the air. He had dislodged the quilt she had put over him, exposing yellow pajamas that had once belonged to his sister, the bulge of his nighttime diaper clear under the knit.

"You want me to cover him up?" Meg asked.

Kathleen turned back to her daughter. She brushed off Meg's forehead a strand of shining black hair that had escaped the barrettes, smiling at her as she did. "Would you? That would be great," she said softly. "And then you better get your jammies on, too."

"Are we leaving tonight?" Meg asked.

Kathleen nodded. "You don't even have to wake up. I'll carry you to the car, just like I used to when you were a baby."

"Then why can't I sleep in my clothes?" Meg asked.

"I think you'll be more comfortable in your pajamas. Don't you?"

"Okay," Meg agreed.

Her small, reluctant feet scuffing against the wooden floor, she walked over to the other twin bed and pulled the quilt over Jamie's bottom. He didn't wake, but turned his head, cherub lips closing around a convenient thumb. Meg bent, as she must have seen her mother do a million times, Kathleen realized, and placed a kiss on her brother's temple.

Kathleen had had to fight tears before, right after the woman at the day care center had given her the news. Those had been tears of anger. Of fear, perhaps. These were something very different, and she almost welcomed the sting at the back of her eyes. When Meg straightened, however, and turned to face her, Kathleen was smiling again.

"You won't forget anything, will you?" Meg asked, entreaty in her eyes. "You won't forget to pack everything."

"I won't forget a thing. I promise you," Kathleen said softly.

She wouldn't. She had done this too often before to be careless about it. And there really wasn't all that much to pack. But she'd be extra careful that nothing of Meg's or Jamie's got left behind, she resolved, smiling into her daughter's distressed eyes. Nothing except some of the intangible joys and securities every childhood should hold.

And there was nothing Kathleen could do about that.

Chapter One

Six weeks later

Although he had never lived here, San Francisco had always been one of Jordan Cross's favorite cities. He hadn't factored into his design for starting over, however, how high the cost of living would be in the city with the Golden Gate. And golden everything else, apparently.

He had planned to take his time finding a job that was not only interesting, but fulfilling. However, watching his savings dwindle while he hunted for something that matched his requirements was becoming unsettling. It wasn't that he didn't have some highly specialized skills. It was just that those assets didn't seem to transfer well to the private sector.

Jordan's lips quirked at that admission. After more than fifteen years spent in government service, in one guise or another, he now found himself in a world he hadn't occupied since law school. *The private sector,* he thought again. Which didn't appear to be looking for someone who could do the things he could do. And which was beginning to be boring as hell, too.

Boredom wasn't something Jordan had worried much about. After having lived so long on the edge of danger, the possibility that he might find "normal" life tedious at times had certainly crossed his mind. His experiences within the agency had been many things, but they had seldom been dull. He had believed, however, that he'd eventually adjust to a life without the excitement and camaraderie Griff Cabot's External Security Team had provided.

Of course, he had lost not only his career, but all his friends as well. And it had been especially hard to lose Griff. There had been no one else in his adult life that Jordan had been closer to. No one who had taught him as much, both personally and professionally. And certainly no one he'd admired more.

But the team, and all it had meant to him, was over. Not by his choice, of course, but through circumstances he could do nothing about.

Other people had made the transition. According to Jake Holt, Hawk had even gotten married. And Lucas Hawkins as husband material was a concept that was pretty damned difficult to accept, Jordan thought, lifting the ale the bartender had just set down in front of him. Jordan couldn't prevent the slight upward tilt of his lips as he tried to visualize Hawk in that role.

"Rob?"

Jordan wasn't usually slow on the uptake, but he hadn't made any friends in the city, deciding that he ought to get used to the persona the agency had provided before he tried it out on anyone else. He wasn't accustomed to it yet, just as he apparently wasn't accustomed to the name they had given him.

He didn't respond to the voice at his elbow, his mind still savoring the image of Hawk coping with the perils of domestic bliss. Despite Tyler Stewart's many charms, Jordan couldn't help wondering if boredom wouldn't be a problem for Hawk, as well.

"Rob?" the man said again, leaning far enough forward against the edge of the pseudo-antique oak-and-brass bar to show up in Jordan's peripheral vision. He glanced to the side, realizing only then that the guy was talking to him.

And realizing also that he had the name right. Robert Sanders was the identity the CIA had created for Jordan, so

"Rob" wasn't that much of a reach. However, the face that went with the inquiring voice didn't seem familiar.

"Sorry?" Jordan responded, deciding that was noncommittal enough to cover any situation. Obviously, he had been mistaken for someone else, which, given his situation, was fairly ironic.

The eyes of the man who had addressed him continued to study his face, tracing over his features with almost the same fascination he himself had felt in the first couple of weeks he'd worn them. Jordan tried to keep his face expressionless, only the faintest hint of polite puzzlement allowed. When the examination continued beyond civility, however, he let one dark brow slant upward in inquiry.

"I think you must have me confused with someone else," Jordan said.

His voice was level, perfectly calm, but for some reason he had felt a frisson of unease at the man's scrutiny. He was becoming accustomed to hiding out behind someone else's features. He wasn't sure, however, that he was comfortable with the idea that those features might already have been occupied.

Slowly the man nodded, but his dark eyes never left Jordan's face. His lips pursed slightly, as if he were considering the possibility that he'd made a mistake.

"Something for you?" the bartender asked, interrupting that assessment. At the question, both men turned to face him, the uncomfortable connection that had stretched between them broken.

"Gotta phone?" the man beside Jordan asked.

The bartender tilted his head toward the back of the room, and the newcomer took his hands off the bar and turned away, heading in that direction. Relieved, Jordan lifted his beer and took another long swallow.

The bartender's eyes followed the man across the room, coming back to Jordan's face only when he asked, "A regular?"

"Not here," the bartender stated, shaking his head. "Never seen him before."

He turned away, moving toward the end of the bar to greet a couple who had just come in, bringing with them, caught in the damp wool of their coats, the scent of the rain-filled night outside. It was fresher than the stale, soured-hops odor of the bar, which Jordan hadn't been aware of until now.

Suddenly he was in a hurry to get out of here. He finished the beer in one long, smooth draft and set the glass back on the bar. The man who thought he had recognized Jordan hadn't come back yet from the phone. And for some reason, it seemed desirable that he get out before the guy did.

Jordan stood, pulling a five out of the loose bills in his pocket and putting it down beside his empty glass. The thought of being outside was growing more appealing by the second, although he had stopped in the neighborhood pub in the first place because the cold rain had seemed to permeate his spirits.

Or maybe that was loneliness. A feeling of being dislocated. Disassociated from his current surroundings. Like a displaced person after some long and costly war.

"Thanks," he said to the bartender as he walked down the length of the bar and headed toward the door. The eyes of the feminine half of the couple that had just come in met his, a subtle glint of interest in them.

Some other time, Jordan thought, *maybe some other place.* Not here. Not now. Because now...

Now, he realized, all he wanted to do was get home. To the place he was temporarily calling home, he amended. He wanted to turn on all the lights, lock the doors and then turn up the heat until the chill dissipated. Not just out of the apartment, but out of his head. Away from his spine. He wasn't sure, even now, why it had settled there.

He opened the outside door and stepped onto the sidewalk. It was both darker and colder than when he'd come in, although the rain had stopped. His gaze automatically searched the area around him, checking the cars parked along both sides of the street. Old habits were dying hard, he had found.

There seemed to be no one sitting in any of the parked vehicles. And few people walking along the sidewalk. Those who were there, probably on their way home after a day's work or shopping, hurried by, their eyes downcast. Which was just what *he* should be doing, Jordan thought. And he wasn't sure why he was scanning the streets for enemies instead. Except maybe what he had thought before: old habits.

Or well-honed instincts? he wondered. Jordan Cross hadn't stayed alive as long as he had in what was a very dangerous profession by ignoring what his instincts told him. He just wasn't sure what message they were trying to convey tonight.

But something had changed in the world he had chosen to inhabit. Something…disturbing. Because a stranger had thought he was someone else? Or because he was beginning to feel like someone else?

Jordan wasn't sure. And he wasn't certain it was important that he figure it out. It seemed more vital right now to get out of the cold darkness and into the warmth and light of his apartment. Maybe, he thought, that in itself was the message.

DESPITE THE PREMONITION he had had that night, despite the sense of danger that had tingled along nerve endings long inured to hazardous duty, Jordan hadn't been prepared when it happened. After all, he had believed what they all told him.

Change your identity, undergo these operations and you can live out your life in peace. None of his enemies, or Hawk's, would be able to find him. The agency would see to that, they'd promised. A new face, a new identity, a new start. And all of it possible without having to live constantly looking over his shoulder.

It should have seemed too good to be true. And now he knew it was, of course. He should have kept looking behind him, every step of the way.

He still hadn't found anything on the job front that interested him. He'd done two interviews this week, presenting the résumé that the agency would back up if any of the companies or references listed on it were checked. He hadn't heard back from either interview and found that he didn't much care.

Apparently, despite the facial surgeries and the new identification, something of the old Jordan Cross still clung to him. Some aura of danger or sense of threat. He wasn't sure what it was, and he also didn't spend a lot of time trying to analyze it. He just knew that he sometimes saw a question or apprehension appear in the eyes of the men interviewing him.

Griff Cabot, his former boss, used to say that meeting with the team was like walking into a room full of predators. Jordan had understood that analogy when it was applied to men like Hawk, but he hadn't recognized that aspect of his own personality.

Apparently, however, it had been evident to some of the people who had considered, however briefly, hiring him. Hiring Robert Sanders, he corrected. Who, it seemed, still had some subtle and invisible connection to a former CIA agent named Jordan Cross.

He slowly drank the ale he'd ordered. He kept his eyes downcast, pushing the glass back and forth through the circle of moisture it had left on the highly varnished bar. The last time he had been here, he remembered, almost a week ago, he had been in a hurry to get home. Tonight, however, his inclination was to linger, listening to the background music and the low hum of conversation that surrounded him. Better, somehow, than the waiting quietness of his apartment.

He took a deep, reflective breath, thinking about the emptiness of the apartment. Thinking that tonight might be a good time to call Jake. Or maybe even touch base with Hawk. Check in on how he was surviving in an environment that would be just as alien to Hawk as this one was to him.

Not a bad idea, Jordan decided. Maybe just a little misery-loves-company deal, but there was really no reason *not* to call. Especially if he used a pay phone.

"Could I get some change?" he asked the bartender. He stood up, putting a ten and a five on the bar. He waited as the man opened the cash register, a big old-fashioned one, in keeping with the turn-of-the-century atmosphere of the place.

Jordan caught movement out of the corner of his eye. He turned toward it, in time to see a man disappear into the shadows at the back of the room. Back where the pay phone was. But there were other phones, of course. Jordan would pass one on the way home, he remembered, pocketing the quarters the bartender handed him.

When he stepped outside, he realized that a thick fog had moved in, settling over the streets like a stage effect in some British-made Jack the Ripper film. Along with it had come a drop in temperature. Jordan turned up the collar of his aviator-style leather jacket and put his hands in his pockets. He might rethink using the outdoor phone, he decided. He could always place those calls tomorrow. Or not at all, which would be safer, he acknowledged.

As he walked, the pleasant clink of the change in his pocket accompanied every step. It seemed to be the only noise in the peaceful, sleeping neighborhood. The fog tended to deaden sound, of course, even that of his own footsteps.

There were fewer people on the sidewalk tonight than there had been the last time he'd stopped in for a nightcap. But it was later, of course. He'd spent several hours this evening at the public library, reading up on a couple of the companies he was considering sending a résumé to.

He had had to force himself to concentrate on the information, and that wasn't like him. He wasn't easily distracted. But maybe Robert Sanders was, Jordan thought, almost amused by the idea that he was taking on personality traits to match the identity they'd given him.

He wasn't sure when he became aware of the footsteps behind him. Maybe it was the effect of the fog, but it seemed as if they were suddenly just there. Someone walking up quickly behind him. Just there and very close.

Jordan fought the urge to turn around. It was a public sidewalk, and he had nothing to fear. He hadn't forgotten any of those hard-earned skills of self-defense, so ingrained that using them would be like riding a bike again after twenty years away from it. And he'd had a lot of time lately to work out at the gym. He knew he was in better shape right now than he had been during his latter years with the agency, when most of his work had involved intellect rather than muscle.

He wondered why he would assume whoever was following him had criminal intentions. Why he was preparing to have to defend himself. Those old habits, he thought again, his lips tilting in self-derision at the paranoia that was an inherent part of his profession. *Former* profession, he reminded himself. Former life. Former dangers.

Just as those comforting thoughts moved through his brain, a hand closed over his shoulder. The pressure that was applied was probably intended to spin him around, but instead Jordan turned in the opposite direction, breaking the man's hold. His brain had already made the assumption that his assailant would be armed, so his left hand swept between their bodies at waist level, encountering what he'd expected.

His sweeping hand carried the pistol with it, forcing the muzzle out of alignment with his body. At the same time, his right fist slammed into the exposed solar plexus of the man who had accosted him. The whoosh of expelled air let him know that he had made a direct hit on his target.

The guy doubled over, almost capturing Jordan's fist in the bend of his body. At the same time Jordan brought his knee up into his opponent's groin. The guy cried out, and

Jordan heard the gun hit the pavement. He pushed aside his attacker, turning so he could kick the weapon out of his reach.

Thinking about getting rid of the gun, Jordan hadn't heard the approach of whoever hit him from behind. Maybe that was because of the fog or because of something as simple as rubber-soled shoes. But suddenly, something hard and heavy exploded with paralyzing force against the side of his neck.

The unexpected blow didn't knock him unconscious, though the shock of it threatened to shut down his ability to think, at least momentarily. Shoving the first assailant away and turning to find the gun had changed his body's position just enough so that the blow that was supposed to render him unconscious missed its intended target at the back of his skull. It had landed instead where his neck met his right shoulder, the thick muscle there providing some protection.

Instinct, sharpened by years of training, had already taken over where his numbed brain was failing. Jordan bent and spun, turning all the way to the side. With both hands, he reached up and grabbed the guy who had hit him around the neck, throwing him over his back. The second assailant landed with an audible grunt almost on top of the first one, who was still keening wordlessly, in agony over the damage Jordan's knee had inflicted.

Unsure whether the second attacker had a gun or not, Jordan kicked out, the toe of his shoe connecting with the side of the man's head. His assailant had already begun struggling to push himself off the ground, but when the kick connected, he fell back, either momentarily knocked out or deciding that he wasn't that eager to continue the attack he'd begun.

Crouching, adrenaline pumping in heart-shattering bursts, Jordan waited for whatever came next. The two men didn't move, and finally Jordan took his eyes off them to search the fog-shrouded darkness around him. His breathing was loud in his own ears, sawing in and out as if he'd just run a race.

There was nothing else. No footsteps. No other attacker hurtling out of the surrounding night.

His eyes went back to the two men on the ground. He wasn't carrying a gun. Robert Sanders had no reason to. It didn't fit the persona, and Jordan hadn't thought it would be necessary. He might need to rethink that particular decision.

He bent, his eyes still on the two men he'd downed, trying to locate by feel the pistol he'd knocked out of the first guy's hand. He didn't think it could have gone far, but there was very little light in the street. Which was probably why they had chosen this spot.

And there was too little light, he realized, to get a good look at the men who'd attacked him. He supposed it didn't matter what they looked like. They were almost certainly hired help. Somebody's hit men. Who hadn't been worth whatever they were being paid, Jordan thought.

His groping fingers finally encountered the cold metal of the pistol, and as his palm closed around the grip, he felt a sense of well-being disproportionate to its firepower. It was a smaller caliber than he liked, but it would serve his purposes tonight, he supposed.

A couple of options had run through his mind as he hunted for the gun. He could try to get some answers from his assailants. Or he could get the hell out of here. Go home, lock the door and call the cops. Report the incident just like an average Joe good citizen named Robert Sanders would undoubtedly do. Or he could call in. Report back to the agency that had assured him no one would find him.

Guess what, he would say to Carl Steiner. *Everybody was wrong about this transformation, because I just got made. Thought you might like to know.*

Of course, he realized, holding the gun he'd picked up trained on the two men, he had no proof of that. Given these clowns' ineptitude this could be exactly what he had been thinking at the beginning. A mugging. A couple of hoods who thought they'd spotted an easy target, alone on a dark, fog-shrouded street.

The only problem with that explanation was that this neighborhood was quiet, well-patrolled and noted for its low crime rate. He had chosen to live here for those very reasons. So it seemed a little too coincidental that *he* should be the exception to all those comforting statistics.

Jordan reached down and closed his left fist around a wad of the second attacker's clothing, jerking him to his feet. The guy didn't offer much resistance.

"Why don't you tell me what this is all about," Jordan suggested.

"Go to hell," the man said.

"Eventually. Not now and not on your terms. Who sent you?"

The man laughed, the sound abrupt and humorless. "You got lots of folks looking for you, buddy?"

The question stopped Jordan for a moment. *As a matter of fact...* But there didn't seem to be much point in debating that there were a whole lot of people who wanted Jordan Cross's head on a platter. Or Hawk's. Or that those who had been after Hawk now believed that things he had done could be laid at Jordan's door. So yeah, there probably *were* a lot of people looking for him.

Jordan tightened his grip in the guy's shirt, lifting the shorter man so that he was standing on tiptoe, his face level with Jordan's. "I asked a single question. But just in case you're too stupid to remember it, I'm going to repeat it. Who sent you?"

"They ain't gonna let it go," the man said instead. "It don't matter where you hide. They may not get it back, but they'll see you in hell before they'll let it do you any good."

"I don't know what you're talking about," Jordan said. He didn't. There was nothing in that threat that made sense to him.

"Maybe it's not gonna be us. But it'll be somebody.

Somewhere. These are *not* people you want to screw. You shoulda figured that. And they got long memories.''

"So do I," Jordan said, pushing the man away from him, "but I don't know what the hell you're talking about."

Even in the darkness, he had been able to sense the punk rebuilding his courage, trying to talk himself into taking Jordan on again. That had been in his voice, which had suddenly been full of contempt.

Jordan wanted to be far enough away that his assailant wouldn't be tempted to do something stupid. He didn't want to complicate the situation by having to shoot this guy. Not a particularly good way to start your life over, he thought. Not in any life.

"Get him on his feet," Jordan ordered.

The man hesitated long enough to make it seem as if he might refuse, but apparently the aura that had bothered the interviewers seated behind the safety of those expensive mahogany desks was just as potent on a dark and lonely street corner. The second attacker finally leaned down and offered a hand to his cohort. Using it, the first managed to pull himself up, muttering crude profanities as he did. It was obvious he wasn't feeling as confident as his friend. He also wasn't making any threats.

"Let's go," Jordan said. Turning them in to the police wasn't something he really intended to do, but he *was* interested in seeing their reactions to the suggestion that he might.

"You taking us to the cops?" the belligerent one asked. His voice was contemptuous.

"You got any reason why I shouldn't?" Jordan asked.

"Sixteen big ones."

Again the words made no sense, and Jordan hesitated, trying to fit them into any possible CIA operation he'd ever been involved in or known about. And then, when they didn't fit, into any scenario he could imagine.

"You think that ain't much to them," the man continued. "Maybe it ain't, but it's the principle of the thing, you know. They let you get away with it, and before you know it, somebody else is trying what you did. They can't afford that. They ain't gonna to let it go, man.''

''Let's see how the cops feel about it,'' Jordan suggested.

''All it takes is one phone call from somebody at the precinct, and you're dead meat. You think you've learned some stuff, that martial arts crap, but once they get their hands on you, none of what you know will do you any good. You'll talk to them, all right. Everybody does. So I'd maybe think again about calling the cops, if I was you.''

''You're not me,'' Jordan said softly, his mind still trying to fit together the clues.

The more the man talked, the less likely it seemed that this was related to the Middle East or to Hawk or even to the agency, for that matter. It didn't seem to have any connection with the international affairs the External Security Team had always been involved with.

''Hey, man, it's your neck,'' the guy said, his voice assuming a patently false nonchalance. ''But you let us go, you can disappear again. And who knows? This time you might get lucky.''

Disappear again. That at least seemed to fit, to make sense where none of the rest of it had. Jordan Cross *had* disappeared, and then reappeared as Robert Sanders. But he couldn't make any connection with the rest.

The one who had been doing all the talking had begun to back away, Jordan realized. Backing slowly toward the shadows of the alley. Because he knew Jordan had already made the decision not to kill them. If Jordan *hadn't* already reached that decision, then he should have put a bullet into them as soon as he had found the gun. Making threats about what you were *going* to do with a gun wasn't ever a smart move because it usually backfired.

Maybe the man recognized that since Jordan hadn't already pumped a bullet into him, he wasn't going to. Maybe he was that smart. Or maybe he was just that scared. In any case, Jordan watched him back away, the gun unmoving.

No threats issued. Tacit approval for them to disappear back into the darkness.

"Come on, man," the second attacker urged, when he realized Jordan was going to let them go.

The strategic retreat suddenly became a stampede, their footsteps slapping softly in the fog as they were swallowed up by the shadows of the alley they had come out of. The entire encounter had lasted less than two minutes. And after it was all over, Jordan knew as little about who had sent them after him as he had before.

His instincts told him they hadn't been looking for Lucas Hawkins or Jordan Cross. They had come into the darkness expecting to find someone who would be easier to take down than an ex-CIA agent. The fact that there were only two of them, and that only one had been armed, argued that they didn't have any idea who—or what—they were up against.

And if they weren't expecting to encounter Jordan Cross and if this wasn't a random attack, which was what the guy's words indicated, then... Then they had been after Robert Sanders, he realized. Robert Sanders, a man the CIA had created less than four months ago. Robert Sanders, who shouldn't have any enemies.

As innocent as a newborn baby, Jordan thought. Or he should have been. The fact that someone thought he wasn't was very interesting. And there was only one place to go to find out more about that possibility.

"I'M TELLING YOU there's nothing. This background is cleaner than the proverbial hound's tooth. I ought to know," Jake Holt said. "I helped build it."

"Then who the hell were they after?"

"Mistaken identity," Jake suggested.

"That's just a little too cute to swallow, Jake. How about you?" Jordan asked sarcastically. "You don't think this is too coincidental to *be* coincidental?"

"I never knew you were so suspicious," Jake said, amused.

"I get real suspicious when somebody puts a gun in my back."

"That's the most interesting part of this whole thing," Jake suggested.

"What is?"

"That they had a gun and didn't kill you. Anybody really looking for you or Hawk wouldn't have fooled around with trying to take you. It would have been a clean hit. From a distance."

"So this is nobody looking for revenge for the assassination in Baghdad? Is that what you're suggesting?"

"If it had been, we wouldn't be having this conversation."

"And Robert Sanders is clean."

"Pristine," Jake said. "You've never even had a parking ticket. No enemies, amigo. I should know."

"Then what the hell?" Jordan asked. It was rhetorical, just thinking out loud, but Jake picked up on the question.

"Let me do some checking. It shouldn't take more than a couple of days. Lie real low," he said, the familiar amusement back in Jake's voice, "and then call me back. I may have an answer for you by then."

"You want to tell me what you suspect?"

"It's not even that far yet. It's…just an idle thought. Something I had nothing to do with. Something I can't verify for you right now, but…maybe. If you give me a day or two."

"Okay," Jordan said, knowing that if anyone could find the information that might explain what had happened tonight, it was Jake Holt.

"And keep your head down," Jake warned, his voice now clean of any trace of humor. "This may have been a mistake. Some kind of isolated incident. Mistaken identity, but don't take any chances. And get back in touch on Monday."

"You got it," Jordan agreed. After all, if Jake had any idea at all what this might be about, it was more than Jordan had.

When he agreed to take the blame for Hawk's actions that day, he had expected to spend the rest of his life lying low. He supposed he could manage to do that for a few days while Jake tried to come up with some answers.

And whatever those answers were, he would deal with them. There was still no regret for what he'd done for Hawk. After all, it had simply been his share of the larger debt they all owed a dead man named Griffon Cabot.

Chapter Two

Whoever they had sent this time was good, Kathleen acknowledged. Good *and* cautious. But after nearly three years she was a much better player than she had been at the beginning.

Three years ago she would never have noticed the car behind her. She wouldn't have been observant enough to spot patterns. Or to be aware that the same car had shown up in her rearview mirror three times in the last two days. In a town this size that might happen by accident. It might. To somebody else. But the fact that it was happening in *her* rearview mirror pretty much removed the possibility that this was a matter of chance.

No accident. No coincidence. The green Buick was following her. So much for the expertise she had thought she was acquiring. They had been here less than two months, and they had already been found.

"We're going to be late," Meg said from the back seat.

"No, we're not," Kathleen assured her, but she realized she had unconsciously slowed, her foot easing off the pedal a little as soon as she became aware of the trailing car. She pressed the gas, speeding up again in response to Meg's reminder. "We have plenty of time."

They did. The rehearsal for the Christmas pageant at the small church didn't start for another ten minutes. Even given the number of red lights that lined Main Street and the afternoon "rush hour" traffic, they had plenty of time.

Kathleen understood how important this was to her daughter, however. Unfortunately, Meg had been right about the Thanksgiving performance at her new school. She was now enrolled in a kindergarten that was part of this rural county's public school system. And just as Meg had feared, all the parts in the Thanksgiving play *had* already been assigned when they arrived. Meg had been allowed to sing in the chorus with the other children, but that wasn't the same, of course. Not the same as having a speaking part. And a costume.

In the church Christmas pageant she had both. Kathleen had volunteered to make the costumes for all the children because she had already learned how things like this worked, especially in a small town. And she had been right. Meg had been chosen as the announcing angel. Gossamer-like wings edged with silver tinsel *and* a speaking part. She had practiced her lines until even Jamie knew them by heart.

And by God, she's going to have a chance to say them, Kathleen thought, indignation building. Meg had a right to things like this. Kathleen wasn't going to let them frighten her away again. This time she wasn't leaving until *she* was ready to make the move.

She took a deep, calming breath, eyes moving back and forth between the traffic in front of her and the big green car in her mirror. He was still back there. Still following them. But, she admitted, that didn't mean they had to pack everything up and disappear into the night.

That was Kathleen's choice. It always had been. Now perhaps it was time to weigh the cost and consider the odds. Time to balance Meg and Jamie's right to a normal Christmas, to their participation in this small Texas community's holiday activities, against the force of her own fears.

The people who were following her wouldn't hurt the children. Not because they had any compunction against doing that, but because they understood it wouldn't do them any good. Not unless there was some way they could be sure Rob was aware of what they were doing. And they had no idea where Rob was.

Neither did she. As long as that was true and, more importantly, as long as they knew it was true, then the children should be safe. Because if no one knew where Rob was, there was no way Meg and Jamie could be used against him.

As long as no one believes I know where Rob is, she thought. That was the important part of the equation. She had no reason to think her husband might be trying to contact his family. No reason at all. She hadn't heard a word from Rob since the night he'd disappeared.

He had been working late in his office at home when she went to bed. He had never come upstairs that night. Or any other, of course. He had simply vanished without a trace, and she had been frantic until his "employers" had finally spelled out for her what her husband had done.

From the beginning, they had been totally relentless in their efforts to locate Rob, convinced he would get in touch with his pregnant wife. They had taken his computer, all the disks and every file from Rob's office. They had tapped Kathleen's phone. They had followed her everywhere, until even Meggie had begun looking over her shoulder to find "those men." Throughout the months of her pregnancy, they had tried threats and intimidation to get Kathleen to tell them where her husband was.

What she had told them instead was the absolute truth. She had no idea where Rob was. She didn't want to know. Once she realized what Rob had done to his family, she really didn't care if she ever set eyes on her husband again. And just to insure that she never would, as soon as Jamie was old enough to travel she had finally packed the children up and disappeared. Running as much to escape the possibility that Rob *might* try to contact them as from the constant harassment of the men who were seeking him.

Rob had taken the mob's money and fled, apparently

without a thought about what would happen to his family as a result. His children, however, one of whom he had never even seen, would always be a blood link to their father. And the people who were following Kathleen hoped she would lead them, someday, to the man who had stolen sixteen million dollars of their money. If Rob Sorrel ever dared try to reestablish contact with his family, those people intended to be in a position to know about it. So Kathleen had kept running.

Maybe, however, it was time to rethink her strategy, she was forced to acknowledge. Meg was old enough that the constant uprooting was deeply distressing, especially if six weeks was the longest Kathleen could manage to keep them hidden, she thought bitterly.

They would stay here at least until after Christmas, she decided. That was less than two weeks away. Surely she could chance staying in one place that long. Chance that Rob wasn't looking for them. Or, even if he were, chance that he couldn't locate them this quickly.

She turned the car off the road and into the paved parking lot of the church. There were several vehicles already lined up in the spaces out front, their hoods and tops dusted with the snow that had begun to fall with the setting of the weak winter sun. This snowfall hadn't been predicted when she'd left for work this morning, and it probably wouldn't amount to anything, but it made her a little nervous to have the children out.

There was no equipment for salting or clearing the roads down here. Snow was very rare, an infrequent enough occurrence to make that unnecessary most winters.

Maybe they would decide to call off play practice, Kathleen hoped, pulling the car into a space between two others, near the front door. Then she could take the children home and try to think about what she needed to do. Try to evaluate more rationally whether she really could afford to stay here until after the holidays or if that were just a dream based on what she knew this was doing to her daughter.

"They've already started," Meg said, worry that she would be late clear in her voice.

"Not yet," Kathleen reassured her, glancing at her watch. It was already five-thirty, but the rehearsal hadn't started on time any other day, so she wasn't concerned. There were always parents straggling in, running late from work or from picking up and delivering children. It would be the same today, especially with the unexpected snowfall.

"You can run on in if you want," Kathleen said. "I'll get Jamie out of his car seat, and we'll be there in a minute."

"Okay," Meg agreed, scrambling quickly out of the back. She slammed the door in her hurry to get inside, eager to perform her part flawlessly in the rehearsal.

Kathleen's eyes didn't follow her daughter as she flew up the brick steps to push open the big white door. Instead, in the mirror, they continued to watch the road behind her, looking for the car that she thought had been following them. It drove past, moving slowly enough that she was sure the driver had spotted them. He didn't turn in, however, but continued along the street, making a right at the end of the block.

When the Buick disappeared, Kathleen began to unbuckle her seat belt and found that her fingers were trembling. Angry at herself for letting them get to her, she climbed out of the car, closing her own door too forcefully, almost slamming it as Meg had done.

Her hands were still shaking a little, despite her determination to keep them steady, as she unfastened the straps and lifted Jamie out of his car seat. His eyes opened, looking up sleepily into hers.

They were more like her own eyes than Meg's, and occasionally she thought she even saw a glint of her dark auburn hair in Jamie's softly curling brown. And like hers, his skin was delicate, thin and pale. Meg, however, was all Rob, from the shining black hair and gray eyes to the very shape of her face. She was even going to have Rob's height, Kathleen thought.

"Going home?" Jamie asked, putting his head on her shoulder. His hair smelled of baby shampoo. There was even a faint hint of her own perfume. Sweet, familiar Jamie smell. Just as she was thinking that, Jamie lifted his face to the sky, looking up at the big soft flakes that were falling around them.

"Snow," he said, his voice filled with ineffable delight.

"Snow," Kathleen agreed, smiling at him.

She turned and took one last look at the road that ran in front of the church's parking lot. The Buick hadn't come back. She had thought he might circle the block, but apparently he was satisfied now that he knew where they would be for the next few minutes. He would probably be waiting for them, hidden somewhere in the darkness, when rehearsal was over.

And he would follow them home. She might see him in her mirror again or she might not. But he would be out there. Somewhere in the darkness. Watching them.

AT THE END of the rehearsal, Kathleen opened the outer door of the church, allowing a rush of cold outside air in to mingle with the heat from the sanctuary. There was now a covering of snow over the cars and pavement, gleaming like spun sugar under the parking lot's security lamps, which had come on while they were inside. She was relieved that the layer of snow wasn't thicker. Maybe they would be home before it caused any driving problems.

She held the door, waiting for Jamie to wander through. He was obviously in no hurry now to go home. There had been other children to watch during the rehearsal, and he had sat quietly in Kathleen's lap, taking everything in, brown eyes wide and interested.

By this time next year he'd be old enough to understand some of the holiday traditions. And the following year it would probably be time for his own participation in a Christmas pageant. Wherever they were living then.

They grew up so fast, she thought, taking his hand to steady him as he made the climb down the high steps. He was growing up too fast. But then life all went by too quickly, at least the good parts. It seemed only yesterday that independent Meg had been Jamie's age, clinging to Kathleen's hand. Only yesterday.

Automatically, Kathleen's eyes swept the parking lot as they started down. From this elevation, she could see all the cars, especially the ones under the tall poles that held the lights. Some of them, their exhausts producing clouds of vapor in the cold, were occupied by parents waiting to pick up children who were still inside the church, putting away the props and costumes.

As soon as the director dismissed the rehearsal, Kathleen had headed out, planning to start the car and let the heater warm it while Meg said her goodbyes. Her gaze had already fallen back down to Jamie, one chubby corduroyed leg extended carefully over a high step, when her subconscious kicked in, her mind finally registering what she had seen. Just to be sure, she raised her head again, eyes straining into the darkness

Parked on the far edge of the lot, just beside the road, was a big car. It was carefully out of the circle of light cast by the lamps, almost hidden in the shadows of the trees. But the size and the shape of it were right. A big car. Dark in color. Deliberately hiding.

Without giving herself much time to think or to plan, Kathleen stooped and picked Jamie up, hurrying with him down the steps, despite the possibility that they might be slick. She peered into her car when she reached it, looking for any sign that it had been tampered with and finding nothing inside but what they had left there an hour ago. Books and school papers and her own work from the office.

She unlocked the back door, and still hurrying, before she lost her nerve or her fury, she set Jamie down in his seat and fastened the straps to hold him there. Then she closed and relocked the back door.

Jamie's eyes met hers through the window, and she smiled at him, nodding reassurance. His expression was puzzled, and he turned his head when she moved away, his gaze following her as far as it could, given the constraints of the car seat.

She didn't look back because she knew that if she did, she might not be able to do this. If she thought about what she was doing, she would get cold feet. She had never, in all these long months, confronted these people. She had never even thought about it. Her instinct had always been to run. And to hide.

But tonight, something—maybe the thought of what this was doing to her children, maybe the season itself, which shouldn't be full of fear—compelled her at last to take a stand. At least to tell them that this time she wasn't leaving. This time, she wasn't running away.

They could follow her around this town if they wanted to, but it was going to be a waste of time. She wasn't going anywhere. Not until after the pageant. Not until after her children had celebrated a normal Christmas.

He had the engine running, she realized as she approached the car. At least the son of a bitch wouldn't get cold, she thought, her redhead's quick temper flaring more strongly with every step she took as she strode across the snow-covered ground.

It was only as she neared the car that she began to have second thoughts. And to realize that this was probably not the smartest thing she had ever done. Not very well thought out, she realized, her quick, furious stride slowing.

She came to a stop just beside the passenger door. It was too dark to see into the car. She couldn't even know if he were looking out at her. She didn't know if he had watched her walk across the parking lot, finally ready to do battle on behalf of her children.

For the moment, now that she was here, she was at a loss

about what to do. Should she tap on the glass? Fling open the door and say whatever she had come to say? Say it before she had time to think about who and what these people were or about the things they did? Incredibly, as she hesitated, the window of the Buick began to lower, the glass moving down as silently as the falling snow.

Decision made. Made *for* her. They had obviously wanted her to know they were here, she realized. They had intended for her to know that they'd found her and the children again. This was a warning, just like at the day care. She should have known that if this man hadn't wanted her to be aware he was following her, then she wouldn't have been.

She bent, putting both hands on the edge of the open window, and looked into the interior of the car. It took a second for her eyes to adjust to the inner darkness. A few more for the pale face to float into focus against the backdrop of night behind it. Another second or two for her mind to make the recognition. And to reach the acknowledgment of all it meant.

Her heart stopped. The breath she had already drawn with which to begin her tirade congealed, unused, in her lungs. None of the words that had formed in her brain came out of her mouth.

Nightmare. Suddenly, she was facing her worst nightmare. Sitting calmly in a dark car in a church parking lot in Cleo, Texas. Just sitting there, looking back at her, his gray eyes exactly as she remembered them. Exactly like Meg's.

Her mouth was still open, moving slightly in shock, but nothing came out. No words. There were no words that could convey what she felt. None that were strong enough to tell him what he had done.

Maybe, she thought, frantically grasping at the possibility, her mind clinging to any small glimmer of hope in this black and hopeless chaos he had again thrown them into, maybe *they* didn't know where she was. And if they didn't, then, pray God, there might still be a chance.

She turned and stumbled away from the car, her body as well as her mind numb with the enormity of what had just happened. And then the adrenaline kicked in, a mother's instinct to protect her children clearing her head and pushing her body to move despite the effects of shock.

She ran across the parking lot toward the picturesque little church, its steeple white against the night sky, the snow settling on its dark roof and on the ground around it, painting the scene with the serenity of a Christmas card.

One of the double doors at the front of the church opened before she reached the car where Jamie waited. Meg and two other little girls came through, laughing together. Seeing her daughter, Kathleen finally remembered to breathe, pulling the wet, cold air into her aching lungs.

"Get in the car," she shouted.

Recognizing her mother's voice, Meg looked up, her eyes searching. Kathleen didn't even think about the image she must be presenting, running across the parking lot, shrieking like a madwoman, screaming orders at her child. The other girls shrank back as if wondering whether to seek sanctuary within the warmth and safety of the building.

"Get in," Kathleen yelled again, uncaring of what they thought. Uncaring about the parents watching from the other cars. Nothing mattered but getting away from here. Getting Meg and Jamie away.

She skidded in the snow, coming to a stop by the driver's door, throwing her hand out to regain her balance. Her shaking fingers aimed the key they held at the lock, but it took several tries before she finally succeeded in sticking it in the elusive hole and unlocking the door.

When she glanced up again, Meg had started down the stairs. Kathleen opened her door and almost fell into the car, leaning across the front seat to unlock the passenger side. Meg scrambled in, eyes wide and frightened, searching her face.

Kathleen didn't have time to explain. She didn't even wait for her daughter to fasten her seat belt. Instead, she started the engine and pulled the car out of the parking space, backing far too quickly for the conditions. In response to the force of her foot on the accelerator, the car slid sideways, but Kathleen eased off the gas pedal and then straightened the wheel.

"Fasten your belt," she ordered.

"What's wrong?" Meg asked.

"Just do it. Do it now."

"Is it those men?" Meg said, her voice shaken, her normally competent fingers struggling with the familiar buckle.

Is it those men? If only, Kathleen thought. If only it was "those men." That was what she had been thinking when she approached the big dark car, anger fueling her reaction. Those men. Men who were ruthless enough to do anything. Even to hurt innocent children to get what they wanted.

She steered the car around the others in the lot, driving too fast for the crowded space. Her eyes frantically tried to watch for children darting from between the parked cars. To watch for any unexpected movements of the vehicles themselves. But normal precautions had become secondary considerations now.

She needed to get her children out of here. The car finally roared out onto the blacktop, worn tires fighting for traction on the slick road. Apparently the temperature had dropped more quickly than she had anticipated. Or the volume of snow had increased.

She switched on the wipers to push the accumulation off the windshield. She hadn't turned on her lights while she was in the lot because she hadn't needed them, but out here on the dark street, away from the security lights, she did.

She glanced in the rearview mirror, expecting to find a matching pair of headlights trailing her. There was nothing back there. Nothing visible in the darkness.

Her eyes found Jamie's face in the mirror, his chin bobbing gently against his chest. He was already asleep. Or almost. She looked to her right. Meg's eyes were still fastened on her, wide and dark in her pale face. *She looks so much like Rob,* Kathleen thought again. The resemblance was clear, even in that fleeting examination.

She pulled her gaze back to the road, peering ahead, trying to make out the lines that had been painted to mark the shoulder of the road. It was snowing harder now, big wet flakes pelting against the windshield.

Her hands were gripping the wheel, knuckles whitened with the force they were exerting. She knew she was going too fast. Her head strained forward, trying to steer by the painted lines, despite the poor visibility.

It wouldn't do Jamie and Meg any good if she wrecked the car, she told herself. She was responsible for their safety. She had to be. They had no one else. Fighting her panic, she forced her foot off the accelerator, allowing the car to fall back to a speed more appropriate for the conditions of the road.

Again she glanced in her mirror. There were still no lights behind her. Dimly she could see the path her own tires had cut in the newly fallen snow, but there was nothing else.

She wondered if he could be back there, lights off, just following her taillights through the darkness. The adrenaline was fading and with that had come a sense of letdown. An urge to cry out against the unfairness of it all. How could Rob do this to them? How could he do this to his own children?

Unconsciously, in response to that unanswerable question, she pressed harder on the gas again. She looked back at the road in front of her just as the car was entering a curve. Another vehicle was approaching from the opposite direction, its lights too bright, glaring off the glaze of moisture on her windshield.

The other driver had obviously not been expecting to meet anyone on this isolated stretch. He was well over the yellow line and going too fast. His horn blared, almost as distracting as the unexpected lights, and Kathleen reacted by turning her wheel to the right.

The nearly bald rear tire hit an icy spot on the edge of

the road, a patch of frozen water under the snow. The car started to slide. Frantically, Kathleen tried to remember what she had been told about this kind of situation, because she didn't have a lot of experience driving on ice. However, as the trees along the edge of the road loomed before her, she followed her instincts, touching her foot to the brake.

Instead of straightening back onto the road, the car began to spin in circles. Kathleen immediately removed her foot from the brake and tried desperately to steer the car away from the trees, but it was too late.

She glanced to her right to make sure that Meg had gotten her seat belt fastened, and so, eyes searching for her daughter, she didn't even know what they hit.

Chapter Three

A rush of cold air brought Kathleen around. She didn't think she had been unconscious long. She could still hear sounds of the car settling, soft metallic creaks, and there seemed to be water dripping from somewhere.

She opened her eyes and, looking out through the spiderwebbed windshield, found the top of the small tree that had stopped their momentum lying across the hood. It had broken in two and the trunk was embedded in the left fender. There was a cloud of vapor rising from the front of the car, and as the other noises faded, she could hear steam from the damaged radiator hissing out into the cold night air.

"Don't try to move. I'm going to call the paramedics," a voice at her elbow said. A deep, pleasant voice, with a hint of a Southern accent. "They'll get you all out safely."

She turned her head to find the speaker, turned it too quickly, so that she had to close her eyes to keep the world around her from spinning off into that black void again. When she opened them once more, Rob was peering in at her through the door he had forced open. He was leaning down, his right hand gripping the top of the car to keep from sliding all the way down into the ditch in which the wrecked vehicle had come to a stop.

Rob was what had sent her running in the first place, she remembered. So panicked by the thought of what would happen if those people realized her husband was here that she herself had put her children's lives in jeopardy. *Her children.*

She turned her head, moving too quickly again because she was desperate to find Meg, to make sure she was all right. Pain speared through her brain, and Kathleen fought to stay conscious.

Finally her gaze found Meg. She had had to look slightly up to do that because of the slope of the bank and the angle at which the car had come to rest against the tree.

"Mommy," Meg said softly, her eyes wide in concern.

My head, Kathleen thought suddenly. She must have banged her head against the side of the car when they hit. For the first time, she was aware of the pain, which seemed centered in her left temple. She lifted her hand and touched the place that hurt, and her fingers came away covered in blood.

"I'm all right," she said automatically, looking down in shock at the blood on her hand, even while she was trying to reassure Meg. "Can you see Jamie?" she asked.

Jamie was in the back seat, she told herself as she waited for Meg's response. He had been securely strapped in his car seat, and that was the safest place he could possibly be.

Besides, they hadn't hit that hard. The tree that had stopped them was small, and the bank they'd slid down hadn't been steep enough to cause the car to roll. She was just beginning to realize how lucky they were. And realize, too, that she could hear Jamie screaming from the back seat.

"He's crying," Meg said unnecessarily.

By that time, hysteria had crept into the little boy's screams. She wondered vaguely why Rob didn't pick him up. Why he didn't comfort his son. Why he didn't do something, damn it.

But of course, he *was* doing something, she remembered. He was going off to call the paramedics. Despite her shock, despite the pain that was pounding mercilessly at the back of her eyes, she knew what would happen if he did. She turned her head, remembering this time to move carefully. Rob had already turned away from the open door, one foot planted cautiously on the slippery bank that led back up to the two-lane road above them.

"Don't," Kathleen said. "Don't you understand? You can't call *anyone*."

She was afraid for a moment that he wouldn't listen. Afraid that, Rob-like, he'd just do whatever he wanted to, with no regard for her wishes.

"Please," she said again, trying to make her voice compelling enough to stop him. "Please don't do that to us."

He turned back, maybe stopped by the desperation of that plea, gray eyes meeting hers. There was something in them she didn't understand. Some emotion she didn't recognize.

"Get the children out," she begged, responding to whatever she saw. Hoping that it meant he was, for once, willing to listen. "Then help me out. We're not hurt. But please God, don't call anyone. They'll find us if you do. Dear God, Rob, you can't let them find us."

Her eyes had filled with tears as she thought of all she had done these long months to keep them safe. And now, with one phone call, Rob was about to destroy everything. To negate all those efforts.

She wasn't exactly sure why she was so convinced calling for help would be disastrous. Because hospitals demanded insurance cards and valid IDs? Because someone might check up on the identity she had assumed? Or simply because of her hard-learned conviction that she couldn't trust anyone?

"Please," she whispered again. She felt one of the brimming tears slip out, its heat running downward over her ice-cold cheek. "Please."

Rob's gray eyes held hers a long moment as he obviously tried to decide. Then they lifted back toward the road above them. Where his car must be parked, she realized. She listened to the snow-shrouded silence, just as he seemed to be doing. There was no traffic on the two-lane above. No whoosh of tires moving through the slush.

Apparently everyone else who had to travel this isolated stretch had either gone home earlier, when the snow had first started, or had decided it was safer to stay in town. Whatever the reason, she was thankful there was no one else out here. No one on the road. No one to see them together.

"Please," she said again, her voice little more than a whisper. She was so tired. Tired of it all. And she was cold. The air that had been reviving when Rob first pulled open the door was now freezing. Her teeth had started to chatter.

Which might mean she was going into shock, she realized, but she couldn't afford that. She had to hold on. She had to make sure that no one saw the children with their father. She tried to convey her urgency to him with her eyes, feeling almost too weak to beg him again.

She knew exactly when he reached his decision. He took one long stride back down the bank. Then he put his foot against the floor of the car and held out his hand.

"Come on," he said softly.

It was what she had asked him to do, and she couldn't imagine why she was hesitant to obey. Slowly, she forced her shaking fingers to release the latch of her seat belt. Then her eyes fell again to the hand he was offering. She didn't want to put hers into it. She didn't want to touch him. She didn't want to be dependent again on Rob Sorrel. Not for anything.

Right now, however, she didn't seem to have an option. And she was finally forced to acknowledge that. So she put her hand in his, turning her body carefully in the slanting car, preparing to step out. His fingers closed around hers.

His hand was callused and very strong, not at all the way she remembered Rob's hands. They had been the hands of an accountant. These were not. But she supposed his life had changed as much as theirs. Maybe, she realized, he was as different a man now as she was different from the woman she had been three years ago.

She had always thought of Rob as having escaped the consequences of his actions. She had pictured him living very well, relaxing somewhere warm and beautifully tropical. Somewhere safe, while she and his children played hide and seek with his enemies. Maybe, she was forced to realize, maybe she had been wrong.

He pulled, and although her knees had felt incapable of supporting her, she managed to make it out of the car. With Rob's arm around her waist, almost carrying her, she also made it up the bank.

Just as she had suspected, the forest green Buick was sitting on the edge of the road, its headlights stabbing the darkness. She wanted to tell him to cut them off, afraid they would attract someone's attention, but she supposed he would need even the faint light they were providing to get the children out.

She could still hear poor Jamie crying. She could also hear the murmur of Meg's voice. Trying to comfort her brother? Poor babies, alone and terrified in the darkness. She didn't know why she hadn't made Rob get them out first. She just couldn't seem to think. Her head was now throbbing so violently that she was nauseated with the pain.

"I have to get to the children," she said. She took a step away from him, back toward the bank, but suddenly she was surrounded by blackness. The world literally disappeared.

When it swam back into focus a few seconds later, Rob had picked her up, holding her against his chest. Despite everything he had done to them, despite his treachery, just for a moment the urge to rest her head on his shoulder was too strong to resist. And her will too weak to protest his right to hold her.

He had forfeited that right, of course, along with so many others, almost three years ago. For a moment, however, the impulse seemed impossible to resist. Just for a moment she needed someone else to carry part of this terrible burden.

But that someone wasn't Rob. He was too weak a vessel for that task, as she of all people had cause to know. She lifted her head, looking up into his face, its planes and angles illuminated by the car lights.

He really *had* changed in the years they had been apart. Searching his features, as if she didn't know them as well as she knew her own, she was forced to acknowledge that there was something different about his face. A subtle realignment of its familiarity. If she hadn't known him so well, she would have said there was a strength that had never been there before. A confidence.

"The children," she reminded him, her eyes still meeting his. Still trying to decide what was so different about them. About him.

Rob didn't respond verbally. Instead, he carried her over to the green car. He bent down and opened the passenger side door with the hand that was under her knees. Then he eased her carefully down into the seat. She was sitting sideways, her feet still on the ground outside the car.

"You stay right here," he ordered softly, leaning down to make sure she heard him. "Don't move until I get back."

She should have resented Rob giving her orders. But for some reason, right now she couldn't. She found she was grateful instead that he had taken charge. She looked up into his eyes, intending to nod agreement.

There was something very compelling in their gray depths. Comfort. Strength. Surety. All those elements she thought she had seen when he held out his hand, offering to pull her from the wrecked car. Once again she was aware of things that had never been in his eyes before.

"Just…just get the children," she said. "I won't move. I promise."

He nodded, and then he turned, climbing cautiously down the snow-covered bank to her car. She could hear him talking. To Meg, she supposed. Giving instructions? His tone was encouraging, and even Jamie's shrieks seemed less panicked. Just the presence of an adult, any adult, would be infinitely reassuring to them both.

Of course, it should have been her down there. She should never have left them alone in the darkness. And none of this would have happened if she hadn't been driving too fast. All of it was her fault. Because, like poor Jamie, she had allowed her panic to overcome rationality. She closed her eyes against the overwhelming force of guilt.

"Mommy," Meg said. She threw herself against Kathleen's legs, small hands grabbing the front of her jacket and clutching fiercely.

"It's okay," Kathleen replied. "Everything's okay." She put her hands on Meg's back, pulling her daughter closer. The little girl was trembling, with cold or with shock.

"He's getting Jamie out," Meg said.

"I know," Kathleen whispered, stroking the silken-smooth black hair, her voice as comforting as she could make it. As comforting as she intended her hands to be.

"You're hurt," Meg said, pulling away to look up at her.

By now, Kathleen knew she had been. She probably had a concussion. At the very least. She had been aware of a small-but-steady stream of warm blood trickling from her temple and running down her cheek. She only hoped the injury didn't look as bad to poor Meg as she felt. Which was pretty awful, she admitted. Weak. Unable to think. Or to plan.

Despite the fact that she could still hear Jamie crying, she didn't seem to be able to figure out what to do about it. Anything but holding on to Meg seemed to be beyond her fragile strength. She should climb down to Jamie. What kind of mother was she to let her baby scream in terror?

But she had promised Rob she'd stay here. She couldn't quite believe she had promised her husband anything, but she clearly remembered giving him her word that she wouldn't move.

"I bumped my head," she said to Meg. "Nothing bad."

"It's bleeding," Meg said, her voice full of a five-year-old's fascinated horror of blood.

"I know, but it's really not bad, Meggie. I promise it's not. I'm okay, sweetheart."

Jamie's crying seemed to be growing in volume. Kathleen looked up to see Rob climbing over the top of the bank. He was moving carefully, his left hand touching the ground occasionally to maintain his precarious balance up the slippery slope. He was carrying Jamie, who was clinging to his neck like a small, terrified monkey.

"Is he all right?" Kathleen called. The sound of her own words throbbed painfully in her head.

"He's fine," Rob said. "Not a scratch. They're both fine." He had reached the car by that time. He bent down, allowing her to see her son, who really did appear to be all right.

"Jamie," she said softly.

The little boy turned, releasing Rob's neck. He leaned out of his father's arms, reaching both arms to Kathleen. Rob bent down far enough that she could take him. Meg refused to be displaced, however, so that now Kathleen was holding both children, which was wonderful, of course.

Jamie clung to her neck now just as he had to his father's, his small, tear-streaked face buried against her shoulder, his sobs reduced to hiccups. Meg was still half lying in her lap, her head against Kathleen's thigh.

Rob was right, she realized. Both children seemed to have survived the ordeal without a scratch. Some of her fear, and her guilt, began to ease, she was so reassured by having them in her arms. Safe. But they weren't, of course. Not as long as Rob was here. She realized that he was still leaning forward, his forearm propped on the top of the car, watching the three of them.

"We have to get out of here," she said.

She meant herself and the children. She needed to get them away from their father before anyone saw them together. He nodded, his eyes still on her face. Although he didn't say anything in response to that plea, she thought he must surely understand her urgency.

"Is there a hospital in town?" he asked.

"A hospital?" she repeated, unable to believe he was thinking about her head rather than about the danger to the children. "We can't go to the hospital," she said scathingly, ridiculing the calm suggestion.

"That needs stitches." He tilted his head forward, toward hers, his eyes examining the wound on her temple.

"Then it will have to go on needing stitches," she said sharply. "We have to leave. I have to get them away before anyone sees us together."

Then, for the first time, she realized the utter impossibility of doing that. Her car was down in that ditch. Wrecked. Undrivable. She had no way to leave. No money to buy a new car. Not even enough money to have that one repaired.

Tears brimmed again at the terrible injustice. She was caught. Trapped by circumstances. And there was nothing she could do about it. After all these months, her worst nightmare had finally come true, and there was nothing she could do.

"Don't cry, Mommy," Meg said. She reached up, small fingers wiping at the tears that were now streaming unchecked down her mother's face.

Kathleen Sorrel had never been a crier. She was a doer. She believed that action, any action, was better than whimpering over fate, but suddenly, for the first time, it all seemed too much. Overwhelming. Too much for her to deal with alone.

The sob that tore through her throat caught her unaware. It was soft, but undeniably a sob. Hers. She was the one crying. She was the one this time who needed comfort. When she realized that, the floodgates of emotion broke open, and everything that she had kept bottled inside for almost three years released. And once she'd started crying, she couldn't seem to stop.

She was vaguely aware when Rob lifted her feet, putting

them gently into the car. Obediently, she turned her body in the seat, no resistance left. No will. No fight. Because for the first time, she understood she couldn't win. She couldn't keep her children safe. Not with Rob around.

She was holding them both, still crying, when he got into the driver's side and started the car. He didn't ask her where they should go. He didn't ask her anything. He just drove.

And she let him. She leaned back against the headrest, her children held tightly in her arms, and closed her eyes, unable to face what she knew was going to happen.

WHAT THE HELL had he gotten himself into now? Jordan Cross thought, listening to the subdued crying of the injured woman beside him.

The children were quiet, at least. Maybe too quiet. Theirs was an unnatural silence, even given the shock that the wreck must have been. Like him, they seemed simply to be listening to the heartrending sounds of their mother's soft sobs. Listening almost as if they had never heard her cry before.

Obviously Jake had been right. His face, the face the doctors had given him, belonged to someone else, as well. They always said everyone had a double. Apparently, the CIA surgeons had unknowingly created one for a man named Rob Sorrel. A man who had two small, beautiful children. And an equally beautiful wife, who for some reason was terrified to be around her husband.

She wasn't terrified *of* him. Jordan had figured that much out from what she'd said. When she had run from his car back at the church, he had assumed she was afraid of Sorrel. Assumed her husband had abused her or the children. Assumed he had done *something* to them to cause her fear, and that that was why she was hiding.

Now he knew that she was afraid of someone else. So afraid that she wouldn't even let him take her to a hospital to have her injury checked out. He supposed he could take her there anyway, especially considering her present state.

Part of Kathleen Sorrel's reaction could be explained by shock. By the concussion he suspected she'd sustained. But he thought there was more to her collapse. Something else he hadn't yet figured out.

"You have to go get our things," the little girl said.

Jordan's eyes again left the snow-covered road to find her small, serious face in the darkness. She was on her knees on the floorboard, looking up at him. When he had lifted her mother's feet into the car, she had scrambled in, crouching beside her. Now she was sitting up, her gaze focused on his face.

"What things?" he asked, his eyes shifting back to the icy road, trying to follow the almost invisible lane markers.

"*All* our things," she said simply, as if that explained everything. "The things from our house. You have to go get them. You *have* to."

She said it as if there were no room for argument, as if what she had asked him to do was an absolute necessity. Jordan glanced at Kathleen Sorrel, hoping for direction or clarification about the importance of the "things" her daughter was demanding he retrieve.

The woman's head was back against the headrest, her eyes closed. The trickle of blood from the cut on her temple seemed to have stopped, and her sobs had diminished. She was quiet now, except for the occasional long shuddering breath. But she didn't appear to be listening to his conversation with her daughter.

"Your mother thought we should leave," Jordan said.

"Not without our things," the child said again. Her chin tilted upward, a little aggressively, perhaps. Determined at least.

Despite his unanswered questions, despite the fact that he seemed to have gotten himself stuck with another man's wife and children, Jordan's mouth also tilted. He wasn't used to taking orders from a pint-size dictator with a stubborn streak that matched her mother's. He had time to wonder why he had decided Kathleen Sorrel was stubborn, before he got another order.

"You turn at Moore's Lane," the little girl directed. "There's a sign that says that, I think."

There might be a sign, but Jordan doubted he would be able to read it in these conditions. However, he supposed the little girl was right. There were probably things the children would need. Clothing. Bottles, maybe.

He had no experience with children, of course, but Jordan's impression was that they required a lot of paraphernalia. Besides, the woman's insistence that they had to leave probably had as much to do with her head injury and shock as with any real danger, he decided.

"Think you can spot that sign for me?" he asked.

"Of course," the little girl answered without hesitation. She managed to turn her small body in the crowded space and ease up to sit on the edge of the passenger seat already occupied by her mother. She put her hands on the dashboard and peered through the windshield, searching.

He had gone less than a mile when she said, "There."

She was pointing to a road about a hundred feet ahead that angled off to the right. At least it was paved, Jordan thought. And when he turned off the two-lane, he could make out the words on the signpost. Moore's Lane, just like she'd said.

Smart kid, he thought, forced to slow the car because the pavement hadn't lasted long. The dirt road was deeply potholed and had ruts he couldn't manage to avoid because of the covering snow. He drove carefully, easing through them.

"How far?" he asked.

"We're almost there," the little girl assured him.

She turned to look at her mother, whose breathing had evened out, as if she were asleep. The baby seemed to be sleeping as well, his arms still wrapped around her neck, his head buried in the crook of her shoulder.

When Jordan rounded the next curve, there was a small

mobile home sitting on the left of the road, its porch light piercing the darkness.

"That's it," the child said, pointing.

The driveway was no better than the road, but at least there was an attached carport. Jordan pulled his rental car into it and cut the engine. Other than the sounds the car made as it cooled, only a rural silence, its totality enhanced by the snow, surrounded them. If he had expected some reaction from the woman in the seat beside him, he was disappointed.

"You have keys?" he asked the little girl, whose eyes were once more fixed on his face.

Without answering, the child opened the passenger-side door and crawled out. She bent down and reached behind one of the concrete blocks from which the two steps that led up to the door of the mobile home had been constructed. She took out a key from its hiding place and slipped it into the lock. One turn of her fine-boned wrist and the door swung inward.

Smart kid, Jordan thought again, opening his car door and climbing out. He closed it and walked around the vehicle. Kathleen Sorrel appeared to be sleeping, but the little boy's head had lifted, and his eyes were open, looking up into his.

Jordan wondered if the kid would start screaming again if he tried to pick him up. And there was only one way to find that out. He bent, reaching inside the car, and put his hands around the little boy's chest, under his armpits. He lifted, and the small body came up.

Soft arms fastened around Jordan's neck, just as they had when he'd lifted the toddler out of the wreck. He had been screaming then. Now he was quiet, big brown eyes solemnly examining Jordan's face.

Jordan turned, carrying him up the block steps and into the warmth of the trailer. The girl had turned on the lights, revealing a central room that was neat and clean. There was a plastic laundry basket full of toys in one corner of what must serve as the family area.

To his right was the kitchen, which appeared to be as spotless as the den. To the left was a hall that would lead, he imagined, to the bedrooms and bath. The mobile home was compact enough to make a man his size a little claustrophobic. But it was warm and welcoming, especially after the coldness of the night.

"You put Jamie down," the little girl said with a touch of self-importance. "I can take care of him."

She had already taken off her jacket, Jordan noticed, a ritual of homecoming. She, at least, no longer seemed so eager to get their things and leave. Of course, this was home. Its familiarity would be especially soothing to the children after the traumatic events of this evening. Its warmth and cleanliness were comforting somehow even to Jordan.

Warmth, he realized, thinking about Kathleen Sorrel. He needed to get her inside. He believed she was in shock, and if he wasn't going to go against her wishes and take her to the hospital, then he had a responsibility to see to her himself.

"It's okay," the little girl said unexpectedly. "I can look after Jamie."

She appeared both confident and competent, Jordan thought, although incredibly small to be left with that responsibility. Of course, it would only be until he got their mother inside. He could hear if anything went wrong. So he sat the little boy down on the floor of the den, holding on to him until he was sure the child had his balance.

"I'll take his jacket off and get him a cookie," his sister said.

"I'm going to get your mom inside. Yell if you need me."

The girl nodded, already unzipping her brother's jacket. Jordan watched a moment, needing reassurance that it really would be all right if he left them alone for a minute or two. But the breath of icy air seeping in through the door they had left open reminded him of the injured woman in the car.

Before he turned away, he saw that the girl had taken the little boy's hand and was leading him toward the kitchen. Getting a cookie *sounded* safe enough. And he really didn't have much choice, Jordan decided, turning and retracing his steps to the car.

Kathleen Sorrel didn't seem to have moved while he'd been gone. Her lashes rested against almost colorless cheeks. Her face was frighteningly pale in the light streaming out through the open door of the mobile home. It touched the dark red of her hair with golden highlights and played over the shape of her high cheekbones and the intriguing hollows beneath them. She looked fragile, but as beautiful as he had thought her to be the first time he'd seen her.

That had been coming down the steps of her son's play school four days ago. She had already picked up her daughter at the public school, and they had gone in together to get the little boy. When they had come out, talking and laughing together, Kathleen Sorrel had had a hand on each child's shoulder.

Her hair had been loose that day, and the wind had suddenly whipped a long, curling strand of it across her cheek. She had raised her right hand to push it away, smiling at something the toddler said, and then she had turned, looking almost directly toward the car where Jordan was sitting. At that moment, at the picture they presented, maybe, something had shifted inside Jordan's chest. Some connection to the three of them seemed to have been forged in that instant.

There had been nothing about Kathleen Sorrel that had seemed out of the ordinary that day. She had been dressed in charcoal slacks and a moss-green sweater, her short camel coat unbuttoned to reveal the touch of color. She had looked, he supposed, like a hundred other busy mothers picking up their children from school.

Except, he acknowledged, there had been *something* that had made her stand out. Some aspect of her appearance that had not allowed him to take his eyes off her. Something that was vital and alive and beautiful. Even now, he thought, looking down at her face, despite the dried blood and the tearstains, she looked like some mythical sleeping beauty. As enticing as that image was, however, he shouldn't be letting her sleep, not if he was right about the concussion. He bent down, leaning into the car.

"Kathleen," he said softly.

Her lids flickered in response, and then they lifted, revealing eyes the color of leaves turning in the fall. They rested a moment on his face, as if she had never seen him before.

"I need to get you inside," he said. "Get you out of the cold. I need to look at your head."

Her face turned languidly away, eyes moving toward the driver's side of the car, and then they came back to his. "Where are the children?" she asked, but she didn't seem overly concerned to find that they weren't in the car.

"They're inside. They're fine."

She nodded, her eyes drifting slowly over his features again. Studying them, almost as if they were unfamiliar.

"Think you can walk if I help you?" he asked.

"Of course," she said.

He smiled involuntarily at the quiet determination he heard in her answer. Her eyes widened a little in response to his smile, a question appearing briefly in their russet depths.

"Come on," he said softly, reaching in to help her out of the seat. She ignored his hand. She might have managed to stay upright with a lot of support, but as soon as she put her feet on the concrete slab of the carport and tried to stand by herself, her eyelids fell. Her head tilted back on the slim column of her neck as her knees began to buckle.

Jordan had almost been expecting that. Without saying another word, he quickly bent, slipping his right arm under her knees and putting his left behind her back. When he picked her up, she put her head against his shoulder automatically, just as she had done before. A gesture that made her seem as trusting as her small son had been when Jordan carried him.

He remounted the concrete block stairs, turning sideways so he wouldn't bump Kathleen's head against the frame of the narrow opening. The little girl was there, and she closed the door behind him, throwing the night latch and slipping the security chain into its slot. The toddler, divested of his jacket, was holding his cookie and watching the proceedings with wide-eyed interest.

"Mommy," he said softly.

"Mama's sleeping," Jordan explained.

He carried Kathleen across the den and down the narrow hallway to the bedroom. The children's room was on the right, scarcely big enough for the bunk beds it contained. The tiny bath was on the left. And at the end of the hall was a double bed taking up the middle of what was supposed to be the master bedroom. Everything back here was as clean and orderly as the rest of the house had been.

"Can you pull down the covers for me?" Jordan asked, realizing that the little girl had followed them.

She managed that task better than he would have thought she could, given her size. Jordan laid her mother on the bed and bent to turn on the bedside light. He pushed back the bloody, matted hair at her temple to find the injury. The area around the abrasion was puffy and beginning to discolor. Jordan had had some experience dealing with wounds through the years—not any that he particularly liked to remember.

This one didn't look all that serious, but you could never tell with a head injury, not within the first few hours. And he didn't like the fact that Kathleen Sorrel seemed to be drifting in and out of consciousness. Just as he thought that, her eyes opened again, looking straight up into his.

"Why are we here?" she asked.

"The children thought we needed to get your belongings," he said. Her pupils were the same size, he was relieved to see, and they were reacting to the bedside light. Equally reactive, which he knew was a good sign.

She nodded slightly at his explanation, then closed her eyes again. Apparently, despite her earlier urgency, she was willing to accept his explanation for the decision to bring them here. The child's decision, Jordan remembered.

He admitted that it had been a good one. Driving any farther tonight was dangerous. Besides, he was certain no one had been following this small family in the four days he had been watching them, and given his experience, he would have known if they had been. No one except Jordan Cross had seemed to have any interest at all in Kathleen Sorrel and her children.

If it hadn't been for Jake, Jordan would never have located them. Jake's computer search had matched his picture to Sorrel's. The information that had come with the picture had been sketchy, almost suspiciously so, Jake had suggested. But then Jake tended to be suspicious. It was a good characteristic in their line of work. One Jordan ought to cultivate, he supposed.

He had left San Francisco and flown down here hoping to get some answers. Was it possible that the men who had attacked him that night had been looking for Rob Sorrel instead?

Since he was evidently now wearing Sorrel's face, and since it, too, seemed to come with a set of enemies, Jordan had thought he needed to know as much as he could about the man. He hadn't learned anything, of course, except that he found Rob Sorrel's wife to be extremely attractive. His eyes again studied the delicate Celtic features of the woman on the bed.

Kathleen, Jordan thought. An old-fashioned Irish name for a woman with red hair and skin so fair as to be transparent. So fair it appeared translucent in the lamplight. Of course, he reminded himself, that might also be from loss of blood. Shock. Hypothermia. All those unpleasant realities that he was disregarding in his admiring assessment.

Jordan turned, intending to make his way to the bathroom to get a cloth to wash the blood away from the cut so he could get a better look. He should also check out the first-aid supplies. Even if the injury wasn't serious, Kathleen Sorrel was going to wake up sometime tonight with a massive headache.

When he turned away from the bed he found the two children standing in the doorway to the bedroom, their eyes wide and concerned. The little girl held her brother's right hand. In the other one, the toddler still clutched his uneaten cookie.

"Mommy," he called, his soft voice tentative, as if he were torn about whether or not he wanted to wake her.

"Mommy's resting now," Jordan said. "I'm going to put a bandage on her head."

"Boo-boo," the toddler said, nodding.

Jordan didn't have a clue what that meant, but he nodded back. He wouldn't have thought kids this young could look worried, but these two did. And why shouldn't they? he acknowledged. They'd been in a car accident, their mother was injured and some strange man was in their home.

"You should fix supper," the little girl said. "Jamie's getting really hungry."

Since Jamie hadn't touched his cookie, Jordan figured Jamie wasn't the one who was anxious about dinner. But maybe they weren't as hungry for food as they were for reassurance. Reassurance that somebody was in charge. That somebody was going to look out for them.

"As soon as I look after your mom's head."

"Okay," the child said.

"You want to take him back to the den?" Jordan suggested.

"No," she said. The word was soft, but determined. The small chin tilted upward. "We're going to stay here. With Mommy."

A reasonable request, he supposed, if you had been

through what they had tonight. And if you were their age. In their situation.

"All right," Jordan said, wondering for the first time what you fed kids this young. His culinary efforts, if he were forced to make any, usually extended to something from a box shoved into a microwave. If Kathleen Sorrel didn't have one of those, he was probably going to be in a whole hell of a lot of trouble.

But at least, he thought, looking down at the two children huddled together in the doorway, he wasn't going to be bored.

Chapter Four

Jordan dipped the washcloth into the bowl of warm water and used it to dab at the dried blood. His hand hesitated when Kathleen made a sound. He glanced at her face, but her eyes were still closed, the tracery of blue veins clear through the delicate skin of their lids.

"Sorry," he said, and waited, hoping for a response.

Although the gash still looked relatively minor to him, he was more worried than he had been when he'd first seen the injury. By now Kathleen should have rallied from the shock of the wreck and even from her emotional outburst. Jordan would have expected her to be asking about the children. To reiterate her demands that they all leave. He would have expected the woman he'd watched for the last four days to be doing *something*, other than lying almost motionless on the bed where he'd placed her.

She said nothing in reply to his apology, however, nor did she open her eyes. Instead, a glimmer of moisture appeared at the inside corner of her left eye, near where his hand hovered, the damp cloth still held in his fingers. Seeing the tear, Jordan's lips tightened, and he fought his anxiety.

Her reactions tonight certainly didn't fit with the impressions he had formed of Kathleen Sorrel. He had admired the way she handled the children, juggling their activities and the demands of her job. Even the cleanliness of her home, despite the fact that two small children lived and played here, testified to her energy and efficiency.

Now she seemed to have crawled into some kind of shell, willing to let him handle everything and to make the decisions. Of course, that wasn't a fair assessment. She had a head injury. Maybe she was even in shock. She was certainly upset that her husband had shown up again, because she believed his presence threatened their safety in some way.

Jordan should have explained who he was at the outset. That he hadn't was a cruelty, no matter what he'd thought he might learn by catching Kathleen off guard. That confrontation hadn't ended at all as he'd hoped it might. After all, seeing his face was what had sent her running onto that icy road, so he felt responsible for what had happened.

But explaining everything seemed a little too complicated right now. He even wondered whether it would make Kathleen feel better to be told he was a stranger. A stranger who was sitting on the edge of her bed, caring for her and the children.

Would it be a comfort to find out he wasn't Rob, or would it be another source of anxiety? Of fear? Jordan wasn't sure, and given the fact that Kathleen didn't seem capable of or interested in demanding any answers from him right now, he decided that it might be better to let things like identifying himself ride for a while. At least for tonight.

He dabbed again at the matted hair at her temple. She didn't offer any protest this time, so he dipped the cloth into the warm water and worked carefully until he had cleaned the blood off her skin and gotten most of it out of her hair, as well. The moisture had awakened its natural curl, so that the fine strands of hair, dark gold in the lamplight, seemed to float around his fingers.

The gash itself was about an inch long and didn't appear to be deep. However, the bruising and swelling around it was pretty extensive, especially given the fine-grained texture of her skin. That was the most dangerous part of the injury, of course, and one he had no way of determining— the force with which she had struck her head when the car hit the tree. And the impact that blow had had on her brain.

He knew now he had been right about the cut needing stitches. Without them, this would leave a scar. Which would be a damn shame, Jordan thought irrelevantly, his eyes again moving over her classic features.

The best he could do to lessen the chances of scarring would be to use a series of butterfly bandages and try to pull the edges of the laceration together. However, given the skin's natural thinness and fragility in this location, those might not have much effect. He wondered again if it would be better to force Kathleen to go to a hospital, but he really hated to take the three of them out again on those treacherous roads. Like a fool, he hadn't taken the baby's car seat from the wreck. He hadn't even thought about it.

Here, at least, they were warm and not in danger of ending up in a ditch. With the snowstorm, he also thought they would even be safe for a few hours from Rob Sorrel's enemies, whoever the hell they were. And if he watched Kathleen carefully through the rest of the night…

The more he thought about it, the more he believed he had made the right decision. If her condition changed dramatically later on, then he could take her for medical help. He wished he'd asked her about directions to the hospital when she had been more communicative. That was something her daughter, as precocious as she seemed to be, probably wouldn't know.

"Is Mommy sleeping?" the little girl asked.

Jordan looked up to find her standing beside the bed, her eyes on her mother's pale face.

"She's resting," Jordan said, "but I think maybe she'd like to talk to you. Why don't you say something to her?"

"Mommy?"

There was no reaction to the whispered word.

"A little louder," Jordan suggested, watching Kathleen's face, hoping to see some response to her daughter's voice.

Hoping for some indication that she was only concussed. "Maybe she didn't hear you."

"Mommy," the child said again.

Jordan dropped the cloth back into the bowl of water and took Kathleen's chin in his fingers, gently turning her head toward him. The closed lids fluttered, but they didn't open.

"Kathleen," he said, his voice more demanding than the little girl's had been. "You have to wake up now."

The translucent lids lifted slowly. Her eyes looked unfocused, but again the pupils reacted to the lamp beside the bed. Her dazed stare lasted only a second or two, and then she seemed to realize who she was looking at.

"Rob?" she questioned softly, as if she couldn't believe he was here.

"Your daughter wants to say hi," Jordan said. He tilted his head to the right, toward the little girl, and Kathleen's eyes followed the movement, finding her daughter's face.

"Hi, sweetheart," Kathleen said, her lips lifting fractionally. The movement might have been slight, but the little girl's answering smile was wide and relieved.

"Is your head all better?" she asked.

Kathleen nodded, but then closed her eyes quickly, squinting tightly in an obvious reaction to the pain engendered by the movement. And when she opened them once more, she focused on Jordan's face again instead of on her daughter's.

"You're sure they're all right?" she asked, her eyes seeking reassurance.

"They're fine. I'm going to try to find them something to eat. Think you could manage to get something down?"

She shut her eyes again, her lips pressed tightly together, and moved her head slightly from side to side.

"Nauseated?" Jordan asked.

"A little," she whispered.

"I think you've got a concussion," he said, wishing again that he had some way to tell how severe it was.

"I know."

"I think it might be safer for you to spend the night in the hospital. They can monitor your condition. Make sure that—"

"No," she interrupted, her eyes almost snapping open. She shook her head again, more forcefully this time, despite the pain. "No, Rob. For God's sake, don't do that to us."

It was clear the very idea agitated her. And, more importantly, clear that she had understood exactly what he'd said. She had apparently even understood the implications of being seen with her husband. All of which, thankfully, seemed to argue that the head injury wasn't too serious.

"All right," he said, making his voice reassuring. "I'm going to wake you up every couple of hours, though. You may hate the sight of me before morning," he added, smiling at her.

She didn't return the smile, but her eyes stayed on his face. There was no response in them to his small attempt at humor. Apparently, he realized belatedly, Kathleen already had ample reason to hate the sight of Rob Sorrel. And she had no way of knowing the man who was trying to take care of her wasn't the husband she seemed to despise.

"THAT ISN'T THE WAY Mommy does it," Meg announced, watching Jordan ladle tomato soup into three bowls.

Meg and Jamie. He knew that now because he had finally thought to ask her. Of course, he also knew a lot of other things about them as well, most of it not nearly as relevant as their names. In fact, once she started, Meg had proved a veritable fountain of information. He knew about her costume and her role in the upcoming Christmas pageant. About her school. A lot about Jamie. What he could and couldn't do. What she, as big sister, had to do for him. What Mommy did. Which was infinitely better than whatever Jordan was doing.

"Well," he said, adding the remainder of the soup in the boiler to his bowl, "this is the way we're going to do it tonight."

He'd be the first to admit he knew nothing about feeding kids. He hadn't been around all that many children. The few times he had been, it had certainly not been in the role of caretaker. However, despite Meg's opinion, he didn't think he had made too big a mess of it so far.

There hadn't been a microwave, but there had been canned soup on the shelf. And crackers. Some peanut butter. That had been another thing he'd learned from Meg. They both liked crackers and peanut butter. Especially graham crackers.

Jordan wasn't sure that the combination of tomato soup and peanut-butter-between-graham-cracker sandwiches was going to get a nod from any child nutritionist, but it was food. The soup was hot. The peanut butter would be filling. And at Meg's direction, he'd already poured three glasses of milk.

Milk, he thought in amazement, as he set a bowl of soup on top of each of the three plastic place mats Meg had put out on the wooden table. He couldn't remember the last time he'd drunk a glass of milk.

"You have to put him on something," Meg said.

"Put him on something?" Jordan repeated, puzzled by the instructions. She was real good at giving those, he thought, still a little amused at her efforts to help him. Maybe because she had figured out he was going to need all the help he could get.

"Something to sit on. Mommy uses books," she said, pointing at several children's books stacked on top of the telephone directory on the counter. He scooped them up and put them on the chair at one side of the table. As soon as he saw the books there, the little boy held up his arms, waiting to be picked up.

Jordan obliged, settling him on the books and pushing his chair up to the table until Jamie's tummy was touching the edge. The toddler laid his cookie down beside the bowl of soup. His brown eyes followed Jordan as he took the place at the head of the table.

Jordan had put all the peanut-butter-and-graham-cracker sandwiches on a plate in the middle of the table, so he took one and held it out to the little boy. The kid was bound to be hungry, Jordan thought. It was nearly eight o'clock, which must be long after dinnertime for these two.

Chubby fingers fastened carefully around the cracker, and then Jamie placed it on the place mat beside his bowl, as well. His eyes lifted again to Jordan's face.

"What's the matter, champ?" Jordan asked softly, smiling at him. "Not hungry?"

"We have to bless it," Meg said.

"Bless it?"

"Say the blessing," she explained.

"Say the blessing," Jamie repeated, nodding, his eyes on Jordan.

"Okay," Jordan agreed. "So who says it?"

"You do," Meg proclaimed.

Which would be all right, Jordan thought, if he could remember any. "Now I lay me down to sleep" drifted through his head, but even as long as it had been since he'd prayed, he didn't think that one was appropriate for mealtimes.

"Think you could help me out here?" he asked, smiling at Meg. His smile usually worked pretty well with women. Of course, he'd never tried it out on a female this young, but maybe...

Gray eyes met gray. Hers held a hint of suspicion.

"That isn't the way Mommy—"

"I know," Jordan interrupted. "I know Mommy does it all differently, but since she's not feeling too well, do you think that just for tonight we might make an exception?"

"An exception?" Meg questioned.

"Do something else," Jordan explained.

"We could sing the one we sang at our other school," Meg offered, after thinking about it.

"I think that would be perfect," Jordan said, hearing the relief in his own voice.

She reached for Jamie's hand, and the little boy took her fingers. And then he held out his other hand to Jordan.

It seemed incredibly small. And not very clean. There was a smear of peanut butter on his thumb. There was something that looked like purple marker on one of his knuckles and a stringy, edge-raveling Band-aid on the first joint of the middle finger.

For an instant there was a strange thickness in Jordan Cross's throat. He swallowed and then reached out, his long fingers enclosing the little boy's hand. As soon as they had, the child bowed his head and closed his eyes, dark lashes falling to lie against the soft rose of his cheeks.

"Bow your head," Meg ordered.

Jordan looked up to find her eyes on him, impatience and disapproval written on her small features. Obediently, he lowered his head. Which had probably been a good thing, he thought, as two childish voices clashed over the almost-familiar melody. Like the bedtime prayer, this, too, had been hiding somewhere in his memory.

Not even the amen was in tune. At least it had been brief, Jordan had time to think, trying to control the twitch of his lips before he lifted his head. After the last wavering note, Jamie's fingers squeezed his. And they didn't release.

Jordan looked up to find the little boy's eyes again on his face. He was waiting, as Meg had been earlier. Only just like before, Jordan wasn't sure what the kid was waiting for. Not until the little fingers tightened again over his.

This time Jordan squeezed back, and the toddler smiled, uncurling his grip. Then Jamie used the same grubby fingers to carefully pick up the peanut butter cracker and bring it toward his mouth.

"We didn't wash your hands," Jordan said. Obediently, the little boy hesitated, although his mouth was already open, ready to take a bite. His brown eyes lifted, questioning.

"I washed mine," Meg said, holding out two very clean and dainty hands, her fingers spread as if inviting inspection.

"But I didn't wash Jamie's," Jordan said. "Did I, champ?"

The toddler shook his head and laid the cracker back beside his bowl. He lifted his arms again to Jordan, waiting to be picked up.

It was a little late now, of course, Jordan thought, remembering the number of times the graham cracker had already come in contact with the fingers in question, but maybe in this, it was still better late than never. And whatever he did, he knew he would probably hear that it wasn't the way Mommy did it. Jordan stood and picked Jamie up from behind, hands under his armpits, and carried him awkwardly to the sink. He pressed Jamie between his own stomach and the counter, holding him there while he turned on the water and waited for it to warm.

"Hold out your hands," he said.

He secured the solid little body around the chest with one arm. Then, using his other hand, Jordan opened the spout of the dish washing liquid and squirted a drop or two on each set of chubby fingers.

After he'd tested the temperature of the water, he said, "Okay, cowboy, scrub 'em down."

A lot of vigorous motions and a sink full of bubbles later, the hands looked *almost* clean enough to eat with. The purple marker and the disreputable bandage hadn't changed, but the general appearance of cleanliness had improved, Jordan thought.

On the way back to the table, a matter of a couple of steps, Jordan grabbed a towel off a rack by the sink and used it to dry Jamie's fingers.

"That's the dish towel," Meg said matter-of-factly. She dipped competently into the soup and brought a brimming spoonful of it up to her mouth without spilling a drop.

"Right now," Jordan told her, trying to hold on to his sense of humor, "it's a hand towel. We'll get another towel out for the dishes later."

"Mommy's not going to like that," Meg warned.

"Probably not," Jordan said under his breath. It wasn't what he wanted to say, but even he knew you couldn't use those words with a five-year-old. Not even an officious one.

He settled the toddler back on the stack of books and sat down again at the head of the table. A shiny, unappetizing skim of red-orange had settled over the top of his soup. Resolutely he put his spoon in it and took a taste.

Not bad, he thought, despite the temperature. He reached across the table for a peanut-butter-and-cracker sandwich just as Jamie's bowl of soup somehow managed to upend itself all over the little boy's stomach. The soup turned the middle section of his knit shirt pink, ran off either side of his rounded belly and began to puddle, drop by thick drop, onto the floor.

Jordan jumped up and pulled the child's chair back, grabbing the bottom of Jamie's shirt and holding it away from his skin. Jamie had begun to sob, the sounds certainly not as piercing as those he had made after the wreck, but pretty loud in the confined space of the kitchen.

"It's okay," Jordan said, peeling the shirt off over the toddler's head and dropping it in a sodden heap on the table. He picked Jamie up, and the little boy's arms fastened tightly around Jordan's neck, the noise of his crying subsiding almost as quickly as it had started.

Jordan carried him back to the sink and set him down on the counter. The small belly wasn't even red. There didn't seem to be a surface burn. Either the soup hadn't been hot enough or the shirt hadn't stayed in contact long enough for it to do damage. Jordan took a breath in relief.

"I tried to tell you that's not how Mommy does it," Meg said. When Jordan looked up, she was still sitting calmly at the table. She took a bite of one of the graham cracker sandwiches. "She puts soup in his cup. The one that has a lid."

Which made sense, Jordan thought, turning back to the little boy. Brown, baby-fine hair was standing straight up with the static electricity that had been generated when Jordan pulled off his top. Several of the strands were streaked with soup, as was his face. There were tear streaks there as well, but at least he had stopped crying. And he wasn't hurt. Probably as scared by Jordan jumping at him as by the spill. Or maybe afraid he'd get in trouble for making a mess.

"It's all right," Jordan said reassuringly. "It doesn't matter. We'll get some more soup."

"Okay," Jamie said.

"Here," Meg said.

Jordan turned and found her standing beside them, holding out the towel he'd used to dry the little boy's hands.

"Thanks," he said. He took it and began wiping soup off Jamie's hair and face. "You want to find me that cup?"

"Okay," she said.

The trace of "I told you so" in her voice was bearable, Jordan decided. After all, she really had.

When the cleanup operation had been completed, Jordan set the toddler back in his chair and poured most of his own soup into the cup Meg had supplied. He put a fresh peanut-butter-and-cracker sandwich on the place mat beside it, disposing of the original one, now soggy with spilled soup.

"I'm going to check on your mom," he said. "Can you watch Jamie for a minute?"

"You need to put his milk in a smaller glass," she said, taking a sip of her own. She did it so neatly there wasn't even a white mustache on her upper lip.

This time Jordan followed her suggestion, filling a small glass he found in the cabinet less than half full, and setting it down by the little boy.

"Watch him," he ordered, grabbing a sandwich off the plate in the middle of the table and sticking it in his mouth. "I'll be right back," he promised around it.

JORDAN HAD TURNED off the light in the bedroom when he'd left earlier, and he paused a moment in the doorway, waiting for his eyes to adjust to the contrast.

"What's wrong?"

He heard Kathleen's voice a few seconds before the pale oval of her face floated out of the darkness. She was half sitting, propped on her right elbow. Her left hand was cupped protectively over the cut on her temple, or maybe that was to block the light coming into the room from behind Jordan.

"Nothing really. Jamie spilled his soup," Jordan said.

"He's not burned?"

There was concern in the soft question. Natural enough, he supposed, even though she believed Jordan was the child's father and had some parenting skills. She'd probably be a lot more concerned if she knew the reality of the situation.

"He's fine. I think I scared him when I jumped up. The soup wasn't hot enough to burn, and I've already cleaned up the mess. They're eating."

Apparently reassured, she lay back against the pillows and closed her eyes.

"How's your head?" Jordan asked.

"Better," she said softly.

He didn't believe her, not judging by her actions. He suspected the truth of the matter was that she was nauseated and had a headache like the worst hangover of all time.

"Still not hungry?" he asked. He didn't believe she'd want to eat, but he was trying to evaluate her condition. She was lucid and coherent, which seemed hopeful.

"No," she said succinctly.

"I don't blame you. I'm afraid dinner wasn't much."

"As long as they're fed. They're *not* picky eaters."

"He used the dish towel to dry Jamie's hands," Meg announced. She was standing in the hallway behind Jordan. He stepped to the side to let her see her mother. Or maybe, he thought, to let her mother see her.

"That's okay," Kathleen said. "It doesn't matter. Things may not be exactly the same around here for a little while, Meg."

"Because he's here?" the little girl said.

"Partly," Kathleen agreed.

"And because you hurt your head?"

"Yes."

"Run on back and watch Jamie for me," Jordan suggested.

"Do I have to do what he says?" Meg asked.

There was a long silence from the darkened bedroom. Jordan understood Kathleen's reluctance to answer, and when she did, he was a little surprised by what she said.

"Yes, you do," she said quietly. "And Jamie, too. You both have to mind him."

"He doesn't know *anything* about taking care of Jamie."

The five-year-old's voice was full of undisguised scorn at Jordan's ineptitude. He couldn't blame her. After all, she was right. He knew nothing about children.

"You can help him," her mother suggested. "Do it for me, Meggie. Will you do that for me, sweetheart?"

It was an appeal that would be hard to resist, Jordan thought, especially given Meg's personality.

"All right," she said. "But tell him to listen to me next time," Meg added.

Instead of issuing that requested instruction, Kathleen said, "Go check on Jamie for me, please."

"Can I kiss you good-night later on?" The tone of Meg's question was totally different from her comments about Jordan.

"Of course you can," Kathleen said.

"And Jamie, too?"

"And Jamie, too."

"Okay," Meg said.

They listened to her skip back down the hall and the low murmur of her voice talking to Jamie. She was probably telling him that they could visit Mommy later.

"Meg doesn't deal well with change," Kathleen said. "I'm sorry if she seems…"

She hesitated and Jordan resisted filling in the blank, although he could come up with a few words that would fit.

He understood, however, that the kids had had a rough night. And he was a stranger. An inept stranger. Meg was entitled to be disdainful.

"I understand," Jordan said, almost amused by her attempt to explain Meg. After all, he was the adult here. He didn't have to score points against a five-year-old, he thought, fighting the urge to smile at his ridiculous resentment of Meg's attitude.

"Your voice seems different," Kathleen said softly.

It threw him for a moment, because he hadn't been expecting that kind of challenge. He hesitated, knowing she'd given him an opening, the perfect opportunity to tell her the truth. For some reason, he didn't take it.

She wasn't capable of taking care of her children right now, he told himself, but if she knew who he really was— what he was and why he was here—she probably wouldn't be willing to let him do it for her. Or to check on her during the night. Maybe not willing to let him be here at all. He was a stranger who had no right to be in this house. Who had no place in the intimacy of this small family.

"It's been a long time," he said instead.

Standing in the shaft of light coming from the hallway behind him, he waited for her to answer. Kathleen said nothing else, and after what seemed an eternity of waiting, he turned and walked back down the hallway, toward the two children she believed were his.

His and hers together, he realized. And that thought had, of course, an intimacy all its own. A totally different sort of intimacy than the one he had recognized before.

Chapter Five

Jordan came awake with a start, disoriented by the unfamiliarity of his surroundings. He lay without moving, listening to the heavy silence, trying to figure out where the hell he was. There was absolutely no sound in the darkness. No traffic. No hum of appliances.

That in itself was finally the clue he needed. Once he had remembered the reason for the totality of the silence, the rest of the night's events began to filter back. The snow. The accident. Kathleen Sorrel's injury.

Kathleen, he thought. He turned his head a little and verified what he had already been aware of on some level. Kathleen Sorrel's head was on his shoulder, her body aligned so that it lay along the length of his, one of her knees bent and resting on top of his thigh. Her right hand, fingers limp and relaxed, was lying on his chest.

When he realized that, he was almost afraid to take another breath. Afraid that any motion would wake her and cause her to move away from him. He didn't want that. He wanted her to stay right where she was. Exactly the way she was. With the fragrance of her hair and body around him, like the scent of wildflowers, sweet and clean and natural.

He closed his eyes, fighting his own body's uncontrollable reaction to the discovery he'd just made. He was in bed with Kathleen Sorrel. He had wanted to be there, probably since the first time he'd seen her standing on the steps of the day care center. And yet this was not what he had intended when he'd come to this bedroom last night.

He had planned to sit up all night, to wake her every few hours, to make sure nothing was going on with her injury that he wasn't aware of and to be alert if there was a need to take her somewhere to get treatment. That's all he had intended, but apparently it hadn't quite worked out the way he planned.

He lay very still, thinking about the events that had led up to this. He remembered getting the children to bed. He had bathed Jamie, washing his hair to remove the last sticky traces of soup.

He had forgotten to take the little boy's pajamas with him into the bathroom, so he'd had to carry him, naked and still faintly damp, wrapped in a towel and the aroma of baby shampoo, across the hall to the bedroom the children shared. Once Jordan had gotten him dressed in his nightclothes, the toddler had settled down on the bottom bunk as if relieved to be there. Meg had been far more reluctant to go to bed, but she had eventually acquiesced after the promised visit to her mother's room.

When they were both asleep, Jordan had found himself alone in the quietness. He had finished cleaning the kitchen, not that, despite his efforts, it looked as spotless as it had when he'd first entered it. Then he went out to the car to get his suitcase and to take a last look around.

The snow had still been falling, and in the shrouded silence it created, the trailer seemed as isolated as if it were standing on the moon. There was literally nothing out here. No sound. No lights. No other houses.

Looking out over the peaceful swirl of wind-driven flakes, Jordan had decided that there were also no enemies. Whoever Kathleen was so terrified of wasn't hiding in this white tranquillity, he thought, as he locked the car again and carried his bag inside.

His weapon was in the suitcase, and that was really what

he'd gone out to retrieve. He was willing to give in to Kathleen's paranoia to that extent. Or maybe to his own deeply ingrained habits. He knew he'd sleep better with the semiautomatic nearby. Except, of course, he wasn't planning on sleeping, he reminded himself, as he turned off the kitchen light.

He had taken the gun and a chair down the hall with him to the master bedroom. He could tell by the regularity of her breathing that Kathleen was asleep. And there was no sound from the children's room. He put the wooden chair down beside the bed and laid his weapon on its seat.

Although he had hated to do it, he'd turned on the bedside lamp. Kathleen didn't stir. She looked as much at peace as the snow-blanketed countryside that surrounded them. And almost as pale, he thought. So despite the fact that she seemed to be sleeping normally, Jordan touched her chin as he had before, turning her head toward the light as he called her name.

"Kathleen."

Her eyes opened. She blinked against the unexpected glare. He again watched the pupils adjust, equally reactive. In his concentration, he hadn't been aware of what else was in her eyes, not until she lifted her chin, pulling it away from contact with his fingers. Only then did the contempt register. And although he knew logically it wasn't directed at him, it stung nonetheless.

"What is it?" she asked.

"I wanted to make sure nothing was going on with that bump that I should know about."

"Nothing's going on," she said, her voice as cold as her eyes.

Considering what he'd been able to piece together about Kathleen's relationship with her husband, this reaction was more normal, Jordan supposed, than the earlier one had been. That had seemed an acceptance of him wrung from her by circumstances. She had seemed defeated and overwhelmed, obviously, by the accident.

This anger and contempt, however, was more what he would have expected. The impression he had formed of Kathleen Sorrel during the days he had spent watching her was that she was a strong woman, used to being in control. Maybe that's why her actions earlier tonight had bothered him so much. He hadn't liked seeing her down.

He nodded, holding her eyes, feeling the bite of their scorn. Feeling an unexpected relief that there didn't seem to be any residual emotional attachment to her husband—no emotions other than those he saw in her eyes right now.

"Go back to sleep," he advised softly.

He reached over and flicked off the light, plunging the room back into darkness. Then he picked up the big semi-automatic and sat down in the chair it had been occupying.

Eventually his eyes adjusted enough that he could distinguish her profile, its purity limned against the blacker emptiness behind it. He believed her eyes were open, staring up into the darkness, and he wondered what she was feeling about having her husband here.

In the morning he would tell her that he wasn't Rob Sorrel, he decided. She'd be even more back to normal. That would be time enough for explanations. His about who he really was and what he was doing here. Hers about what her husband had done that had put both his family and Jordan at the center of a manhunt.

After that decision, Jordan had sat in the uncomfortable kitchen chair a long time, remembering the last four days. Thinking about tonight. About what a disaster the dinner he'd fixed for the kids had been. Thinking about bathing Jamie and the feel of arms around his neck. Thinking about Kathleen. Trying to explain why he felt such a connection to a woman whose existence he had been totally unaware of until four days ago.

That was the last thing he remembered until he woke up and realized he was sharing a bed with that woman. Her head was resting on his shoulder. Her fingers lying on his chest. Her breathing slow and regular, causing the softness of her breast to move tantalizingly against his body.

Was she curled at his side because she believed he was her husband? Somehow he doubted that. More than likely this closeness was simply a reaction to the once-familiar feel of another warm body in the bed on a cold night.

She was a married woman with two children. At one time, she had been accustomed to snuggling up against a man as she slept. Apparently those physical responses had not been completely forgotten, no matter what had happened later to drive her and Rob Sorrel apart.

Jordan took another slow, careful breath, wondering if he should attempt to crawl out of bed without waking her. Or if he should just close his eyes and go back to sleep, giving in to the reality that sitting up in a chair all night when there was half a bed available right in front of him wasn't very bright.

Kathleen was the one who moved, however, her breath sighing out strongly enough that he could feel the moist heat of it against his neck. He closed his eyes, fighting the urge to respond. To turn his body so that it would be even more intimately aligned with hers. An alignment that, asleep, she might even unconsciously accept, but one he had no right to seek. Just as he had no right to be lying beside her in this bed, cradling her body in the curve of his right arm.

He opened his eyes again, carefully turning his head enough to the left that he could see the clock on the bedside table. It was a little after 5:00 a.m. The last time he remembered waking Kathleen to check on her was around midnight. Which meant…

Unconsciously he tensed, preparing to make the attempt to slip out without disturbing her. He knew that finding him—finding Rob, he amended—in her bed wasn't going to be a pleasant surprise. He turned his head back toward Kathleen to check for any signs of waking as he prepared to move.

He found her eyes already open, watching him. His

breathing stilled, all thought of movement suspended. The low light of dawn, which was beginning to seep into the bedroom, had been brightened by the snow-whitened landscape outside. It still wasn't enough, however, to reveal exactly what was in her eyes.

"What the hell do you think you're doing?" she said.

Jordan fought a surge of disappointment. And yet, considering who she believed him to be, he didn't know what other reaction he might have been hoping for. Actually, it would have been a lot worse, he acknowledged, if she had been welcoming toward the man she believed to be her husband.

"This isn't what you think," he said softly.

It was probably *worse* than whatever she was thinking. She didn't want Rob Sorrel in her bed. She wouldn't want a stranger there, either.

"What I think is…"

She hesitated, and he felt the depth of the breath she took, her breast again moving against his body. She became aware of that at the same time he did. She pushed violently away from him, as if she couldn't bear to have any contact with his body.

And *that* was what had been in her eyes, he realized. Disgust. Revulsion. Despite the fact that her revulsion wasn't directed at him, Jordan again felt the force of it. And it was in her voice when she spoke again.

"Get out of my bed, Rob. You forfeited any right you ever had to be here."

"It's not—" Jordan began, trying to think how to phrase an explanation he knew he should have made last night.

"Get out," she ordered, her voice low and vehement. "I don't want you here. I don't want you around us at *all*. I certainly don't want you in my bed."

She pushed at a lock of hair that had fallen across her eye, wincing a little when her fingers brushed the abrasion on her temple. The butterfly bandages he'd applied last night had held, but even in this light, the bruising and swelling around them was obvious. Even the area under her eye was discolored.

She looked tired. A little frail. Sleep deprived. And as if last night's headache had grown in size and scale. But at least she didn't look defeated, Jordan thought in relief. And she didn't look or sound as if she were willing to let him make any more of the decisions.

Without another word, he crawled out of the bed they'd shared for some part of last night. That had not been one of his better ideas. Not because of her anger, but because it had made him hungry. Hungry to feel the weight of her head on his shoulder again. To have the fragrance of her body drifting around him once more.

And the next time it did, he wanted that to be because Kathleen Sorrel wanted it. Because she intended to be there. Not by default. Or because of illness or simple proximity. Or by the force of a physical memory.

Schooling his features so that none of that newly awakened desire was in them, Jordan turned around, looking down on the woman who was lying on the bed. She was again propped on one elbow, watching him.

"Why did you come back?" she asked. "Why couldn't you just leave us alone? My God, Rob, haven't you done enough to us?"

Jordan had opened his mouth to answer her when he heard a sound that didn't belong. Not in this isolated location. Not at this time of day. It might not have been loud enough to wake them if they'd still been sleeping, but it was obvious Kathleen heard the same thing he had—the unmistakable crunch of tires pulling onto the gravel driveway.

Her eyes had widened, the pupils changing as quickly as they had when he'd turned on the lamp last night. Her gaze moved to the doorway that led into the hall, and then came back to meet his. In them was sheer, stark terror. And he understood that her fear was for her children.

"Get into the kids' room. Keep them in there and keep them quiet," Jordan ordered.

He didn't wait to see if she obeyed. Instead he grabbed the gun off the chair where he'd placed it last night, right beside the bed, and moved silently on bare feet to the door. He was aware of her scrambling out of bed, but he didn't look around. When he heard her breathing behind him, he reached back and touched her, just to be sure exactly where she was.

Then he took a step into the hall, motioning with his unencumbered hand for her to follow him. When he reached the door to the children's room, he glanced inside. They were both still asleep. Jamie was out from under the covers, his bottom in the air and his thumb firmly planted in his mouth.

Jordan motioned Kathleen inside. When he heard her slip into the room, his eyes still locked on the end of the short, narrow hall that led to the den, he caught the knob of the children's room door in his left hand and pulled it closed.

There was no other sound. Not here in the hall or in the rest of the small mobile home. Not even from outside, where they had heard the noise of the arriving car. Jordan listened to the silence a few heartbeats and then moved farther down the hall, his bare feet as noiseless as the falling snow.

The den looked just as it had when he'd left it last night. The security chain was still on the door. Now that he was this close, however, he could plainly hear someone moving outside—quiet footsteps on the concrete slab of the carport. Someone was walking around his car, moving stealthily, perhaps, but even if that was what they intended, not quite soundlessly.

There would probably be someone coming around the back of the trailer as well, Jordan thought. He wished he had checked the locks on the windows in the children's room when he'd put them to bed last night. He hadn't, of course, because he hadn't believed there had been any real reason to be worried.

He would just have to trust that what he had almost been considering Kathleen's paranoia would have kept those windows permanently locked. He moved across the carpeted den, stopping beside the door that led out to the carport. He could hear the movements even more clearly than before.

Jordan put his hand on the knob of the chain and began to slide it slowly out of its slot. He was surprised to find that his fingers were trembling. *I must be getting old,* he thought, the corners of his mouth lifting in amusement despite what was happening. His imperturbability had been a standing joke on the team. It hadn't been entirely true, but that had been his reputation. Unshakable coolness under fire.

Of course, a lot of things had happened in the last twenty-four hours, he thought, watching his fingers pull the metal knob of the chain along the track that held it. A lot of things he had never expected when this had started.

Things like seeing Kathleen Sorrel's car careen off the road and into the ditch. And then racing down that bank to reach it, his heart in his throat. Playing daddy last night to a couple of little kids, one who seemed to like him and one who definitely didn't. Waking up with Kathleen's head on his shoulder, the fragrance of her hair filtering through his consciousness.

A lot of things had happened that for some reason were rushing through his head like outtakes from a movie. He knew that all he *should* be thinking about was whoever was on the other side of this door. And what kind of hell was going to break loose when he opened it.

He had the chain out now, and he held it lightly with his thumb and fingers, trying to keep it from touching the metal door as it swayed back and forth. When its motion finally stilled, Jordan put his hand on the doorknob, ears straining to follow the movements of whoever was outside, trying to picture the layout of the objects in the carport in his mind's eye. Trying to decide exactly where the guy was. Trying to figure out what he might do when the trailer door slammed open and Jordan came out, weapon held out before him, its weight steadied with both hands.

Suddenly the image of Jamie holding up his arms to be

lifted out of the bath last night was in Jordan's head instead. It had no place here. No place in what was about to happen. So he deliberately destroyed the memory. Then he watched his fingers tighten around the knob and begin to turn.

KATHLEEN WAS AFRAID to even touch the children, although the urge to hold them to her was almost overpowering. She didn't want to wake them and chance that they might make a noise that would give away their location.

What was happening now was what she had dreaded these long months. And yet now that it *was* happening, she couldn't seem to grasp the reality. Just as she hadn't been able to make the sight of Rob handling that big gun as if he knew exactly what he was doing gibe with her memories of the man she had married.

Since Rob seemed to be all that stood between them and his enemies, however, she supposed she should be glad that was a skill he had learned during their separation. The man who had sent her to this room and had then gone to confront whoever was outside wasn't the Rob she had known. Not the Rob she had married. He had changed, as much or maybe more than she had.

She closed her eyes, still crouching on the floor beside the bottom bunk. It seemed she had been here an eternity, without a clue as to what was going on. It was gradually growing lighter outside. The sun was coming up, and pale, lemon-colored streaks slid through the miniblinds that covered the windows.

Were they locked? she wondered suddenly, fighting a renewed spurt of terror. They were always locked, she reassured herself. She and the children had learned to live with everything locked and bolted. Their very lives were locked and bolted into this nightmare. A nightmare that was finally about to become reality.

The sound she heard was faint. Indistinct and unidentifiable. If she hadn't already been straining so hard to hear whatever was happening at the front of the trailer, she might not even have been aware of it.

Both heartbeat and breathing suspended, she listened until she heard it again and knew she hadn't been mistaken. Someone was walking outside. Just beyond the wall against which the bunk bed was placed. Just beyond the sleeping children, someone was walking on the snow and underlying ice, his footsteps careful, but unable to avoid the soft crackling of the frozen grass.

She wondered if she should get the children and carry them to Rob. He had the gun. He was the only one who might offer them protection.

Rob, she thought, realizing the possibility. It might be *Rob* walking around outside the trailer. Maybe he was already outside, trying to identify what they had both heard earlier.

It had sounded like a car pulling into the driveway, but it *could* have been something else, she realized. A snow-laden branch falling onto the gravel? Someone from the county out on the road evaluating conditions? Just because they'd heard a noise, she thought, didn't mean that the men Rob had taken the money from had found them. That was panic and not logic. She had given in to that last night and the results had been disastrous. *Think,* she urged herself. *Just think, damn it.*

She began to ease up into a standing position, holding on to the railing of the bed to maintain her balance. Her eyes touched briefly on Jamie, sleeping peacefully, his dark, baby-silk hair almost standing on end around his exposed ear. His mouth was open, the thumb half in, half out, and his lashes occasionally fluttered as his eyes twitched behind his eyelids. He was dreaming, she realized. Not her familiar nightmare, but something else, she prayed. Something besides this terror.

Other than that movement, Jamie didn't stir as Kathleen stood up. She could now see into the top bunk. Meg was still sleeping, too, her black hair spread over the white pillow, the sun gleaming in the ebony strands. Her usually animated features were relaxed and still. Again Kathleen could see the imprint of her father's heritage underlying the feminine daintiness.

Rob, she thought again. *Please, dear God, let it be Rob outside.*

She took one noiseless step toward the window at the head of the bed and then another. She put her eye against a crack between the slats of the blind. She couldn't see anything but the reflected sunlight from the snow. But she had to know. And to do so, she would have to take a chance. She lifted her hand and touched the slat that was at eye level, raising it minutely.

A man was standing behind the trailer, just as she'd expected. His back was to the window, but despite that, her mind had made an instantaneous recognition.

Not Rob. Shape and size were wrong. And he was wearing a jacket. A heavy brown jacket.

Kathleen gasped a little and her fingers released the slat she had raised. She whirled from the window, no longer worrying about waking the children, and ran across the room to fling open the bedroom door.

Chapter Six

The hall was much dimmer than the bedroom, but there was enough light to see that Rob wasn't at the end of it. Without stopping, Kathleen rushed into the den. "Sheriff," she said.

The single word was soft, breathless, but it broke the silence and destroyed Rob's waiting stillness by the door. He swung around, the dark muzzle of the gun he had taken with him from the bedroom focused on her.

His features were hard, uncompromisingly set. The look on his face was one she had never seen there before, so that for a moment he seemed almost a stranger. The gray eyes were narrowed and gunmetal cold. They appeared almost feral, but even as she watched, they began to change. Then the lean, taut features relaxed, and he nodded.

With a movement of his head he motioned her toward the door he was standing beside. Without hesitation, without even thinking about whether or not to obey, she moved, walking across the short expanse of the den carpet to stand beside him.

With the gun held in both hands, he pointed the barrel downward at the doorknob he'd been touching when she'd entered the room. Her eyes met his, questioning. He nodded, gesturing toward the knob again. She wondered briefly if the uniform she had seen could be a trick. Would they dress up as law enforcement officers to gain her trust? To make her let them in so they could get to the children?

But even as she thought about the possibility, she knew Rob was right. They didn't have a choice. If this really was the county sheriff, not coming to the door would only call more unwanted attention to them. She reached for the knob and turned it. Rob had flattened himself against the wall behind the door, the big gun still held in both hands. He wasn't watching her. His head was turned so that he could see through the crack that would appear between the door and the frame when she opened it. Taking a deep breath, Kathleen did just that.

There was another deputy in the carport. He was writing down the license number of the rental car Rob had been driving last night, but he looked up as soon as he heard the door open.

"Mrs. Simmons?" he asked.

"Yes," Kathleen answered. "Is something wrong, Officer?"

"That's what we came out here to find out," he said. His pale blue eyes were studying her face with undisguised interest.

"I'm afraid I don't understand," Kathleen said.

"We found your car this morning. Daylight patrol because of the snow. We saw marks where something had gone over the bank. When we got down to the car, there was blood on the seat. And we found your pocketbook," he said. He nodded to her purse, which he had put on the trunk of the Buick while he wrote down the license number.

Of course, Kathleen thought, relief spreading through her body, easing the anxiety. Why hadn't she realized they were here about the wreck? Apparently the effects of the blow to her head hadn't completely disappeared. And like Rob, she had been expecting something very different.

"When we saw that blood," the deputy continued, "we thought we should come out to check and make sure you're all right."

"I'm all right," she said.

''Bumped your head,'' he suggested, his eyes cutting up to her left temple.

Kathleen nodded and then was sorry. She hadn't been aware of the headache before. Now, however, the adrenaline that had flooded her system since she had awakened in Rob's arms, the last place on earth she ever intended to be again, was beginning to fade. The pain was a distraction, making it a little difficult to think coherently.

''We checked the hospital first thing when we found your car, but they had nothing but a case of false labor brought in during the night. That's when we got really worried about you.''

His eyes left her face and returned to his notebook. He checked whatever he had written there against the plate, and then he folded the small notepad and returned it to his jacket pocket.

''Looks like you had some help, though,'' he said, the blue eyes coming back to hers. The question he hadn't really asked was in them.

''Yes, we did,'' Kathleen said.

''You're lucky somebody came along. That's an isolated stretch.'' His eyes moved toward the dirt road in front of the lot. ''Far as that goes, so is this. Real isolated. For a lady living alone,'' he said, looking back at her. ''Nice and quiet, I'll bet,'' he added, his lips moving slightly, almost a smile.

''Yes, it is,'' Kathleen agreed.

''Friend of yours?'' he asked, his eyes indicating the Buick.

Kathleen tried to think of what she could say, other than ''That's none of your business,'' which probably wouldn't be the smartest choice. She didn't want to antagonize him, and he had asked nothing that was too out of line. However, he seemed overly interested in a minor accident in which he'd already verified that no one had been seriously injured. And it really wasn't the county's business whose car was parked in her carport.

"May I have my purse, please?" she said, instead of addressing his question. She had never thought of herself as a good liar, so it probably wasn't wise to start lying now. Besides, she didn't owe him or anyone else an explanation of who was staying at her house.

"Sure," he said. He picked the purse up by the handle, holding it with two fingers as if coming in contact with it might in some way emasculate him.

Too macho to carry a woman's handbag, Kathleen thought, almost amused by the silliness of that display.

He carried it over to the door and handed it up to her. Which, considering Rob's current position, probably hadn't been a good idea on her part, Kathleen realized.

"Thanks," she said.

With her standing in the middle of the doorway, conspicuously uninviting, the deputy didn't mount the concrete block steps and try to come inside, but he didn't move away, either. He stood looking up at her instead. His eyes examined the bloodstained top she was still wearing before they returned to her face.

"Nasty cut," he said. "Must have hurt like hell. But it looks like somebody did a good job with those bandages."

She nodded again, her sense of uneasiness building. There was definitely something wrong here. He had done his job. He had brought her the purse, verified she didn't need his help, and there was nothing else he was needed to do. There was no reason for him to still be standing in her carport making conversation.

"Thanks again for bringing this all the way out here," she said. She took a deliberate step back, her hand finding the doorknob, trying to signal an end to the exchange.

"Want me to send someone from town to tow your car out of that ditch when the roads thaw?"

Another legitimate question. For which she didn't have an answer. She and Rob hadn't talked about what would happen next. She knew it would take days to get her car operational, even if she had the money to have it fixed. Which she didn't, of course.

She hated to ask someone to tow the car in and repair it, and then leave town before they finished. Leaving them the old car might not even be enough to pay for the repairs. It wasn't worth more than a few hundred dollars. It probably wasn't even worth having the damages fixed. And the deputy would know that.

However, she and the children would still have to leave. Some way. Somehow. Now that Rob had shown up and there was the chance someone had seen him, they really had no other option.

"I'll call someone later," she said. "When I'm feeling a little more up to dealing with it."

"Maybe your friend could do the calling for you."

Again Kathleen nodded. She met the deputy's eyes, trying to convey to him that whatever information he was fishing for she wasn't planning to provide. As she watched, the corners of his mouth lifted, and finally he touched the brim of his hat.

"You take care now," he said simply, apparently giving up his attempt to find out who else was staying here.

He turned and walked across the carport and down the driveway to his patrol car. He had left it running, the exhaust producing a small cloud of white fog in the sharp dawn air. He climbed into the driver's side and tapped the horn. Then, as Kathleen continued to watch from the open doorway, he picked up the car's two-way radio and began talking into it.

After a few seconds, the other deputy, obviously the one she had seen at the back of the trailer, reappeared. He climbed into the passenger side of the patrol car and seemed to be listening to his partner's conversation. After another moment, apparently in response to something that had been said on the other end of the connection, both of them glanced back up at the trailer. Finally the driver nodded and put the radio down. He said something to the other man, and they both looked again toward the open door where Kathleen was standing.

The driver lifted his hand to her in a farewell salute and then, looking over his right shoulder, began to back the car out of the narrow drive. Kathleen watched until they had disappeared down the snow-covered dirt road. Only then did she close the door, automatically throwing the night latch and slipping the chain into place.

"Gone?" Rob asked.

"They're gone," she agreed, turning to look at him.

He still seemed poised for action, wound tight as a spring, almost as if he didn't believe her. His eyes were cold, their gray still bleak as the winter sky outside. Despite what she had just told him, there seemed to be no relaxation of the tension with which he had listened to her conversation with the deputy. He seemed still vigilant. Still waiting.

He had lowered the gun, but he was holding it with both hands. He moved in front of her, and with his left hand he lifted one slat of the blind that covered the window beside the door, much as she had done in the bedroom.

"They were checking the plates of your car," she said.

It was a warning, of course. And a question. Because she was wondering if there was any way the information that check would reveal could lead the deputies to an identification.

"They won't find anything even if they run it," he said after a small hesitation.

There was something in his voice that made her think that might not be the complete truth. Something that made her believe he wasn't being totally honest with her. Which, given his past behavior, shouldn't be surprising.

Kathleen thought about her determination not to move the children again before Christmas. She had wanted to create some normality in their lives. She thought of Meg's role in the pageant at the church. Of Jamie's wide-eyed fascination with the children and the story they acted out. Of all the other things her children deserved that had been taken from them by their own father.

Now she knew they would have to move again. They should do it immediately, she acknowledged, fighting the bitterness of that realization. Even if Rob left right now, she couldn't afford to take the chance that someone might have seen him or that the inquiry she believed the deputies had just put into effect might not somehow notify his enemies that he had been here with them.

His back to her, Rob turned his head slightly, trying to get a better view of the road out front. The muted light from the slat he was holding up touched the side of his face, illuminating a small portion of it. For the first time she noticed a faint scar, so straight it resembled an incision, near his ear. She didn't remember Rob having a scar like that.

There had been other things she hadn't remembered. How deep his voice was. That his eyes could turn so cold, opaque and shuttered.

The years they had been apart had wrought changes in them both, she knew, but Rob was *so* different now. His competence in handling the gun. The confidence with which he moved. The way his once-so-familiar features sometimes seemed...unfamiliar. Strangely alien.

Unfamiliar. Alien. Suddenly the words beat at her brain, demanding that she pay attention to them. As if in response, she leaned forward, moving carefully, eyes focused on the faint line she had just noticed. It was definitely an incision, healed, but, judging by the color, fairly recent. And it had been carefully—deliberately even—hidden in the natural contours of his face.

Now, without the concealing darkness that had blurred his features last night, without the effects of her concussion, which had made it too difficult to think, the significance of all those things, some of which she had been vaguely aware of from the beginning, finally began to sink in. She took an involuntary step back. Moving away from the man at the door. Trying to put distance between them.

Just as she did, he released the slat, letting it fall back in line with the others. He turned, his eyes assessing her face, and she wondered how she could possibly keep it from revealing the incredible thought she had just had.

"I don't think that was anything but what they said it was," he said. "Just checking on you after the accident. Making sure that whoever had stopped to help you wasn't out here doing you harm."

She nodded, not trusting her voice. She forced her eyes to hold on his. She refused to allow them to study his features, to search for confirmation of the bizarre scenario that small hairline scar had suggested. Maybe the blow to her head was still affecting her thinking. The fact that she could even consider the possibility she was contemplating seemed to argue against her rationality.

She tried to remember the exact color of Rob's eyes, but despite the years they had been married, she couldn't be sure that these were the same. And not sure that they weren't.

"I could use some coffee," he said. He was still examining her face, and finally his lips moved into a slight smile at whatever he found there. "How about you?"

Almost three years, she reminded herself. People change in that length of time. There could be a lot of changes in three years. *In his eyes? In the very way he carries himself? In the sound of his voice?* her consciousness mocked.

"Okay," she said aloud.

She turned and walked into the kitchen. Things were vaguely disarranged, but then she remembered that Rob had cooked dinner for the kids last night. Rob, she thought. *Rob.* Was this Rob? And if this man was *not* her husband, then who the hell was he? And even more important, what was he doing here and why was he wearing Rob's face?

The ritual of making the coffee was a welcome occupation for her hands. It was something she could do without thinking, leaving her mind free to go back over everything that had happened since he had shown up last night.

She was aware as she worked that he had gone to the back of the trailer, maybe to the bedroom, perhaps looking out the windows there as she had done. Maybe making sure that the deputies hadn't left anyone behind to spy.

As her hands moved through the familiar sequence, her mind moved again through all the things that had happened since he'd shown up. Reliving and reexamining each occurrence. Analyzing them. Trying to decide.

When she had finished putting the coffee on, she opened the cabinet above the sink and took down two mugs, which she placed beside the coffee maker. Then, still trying to work out in her mind any logical reason for the anomalies she had noticed, she took the carton that held the children's milk out of the refrigerator. She set it down beside the two mugs and retrieved the sugar bowl from the center of the table and put that beside them as well, listening for his return. She was taking a spoon out the drawer when she heard him come into the kitchen, his footsteps loud over its tile floor.

He'd taken time to put his shoes on, which he hadn't done earlier when the threat had seemed real and immediate. Apparently he had taken them off before he'd lain down on the bed last night. She had been furious that Rob thought he could climb back into their bed after what he had done. But somehow that was even worse if this man wasn't Rob.

She pushed the sudden anger the thought caused from her mind, trying to deal instead with that possibility and its implications. She picked up the coffeepot. She filled the two mugs, then lifted one of them, holding its warmth with both hands, and turned around to lean back against the edge of the sink. She took a sip of the scalding liquid, watching him, unobtrusively she hoped, over the rim of her cup.

He laid the gun he had been carrying down on the end of the counter and walked over to the coffeepot. Once there, it seemed to her he hesitated, at least for a second or two. He didn't look at her, however, appearing to be unaware that she was watching him. He picked up the second mug, ignoring the milk and sugar.

"What are you going to do about your car?" he asked, finally looking at her.

"I'll figure something out," she said.

"We need to talk," he suggested. He walked across the kitchen and pulled out the chair at end of the table nearest to where she was standing. Instead of sitting in it, however, he went to the other side and pulled that one out as well. When he had, he looked back at her again. "There are some things I need to tell you."

Was this it? Was this where he made whatever suggestion he had been sent here to make? Where he tried to talk her into coming with him? Or maybe that wasn't what he was about to suggest. She couldn't know what their plan was. But there was one thing she was sure of. One thing she was now *very* sure of. She had been since he'd ignored the milk and sugar.

She drank her coffee black, but Rob had never acquired the taste. He always added both milk—cream if possible— and sugar if available. For some reason that small detail hardened all her other doubts into certainty. The man sitting at her kitchen table wasn't Rob Sorrel.

"Okay," she said. She took a swallow of her coffee, then pushed away from the edge of the sink and walked back over to the coffeemaker. She set her mug down and lifted the glass carafe as if she were going to add more coffee to her cup.

Her back was to him, and she wondered briefly if he were watching her. She supposed it didn't matter. He was too far away to do anything about what she was planning.

She put the glass carafe back in place, but she didn't pick up the mug. Instead, she took the two steps that would take her to the end of the cabinet, to where he had put down the gun. It was obvious by the fact he'd left it there that he didn't have any idea she had figured out what was going on.

She picked up his weapon and realized why he had held it with both hands. It was far heavier than she'd expected. Of course, she hadn't known what to expect. This was the first time she had held a handgun in her entire life.

At no time in the long months she'd hidden his children from her husband's enemies had she ever considered buying a gun to protect them. The whole notion was foreign to who she was.

Now, however, the enemy was in her home, and her children were sleeping in the next room. She had always known she would do anything to protect them. Even this.

She turned, holding the big gun out before her, just as she had seen him do. At her sudden movement, his gaze lifted from the coffee cup that was between his hands on the table in front of him. His eyes widened slightly, but other than that, there was no reaction revealed in the dark, handsome face. Certainly not the one she had expected. The one she had almost been anticipating putting there.

Whatever he was, whoever he was, he wasn't afraid. Not even with his own powerful weapon pointed directly at him.

"Now why don't you tell me what this is really all about," Kathleen said softly.

It sounded like a line from a bad thriller. With the gun in her hands, she even felt as if she were in the middle of one, but she had burned her bridges pretty spectacularly, she supposed. It was a little late to put the gun down because the dialogue was embarrassing.

"You know how to use that?" he asked calmly.

She could have sworn there was a breath of amusement underlying the question. A hint of mockery. Belittling whatever danger she might represent, and that was something she didn't like hearing. She could feel the heat of blood burn under the skin of her cheeks. Anger or embarrassment? she wondered.

"I can probably figure it out," she said. "I think it has something to do with putting pressure on the trigger and holding my finger on it until it's empty. I think that's exactly how it's done,'' she challenged. *At least in the movies.*

He still didn't look intimidated, and she had really wanted him to. It would have been so damned satisfying to perform the tricks and have the fear on their side for a change. But at least there no longer seemed to be that trace of amusement hiding in the gray eyes. For the first time they were very open, meeting hers without any attempt at subterfuge.

''I told you we needed to talk,'' he said.

He pushed the coffee away from him and put his hands, their fingers interlocked, on the table in front of him. *They don't even look like Rob's hands,* she realized, watching him. His fingers were longer. The hands themselves were stronger, somehow. More masculine.

She had even thought that when he'd pulled her from the wreck, she realized. She must really have been out of it last night to have bought into this. He didn't seem stupid, so she wondered how he thought he was going to carry this charade off.

After all, she had been married to Rob Sorrel, had lived with him for over four years. They knew that. Whatever this little stunt was intended to accomplish, surely they knew she'd figure this impersonation out sooner or later. And if it hadn't been for her head injury and the darkness, it would certainly have been sooner than this morning.

''You start,'' she suggested. Already her forearms were tiring from the weight of the gun. She thought briefly about sitting down opposite him and resting her elbows on the table, which would give her some support. However, she didn't want to be that close to him. She didn't intend to give him a chance to take the gun away from her.

''My name is Jordan Cross. I'm a CIA agent,'' he said.

She laughed. She couldn't help it. She might have been pretty naive when she'd started this, but she had never been a fool. And she had learned a lot about survival. Learned all of it the hard way.

''The CIA?'' she repeated mockingly. She was pleased

to hear that the sarcasm she'd intended to convey in response to that claim came through loud and clear. Mocking him, this time. "I think you're going to have to do better than that," she said.

He took a breath, its depth expanding his chest. Broader and more muscled than Rob's. As were his shoulders.

"A few months ago," he said, "I was involved in an operation that became public. It went wrong enough that…it made the papers. So did I."

"I'm sure this is fascinating," she said when he paused, "but I don't understand what it has to do with us."

"Neither do I."

Again, his tone seemed without sarcasm. That denial had sounded like a simple statement of fact.

"That's what I came here to find out," he added.

"I don't understand," she said again. She didn't have a clue where he was heading with this cock-and-bull story.

"Put the gun down, Mrs. Sorrel. I'm not going anywhere. I'm not here to hurt you or the children. If I had intended anything like that, you'll have to admit last night would have been the perfect opportunity."

He was right, of course. They had been more vulnerable after the accident than they had been in all these long months of hiding. And instead of doing them harm…

"I know about your face," she said. "Somebody went to a whole lot of trouble to try to make you look like my husband."

"I'm not sure that's the case."

"You've had plastic surgery," she said. An accusation. And the basis for her suspicions, so she expected him to deny it.

"Yes," he agreed instead.

"Surgery designed to make you look like Rob."

"That was the result. It wasn't the purpose."

She thought about that, evaluating his tone and demeanor as well as what he had said.

"Then what *was* the purpose?" she asked. She could lis-

ten to this fairy tale as long as he wanted to tell it. She had
the gun. Whatever he said couldn't change that situation.

"To give me a new face. A new identity. One that wasn't
public property."

"Why?" she asked.

"I told you. As a result of having my cover blown, I had
become too well-known to people…who had reasons not to
like me very much."

The CIA, she thought again. That line was almost a joke.
The standard con for the gullible. *Hello, ma'am, I'm with
the CIA.* Only Kathleen wasn't *that* gullible. Not anymore.

"I'm not buying this one," she said. It was only fair to
warn him. "So why don't you try again? Maybe something
a little less colorful this time. Something more believable,"
she suggested softly. "Like what are you supposed to do
here?"

"Someone attacked me in San Francisco. Apparently because they believed I was your husband."

"How did you know that?" she asked, wondering if this
new explanation could be true. At least it was more plau-
sible than the other.

"A friend who's still in the agency ran my new face
through the computers. It matched that of a man named Rob
Sorrel. Someone in San Francisco had called me Rob a few
days before the attack, so that seemed to make sense. But
when my friend tried to track Sorrel down, he ran into a
dead end."

She held his eyes as he talked, and she couldn't see any
sign of deception. It was even possible, she acknowledged,
that the attack he had told her about had happened. If it had
taken her twelve hours to figure out this man wasn't Rob,
she supposed it was possible her husband's enemies had
made the same mistake she had made last night. Possible,
she thought again.

"So how did you find us?" she asked.

"My friend found out that Sorrel had a wife. And children. The public schools keep all their data on computer.

We traced you through the children's immunization records.''

She had never even thought about the danger of using those when she had enrolled Meg in public school. They demanded verification that she'd had all her immunizations, and Kathleen presented it. She had explained the discrepancy between the name on that document and the name they were using by the common enough scenario of divorce and reversion to her maiden name.

No one had questioned her story. But she had never thought about the possibility that anyone could trace her through something like that. Another mistake. She couldn't afford to make those, so it was a lesson, as well, of course. That was one error she wouldn't make again.

"So you just decided to come and check us out," she said bitterly.

"I thought maybe you had some idea where your husband might be. Failing that, I thought I'd at least get an explanation of why someone's looking for him," he said. "An explanation of why I'd been attacked."

"You knew you looked like him when you rolled down your window last night," she accused.

He had done that deliberately, she realized. Since he'd been attacked in San Francisco, he must have known someone was after Rob. And when his friend couldn't find him, he must also have realized that Rob was hiding. Putting those together should have given him enough information to know she was probably going to be pretty shocked to confront her husband in a parking lot.

He hesitated again, and his eyes fell for the first time since she'd started questioning him. They rested on his hands a moment before they lifted again to hers.

"I knew that much," he admitted. "But...I didn't understand how frightened you are. I didn't mean to make you more afraid."

"You don't even know what you've done," she said, her

anger building. "You don't understand, even now, what you've done."

"You think that if whoever's after your husband sees me, they'll believe I'm him," he suggested quietly, his eyes still on her face. "Is that what you're afraid of?" he asked.

"What I'm afraid of—" she began angrily, only to be interrupted.

"Why are you trying to make Daddy go away again?" Meg asked.

Chapter Seven

They both looked around at the sound of the childish voice. Meg and Jamie were standing in the doorway that led from the hall into the den. Jamie's thumb was in his mouth, a sure sign of distress, since he usually took great pride in having conquered that habit, at least in the daytime. Kathleen wondered how much of the conversation they had overheard. And more importantly, how much of it Meg had understood.

"Meg," she said softly, turning to face her daughter.

Unthinkingly, she brought the gun she had forgotten she held around with her. Meg's eyes widened, locking on the weapon in her mother's hands. And no wonder, Kathleen thought, feeling despair that they had come to this. Despair that this was happening to her children—the constant disruption of their lives, and now seeing their mother holding a gun on someone.

Despite the doubts she had about the man seated at her table, Kathleen quickly laid the gun on the counter and started across the room toward the two children. Then, realizing that giving him access to that weapon would put Meg and Jamie at the mercy of a man who had brought this gun into her home, a man about whom she knew nothing, except that, incredibly, he claimed to be a CIA agent, she hesitated.

"Daddy?" Jamie said. It was obviously a question, but

the tone in which it had been asked was just as obviously hopeful.

"No," Kathleen said, fighting a sudden tightness in her throat. "This isn't Daddy."

But Jamie's big brown eyes had already found the man who had fed him last night, and undeterred by her denial, he started across the den. Kathleen wasn't sure where the little boy was headed, but when he reached the end of the kitchen counter, she took a couple of steps forward and picked him up before he could get any closer to the stranger with his father's face.

"I remember him," Meg said stubbornly. "From his picture. From when he went away before."

"This is someone who…just looks a lot like your father," Kathleen explained. She brushed Jamie's bangs off his forehead with her fingers. Like making the coffee, that was something to do with her hands while she tried to think. "I promise you, Meg, this isn't Daddy."

"But you were trying to make him go away again," Meg argued.

Kathleen didn't understand why this man was here, or why he had had plastic surgery to make him look like her husband. So she didn't know how she could possibly explain to her daughter what was happening.

"Is it because of those men?" Meg asked in the silence.

Slowly, Kathleen nodded. "In a way," she admitted. It seemed as good an explanation as any. Something Meg had already dealt with and accepted.

"Is he one of those men?"

Was he? Kathleen wondered. Was this some kind of elaborate trick? Like the one they had pulled at the day care center? If so, she hadn't had time to figure out all the possible ramifications of what they were doing this time.

"Is he going to hurt us?" Meg asked. "Is that why you have a gun?"

"He's not going to hurt anybody," Kathleen said quickly.

She glanced toward the man seated at the table. His eyes were on her, or maybe on Jamie. "Tell her," she ordered.

"I'm not here to hurt anyone, Meg," he said. "I'm trying to convince your mommy to let me help you."

"Don't," Kathleen ordered. "Whatever's going on, they're not part of it. You damn well aren't going to use them," she said angrily. "I won't let you."

"I'm not trying to use them. I'm trying to take care of them. Just like I did last night," he reminded her, his voice quietly reassuring.

So much so that, incredibly, Kathleen found herself wanting to believe him. She wanted to believe that he really *was* some kind of agent and that he wasn't involved with the Mafia or Rob and what he'd done. But if there was one lesson she had learned from all they had gone through, it was that she couldn't trust anybody. No matter how appealing it might be to do so.

"And I'm just trying to understand what's going on," he said, his eyes seeming open and sincere. "When I do, maybe I can help you. Help all of you," he said, his gaze moving to Jamie's face before it came back to her. "But first *you* have to help me. Before I can do anything to change their situation," he said, his eyes touching on each of her children in turn before they came back to confront hers, "I have to know who's after your husband, Mrs. Sorrel. And I have to know why."

SHE STILL HADN'T told him what was going on, but after the demand he made had hung in the air between them for a long time, she finally nodded. And Jordan had taken that to mean Kathleen intended to answer his questions. Given Meg's reaction to what had been going on between them when the children interrupted, he understood that Kathleen wouldn't want to make those explanations while they were listening.

Jordan didn't blame her. She had apparently tried to protect them as much as possible from the fear she herself lived with constantly. And judging from the normality of her children's behavior, she must have been successful. They had seemed remarkably trusting last night as he'd fixed dinner for them and then gotten them ready for bed.

They appeared to be bright, confident and well adjusted, despite what had been going on throughout their young lives. And Kathleen Sorrel was to be commended for that remarkable accomplishment. Jordan could only wonder, however, what that achievement had cost her.

While she fixed the children cereal, he removed his weapon from the counter and put it on top of the refrigerator, close enough if he needed it, but out of the way of small, curious fingers.

The children seemed far more subdued this morning than they had been last night. Of course, Meg had thought he was her father. And they both had seen their mother holding a gun on him, which would be more than enough to disturb most kids their ages. As he watched Kathleen set the table and fix the cereal, Jordan kept finding Jamie's big brown eyes on his face.

Jordan wasn't sure how much a kid that young understood about family relationships, but Jamie had repeated the word Meg said as if he knew exactly what it meant. *Daddy?* There had been something heartbreakingly plaintive about the little boy's question.

Something about that softly spoken word haunted Jordan, especially when he remembered how Jamie had responded to him last night. Maybe, despite Kathleen's efforts, the kid missed his dad. Missed having a man to take care of him. A masculine presence that could make him feel secure, despite their nomadic existence.

Jordan resolutely clamped down the surge of emotion that thought caused. It would be tough for a little boy to grow up without a father, but this wasn't his problem. Kathleen Sorrel was doing a damn fine job of being a single parent. Changing that particular situation wasn't why Jordan had come here. And it was definitely out of his realm of expertise.

The other, however, wasn't. It was possible that he *could* do something about the people who were hunting Sorrel. That in itself would give these kids more real security than they had ever known.

After she'd fixed the children's breakfast, Kathleen walked to the coffeemaker and refilled her mug. She looked over her shoulder at him, a subtle inquiry in her eyes, so he moved away from where he was standing near the refrigerator and joined her. He leaned against the counter, facing her. Her back was turned to the children.

"I meant what I said about wanting to help," he offered, keeping his voice low. "But before I can, I really do have to know what's going on."

"I think maybe you *already* know," she said, russet eyes examining his face. Her distrust was almost palpable. "I *will* tell you, however, the same thing I've told everyone else from the beginning. I don't know where Rob is. I don't know where the money is." Her eyes were challenging. And uncompromising. "So if either of those is what you're after, you're wasting your time here."

"Your husband stole money from someone," Jordan suggested. "And whoever he took it from wants it back."

"Did you figure that out all by yourself? I guess the CIA really *is* an intelligence agency," she said mockingly.

"And whoever he stole it from thinks you can lead them to your husband. Or," Jordan continued, piecing together what he had managed to figure out, "they believe that eventually he'll contact you. To try to see his children. When he does, they'll be waiting for him."

"Congratulations. Right on all counts," she said. "I guess that means you get an A in deduction."

"But he *hasn't* tried to contact you," Jordan said, again ignoring her sarcasm.

Figuring things out, arriving at the whys and wherefores, was exactly what Jordan Cross had done for Griff's team through the years. His self-esteem certainly wasn't fragile enough to be bothered by Kathleen's mockery of the process he'd just used to arrive at his conclusions.

"And he won't," she replied, her voice filled with conviction. "Wherever Rob is, he *isn't* pining to see his children. I can promise you that."

"Then why are they still following you?"

"Because they can't find him," she said simply. "And I think they've really tried. That's something I eventually figured out. Why they're so persistent in their efforts to keep track of us. I guess you could say we're their last hope."

"How much?" Jordan asked.

The corners of her lips moved, tilting into a smile that held no amusement. "Sixteen million dollars," she said, enunciating each word distinctly, yet her voice was so low he had to strain to hear. "I guess that makes it more understandable that they'll do anything to get it back."

He already had been given a clue to that amount, Jordan realized, remembering what the punk had said. *"Sixteen big ones."* That much money was a hell of a reason for what they were doing. More than enough to make someone very determined to find it.

"How did he manage it?" he asked.

"Rob was an investment consultant in New Orleans. That's where we lived. Apparently..." She hesitated, taking a deep breath before she finished. "He was laundering money for them. I think he had been doing it for some time. They were using him to channel their profits from drugs and gambling and prostitution into legitimate investments. Construction, shipping. Things like that. I discovered that later, from the FBI."

"They?" Jordan asked, but by now, from what she had said and from his own background, he had figured that part out, too.

Her lips tightened. For some reason she still seemed reluctant to put into words what he suspected. Her eyes held on his, however, seeming more open than they had before.

Finally she shrugged, slender shoulders moving upward quickly as if to acknowledge there was nothing she could do to change the reality of what her husband had done.

"The Mafia," she said. "The mob. Even now, even after all I know, I still can't believe he was that stupid. Rob was good. Good at what he did. He didn't have to get involved in that. We were…we were doing all right. Financially, I mean. I thought our real problems were…all personal."

Jordan didn't comment on the last, but he noted it. He filed it away for future reference, encouraged for some reason by what it revealed. Apparently, their marriage had been troubled even before Sorrel had absconded with the Mafia's money.

"You were doing all right until he got greedy," Jordan suggested.

She nodded. "I guess so," she said softly.

"Did you know what he was planning?"

"Did I know he was going to steal their money?" she asked, her tone incredulous. "Rob wasn't exactly confiding in me about anything he was doing. He knew I'd never put up with any of that. I didn't know he was involved with them at all. I guess that seems unbelievable…." She shook her head and her eyes fell. "We didn't talk about his business. Rob didn't want to, and I didn't know a lot about what he did. He didn't seem to want to explain it. And frankly, that was all right by me."

She raised her eyes, searching Jordan's face, probably trying to determine if he believed her. And he did. Someone who was doing what Sorrel had done wouldn't take a chance on talking about it to anyone, probably not even to his wife. Not until he was ready to make his move. Then he would just disappear. Which was apparently exactly what had happened.

"Your turn," she advised.

He looked up and realized she was waiting for an explanation he'd already given. One she obviously hadn't believed.

"My name is Jordan Cross," he said, doggedly repeating exactly what he had told her before because it was the truth. "I was a CIA agent whose cover was blown in a very public way. They gave me a new identity and a new face to go with it. This is it," he finished softly, watching her eyes and well aware of the disbelief that was still in them.

"Why would they give you Rob's face?"

"I don't think they did. Not intentionally. They tried to modify my appearance, but with minimal structural changes. There was probably some resemblance between us to begin with, and when they got through…" He shrugged, aware that her eyes were again studying his features. Her husband's features.

"When they got through, you just *happened* to look like a man who had stolen sixteen million dollars from the Mafia?" she suggested. That mocking half smile touched her lips again.

"Stranger things have happened," Jordan said.

"Not to me," she denied, and then she shook her head, the motion small and quick. "Maybe they have. I don't know anymore. Sometimes this all seems like a nightmare. I keep thinking that one day I'll wake up, and it will just all be over. We won't have to run anymore. We won't have to hide. They can have a normal life. A childhood. Is that too much to ask?"

She turned her head, looking over her shoulder at the two children sitting at the table, before her eyes came back to focus on his face. "You said you wanted to help us," she said. "How?"

Jordan thought about it before he spoke. He tried never to promise more than he could deliver, and given Jake Holt's inability to find any information about Rob Sorrel, he knew it would be a long shot that he could change anything going on here. Change it for the better, he amended. He might already have changed the dynamics of this in ways he had never intended.

"I can take you and the children out of here," he offered.

"*I* can take them out of here," she said. "That's what I've been doing for almost three years. Just...running away."

She had obviously been hoping for something more, and Jordan really wished he had something else to offer. He was a realist, however. A pragmatist who understood the ruthlessness of the enemy she was facing. If the mob and the money it had put out on the street to get Rob Sorrel couldn't find him, then Jordan probably didn't have a chance in hell of working that particular miracle.

And he knew they both understood that was the only thing that would put an end to this nightmare, as she called it. To find Rob Sorrel and make him give back the money. Or what was left of it. Jordan found himself wondering how much of it the bastard had spent while his family lived like fugitives.

"I had hoped we could stay here at least until after Christmas," Kathleen said softly. "Meg has a part in the Christmas pageant at church."

"She told me," he said.

Kathleen's eyes found his again, and surprisingly, she smiled at him. "Did you get the blow-by-blow?"

"Tinsel, wings, halo and recitation," he said.

"I know it doesn't seem like a big deal...."

She hesitated, her gaze again briefly visiting the children. This time Jordan allowed his to follow. Meg was talking to Jamie, her big-sister bossiness back in place.

"But it means a lot to *her*. And they *should* be able to have a normal Christmas. It's little enough."

"Does that mean you intend to stay here?" he asked, thrown by her about-face. That didn't fit with what she'd told him. Or with her fear. She thought he had intensified the danger they were in by coming here. By being with them.

"No," she said. Her voice seemed resigned, but it was clear she was deeply troubled by the thought of moving the children again. She put her hand against the bandages on her temple and closed her eyes. "I know I don't really have a choice," she said, her voice little more than a whisper.

"Because you're afraid someone has seen me."

"If someone in California thought you were Rob, then anyone who sees you around us..."

"Is bound to make that same assumption," he finished.

She nodded.

"What do you think they'll do?" he asked, wondering about the particulars of her nightmare. Knowing who and what was involved, Jordan agreed they would stop at nothing, no matter how brutal, to find Sorrel. He just wondered if she realized that.

"They'll use Jamie and Meg," she said softly. "They'll use his children to force Rob to tell them where the money is."

Jordan nodded, his eyes involuntarily finding the small dark head bent over the cereal bowl. Soft brown hair that had felt like silk against his face and would still smell of the baby shampoo he had used last night.

"Do you want to know the worst part?" she asked.

Jordan's gaze came back to her face. In her tired eyes was reflected the horror of the last three years.

"I'm afraid that given a choice between handing over the money or saving the children—" Her voice broke suddenly, but her eyes were dry. Resolute. "—I'm not sure anymore which one Rob would choose."

SHE DIDN'T HAVE A CHOICE, she told herself over and over as she worked. The decision had been taken out of her hands. She no longer had a car. And she had too little money.

She didn't quite believe what the man who called himself Jordan Cross had told her. The CIA angle was as hokey as UFOs and alien abductions and conspiracy theories. But the only other explanation she could come up with for the plastic surgery and his resemblance to Rob was even harder to believe. And far more frightening.

If he wasn't telling the truth about the CIA, then he was one of them. Someone who had been sent here to do exactly what he appeared to be achieving. Sent to gain her trust. Sent to convince her to put herself and the children under his protection. And then...

She shook her head, denying that possibility. Her hands moved quickly, folding and packing the children's clothes. It was a ritual that was too familiar. One she had hoped she would never have to do again. And if Jordan Cross hadn't shown up...

Maybe he was exactly what he said, she thought, arguing with her cynical side. He *had* helped her last night. He had taken care of her and the children when they had been, as he'd pointed out, highly vulnerable. Or maybe that's just what he was supposed to do, she mused, coming full circle. Maybe he'd been sent here to win her trust in exactly those kinds of ways.

She closed her eyes against the force of the headache that had been pounding behind her eyes almost since she'd awakened this morning. In bed with Jordan Cross, she remembered. Curled up next to his warmth, lying against the solid strength of his shoulder and chest. And it had been a long time since she had slept in a man's arms. Or had wanted to.

The fact that she had been there—the fact that she had liked being there, she amended, at least in the first few seconds after she awakened—had shocked her. And then it had as quickly repelled her. Of course, at the time she had thought he was Rob, who had betrayed them.

Now she knew he was not. She just didn't know exactly who or what he really was. She had to admit, however, that her instincts were telling her to trust him. There were probably strong psychological reasons for that instinctive desire to give in to his surety. An urge just to let him take care of them.

And after all, she acknowledged, she had a long time ago fallen head over heels in love with a man who had worn this same face. She saw it constantly repeated in Meg's features whenever she looked at her daughter. And occasionally even in Jamie's. It was almost inevitable that she would be drawn to this man, even as she questioned his motives.

But she didn't have a choice, she repeated, folding the last of Jamie's clothes and shutting the lid on the suitcase. She had no one else to turn to. She certainly couldn't depend on the authorities. Her reaction of distrust to the sheriff's deputy this morning had been as instinctive as her opposite response to Jordan Cross.

There had been something wrong about that visit. She had known it the whole time she had been talking to the deputy. And that knowledge simply reinforced the urgency she had felt since Jordan had shown up last night. Despite the approach of Christmas, despite the pageant, despite her hopes, she knew they had to leave.

She could still hear Meg's soft sobs from the other room. Kathleen had packed the angel costume, carefully arranging the wire-framed, gossamer-covered wings so they wouldn't be damaged in Meg's suitcase. It seemed such a small sacrifice to give up the pageant, but she knew it wasn't. Kathleen understood the heartbreak the unused costume represented for her daughter, but there was nothing else she could do.

No choice. She had no other choice. She repeated it like a litany as she efficiently destroyed her children's lives once more, closing their dreams into the small battered suitcases she had dragged with them through state after state.

She didn't even allow herself to think that what Jordan Cross had told her was true. She would love to believe he could help them, but that was almost too much to hope for. If she allowed herself to put any stock in his promise, as appealing as it was, she would end up like poor Meg, dreaming of the impossible. A Christmas miracle. A normal life.

Meg was a child. And children still believed in miracles. And Kathleen…Kathleen was a woman who had learned the hard way that there was no one on this earth she could depend on to keep her children safe. No one but herself.

She was leaving here with Jordan Cross because she had no other options. No choice. Not because she trusted him. Not because…

She stopped that thought, drawing in a slow, calming breath. That was something else she couldn't afford to allow herself to reach for. Elusive. Tempting. So damned enticing to someone who had been alone for so long.

Like the sad, tinsel-edged angel wings she had packed, those fragile, almost forgotten feelings were something that must be put away. She had no right to imagine they could ever again be part of her life.

Until she had slept in Jordan Cross's arms last night, until she had awakened with his hard, masculine body next to hers, she had not realized she had been just as deprived as her children of relationships and experiences they were entitled to. And in her case there had been no one around to try to make up for any of those losses.

Her hands stopped moving, hovering motionless over the next garment she needed to fold and pack as she replayed over and over in her head, like an old record with a scratch, the scene that had occurred in her bedroom at dawn.

The warmth and strength of his body. The pleasantly masculine scent of it. His arm curved protectively around her shoulders. Her breast moving erotically against the hard muscle of his chest as she breathed.

Even while believing he was Rob, who had put them all in such danger, that awakening had had an unwanted effect. The feelings it produced had curled like smoke throughout her lower body, making her ache with the realization of how long it had been since a man had touched her. And now that she knew this man was not Rob…

She closed her eyes, trying to deny the images that were forming in her brain, but the same sweet heat that had invaded her sleep-dazed senses so briefly this morning was there again, moving like a molten river of sensation. Sexual. Undeniably sexual.

He was a stranger. With a stranger's long-fingered and unfamiliar hands, strong and yet gentle while he had taken care of her. And a stranger's arms, which had carried her through pain and injury and had cradled her as she slept. A stranger's eyes, which made promises she wanted so desperately to believe.

And with her husband's betraying face, she remembered. Maybe she didn't know exactly who this man was or why he was really here, but she had learned through bitter experience that she could never trust any man again. Not even Jordan Cross, she thought. No matter how much she wanted to.

Chapter Eight

"Ready?" Jordan called, his voice coming from somewhere at the front of the trailer, echoing a little down the dark, narrow hall that led to the bedrooms.

As ready as I ever am for this, Kathleen thought, taking one last look around the children's bedroom. The beds were stripped, the closet standing open, the drawers of the small chest emptied of their few belongings. Her eyes made a slow and careful survey, determined not to forget anything of Meg's and Jamie's.

And when she spotted what she had forgotten, she was glad she had made that last effort. On the shelf at the top of the closet, barely visible, was a touch of red. It was the foot of Meg's old Raggedy Ann.

Kathleen's mother had made the doll shortly before her death. It had been part of Meg's gifts the Christmas before Rob's disappearance. For a long time her daughter had slept with Ann, but now she was simply part of the emotional baggage they carried around with them.

Still, it wouldn't do to leave her behind, Kathleen thought, walking over to the closet and reaching up, stretching on tiptoe, to pull the soft, familiar body off the high shelf. For just a second, she unconsciously hugged the limp form, drawing comfort from this tangible connection to her own safe childhood—one of the last things her mother had made with her own hands. Kathleen glanced up to find Jordan standing in the open doorway, watching her.

"I think that's everything," she said softly, a little embarrassed to have him see her clutching the doll.

He nodded, his eyes dropping to the disreputable rag baby she held. "Meg's?" he asked unnecessarily.

Kathleen smiled, thinking that this was probably as much her talisman now as her daughter's. Meg had moved on to more sophisticated toys. Kathleen was the one who would have missed this most if it had been left behind.

"My mother made it," she said by way of explanation.

He nodded again, his gray eyes coming back quickly to her face. "You okay?"

It had been so long since anyone besides the children had evinced concern for her feelings or for her well-being that his question caught her off guard. And his interest was sincere, she realized, judging by what was in both his eyes and his voice.

She wondered again how she could have thought this man was Rob. There were so many things that were dissimilar, including the timbre of his voice. It was deeper than her husband's had been. Even the Southern accent was subtly different.

"I'm okay," she said softly. "Just…eager to go and yet so sorry to disrupt them again. I know how much Meg was looking forward to the play."

"Maybe it's possible—" he began, before she cut him off.

"No," she said. "No, it's *not* possible. I'd never forgive myself if I made that decision and as a result…" She swallowed, unable to express the unrelenting horror of the rest. "I can live with this if I have to," she said. "I couldn't live even one more day with…that."

He nodded again, and they stood a moment, the silence of last night surrounding them, before he held out his hand to her. "Come on," he said. "I'll help you get the kids into the car."

She hesitated, wondering about the gesture, but when she walked across the room, she ignored his outstretched hand. As she brushed between him and the frame of the narrow doorway, the same scent that she had awakened to again surrounded her.

And the same forbidden sensations suddenly moved within her. She ignored them, too, walking down the dark hallway and into the muted sunlight of the den. But she was too aware that he followed her down the hall. Too aware of him entirely for her own peace of mind.

Jordan had already put the suitcases she'd packed into the car. The cardboard box she kept under the sink now sat on the kitchen table, filled with dishes and kitchen utensils. Only that and the laundry basket full of toys remained to be loaded.

Whenever she got everything packed, she was surprised at how little they possessed. That had not always been the case. She seldom thought about the huge four-bedroom home outside New Orleans she had run away from two years ago. That life was gone, and these meager belongings were the sum of what she had now. These and her children.

"Are the kids in the car?" she asked, realizing she hadn't heard them during the last few minutes.

"They're investigating the snow," Jordan said. He picked up the box from the table and headed toward the door.

"By *themselves?*" she asked. She could hear the note of panic in her voice, and apparently he could, too. He stopped, turning back to face her.

"They're fine, Kathleen," he said. "I made them promise to stay in the carport. I told them they could make a couple of snowballs as soon as we got everything outside."

She nodded, knowing she was being absurd. He wouldn't have let them out there until he'd checked everything. He was going to help them. He had taken care of the children last night, she reassured herself, and had been prepared to defend them this morning. He wouldn't let anything happen to them now.

"You want to open the door for me?" he requested, shifting the box onto his knee to get a more secure grip on the bottom.

His eyes were on her face, and she knew he was watching her as she walked across the room to the door. As soon as she opened it, she heard the children's voices—Jamie's soft giggles and Meg's excited, high-pitched tones, talking about the snow. Or maybe she was explaining to Jamie, in her best little miss schoolteacher manner, how to make a snowball.

Kathleen could see that there was no one else out there. The drive stretched long and empty to the road, which was still snow-covered except for the dark tracks the deputies' tires had made. Everything was fine. No threats. No tricks this morning.

"You take care of the snowballs," Jordan said from behind her. "I'll get the rest of this into the trunk."

"Don't forget the toy basket," she reminded him, her eyes still on the children. As she watched, Jamie squatted down on the edge of the concrete and reached out to poke his fingers into the snow. He giggled again, and Kathleen's lips relaxed the anxious compression they had held to all morning.

She met Jordan's eyes and realized he was smiling, too. There was something infectious about Jamie's giggle. He took such delight in the world surrounding him that it was hard not to savor it along with him, no matter what else was going on.

"I told you they were fine," Jordan said, stepping past her. He carried the big box carefully down the concrete steps.

He *had* told her that, Kathleen acknowledged. And he'd been right, of course. They *were* fine. They had on their coats and mittens, and since Jamie never remembered those, she knew Jordan had helped him dress.

The cold air coming in through the open door reminded her that she needed to get her own coat. She had laid it over

the back of one of the kitchen chairs before she'd packed
the rest of their clothes.

That had been after she bathed and changed out of the
outfit she'd worn yesterday, the same clothes she'd slept in.
She had thrown away the bloodstained top, not because she
thought it couldn't be cleaned, but because the wreck was
a memory she wanted out of their lives as soon as possible.
Her panic last night had had serious consequences, which
could have been much worse, of course. She would never
forget that, but she did want to banish the horror of listening
to Jamie's heartbroken sobbing in the darkness, unable to
do anything for him.

She slipped on her coat, taking a last glance around. The
trailer looked just as it had the day they had moved in, little
more than six weeks ago. It was bare and lifeless without
their belongings scattered around, no longer a home, but
only a shell.

She had dropped the key, along with a note of explanation, into an envelope Jordan had taken out to the mailbox.
She had already paid this month's rent, so her landlord
wouldn't be out any money, even if she were breaking the
lease. She always worried about doing things like this. She
hated to deceive people who trusted her, but she didn't have
any choice. *No other option,* she told herself again, just as
she had been all morning.

"I thought you were going to give the snowball-making
demonstration," Jordan said. Empty-handed, he had reen-
tered through the still-open door while she'd been worrying
about running out on her lease.

"I'm on my way," she said.

She had begun to turn, but almost without her conscious
volition her eyes lingered on Jordan, watching as he stooped
to pick up the heavy basket of toys. He had changed into
jeans this morning, and the aged denim stretched revealingly
over the shifting muscles of his thighs and buttocks as he
bent and then lifted. Her eyes followed the fluid movement,
and her throat suddenly went dry.

As he shifted his grip on the basket, the muscles in his shoulders flexing now, she pulled her gaze away, turning back to the open door. She walked through it, cheeks burning, and then down the steps and into the welcome chill of moisture-laden air. She hoped it would help suppress the heat that had just flared through her body.

She was both surprised and embarrassed by her reactions to Jordan Cross. She couldn't explain them, and she thought she would rather die than have him become aware of the effect he was having on her. But after all, she admitted, it had been a long time. Too long without the physical intimacies of marriage she had once cherished. What was happening within her body was just another result of her situation, another deprivation, she supposed.

She didn't find that a very satisfactory explanation, of course. After all, she had been around other attractive men since Rob left, and she had never reacted to any of them this way. Maybe, as bizarre as the possibility seemed, Jordan Cross's appeal was partly because he looked like her husband. He wasn't Rob, of course, and she knew that. But perhaps the familiar face, a face she had once loved, a face that Meg's was a dear reflection of, was the catalyst for whatever was going on.

The stain of blood in her cheeks had surely receded enough to be blamed on the cold, she hoped, as she heard Jordan come down the concrete block steps behind her. By that time she had crossed the carport to the children. She knelt down between them, kissing Jamie on top of his head. He lifted his face, his eyes alight with joy at the unfamiliar miracle of snow.

His fingers brought up a bit of it, and he touched it to her cheek. Kathleen smiled at him, catching his hand and turning her face to kiss the cold, wet fingers pressed against her skin.

"Snowball," he said.

"Want to make a snowball?" she asked.

He nodded so vigorously that he upset the delicate balance necessary to maintain his squatting position. She grabbed his coat before he could topple over. He and Meg thought that was hilarious, and their laughter rang out into the winter stillness.

She couldn't help smiling at them. Despite Meg's tears and protest, she was again able to laugh. There would be other tears, Kathleen knew. Just now, however, the loss of the angel costume and the pageant had momentarily been forgotten.

Kathleen reached down with her bare hands and picked up enough of the melting snow from beside the concrete slab to make a passable snowball. Because of drips from the carport roof, this one would have bits of dirt and pieces of grass in it, but it was a snowball just the same. A winter miracle. Not angel wings, of course. Not a real home. But still, a small, perfect memory to be treasured.

She put the packed snow into Jamie's mittened hand and pulled his arm back. She helped him make the throwing motion, but he failed to release at the apex of the arch so that when he finally did, the snowball didn't go very far. It landed with a splat a couple of feet in front of them.

Jamie turned his face up to hers again, both his eyes and his grin wide with delight. She smiled back at him, just as if he'd hit some mythical bull's eye.

"Pretty good toss, champ," Jordan said.

Kathleen looked up to find him towering over them. His black hair was ruffled by the wind. The tip of his nose and his lean cheeks, despite the natural darkness of his complexion, were touched with pink. His gray eyes were filled with light, laughing down into hers and Jamie's.

Although she was almost unaware of what was happening, her smile slowly faded. Her eyes didn't release his, and gradually the amusement that had been in the steel-gray depths disappeared, to be replaced by a look she recognized. A look she had seen before in eyes exactly like these.

She took a breath, short and aching with the sudden tightness in her chest. She lowered her head, hiding her too-

revealing face against the softness of Jamie's hair. The toddler caught her hand with his mittened fingers, pulling it
down again.

Obediently, she began to gather up another handful of
slush. This time she guided his fingers in shaping, and together they threw the snowball, their combined aim a little
better on this throw. Kathleen waited for Jordan to make
some comment, but there was only Meg's chatter beside
them as she happily shaped her own missile.

Kathleen looked around, but the man who had been standing behind them was gone. Almost at the same time she
made that realization, she heard the engine of the Buick
start. He was warming the car for the children. Or maybe,
as she had just done, he was fashioning his own escape from
whatever seemed to be happening between them.

"YOU STAY IN THE CAR," Jordan said. "I'll go down and
get the car seat. Anything else down there you need?"

At least he was looking at her again, Kathleen thought.
He hadn't, not since he had stood over them as she and
Jamie made snowballs. And, she realized, whatever emotion
she had seen in his eyes then was no longer there. Maybe
she had even imagined it. Wishful thinking.

"Check the trunk," she suggested, trying to remember
anything valuable the old car might contain. Whatever it
held would be valuable only to them, of course.

"I will. You stay right here," he said again.

Of course they would. They had nowhere else to go, she
thought. No money. No transportation. No choice. She nodded agreement, however, and watched him disappear over
the same bank he'd climbed down last night to get them out
of the wrecked car.

Thank God he had. It would have been a long, cold night
if they had had to wait here for rescue until the deputies
arrived on the scene this morning. She wondered idly how
they had found the wreck, since the falling snow would have
covered whatever marks the tires had left on the bank. When

GET 2

HOW TO GET YOUR
2 FREE BOOKS AND FREE GIFT!

1. Peel off the MIRA sticker on the front cover. Place it in the space provided at right. This automatically entitles you to receive two free books and an exciting surprise gift.

2. Send back this card and you'll get 2 "The Best of the Best™" novels. These books have a combined cover price of $11.98 or more in the U.S. and $13.98 or more in Canada, but they are yours to keep absolutely FREE!

3. There's <u>no</u> catch. You're under <u>no</u> obligation to buy anything. We charge nothing – ZERO – for your first shipment. And you don't have to make any minimum number of purchases – not even one!

4. We call this line "The Best of the Best" because each month you'll receive the best books by some of today's most popular authors. These authors show up time and time again on all the major bestseller lists and their books sell out as soon as they hit the stores. You'll like the convenience of getting them delivered to your home at our special discount prices . . . and you'll love your *Heart to Heart* subscriber newsletter featuring author news, horoscopes, recipes, book reviews and much more!

5. We hope that after receiving your free books you'll want to remain a subscriber. But the choice is yours – to continue or cancel, anytime at all! So why not take us up on our invitation, with no risk of any kind. You'll be glad you did!

6. And remember...we'll send you a surprise gift ABSOLUTELY FREE just for giving "The Best of the Best" a try.

SPECIAL FREE GIFT!

We'll send you a fabulous surprise gift, absolutely FREE, simply for accepting our no-risk offer!

Visit us online at
www.mirabooks.com

® and TM are trademarks of Harlequin Enterprises Limited.

BOOKS FREE!

The Best of the Best™ — Here's How it Works:

Accepting your 2 free books and gift places you under no obligation to buy anything. You may keep the books and gift and return the shipping statement marked "cancel." If you do not cancel, about a month later we will send you 4 additional novels and bill you just $4.49 each in the U.S., or $4.99 each in Canada, plus 25¢ shipping & handling per book and applicable taxes if any.* That's the complete price and — compared to cover prices of $5.99 or more each in the U.S. and $6.99 or more each in Canada — it's quite a bargain! You may cancel at any time, but if you choose to continue, every month we'll send you 4 more books, which you may either purchase at the discount price or return to us and cancel your subscription.

*Terms and prices subject to change without notice. Sales tax applicable in N.Y. Canadian residents will be charged applicable provincial taxes and GST.

Jordan had pulled off the road just now near the scene of the accident, they had been able to see clearly where the deputies had parked, but by dawn, the time they said they'd arrived, the snow had stopped.

It was a minor puzzle, however, and not one Kathleen was overly concerned about. She just wanted Jordan to get Jamie's seat out of the wrecked car and then return. The longer they stayed here, the more nervous she became. The sense of urgency that the effects of her head injury had somehow negated last night seemed to be back with a vengeance this morning.

They should have left then, she thought. Under the cover of darkness. This was taking too long, and therefore was dangerous. Kathleen fought the sense of dread that began to build as they waited. She tried to concentrate on the words of the song Meg was singing in the back seat, obviously something she had learned at school because it was unfamiliar.

Kathleen wasn't aware of the car that pulled up behind the Buick until she heard a door slam. Her gaze flew to the side mirror, and she watched as one of the two deputies who had come to the trailer this morning, the one who had stood in the carport asking questions, walked up beside the car, approaching it on her side.

She heard another door slam about the same time he rapped his knuckles on her window, but from her limited view through the side mirror she couldn't see who else had gotten out of the car. She didn't know if her door was locked, but she supposed it didn't matter. Even if it were, Jordan's probably wasn't, so they were vulnerable. She could lock them now, but that gesture might make the deputies even more suspicious than they had appeared to be earlier.

Given the deputy's imperious rap on the glass, she didn't think that she could refuse to roll down her window. Jordan had thought these two were simply being protective of a woman living alone. And she remembered that the deputy had been concerned about her getting her car towed in. Maybe that's what this was all about. *Please, God, let it be what this is about.*

She pushed the button, and the window slid downward. The deputy was already bending to peer into the car. When the window disappeared into the door, he put the fingers of both hands over the slot into which it had receded.

"Mrs. Simmons?"

"Yes," Kathleen said, trying control the tremor in her voice that threatened to break through.

"Would you step out of the car, please?"

Her heart dropped. That line wasn't in the script she had been writing in her head. And it was frightening.

"What's this about, Officer?" she asked, trying to delay obeying his request long enough to think. She was aware that Meg had stopped singing in the back seat. Even in the sudden silence she couldn't hear the other deputy. She had no idea where he was. Maybe down in the ditch looking for Jordan?

"We need to ask you some questions, ma'am. Just step out of the car, please."

She wanted to refuse, but she didn't know how much they knew. Or what they suspected. This might have nothing to do with Rob. They might have found something suspicious when they ran the plates on the Buick, she realized.

After all, she didn't know that what Jordan had told her was the truth. She had been highly skeptical of his story at first and had finally accepted it simply on the basis of instinct. But if it *weren't* true, then the officers might have found something in their background check that made them want to talk to him. Something to connect Jordan to the people who were trying to find Rob? A criminal record? A warrant?

After all, these men were law enforcement officers, she reminded herself. It was possible the deputies were simply trying to protect her and the children from the stranger she had entrusted them to. Foolishly entrusted them to?

She hesitated another few seconds, still trying to decide the best thing to do. The deputy didn't move until she reached for the handle of the door. Then he stepped away from the car, his back toward the front right fender, keeping his hand on the door as she opened it.

"Is something wrong?" she asked when she was standing, the car door between them. Her knees were weak, and she had to mentally command her body not to tremble. The cold after the warmth of the car was a shock, and the urge to shiver was strong.

"That's what we're trying to find out, ma'am," he said. "Would you step away from the car, please?"

"Why?" she asked, upset by that request. Her children were inside the car. She didn't want to move away from them. And as yet, he hadn't given her any valid reason to do so.

"Just move away from the car, please."

He released the snap that secured the strap across the top of his holster and lifted his gun out. He didn't point it at her, but he might as well have. Her heart seemed to stop, the flow of blood through it thickened and congealed.

"You don't need that," she said.

There should be no guns around the children, she thought. Again, she knew instinctively that something was wrong here. Wrong with what he was doing. And with what he was saying. Threatening her made no sense if they had found out something suspicious about Jordan. And this didn't feel like any rescue attempt she could imagine them trying if that were the case.

"Where's your friend?" he asked, ignoring her protest.

His gaze searched the roadside, between quick glances back at her. Involuntarily Kathleen's eyes followed his, finding the spot where Jordan had disappeared. Her attention was still focused there as the second deputy, the one who had been behind the trailer this morning, climbed up out of the ditch, almost exactly where Jordan had gone down. He, too, had his gun out, and his eyes began to move up and down the isolated road as soon as he topped the bank.

"Find him?" the deputy who had tapped on her window questioned.

"He's not down there," the second one called.

Kathleen remembered to breathe, feeling a glimmer of hope in the midst of the paralyzing crush of terror. Her chest was too tight, the cold wet air hard to pull into her lungs. Apparently the breath she managed to draw was deep enough to be audible. The deputy's gaze swung back to her.

"I asked you a question," he said, his tone menacing for the first time. "Where's your friend?"

Kathleen looked him straight in the eye. "Who?" she asked. She was surprised that her voice seemed so calm and genuinely puzzled, considering what she was feeling.

The deputy laughed, the sound short and biting. "Whoever the hell was driving this car," he said.

"I don't know what you're talking about."

"Don't get cute," he warned. "You weren't driving it from this side."

"I was putting the registration I got out of my car into the glove compartment," Kathleen said. "I thought I might need it."

His eyes held on her face, long enough for Kathleen to wonder if he could possibly be stupid enough to buy that.

"Play time's over, Mrs. Sorrel. Why don't you just tell me where your husband is, and then nobody will get hurt."

"I don't know where my husband is. I haven't known where he is for three years."

"Then who was that with you this morning? Who got you out of the ditch last night?"

"Not Rob," she said. "No matter what you believe, that wasn't Rob."

"Get the kid," he ordered, the words thrown at the other deputy. By this time his gun was pointed at her, of course. Despite that, however, Kathleen took a step toward him, an automatic protest of his command.

"You move one more inch," he threatened, "and I swear I'll kill them both. I'll kill you all, Mrs. Sorrel. And nobody will ever know. There's a lot of empty real estate around here. Places nobody ever goes. Places where nobody would even think to look for you."

His voice was too high, she thought. Higher and tighter than it had been this morning at the trailer. He might just be on edge enough right now to do what he'd threatened. Obviously, he was upset and worried because his partner hadn't found Jordan. Things weren't going exactly as they had planned, and that was making him nervous.

"You're wrong," she said softly, trying to make her tone reasoning, reassuring. The black hole of the muzzle held her motionless, but her eyes followed the other deputy as he began to walk toward the back of the Buick where the children were. "I don't know anything about the money. I can't tell you where it is. I don't know where Rob is," she said.

The other deputy was almost to the car, approaching the back of the driver's side, the side where Jamie was sitting.

"And unless you know where Rob is, taking the children won't do you any good," Kathleen said, her gaze swinging back to the one beside her. "You could kill us all, but you still won't be any closer to the money. We know nothing about where he hid it. Only Rob knows that, and Rob's not here."

She could see in his eyes the impact her words had made. A moment of hesitation, at least, to think about what she'd said. Emboldened by that, she took another step forward, despite the gun, expecting to be shot, but knowing that she couldn't just stand by and let them take Jamie.

"I told you not to move," he said, adding a profanity. "I meant what I said." He put his other hand on the gun.

Where in the world is Jordan? she wondered frantically. He had promised to help them. To protect them. Surely he wouldn't let these men take Jamie.

"Get out here right now, Sorrel," the deputy shouted, his voice painfully loud because she was so close to him. De-

spite the wind, it seemed to reverberate through the cold
silence along the roadside. ''I'll kill your boy if you don't.
I swear to God I will. I'll kill him slow and make you listen
to him dying.''

The words echoed among the snow-covered trees. When
they died away, the two deputies seemed to be listening
intently for an answer, their breathing suspended. Kathleen
listened, too, but she didn't know what she was hoping for.

Even if Jordan answered, she knew they would still use
the children to try to get him to tell them where the money
was. And he didn't know. He couldn't tell them anything
because he wasn't Rob. They wouldn't believe that, of
course. Not looking at him.

''Get the boy,'' the deputy ordered again. Obediently his
partner moved, his hand reaching toward the handle of the
back door.

Chapter Nine

It was a move he never completed. In the middle of it, the deputy's body was thrown backward, away from the car, almost as if it had been jerked by an invisible hand. The crack of sound that followed the movement echoed through the winter stillness, just as the first deputy's shout had done. *Gunshot,* Kathleen realized.

And as soon she had, she turned to face the man who was holding a gun on her. That weapon had automatically swung away, pointing now in the direction the shot had come from. She watched his mouth open and close, moving almost in slow motion, his eyes scanning the wooded terrain, searching for the shooter.

Taking advantage of his lapse, Kathleen dropped to the ground, putting the car door between them. From where she crouched inside of it, she looked up. Through the open window she could see the deputy's chest, the badge he wore flashing in the sunshine as he began to turn.

Apparently, instead of focusing on an attacker he couldn't see, his attention was coming back to Kathleen. He stuck the gun through the open window, its barrel pointing downward.

Kathleen cringed closer to the door, trying to offer him the smallest possible target. Her movement inadvertently pushed the door into the deputy's knees. He staggered backward and then seemed to regain his balance. The gun, which had been sticking through the window during the entire incident, never disappeared from sight. Then it began to lower again, the dark eye of the muzzle once more seeking.

This time the sound of the gunshot came simultaneously with the reaction. The deputy's body flew backward, and his hands, both of which had been fastened around the grip of his own gun, struck the top of the window frame. The weapon went off, unaimed, but it took a heartbeat or two for Kathleen to grasp that she hadn't been shot.

The hands, and the gun they held, disappeared from the opening above her head. In the same second, Kathleen heard the sound of the deputy's body hitting the ground on the other side of the car door, a soft boneless thud. She waited, her heart trying to tear through her chest, her ears straining for any sign that he might be getting to his feet again.

Those sounds never came. When the echoes of the second shot finally faded away, Kathleen was aware of the children crying. Aware again of the wind moving through the heavy branches of the trees along the highway. Aware for the first time of the wetness of the melting snow under her knees, ice-cold and soaking through the material of her slacks.

Finally aware of footsteps. Someone was running toward her along the blacktop. By the time she heard that sound, however, reaction had already set in. Her whole body was shaking. Dry, aching sobs racked her chest, too strong for tears.

Between these spasms, she fought to pull oxygen into her lungs. She could still hear Jamie and Meg crying, and with one part of her brain she knew that she needed to go to them, to offer comfort. Another part thanked God that they could still cry. And that she could still hear them.

Now that it was all over, her terror for what *might* have happened seemed too powerful to overcome. As she had been after the wreck, she was almost paralyzed. Unable to move. Unable to think. She put her hand up, feeling blindly for the bottom of the window, where the deputy's fingers had rested only minutes ago. Gripping the door, she pulled herself up. Her legs were trembling, bone and muscle as fluid as water.

When she was standing, she could see the body on the other side of the door. The deputy's hat had been caught behind the back of his skull when he fell. It was still in place, but it was standing away from his head at a ninety degree angle. His pale blue eyes were wide open, staring up at the overcast sky. And there was a small dark hole in the very center of his forehead.

A bullet hole, she realized. *There's a bullet hole in that man's forehead. Which means...*

She closed her eyes, turning her face away at the same time, holding on to the car door because she knew if she didn't, her knees would collapse.

"Kathleen."

She forced her eyes open. Jordan was standing two feet from her. The raven's wing hair was disordered, again ruffled by the wind. The high cheekbones were stained with color, his mouth was open and he was breathing through it. His eyes traced carefully over her body, looking for an injury, before they came back to her face. He still held his gun in both hands, ready to fire again.

Jordan had been the one she heard running, she realized. Running to her. Running to help her. And of course, he was the one who had shot the two deputies. Who had kept them from taking Jamie. Who had kept them from killing her children.

Without a word, she took the two steps that separated them. Just in time, his left hand released the gun and his arms opened to enclose her body. She moved within their circle, into their protection, and felt his strength surround her, just as it had when she'd awakened this morning. A man strong enough to protect her. To protect her children.

She felt his mouth moving against her hair, his lips caressing the top of her head. Comforting. Very much like the gentle kiss she had placed against Jamie's soft brown hair in the carport a few minutes ago. Had it really only been minutes since she had helped those small mittened fingers shape and throw a snowball? she wondered. And if it hadn't been for what Jordan had just done, she realized…

She laid her cold cheek against the solid warmth of his chest, the softness of the navy pullover he wore offering its own reassurance. A sense of familiarity. A return to normalcy. To normal sensations. Normal reactions.

"You're all right," he said. "It's over."

She listened to the words rumble through his chest, the sound of them beneath her ear. She could feel his heart beating there as well, its rhythm hard and very fast. From the exertion of his run or from fear, she didn't know. She didn't care.

"The kids okay?"

This one was a question, and she answered it by nodding. They were. Jordan had never allowed the deputy to get near enough to open the back door. The kids were still strapped in, and she could hear them crying, the sounds of their distress different and distinctive. Crying, but unhurt. There was no doubt in her mind about that.

"Come on," he said.

He took a step, and she had to turn a little to walk beside him. She didn't want to move away from him. Not away from his strength. From the safety he represented. He had saved her life. And Jamie's. Meg's. Kathleen was just realizing the scope of what this man had done for them. He had saved them all. There was no melodrama about that, as melodramatic as the words seemed.

He had killed two men to save their lives. Suddenly, she was crying, the tears streaming unchecked down her cheeks. This had been as close as it could get. As close as they would ever come, she prayed, to the nightmare she had so often imagined. As close as they *could* come and still be alive. And they were, incredibly, all still alive.

At the sound of her sobbing, partially stifled against his chest, Jordan pulled her closer. He didn't stop, however. He guided her blind steps, leading her, trembling and unseeing, around the open car door. He paused to look down at the deputy.

Kathleen didn't need to verify what she already knew. He was dead, the bullet hole in the middle of his forehead neat and precise. *Bull's-eye,* she thought, remembering Jamie's attempt at throwing a snowball. A real bull's-eye this time. For Jamie. And for Meg.

"I have to check the other one," he said softly.

She realized that she had turned her face more firmly into his chest. Somehow her arms were now around his waist, the right one under his sweater. The skin of his back was warm and smooth. Warm because he was alive. They were all alive.

She nodded, her head moving up and down against his body. Whatever he said, she thought. Whatever he wanted her to do. Now and forever. Because he had kept her babies alive.

SHE COULDN'T STOP SHAKING, and Jordan was beginning to worry about her. Too much had happened in the last twenty-four hours. Too much for anyone to deal with. First, he had shown up last night and scared the hell out of her. Then there had been the wreck. Her head injury. And this morning…

Jordan's lips compressed, and he glanced over at her again. The tears had stopped, but her body was still vibrating slightly, trembling as if she were standing out in the cold without any clothing on.

He pulled his eyes away from Kathleen in order to glance into the back seat and check on Meg. The little girl was clutching the old Raggedy Ann Kathleen had retrieved from the closet just before they left the trailer. Her eyes were almost as glazed as the dead deputy's. All the light and joy from the carport and the snowballs had gone out of them.

These were eyes that had seen too much in their few short years. This was a five-year-old child who had had to deal with the evil of the world. Evil she should know nothing about. A father who had deserted her. Strange men who followed and harassed her family. And now, law enforcement officers who tried to kill them. Men he had killed, Jordan acknowledged. And Meg Sorrel had seen all of it.

She had understood what was happening. Too damn bright *not* to have understood, he thought. Jamie would be all right. He was too young, probably, for this to leave permanent scars or memories. Hopefully, he was too young, Jordan amended.

But Meg and Kathleen needed to be somewhere where they could feel safe. Not only feel safe, but *be* safe. So that what had happened this morning could never happen to them again.

The deputy's threat echoed over and over in his head as he drove. *"I'll kill him slow and make you listen to him dying."* The thought of it made him sick, and Jordan could only imagine what those words must have done to Kathleen.

He glanced at the passenger seat again. Her face was turned away from him. She seemed to be looking at the passing scenery. He knew, however, that her eyes were as unseeing as Meg's. That she was reliving over and over again the horror they had just escaped.

"We have to get rid of the plates," he said, pulling his own eyes back to the road.

He didn't need to tell her this, but he needed to hear her talk. He needed some indication that she was strong enough to deal with what had happened back there. Strong enough to accept that what he had done was necessary.

Jordan had killed men before, probably none of them more deserving of death than those two. They were the ones who were supposed to protect people like Kathleen Sorrel and her children. Instead, they had become the instruments of those who threatened them. Or maybe instruments of their own greed. Just as Rob Sorrel had.

Given the scope of the betrayals she had faced, Jordan wondered how Kathleen would ever be able to trust anyone again. He honestly couldn't figure out why she trusted him.

He was just grateful that she had. And grateful that he had been there this morning, especially since what had happened was almost certainly a result of his showing up in their lives.

He had no idea about what had been going on when he'd arrived, of course, but he recognized that some part of his original reason for deciding to track Sorrel's wife down had probably been boredom. He had needed to get to the bottom of the attack in California, of course, but that determination had had a profound and dangerous impact on Kathleen's life. All he could do about that now, however, was attempt to minimize the effects of what he'd done and keep them safe, he thought, sickened when he remembered the threats the deputy had made.

Although the interstates would certainly have been faster, Jordan had deliberately kept to the back roads since they'd left that grisly roadside scene. He didn't think those two deputies would have filed an official report on him or the car, because of their own greed. They wouldn't want to chance having to share the payoff they were working toward. He couldn't be certain of that, of course, but he was hoping.

He was driving east, heading instinctively, he supposed, back to his home territory. Back to friends. To other members of that elite brotherhood of CIA specialists he had once belonged to. To Jake Holt, with his genius for pulling seemingly nonexistent information out of the computers.

Jordan knew he could appeal to any of the others on the team as well. Hawk, of course. Grey Sellers and Drew Evans. Or Mark Lindsey, another soft-spoken Southerner like Jordan and Griffon Cabot. The sudden memory of Griff stopped those circling thoughts, reminding Jordan of that loss and of what it meant now.

Griff would have had the connections to arrange some sort of protection for Sorrel's family. They weren't federal witnesses in any criminal case, of course, but Cabot would have been able to figure some way to use the system to their advantage. Jordan wasn't sure that Carl Steiner, who had taken Griff's place as the head of what had been called the External Security Team, would go to that much trouble for him. Or for them, Jordan thought.

"How do we do that?" Kathleen asked.

He turned toward her voice and was glad to see she was no longer pretending to be focused on the scenery. Her eyes were on him, and she seemed willing to think about the problem the license plates represented. Maybe glad to have something to think about, other than what had happened this morning.

"We ditch this set somewhere and pick up another."

"The deputies ran the license number on this car, and that led them…" She hesitated.

"To a man named Robert Sanders," Jordan supplied.

"I don't understand," Kathleen said.

"That's the identity the CIA provided. The connection between Sanders and your husband had already been made in California."

"By the men who attacked you?" she asked.

"It must have been. They didn't succeed, but they probably collected something for identifying Robert Sanders as Sorrel. And then the word was out. I should have realized that would happen."

"The plates on this car could be traced back to Sanders."

"I think that's the only way they could have made the connection," Jordan agreed, because he had already worked some of this out. Too late, he thought bitterly, chastising himself for not taking the necessary precautions. Of course, when he'd rented the car he hadn't known what Sorrel had done, and Jake had just assured him the Sanders ID was clean.

"Unless somebody saw your face when you were following me," she suggested.

"Nobody saw me," he said.

Jordan had already considered that possibility, but he knew he had been careful, remaining as unobtrusive as possible, right up until he had decided to confront Sorrel's wife and see what kind of reaction he got.

"I did," Kathleen said.

He turned his head, again meeting her eyes. In them was a hint of amusement. Or challenge. He liked seeing it there, relieved that her spirit seemed to be reemerging.

"You're the exception," he acknowledged.

He had thought that from the first. He had admired her from the first day he had watched her and the children. He had admired the way she handled everything.

He hadn't had any idea then of the magnitude of the strength that must have been necessary to carry Kathleen Sorrel through this years-long ordeal. Now, of course, he understood something of what she had gone through, and the admiration her struggle evoked made her courage and character more appealing.

And it made what Sorrel had done even less believable. Maybe not stealing the money. A lot of people might be tempted by that much money, especially if they thought they could get away with it. And apparently, Sorrel had.

What Jordan couldn't believe was that the man had deserted his family. This woman, whose strength of character shone through her every action. A daughter as bright and beautiful as Meg. Sorrel had never known Jamie, of course, whose small fingers had taken a grip on Jordan's heart from the beginning.

These children weren't Jordan's flesh and blood. He didn't even like kids. Or, he corrected, he had never thought he did. He sure as hell liked these, he acknowledged.

And he liked Kathleen Sorrel. *Like* wasn't quite the right word, but he had deliberately guarded against using any of the others that invaded his thoughts from time to time. Such as what he had been thinking—and feeling—in the carport this morning. And then outside the car, after he'd killed the deputies, when she had walked into his arms as if she belonged there.

That had been shock, maybe. Gratitude. A hundred emotions could explain that action. But what had been in her eyes as she knelt beside Jamie, making those dirty, lopsided snowballs could not be so easily explained away. Or so easily forgotten.

"So what do we do about the plates?" she asked.

He realized that in thinking about things he had no right to think about, he had neglected an explanation of what he meant.

"We steal a new set," he said.

"Steal them?" she repeated, her voice tinged with disbelief.

"Unless you have a better suggestion."

As it turned out, she didn't. He dropped them at a McDonald's for lunch. He could see the fear in her eyes, but she didn't protest his plan, which would leave them alone and unprotected at the restaurant for as long as it took him to find a suitable candidate for the tag swap.

Jordan didn't like leaving them alone any more than she did, but it seemed that having them with him while he stole the plates from another car put them even more at risk than leaving them at the busy restaurant. Getting transportation that wouldn't betray them necessitated his taking that chance.

Besides, he knew no one had been following them. The roads they had used were all deserted enough, given the freak snowfall, that he could be absolutely certain of that. And if anyone was looking for them, then all they would have to go on was the description of the car and the license number, both of which would be with Jordan.

It hadn't taken him long to find a car parked in an isolated location and switch the plates. There wasn't much danger that the ones he put on the Buick would be reported as stolen anytime soon. Most people never looked at their tags. It might be weeks before the owner of the car would even notice that his had been changed. And the red Honda Accord was different enough from the Buick that anybody who had been given a description of what Robert Sanders was driving wouldn't look at it twice. Not long enough anyway, Jordan hoped, to compare the numbers on the plates to the ones they were looking for.

And if they spotted a dark green Buick traveling east, then the plates it sported wouldn't match the numbers of the one Sorrel's enemies might already be looking for. It seemed the best he could do, at least for the time being.

Time, he thought again, the word seeming to stick in his worried mind. That was really all he had managed today, Jordan knew. Just to buy them a little time.

Chapter Ten

"The only solution is to find Rob Sorrel," Jordan said softly, his mouth close to the receiver. His gaze again circled the area around the isolated phone booth he was using.

"You want me to do that before or after lunch?" Jake asked.

"I wanted you to do it *yesterday*. I was hoping for some good news when I called you."

"Look," Jake said patiently, "the mob's been looking for this guy for nearly three years. There's been a street price for information about him on for at least the last five months. Nobody's found him. And you've given me less than a week to work on it?"

"But you're the best," Jordan said, his lips lifting slightly at the corners. "Everybody knows that."

Although what he had just said had a deliberately mocking tone, it wasn't an exaggeration. Jake *was* the best at this kind of needle-in-a-haystack search, and they both knew it.

"I can't find something that's not there. No matter how much you want me to."

"What does that mean?" Jordan asked, reading the warning implicit in both tone and statement. "You've always said there'll be something," he argued. "A receipt for a favorite purchase, some ingrained pattern of behavior they can't help repeating, a phone call they couldn't resist making. You said there was always something. Nobody lives in a vacuum.'' The last was a direct quote from Jake, and one the team had heard often enough that it had stuck.

"It's nice to know you've listened to the wisdom I've tried to share with all you hotshots through the years,'' Jake said. The familiar trace of amusement was back in his voice. "And you're right. *I* was right,'' he amended.

"So you did find something on this guy.''

"Not a damn thing,'' Jake said. "There's not a blip of information anywhere.''

"Then how the hell am I right?''

"Nobody lives in a vacuum,'' Jake repeated softly.

It took a second for that to sink in, and when it did, Jordan waited another couple before he attempted to verify what he thought Jake meant. He didn't want to jump to any conclusions, even as appealing as this one would be.

"Sorrel's dead,'' he said.

It was not a question, but an explanation, and as he pronounced it, Jordan kept his voice flat, carefully unemotional. That wasn't the way he felt. No matter the circumstances or the consequences, he couldn't help the small surge of relief caused by the thought that Kathleen Sorrel's husband might no longer be alive.

"Maybe,'' Jake said.

"Other possibilities?'' Jordan asked, trying to imagine one.

"A desert island,'' Jake said. "Somewhere where he is *not* spending his ill-gotten gains. The money also wasn't reinvested. He took it from them a little bit at a time and stuck it away in a lot of different places. But when he decided to make his move, he took it all with him.''

"He cleaned out the accounts where he had been hiding their money.''

"Down to the last nickel. And he did it physically. No electronic transfers were made out of those accounts. Not to Switzerland or anywhere else. And after studying Sorrel's patterns of investing, I don't think he's done anything with it since it disappeared.''

Jordan didn't even ask how Jake could know that. Everything was done by computers these days, and Jake was the master at reading the information they contained. He could get in anywhere. That's why he had been so valuable to Griff's team.

"You think if he *were* alive, he'd be investing it?"

"Or spending it," Jake said. "How many people do you know who could sit on sixteen million dollars for three years? Especially some guy who calls himself an investment consultant." The ridicule was strong in the last two words.

"Maybe they could if they knew the people they stole it from were after them? And if they knew those people play hardball."

"Maybe," Jake said agreeably. "But people who do what Sorrel did are risk takers. They have a very healthy ego and a highly inflated idea of their own smarts. Neither of which argues he's going to lie low for this long."

"If he's dead, who killed him?"

"That, my friend, is *your* area of expertise. You're the puzzle man. I just read the trails they leave. And ours."

Jordan hesitated, knowing that everything the normally laconic Jake said meant something. It wasn't always apparent, but then Jake liked for you to follow the logic of what he was telling you. Maybe that was a natural result of what he himself did with those telltale patterns he found in the computers.

"Somebody *we* know is tracking Sorrel?" Jordan asked. That someone in the CIA was also looking for Sorrel seemed the only explanation for that last cryptic addition.

"At least somebody with access to our systems."

"Have any idea who?"

"All I can give you is a time frame. They started looking about five months ago."

"An expert?" Someone like Jake? Jordan wondered. Someone who, given enough time, could find out anything about anybody?

"Hard to say. Maybe somebody who has the codes."

"So you're saying either a very good hacker or someone from inside the agency?"

"Make that an *extremely* good hacker," Jake emphasized. Jake had set up much of the agency's systems security, but there wasn't a system built that couldn't be invaded. "And by the way, Sorrel's not the only thing somebody is looking for," Jake added.

"What else?"

"Somebody's looking real hard for Robert Sanders."

"You told me that ID was clean."

"It is. Whoever this is is not looking into your past. They're looking *for* you, my friend. And there's something very interesting about how they're doing it."

"Interesting how?" Jordan asked.

"Every system I build has a back door," Jake said.

"And…" Jordan prodded when Jake paused.

"Whoever this is came in that way."

Again, Jordan thought about what Jake was saying, trying to be sure of the significance. Nobody could find that hidden way into a system by accident. Jake was too good for that. "So who knew about the back door?" he asked finally, having worked his way to that question. Just to where Jake wanted to lead him.

"Me and Griff," Jake said softly.

And Griff Cabot, of course, was dead.

THE CONVERSATION with Jake hadn't been reassuring, Jordan thought. There had been no good news at all, other than the suggestion that Rob Sorrel might be dead. Considering how Jordan felt about Sorrel's wife, that possibility should have been real comforting.

He had finally realized, however, after the first sense of euphoria faded, that it just presented a whole slew of new problems. If Sorrel *were* dead—and Jordan had known Jake Holt long enough to know he wouldn't make that kind of suggestion without being ninety-nine percent sure he was right—that didn't mean the people who had been looking for him would stop. Not even if they *knew* he was dead. Not with the sixteen million dollars still unaccounted for.

The money Sorrel had stolen was hidden somewhere, and with Sorrel out of the picture, a whole lot of people were going to believe that the only remotely possible route to locating it now ran through his wife. Through Kathleen. And Jordan knew the two innocent weapons they would use to try to force that information out of her.

He slipped the key into the motel room door, but before he opened it, he took another look around the nearly deserted parking lot. It was late afternoon, still too early for people to be checking in for the night, but the children had been irritable, tired of being confined, and maybe acting out their distress over what they had witnessed this morning. Besides, Jordan had known he needed to get in touch with Jake to see what he'd found out since the last time they'd had a chance to talk.

Unfortunately, what Jake had found out wasn't much help, he thought, his gray eyes carefully scanning the scattered cars. The Buick wasn't there, of course. He'd parked it on the other side of the building, just in case. He was registered in the motel office as Michael Davis, and he was supposedly staying alone. Paying cash for the room had simplified the process.

No one was watching him from the parking lot, he decided. Just as no one had followed them on the road today. Kathleen and the children were as safe as he could make them. Safe at least for tonight.

He turned the knob and stepped inside. Shoes off, Kathleen was stretched out on the bed, her back against the pillows stacked against the headboard. There was a child on either side of her, their small bodies encircled by her arms. Across her lap lay one of the big children's books from the laundry basket Jordan had set inside the room before he'd gone to make his call.

Three pairs of eyes lifted to the door when it opened.

Only Jamie smiled at him, his grin wide and wet because he had been sucking his thumb again.

"Hey, you," the toddler said.

Both Jamie's voice and those brown eyes expressed true delight at seeing him again, and a little of the tension Jordan had been carrying around over what the children had witnessed this morning eased. Compared to Meg and Kathleen, who still looked shell-shocked, Jamie appeared to be bright eyed and bushy tailed. Of course, he'd slept away a lot of the hours of the drive. Kathleen had tried for a while to keep him awake, but finally even she had given up.

"There'll be hell to pay tonight," she had warned.

"Let him sleep," Jordan had advised, watching the little boy's chin bob gently against his chest in the rearview mirror a moment before he had brought his eyes back to hers. She had looked exhausted, but he knew that was as much an emotional reaction as a physical one.

She still looked exhausted, he thought, and it was still probably emotional. After what had happened this morning, he wasn't sure how she was managing the calmness she had displayed all day in front of the children. Her courage had broken only that once, when the actual threat was over, and her breakdown had lasted only a few minutes. During that too-short time when he had been allowed to hold her trembling body against his own.

Then she had set about calming the children. She seemed to have succeeded with Jamie, but Meg's eyes still expressed the horror of what she had seen. And they were looking at him now, he realized, with a dislike that hadn't been there the night she had bossily given him directions for fixing dinner. But maybe that was because she knew he had been the instrument of the deputies' deaths today. And she was old enough to understand the concept of dying.

Meg would probably never look at him the same way, Jordan acknowledged, but at least they were alive. That was really all that mattered—not what Meg felt about what he had had to do, the reason for which he sincerely hoped she hadn't understood.

Jordan walked across the room and put the sacks of food he'd picked up at one of the fast-food places in town down on the foot of the bed. He didn't know if they were hungry, but since he'd missed both lunch and breakfast, he knew he was.

"Hand-burgers," Jamie said, mutilating the word, but instantly recognizing the familiar logo. He scrambled out of Kathleen's arm and crawled across the expanse of the mattress to open one of the bags and peer inside.

"Chocolate for Jamie?" he questioned hopefully, looking up into Jordan's face.

Jordan glanced at Kathleen for explanation.

"An unexplainable addiction to milk shakes. Probably genetic," she said, her smiling eyes falling back to her son, who was carefully removing the contents of the bag and laying them out on the bed in a relatively neat row. Luckily, the sack he had chosen was the one with the burgers, each of which was individually wrapped.

"Sorry," Jordan said. "I didn't know. I got them sodas."

"Caffeine free, I'm sure," Kathleen said, but her voice was both amused and resigned. She stopped watching what Jamie was doing and looked up at Jordan again.

There was a hint of a smile hovering around her lips. Jordan thought she was probably the only woman he had ever known who could go through what she'd been through today—could watch what he had had to do today—and still manage a smile. And manage to tease him over his ignorance about the care and feeding of children.

"I wasn't planning on sleeping," he said.

"Which is probably a really good thing," she said softly.

He laughed. Her smile widened a little in response. Then, reading what Jordan knew must be in his eyes right now as he listened to her laughter, her smile faded slowly, just as it had this morning. Unlike this morning, however, she didn't duck her head or break the undeniable sexual pull that had just arced between them.

That lasted until Jamie, having succeeded in emptying the contents of the first bag, reached for another. The next one in the line of fire held the drinks, however, and Jordan moved it quickly out of range of the little boy's fingers.

"Wait a minute, champ," he said. "You're going to spill something."

The look that had been in Kathleen Sorrel's eyes was still flooding his body with heat, despite his attention to Jamie. These were the same feelings he'd denied before, because he had no right to feel them. Maybe he still didn't, but now at least...

Except she doesn't know, he realized suddenly. Here he was, thinking about the possibilities that her husband's death could open up for them, and Kathleen didn't have any idea that her long-missing husband might be dead. And since Jordan himself had no tangible proof of that, nothing beyond his confidence in Jake's uncanny ability to read all those scattered bits and pieces of information, he wasn't sure he had the right to even suggest the possibility to her.

"Chocolate?" Jamie inquired, interrupting that unwanted realization.

The toddler had gotten to his feet in an attempt to find milk shakes in the sack Jordan had moved. Trying to maintain his balance on the less-than-stable mattress, Jamie took a couple of staggering steps, which brought him perilously close to the edge.

Kathleen and Jordan reacted at the same time. Jordan was closer, of course, so he reached down and grabbed the little boy by the shoulder before he could fall off. Jamie's eyes widened at Jordan's sudden lunge or maybe at the tightness of his grip. Then they began to look suspiciously damp.

Seeing that tearful reaction, Jordan reached down and picked Jamie up, settling the little boy on his hip as he'd seen Kathleen do. The toddler leaned back to look at his face, and then he put both arms around Jordan's neck in a hug. Automatically Jordan squeezed back, holding the small, sturdy body close, fighting again the unwanted images that had kept appearing in his head all day, horrors that had been put there by the words the deputy had shouted into that cold roadside emptiness.

Jamie struggled a little, maybe at the fierceness of the hug. Jordan loosened his grip, and the little boy leaned back again, once more looking at his face. Finally he reached out and patted Jordan's cheek.

"*My* daddy," he said clearly, small wet fingers leaving their sweet, warm message on the skin of the man who held him.

"*Nobody lives in a vacuum,*" Jake had said. Everything a person did, every unthinking and unplanned action, touched and changed the lives of others, maybe forever.

Jordan's gaze dropped from Jamie's face and found Kathleen's. Her dive for the toddler had taken her almost to the foot of the bed, and propped on one elbow, she was still lying there, surrounded by the scattered hamburgers. She was completely motionless, looking up at the two of them.

There was no possibility that she hadn't heard what Jamie had said. And no doubt about what was in her eyes. Longing. Maybe even an unspoken invitation to make what her son had just suggested a reality.

Then, as quickly as it had appeared, she hid what had been in her eyes. She reached up and touched Jamie's arm, her attention focused deliberately on him now, and not on Jordan.

"That's Jordan," she said. "Can you say Jordan?"

"Jordan," Jamie repeated agreeably.

Then, suddenly, he flung his small body backward, his head hanging down and his arms reaching toward the floor. He squealed in delight, as if he were on some sort of carnival ride. Jordan managed to hang on by tightening his grip around the little boy's knees, but despite his quick reflexes, it was a near thing. Kathleen laughed, at the child or at his own expression, Jordan wasn't sure which.

''That's one of his favorite maneuvers. I should have warned you,'' she said.

About a lot of things, Jordan thought. *Like how seductive this can be. The feel of Jamie's arms around my neck. And about whatever is in your eyes when you look at me.*

Somebody damn well should have warned him, Jordan thought, before he got in way too deep to ever want to get out again.

''I THINK YOU CAN put him down now,'' Kathleen said.

The words were very soft, whispered in the darkness of the motel room. Jordan had thought she was asleep. She and Meg were sharing the double bed, but just as promised, Jamie hadn't managed to settle down.

Jordan, who had already decided that he wasn't going to take any chance of being caught off guard as he had been this morning, had volunteered to entertain him. They had played on the floor for a while with Jamie's trucks, but the last hour or so, Jordan had turned off the light and told stories and sung songs until he was hoarse, dredging up forgotten tales from his own childhood. The parts he couldn't remember he made up, but Jamie didn't seem to know the difference. If he did, apparently he didn't care.

Gradually the small body had relaxed, and now the little boy's head was lying against Jordan's shoulder, a growing circle of warm dampness spreading over Jordan's shirt as Jamie found comfort in his thumb. The soft, rhythmic noises he made were relaxing, and Jordan's own eyes had drifted closed a few times before he forced them open, the deputy's threat too real, too close.

Safe, he told himself over and over again. He had taken all the precautions. The door was locked and bolted. His gun was lying against his right thigh, the hard bulge of it not uncomfortable, but infinitely reassuring instead.

If Kathleen hadn't spoken, he probably would have drifted off to sleep himself in a few minutes. He debated about answering her and about doing what she'd suggested, but he wasn't sure how soundly Jamie was sleeping.

After a few seconds, he heard her moving in the darkness. Then she was suddenly just there, standing beside the chair he was sitting in. She bent toward him, the faintest hint of whatever fragrance she had applied after her bath this morning reaching him a fraction of a second before she did.

She took Jamie out of his arms, and although the toddler stirred drowsily, he didn't protest, going into his mother's embrace without a sound. Jordan listened to the soft rustling as she carried him back to the bed.

Freed of his responsibility, he stood up, flexing muscles that had become cramped from sitting too long in the same position. Once he'd finally gotten Jamie to sleep, he had almost been afraid to move. Now he put both hands behind the back of his head and stretched out his spine, arching into the ache that centered just below his waistline.

He had just straightened when Kathleen touched him. She laid her hand flat against his chest, and then she lifted it away quickly. Her laughter was a breath of sound, so quiet it was intimate. Shared only between the two of them.

Her fingers again lightly touched the wet spot on his shirt, and then they caressed it, moving slowly over the underlying muscle. Arms held out to his sides, Jordan waited, not breathing. Thinking about what was happening. Wondering about her intent. Was this the invitation he had seen in her eyes? Made now when they were alone, here in the darkness together?

Except they weren't alone. Whatever she intended, it wasn't seduction. Kathleen would never even consider making love to him in the same room where her children were sleeping. He didn't know why he was so certain of that, but he was.

Maybe she needed what she had needed this morning. The comfort of a human touch. Maybe those words that had echoed obscenely in his head all day were what haunted her eyes. Comfort wasn't all he wanted to give, Jordan acknowledged, but if that was what she needed from him tonight…

Slowly he allowed his arms to lower, enfolding her body, but not tightly. His right hand soothed up and down her spine, trying to ease the tensions of the long day. Trying to tell her, without speaking words that might wake the sleeping children, that everything was going to be all right. He hadn't quite yet figured out how he intended to insure that it would be, but if he thought he could possibly bring that about, he was willing to devote the rest of his life to doing it.

She rested a moment against his body, and then her right hand found his left. She began to move, pulling him with her, guiding him through the unrelieved midnight blackness that surrounded them. Into the bathroom, he realized.

Once there, she slipped away from him, and he listened, trying to figure out what was going on. His breathing hesitated, his heart started to hammer when she eased the bathroom door closed.

Then the light came on. He blinked at its shocking brightness. She was, too, he discovered, when his eyes had made the adjustment. She was standing by the door, one hand still on the light switch. The other hand had lifted to shade her eyes from the glare, and she was looking at him.

"You were going to call a friend," she said.

It took a moment to adjust his thinking. He had been anticipating something else, so this abrupt departure took time to react to. Less for his mind than for his body. And his jeans were probably old and thin enough, he thought, that exactly what he had been anticipating when she'd brought him here was pretty damn evident. Kathleen's eyes stayed on his face, however. In them now was the anxiety she had hidden all day from the children.

Reading her distress, he felt the hard physical ache in his groin ease a little. She hadn't asked before about what Jake had said because they had never been alone. Now, hopeful for good news, she wanted to know. And what he had been told…

"Jordan?" she questioned softly.

Still he hesitated, trying to figure out what, and how, to tell her.

"What did you find out?" she prodded.

"Nothing good," he admitted.

Her eyes widened a little, but she slowly lowered the hand that had been shading them from the fluorescent glare.

"Tell me," she ordered.

"The friend I was hoping would be able to give us some information about your husband couldn't find anything."

She waited, her eyes on his face. And then she shook her head, puzzled it seemed by what he'd said or by what it meant.

"What were you hoping he could tell you?" she asked finally.

"Where Rob is," Jordan admitted.

Her face didn't change, but her eyes widened again. "Nobody knows where Rob is," she said. "Why do you think your friend—"

"It's what he does," Jordan said. It was hard to explain his faith in Jake's expertise. It would be harder to justify the fact that he had accepted Jake's opinion that Rob Sorrel was dead based only on that same faith. "For the agency," he added.

"He finds people who are missing?" she said doubtfully.

"If someone *can* be found, then Jake can find them."

That was skirting very close to what Jake had said, of course. And there really wasn't going to be an easy way to tell her this, Jordan realized. Not easy because Sorrel had been both her husband and the father of her children. And not easy because it probably meant they were in even more danger than they had been before. Maybe, he thought, she wouldn't realize that.

"What does that mean?" she asked, her voice still puzzled. "If they *can* be found…"

He didn't respond immediately, hoping that she would figure it out, as he had. Hoping that he wouldn't have to be the one to put this into words. Hoping for something that would make any of it easier. Her eyes didn't falter, however, holding his, her inherent honesty demanding the same from him.

"It could mean a couple of things," he said.

She didn't respond, still waiting. And he didn't soften it.

"Jake thinks he may be dead."

Jordan's voice was as carefully unemotional as it had been this afternoon. And now he was the one who waited. Her mouth was strained, the fine, faint lines under her exhausted eyes apparent in the harsh light of the bathroom fixture.

Her lips tightened suddenly, and she swallowed, the movement strong enough to be visible. She drew a breath, her mouth opening at the same time so that the inhalation sobbed inward, almost a gasp. As if she were in pain.

"Or?" she said.

She wanted to hear the other option. Jordan didn't like that…because maybe that meant she didn't want to accept the first one. Maybe she wasn't ready to think of Sorrel as dead.

Even considering that possibility created a knot of disappointment in Jordan's stomach. He knew he had no right to be disappointed. What the hell had he expected? That she would celebrate her husband's death?

"Maybe he's…gone underground, somewhere where he can't ever be traced. Somewhere where he's *not* spending the money."

She laughed, the sound as low as when she had discovered the damp circle Jamie had made on his shirt. But the tone of this was totally different. It held no amusement. And no intimacy.

"I always pictured him somewhere warm and tropical," she said. "Enjoying the hell out of spending all that money while they hounded his children. While they robbed them of their childhood. It was so easy to hate him," she added, her voice only a whisper. "Too easy to hate him, I guess."

"I don't have any proof," Jordan said. "Nothing other than the fact that Jake's…exceptional at what he does, so when he says something like that…"

His voice trailed away. There was no need to say it again.

"*You* think he's dead, don't you?" she asked.

"I think the odds are Jake's right."

"And the money?"

Jordan let the words hang in the air between them. The money was, of course, the key to freeing Sorrel's family from the trap they were in. And it was a key that apparently nobody possessed. Because it seemed that Rob Sorrel must have taken that secret with him to the grave.

"Your friend couldn't find the money, either," she said. "He couldn't find it, could he?"

It sounded almost like an accusation, but however she meant it, Jordan had to acknowledge it was the truth. He shook his head, one slow negative movement, holding her eyes.

"So what do we do now?" she asked, her voice sounding almost defeated again.

But he had liked hearing the "we." That meant she was assuming they were in this together. Assuming he wasn't planning on abandoning them. And probably assuming he had a clue about what they should do next. Which he didn't, of course. He hated to admit it, but he really didn't.

"We start back at the beginning," he suggested, partly just to have something to say.

But as the words came out, he realized that that was exactly what they needed to do. It was something he had learned from Griff. "*When you reach a dead end,*" Cabot used to say, "*you can stand at the brick wall and curse, or you can find a way around.*" Find another way around the obstacle.

"And where is that?" she asked.

"With him," Jordan said.

It sure as hell wasn't that he was eager to hear about her husband. Especially not from her. But as much as Jordan hated to admit it, the people who would be looking for the money, even if they found out Sorrel was dead, would be right in thinking she might have the answers.

After all, she had lived with the man. Slept with him. Borne him two children. Shared with him the kind of intimacy Jordan didn't want to think about.

Because he was jealous of a dead man, he thought. Jealous of a man he *hoped* was dead. At least dead to her.

There was one good thing, he supposed, in making her talk about her husband—and in making himself listen. He thought that when they both got through saying whatever needed to be said about Rob Sorrel, he would have a much clearer idea of what Kathleen still felt for her husband. And he supposed now, given what he felt about her, that was something he really needed to know.

Chapter Eleven

"No letters. No...unexplained keys or tickets. No computer disk. No messages of any kind?" Jordan asked again.

She laughed. "How many times are you going to want to hear this? Nothing. Rob left me nothing. He sent me nothing. I found nothing after he was gone."

With each repetition, her voice had gotten louder, until suddenly it was echoing off the cold white tiles of the small bathroom. When she realized that, her eyes shifted guiltily to the door that led into the bedroom. They both listened, but the stillness from the room where the children slept was unbroken. The stillness between them, when she turned back to face him, almost matched it, until finally she spoke again.

"There was *nothing*," she said softly. Her voice was controlled, wiped clean of the anger she had just expressed. Wiped clean of emotion.

Brick wall, Jordan thought. *Another frigging brick wall. So what the hell am I supposed to do now, Griff?*

"How about something he sent the kids?" Jordan asked patiently, knowing this seemingly pointless inquisition might be their only hope. "A postcard. A birthday present. Christmas—"

Before he could get the rest of it out, Kathleen pushed herself off the counter where she had been sitting and walked toward the door, determined to escape the questions he had thrown at her during the last hour. Her body was rigid with anger.

He couldn't blame her. They had been over and over this, over every question he could possibly think to ask her that might lead *somewhere*. He knew he had been relentless, but he thought she understood that this was the only way to protect the children. And her. At least the only way he could think of. They had to find the money her husband had stolen, so no one would ever look for it—or them—again.

Just as her hand reached for the knob, it hesitated. Then it changed direction and, finding the light switch instead, it swept downward, plunging the room into darkness. Jordan had grabbed her wrist at the same instant, gripping hard enough to stop the retreat he understood, but couldn't allow. She tried to shake off his hold, twisting her arm and using her free hand to pry at his fingers.

"Let me go," she ordered, her voice low but furious, each word carefully enunciated, separate and distinct. "I don't know anything to tell you. There *is* nothing to tell you, damn it."

She was tired. And frightened. And this was a brick wall she had been confronting for a long time. That frustration was the real root of her anger, of course, not his questioning. He knew all those things. He understood them. Because he was tired and frustrated also. But he needed to be very clear that what he was trying to do was necessary. And maybe their only hope.

"Listen," he said harshly, pulling her around to face him. Fighting to control his own frustration and helplessness, he put both hands on her shoulders, again gripping too hard because it was so important. He shook her slightly as he said it again. "*You* listen to *me*, damn it."

She stopped struggling, but in the darkness he could hear her breathing, uneven, ragged. With his hands holding her prisoner, he was near enough to be conscious again of the fragrance that had surrounded him when she had come, unexpectedly, out of the blackness of that silent bedroom to touch him. To put her hand against his chest, setting off a chain reaction of desire.

That was what he wanted. To make love to her. Not to fight with her. Not to browbeat and frighten her.

Except, he realized, that was exactly what he had intended to do. He had been intending to drum into her head that if she didn't come up with *something,* and do it pretty damn quick, then she was going to have the whole pack of scavengers down on her and the children. And they would be far more relentless, and far more ruthless, than Jordan had been.

There was a street price on Sorrel. Payment just for information about him. And like the two deputies this morning, there were a lot of people out there who wouldn't care what they had to do, or to whom they had to do it, to collect.

"I am listening," she said bitterly. "I *have* been listening. For hours. And this is getting us nowhere. I don't know anything. Don't you think if I did, I would have told them before now? Told somebody? Don't you think if there were anything, any clue to what Rob did with their money, I would have figured it out by now? Do you have any idea how many nights I've spent doing nothing *but* trying to think about that? Trying to think of something—anything— that might make it possible for me to get my children out of this insanity?"

Again her voice had risen, her frustration far greater than his own. Disgusted with himself, Jordan released her. She couldn't tell him what she didn't know, and Kathleen was certainly smart enough to know that the money was the key. If Sorrel had left her a message of any kind about its location, she would already have figured it out. But she couldn't provide information she didn't have, as much as Jordan needed it.

"Go on," he said softly, regretful, but knowing there was nothing he could say that would make this any easier. "Go back to bed. We can talk tomorrow. We'll figure out what to do."

She didn't move, although his hands were no longer holding her prisoner. Gradually his eyes had begun to adjust to the darkness. Not enough to see her features, but enough to know exactly where she was. Still close enough that he could reach out and touch her. If he had had that right.

"I'm sorry," she said finally. The exhaustion that had haunted her eyes was in her voice.

"I know," he said softly. "Go on back to bed."

Suddenly his own fatigue seemed overwhelming. Maybe because he didn't know where else to turn. Or who to turn to. He had been counting on Jake's magic to get them out of this, and it wasn't there. Nor was Griff, who would have helped him find some way to protect them.

"And when I go back to bed, what are you going to do?"

"I'll be okay," he said.

Just as long as I don't think about this morning. As long as I don't look at you. Or at Jamie and Meg.

She nodded. He wasn't even sure how he knew that, but he did. But she didn't move away. They were still standing together in the darkness. No longer touching. No longer connected. Still, despite the issues of life and death they shared, almost strangers. Listening to the silence.

"I wanted him dead," she said, her tone totally changed, whispering out of the darkness.

It was a non sequitur, but it took only a second for him to understand. She had wanted her husband to be dead, and now that she knew he might be, she felt guilty.

"I would have wanted him dead, too," Jordan said truthfully. In fact he did, and he didn't even know Sorrel. "Anybody would have."

"He was my husband," she whispered, "the father of my children, and I can't find a shred of regret inside me that he might be dead."

Jordan nodded, not remembering she wouldn't be able to see him. He reached out and found her shoulder again, his fingers no longer cruel. In their touch was compassion for what he heard in her voice. And understanding.

The son of a bitch didn't deserve to have her grieve. Rob Sorrel had forfeited that right. And she shouldn't feel guilty because of what her husband had done. What had come between them was Sorrel's guilt, and not Kathleen's.

Jordan didn't say that, of course. He wanted this woman, a woman who still legally belonged to a man who had ruined her life with his greed. And because Jordan now wanted to take and protect what belonged to Sorrel, he knew he couldn't urge her to forget her husband, no matter how much he hoped that she would. That would have to be her decision. And it would have to be made in her own time.

He heard the breath she drew before she leaned against him. There was no doubt now of her intent. She laid her cheek against his chest, and her arms came around his waist. Without hesitation, Jordan enfolded her again, simply holding her.

He expected her to cry. He waited for the sounds to start, for the small movement her body would make against his just before her sobs broke through those barriers of calmness and courage she had built in order to keep functioning.

But nothing of what he waited for happened. There was only her body, resting against his. Finally, he put his hands on her shoulders again and forced her away from him a little, holding her so that he could look down into her face. He wanted to read what was there, and with the darkness, he couldn't. But he also couldn't bear the intrusion of the fluorescent light again.

"Whatever you feel about him," he said softly, "is your right. You've earned that right."

"I don't feel *anything* about him," she said. "I just don't feel anything...." The sentence trailed off, the whisper fading away in the darkness. And then she added, low enough that he almost didn't understand, "Make me feel something," she said. "Please, just make me *feel* something again."

Jordan thought he had read this plea in her eyes before, but he had denied himself the possibility of responding.

Now, whether because of what Jake had told him or because of what she had confessed, something had changed. The rules were different.

For almost three years she had been Rob Sorrel's victim. That seemed a long-enough punishment for a crime she hadn't committed. A long-enough sentence of loneliness, which she had served in the dark isolation of an unspeakable terror she fought alone. It didn't matter what anyone else might think, Jordan knew that whatever happened between the two of them, Rob Sorrel could demand no reparation, no atonement. Not from Kathleen.

And Jordan had learned long ago to deal with guilt. At least with whatever guilt was occasioned by the demands of duty. *Standing guard over those we love,* Griff Cabot had once said, trying to make the nearly unbearable burden of what the team sometimes had to do for their country make sense. As this did.

"Make me feel something," Kathleen had begged. *"Just make me feel something again...."* And he wanted to. Dear God, how he wanted to.

He lowered his head as his hands, locking on her shoulders again, pulled her upward. Her head tilted, falling backward on the slim column of her neck, exposing her mouth. His lips descended, aligning themselves over the trembling softness of hers.

The first movement was tentative, almost questioning, and for an endless heartbeat he thought she might not respond. And then her mouth relaxed under his, her breath sighing outward in release. Tension, guilt and fear were dissipated in an instant by that surrender.

In response, his tongue invaded, and hers answered. The sweet heat of her reaction surged through his body, a rage of blood rushing to make the satisfaction of what he had never demanded from her possible. Suddenly he was incredibly hard and tight, aching with need. With desire. With love.

He was a man who had learned exactly what qualities of

the human spirit he valued. And those were the very ones Kathleen Sorrel possessed. Courage in the face of unrelenting horror. The intelligence required to face and outwit an unforgiving enemy, as brutal as any Jordan himself had ever faced. And enough tenderness to keep two small children from being affected by the madness of the world they had been forced to inhabit.

It hadn't taken long for Jordan to fall in love with her. Kathleen embodied all that he had worked so long "to preserve and protect." All the nameless, faceless thousands who depended on men like Jordan Cross and Griff Cabot and Hawk and the rest of the team to fight these kinds of battles for them. She had fought hers alone. At least until now.

His hands released her shoulders and cupped her hips, lifting them into his arousal. When she realized what he was doing, her gasp was audible, and he hesitated until she moved again. That movement was not away from him. She pushed into his body, seeking a deeper contact.

He picked her up, his palms sliding under her thighs to support her weight. Her arms quickly fastened around his neck. Jordan took one step forward and set her on the counter where she had been perched earlier.

As soon as he did, he moved against her, positioning himself between her legs. But there were still too many barriers, he realized. Barriers to what he wanted to give. Barriers to what she had said she needed.

His left hand found the back of her neck, his fingers spreading and then sliding upward through her hair, pulling her head toward his. Her mouth met his again, and their tongues engaged in a slow, primitive waltz that mirrored the intensity of what they both really wanted.

His right hand slipped between their bodies, struggling to unfasten the metal buttons of his jeans. The hard bulge of his erection slowed the process, but trembling with need, his fingers finally succeeded. The sudden freedom from constriction seemed to intensify his arousal.

His left hand, the one at the back of her neck, shifted forward, stroking the smoothness of her skin. His fingers drifted over the fragile ridge of her collarbone and then into the shadowed valley between her breasts.

Her hands lifted, quickly finding the buttons of her shirt. Shaking, apparently as driven by need as his, her fingers hurried to undo them, one by one, and then she shrugged out of the garment, letting it fall off her shoulders and slipping her arms out of the sleeves almost in the same motion.

Jordan was aware of what she was doing, and his other hand came up to help. His fingers fumbled briefly over the clasp at the back of her bra and then released it. He pulled the bra away, dropping it to the floor. And then the heaviness of her breasts was supported only by his hands, cupping their softness.

His lips deserted her mouth, already plundered, and fastened over the peak of one nipple, which pearled instantly under the caress of his tongue. Circling, taunting and demanding. She lifted into his touch, her head falling back against the mirror behind her, and the gasping breath she had drawn at his first touch harshly expelled.

He let that nipple go and turned his head, beginning to nuzzle at the other and then to suckle it. His mouth pulled and released, the soft rhythmic sounds of what he was doing almost the same as the ones Jamie had made in his sleep.

And yet so different. Not the innocence of childhood, but the heated frenzy of adult need. A desperate need to banish loneliness. To reaffirm life in the midst of the deaths he had caused this morning.

His head was bent over her body, and the quality of her breathing told him what she might never put into words. But he knew from it that he had given her what she had said she wanted. The ability to feel.

To know again what she had once known? The worshipping touch of a man's hands on her body? The pressure of his mouth against her nipples, strongly suckling as her children had done?

Her fingers tangled suddenly in his hair, gripping hard, demanding now, holding him to her. His mouth still moved, roaming from one breast to the other, as her breathing deepened.

Finally, Jordan's right hand found the button at the waistband of her slacks and then the tab of the zipper. He pulled it down and slipped his hand inside, his fingers pushing downward, his palm moving over the smoothness of her belly.

He couldn't reach what he sought, and apparently she realized that. She began to push her slacks down, rocking a little from one hip to the other. As soon as their constriction eased, Jordan's fingers completed the journey.

Her body jerked with his first caress. She was incredibly slick, the hot, wet heat of her arousal preparing for his entrance. And he wanted nothing more than to drive into her. To bury everything that had happened today in the fulfillment of this. Something they controlled. Something they had chosen. Something born of life and not death. Of hope and not despair. Of love and not hate.

"Yes," she whispered, her voice low and harsh, her need as great as his.

And more easily satisfied, he realized.

"Yes," she whispered again, writhing against his hand.

His fingers moved, and she arched into them, her body blindly seeking what his, too, sought. Release. Forgetfulness. The freedom, for one brief moment, not to have to think or worry or plan. To know nothing but the loving touch, the shivering ecstasy. To remember nothing of fear or betrayal. To become, briefly, only the woman he loved. Someone without her terrible responsibilities. Without duty. Without a past.

Her breathing crescendoed as he tried to give her that freedom, his effort now as relentless as his questioning had been before, but motivated by love and not fear. She tried to hurry him, straining wildly against the building sensations, but he was in control, setting the pace. Taking her to the peak and then refusing to let her go. Refusing her culmination, each summit higher and yet more easily scaled than the last.

Until finally there was no way to stem the tide of sensation. He held her as shuddering tremors racked her body, her small outcry hoarse and guttural, gasped first into the darkness, and then buried against his shoulder as she arched. When it was over, her body collapsed in his arms, limp and spent.

He had succeeded. He had given her what she had asked him for. He had made her feel. And he could only hope he had shown her, too, what he felt.

KATHLEEN THOUGHT that they probably heard the sound at the same instant. Just as she became aware of the noise, Jordan's body stiffened. Then he stilled and waited, unmoving, listening just as she was, to Jamie's muted sobbing.

Neither of them responded. Her head was lying on his shoulder, his arms around her, her heaving breasts crushed against the wall of his chest. His breathing was almost as uneven as hers.

"Kathleen?" he whispered.

Unwilling to answer, she shook her head, and her fingers found his mouth, pressing against it in a silent warning. She waited, praying that Jamie would go back to sleep.

"He'll wake Meg," Jordan said finally.

His breath was warm and moist, stirring against the perspiration on her temple, and then his lips caressed that same spot, pushing the gentlest of kisses into her damp skin. There was no anger in his voice. No impatience at the interruption.

"I know," she said.

Still she didn't move. She didn't think she *could* move. Not away from him. Away from what she had just discovered with Jordan Cross. And it was not the physical release, as incredible as that had been. She just wanted his arms around her, holding her. Protecting her. Loving her.

The soft whimper from the bedroom seemed to grow in volume, its tone becoming more desperate. *Go back to sleep,* she begged silently. *Just go back to sleep.*

It wasn't so much to ask, considering that this was the first time she could remember *not* rushing to resolve the children's needs. Either one of them. They had always come first. They still did, but it seemed that just this once…

"Kath?" Jordan questioned, his tone amused, or at least resigned. But she couldn't bear what he had just said.

"Don't," she said. "Don't ever call me that."

Kath was what Rob had called her, and she didn't want to hear the diminutive because it reminded her too strongly of the very things she was trying to forget.

Like her marriage vows? her conscience demanded. Till death do us part? In sickness and in health? Rob was sick. She had known that. He would have had to be sick to do what he had done. To have put Meg and Jamie in this danger, to be so callous and uncaring of what happened to them.

Jordan's hand smoothed over her back, caressing, and again they listened together. Jamie's whimpering seemed to be fading, and Kathleen's mind began to leave the darkness where the children slept and return to this.

There was no heat in the slow glide of Jordan's hand across her back. His palm was a little rough, callused and very exciting. She savored the almost forgotten feel of a man's hand moving against her body. Sensual. Arousing.

"Mommy?" Meg called. Her voice was muffled by the distance and the closed door, but the small quiver in it indicated her unease at waking in the big bed alone.

What kind of mother was she? Kathleen wondered, just as she had wondered the night she let Jordan bring her to the top of the embankment, leaving her children in the wrecked car below. What kind of mother would let a stranger make love to her while her children slept in the room next door? When she had just learned that their father might be dead? What kind of woman did either of those things?

Finally, drawing strength from somewhere—probably that same small reserve she had drawn from so many times these last few years—she lifted her head and leaned back against the mirrored wall behind her. The glass was cold against her back.

Because she was naked, she realized. Bare from the waist up. Embarrassingly aware now of her nudity, she crossed her arms over her breasts, shivering slightly in reaction to the cold. Or to the realization of what she had done. Had allowed him to do.

"Mommy?" Meg called again, a hint of panic creeping into her voice.

Jordan stepped away from the counter she was sitting on. She heard him take another step on the tiled floor, but she wasn't prepared for the sudden blaze of light. His eyes sought hers and then traveled slowly over her face and down her neck, resting a long moment on her exposed body. She could only imagine what he was seeing. And thinking.

One hand still protectively covering her breasts, the other groping beside her, she found the shirt she had discarded. The right sleeve had fallen into the sink, and it was wet and cold, unpleasant against her skin as she struggled to pull it on.

Suddenly the dampness reminded her of the small ring of moisture on Jordan's shirt, left there by Jamie's mouth as he slept against the same hard chest that had just sheltered her. While Jordan gave her what she had told him she needed. While he cared for her, just as he had cared for Jamie.

And probably for the same reasons, she thought. Because they had both been crying against the darkness, fighting it, too tired to give in. For some reason that realization made her eyes sting. She fought the burn, denying an urge to give in to tears she couldn't afford.

Instead, she slid down off the counter, and as soon as she was standing, pulled her slacks up and zipped them. She even took time to make her trembling hands push the button through the hole. At least that gave her something to do so that she didn't have to look at Jordan. So she didn't have to see what she knew would be in his eyes.

"Mommy, Jamie's crying," Meg called again. Now the threat of tears was in her voice, too, and Kathleen made herself answer.

"I'm coming, Meggie. Tell him I'll be right there."

She stepped across the white tile—cold against her bare feet. Everything was so cold. She pushed down the handle of the commode, and the toilet flushed noisily. When she turned back, hurrying now to get to the bedroom, or maybe just to get out of here, she caught a glimpse of herself in the mirror.

Her hair was a tangled mess from the few restless hours she had slept. Her cheeks were flushed, whether reddened from embarrassment or from Jordan's late-night beard, she didn't know. Even her lips seemed swollen and used. She looked like a woman who had just made love. Or had been made love to, she amended.

Not love, she corrected. That wasn't what this had been, of course. She had made a request, a plea, and Jordan had fulfilled it. Any man would have. And it would have gone further, she acknowledged, if Jamie's crying hadn't interfered. She had been ready for this to go further. She had wanted it to.

Jordan was watching her, she realized suddenly, meeting his eyes in the mirror. She couldn't read what was in them, but whatever was there, she knew she didn't really regret what had just happened. No matter what kind of woman that made her, she couldn't regret that brief mindless ecstasy, which had taken her somewhere beyond fear and guilt.

A needed release that he had been denied. But there was nothing she could do about that. Not now. Her children were crying. They needed her, and their needs had always come before her own. Or before Jordan's. Because she was their mother.

And she was Rob's wife. She was married. Still married to Rob Sorrel, who was, as far as they *knew*, still alive. And no matter what she felt for Jordan...

Her eyes lifted again to meet the steady reflection of his. He looked almost as bad as she felt. His mouth was a thin, flat line, so tightly compressed a muscle twitched beside it. His eyes were cold and dark and empty. And his face seemed set in stone, the angles of the lean, handsome features, so much like Rob's, hard and sharp in the harshness of the bathroom light.

But then, Jordan Cross was a hard man. She knew that. She had certainly seen evidence of that this morning. He had to be hard, of course, to do what he had done. To be what he was.

"I'm sorry," she said softly.

She was. She had cheated him. By her actions she had promised something, and then she had reneged on that promise. That didn't work with children. It wasn't the kind of mother she was. And not the kind of woman. But all that was too hard to explain right now, and she was too tired to try.

"I am *so* sorry," she whispered again.

Then, without waiting for his reply, she pushed the light switch downward, plunging the room back into forgiving darkness, and opened the door.

Chapter Twelve

They probably hadn't said more than two words to one another this morning, Kathleen realized, as she folded Meg's nightgown and pushed it into the side pocket of the suitcase. Jordan had tried, however. She would give him credit for that.

Once he had even touched her arm, his thumb sliding slowly over the soft flesh inside her elbow, sending aftershocks of last night's eruption spiraling through her body. He had smiled at her above the children's heads, that small, secret morning-after smile lovers shared. But when his mouth opened to say something, she had turned away like a coward, unsure that she was ready to listen. Unsure how to respond if she did.

She'd been thinking about what had happened between them the whole time she dressed the children and picked up the toys that had somehow gotten scattered throughout the room, tossing them methodically back into the laundry basket. It had been especially hard going back into the bathroom. Brushing the children's teeth at the same sink where her discarded shirt had fallen last night. Washing their faces and at the same time avoiding looking at her own in the mirror.

The children had been subdued, just as they had been after the shooting, their eyes questioning and a little confused. Or maybe they were both just tired, which was understandable after the sporadic nature of their sleep last night. Or maybe they were disconcerted by waking up in strange surroundings again. By watching another round of packing. Leaving. Destroying.

Of course, they should be used to that by now, she thought bitterly. Usually, however, she was able to help them make the transition. Able to help them find something to look forward to. Today she couldn't seem to muster cheerfulness, not even the false kind, which might have helped to reassure them.

Only after she had gotten back into bed last night, a sleeping child snuggled warmly on either side of her trembling body, did the significance of what Jordan had suggested hit her. If Rob *were* dead—and she thought Jordan really believed that—then this was truly a nightmare without end. An eternal damnation of someone always hunting them. Always looking for the money Rob had taken. And because she had no idea where that money was, there would now be no way to get them off the merry-go-round ride of terror her husband had set his family on nearly three years ago. No way.

She had tried to change her identity, tried to get lost in the ordinary sameness of small-town life. She had made mistakes because she had had to learn the necessary skills to do that as she went along. Mistakes like using Meg's old immunization records. She had never even thought about that being dangerous.

Just as she had never thought about the computers that stored everything, all that information just waiting for someone to find it. Every medical record. Every purchase made on a credit card. Every phone call.

But she *should* have realized those things, she thought fiercely, damning herself for her stupidity, her naiveté. She couldn't afford either. She was the one who *had* to think of everything. Everything that could possibly put her children in danger. Every detail. That was her responsibility. Her job. Because if she failed them again…

She had blocked the unthinkable consequences of that, her mind racing over the same possibilities of escape she had considered for almost three years. She knew there were programs, things like Witness Protection, where the government made people disappear. She wasn't a witness to anything, however, and until the deputies' attempt this morning, there had been no overt violence.

That attack, the one she had been expecting for nearly three years, had finally come from law enforcement officers themselves. So who did she turn to to seek protection for her children? The FBI? she wondered. But if even the CIA couldn't successfully manage to change Jordan's identity...

Those thoughts had circled endlessly, always coming back to the central question. The same one that echoed again in her head this morning. What should they do next?

She wondered if those who believed it was sport to kill a defenseless animal could possibly imagine what this was like. Forever on the run. Being stalked, so that there was no place of safety. No place to rest. No sanctuary.

"Ready?" Jordan asked.

She looked up to find him standing in the doorway, the morning light coming into the room from behind him, so that he was little more than a silhouette against it. She realized that she had been looking down, unseeing, at her hands, which had stilled over the suitcase she was supposed to be repacking.

She wondered again, just as she had all morning, what Jordan thought about what had happened last night. What he thought about her. About what she had let him do.

What she had asked him to do, she amended, always honest with herself. Because he hadn't touched her until she had asked him. He had held her. Comforted her. And that had been all—until she had begged him for something more. *"Just make me feel something...."*

"I think that's everything," she said, taking one last look around the room. It gave her an excuse to turn away, to hide from his eyes, to hide whatever he might be able to read in her face.

Out of habit, she tried to think of all the places where something might have been left behind. "I guess I'd better check the bathroom," she said. Then, remembering what had happened in that small cold room last night, she wished she hadn't.

"I'll take the kids out to the car," Jordan suggested.

She nodded agreement, her gaze finding the two children. They were on sitting on the floor in one corner of the room, out of the way. Kathleen had asked Meg to help Jamie with one of the puzzles she had picked out of the laundry basket. The pieces were almost big enough for him to manage on his own, but sharing the task had given them both something to do.

Kathleen had thought it might help if she could have just a minute or two alone. Some time to put what had happened between her and Jordan into some kind of perspective. It probably didn't loom nearly as large in his consciousness as it did in hers.

Men were different. They didn't think the same way women did about initiating intimacy. But she had never done anything like that. Not even in the beginning with Rob. He had been the one who'd always tried to push her toward making theirs that kind of relationship.

She took a deep breath and walked across the room to the bathroom door. It was standing half-open. The light that had seemed painfully bright last night, especially after the quiet darkness, didn't seem nearly so intense this morning.

She walked over to the shower stall. The sound of her steps echoed slightly off the hard tile, and she remembered its coldness against her bare feet. She pulled back the curtain, checking for anything that might have been left there.

Jordan had taken a shower this morning. There was still a faint hint of steam in the room, and the scent of the motel's soap clung to the curtain and the enclosure. But he had left nothing behind. Nothing but memories had been left in this room.

She turned around and, as she had last night, caught a glimpse of her reflection in the mirror over the counter. The physical evidence of what had happened between them, which she had seen so clearly then, had been erased by the intervening hours. Her cheeks were pale now. If anything, they were too pale, no longer marked by the abrasion of Jordan's unshaven skin. Her hair was neatly combed, and she was fully clothed.

Surprisingly, she looked exactly the same as she always did. The same way she looked every morning when she dressed for work. Before she loaded Jamie and Meg into the car and drove them to school and to day care.

She didn't look like a woman who had begged for a man's touch only minutes after she had been told her husband was probably dead. *"Make me feel,"* she had pleaded, and Jordan had done exactly what she had asked him to.

He had made her feel. Emotions and sensations she hadn't thought about in months. In years. And more tellingly, he had made her hungry to feel them again. Still hungry. For his touch. For his hands. His concern. His strength.

She was a woman. In all that had happened in her life, she had almost forgotten that. And yet, despite her situation, she had the same needs and desires every woman did. Jordan had simply reminded her of them.

Because he looked like Rob? Because she was so grateful to him for what he had done yesterday morning on that isolated stretch of snow-covered road? Because she really thought that he might be strong enough, and smart enough, to keep her children safe? Or maybe because...

The eyes of the woman in the mirror stared back at her, that incredible thought revealed in their sudden widening. *Because she had fallen in love with a stranger?* A stranger who had touched her in the darkness. Who had held her. And who had made no promises.

She hadn't understood, not even then, all the reasons she

had whispered that soft plea last night. Or why she had allowed this man make love to her. Allowed him to touch her. To caress her in one of the most intimate ways a man can touch a woman.

But she had, because, just as she'd told him, she had needed to feel *something*. Just to be certain that it was still possible to feel those things after such a long, aching loneliness?

As she watched, the too-thin body of the woman in the mirror seemed to straighten. Her chin tilted upward and her eyes, which had looked so empty only a moment ago, suddenly filled with moisture. She closed them tightly, blacking out the image and denying the hot spill of tears.

Denying, just as she always did, she supposed, her right to feel. The right to express her needs. To put them, if only for a moment, above the needs of her children. She had always denied herself the right to do that.

Except last night. And in spite of what she thought she *should* feel about what had happened between her and Jordan Cross, who was a stranger, she really didn't feel it. Maybe that was why she hadn't known what to say to him this morning. Because she thought there wasn't enough remorse in her soul for the sin she had committed—betraying the vows she had made to Rob. She wished she could find more, but this betrayal, measured against the one Rob had made…

She turned away from the mirror and left the room. As she crossed the bedroom, she resisted the inclination to straighten the disordered bed. That had been her failing, Rob said. She always wanted everything to be perfect. She wanted to fix all the rough edges. To smooth and straighten the very fabric of their lives.

And maybe that's why Rob hated her so much, she thought. Only after the words had formed in her head did she realize the significance of them. She had never acknowledged that thought before, but now she realized that it must be true.

Rob had hated their life together or he would never have done what he had done. And whatever he had hated must have been generated by his feelings about her.

But it was far too late, she supposed, to change anything. Rob had left, and whatever blame she bore for what had gone wrong between them, it couldn't be fixed now. And the results of it couldn't be changed.

It seemed that there was nothing about this situation that could be changed. Not, she acknowledged, unless Jordan was somehow capable of doing it.

JORDAN WATCHED KATHLEEN cross the parking lot toward the car. He had put the children in the back, Jamie in his car seat and Meg strapped in with the shoulder harness. She hadn't wanted his help, pushing his hands away from the seat belt.

Apparently Meg was afraid of him now. That was something else he'd have to work on. Right now the important thing was keeping her safe. He'd worry about winning her trust when he got them out of this. *If* he got them out of this.

He erased that caveat, denying it, as his eyes followed Kathleen's progress. He knew the exact moment when she looked up and realized he was standing by the passenger-side door. Waiting for her. A meeting between them unavoidable.

Her stride checked briefly, an almost undetectable faltering. Undetectable, maybe, if he hadn't been looking for it. He had been, of course, because after the way she acted this morning, he knew she didn't want to talk to him. And he had decided that wasn't going to be an option any longer.

After the small hesitation, she continued walking, her eyes holding his as she approached. This was more the attitude he associated with Kathleen Sorrel, he realized, still watching her. A willingness to meet things head-on.

Just like her angry approach the night he had parked his car on the edge of the church parking lot. He hadn't known what to expect at the time, because he hadn't understood the situation, but still, her decision on a face-to-face confrontation with a stranger who was following her had surprised him. Now that he knew her, it wouldn't have, of course.

"What's wrong?" she asked when she was within a couple of feet. Her voice was low, maybe to keep the children from overhearing their conversation, but it seemed there was an edge of uneasiness in it as well.

"Nothing's wrong. I just thought we ought to talk."

Her mouth tightened, but she nodded, her eyes never leaving his.

"You're uncomfortable about what happened last night," he said. It had taken him awhile to figure that out. He had thought at first she was angry, but eventually he had been able to read her body language a little better than that, despite her refusal to look at him. That had been a good clue, of course. If she'd been angry, he decided, she would have confronted him.

She didn't answer immediately. Her eyes examined his face, but he wasn't sure what she was looking for. Or whether she had found it.

"What happened last night..." she began. She took a breath, and when she released it, she shook her head. "I'm not like that," she said finally.

"Like what?" Jordan asked, controlling the urge to smile. He couldn't believe she was embarrassed, but a soft rose that certainly looked like a blush was creeping into her cheeks.

She had wanted his touch last night as much as he had wanted to touch her, and she was having a hard time dealing with that this morning. She didn't say anything for a moment, but her lips compressed, tightening into a line, and her eyes fell. He felt guilty about teasing her.

"Not sensual?" he suggested softly.

Her eyes lifted, searching his face.

"Desirable?" he said, his tone softer, even more intimate.

Her eyes widened slightly, but they clung to his, and he let the silence build, using it. And finally the tactic worked.

"I thought you would..." Again her words trailed away.

Finally he smiled at her. "You were afraid I'd embarrass you in front of the children?"

She shook her head, a crease forming between her brows.

"Because I wouldn't be able to keep my hands off you," he suggested.

"Be angry." She finished the sentence she had begun, but of course it didn't fit into the context he'd just created. Or with the low sensuality of his deep voice. And it certainly didn't fit with the words he'd just uttered.

"Why did you think I'd be angry?" he asked, puzzled.

He really didn't understand what she meant. Maybe he'd been wrong about the source of her silence, he thought. Was she, like Meg, afraid of him?

Except she hadn't been last night. She had been tired of his questions and frustrated that he was still asking them, long after she had told him everything she thought she knew. That's why he had kept on, of course. On the off chance that she knew something she didn't realize she knew.

"Because you didn't want to answer any more questions?" he suggested. "I understood that. I knew you were tired."

"Not that," she said.

"Then what?"

"I guess...because of what happened afterward," she whispered.

"Believe me, Kathleen. What happened afterward made me feel a lot of things. I don't remember anger being one of them."

"When I left," she said.

He nodded, still trying to understand, and then he did. "You thought I'd be angry because...there was some unfinished business between us," he said. He tried to inject enough amusement into his voice so that she'd understand that he hadn't been. And still be very clear that he had been disappointed.

He had never expected to make love to her last night. He had known that with the children there, it wasn't an option. Then she had taken his hand and led him into the bathroom, and his expectations had, he admitted, suddenly gotten a little out of control. But he had always understood her children would come first. Certainly before whatever was starting to grow between the two of them.

They had known one another only a few days. And Jordan was certainly experienced enough to know that just because *he* had finally found someone who was the essence of what he believed a woman should be, it didn't mean she was in love with him. He intended to do everything to ensure that eventually she would be, of course.

Judging by her reactions last night, that hadn't been a bad way to start. He hadn't counted on having her worry about him. Or worry about his reaction to the interruption. He hadn't dreamed she would think he was angry because the kids woke up.

"Are you saying you weren't?" she asked.

"I'm saying that I wanted to make love to you last night. And I would have, if that was what *you* wanted. What you were ready for. I'm a patient man, Kathleen. I'm not going to rush you. Not into anything," he said softly.

He let her see what was in his eyes, and hoped that she'd be able to read the truth there. He had learned a lot of things working for Griff. Patience was only one of them, but still, it had been a major part of the specialized service he performed for the team. It had to be. So he had cultivated it. And practiced it.

There was nothing that would delight him more than demonstrating to Kathleen exactly the scope of the patience he possessed. It might take him a lifetime, but he had known last night, maybe even before, that he was in this for the long haul. Kathleen was the one who apparently needed some time to understand that.

"Thank you," she said, russet eyes locked on his, a suspicion of tears in them, so that they looked a little like Jamie's.

"As fast or as slow as you want this to happen. I'm not going anywhere," he promised.

I'm not like him. I'm not the running kind. He wanted to tell her that, but saying the words would be a reminder of something he wanted her to forget. A reminder of another man who had done exactly that.

Despite the threatening tears, suddenly the corners of Kathleen's mouth tilted slightly, the movement a little tremulous, but obviously a smile. "I didn't mean that," she said. "I wasn't thanking you for that."

He tilted his head and allowed one dark brow to lift, inquiring, and watched her smile widen.

"I meant to say thank you for last night," she said.

Suddenly, the heat pushed through his body in a long, slow wave of flame, his arousal seeming even stronger than when he had held her in the darkness last night. Because now he also had the memory of her body arching, reacting so strongly, so incredibly to his touch.

He also remembered her relaxing into his arms when it was over. Trusting. Trusting enough to allow him to take control away from her. Especially trusting for Kathleen since that rigid control had been all that had kept her children safe for three years. Last night she had given herself— and at least part of that responsibility—into his keeping. Maybe, however, she hadn't fully realized that.

"I think I'm the one who should say thank you," he said. "And you have nothing to apologize for. Nothing to regret," he added.

He touched her chin, catching it between his thumb and forefinger. He wanted to kiss her, to claim her mouth again, but that probably wouldn't be the best idea with the kids in the car beside them. Especially Meg. So instead, he ran his thumb along the fullness of Kathleen's bottom lip, the smallest caress.

Her mouth opened slightly, and then her tongue touched the pad of his thumb. His hand froze as he savored the sweet heat of her mouth. Wanting it moving under his again. Wanting to have her alone somewhere. Just the two of them.

Somewhere safe. When this was all over and when there was time to explore all the ways he could make her say thank-you. Surely that wasn't too much to ask.

But not here. And not now.

"I think you better get in the car," he said. "Meg's not real fond of me this morning. I don't think she'd be pleased if I did what I want to do right now."

"What is that?"

"Kiss you. For starters," he added.

"I don't think that would be any of Meg's business," Kathleen said softly, smiling at him. "Despite how she acts, she isn't really in charge."

"I know," Jordan said. "But all the same, she's got a stake in this. I need to consider mending a few fences with her instead of making her any more unhappy to have me around."

"And why is that?" Kathleen asked.

He wasn't sure if she really hadn't figured it out or if she just wanted to hear him say it. "Because I'm very much in love with her mother. And because I really am in this for the long haul. I'm here for as long as you want me to be, Kathleen. As long as you'll let me be."

Her eyes widened and her lips parted, but she didn't say anything. Her eyes held his, her very breathing suspended.

And he wanted again to put his mouth over hers, to kiss her until she melted into his embrace as she had last night. Instead, he released her chin and turned to open the door of the car.

When he looked at her again, he realized that she really hadn't known how he felt. He would let her think about it awhile before he gave her the opportunity to say no. After all, there were still a few problems to be solved before any of what he had been talking about could happen.

Problems like Sorrel and the money he had stolen. And what to do about all the people who were determined to find it. People who believed that the best way to do that was to go through Sorrel's wife. Once he'd worked his way through those obstacles—or around them, Jordan thought, remembering Griff—then the rest of this would fall into place. But first, before any of what he wanted could happen, they had to find Sorrel. Or find the money.

Chapter Thirteen

"Are you sure we're safe here?" Kathleen asked hesitantly.

It had been a long day, and she didn't know how Jordan had managed the mileage they had achieved during the course of it. They had stopped only twice, once for lunch and again for dinner, but other than those brief intervals, they had been driving since they'd left the motel this morning. All the way to Virginia.

She had done some of it, of course, while Jordan grabbed a few hours of much-needed sleep, but he had driven the last four or five hours straight. His eyes, red rimmed with fatigue, bore evidence of how exhausted he was.

"As safe as anywhere we could be right now, I think," he said, his voice reassuring. "The security here is as good as it gets."

She nodded, although she hadn't been able to tell much about the big house in the darkness. She had carried Jamie on her hip as they climbed the long flight of steps leading up to the front door. Jordan had carried Meg.

The little girl had fought against sleep as they drove through the long hours, refusing to give in to her exhaustion, even after nightfall. When she finally succumbed, it seemed that nothing could wake her—not even Jordan taking her from the car and carrying her up the wooden steps that had been laid along the oceanside cliff on which the house perched.

That was not the case with Jamie, of course, who had again slept through too many hours of the day. Now that they were inside, he was wide awake and interested in his new surroundings. Kathleen was afraid to let him explore, since so many of the objects on the tables and shelves of the Victorian summer home seemed to be old and valuable. The decor had not been designed with an active and curious two-year-old in mind.

She glanced over to where Jamie was pushing his trucks over the Oriental rug that covered the wide-plank hardwood floor in the study. He was happily making truck noises, obviously relieved to be out of the confinement of the car seat.

Jordan had built a fire in the fireplace, and the damp chill that had pervaded the old mansion when they'd arrived was finally beginning to dissipate, at least from this room. She should take off Jamie's jacket, Kathleen thought, but she was almost too tired to move, and she thought he'd be all right for a few more minutes. The room could not yet, by any stretch of the imagination, be called too warm.

Jordan was typing something into the computer on the desk, which he had booted up as soon as he finished building the fire. Kathleen wondered if he was contacting his friend at the CIA, the one who had suggested Rob might be dead.

That was something else she had thought about all day— the possibility that her husband was dead and the implications of that for their lives. Which were frightening enough that she decided she didn't like to think about them. Right now, she just wanted to enjoy the sanctuary this house seemed to offer.

Her eyes drifted around the big room, with its mix of antiques, comfortable overstuffed furniture and books. The computer that occupied a good portion of the desk seemed incongruous, an unlikely mix of the new with all the old that surrounded them.

There was also a photograph on the desk, a simple snapshot in an ornate silver frame. It was a picture of a little girl with long blond hair. She appeared to be about Meg's age, maybe a year or so older, judging by her gap-toothed smile.

Kathleen's eyes moved from the photo to find her own daughter. Meg was sleeping on the sofa where Jordan had laid her, clutching the rag doll Kathleen had almost left behind in Texas. Apparently, in the stress of the last two days, Raggedy Ann had become something of a security blanket, a reminder of a more stable time in her daughter's life. A happier time.

Kathleen wondered if the laughing child in the picture was the daughter of the house's owner, who was apparently another of Jordan's friends. He hadn't offered any explanation other than that of why he had brought them here. Or of why he believed they'd be safe here.

"Why don't we go upstairs and sleep out what's left of the night," Jordan suggested. "I don't suppose I'll get an answer to that tonight."

Lost in thought, Kathleen hadn't been aware when he moved away from the computer, but he was now standing close to the wing chair she was sitting in. She thought again how tired he looked. And about what he had said this morning. The promise of it. Those words, too, had run endlessly through her mind during the day.

"They're probably asleep. Whoever you're trying to contact," she clarified. "I guess everybody should be at this time of night."

"Everybody except Jamie," he said.

Her gaze followed his to the little boy, still varooming his trucks across the rug. Jordan had gone back down to the car to get their suitcases and then the basket of toys, so at least Jamie had plenty of things to play with.

"My night to entertain him," Kathleen said, turning back to face Jordan. "You need to sleep."

He nodded, not even bothering to deny his tiredness. "I'll carry Meg up when I go. As I remember, there are three suites on the second floor. I imagine you'll want the children in the same room with you."

"I think I'll feel better if they are."

"Nobody followed us, Kathleen," he said. "You don't have to worry about them finding us. Not here. I turned the security system back on after I got your suitcase."

"What if someone else knows the codes?" she asked. That's how Jordan had gotten in past the system he claimed was state-of-the-art. She supposed it might be, but he hadn't seemed to have any trouble.

"The people who know these codes *aren't* the ones we have to worry about," Jordan said.

His eyes had lightened, and he seemed almost amused, but she didn't take that to mean he was belittling her concerns. The amusement seemed more a reaction to the thought of the people he'd mentioned. The others who, like him, knew all about this house and its security systems. The people they *didn't* need to worry about.

"I guess I've been conditioned to worry about everything," she said. "To consider every possibility."

"I know. I know you've had to do that. But for tonight at least…" He hesitated, and when he finished, it was almost the same promise he had made this morning. "Let me do the worrying tonight."

She nodded, smiling at him, not reluctant to share the burden she had carried alone for so long. Two or three slow seconds ticked by, their eyes holding.

She wondered if he were remembering, as she was, what had happened last night. After their conversation by the car, that was now a memory she could savor, even if their situation, and the children, precluded anything like that happening tonight, she acknowledged. And in all honesty, that was something she regretted.

Trying to hide that sudden thought, which she was sure would be reflected in her eyes, she stood and began to gather up the things she would take upstairs. Trying to think about something besides Jordan and what had happened between then. Trying to think about almost *anything* else.

They couldn't get the children and all their paraphernalia

upstairs in one trip. Of course, letting Jamie climb the long staircase that led to the second floor might work off some of his excess energy. She could manage the suitcase and hold his hand at the same time. The toys could stay down here. That would leave Jordan with only Meg to carry.

Kathleen's gaze again found her daughter, and she was grateful the little girl was sleeping so soundly. Meg's near-hostility to Jordan had been obvious during the course of the long day, and yet Kathleen had had no opportunity to talk to her about it. Maybe tomorrow, she thought. Maybe when they weren't all so exhausted.

"Ready?" Jordan asked, just as he had this morning.

At least they had a safe place to sleep, she thought. Sanctuary, if only for a little while. And so she nodded, reaching for Jamie's hand.

SHE WASN'T SURE what awakened her. Maybe nothing more than the morning sunlight pouring through the sheer curtains that covered the windows of the suite she had chosen. Jordan had built a fire in the sitting room, and she had watched Jamie play with his trucks until he had become sleepy enough for them to join Meg in the big bed.

Which was exactly where they all were now. Usually Jamie was the early riser, but he was sleeping, the sun touching his baby-fine hair with a tinge of copper. Kathleen turned her head and realized that Meg was sound asleep, as well. Neither of them had been what awakened her.

She lay in the unfamiliar bed a few minutes, listening for some noise that might be repeated. Only the quietness of the old house surrounded them. Still...

She slipped carefully out of bed, climbing over Jamie, who was usually a much deeper sleeper than Meg. Kathleen had put on her nightgown last night, opting not to sleep in her clothes as she had at the motel. Jordan had said they would be safe here, and she trusted him. Apparently, since it was late morning, he hadn't been mistaken.

She walked over to the windows and pushed one of the

curtains aside. The Atlantic foamed gray-green against the rocks below. The water looked choppy and cold, even for midwinter. And it seemed she could feel the ocean's chill, especially here beside the wall of glass.

She let the curtain fall back into place, and stood a moment, arms crossed over her breasts, unconsciously rubbing the palms of her hands up and down from shoulder to elbow. Whatever had awakened her had left a sense of unease. And was still unaccounted for.

She wondered if Jordan could already be up. Given the amount of sleep he'd lost in the last couple of days, she would be surprised if he wasn't, like the children, still dead to the world. Not a good choice of words, she decided, shivering before she turned away from the expanse of cold glass.

She couldn't quite decide whether the chill of the room was invigorating or whether she had simply slept long enough. The bed, despite the two small occupants she loved so dearly, didn't seem half so inviting as the prospect of a cup of coffee. Given that the house seemed to have been occupied in the not-so-distant past, she thought it was possible that there might be a canister of coffee still around the kitchen. She was always better in the mornings after some caffeine to jump-start her system.

She thought about rousing the children to go downstairs with her, worrying briefly about the possibility of their waking alone and frightened in a strange place. But it wouldn't take her ten minutes to make coffee—if there was any in the kitchen. And if there wasn't, then she would be back up here sooner than that.

Ten minutes, she thought, watching the regular rise and fall of their breathing. Neither child had stirred, not even when she'd climbed out of bed. They appeared to be in a state of deep sleep and, based on all her previous experiences with them, they would remain so—at least for ten more minutes.

KATHLEEN DIDN'T TAKE TIME to dress. Her gown was flannel, full and substantial enough to be modest, even if Jordan were already up. Not that it wasn't a little late to be worrying about modesty, she thought, her lips tilting in remembrance as she descended the stairs. And in anticipation. With one hand she held up the hem so her feet wouldn't get tangled in its voluminous folds.

"Mrs. Sorrel?"

The inflection seemed questioning, but when she lifted her shocked eyes to find the speaker, she knew that was an illusion. The man who stood at the foot of the stairs knew exactly who she was. His surety was revealed in his eyes.

She hesitated, one bare foot extended. She was probably seven or eight steps from the bottom, far enough away from him that he wouldn't be able to reach her if she tried to run. Of course, given the length of her gown and his longer stride, he would probably catch her before she could reach the second floor and the children.

Besides, there was always the possibility that he didn't know where Meg and Jamie were. And the possibility that, just as he had been two days ago, Jordan was already aware of what was going on and even now preparing to do something about it. Preparing to protect them.

Please, dear God, Kathleen prayed. *Let him be. Please let Jordan be awake. Let him know what's going on. Please keep my babies safe.*

The wordless prayers were a jumble, emotional outpourings that formed in her brain with lightning rapidity, as did the decision not to run. As she prayed, the man standing at the foot of the stairs began to reach into his inside coat pocket.

Kathleen's heart dropped, its too-sudden descent into the cold pit of her stomach nauseating. Instead of the gun she'd been expecting, however, he removed a flat leather case from his pocket and flipped it open with a practiced twist of his wrist.

"Special Agent Donald Helms, Mrs. Sorrel. New Orleans. FBI Organized Crime Division."

Her eyes moved to focus on what he was showing her, and then she wondered why she had bothered. What he held looked official enough, but despite the fact that she had talked to a couple of FBI agents after Rob disappeared, she had not looked too closely at the identification they'd showed her. All she knew for certain was that this middle-aged, slightly overweight man had not been one of those she'd talked to back then.

"Thank God we found you," he said, smiling at her in an almost avuncular way. He seemed genuinely relieved.

Wary, trying not to make a mistake when it was so important, Kathleen didn't return the smile, concentrating on reading his eyes instead. After a moment, his smile faded. He closed the leather case, slipping it back into his coat pocket.

He was wearing a beige raincoat over a dark suit, a white shirt and striped tie. If she had had to dress someone up to pretend to be a government agent, this would be the costume she'd choose. The same one that had been used in every movie she'd ever seen. Every TV show. And almost exactly like the other FBI men she'd talked to, she acknowledged.

"It's over, Mrs. Sorrel," he said. "We're going to take care of you and the children from now on."

She allowed her eyes to scan the hall behind him, even glancing at the open doors that led into the parlor. There was no sign of Jordan. But there was also no sign of anyone else. No partner, she realized, although he kept saying "we."

And FBI agents didn't work alone. She supposed that they could be doing something like the deputies had done out at the trailer, one coming inside and the other checking the grounds. Of course, the deputies...

And her heart, which had begun to slow a little, began to race again, adrenaline flooding her system. Deliberately, she brought her eyes back to focus on the face of the man standing below her. She fought for control, fighting harder, it seemed, than she had ever been forced to fight at any other time in this long dark battle.

"My name is Barbara Simmons," she said. Her voice was low, and there was nothing in it, she prayed, to betray her panic. "If you're looking for someone named Sorrel, then I'm afraid you must have the wrong house."

"We know everything," Helms said reassuringly. He smiled at her again, amusement touching his brown eyes. They appeared compassionate. And friendly. And surprisingly honest. "We can keep you safe, Mrs. Sorrel. You and your children."

"I don't know what you're talking about," Kathleen said stubbornly.

His mouth tightened a little, but his eyes didn't leave her face. He seemed to consider a moment, and then nodded, the movement slight.

"I don't know what he told you, ma'am. I can only guess what kind of story they made up to fool you with, but whatever it was, the man who brought you here *wasn't* telling you the truth. He was sent to gain your trust. That was his job. And…I guess he did it pretty well." He hesitated, brown eyes still patient, still compassionate. "But he's not your husband, Mrs. Sorrel, and I think you must know that by now."

Kathleen still said nothing, trying to piece it together. Jordan wasn't her husband, of course. She had known that almost from the beginning. But if this man knew that Jordan looked like Rob, and yet wasn't, then…

Then what? she wondered. She didn't know what that meant—the fact that this man understood that although Jordan looked like her husband, he wasn't.

"It was a scam," he said, almost as if he had read her mind, had followed that train of thought. "You were supposed to do just exactly what…" He hesitated again before he started over. "You were supposed to believe just what I guess you did believe. Who did he tell you he was, Mrs. Sorrel? Someone who had come to help you, obviously.''

The nausea pushed into her throat, but she forced herself to go over everything Jordan had said that first morning. Remembering it all. And, despite what this man had said, remembering the night they had spent in the motel as well.

All the images ran through her mind. She tried to sort through them unemotionally, because she couldn't afford to make a mistake. She remembered the first time she had noticed the faint scar, and what she had thought then, deliberately recreating her initial suspicions, examining them.

''Whoever he is, he must be pretty good,'' Helms said. ''He's made you believe he's really trying to get you all out of this, hasn't he?''

Just like you're trying to make me believe, Kathleen thought, fighting her sickness. Fighting against the steady confidence in this man's voice. Fighting because she didn't think she could bear another betrayal.

''They set you up, Mrs. Sorrel. They need your cooperation because they've run out of options, and they realized, belatedly I guess, that they had made a dangerous mistake offering money for information about your husband. Dangerous for you. So they sent this guy. If he could make you trust him, then maybe, they figured, you'd spend some time with him. Be willing to answer some questions. They're hoping you'll tell him something that would allow them to find what they're looking for. And you know what that is.''

''Be willing to answer some questions for him.'' And she had. A lot of questions. Endless questions about almost everything that had happened to them since Rob left. A detailed questioning that had been both relentless and unceasing, until she'd gotten angry and tried to walk away.

''They figure you have to know something,'' Helms continued, his voice still calm and so reasonable. All of it was reasonable. More so than the story Jordan had told her. That he was CIA. That during plastic surgery they had given him Rob's face by accident.

And yet she *had* believed him, she realized. Despite her doubts at the beginning, eventually she had swallowed it all, hook, line and sinker. Agent Helms was right. The man who called himself Jordan Cross was very good.

"They want to find out whatever you might know," Helms added. "Even stuff you maybe don't realize you know. They figure you're their last shot at getting back the money your husband took. They aren't going to leave you alone until they find it. You need to understand that."

If she accepted what he was saying, then she had to accept that Jordan was the enemy. That nothing he had told her was true. That everything he had said to her from the very beginning was a lie. That he had lied so he could interrogate her. And that someone was paying him to do it.

Paying him? she thought, sickened again when she remembered the cold mirror against her naked back. And the way she had looked when she'd caught a glimpse of herself afterward.

But he hadn't touched her until she had asked him to, her heart argued, fighting against what her mind was slowly being forced to accept. But maybe he was that smart. Smart enough to understand both her need and how she would interpret his restraint. Maybe just that smart...

"Are your children upstairs, Mrs. Sorrel?" Helms asked softly.

She should answer him, she knew, but somehow she couldn't force the words past the nausea in her throat. Were her children upstairs, sleeping in a room next door to one of the scavengers who had hunted them for three years? Next door to a man who was ruthless enough to endure plastic surgery in order to trick her into talking to him, into answering his questions?

And then, sickened anew, finally she remembered the other. The thing that had made him a hero in her eyes. That had left no doubt in her mind that his story was true, and that he was exactly who and what he had told her he was.

She remembered the dark hole that bullet had left in a

dead man's forehead. Was Jordan Cross, or whatever his name was, ruthless enough to kill those two men, when he himself had the same goals?

If he were one of them, she acknowledged, then of course he was. He would do anything to get back the money Rob had stolen. He'd try to get information any way he could, even if it meant using her. Using her children.

"Is *he* up there with them, Mrs. Sorrel?" Helms asked.

Slowly she nodded, and he nodded in reply. "You want to come on down here, ma'am, out of the way, and let us do our job?" he suggested.

"I want my children," she whispered. "I want to get them out of there first."

"I'm not sure we can do that right now," he said. There was genuine regret in his voice, and his eyes held steady on hers.

"Let me get them and bring them down here before you go up."

"That might wake him."

She shook her head. "He hasn't had much sleep," she said.

Because he had held Jamie. Some small part of her trust in Jordan must have remained intact to remind her of that. He had held Jamie most of the night. He had sung to him, silly little songs, making up half the words he had obviously forgotten. And he had told him stories until he was almost hoarse. And then the rest of the night—

"He's a very dangerous man, Mrs. Sorrel. He's a real danger to your children. He killed two deputies in Texas. Gunned them down in cold blood. They never had a chance. We figure they must have gotten on to him somehow, and so he took them out before they could let you know what was going on."

That hadn't been what happened, of course. But maybe the FBI didn't know what had really happened. Maybe they didn't know that the deputies had also wanted the money Rob had stolen.

A whole hell of a lot of money that everyone wanted, she thought. Enough money to make Rob willing to betray his family. And enough to make Jordan do what he had done?

Or enough to set this trap. Another trick. A ploy that she was being rescued. A scam. Maybe one even more elaborate than the one he was accusing Jordan of setting up.

"Why don't you come on downstairs, Mrs. Sorrel. Let us do our job," he urged softly. "Then this thing will be finished. You come on down, and let us take care of him. We'll put you into protective custody, and this will finally be over. Your children will be safe. All you have to do is come downstairs."

Chapter Fourteen

She didn't, of course.

She whirled instead, running back up the staircase. She had expected Helms to catch her on the landing, and when she reached it and realized she was still free, exhilaration broke through whatever restraint had been holding her. Or maybe it broke through the last shred of doubt he had created.

"Jordan," she screamed, hands clutching the flannel gown, holding it high, exposing her legs up to her knees as she flew up the second half of the staircase. "Jordan," she yelled again when she neared the top.

She could hear Helms, or whoever he was, his breathing labored as he pounded up the stairs behind her. Suddenly she was in the hall. The room she had shared with the children was the first one on the right, but she passed it by without even slowing, bare toes digging into the carpet runner, frantic to stay ahead of her pursuer. Frantic to wake Jordan.

"Jordan." She called his name again as she flung open the door of the room next to the one where the children were sleeping.

It was empty. The morning sun poured through its windows, as tranquil as it had five minutes ago in the room next door. Like a spotlight, it illuminated the bed, which she could see through the doorway across the sitting room. The bed was made, she realized, the blue silk coverlet as smooth and undisturbed as even she could have wished it.

The next room, her mind suggested. Her feet had already responded to that decision, skidding a little on the waxed wood as she tried to get traction to make the turn away from this doorway. Then, out of the corner of her eye, she caught movement in the direction she'd come from.

Helms had topped the stairs and started down the hall. In his hand was the gun she had expected before. Her brain registered that fact, and then acknowledged she had wasted time in looking at him. She'd begun to turn, heading for the next room, when she became aware of something else. Another movement.

And, realizing what it was, she froze, horror holding her motionless. Helms's headlong rush had also slowed. He was gripping the gun with both hands now, steadying it in preparation for firing, obviously expecting the appearance of the man whose name she had been calling. Expecting to face Jordan, because the door of the room where she had left the children asleep had begun to move, swinging inward.

Jamie stepped through it, the seat of his yellow pajamas drooping under the weight of a soggy disposable diaper. Meg was right behind him, still clutching Raggedy Ann. She hesitated in the doorway, her hand on her brother's shoulder.

"Mommy," Meg called tentatively.

She leaned out past the door frame, her face turned toward the stairs. Kathleen knew exactly when Meg saw the man with the gun. The little girl shrank back, trying to pull Jamie with her, but by that time the toddler, who had been looking in the other direction, spotted Kathleen. He jerked forward, and Meg's fingers slipped off his shoulder.

"Don't move," Helms shouted.

No one listened to him. Kathleen started toward her children, trying to get between them and the gun. She knew there was probably no power on earth that could stop Jamie from running toward her, not once he had seen her. Desperate, Meg reached for her brother again, stepping into the hallway, grabbing at the back of his pajamas. She missed.

So did the bullet. It plowed into the floor beside Jamie's feet, sending slivers of wood upward and leaving a long, light-colored scar in the plank. Kathleen heard the ricochet hit somewhere behind her.

Maybe that had been Helms's intent. Just a warning shot. But the hall was narrow and the children so close, both of them moving, that it was a miracle they hadn't been hit. Or an accident. The shot reverberated in the confined space. Before its echo died away, Helms's voice joined it.

"Tell them not to move again, Mrs. Sorrel. I don't want *anyone* moving."

Like the deputy's voice, this one was full of stress, high-pitched and strained. Helms was on edge because he hadn't been expecting the children, of course. He had been expecting Jordan instead, and it probably *was* a miracle that he hadn't shot the little boy when he had first appeared in the doorway.

"Stay right there, Jamie," Kathleen yelled, realizing that in his tension and fear over not knowing where Jordan was, Helms might do anything. They couldn't afford to upset the delicate balance of the situation. He was still looking for Jordan to come out of one of these doorways, and any movement, however innocent...

"Don't take another step," Kathleen said to Jamie.

The little boy's eyes lifted from the gouge the bullet had cut in the floor less than six inches from the toes of his footed pajamas. His eyes were wide with shock, but he grinned when Kathleen spoke to him. And he took another step toward her.

"I told you not to move, damn it!" Helms shouted. His words came on top of Kathleen's.

"Stop, Jamie," she ordered. "Stop right there. Not another step."

She tried to imbue sternness into the command, that familiar "I really mean business this time" mother timbre that

Jamie might obey. Her voice quavered instead. Like Helms's, it was high-pitched and unnatural. Jamie's eyes lifted, questioning.

"Don't move," she said, working hard to modulate her tone and at the same time let Jamie know he had to obey. "Stay right where you are."

His expression was a combination of surprise and puzzlement, but he was listening. He was obviously thinking about what she was saying, but the understanding of a two-year-old, even a bright one, was always uncertain. Jamie might decide they were just playing a game. Some interesting new version of Mother, may I.

One that could have terrible consequences if he forgot to ask the magic question, Kathleen knew. She swallowed the fear engendered by that thought, wondering if this graying, grandfatherly man would really shoot a two-year-old because he made a break for his mother's arms. That was insane. But then she had known that all along. This was all insanity.

"Now you," Helms said. "You get over there with him."

Surprised, Kathleen tore her gaze away from Jamie, looking up quickly, afraid the toddler would take her wavering attention for permission to move. Helms wasn't talking to her. He was looking at Meg, the gun pointed at the little girl hovering in the doorway. As Kathleen watched, he gestured with the barrel, urging Meg to join her brother in the middle of the hallway.

Meg's gray eyes lifted, just as Jamie's had, to her mother's face. Kathleen nodded, the movement very small, but even so the gun swung back to her. At least it wasn't focused any longer on Meg, who took one hesitant step out of the semiprotection of the doorway and then another.

Unlike Kathleen, Meg had remembered to put on her bedroom slippers. They were shaped like bunnies, and the pink ears trembled as she walked carefully across the hall to stand by Jamie. When she got there, she put her arm around his shoulder, pulling him protectively against her side.

Kathleen's eyes filled with tears at the gesture, but she blinked them away because she couldn't afford to cry. She had to know what was happening. She had to keep watching this terrible drama unfold, no matter what.

She had made another mistake. Just as when she had used the old immunization record, this, too, was all her fault. She had run screaming up the stairs, yelling for Jordan to save them. Instead, the sound of her voice had awakened the children, drawing them into the hall and into the line of fire. Putting them finally where she had known all along they must not be.

"Now, Mrs. Sorrel, let's you and me talk," Helms said softly.

The near hysteria seemed to have faded from his voice now that he had them all together where he could see them and nothing was moving in the upstairs hall. His tone sounded almost as reasonable as it had downstairs. Back when he was trying to convince her that Jordan was her enemy.

"All right," she said. She had nothing to talk about. She had told everyone that for nearly three years, but as long as he thought she might, maybe she could keep them alive.

"Where's your friend?" he asked.

"I don't know. I thought…" Involuntarily, she looked again into the suite where she thought Jordan had slept last night. It was undisturbed. Unoccupied. "I don't know," she said again.

"Looking for me?" Jordan asked. His voice came from the staircase at Helms's back.

Instinctively, Helms turned, carrying the gun with him, away from the children. Which was, Kathleen realized, exactly what Jordan had intended. As soon as she understood that, she was moving, too. Keeping low, she ran the few feet that separated her from the children and scooped them up, one in each arm. By then, however, the shooting had started.

Kathleen dived into the open door of the bedroom the

children had come out of. She used her body to cover theirs on the floor where she had thrown them. She lost count of the number of shots. Too many bullets, she knew. A couple ricocheted, as the first one had done, whining into a wall or the ceiling.

Too many shots for some of them *not* to reach their targets. Those that came into the upstairs hall were Jordan's. Misses. And the others…

Almost as that terrifying thought formed, the battle was over. The gunfire had lasted only seconds, but as she listened to it, it had seemed to go on for an eternity. Even when the noise died away, she couldn't seem to move. She waited, wondering which of them would come through the open door. Wondering which of them was left alive.

"Kathleen."

She opened her eyes and slowly turned her head so she could see the doorway. Jordan was standing in it, his right shoulder propped against the frame. With his right hand, he was holding both his gun and his left arm, right above the elbow. There was a splotch of blood there, but he was alive.

Thank God, Jordan was still alive. In the midst of that overwhelming emotion, the sense of gratitude and relief that was flooding her body, there was another emotion as well.

"Why didn't you just shoot him?" she asked angrily. "You could have shot him in the back. Why did you give him a chance to turn around and shoot *you?*"

The look of deep concern cleared suddenly from Jordan's face, and he laughed. The sound of it, surprised and spontaneous, seemed out of place with the blood and her terror. Terror for him as well as the children. Fear that was almost paralyzing in its intensity, even now that it seemed to be over.

Not over, she thought. Only this. Only this part of the nightmare. It would never be "over" unless Rob or the money could be found. And they were no closer to doing that than they had been three years ago.

Hearing Jordan's laughter, Jamie began struggling to get

out from under her, so she pushed up onto her knees. Once there, however, she didn't think she could make it the rest of the way, as weak as her legs felt, so she sat there, just looking at Jordan and crying.

Once free, however, Jamie quickly got to his hands and knees. Then he stood up and ran straight to Jordan. When he reached him, he threw his arms around one long, jeans-clad leg, looking up into his face.

"Hey, champ," Jordan said softly. "How you doing?"

He reached down with the hand that didn't have blood dripping off its fingers, obviously intending to ruffle the little boy's hair. Except the hand he extended still held his gun. When he realized that, it hesitated in midair, hovering over Jamie's head.

"And if I'd shot him in the back and *hadn't* killed him?" Jordan asked, his eyes still on the toddler hanging on to his leg. "What if the muscles in his dying finger had squeezed that trigger? What if he'd gotten off even one round?"

He looked up at her then, and in his eyes, just as it had been in his voice, was the reason he hadn't shot Helms in the back, despite the danger to himself of doing it the other way.

"That wasn't a chance I was willing to take," he said softly, glancing down again to smile at Jamie. "I knew he'd turn around. It's too strong a reflex to ignore—that urge to find the threat you can't see."

"He could have killed you," Kathleen said. Jordan had saved their lives, and he had taken a bullet in order to do it the way he believed would put the children at the least risk.

"I wasn't going to let him do that," he said, looking up at her again, his eyes lightening. "I still have some unfinished business to take care of. A lot of unfinished business."

"You missed," she accused ridiculously.

"Not the first one," he said. "The first one was the important one. The rest were…just insurance."

She took a deep breath, hearing the absolute certainty in his voice, and then she nodded. His eyes held hers a moment longer, before they fell to watch her fingers wipe at the tears on her cheeks.

"How bad is that?" she finally asked, tilting her chin at his injured arm.

"Survivable," he said, his lips lifting again. "Like it or not, you're stuck with me."

Inanely, she nodded, trying to come to grips with the fact that they were all still alive, despite that hail of bullets. "Is he dead?" she finally thought to ask.

"I didn't have a choice," Jordan acknowledged. There seemed to be genuine regret in his voice.

"You sound as if…as if you'd like it better if he wasn't dead."

"I want to know how the hell he found us."

Kathleen hadn't even wondered about that. After all, they had always found her. Eventually. Obviously, Jordan had made a mistake. He had done something that alerted someone to the fact they were here. That had to be it, because Jordan had been so sure no one had followed them. And just as sure of the house's security system, she remembered.

"How did he even get in?" she asked. The alarms hadn't sounded. At least she hadn't heard any.

"I don't know," Jordan said. "How did you realize he was?"

"I was going down to make coffee, and he was just there at the bottom of the stairs. I kept yelling for you."

"And wondering why the hell I didn't respond," he suggested. He transferred the gun to his other hand, and finally put his right one, palm down, on top of Jamie's head. "I decided to sleep in the study last night. I thought that might be a little more protection. I woke up when I heard you yelling, but it took awhile to get into position. And then I heard that shot.…" He paused, but what he had feared was revealed in his eyes.

"I was beginning to wonder if what he said could be true," Kathleen confessed, knowing now how wrong she had been.

"What he *said?*" Jordan repeated.

He looked down to smile again at Jamie, who was trying to attract his attention by patting his thigh. Jordan tweaked the little boy's nose between his first two fingers and then slid his thumb where Jamie's nose had been. It was a game the toddler had played before, of course, and laughing, he reached up and grabbed at Jordan's fingers.

Watching them, Kathleen remembered the long moment of doubt she had had standing on the staircase, wondering if what Helms had told her could be true. This was what had convinced her it was not. The images of Jordan and the children together were stronger than any of the logic Helms offered. The endless patience Jordan had shown dealing with Jamie that night. Coping with Meg as he tried to fix dinner for them and keep his sense of humor at the same time. Nobody was that good at hiding his true character. Nobody.

She stood, her legs still shaky as she got to her feet. That weakness was unimportant beside what she needed to do. She walked over to Jordan and put her arms around him. His good arm tightened around her, and he pulled her against his chest.

"I love you," she whispered. "No matter what happens…about Rob, I want you to know that."

Her fingers touched the edge of the bloodstain on his shirt. She looked up into his eyes, trying not to think about the bullet that had plowed into the wooden floor only inches from Jamie. Trying not to think about what might have been.

Jordan's mouth lowered to hers. As he kissed her, Jamie put his arm around Kathleen's leg, too, pressing his face into the narrow space between Jordan and his mother. The three of them stood, clinging to one another for several seconds, at least two of them realizing what a close thing this had been.

"Mommy," Meg said.

Interrupting because she felt left out, Kathleen realized.

She had been too concerned about protecting them, and then too concerned about Jordan and too eager to confess what she felt, to offer comfort for what Meg had been through.

Slowly Kathleen broke the kiss, but she held Jordan's eyes a heartbeat longer, smiling at him. Then she walked over to the little girl, still huddled alone on the floor of the bedroom. Kathleen knelt down and then sat back on her heels, pulling her daughter into her lap. Willingly, Meg came into her arms.

What had happened this morning had again been much harder on her than on Jamie. Meg had understood what was going on. At least she was aware of the danger the gun posed. She was still trembling, her small body vibrating as if she had a chill, even as Kathleen held her. Just as Meg had held her little brother out in the hallway.

"You were so brave," Kathleen said softly. She cupped her hand around the back of Meg's head, pressing it against her shoulder. She turned her face to kiss her daughter's temple as she stroked the shining black hair. "I was so proud of you, Meggie, for taking care of Jamie."

"Did he shoot that man?" Meg whispered, her mouth moving against Kathleen's throat.

After Meg's reaction to the deaths of the deputies, Kathleen wasn't sure if this was a plea for reassurance or something else. Something that would only feed Meg's hostility to Jordan. She hesitated and then finally settled for reassurance rather than an answer.

"It's all over, sweetheart. You really are safe. You and Jamie are both safe. We all are."

She thought about that for a moment. They were safe. For the time being. Thanks to Jordan. But at what cost…

Her eyes lifted to his. He was watching them, his mouth set, his eyes shadowed. His skin looked gray beneath its natural darkness. She needed to stop the bleeding. She needed to do something for *him,* after all he had done for them.

"What did he tell you?" Jordan asked.

She didn't know at first what he meant. Then she realized he was still asking about what Helms had said. And maybe it was important.

"He said you'd been sent to trick me. To win my trust and to get me to answer questions."

"And you believed him?" Jordan queried, a hint of amusement in his voice.

"For a minute or two. At least...I thought it was possible," she admitted.

"Was this before or after you screamed my name?" he asked.

She laughed, the sound of it a little shaky, thinking he was mocking her moment of indecision.

"Before or after, Kathleen?" he asked again, his voice no longer amused.

He was serious, she realized. She wondered why it mattered. But she had made her decision about who to trust before she had gone rushing up the stairs.

"Before. I didn't call you until *after* I'd decided that it didn't make any sense. What he said, I mean."

"So he didn't hear my name until after he'd given you that story."

She shook her head, still not sure what Jordan was getting at.

"But he definitely knew I was here?"

"He even knew about the deputies," she said, remembering. That was another part of his story that hadn't made sense. Trying to paint those two as good guys. "And he knew you'd shot them. He said that."

"Then he knew I was with you when you left Texas," Jordan said. "So somebody must have seen me with you."

"I guess so," she agreed. It was the obvious conclusion.

"Then how the hell could they know for sure that I wasn't Rob?" Jordan asked softly.

He didn't expect an answer, she realized. Because there was none. The Mafia had been waiting three years for Sorrel to show up. When he had, why hadn't they done something?

Why had they waited until now, until Jordan had brought her and the children halfway across the country?

Why hadn't they just grabbed the man they had been looking for? Why had they followed them here and then tried to question her? They had accepted that she really knew nothing. Why, then, after all this time...

"He said he was FBI," she whispered. "He showed me an identification. Do you suppose it's possible..."

Almost before she had finished speaking, Jordan reached down and began to untangled Jamie's arms from around his leg. "Gotta go, champ," he said. "But I'll be right back."

He was going to check on the identification, Kathleen realized, wondering if this, too, had been a terrible mistake. But Helms had shot at the children. And what he had told her about the deputies had been a lie. So even if he were FBI...

"Come over here, Jamie," she suggested, still worried.

Jordan ruffled the little boy's hair again, smiling at him, before he put his hand on the back of Jamie's head and gave him a gentle push to get him started. As soon as Jamie reached Kathleen, sitting down on the floor beside her, Jordan turned toward the hall. Then he hesitated.

He stooped down, and when he turned around, he was holding Meg's Raggedy Ann, apparently dropped when Kathleen had grabbed the children and thrown them into the safety of the bedroom.

"Here's your baby, Meggie," Jordan said. "You must have dropped her."

He took a couple of steps into the room and bent, balancing on his haunches, holding out the limp, faded rag doll. Meg lifted her head from Kathleen's shoulder far enough that she could see him, but she didn't reach for the toy.

"Don't you want Raggedy Ann?" Kathleen prodded, hoping that the little girl wouldn't reject the effort Jordan was making. Despite her seeming maturity, Meg couldn't possibly understand what this was all about or why Jordan

had done the things she had seen him do. She couldn't realize that he had only been protecting them.

She was simply a little girl who was very much afraid.
And she wasn't sure who, except for Kathleen, she didn't
need to be afraid of. *Give her some time,* Kathleen pleaded
silently, meeting Jordan's eyes, so much like Meg's.

"You give it to Jamie this time," Meg said unexpectedly.
"I don't want it. I'm not a baby anymore." Her voice was
defiant, almost challenging.

"I know you're not," Jordan said easily.

He laid the doll on the floor and stood up, looking down
a moment on the three of them. Then he turned and walked
back through the door to check on the ID Kathleen had told
him about.

"Jordan was trying to be nice to you," Kathleen said.

She didn't want to reprimand Meg, not after all she'd
been through, but her hostility probably shouldn't be allowed to harden. Not if one day, as Kathleen hoped...

She took a deep breath, admitting how many things stood
in the way of what she hoped. Not only for herself, but for
Meg. And for Jamie, who had already formed such a strong
attachment to the stranger who had come out of nowhere to
protect them. Unconsciously, she put her hand on the little
boy's head, just as Jordan had done, smiling at him.

"He just came back because of Jamie," Meg said, her
eyes focused on the doorway through which Jordan had disappeared.

"Came back?" Kathleen repeated, puzzled.

"He just came back to get Jamie," Meg said again, her
voice bitter.

"Oh, Meggie," Kathleen said softly, her throat tightening
painfully when she made the connection. "Meggie, that's
not true. I told you this isn't Daddy, darling."

"I remember him," Meg said, nodding with conviction.
"I have our picture."

Despite what had happened three years ago, Kathleen
hadn't done any of the things she had felt like doing. She

hadn't tried to destroy the bond that had existed between Meg and her father. She hadn't forbidden Meg to talk about how much she missed Rob or to question when he was coming back for them. And she hadn't gotten rid of his pictures. Every time they moved, she had packed the photograph Meg was talking about, one in which their dark heads were close together, their nearly identical eyes and mouths laughing into the camera.

"But this isn't your daddy," Kathleen said again. "I promise you it's not."

"You're just saying that because of those men," Meg declared accusingly. "Because you don't want them to find him."

"I'm *saying* it because it's the truth," Kathleen said carefully. "I know he *looks* like Daddy...."

She hesitated, wondering how in the world she could explain it all now. The fact that Rob might be dead. That Jordan wasn't Meg's father, but that someday, if they could figure a way out of this, he might be.

"I don't want that old doll anymore," Meg said again. She reached out with one small, pink-bunny-slippered foot and poked at the toy, pushing it away from her. "I'm too old for that."

"I know," Kathleen said. "I know you are. But *I'd* like to keep her. My mommy made that baby," she said, finding a smile for the confused little girl with the stormy eyes. "So Daddy didn't really give it to you, you know. Gramma did."

"He told me to keep up with Annie," Meg said, taking another, stronger poke at the rag body with her toe. "But I don't want to anymore. He can just give her to Jamie. He loves Jamie, so Jamie can keep up with her for him."

And suddenly, just as if Rob himself had told her, Kathleen understood. She could almost hear him saying it. She could see him handing the rag baby to Meg, who, at that time, had adored it. And who had also adored her father.

"Take care of your baby, Meggie," Rob would have said, pulling a strand of her hair around to tickle her nose. *"Don't*

you let anything happen to Raggedy Ann. Keep up with her for Daddy.''

And for almost three years Meg, being Meg, had done exactly that.

Chapter Fifteen

"It's genuine," Jordan said.

Kathleen pulled her eyes away from the rag doll. Jordan was again standing in the doorway. She didn't even know what he was talking about because her whole intellect was focused so intently on what Meg had just said.

"At least it appears to be," Jordan added, when she didn't respond.

"What does *that* mean?" Kathleen asked, finally realizing what he meant.

"Maybe nothing. Even if he really was FBI, that doesn't explain how Helms could know I wasn't Rob."

That was a question she couldn't answer, of course, but now there was something that seemed far more important.

"Meg says her daddy told her to take good care of Raggedy Ann before he left," she said.

She held Jordan's eyes, trying to convey the importance she had attached to that information without spelling out in front of Meg what she believed. Suddenly Jordan's eyes narrowed, a small crease forming between the dark brows. His gaze fell to the rag doll, still lying on the floor. When his eyes came back to Kathleen's, the question in them, she nodded carefully.

Shifting his gun to his left hand, Jordan bent, picking up the doll and examining it. When his eyes lifted again, he said, "I need the scissors from the desk downstairs. And I need to use the computer down there."

"Maybe that's how he found us, Jordan. The message you sent last night."

"This place belongs to one of the CIA's assistant deputy directors. Someone...someone who used to be," he amended. "That was an encrypted e-mail, the same kind the agency sends and receives from its stations all over the world. There's no way—"

"Helms got in past your friend's security system," she interrupted, reminding him that apparently none of the fail-safes had worked.

Jordan seemed to be thinking about what she'd suggested, but finally he said, "It may be a chance we have to take. Especially if..." He gestured with the rag doll by lifting it slightly. "If you're right about this, then we're going to need help, and we're going to need it as quickly as possible."

"WHAT IS IT?" Kathleen asked.

Her voice was too controlled, Jordan thought. She was probably afraid to hope. Just as he had been. Until now.

"It's a key," Jordan said softly, holding up what he'd found. It had been inside a tiny red envelope fastened with a safety pin in the very center of the stuffing of Meg's doll. That's what he had noticed upstairs—the uneven seam where the original stitches had been removed and then ineptly resewn.

"A key to what?" Kathleen asked.

"A safety deposit box," Jordan said. Helpfully, the name of the bank was printed on the red envelope. Of course, this was the key to a lot more than that, he believed. He looked up, wondering if Kathleen realized what this meant.

But of course she did. After all, she was the one who had kept her children safe for three years. First by convincing some very ruthless people that she truly didn't have any idea of her husband's whereabouts, and then by hiding her children, more to prevent her husband's unwanted reappearance from endangering them than to conceal them from the mob. And she had done that pretty successfully, until Jordan had shown up and unintentionally intensified the hunt.

"And you think the money's there?" she asked. "In that box?"

"I doubt it would hold it. The box probably contains something that indicates where he hid the money. Maybe an account number."

Jordan was trying to think what else might be in the box. Sorrel could have bought diamonds or something equally as valuable and portable, but it seemed that kind of purchase would have been traceable, especially for someone like Jake.

"But why would he give it to Meg?" Kathleen asked. "That seems so…"

"Maybe he needed a hiding place in a hurry," Jordan suggested, "and the doll was the best one he could think of on the spur of the moment. He knew Meg. He knew she wasn't going to be separated from her baby. He'd always know where it was."

"But if he was planning to leave us…?"

Jordan had already reached that point, and he almost didn't want to tell her what he'd concluded. However, given Sorrel's hiding place in Meg's doll and the way this was starting to play out, she deserved the truth.

"Maybe he wasn't," he said.

He watched as the implication impacted in her eyes—the realization that what she had believed about her husband for nearly three years might not be true. Jordan couldn't tell what she was feeling, however, until the russet eyes glazed with tears. She blinked them away, refusing to cry.

"What do we do?" she asked instead.

"I make a couple of phone calls," Jordan said, remembering her concern about last night's e-mail.

"Aren't you afraid that whoever you call…" She hesitated, seeming reluctant to suggest that sixteen million dollars was still a hell of a lot of incentive to betrayal.

"Not these people," Jordan said. Griff would have been the one Jordan would normally turn to. The one any member of the team would have turned to when in trouble.

But since Cabot had been killed in the massacre at Langley, Jordan would have to rely on someone else. And he needed Jake to find out what information he could on Helms. Then they needed someone from Justice to pick up the key and arrange to put Kathleen and the children into protective custody until the money had been recovered.

As soon as those arrangements were agreed to, Jordan would call Claire Heywood and ask her to alert the media. The glare of the cameras was the best way to insure that the money wouldn't disappear again. Media coverage would also alert the mob that it was over. Going public was the only way to drive all those scavengers back into their holes and away from Kathleen and the children, and Claire had the connections to see that done.

"Friends of yours," Kathleen suggested.

He was relieved that the moisture had disappeared from her eyes and that her lips were tilted. Almost into a smile.

"Friends I'd trust with my life," Jordan said. "Some of them I *have* trusted with it."

"Don't you think I ought to take a look at that first?" Kathleen asked.

Her eyes were on his arm, he realized. He had almost forgotten about the injury, considering everything else. The initial pain had subsided to a dull burn. Since the bleeding had stopped, and he could still move everything, he wasn't too concerned. But it was nice to know she was.

"After I call Jake," he promised. "We need to get someone trustworthy out here. And I want Jake looking into Helms's involvement with your husband."

"He was looking for that," Kathleen said simply, nodding toward the key Jordan was turning over and over in his fingers. "If you're right about what's in that safety deposit box, then that's what they've all been looking for."

"If I'm right about this," Jordan said, holding the key up, "then it's over. If this is what I know in my gut it has to be, then you're free. You *and* the children," he said.

No more running and hiding. And no need for protection. They might want to start over somewhere, but that move would be from choice and not necessity. And wherever they went, Meg and Jamie would have a chance at a normal childhood. At least, Jordan amended, a more normal childhood than they had had up until now. Because they would still be without their father. Unless…

That would be Kathleen's decision, of course. He had already told her what he felt. He needed to give her time to rediscover what it was like not to live in fear, and time to deal with the fact that Rob Sorrel's betrayal of his family had perhaps not been as cold-blooded as she had always believed.

Jordan's eyes moved to the children. They were sitting together on the couch where he had laid Meg last night. She had her arm around her little brother, but her eyes were on him. Still wary. That was another battle he'd have to fight if he intended to get what he wanted. He would have to win Meg's trust. He already had Jamie's. And if he could convince Meg…

Kathleen's decision, he reminded himself again. One step at a time. And the first one, as always, was just to make sure they were safe.

FOR SOME REASON he called Claire Heywood before he got in touch with Jake. As he'd told Kathleen, the spotlight of the media would be the best insurance they could have that the money would get into the right hands and that the mob would understand it was all over.

All over, he thought again, almost in disbelief, as he listened to the ringing of the phone at Claire's office.

He had appealed for her help once before, to set up

Hawk's meeting with Carl Steiner. Jordan had been surprised when she'd agreed, but maybe she felt she owed Hawk for avenging Griff's murder. And even if that gratitude didn't extend to this favor—

"Hello."

The voice sounded exactly like Claire's. Jordan had been expecting her secretary's, of course, and it threw him.

"Claire?" he said questioningly.

The pause that followed was long enough that he wondered if he'd been mistaken. Or gotten the wrong number.

"For just a couple of seconds there," Claire Heywood said softly, "I thought you were Griff."

The result of the Virginia accent he and Griff had shared, Jordan realized with real regret. He should have identified himself.

"Sorry," he said.

It was probably an inadequate response for what she'd felt, but he didn't know what else to say. He certainly hadn't intended such a cruelty.

"Don't be," she said, and Jordan was relieved to hear that her tone had lightened. "Actually...actually those were a couple of very nice seconds."

There was another brief silence, and he knew they were both thinking about Griff. About how much they missed him.

"What can I do for you this time?" she said finally, her voice touched with amused resignation.

"What makes you think I'm calling to ask for a favor?" Jordan queried, allowing his own amusement to show. She was right on target, of course.

"Um, let's see. Maybe that I haven't heard from you since you asked me to arrange that meeting."

"I've been busy," he said.

"I know. I saw the papers. I'll bet Mr. Steiner wasn't too happy with that."

Jordan laughed before he admitted, "You can't imagine."

"I probably can," Claire corrected. "I know..."

She hesitated, maybe reluctant to reveal over an unsecured line exactly how much she did know about the agency. Jordan guessed that would be a lot, not only from her association with Griff, but because her grandfather had once been the director.

"I know they wouldn't like what happened," she finished.

"They didn't," he said succinctly.

"Reprisals?"

"No," Jordan said.

A new face. And a new name. New problems. But no reprisals. Although he knew they hadn't approved of what he'd done to help Hawk, he hadn't disobeyed any direct orders. That was what had made them go after Hawk.

"But you're right. I do have a favor to ask. Another favor," he said.

She laughed, the sound soft and very pleasant. Genuine. The more dealings he had with Claire Heywood, the more Jordan understood Griff's feelings for her. She was a woman who was probably as powerful in her world as Griff had been in his. As bright. As honorable.

"I'm keeping track, you know," Claire said, her voice amused.

"Quid pro quo," Jordan said.

"Something like that. What do you need this time?"

"Media types. A lot of them. Big enough names that a few Justice Department officials won't be able to scare them away."

"You don't know the same media types I do if you're worried about that," she said. "Where to and what for?"

"Griff's summer house. To watch somebody be given the key to sixteen million dollars. Is that tantalizing enough?"

"Probably. You want to tell me whose millions you're handing over to Justice?"

"The New Orleans mob's."

"Now that *is* tantalizing," Claire said. "So why do you

want coverage? I wouldn't think Justice would be interested in having that on the evening news.''

"*I* am," Jordan said.

"Care to tell me why?"

"Because of this money somebody almost killed a two-year-old and a five-year-old this morning. A couple of kids I happen to like. A lot," he added, remembering how close it had been. Remembering the deputy's threat. Remembering everything that had happened to Rob Sorrel's children because of that sixteen million.

"I see," Claire said, her voice very quiet.

She probably didn't. At least not like he did, Jordan thought. Or like Kathleen. You probably couldn't really imagine what that felt like until it was your kid being threatened. Your loved ones being hunted.

Of course, in Claire's case, he remembered belatedly, maybe she would understand. Because she had lost Griff.

"Can you do it?" he asked.

"Give me the time you want them," she said, "and I'll have them there. And the people I'm thinking about aren't afraid of the Justice Department *or* the mob."

"That's just exactly what I had in mind," Jordan said.

JAKE PUT MOST of the rest of it together for him. That happened much later, of course. Several days after the Justice Department sent their people out to the summer house to pick up the key.

They hadn't been happy about the media being there when Kathleen handed over the key. Jake had warned him that they wouldn't be, but the cameras, which Jordan had avoided, had accomplished exactly what he had been hoping they would—enough publicity to insure that the money would go where it was intended and that anyone who needed to know would realize the hunt was over.

Jordan found out he'd been right about some of what he'd speculated about Rob Sorrel's last days. The safety deposit box that Meg's key opened held not an account number, however, but another key, this one tagged with the address of a rented warehouse in Matamoros, just across the border from Brownsville, Texas. And that's where they found the money, which Sorrel had probably transported across in the family station wagon. No border crossing guard ever checked what someone might be trying to smuggle *into* Mexico, so a couple of weekend trips down there, and Sorrel was set. Set for life, it seemed.

In addition to the warehouse key, there was an unmarked brown envelope in the bank box that contained three passports. Sorrel's, Kathleen's and Meg's pictures were on them, but they had been issued in other names, of course. Whatever escape Sorrel had planned hadn't included leaving his family behind.

Eventually Jake had tied up the other loose ends, as well, including Helms's involvement. Apparently, the local FBI office in New Orleans had caught on to Sorrel's money laundering operation. That might even have precipitated his decision to take the money and run rather than face a long prison sentence. But Helms, who had not been the agent in charge, had moved in very quickly, before Sorrel could put his plan into effect.

Bringing Sorrel to justice hadn't been what Helms wanted, of course. He was far more interested in the money Rob had hidden and had apparently tried to force him to reveal its location. Unfortunately, he had been overzealous in his methods of questioning. Or Sorrel, being the arrogant risk taker he was, had maybe tried to resist giving up the location a little too long.

They would probably never know exactly how those final hours had gone, but the authorities found Sorrel's tortured body in a shallow grave in southwest Louisiana, very near a cabin Helms used for hunting. A location isolated enough to use to solicit information from someone who had refused to give it.

As Rob Sorrel must have. For whatever reason, he had carried with him to that lonely grave the secret of where he had hidden the money. Greed, arrogance, stubbornness or stupidity. Or perhaps… Perhaps, Jake acknowledged, he believed he had been protecting his daughter, with whom he had left the key.

Even Jake hadn't quite been able to explain why Helms had gotten back in on the search at this late date. Maybe he had been watching what was going on all along, keeping tabs on Kathleen through the bureau's informants inside the Mafia. Or maybe from those same informants he had learned that Sorrel had finally been spotted in San Francisco, masquerading as someone named Robert Sanders, who had turned up later in Texas with Kathleen Sorrel.

"Since Helms knew Rob was dead, he must have been the one searching for information about Sanders, trying to figure out who he was and what he was after." That was the first comment Jordan made when Jake had finally laid everything out. "Or he had the bureau's experts searching for him. They're the ones who discovered Sanders's connection to the agency."

And from there it would only be a short leap to Jordan Cross. And to Jordan's connections to Griff. Or to Jake himself. And Jordan, of course, had made several phone calls to Jake, as well as sending an e-mail, after that connection had been made.

There was a long pause, as if Jake was having to think about the possibility. The bureau would have their own Jake Holt somewhere, who might be good enough to ID Sanders and to get past the CIA's security system. Helms was an agent, with access to the bureau's expertise, and the fact that he'd worked on the Sorrel case gave him a legitimate need-to-know about Sanders.

"If those guys were able to read our stuff, then I'm getting old," Jake said finally.

Jordan knew, however, despite Jake's halfhearted disclaimer, that that must have been how it happened. Jordan had fallen into the trap Jake had warned them all against—

making that irresistible contact. And it had led Helms straight to Kathleen and the children.

"We're all getting old," Jordan acknowledged, laughing. "Maybe they were right about standing down the team."

"The bureaucrats are *never* right," Jake said, his voice richly sarcastic. "They used Griff's death as an excuse to get rid of people who were too good at what they did. And who knew too much about how things really work here in Washington."

"You're still there. Or doesn't that description include you?" Jordan asked, laughing.

"They can't do without the computers, so they still need me. They haven't quite figured out that someday they're going to need you guys as well."

Hawk's ability to take out a selected target. Or Jordan's skill in finding the scattered pieces of a puzzle and putting them together. That uncanny knack of seeing all the separate parts and fitting them into a whole.

Only in this case, it had been other skills he had learned during his tenure with the CIA's External Security Team that had been most useful. Ones that involved using weapons other than his brain. Ironically, Kathleen and Jake had done all the mental work on this one.

"What's happening with Sorrel's wife and children?" Jordan asked, keeping his voice deliberately neutral.

He had requested that he be kept informed, and Justice had politely told him that since he had no official status, what happened to the Sorrel family was no longer any of his business. He had done his patriotic duty in turning over the Mafia's money, and now he could leave the rest of it to them. Except, of course, his involvement with the Sorrel case was far more than professional.

"With all the publicity surrounding the recovery of the money, they ought to be in the clear. You owe Claire Heywood big-time for that."

They both knew why Claire had been so willing to cooperate. Hawk had taken out the man who had ordered the massacre in which Griff Cabot had been killed—the man Claire Heywood had been in love with. And Jordan Cross had taken the heat on that assassination, which had ultimately put him into the middle of this.

"Just like I owe you," Jordan acknowledged softly.

"The identity I helped create got you into this. The least I could do was try to get you out."

"However you want to justify it, Jake, I won't forget what you did."

"Yeah, well…" Jake said awkwardly. He was no better than Hawk at accepting gratitude. Probably no better than Jordan himself would be. "By the way," Jake said, in an obvious change of subject, "I've got that other information you wanted."

"Other information?" Jordan repeated, trying to think what they hadn't covered.

"Where they're holding Sorrel's family. I just thought you might be interested. Cute kids and all. The wife ain't too shabby either, or so I heard. I guess you'd know more about that than I would," Jake suggested, his voice again amused.

"Nobody knows more than you, Jake. About anything," Jordan said, laughing.

JORDAN DECIDED it would be better to make his request officially, through channels, so he called Carl Steiner first. And he was aware of the definite hint of displeasure in Steiner's voice when he agreed to his request.

Steiner had inherited the thankless job of dismantling the elite CIA team Cabot had painstakingly put together, and had had plenty of problems in the process. There had been quite an uproar in the State Department because of Hawk's unauthorized assassination of the terrorist who had ordered the Langley massacre. And now Jordan had been involved in an operation that had revealed corruption within the bureau. Neither of those bureaucratic nightmares could have been pleasant for Steiner to deal with.

Apparently, they hadn't been enough, however, to prevent the new head of external security from arranging with the Justice Department for Jordan to visit Kathleen and the children. When he arrived at the safe house, nobody asked him for anything but an ID. They ushered him into the room where he was now waiting just as if he were still working for the agency. And maybe he should be, he thought. There he had known exactly what he was doing. And here...

"Hey, you," Jamie said, his grin lighting up his small face.

At least somebody's glad to see me, Jordan thought.

But it was obvious by Kathleen's eyes that she was, too. Her face seemed a little more tense than he'd expected, considering that for the first time in years she and her children were safe, but her eyes were warm and welcoming.

Meg's, however, were definitely wary. Given what she'd witnessed, her distrust of him was something he might never be able to overcome, Jordan acknowledged, but it would be worth a try.

More than worth a try, he decided, as Jamie tugged free of Kathleen's hand and ran across the room to fling himself against Jordan's legs. He reached down and scooped the little boy up, swinging him in a circle before he hugged him.

In the few days they'd been separated, he had almost forgotten how it felt to have Jamie's arms around his neck. Almost forgotten the heady scent of baby shampoo against his cheek. Forgotten how good it felt to be loved this much.

"How's your arm?" Kathleen asked.

"Almost as good as new," Jordan said truthfully. Today, he had left off the cloth harness contraption he'd been wearing because it was a graphic reminder of what they'd been through. A reminder none of them needed.

"I'm glad," she said softly, her eyes meeting his.

"They been treating you well?"

Pretty inane conversation, he supposed, considering all he wanted to say. But after all, he and Kathleen would have a hard time making small talk. They knew next to nothing about one another. What they did know was how the other would react in moments with life-and-death consequences. That was enough to build a future on, but it was tough to make superficial conversation about.

Kathleen nodded. Her eyes, however, were still examining his face, almost as if it had been months instead of days since they'd been together. Despite the tension he'd noticed, she looked rested. And beautiful.

Of course, he'd thought that from the first time he'd seen her, shepherding the two children down the day care steps. And he'd thought it almost every moment since. And he knew now that whatever happened, Kathleen would be all right because she was tough. She wasn't the one he had to worry about. Nor was Jamie, of course.

"Hello, Meg," he said softly. "I've been thinking a lot about you." He had. While they had waited at Griff's for everyone to arrive, Kathleen had told him what Meg believed. And that had, of course, explained her hostility.

"Mommy says you aren't my daddy," Meg said.

Trust Meg to cut right to the chase, Jordan thought, controlling the urge to smile. She had been up-front with him from that first night. Especially about his shortcomings and mistakes. And there had been a lot of those, he admitted. Like not realizing how Meg might interpret his response to Jamie's obvious infatuation with him.

"That's right," he said.

He stooped, balancing on his toes, and set Jamie down. When he had, Jordan didn't stand up again, wanting to be at eye level with Meg as they talked. He glanced up at Kathleen, hoping she'd understand his unspoken request.

She walked over, took Jamie's hand and led him a few feet away, giving Jordan the opportunity to speak to Meg one-on-one. After all, he had some important fences to mend.

"Mommy told you the truth, Meg. I'm not your daddy."

"You look like my picture of him," she said, her eyes

traveling slowly over his altered features, as if to prove that she hadn't been mistaken.

Jordan Cross didn't believe in coincidences. His background made him suspicious of anything that smacked of happenstance. There seemed to be no other explanation, however, for how he had ended up with Sorrel's face. And he knew that what had happened as a result of that coincidence wasn't anything he could regret.

Standing guard over those you love. That had been Griff's phrase for what the team did. Looking into Meg's face, almost a mirror image of his own, Jordan understood for the first time what those words really meant.

That's all he had done. He had guarded those he loved. Kathleen. Jamie, who had returned that love unconditionally almost from the first moment he'd met him. And prickly Meg, who certainly intended to make him earn hers.

But that was her right, he acknowledged. And after all she'd been through, she had the right to some explanations.

"I don't know why that is, Meg. But I'm glad I do. Looking like your daddy gave me a chance to meet you. And your mommy. And Jamie, of course."

Her gray eyes held his, as openly assessing as her mother's could sometimes be. Jordan didn't flinch from her appraisal. He had nothing to hide. He wouldn't try to take her father's place. He didn't want to destroy any of the good memories she had of Rob Sorrel. Jordan just wanted to create a place for himself within the small circle of this family.

"Mommy said you're like a policeman and that you stopped those men who were following us. She said we won't ever have to move again unless we want to."

"That's right," Jordan confirmed, his eyes lifting quickly to Kathleen's. She was holding Jamie on her hip now, her attention focused on the conversation he was having with Meg.

"Was my daddy a bad man?" Meg asked softly. "Is that why you came? Because you're a policeman, and he did something wrong?"

Jordan's eyes came back to her face. It had taken courage to ask that question. Kathleen's kind of courage. And it deserved an honest answer.

"Your daddy did something that...he shouldn't have done, Meg, but he wasn't a bad man. He loved you very much, and he didn't want to leave you and Mommy."

"Then why did he?"

Maybe because he really loved you, sweet Meggie, just as much as he was supposed to.

"He didn't want to leave," Jordan said again, fighting an unaccustomed tightness in his throat. "But he couldn't help it, sweetheart. He had to go away. Sometimes daddies do. Even from the people they love."

"Mommy says he's dead now."

Deliberately, Jordan didn't look up at Kathleen. He nodded instead, keeping his eyes on Meg's through sheer force of will.

"So Jamie won't ever have a daddy," she said.

Jordan let the silence stretch, not exactly sure what she meant by that. Not even sure at this point if Meg considered that cause for regret.

"I had a daddy when I was a baby," she said finally.

"I know," Jordan said softly. "I know you did."

"Jamie probably needs one. Especially him being a boy."

"I think you're right. But I think everybody needs a daddy. Not just boys."

"Not for me," she said, her voice very low. "For Jamie."

"Are you talking about *me* being Jamie's daddy, Meg?" he asked. "You think Jamie would like that?"

She nodded. She turned to look at her little brother. And then her eyes moved to find her mother's face, maybe, as she always had, seeking Kathleen's approval.

"And Mommy?" Jordan asked. "You think she'd like for me to be Jamie's daddy?"

Meg nodded again.

"I'd like that, too," Jordan said. "I want to marry your

mommy and take care of her so she never has to worry or be afraid again.''

Meg nodded, her eyes still on her mother's face.

"But I won't do that," Jordan said softly, and watched the small dark head turn again to face him. And when her eyes were on his, he said what he had come here to say. The only thing, he thought, that still had to be put into words. "Because that's not enough, Meg—taking care of your mother and being Jamie's daddy. That's not all I want."

Her eyes widened a little, but she didn't say anything, so Jordan wondered if he was making it too complicated. But Meg was bright, and like Kathleen, she had earned the right to have a say in what happened in their lives. Just as he wanted time to learn all about Kathleen, he was asking for time with Meg, too. And only she could decide if she wanted to give him that.

"What else do you want?" she asked softly.

"I want you, Meg," he said, knowing how true that was. Her spirit was the same as Kathleen's, as much a reflection of her mother's character as she was of her father's features. "If not to be your daddy…" He hesitated, knowing this was too important to chance saying the wrong thing. "If you don't want me to be your daddy, too, then I'd really like to be your friend."

Meg held his eyes a long time. Then she turned her head, looking toward Kathleen, who smiled at her despite the tears that were slowly making their way down her cheeks. But Kathleen didn't nod or encourage her in any way to accept the offer Jordan had just made. Meg's decision.

Again the gray eyes found his, and Jordan realized he had been holding his breath as he waited.

"You don't know a lot about being a daddy," Meg said, the edge of accusation clear in her voice.

"No, I don't," Jordan admitted. *More than when we started,* he thought, but like Kathleen, he didn't try to influence whatever was going on in the little girl's head.

"I guess I could help you," Meg said softly. "I had a daddy when I was little. I know what they're supposed to do."

Standing guard over those we love. I know what they're supposed to do, too, Meggie, Jordan thought, but that wasn't what he said.

"I'd really appreciate that," he whispered, pushing the words past the hard knot that blocked his throat.

He waited, but she didn't seem inclined to any more pronouncements, neither criticism nor acceptance. And that was all right. She had come a lot further than he'd expected her to. Like Kathleen, she had a solid core of courage and honesty inside. And that was one reason he loved them both.

He had already begun to stand when her fingers touched his hand. He waited again, giving her time. But when her hand slipped into his, he couldn't resist. He picked Meg up and hugged her tightly. She didn't respond as Jamie always did, clutching him as if he couldn't bear to let go. Finally, however, she laid her head against his shoulder and her fingers found his cheek, resting warmly against the unaccustomed moisture there.

Over her head, Jordan's eyes met Kathleen's. In them was more than a promise. It was a trust instead.

Standing guard over those we love.

Epilogue

When the doorbell rang, Claire Heywood was immersed in a brief. She looked at the clock on her desk and realized she had missed dinner again. And a lot of the rest of the night as well. It was after ten o'clock. Pretty late for company.

Dad, she thought. Sometimes her father stayed over with her when he had been working late and didn't relish making the long trip home. They'd have a nightcap and talk before he went up to the guest room.

She uncrossed her legs, and realized only as she stood that they were stiff from sitting in the same position far too long. She walked to the front door, stretching out cramped muscles as she moved.

"Who is it?" she called, turning on the outside lights.

"Delivery for Ms. Heywood."

Her view through the peephole revealed a man dressed in a black uniform, suspiciously like a chauffeur's, even down to the billed hat. And a huge black car in the drive. A Rolls, she realized. *If he's a burglar,* she decided, *he's doing real well for himself.* She opened the door, leaving the security chain in place.

"Ms. Heywood?"

"Yes," she acknowledged.

"I have something for you."

Into the opening allowed by the length of chain, he held

a single, long-stemmed rose. There was no florist wrapping. No ribbon. No card. Simply a dark red rose, its petals still touched with dew. Without thinking, Claire took the flower. The man touched the brim of his hat and began to turn.

"Is there a message?" Claire asked.

"I almost forgot," he said, smiling apologetically. "I was to tell you thank you." He turned away from the door.

"But...who? Who said to tell me thank you?"

"I think he believed you might know, Ms. Heywood," the man said. He touched his cap again, and this time Claire didn't attempt to stop him as he went down the steps.

She closed the door and walked back to her study, carrying the rose, occasionally bringing it to her face and breathing in its sweetness. *I think he believed you might know.* Obviously someone who liked to play games, she thought. Someone who didn't have nearly as much to do tonight as she did.

She laid the rose on top of the papers on her desk. Its fragrance drifted through the room. A thank-you from Jordan Cross, perhaps?

She had watched the media coverage she'd arranged for the exchange at Griff's summer house. And the memories the pictures of those familiar rooms evoked had been painful. But if this was from Jordan, how could he possibly know about the significance of such a flower?

She didn't even remember why Griff, who could have afforded hundreds of florist roses, had begun sending her a single red rose from the gardens of his big country house in Maryland. So how in the world could Jordan Cross have known that? No one but she and Griff...

She shivered, crossing her arms over her breasts, running her hands up and down her upper arms, trying to find some warmth in the sudden chill that had fallen over the room.

The vivid red against the white paper reminded her of the rose she had laid on the smooth green of Griff's grave. She had done that as soon as she'd returned to Washington. In memory. In regret. And then tonight...

She picked the rose up by the long stem and lifted it, again breathing in the scent. Unlike Griff, she was no expert, but she would vow that this was the same variety he had always sent. The same color. The same haunting fragrance.

Haunting, she thought, smiling a little at the thought. *If you're haunting me, Griff, I sure as hell wish you'd be a little less subtle about it. Because, my darling, it's so bloody lonely without you.*

The tears she had denied burned suddenly at that admission, but determinedly she blinked them away. Maybe by helping Hawk and Jordan she had made up for what she hadn't done while Griff was still alive. And for the hurtful things she had said.

She lifted the rose again, inhaling deeply. Remembering. The dew that had clung to its petals touched her cheek, the sensation as soft and moist as a lover's kiss.

Claire looked down at the papers on her desk, which only moments before had seemed important. Then moving slowly, she reached out and turned off the desk lamp, and carrying the rose with her, she went upstairs to check on her daughter. Griff's daughter.

And when she looked down on the sleeping baby, who already looked so much like her father, she admitted it again. *So bloody lonely without you.*

HER BABY, HIS SECRET

Prologue

It was always night in the dream. And she was running. It felt as if she were running away from someone, but she knew that couldn't be right. At least at some point in the sequence she knew that.

Running. And the maze of rose bushes that surrounded her tore at her arms and her face as she ran. The light ahead was so dim and distant, but she knew she had to reach it in order to be safe. If she could only reach the light...

And then the house would materialize in front of her, looming up out of the gray netherworld of the dream. She always stopped when that happened, her feet suddenly reluctant, her passage through the maze and the darkness slowed by an unbearable pressure she didn't understand.

If she could only reach the house... She knew that she'd be safe there, and yet invariably her footsteps slowed until she was walking, the sound of her shoes on the gravel path disturbing the soft, surrounding stillness of the night.

She would climb the steps, and as she neared the door, the scent of roses from the maze she had escaped would pervade the air. She knew that their fragrance meant something, but she could never decide exactly what, or how she felt about it. Her emotions about the roses were as confusing, as nebulous and unformed, as her reluctance to approach the door.

She always raised her hand to knock, but the sound she made, if there were one, was muffled by the darkness and the now-overpowering scent of the roses. Then the door silently opened anyway. And behind the man who stood within its frame was the light she had been running toward.

It was only after she put her cold, trembling fingers into the hand he held out to her that she could see his face, materializing before her, just as the house always did. His eyes were dark and compassionate, and although she expected him to, he never seemed to judge what she had done.

As soon as she looked into his eyes, all the doubt and reluctance vanished. Spiraled away in the darkness, to leave only the feel of his hand. Warm and so strong. Strong enough to pull her out of the maze in which she had been lost, and into the light. Strong enough to keep her safe.

Then he was leading her up the staircase, although she could never remember crossing the threshold. And because she knew so well what lay at the top of the stairs they were climbing, anticipation increased with each step.

Ascending together. Hand in hand. Somewhere in her heart she knew that this was the way it was supposed to be, and that this place was where she was supposed to be.

She didn't understand how she could have gotten so lost. So lost in the maze. In the clawing pain of its thorns. She had been so alone.

Never again, *she thought.* Not as long as she held on to his hand. *Then, even as the thought formed, it was all gone. His hand. The staircase. The house.*

And once more she was running through the maze, in the cold, dark sickness of her grief and despair, toward a light she knew she would never be able to reach again.

Chapter One

Claire Heywood opened her eyes slowly, climbing out of sleep as if it were a pit. Too little sleep, she diagnosed groggily, automatically analyzing the weak winter sunlight that was filtering into the room.

It was too early to think about getting up, but there had been something... She listened to the dawn stillness that surrounded her, waiting for whatever had disturbed it to be repeated. When it wasn't, her eyelids dropped downward again, her body returning to that blessed state of relaxation possible only when she knew everything was right within her small world.

Nothing alarming had intruded into its safe and well-kept familiarity. Nothing was here that shouldn't be. Only the accustomed quietness of the exclusive Georgetown neighborhood where she lived. Peaceful, apparently, even on New Year's Day.

Because of the holiday, Claire had been up much later than usual last night. At least later than was now the norm. She had let her sister goad her into attending one of the embassy parties. Of course, no one could provoke Claire like Maddy could. In her anger over her sister's repeated accusations that she was turning into a hermit, Claire had also agreed to the oh-so-eligible escort her sister's husband had casually suggested.

The two of them had ridden over to the embassy with

Maddy and Charles, but still, Claire acknowledged, there was no way around the awkward reality. She had had a blind date, more commonly known now as a fix-up. And even if she argued that last night hadn't technically been a date, it was still as near to one as she had come in a long time.

And in all honesty, the experience had been relatively painless. And relatively meaningless as well, of course.

Claire rolled restlessly onto her side, pushing her pillow into a more comfortable shape under her cheek. For some reason, despite the lateness of the hour when she'd gone to bed, she didn't seem able to slip back into sleep this morning, as much as she wanted to.

Too much champagne? she wondered. A little hung over? She must have been the slightest bit tipsy when she'd gotten home last night. Giddy enough to let John Amerson kiss her at the door, she remembered with a pang of remorse and embarrassment. She hadn't meant for that to happen, but in all honesty she couldn't say that the kiss had been unpleasant. Actually, there had been nothing about the whole evening that had been unpleasant.

She opened her eyes again, studying the familiar pattern of light that the rising sun, reflecting off the carpet of her bedroom, threw against the wall. White wool had not been a practical choice for carpeting, she supposed. When she had decorated the house, however, not only had practicality not been a priority, it had not even been much of a consideration.

Now, of course, it was both. Another aspect of her life that had drastically changed in the course of the last year. More than enough changes, she thought, her lips tightening reflexively.

She lay, watching the spill of sunshine and willing her mind to disengage from that familiar litany of regret. There was nothing she could do about any of it. Nothing she could change. And of course, there were a great many things about the last twelve months that she wouldn't change, even if she could.

Her lips relaxed into a smile, envisioning the room next door. Its occupant was apparently still sleeping, cuddled under the heavy warmth of the quilt her Great-grandmother Heywood had hand-stitched to celebrate her birth. It would be stretched tightly over a small, rounded bottom that at this time of the morning was usually sticking straight up in the air.

And that air, Claire realized, despite the normal efficiency of the central heating unit, was decidedly chilly. She pulled the covers up over her exposed shoulder, trying to relax again into the peaceful cocoon of oblivion. Trying not to think about last night. Or about New Year's Eves past. Trying not to think about anything.

After a few minutes devoted to that fruitless endeavor, she determinedly directed her thoughts back to the nursery next door. Gardner was a distraction from regret that almost always worked, except on those rare occasions when Claire let herself acknowledge how much her daughter looked like her father.

But this wasn't going to be one of those times, she decided doggedly. Not after last night. Her first date, she thought again, almost amused by the phrase.

Maddy, as usual, had been right. It *hadn't* killed her to go out with John Amerson. Her lips tilted at the memory of her sister's familiar arguments. And Maddy would, of course, be calling this morning for a report.

"Yes, I survived. Yes, he seems to be very nice." A firm *"It's none of your business"* to the rest.

And for herself? she wondered. An acknowledgment, maybe, that although he wasn't Griff…

But then, no one else ever will be Griff, she thought. *And here I am, right back where I was determined not to be. Especially not today, the beginning of a brand-new year.*

Disgusted, she pushed the covers off and sat up on the side of the bed. If she wasn't going back to sleep, she might as well get up and get some work done before Gardner woke and began demanding attention.

The whole wonderful day lay before them. A rare one that they could spend totally together. Claire had a couple of things to take care of, but she didn't have to go into the office, of course. She had given the nanny the long holiday weekend off, so it would be just the two of them.

She slid her feet into her mules, standing up and stretching out the kinks. Her watch confirmed her guess that it was early—only a little after six. Considering the time she'd crawled into bed last night, it was no wonder she was feeling rocky. *Not* the champagne, she decided. Just lack of sleep.

Shivering, she crossed the expanse of thick white carpet, rubbing her palms up and down the sleeves of her pajamas. Maybe the baby-sitter had turned down the heat last night and forgotten to mention it before she left.

Claire always kept the house warm because of the baby. Mrs. Crutchen, the nanny, was cold-natured, so she never complained, but maybe Beth, being younger, had decided it was too hot. In any case, Claire was glad she'd gotten up. If Gardner had managed to kick her covers off, she was probably freezing her sweet little tush by now.

Claire opened the nursery door and was met by a damp coldness that sent a frisson of alarm through her. If her room had seemed chilled, then this one…

The damn window was open, she realized, hurrying across to pull down the sash and lock it. Why in the world would Beth, the most reliable sitter in existence, despite her age, leave the window open in the baby's room? It made no sense. Not in the dead of winter. Not in this freezing cold. It was a miracle that Gardner wasn't screaming her head off….

Claire's gaze automatically found the crib. There was no rounded bulge of baby bottom visible. Gardner had probably retreated from the cold, burrowing deeper into the warmth of the covers.

Claire took the three or four steps that separated her from the baby bed and looked in. That was when her heart stopped, congealed by a cold that owed nothing to the temperature of the room. In spite of the evidence of her eyes, she frantically pulled the covers back, flinging them to the end of the bed. And then she jerked them up, ripping them loose from the mattress and throwing them to the floor.

Which didn't change the harsh reality. There was no baby in the crib. Knees trembling, Claire bent, crawling under the bed, as if she thought her six-month-old daughter might suddenly have mastered the art of climbing out over the rails.

Still on her hands and knees, she picked up the wadded quilt and sheet, knowing immediately by their weight that there was nothing else in the pile. When she had physically confirmed that face by pawing through them again, she dropped them, her eyes searching every corner of the room.

Shock and disbelief clashed with acceptance of the unacceptable, so her mind sought another explanation. Any other explanation. Maybe Beth had taken Gardner home with her for some reason. But Claire had seen the sitter out last night, locking the door behind her. And there had been no one else in the house. No one…

Her gaze flew again to the window. Which had been open on this bitterly cold night. A window that shouldn't have been left open, unless…

No note, she told herself, scrambling up and running her hands over the mattress. She picked up the sheet and quilt again, shaking them, almost relieved when nothing fell out. She examined the top of the chest and then the changing table, but there was nothing on either of them.

If someone had taken the baby, she assured herself, they would have left a note. So Gardner had to be here. She *had* to be here.

Claire ran across to the closet and opened the door, as if she believed Gardner might be playing some macabre game of hide and seek. With trembling fingers, Claire pushed aside the hangers that held exquisite, doll-size dresses, her mind denying what her heart had already been forced to acknowledge.

The closet, too, was empty. As empty as the room. As

empty as her life had been before her daughter had been born. *Gardner,* Claire thought, the images of the short months since her birth flying through her head like a video tape on fast forward.

But if someone had taken her daughter, then surely... Surely, dear God, they would have told her what to do to get her back. They would have told her where to go. What they wanted. They wouldn't take her baby and leave nothing behind, not even a threat, a demand for ransom, a stereotypical warning about not calling in the authorities. Surely they hadn't taken her baby and left her nothing.

And yet, as she stood trembling in the center of the room, surrounded by its joyfully chosen furnishings and toys, Claire Heywood realized that that was exactly what they had done. Someone had opened the nursery window last night and had taken Gardner away from her. And had given her no idea of what she should do to get her back.

"MY NIECE," he said, smiling as he carefully placed the sleeping baby into her arms. "I'm afraid my sister is having some...problems," he said hesitantly. "Nothing serious, I think, but caring for Karen right now is proving to be...difficult. A little...more than she's up to handling at the moment. I think that's not uncommon for first-time mothers," he added, his eyes seeking her assurance that that was so.

Poor man, Rose Connor thought, holding the baby he had given her cuddled against her ample bosom. *He sounds as if he's afraid I'm going to judge. And Rose Connor judges no one. I've enough sins on me own head.*

"Oh, not uncommon at all," she said aloud, eagerly turning back the blanket in which the baby was wrapped to look down at her face. She seemed to be sleeping very soundly, but then it was morning nap time.

"This is my number in case you need to get in touch with me. You can leave a message if I'm out, and I'll return your call as soon as possible. The pediatrician's number is there as well, but…I'm afraid I would prefer that you call me first.''

"Of course," Rose said. "Unless it's an emergency," she added.

Rose always made an effort to follow her employers' instructions, strange as some of them seemed to be, but she wouldn't do anything that might compromise her ability to give the care her babies needed. She made no promises on that.

"She's a healthy little thing. I doubt you'll have any problems you yourself aren't capable of handling. You come very highly recommended, Ms. Connor."

"Just Rose," she corrected, still examining her new charge.

This one certainly appeared to be well taken care of, Rose decided. Whatever problems that poor girl might be having, they hadn't affected the baby. What she had told her new employer was certainly true. She herself had, of course, worked on more than one case where a new mother's emotions created problems. The stresses of modern living, she supposed. Not having a granny or an aunt nearby who could help out.

When those baby blues struck, it was always wise to have someone else step in and take over care of the baby. If only temporarily. *If* the parents could afford it. As these apparently could. Or at least the child's uncle apparently could, she amended.

"She's a real little darling," she said, smiling down unthinkingly, as if the sleeping baby might be reassured by her face or her tone.

After all, Rose was a stranger. And this sweetheart would miss her mother. They always did, even when they were as young as this one.

"She's a good little girl," Mr. Kimbrough said softly. "I'm sure you won't have any trouble."

"Don't you worry your head none, sir, about this dear rosebud," Rose said, her warm heart already engaged by the baby in her arms. "I'll take good care of her, I will. I'll keep her right as rain, I promise you," she said.

The soft lilt of her native Ireland always came back a bit more strongly when she held a baby. Maybe that was because of the memories of her own mother's gentle hands and voice. Maybe that was why Rose had chosen to do this. To care for other people's children.

She had never had any of her own, of course. No man had ever asked Rose Connor to marry him, but her broad, homely face and her softly rounded figure didn't frighten the little ones. They didn't care, bless them, how you looked, as long as you saw to it that they were fed and warm and dry. And as long as you held them when they cried. As long as you loved them. And she always did. No matter how long or how little a time they were in her care, she always loved them as if they were her very own darlings.

Smiling, she touched the soft cheek with her blunt forefinger, delighting in the smoothness of the skin. Savoring again the sweet aroma of baby powder. She would give that poor woman credit. No matter how bad she was feeling, she had taken care of this one.

And so would she, Rose thought, turning away from the man who had brought the baby. He had already been forgotten as she laid the little girl into the crib, smoothing its freshly laundered sheets and soft blankets with her fingers. She looked down on the sleeping baby with a satisfaction that verged on possessiveness.

And so she missed *his* smile. Satisfaction as well, perhaps, but for entirely different reasons. And Rose Connor was intuitive enough that she might even have been bothered by that smile, had she seen it.

It was probably just as well that her total attention was on the baby who had just been given into her very capable hands. Probably just as well for her peace of mind.

"LET'S GO OVER IT AGAIN, Ms. Heywood," the detective said patiently.

His round face was perspiring, and the top of his damp head gleamed bone-white through the strands of thinning hair he'd combed across it. He had patted at his forehead with a folded handkerchief a couple of times in the course of the interview, but so far he hadn't complained about the heat.

Claire had turned the thermostat up after she'd made the phone calls. She was still shaking, however, despite the rising temperature. And the small internal clock that had begun ticking inside her head as soon as she discovered Gardner was missing had turned into a jackhammer. Almost blinding in its intensity, the pain of the headache made it hard to think. Hard to talk. Hard to hope.

"I got home around two," she said, wondering how many times he would want to hear this. And wondering when her grandfather would arrive. That had been the first call she had made, of course, and he had been the one who had told her that she had to notify the police.

"And the baby-sitter was here?" the detective asked, referring to the notebook where he had carefully written everything down the first time she'd told her story.

She nodded, her eyes moving back to the staircase. She wished she weren't sitting where she could see the stairs and the parade of people who had climbed them in the last half hour. The detectives first and then the crime scene technicians, carrying the boxes and cases that held their equipment.

To all of them, this was just another case. Annoying, perhaps, because they had been called out on a holiday. Interesting, maybe, because her face or her name might be familiar. But still, just another job. And for her... For Claire, this was her baby. Her life. Her heart.

"You paid the sitter," Detective Minger continued, his calm voice interrupting that loss of control, "and then you let her out the front and locked the door."

"I turned off the lights down here, and I went upstairs,"

Claire said, trying to gather her thoughts as she pulled her gaze back to his face.

Which seemed devoid of suspicion. Whatever else they thought, apparently the police had decided that she hadn't had anything to do with her daughter's disappearance. She wondered if she should thank her minor celebrity for that conclusion.

"But you didn't check the back?" he asked, referring briefly to his notes again before he looked up, waiting, lips pursed as if in thought. As if he didn't already know the answer to this.

"There was no reason to," she said.

That was exactly what she had told him before. Beth wouldn't have unlocked the back door. Claire knew that. The teenager wasn't careless, and despite the much vaunted safety of the neighborhood, it would be a rare teenage girl who would want to be alone in a big, empty house at night with the doors unlocked. Not given the state of the world these days.

"And when you went upstairs…?"

Claire swallowed, feeling the despair build again despite her attempt to hold on to her rationality, at least until she had told them every detail, as many times as they wanted to hear it. Only then would she be free to collapse in self-reproach.

Perhaps there was no logical reason for the overwhelming sense of guilt she felt. No reason to believe that if she had done something differently, this might not have happened. She hadn't, and it had. And there was nothing she could do about that now. Nothing but help the police as much as she could. Nothing but answer whatever they wanted to ask, as many times as they needed to hear it. Nothing but tell them the absolute truth, and then pray they could find her daughter.

"I stopped at Gardner's door and listened," she admitted.

She hadn't gone in. She had had her hand on the knob, but for some reason—the lateness of the hour, the peaceful silence emanating from the closed door, or the fact that her feet hurt—for some unknown reason, she hadn't turned the handle.

She hadn't looked in on her sleeping daughter. Something she had done hundreds of times in the past, but not last night. Not the one night out of those hundreds when it might really have made a difference.

"But you didn't look into the room," Minger continued.

There was no trace of condemnation in his voice. Of course, it didn't matter what he thought. Not about this. Ultimately it only mattered what *she* believed.

If she had turned that knob, could she possibly have prevented what had happened? Or if her daughter had already been taken, how many hours might she have won back from the cold, empty darkness? Hours during which the searchers might have found a fresh trail or a clue. Might have found something.

"I went to bed," she said simply, unwilling to elaborate on her guilt.

She had undressed, slipping out of her shoes first and then throwing her clothes over the chair in her room, too tired to think about hanging them up. She hadn't even removed her makeup. It hadn't seemed important. Nothing had seemed as important as crawling between the welcoming smoothness of the cold sheets and relaxing.

Maybe even a little tipsy, she thought again, hating herself. *Sleeping off the effects of those two glasses of New Year's Eve champagne while someone took my baby.*

"And you heard nothing until you woke up this morning…at 6:10?" Minger asked, referring to his notes for the time she'd given him.

"Nothing," she confirmed simply.

Of course, she wasn't sure that she had heard anything this morning, either. Although that had been the implication of his question, she didn't bother to correct him.

"And you don't know what awakened you?"

"Maybe the cold. The cold from the window in the

baby's room," she suggested. She couldn't be certain about that, but there had been nothing else that she could swear to.

"When you went into the room, the window was open, and the baby was gone."

"That's right," she whispered.

"Is it possible, Ms. Heywood, that for…some reason the baby's father might have decided *he* should take custody of your daughter?"

Claire knew that what he was suggesting was the most familiar scenario that played out with missing children, one the police would probably feel obligated to investigate. Only this time, of course…

"Gardner's father is dead," she said.

Nothing more. No other explanation. She had never made any. Not even to Maddy, who had certainly demanded one. Only to her grandfather had she admitted the truth. And it was also to him, of course, that she had turned this morning.

The silence that fell after her clipped statement was awkward. She wondered if Minger believed her. Not that it mattered, not unless the thought that Gardner's father might have had something to do with the kidnapping slowed down their investigation.

"And you say you found no note," Minger continued, apparently willing, at least for now, to drop the possibility that this was a noncustodial-parent snatch. "Nothing that would give you any indication as to why someone had taken your daughter."

Taken your daughter. With his words, the nightmare images she had fought invaded her head. Wondering if they were taking care of her. If she was warm. If she'd been fed this morning. She was used to having her breakfast before now, and if they didn't know that…

Claire took a breath, again denying the devastating worry. Denying it at least until she had done this job. Until she had done everything she could do to help them find Gardner.

"I didn't find anything," she said. "Do you suppose it's

possible the note might have blown outside?'' she asked, the thought sudden. ''I mean, with that window wide-open…''

As she made the suggestion, she felt a spurt of hope, one that she tried to control because it made no sense. They wouldn't be that careless. Whoever had gone to all this trouble wouldn't leave a message where it might blow away.

Minger, however, methodically made a notation on his pad. ''I'll have them look. You haven't been outside?'' he asked, his eyes coming back up to examine hers.

''This morning?''

He nodded.

''You think there might be prints?'' she asked instead of answering, realizing where he was heading with that question.

''Anything's possible. If they *did* get into the room through that window, then there ought to be some evidence of that outside. If not footprints, then impressions made by the ladder they used. Something. At least we'll hope so.''

She nodded, although she wasn't sure what those things would tell them that might be useful in finding Gardner. There might be evidence outside that could eventually be used in court. She understood that, of course, but evidence of that kind wasn't what was important right now.

''Any idea why your alarm didn't go off?'' he asked.

Surprised, she looked up at him, wondering why they hadn't checked that for themselves.

''I assumed it had been cut. Tampered with in some way.''

Minger shook his head. ''We checked. As far as we can tell, it should be working. When they opened that window, the system should have gone off here and at the security office. Apparently, it didn't.''

''But…how could that happen?'' Claire asked. If anything, the system had been too sensitive. So why last night, when it would have made such a difference…

''We don't know. It's something else we'll be looking

into. We're also in the process of questioning your neighbors, at least those close enough that there's a chance they might have heard or seen something. We've already set up your phone to record incoming calls, of course,'' Minger said. ''And an extra line to handle our calls or any you might need to make.'' He had begun to unfold his bulk out the chair as he talked.

''How likely would it be that someone might have seen something?'' Claire asked. ''I mean…it was the middle of the night.''

Claire suddenly wished for a neighbor who was a busybody or an insomniac. As far as she knew, however, she had neither. So she didn't hold out much hope that the cops' strategy in canvassing the neighborhood would yield anything useful.

''It was New Year's Eve,'' Minger reminded her. ''Somebody might still have been up. Or coming in from a party. Besides, we don't know that it was the middle of the night when your daughter was taken,'' the detective said. He folded his notebook and stuck it into his inside coat pocket, his lips pursing again. ''Your sitter put the baby to bed a little after ten. Apparently nobody saw or heard anything out of the ordinary after that.''

''Beth says she didn't hear anything, either?'' Claire asked, knowing, because he had told her, that they had already talked to the teenage sitter, who lived only a couple of houses down the street.

''Not a sound. No noise of a ladder being put against the house, although that's on the other side from where she was watching TV. No alarm. And not a peep out of the baby, although the monitor was on down here. Would that be unusual, Ms. Heywood? For the baby not to wake up after she was put down, I mean?''

Gardner had begun sleeping through the night—at least most of it—early on. Sometimes she awoke if she were out of sorts or teething, but the fact that she hadn't cried after

Beth put her to bed wasn't all that surprising. Or that helpful, Claire supposed.

"Not really," she said.

Minger nodded, holding her gaze. "Well," he said, drawing the syllable out as an obvious indication he was through with the questions. "You think of anything else, you be sure and let us know."

"What are you going to be doing in the meantime?" she asked.

Surely he wasn't leaving. Surely there was more to what the police needed than this? More than to ask her some questions, dust the nursery for prints and examine the flower beds. Surely to God there was something else they all ought to be doing.

"Asking questions," he said. "Running a match on anything they find upstairs. Checking this one against the details of other kidnappings we have on file. And waiting," he added after a moment. "Waiting for somebody to get in touch with you."

"But you think they will?" Claire asked, seeking his reassurance.

He looked around the room, evaluating. "Most kidnappings that aren't parental are carried out for profit. In this case, your family, both sides, are pretty well known in this town. It wouldn't be hard for somebody to dig out enough information about you to carry this off. They'll be in touch, Ms. Heywood. My take on this is that somebody figures to hold you up for a nice, tidy sum in ransom."

"Then…you think that means they'll take care of her?" she asked.

She was aware that that didn't always happen. Things could go wrong. There was the Lindbergh baby, for example. But if all these people wanted was money…

"They got no reason not to," he said softly. "And a lot of reasons to. At least that's what we're hoping for."

"How long?" she asked. "How long before I'll hear something?"

He shrugged, thick shoulders rising and holding a second, lifting the ill-fitting suit coat with them. "The sooner the better for them. It won't be long," he said reassuringly.

The last was meant to be kind, she supposed, but the impression she was getting was that the cops were willing to play the waiting game, maybe because they didn't know what else to do at this point. She wasn't willing. Not with Gardner as the stakes.

Claire didn't get up and escort him out when he walked past her chair. She wasn't sure if he would be going out the front door or back upstairs, but she was certain that *she* was going to stay right here, near the phone. After all, he had said it wouldn't be long before she'd hear something.

"Are you by any chance working on a story right now, Ms. Heywood?" the detective asked.

She turned in surprise at the question, looking at him over her shoulder. Minger was standing in the archway that led into the front hall. His face was bland, only polite inquiry in his eyes, but as it had when she'd opened the nursery door and felt the unexpected cold, a shiver of apprehension slipped along her spine.

"I'm a lawyer, Detective Minger. I'm not really a journalist," she said. "The networks sometimes ask me to do analyses of their political stories. Those that have legal overtones."

"Guess there are a lot of them," he said, his lips moving into a smile. "I see you on TV sometimes," he said. "I just wondered if you were working on something right now."

"I'm not working on anything," she said, but Claire understood what he was getting at. And it frightened her. The possibility that this might not be about money at all but about…anger? Retaliation? Something personal.

Mentally she reviewed the features she had done in the last six months. Although there was always the chance that someone who had been touched on in one of her analyses might be unhinged enough to do something like this, it seemed unlikely, as most of them were highly respected figures on the national scene. People she knew personally. And who knew her or her family.

Politics in this town were many things to many people, but seldom did they involve violence. The only things that she could think of that she had been involved in lately that might possibly be connected to anything violent…

Had to do with the members of Griff's team, she realized.

She didn't know how that sudden thought was reflected in her face, but it must have been. An involuntary widening of her eyes, perhaps. A hesitation in her breathing. There must have been some reaction, obvious enough that Detective Minger hadn't missed it.

"You think of something, Ms. Heywood?" he asked softly. "Something we ought to know about?"

Slowly she shook her head. Even if it were possible that Gardner's disappearance might in some incredible way be connected to what she had done for Jordan Cross or for the man they called Hawk, Minger wouldn't be the one to deal with it. She understood that. Minger wouldn't get to first base with any inquiries he tried to make concerning Griff Cabot's External Security Team.

"No," she said softly. "I can't think of anything else I can tell you, Detective Minger."

He nodded, still holding her eyes. He knew she was lying. Apparently Minger was better at his job than she had given him credit for. For a second she thought about telling him the truth, afraid that if she didn't, he would draw his own conclusions about what she was hiding.

She resisted the impulse because she knew she had been right before. The things she had gotten involved with in helping the CIA agents who had once worked for Griff Cabot couldn't be handled by the cops.

And she wasn't exactly sure who might be able to inquire about them within the dark and dirty bowels of the agency itself. Perhaps her grandfather, although the people he had been associated with there were, like himself, long retired from the intelligence agency.

And Claire herself probably wouldn't get any further within the CIA than Minger could. Not unless she could contact Jordan or Hawk directly. Again, as she had earlier, she felt a surge of hope at that thought.

There would be no one better to find Gardner than the men of Griff's team. There was no one with more expertise at tracking someone down, as Hawk had proved in finding Griff's assassin. No one more experienced at putting the pieces of a puzzle together, as Jordan Cross had done in coming up with the location of the millions that had been stolen from the Mafia.

And they both owed her. *Quid pro quo,* she thought. They owed her. And, of course, they owed Griff Cabot even more.

With her daughter missing, Claire knew that she would call due every favor she had ever been owed by anyone in this town. With these men, however, she also knew that wouldn't be necessary. All she would have to say to them was that Griff Cabot's daughter was missing. And that she needed their help to get her back.

Chapter Two

"And what the hell makes you think someone within the agency had anything to do with what happened?" Carl Steiner asked angrily. "You have to know better than that, damn it. You have to know *us* better than that."

When Griff Cabot didn't answer, Steiner shook his head in disgust. After a few seconds he closed his eyes, rubbing his forefinger tiredly up and down the bridge of his narrow nose, as if his week had already been too long, and this at the end of it was too hard to deal with.

And then Carl had driven out to the wilds of southern Pennsylvania, fighting the holiday weekend traffic, Griff remembered. He supposed he should be grateful for the swift response to his message. However, he was having a tough time evoking gratitude for anything right now.

His leg hurt like a son of a bitch. And he was furious. Steiner had certainly known him long enough to read that fury, although Griff was working hard at presenting his case calmly and rationally, just as he would have done when making any professional argument. After he had allowed the echoes of Carl's anger to fade into silence, he again ticked off the points he had already made in his original message to the director.

"One of my men is fingered for an assassination he didn't carry out. As a result, he almost ends up on the most wanted list. Another is set down in the middle of a deal that's an open invitation for somebody to murder him, in a very slow and extremely painful way. Those things happen within weeks of each other and within a few months of my agency-engineered death. So I find all these incidents to be just a little too coincidental, Carl. Those kinds of things don't happen by chance. Not in our world.''

Griff watched as Steiner's lips tightened, but thankfully Carl resisted reminding him that it wasn't exactly ''our'' world any longer. When he had agreed to go along with the story they had put out after he'd been injured in the terrorist attack at Langley, Griff hadn't believed they would use his ''death'' as an excuse to cut his people loose. Or that if they then got into trouble, the agency would refuse to help them.

''Normally I'd agree,'' Steiner said, his voice carefully moderated to sound calm and reasonable. ''However, in those two particular cases—''

''Spare me the crap, Carl,'' Griff said succinctly.

He pushed up out of the chair he was sitting in, the one *behind* the desk, of course. Assuming that position of power hadn't really been intentional, however. It was simply force of habit.

For too many years Griff Cabot had been the one in charge. The one people reported to. Now he was on the outside looking in, having to depend on old friendships to get to the bottom of what had been happening to his team. And he found he didn't like that position worth a damn.

He limped across the library, leaning on a silver-headed cane. Griff Cabot had hated all the restrictions his injuries had imposed, but most of all, he had hated this damn cane, a constant reminder that he was no longer the man he had once been. So he had worked particularly hard on being able to get along without using it. Most of the time he succeeded.

Today, however, he'd had another poking and prodding session with the surgeons, who had spent the afternoon putting him through their tests and congratulating themselves on their latest handiwork. The combination of that and the cold rain he'd been out in most of the day had had its effect.

As a result, he had been forced to acknowledge that if he wanted to be mobile during Carl's visit, then the hated cane was his only option.

It seemed to him to be a symbol of everything that had happened. The attack. The agency's reaction to his injuries. Their lingering effects. The sooner he accepted those, one of the doctors had told him this afternoon, the quicker he would make peace with his limitations.

Screw them. Screw them all, Griff thought, looking out the window at the rain-drenched garden below.

Not that it was much of a garden. Not at this time of year. In the winter downpour it looked exactly like what it was—cold and gray and dead. Just like him.

His eyes flicked upward, expecting to catch the reflection of his guest in the glass, which had been darkened into near opaqueness by the twilight outside. Instead he found his own image, distorted by the streaks of rain. He could see enough to know, however, that he didn't like what he was looking at.

His body canted slightly to the side because of the cane. His hair was too long by his own once impeccable standards. And the eyes reflected in the glass appeared to be without color. *Cold and gray and dead* echoed again in his head. He watched his jaw tighten in frustration, and he forced it to relax.

He turned around to face his visitor, propping his left hip on the deep ledge of the windowsill and leaning gratefully against the glass behind him. Standing probably hadn't been such a hot idea, he acknowledged.

He realized gratefully that his leg was protesting a little less, now that some of his weight was borne by the ledge. He hadn't taken anything for the pain, but he knew he would have to eventually. *If* he intended to sleep tonight.

And to him that would be another triumph for the terrorist bastard whose bullets had shattered his leg. Another small defeat in a battle he had fought every day of the past year.

"I know you're concerned about your people," Carl said quietly.

Griff looked up to find Steiner watching him, compassion evident in his eyes. He hid the emotion as soon as he realized Griff was looking at him, but the fact that it had been there angered Cabot anew. He wasn't even sure whether the cause of that pity was his injury or the concern for his men Carl had just referred to.

"But I can assure you," Steiner added, "and the director has asked me to give you his assurance as well, that those were totally unrelated and coincidental events. They had nothing to do with the team or with operations."

"They've both been retired. Two of the best people we had, Carl, and you let them go."

"Their choice. They *chose* to leave. And we gave them all the help we could to successfully make that transition. All the help they would accept from us."

"Things just...went wrong?" Griff asked, his voice as low as Steiner's, but edged with sarcasm.

"In Hawkins' case he tried to help a woman. Chivalrous perhaps, but foolhardy as well, given his profession. And it put him in the wrong place at the wrong time. You'd have to admit that when we saw Hawk on camera at the scene of a political assassination, we had a right to be a little...shall we say wary? Even suspicious?"

"Not unless you sent him there," Griff argued. He stretched his aching leg out in front of him, using the cane to push himself farther back onto the deep sill of the window.

"We didn't send him to Baghdad, either," Steiner reminded him.

Griff supposed he should have known Hawk would undertake that mission, but he hadn't been in any condition to make that assessment at the time. Even if he had been, Griff suspected he wouldn't have attempted to dissuade Hawk. After all, five people had died in the terrorist attack for which Hawk's mission had been payback. But the sixth...

Like Mark Twain, he thought, *the reports of my death have been greatly exaggerated.* The firm line of Cabot's mouth moved slightly in amusement. "That was personal," he said softly. *Because Hawk was my friend. And because I was his.*

"We had no way of knowing that the other wasn't personal as well. When we saw Hawk on the videos, we assumed al-Ahmad had some connection to the terrorists responsible for the Langley massacre. We couldn't afford to have an agent operating on his own agenda, not on an international level. Not as volatile as the region is. You know that. You would have been the first to rein Hawkins in."

He would have been, too. Griff would never have allowed a member of the team to make that kind of decision. Not even someone like Hawk, whom he trusted implicitly.

Steiner's explanation made sense. And from everything Griff had been able to discover about her, Tyler Stewart had really been an innocent pawn in that assassination. Griff knew he was one of the few people who could believe Hawk was romantic enough to have done what Steiner claimed he had—played knight errant to protect a woman.

"But that doesn't explain why you let Stewart out of protective custody," Griff said.

"Obviously," Steiner said, his own anger creeping out again from under the surface calm he had imposed, "we let her go because we thought it was over. When Holt confirmed what we'd been told about the assassination being an extremist plot, we didn't see the need to protect Ms. Stewart any longer. We were wrong, but what happened as a result of that error didn't impact on Hawk. He was never a target for retaliation. Not by us."

"And what happened to Jordan?" Griff asked. "Are you trying to tell me that was *another* coincidence?"

"After the fiasco at the airport, Cross needed a new face," Steiner said simply.

His voice, however, reflected his displeasure with what had occurred in Mississippi that day. Again Griff couldn't blame him. Any time an agent was exposed, the organization suffered, especially if it were someone whose responsibilities were as sensitive as Jordan's had once been.

"And so the agency gave him one that belonged to a man who was the target of a Mafia manhunt," Griff said softly.

He was careful to keep any accusation out of his tone. Antagonizing Carl wouldn't be smart, since Steiner was one of the few people within the CIA who knew Cabot hadn't died in that attack on headquarters. One of the few people he could still talk to about the operations of the agency whose missions had occupied more than half his life.

Griff admitted that he missed being in on policy decisions and on the day-to-day running of the intelligence unit once known as the External Security Team. His job had encompassed a lot of diverse and fascinating activities during the dozen years the team had been in existence.

Now he had been put out to pasture, and the men he had trained were slowly being reassigned or dismissed or, like him, forcibly retired. Griff didn't have a right to object to that process, he supposed. Not when he got down to the bottom line, which was that he *had* agreed go along with their announcement of his death.

He had done that because he had known the director was probably correct in what he'd suggested. That *was* the safest way to protect Griff from the possibility that someone might try to retaliate for the team's past operations. At the time, the agency had viewed the terrorist attack at Langley as just such a retaliation.

Griff's life had already been a shambles. Given the extent of his injuries, it had been evident that his professional life was over. And then, considering what had happened between him and Claire... He took a deep breath, remembering.

At the time, it had seemed like the simplest thing to do. Maybe it had been just following the path of least resistance. Allowing them to ''retire'' him with a gravestone rather than a gold watch as his monument. After all, they all knew there weren't that many special operatives who lived long enough to collect on the watch, anyway.

And there had been increasing pressure within the agency to do away with his particular branch of the Special Operations Group. The External Security Team had been Griff Cabot's brainchild, although the concept behind it certainly wasn't new. Just more politically unacceptable with each passing year.

However, despite the strictures and limitations now in place on CIA operations, there was still occasionally a need for the so-called quiet option. The need to do away with a dangerous madman whose continuing existence threatened the security of the nation. That was one of the primary jobs of Cabot's group.

One of the last assignments the team had undertaken under his direction had been to find a Russian gangster who had somehow acquired a handful of suitcase nukes. To find him, to take him out and then retrieve the weapons.

With the collapse of the Soviet Union, a lot more nuclear devices were showing up on the international black market. Most of the world couldn't begin to conceive of the kind of terrorism that would engender. It would soon be able to, however, and Griff wondered who would be around then with the mandate the team had once had. A team that, with his retirement, was slowly being destroyed.

Griff hadn't realized, of course, the implications his "death" would have for his people. And although he would certainly have argued against standing down the team, whether the agency's agenda where his men were concerned was smart or not was not really the question.

Mothballing them was one thing. Getting rid of agents who knew too much was another. From the outside looking in, Griff Cabot had begun to suspect that was what was being done, especially in Jordan Cross's case. And Griff wasn't about to let them get away with that.

"You know how it works, Griff," Steiner argued. "We don't make the decision as to whose face someone gets. The surgeons do that, based on existing facial structure, coloring, whatever. Why the hell would anyone want to expose Cross to something like what happened to him?''

"I don't know," Griff said. "I've been trying to decide that since I found out what was happening."

"And frankly, I'd like to know exactly *how* you found out," Steiner said quietly. For the first time there was a hint of challenge in his eyes. Of personal affront.

Again Griff didn't respond, but he didn't allow his gaze to drop. It was a legitimate demand. One he certainly would have made had he been in Carl's position, probably a lot more forcefully. That didn't mean, however, that he intended to answer it.

"If you're in touch with someone in the agency, then that's a breach of security," Steiner continued. "You know that. If you were still in charge of the division, you wouldn't put up with it, and you know that as well."

Carl was right, of course. He wouldn't have.

"I can't allow it either, Griff. No matter how well intentioned you are—and I believe that, by the way—I can't allow you to interfere with the functioning of the division."

"I was not aware that I've interfered with anything," Griff said. "Are you?"

Steiner's eyes assessed him before he answered, his voice softer now. "For a lot of the members of your team, their primary loyalty was never to the agency. Or even to their country. It was to you. That's a dangerous situation, Griff, and we both know it."

"Is that why I was retired?" Griff asked. He could hear the bitterness in his question.

"You were retired because you could no longer function as the head of a vitally important intelligence division. At the time, no one was willing to predict that you would *ever* be able to function in that position again. The DCI made the decision that was in the agency's best interests. He always will. That's the director's responsibility. And you felt that way, too. At the time," Steiner reminded him.

"And now you think I've changed my mind. Is that it?"

"I don't know. You tell me, Griff. Are you drumming up a conspiracy because you miss it? Because you miss the team? The excitement? The thrill of the chase?"

"Which effectively reduces what I did for the past ten years to some macho bull-crap exercise in self-aggrandizement."

Steiner's snort of laughter relaxed the tension his previous questions had created. "Yeah? Well, there are a lot of people who think that about all of us in the agency. It wasn't a personal accusation."

"I want my people taken care of," Griff said softly.

"We're trying," Carl said. "They are sometimes…shall we say, difficult to protect."

"Difficult to control," Griff suggested, again fighting an urge to smile.

"I told you. Their loyalty was personal."

"Is that what this is about? Getting rid of them because they were *my* men?"

"As far as I can ascertain—and believe me, I've tried—no one is trying to get rid of *them*. The team itself is a different story. You're aware of the current thinking about its function."

"Yeah, I'm aware," Griff said mockingly. "Suddenly everybody in the world loves one another. No more bad guys. No more madmen."

Steiner looked down at his hands, which were lying, totally relaxed, in his lap. Night was falling outside, and the room had darkened. Griff supposed that as a good host he should turn on some lights, but there was something about the dimness that invited confidences.

Griff Cabot's position meant he had been well trained in all the psychological tricks. In getting people to do what he wanted. In bringing out the best they had to offer in any situation. And sometimes in pulling things out of them that they didn't want to reveal. It was always easier to be truthful about painful things in the darkness.

When Carl looked up again, Griff's eyes were on his face. Carl didn't look away. It was obvious to Griff that Steiner was assessing him as well, maybe assessing his motives, even across the distance that separated them.

"A lot of people think the members of your team *are* the bad guys," Carl said.

"Not a lot of people," Griff said, fighting the familiar rush of rage at the old argument. "*Most* people don't think about what we do. *Most* people don't care."

"The ones now making the decisions do," Carl said.

Again, neither of them said anything for several long seconds. The era of intelligence in which Griff Cabot and his team had functioned was over. They both knew it. One of them didn't want to accept it. Which didn't change anything.

Finally, Steiner stood up. The raindrops that had glistened in his dark hair hadn't completely dried, but it was obvious he believed he had said everything he had come here to say.

And it was obvious that this had been a warning as well, Griff thought. A warning sent by those in charge, and deliberately, it had been delivered by a friend. They had hoped, apparently, that the message would have more effect coming from Carl, who *was* his friend. As well as his successor.

"If you're having second thoughts about your retirement, I'd advise you to keep them to yourself," Steiner said, almost as if he had just read his mind.

He walked across the room, however, and held out his hand. Cabot could see, despite the low lighting, that the skin under Steiner's eyes was dark with fatigue, discolored like old bruises, and the lines in his face were deeper than they had been twelve months ago. Of course, it was the end of a long, hard week. The end of a long hard year, Griff amended.

Griff remembered what that felt like. Suddenly, unexpectedly, he envied his successor those days of turmoil and hard decisions. Maybe Steiner was right. Maybe his anxiety and anger were simply the result of being so far out of the loop. Out of the seat of power he had occupied for so long. After a moment Griff leaned his cane against his thigh and took the outstretched hand.

"My advice is to keep any future accusations to yourself as well," Steiner added softly. "The days of running the world to suit ourselves are over. It's a new ball game."

"With new players," Griff said. "Is that what you're suggesting?"

"With new players," Steiner repeated. "New rules. And like them or not, we'll have to learn to play by them."

"I won't," Griff said.

Steiner took a breath, and his lips flattened again. Then they relaxed into a smile. "Get a hobby, Griff. Something besides this. Besides living in the past. If your men are as smart as I think they are, they'll do the same. But don't be looking over your shoulder. Nobody from the agency is after them. Or you. Boredom's not an excuse for paranoia."

Griff Cabot's eyes narrowed at the last comment, but after a second, he laughed, the sound of it again breaking the tension that had grown with the darkness. Then he nodded, releasing his friend's hand.

"Thanks for coming all the way up here," he said.

"I didn't mind. I know what you meant to the agency. I don't want to see you do anything to destroy the memory of what you accomplished there."

"I appreciate that," Griff said.

"And I know the way out," Steiner said. "So don't even offer."

It was the closest Carl had come to referring to his injuries, and Griff appreciated his sensitivity. Maybe Carl was even right about the other, he thought, as he watched his guest open the door to the study and then close it softly behind him. Maybe Griff *had* read too much into a couple of unrelated incidents simply because he didn't have enough to do. Or enough to think about.

Hawk and Jordan Cross were certainly capable of taking care of themselves. Even in intelligence work, he acknowl-

edged, there had always been the occasional chance mishap.
Now, like a bored old maid with a new pair of binoculars,
he had created himself some excitement. Imagined a mystery.

Old maid, he thought again, the phrase especially unpleasant. Maybe *hermit* was a better choice of words. But
that life-style wasn't really necessary. His isolation had been
a matter of choice. Probably an unhealthy one, he admitted.

He hadn't gone the route they had chosen for Jordan. His
face had never been that well known, not outside the inner
circle of the intelligence community. He was not a public
figure, so a change in appearance hadn't been considered
necessary.

The other had been easily accomplished. A change of
location. A new identity. He had done that countless times
for other people. Now the agency had done it for him.

He stood up, wincing at the resultant protest from his leg,
and walked away from the window. Looking out at the rain
was almost as depressing as the isolation. Despite the subject of their conversation, he had enjoyed Steiner's brief
visit. Someone to talk to. Someone who...

He blocked the thought, knowing from long experience
that thinking about Claire wasn't something he could afford
to do tonight. And after all, it had been quite a leap from
Carl Steiner and the team to that other lost relationship.

He supposed it was the holiday. Holidays always seemed
a time for nostalgia. For remembering.

Grateful he didn't have to hide his discomfort anymore,
he eased carefully down into the chair behind the desk, looking at the blank computer screen. Carl's question about how
he had known what was happening to his men had been
legitimate. He had just been headed in the wrong direction.
Steiner had been right, however, about the ethics of what
Griff had been doing.

Old spies don't die, he thought, paraphrasing badly. They
just lose their integrity. But of course, most people thought

that was an oxymoron to begin with. Spies and integrity. The CIA and ethics.

He swiveled the chair away from the temptation of the keyboard. He supposed he should have been expecting Jake Holt, the team's systems expert, to show up out here, instead of Steiner. Jake had taught him all he knew about getting information out of the system, even how to get in and out without leaving footprints. At least, Griff amended, without leaving a trail that would be obvious to anyone except the Jake Holts of the world.

And if Jake had found his footprints, he was probably going crazy trying to figure out who had left them, Griff imagined. Which meant that at least Jake had something to do. "Get a hobby," Steiner had advised.

And screw you, too, Griff thought.

He savagely punched the remote button, and the TV screen across the room blinked into life. It was almost time for the evening news. He could watch what was happening around the world just like everyone else. No longer a player, but an observer. That message had come through loud and clear.

Despite the pictures flickering across the screen, his mind began wandering again, mulling over the recent conversation. Then something the announcer said connected, and suddenly Griff's entire concentration was engaged by the picture on the TV.

The house they were showing was familiar. Too damned familiar. His finger found the volume control, his eyes never leaving the visuals marching across the screen as the announcer talked.

Images of a woman now. The same woman in a variety of settings and backgrounds. In different groups. Or looking straight into the camera. Talking. In one scene she was standing outside the Supreme Court building, the wind whipping strands of blond hair out of the neat chignon into which it had been confined.

With a gesture so familiar it closed his throat, she lifted

a slender hand to brush a tendril away from the oval perfection of her face. *Claire,* he thought, unable to draw another breath as he watched. Claire.

And finally, when the words the reporter was intoning managed to break through the spell Claire Heywood had cast over him since the first time he had seen her, Griff began to realize what had happened. And why the face of the woman he loved, a woman who believed, along with the rest of the world, that he was dead, was once more appearing on his television screen.

As soon as he had, Griff Cabot picked up the phone on his desk and, without hesitation, without considering the wisdom of what he was doing or its possible effects, punched in the number Carl Steiner had just warned him never to call again.

Chapter Three

"Because according to the agency, those men you asked me to find don't exist," Claire's grandfather said. "Apparently, they never have," he added softly.

"But…that's not true," Claire said, feeling despair seep in. It dampened the hope that had been created by the thought of being able to put the nightmare of her daughter's kidnapping into Hawk's and Jordan Cross's capable hands. "I met them. I talked to them. They worked for Griff."

"If they did, there's no record of it now."

"He told me they were going to do that," she said, remembering the meeting she had helped Jordan arrange when the man called Hawk had been targeted by his own employer.

"They were going to do what?" her grandfather asked, obviously puzzled by the reference he couldn't possibly understand.

"Destroy the records. At least…destroy the ones on Hawk."

"Cabot told you that? Even if that were true, it sounds like something that wouldn't be discussed outside the agency."

"Not Griff. A man called Steiner. An assistant deputy director. He told Hawk that when he got through, there wouldn't be anything left there with his name on it. Not a pay voucher. Not a memo. Nothing."

''It seems he was right,'' her grandfather said, his eyes bleak.

Tonight he looked every one of his seventy-eight years, Claire realized, and that was something she had never thought before. Montgomery Gardner's slender, erect figure, with its almost military bearing, never seemed to change with the passage of the years. To Claire, he had never seemed to age, appearing no different than he had been in her earliest memories of him.

Although his hair was white and the lines in his beloved face were deeply drawn, she had never thought of him as an old man. Not until now. Tonight his shoulders were slumped, his normal confidence subdued.

But she didn't know how she would have managed today had he not come to help. Her parents had been spending the holidays in Europe. Although they had begun scrambling to get a flight home as soon as she had gotten in touch with them, they hadn't yet been successful because of the holiday traffic. And she wasn't sure when they would finally arrive.

But she could bear even that, Claire had thought when her father called to tell her. She had been reared in her father's highly liberal ideology, but her sternly conservative grandfather had always been the calm, stable rock in her world. He had seemed prepared to fill that role again when he had opened the front door this morning, full of plans and suggestions.

Now, however, despite everything they had done, they were no closer to a solution to Gardner's disappearance than they had been then. And her grandfather appeared almost defeated. As despairing as she was.

It hurt her to see how much this had shaken him. And it frightened her even more to realize that the clever and ruth-less Monty Gardner was afraid. Afraid for Gardner.

All day Claire had fought the images. Pushed them from her head because she couldn't stand to have them there. Images of her baby. Would there be someone to comfort her when she cried? If she were cold or hungry? Did she miss her mother?

And yet Claire had been forced to acknowledge that there was nothing she could do about any of those. She was powerless to change a thing about Gardner's situation. So she had fiercely concentrated on doing everything she could to get her back from the people who had taken her. Whoever they were. Whatever they wanted. And Hawk and Jordan Cross had been her best hope—the one she had clung to throughout the afternoon.

"So…what can we do now?" she asked her grandfather.

The idea that they might be able to appeal to Steiner for the information they needed had crossed her mind. But remembering the cold fury in his eyes the day Hawk had tried to bargain for Tyler Stewart's life, Claire believed he wouldn't tell her anything. The agency had made its decision where Lucas Hawkins was concerned. Apparently they had done the same thing with Jordan, as well.

"I've requested that the DCI put me in touch with any members of Cabot's team who are still working for the agency, but frankly…"

Her grandfather's lips tightened. He shook his head slowly, revealing his frustration with his contacts within the intelligence community, about whom he had been so hopeful this morning.

"You don't think he will," Claire suggested softly. "Not even for you."

"As far as they're concerned, this is a private matter, Claire. Something that has nothing to do with the agency, of course. The people Griff Cabot worked with aren't detectives who can be called in to solve the odd crime or two. I suppose I should have known better than to ask him. I would probably have done the same thing—given a polite brush-off to someone asking a personal favor that has nothing to do with the mission of the agency."

She knew that was over thirty years of intelligence work speaking. And a desire to be fair. It had nothing to do with his love for her or her daughter. Her grandfather would do anything to get Gardner back, but apparently he, too, had no idea where else to turn. And despite Detective Minger's assurance this morning, no one had called demanding ransom. Or demanding anything else.

This had been the longest day of her life, Claire thought. Every minute had been a battle to contain her frustration and control her growing terror, at least enough to be able to function, enough to think, enough to give information to all the people who had asked for it. Now, as night fell, she had no more idea of who had taken her baby or why than she had had this morning when she'd opened the door of that empty nursery.

Since he'd arrived, her grandfather had spent hours on the phone line the police had set up. And he was the one who had urged her to call the FBI. To talk to the media. To issue a plea to the public for their help in finding Gardner.

Maddy and Charles had agreed with that idea. After all, they had argued, her celebrity might be a blessing in this situation, despite the fact that Claire had chosen to keep her daughter out of the spotlight.

Only her family and closest friends even knew of Gardner's existence. That had been fairly easy to accomplish, since Claire had been out of the country during all but the earliest stages of her pregnancy. She had always tried to keep her private life separate from her professional one, and up until now, she believed she had been successful. But maybe, she had been forced to acknowledge, she had been wrong about that.

So she had gone over and over each case she had worked on. And she had thought through every on-the-air pronouncement she had ever made. Reviewed mentally every political story on which she had commented.

Since she wasn't a criminal lawyer, the odds of a client or someone connected with a client having had anything to do with Gardner's kidnapping seemed so small as to be inconsequential. As for the bits and pieces she had done in front of the camera, there was nothing in the fairly dry political commentary that seemed threatening or dangerous. Nothing that should provoke this kind of outrage. And she was again right back to where she had been this morning.

"Griff's people would help me find her if they knew," she said.

She was still as certain of that as she had been when she'd suggested to her grandfather that they should try to contact Hawk and Jordan. But if they couldn't reach them, the only hope she had was that they would see the TV interview she had done this afternoon and contact her. It seemed the one remaining chance to solicit their help.

She tried to think of anyone else they might appeal to. If only she knew what had triggered this. If only she understood the seemingly senseless motivation in taking a six-month-old baby. If it had not been done for money—

The shrill of the phone interrupted those circling thoughts. Her eyes lifted quickly to meet her grandfather's, which had widened in shock at the unexpected sound. She found the same sense of expectation she felt reflected in his face.

But when it rang again, she realized that this was the extra line the police had set up, and not her regular number, where any call from the kidnappers could be expected to come in. Her hand still shaking from that first mistaken impression, she finally picked up the receiver.

"Claire Heywood," she said.

"I have a message for you, Ms. Heywood."

"A message?" she questioned, trying to think if she had ever heard this disembodied voice before, trying to place the caller. No one had this number, unless her grandfather had given it to whomever he had talked to today. She certainly hadn't. Except to her father, whose voice she would have known immediately.

"From a friend," he said.

A message from a friend? None of whom had this number? From a man whose voice she didn't recognize?

Her pulse began to race, as her mind discarded those possibilities. And as it did, the thought that this might finally be word from whoever had taken Gardner began to grow in her heart.

Please God, let this be what we've waited for, she prayed, motioning to her grandfather that she needed something to write on. "All right," Claire said into the receiver when she was sure he understood her gestures.

Then she brought her entire consciousness to bear on listening and remembering—tone, accent, word patterns. It was almost an intellectual exercise, deliberately undertaken because the rest of it was too important—waiting for those words she so desperately needed to hear in order to set her world back on its axis.

"He wants you to meet him in the rose garden," the voice on the other end of the line stated.

Her grandfather had placed a notebook and pen beside the phone. Claire had picked up the pen, automatically turning the pad to face her. It reminded her of Minger's meticulous note-taking this morning, of how careful he had been. And she must be just that careful, too.

But when her caller said those words, her hand hesitated over the paper. For a moment all she could think of was the one at the White House, but of course that couldn't be right.

"The Rose Garden?" she repeated, her inflection questioning. If this was someone's idea of a prank...

A hint of laughter whispered across the distance. "He said to tell you not *that* one."

As if the caller had read her mind. *Not that one.*

"I'm afraid I don't understand," she said carefully, aware of the slow deflation of the hope that had blossomed with the ringing of the phone.

The rose garden? she repeated mentally, bewildered by the instructions. Her mind ran through every connotation that phrase might have. Every reference. And came up with nothing that made sense. This seemed too bizarre to be the real thing. Someone's idea of a cruel joke? Someone who had seen her on TV?

"He said you'd know. If you really think about it."

"Is this about my daughter?" she asked bluntly.

Cut to the chase, she had decided. Ignore the taunting suggestion that if she were only brighter she would be able to figure out what he meant.

"Indirectly," the man said softly. "But it *is* important, Ms. Heywood. I can tell you that."

"Then don't play games," Claire said sharply, all the anger she had hidden during the long day boiling up within her, surprising her by its intensity. "I don't have time for tricks. I want my daughter back. And I want her back *now*, damn it."

Her voice climbed as she made the demand. Her grandfather put his hand on her arm. Her eyes lifted to his again, reading in them a warning.

"Please," she added, struggling to modify her tone. "Please, just tell me what you want me to do."

"Go to the rose garden," the man repeated. "As soon as you can. He'll meet you there."

She thought she could read a hint of regret, even apology in his tone.

"He said surely you remember the rose," he added.

Then, unbelievably, the connection was broken. Claire gripped the dead phone, willing it back to life. He couldn't have hung up, she thought. If they had gone to the trouble to call, they would want to tell her something that made sense, and this didn't. The only roses...

Her racing thoughts slowed, hesitating over the word *rose*. "He said surely you remember the rose." Singular.

And she did, of course. Someone had sent her a rose after she had helped Jordan Cross. There had been a message then as well. Something to the effect of thank you for your help.

She had thought the flower must have come from Jordan. Or Hawk, although the gesture had seemed somehow out of character for him. Too romantic. Too soft for such a cold, hard man. Too...sentimental.

Of course, Griff had often sent her a single rose, and there was not a sentimental bone in his body. He'd been hard, pragmatic, brilliant, but hardly what most people would consider romantic.

Suddenly, the memory of the vast gardens at Griff's Maryland estate was in her head. The lovely hybrid tea roses there were his hobby. Their care, and his love for them, were something he'd learned from his grandmother, who had started that rose garden. At least the flowers were something he could control, Griff used to say, smiling.

Eventually, she had understood what he'd meant by that. So much of what he had to deal with was beyond his control. World situations. Politics. The inner workings of the agency itself.

Griff Cabot had had a rose garden. One that she had visited. One she remembered.

"Was that...?" Her grandfather hesitated.

The soft question faltered as she looked up at him, her attention once more brought back to the present. Her fingers released the pen, laying it carefully on the pad, blocking the painful and unwanted memories of Griff.

"I think that was one of the team," she said.

"Cabot's team?" he asked, obviously surprised.

He sounded as if he had thought they were mythical. Maybe the product of her imagination. Her desperation. What they did *was* a little unbelievable, but they themselves were very real. She had met them. At least two of them.

She nodded. "I think that was a message from Jordan Cross. Maybe...maybe he saw the interview. Or maybe the director *did* forward your request, despite your doubts."

"And this Cross is willing to meet you?"

She nodded again, thinking about the instructions she'd been given. Nothing else made sense. Griff's rose garden. That was someplace she certainly knew, and a clue that was a dead giveaway for anyone who *really* knew Griff. A connection. Even more of a connection if, as she suspected,

Jordan had been the one who'd sent the rose after she had helped him. It all made sense because it fit.

"I have to go," she said, standing. "Will you stay here and take any calls?"

"I'll go with you," her grandfather said, starting to rise. "Maddy can answer the phone. Or Charles."

Her sister and her husband were in the kitchen trying to put together something for supper. Maddy had suggested that, glancing pointedly at their grandfather when Claire had said she wasn't hungry.

She hadn't been, of course, and no matter what Maddy said, the thought of sitting down to eat while Gardner was missing was unthinkable. Nauseating.

It would be much better to be doing something that might help find her. This was the only thing all day that had made sense to Claire. Secure the help of someone like Jordan Cross. Take advantage of the offer she thought had just been made.

"No," she said, putting her hand on her grandfather's shoulder to urge him not to get up.

They hadn't told her to come alone, but if this were Jordan, she thought he might object to her bringing someone like her grandfather, who still had ties to the agency he had once worked for. Especially if the director *hadn't* been the method by which Cross had learned she needed his help.

"I don't trust anyone else to answer the phone," she said, smiling at him. "Not Maddy. You know she'll be too nervous to get it right. And Charles...Charles isn't *really* family."

She said the last only for her grandfather's benefit, to convince him that he had to stay here. He had never approved of Maddy's choice of a husband, who held a minor position in the diplomatic corp. She knew Monty Gardner wouldn't want Charles in a position to make any decisions.

"I don't like the idea of you going by yourself," the old man argued. "You ought to at least notify Minger or the bureau. You can't be sure that this is—"

"I'm sure," she said, bending down to place a kiss on the top of his head, lightly touching the gleaming sweep of white hair with her fingers as well, a small caress.

She *was* sure. The more she thought about what the man on the phone had said, the more certain she was that this had to be one of Griff's agents. Certainly someone who knew Griff Cabot well enough to know about his hobby, an avocation that seemed so out of character for a man like him.

And apparently this was someone who was willing to help. Offering her assistance would be "indirectly" connected to her daughter's kidnapping. The wording of that had been very careful. They didn't want to mislead her into believing they were the kidnappers, so they had chosen that telling phrase with which to answer her question. Maybe they had even thought out the wording before they'd placed the call.

But the voice hadn't been Jordan's. She would have recognized the soft Southern accent he had never quite lost. It had always reminded her of Griff's.

The voice on the phone hadn't. But it hadn't been Hawk either, she decided, replaying the conversation in her mind. A friend who had been asked to convey a message. Just exactly as he had said.

"You stay here," she urged her grandfather. "I'll call you as soon as I've talked to whoever this is. I promise I will."

"I don't like this, Claire," the old man argued. "You can't be sure this is one of Cabot's men. It could be anyone. Someone trying to lure you out of the house. Maybe even the people who took the baby."

"All the more reason then for me to go," she reminded him gently. "But it's not them, Grandfather. I *know* who this is. It has to be. Too many things fit. Things that only someone who knew Griff very well would know. And besides, I don't know anything else to do. Neither do you. This is a chance we can't afford to pass up. You know these people. Or at least you knew agents who were like them. If *they* can't find Gardner..."

She let the sentence trail, knowing that was the reality. Her grandfather would know it, too. But putting into words the possibility that they might *not* be able to find Gardner was unthinkable. Therefore, so was a rejection of this offer.

"Be careful," Monty Gardner said softly. He reached out and took her hand, squeezing it gently with his long aristocratic fingers. "Be very careful. I couldn't bear it if anything happened to you, my dear."

"I know," she said. "But nothing will happen to me, I promise you. These people are friends."

Who owe me something, she thought again, *and are apparently willing to acknowledge that debt. Quid pro quo.*

She freed her hand. Lifting the tips of her fingers to her lips, she touched them to his cheek in farewell. She wasn't afraid of what she might find at Griff's estate. She knew in her heart that whoever met her there would be someone who wanted to help her get Gardner back and put an end to this nightmare.

GRIFF HADN'T BEEN CERTAIN she would come, not until he saw the lights of the car approaching down the long curving drive that led up to the house. And when he did, the once familiar anticipation began to stir in the pit of his stomach.

Just the thought of seeing Claire again, even in these circumstances, had the power to rouse all the old feelings. Emotions he had spent the last year and a half denying. And so he denied them again, concentrating on why they were both here tonight. Together again...and yet farther apart than ever.

He had tried to picture Claire with a baby since he'd seen the news report of the kidnapping, but somehow the images wouldn't form. That was not the way he was accustomed to envisioning her. In his memories, she still moved, as he once had, in a world peopled by the powerful, the influential, the political. Somehow he couldn't quite reconcile the woman he had known so well with motherhood.

He had never even thought that she might want a child. They had never talked about having children. He had never considered the possibility. He supposed that if their relationship had gone further—

The distant slamming of a car door broke the stillness, and he knew that it would only be a moment or two before she made her way around the house and into the winter-devastated rose garden. Asking her to meet him here had been a ridiculous idea. He had known that since he'd lowered himself more than an hour ago onto the cold, damp concrete slab of the garden bench.

It was a frigid January night, and like a fool he had suggested an outdoor meeting. Somehow, his memories of Claire had interfered with all the realities of the present. This garden was somewhere he knew she would remember. A place she would associate with him. That had been a warning of sorts. An attempt to prepare her for what she would find here.

When he arrived, however, he had realized at once that this garden was as cold and dead as the one he had looked out on only a couple of hours ago in Pennsylvania. He had known that if Claire did come in response to the message Jake Holt had delivered for him, she would drive. And the chopper he'd hired would, of course, get him here long before she arrived.

It had. Long enough that the chill had crept into his bones as he waited. Along with the dread. Dread of the meeting he had been eager to set up when he'd first called Jake.

Griff could hear her steps on the loose gravel of the path, and he felt his heart rate accelerate. He couldn't be sure how she would react to seeing him again. Not given the things she had said to him the last time they'd argued. And not given the fact that as far as she knew, he was dead.

He had tried to tell her that he was not. The message he'd sent with the rose, thanking Claire for helping his men, had been a pretext for reestablishing contact. He had even understood his motives at the time.

But of course, there had been no response. Either she had not understood the gesture, not understood the single blood-red rose was from him, or...she had chosen to ignore it. And now he knew that even if she *had* suspected the flower was from him, she had already become involved in a relationship with someone else. A man by whom she had had a child.

"Jordan?" she called softly, her voice hesitant, a little breathless, full of anxiety or fear.

He had known Claire Heywood in many moods. Fear had never been one of them. But then never before had someone kidnapped her baby. He was still having a hard time coming to grips with the senseless cruelty of that.

It was not that he wasn't intimately acquainted with the depravity human beings were capable of inflicting on one another. With his background, he was well aware of their endless brutalities. But things like this happened to other people. Not to those he loved.

The word reverberated inside his head, echoing through all the memories. He didn't bother to deny it. He had loved Claire Heywood almost from the beginning. Almost from the first time he had seen her.

And, he acknowledged, he still did. What other reason would there be for his being here tonight? Alone in a cold, dark garden, waiting with incredible anticipation for a woman who might believe he was dead. A woman who was, in any event, involved with another man.

"Jordan?" she called again.

Griff hadn't realized how near she was. He had been lost in the past, something that was always dangerous when there was a job to be done. In this case their shared past was incredibly painful, as well.

No matter what she had said to him before, no matter if she had chosen to ignore the rose he had sent, he knew that having to confront him tonight would be another blow on top of the kidnapping. Especially if she hadn't realized from that gesture that he was alive. This meeting would be something else for her to deal with on a terrifying and terrible day.

This was a mistake, he realized belatedly. A stupid and cruel error of judgment, although neither of those had been his intent. He should have contacted Jordan and asked him to help Claire find the baby. It was obvious that was who she had come here expecting to meet.

Instead, he had rushed in to play rescuer as soon as he had seen her on TV. And he had not once considered that he was not in any position to undertake that role.

He could no longer call on the resources of the agency, at least not officially. Only on his people, the few who were still working there. Who were still loyal to him. People like Jake, he acknowledged, remembering the shock in Holt's voice when he'd identified himself and asked for his help.

"Jordan?" Claire said again, more softly this time. She sounded more focused. No longer searching.

He realized she was standing at the top of the steps that led up to the gazebo where he was sitting. There was enough moonlight, in spite of the drifting pattern of broken clouds, to outline her figure against the lesser blackness of the night. He knew that she had seen him, but he also knew he would be no more than a shadowed hulk across the wide floor of the gazebo.

"If you're not Jordan," she said finally, "then…who are you? Why did you bring me here?"

"I want to help you," Griff said softly.

He wondered if she would recognize his voice. She had heard it a thousand times whispering from the darkness. Despite his determination to reveal nothing of what he was feeling, he had been aware of a telltale breathlessness in his response, which had changed the normal timbre of his tone. The strength of her effect on his emotions had always been incredible. His physical responses to Claire Heywood had been stronger than to any other woman he had ever known.

She took another step, moving nearer. He knew that she still wouldn't be able to distinguish his features. Not in this light. He even thought about asking her not to come any closer.

Then he could stay hidden in the darkness. He could offer to help and never reveal that the man she had been told was dead was really alive. And not reveal that he was still as caught in the spell of love and desire she had woven about him as he had always been.

Perhaps she couldn't make the leap of logic it would require to recognize his voice if she still believed he was dead. Dead and buried for more than a year. It *should* be inconceivable to her then that he could be sitting in the gazebo of his own rose garden.

He had lied to people on occasion. Everyone had, he supposed, but especially in the position he had once occupied. It went with the constraints and requirements of his job. But he had never lied to Claire.

Sometimes, after it was over between them, he'd wished that he had. At least lied about what he did. What the team did. And especially what he believed about the necessity of those actions. Instead, he had finally told her the truth, because he'd thought he could do no less. Because he'd thought he owed her that truth.

Eventually he would have to do that now. No matter how difficult that might be. For her. And for him.

"Do you know something about Gardner's disappearance?" she asked.

A logical question. He wished to hell he did. But the truth was... The truth was that until tonight he hadn't known of the existence of Claire's child. That knowledge had hurt, making him burn with a jealousy he had no right to feel. Burn even after all this time.

"I'm sorry. That's *not* why I asked you to come," he said.

"Then...why? How did you know about the rose? Are you the one who sent it?"

In the darkness, Griff Cabot's lips moved, tilting into the slight, enigmatic smile Claire would certainly have recognized. If she had been able to see it.

"I sent you the rose," he said.

"Because of what I did for Hawk and Jordan?"

"Partly."

"I don't understand," she said.

"It was intended to be…a message as well."

A single bloodred rose, like those which grew here. That one had been a hothouse variety because of the season. He had chosen it himself that same evening, and then he had sent it to her, the dew still beading its silken petals.

Because he had wanted her to know he was alive. And because of what he had felt when he'd found out she had been helping his men. Men who carried out the missions she had once professed to despise. If Claire's feelings had changed enough to allow her to do that—

"What kind of message?" she asked, interrupting that thought.

She took another step, the wooden boards creaking under her weight. Coming here tonight had taken courage. That was something Claire had in abundance.

Of course, what she had done before had taken courage as well. Almost eighteen months ago, at the same time she had made him promise that he would never try to see her again, she had openly confessed how she felt. She had told him how much she loved him. And needed him.

She herself had broken the agreement they'd made. Only once. As he had broken it in sending her the rose.

Broken it only once. Before tonight.

"Who are you?" she asked again.

Before he could answer, however, she raised her hand, bringing up the flashlight she had carried from her car. She turned it on, directing it toward the darkness where he was hidden. And unerringly, its beam found his face.

Chapter Four

For an endless moment Claire couldn't breathe. Couldn't think. Couldn't move. Couldn't have done any of those things had her very life depended on it.

Griff's eyes had narrowed against the intensity of the light, and he lifted his hand, placing it protectively, palm outward, before his face. At the same time he lowered his head, effectively hiding the features she had once known as well as she knew her own. More intimately than her own, perhaps, because they had appeared so often in her mind's eye.

As they did now. They had been captured like an image on film, burned on her retinas, frozen to stillness by the cold, piercing finger of the flashlight's beam. That first image played over and over in her head, blocking questions. Blocking reaction. Blocking thought.

"Turn it off, Claire," Griff said quietly.

How had she not recognized his voice? she wondered, hearing it now. Knowing it. Knowing it instantly.

Because he's dead, of course. Griff Cabot was dead. She had grieved for him. Every day of this endless year, she had grieved for him. Grieved for the all the foolish, meaningless things she had once said to him. And now...

"Turn it off," he said again, this time in a tone of command. The voice of a man accustomed to being obeyed.

Why shouldn't it be? Everyone obeyed him. They always

had. Just as they listened to his opinions and respected them. Everyone, it seemed, except Claire Heywood.

Now, however, her finger pushed the switch in unthinking obedience. The powerful light blinked out, disappearing as suddenly as it had appeared.

As suddenly as he had once disappeared, she thought. *Dead.* They had told her he was dead.

"I'm sorry," Griff said softly. "I did try to warn you."

I'm sorry. She couldn't fit the understated simplicity of that apology into the scope of her pain. *I'm sorry?*

Sorry they had told her he was dead? she wondered. Sorry he had brought her here to find out in this brutal way that he was not? Or sorry he had done this whole despicable…thing to her? Or had let the agency—

The thought was so sudden, she gasped a little with its impact. Almost too great a shock after the last.

The CIA had given Jordan Cross a new face after the incident at the airport in Mississippi, because his picture— his face—had been spread out under the banners of a thousand newspapers. Had they done it again after Kathleen Sorrel had turned over the Mafia's money? That had been only a couple of weeks ago. But maybe…

"Jordan?" she asked, pushing the question past the hard constriction of her throat. "Is that you?"

The man in the shadows laughed, the sound deep and soft, but *known.* Familiar. So familiar.

"You seem to have some sort of fixation with Jordan Cross. I think I might be jealous, Claire. If things were… different."

His voice. Griff's voice. And despite her shock, its sound flowed through all the places in her mind and body that had once known his touch. Known him so intimately that there could be no longer any doubt about who was sitting in the darkness of the old gazebo. No longer any room at all in her heart for doubt.

Tears stung her eyes, still widened with the shock of what the flashlight had revealed. They had now adjusted to the moon-touched darkness enough to be able to watch as he slowly lowered the hand he had raised.

Griff Cabot was alive. This was not someone pretending to be Griff. Not a figment of her imagination, brought on by the incredible stresses of this day. And not a phantom.

"Why?" she whispered, trying to understand. "Why did they tell me you were dead?"

And then, before he could possibly have answered the first, even if he had wanted to, the more important questions followed.

"How could you *let* them tell me that, Griff? How could you let me believe you were dead?"

"I wasn't in any condition to stop them," he said softly.

Condition? Because he really had been a victim of that massacre? she wondered. But if that part was true—

"And besides..." His words had interrupted that thought, but then he hesitated before he completed the sentence. "You and I had already made our agreement."

She knew at once what he meant, although she didn't know why he would bring that promise, *his* promise, into this discussion. Why he would think that had any bearing on what he had done.

"Our *agreement* never included lying to each other," she accused.

Her knees were weak, her palm clammy as her shaking hand clenched the heavy flashlight. Reaction to finding out that the man she loved, the man she believed had been killed more than a year ago, the man she had grieved for every day and every night of that year, was still alive. *Still alive.*

"Didn't it?" he asked calmly. "Somehow, I thought that was *exactly* what our agreement was about. We pretend that how we felt about each other wasn't as important as..." Again he hesitated, maybe reluctant to dredge up the old arguments. "As the other things in our lives," he finished. "Or wasn't that a lie as well, Claire?"

He was right, of course. It had taken her only a few days after his death to reach that conclusion. And for the rest of the time, from that day to this, she had been forced to live with the reality of what a falsehood it had been.

They had disagreed about politics. About their view of the world. About which solutions to its problems they valued. About what he and his team did.

Senseless arguments. Intellectual. Cerebral. But without any merit at all, without value, when she had lost him. When she *thought* she had lost him, she amended, because all along that, too, had been a lie. She still found it hard to believe Griff would let her think he was dead. That was larger and far more hurtful than whatever sin he was accusing her of.

Moral arrogance, she remembered. That had been one of the phrases he had thrown at her in their last, most bitter argument. Morally arrogant because she thought there were other ways to protect this country. Other ways to settle the problems of the world than those he had chosen, which were both violent and clandestine. And abhorrent to everything she just as vehemently believed in.

"What do you want?" she asked finally, almost numb from the battery of shock, pain and grief she had endured today. "Why did you bring me here?"

She had been forced to accept the fact that Griff Cabot was alive, but she didn't know what that meant. Or why he had, after all these months, decided to tell her the truth. To *show* her the truth in this way. At this particular time.

"I want to help you find your daughter," Griff said.

Your daughter. He had given the words no special emphasis, but they impacted in her mind. Not *our* daughter. And of course, Griff had had no hand in her upbringing. He had been alive, and yet he had never once acknowledged his daughter's existence. He hadn't done that even now.

"Why?" she asked.

She had no idea what answer she expected. *Because she's my daughter as well. Because I want her to be safe. Because I love you.* All the answers she thought he might give her echoed inside her head as she waited, not breathing, wondering which one of them he would say.

"Because I have the skills," he said.

None of the things she had been prepared to hear. *I have the skills.* The most mundane and rational of reasons. He did, of course. Resources she couldn't possibly match anywhere else in the world. His team. His contacts. His knowledge.

Which it seemed he was willing to use on his daughter's behalf. As long as she was safe, Griff had apparently been content to stay out of their lives. Content to live out the lie the CIA had created. But now...

Despite the way she felt about the things Griff Cabot had once done for the CIA, she had always known that inside him was a solid core of decency and honor. That unshakeable belief was one of the things that had made the decision she had ultimately come to so difficult. And one reason she had never understood how he could do the jobs he did.

How could he issue orders for someone to be assassinated and close his mind to the reality of the human suffering that caused? How could he order a commando raid? How could he argue the virtue of the taking of one life to protect another?

To her that always sounded like the twisted statement someone had made during the Vietnam War—that the U.S. must bomb a particular village in order to save it. That was both senseless and destructive, as if violence could ever be defeated with more violence.

The old questions and arguments beat at her, as if she and Griff had made them only yesterday. Just as they had beat at her eighteen months ago when she had finally told Griff she couldn't see him anymore. That she didn't ever want to see him again.

That, too, had been a lie, of course, but at least she had known it was when she said it. She had even admitted to him the enormity of its untruth.

And that was the reason for the promise she had elicited

from him. She knew how weak her will was when confronted with the reality of this man. Because she also knew
how much she loved him.

So she had made him swear that he would never seek her
out again. That he would never call or write her. Or come
to her. Or ask her to come to him. Because if he did, she
had known she wouldn't be able to resist—or deny him.

Griff had kept his word, of course. But he hadn't refused
her the night *she* had come to *him*. The one night when the
seemingly endless longing for the caress of his hand and
the heated touch of his mouth against her body had drawn
her here, unable to bear the loneliness and deprivation of
living without him any longer.

Here to this house, she remembered, her gaze lifting,
searching for and finding through the wooden filigree of the
old gazebo the dark, familiar shape of the mansion. *She* had
come to *him*.

And when he had opened the door and found her standing
there, he had taken her cold, trembling fingers into his warm
ones and drawn her inside. He had not released her hand,
leading her through the silent house like a child. Or a blind
man. Leading her up the wide curving staircase to his bedroom. So familiar, even in the sheltering night.

They hadn't spoken a word. The ghosts of the old arguments had not been released to haunt those hours. They had
met almost as strangers, coming together physically in a
deliberate denial of all the intellectual barriers that had kept
them apart.

That night Gardner had been conceived. And Claire had
not yet had a chance to tell Griff that before she had been
informed of his death. She would have told him, of course.
Eventually. At least it had comforted her through these long
months to believe that she would have. Comforted her
through those bleak, lonely months when she had believed
he was dead. And now...

"Why would you *do* that?" she asked again, unable to

move beyond the agony of what he had done. Unable to forgive him. "Why would you let them tell me that?"

He drew a breath, so deep the sound was audible in the stillness. And it was obvious when he answered that he understood what she was asking.

"It had *already* been done. And long before they did, what had been between us was over. Because *you* decided it should be. *You* decreed it was over, Claire. Because of who I am."

She shook her head slowly, trying to understand that reasoning. *What had been between us was already over.*

"That's not the same as *death*," she whispered.

It wasn't. Not the same as letting someone that you knew loved you believe you were dead. Nowhere near the same cruelty.

"It was to me," Griff said simply, his voice as low as hers, without any emotion she could read.

She examined the claim, trying to understand. And when she thought she did, she shook her head again. This time in denial.

"No," she said.

"No?" he questioned.

"I didn't tell you I was dead," she said.

"What was the difference in what you did, Claire? You wanted me out of your life. So what was the difference in the distance you created between us? In the separation?"

"You *know* the difference," she said, her anger that he would try to deny responsibility for what he had done building. "You *have* to understand the difference."

"What I knew was that you weren't here," he said simply.

"That's not *dead*," she accused, furious with what he was saying. With equating his supposed death with what she had done. She closed her eyes, hearing the growing stridency in her voice. No one but Griff could make her so angry. Or so confused.

Confused because as much as she wanted to deny it, there

was some grain of logic in what he was saying. If they were never to see one another again, as she had demanded, then what *did* the cause of that separation matter? How could it matter what he had let them tell her?

"I'd like to help you find your baby," he said again, but only after he had let the painful silence lengthen unbearably. "What have they asked you for?"

"Nothing," she said truthfully.

And with that word, the remembered despair of the long day broke through her anger. His question reminded her of why she was here. She couldn't believe that devastating reality had left her mind even for a moment. For a second.

Even now, Gardner might be frightened or cold or alone. And unless Claire found her soon... Her mind shied away from that word *unless*. She couldn't bear it, just as she couldn't bear the thought of what Gardner might be going through. She had fought those images all day, pushing them into a tightly locked corner of her mind. Fighting panic and despondency because they would cripple her at a time when she needed all her strength.

But she didn't feel strong right now. There had been too much to deal with. Her emotions were shredded. Griff, whom she had thought was lost forever, was alive. And their baby... Their baby.

"There was no note. No phone call. No demand for ransom."

She made herself enumerate the list of negatives, feeling despair well up as she realized that she knew nothing more than she had known this morning when this had all begun. This morning when someone had destroyed her world.

"I thought when the phone rang tonight..." She stopped, wondering again who had called her. She had been certain it wasn't either of the agents she'd met. And it wasn't Griff. "Who called me?" she asked.

"Jake Holt," Griff said. "I contacted him because I thought he could help. Then I asked him to arrange for you to meet me here."

"You thought he could help how?" Claire asked carefully.

"He finds people," Griff said simply.

For the agency, Claire realized. Or for the team. Jake Holt was another member of Griff's External Security Team, she realized. Like the man they called Hawk, and Jordan Cross.

"And you think he can find Gardner?" she asked.

"It would help if she were using a credit card," Griff said softly.

His voice had been touched with the familiar sardonic amusement she had heard there so often before. She knew he used humor as a defense against the painful realities of his world, but of course this time those realities were too personal for this cool detachment. Or they should be. There should be nothing amusing about someone taking your child, even a child you didn't know.

"I don't understand," she said, her voice stiff, offended.

"I'm sorry," he said softly.

The unforgivable humor had been wiped totally from his deep voice. And she realized Griff could still read her every mood, every nuance of her tone.

"Jake uses the computers to find...patterns," he explained. "In purchases, phone calls, bank withdrawals. In a thousand different ways we leave footprints of our movements in the computer. We do it a hundred times a day without even thinking about it. Without ever being aware that if someone wants to find out about us, the computers that handle our every transaction offer a wealth of information."

"And he...this Jake...finds that information."

"Compiles it. Examines it. Sorts through it until he discovers a pattern. Something recognizable."

She thought about the process Griff had described, trying to see how Jake's expertise might be applied to her daughter's kidnapping.

"I don't understand how that will help," she said finally. "How will that help find Gardner?"

"I'm not sure. But that's always where we start any search. With Jake. With the computers."

"You think they aren't going to contact us," she said, fear making her voice flat.

That was the only explanation that made sense out of Griff using someone like Jake Holt. They would only need to do that if the kidnappers didn't issue any ransom demand.

"No," Griff said quickly. And reassuringly. "They'll call. They want something or they wouldn't have taken her. You'll hear from them. Making you wait is simply part of their strategy. Because they know the longer it goes on, the more eager you'll be to agree to whatever they ask. They'll be in touch. I promise you that, Claire."

The calm surety in Griff's voice comforted her, lessening the urge to hysteria she had hidden during this endless day. Hours during which she had pretended to be rational and controlled. And she realized she had found his promise to be far more reassuring than Minger's professional opinion or her grandfather's earlier buoyancy.

Because, of course, this was Griff. If he told her everything would be all right, it would be. And if *he* told her he would get Gardner back, then he would.

"I knew your team could find her. I was trying to get in touch with Jordan," she said, remembering the hope that idea had given her. Almost as strong as the one Griff had just planted in her heart. "Or with Hawk. I thought that if anyone could find her, they could. Of course, I didn't know that you…"

Her voice faded. *I didn't know that you were alive.* Alive, she thought again, almost unable to deal with that on top of all that had happened.

"They're very good at what they do," Griff agreed.

They were his men. Accustomed to working under his orders. He had trained them. He didn't remind her of that. And, of course, he didn't need to.

"When Grandfather tried to locate them through the agency, he discovered all their records were destroyed. According to the CIA, those men never existed," she said, wondering if Griff had known what the agency had been doing.

"Because they have found them to be...difficult to control," he said.

She recognized the care he had taken in that choice of words. And underlying them, she heard amusement again. *Difficult to control.*

She knew from her grandfather that among some elements of the intelligence community, Griff himself had been considered difficult. But he had also been brilliant and insightful and incredibly successful, his operations so well planned and executed there were seldom problems for the agency to deal with. No collateral damage.

And so they had been willing to put up with him in exchange for what he could do. Even willing, it seemed, to put up with Griff's arrogance.

Moral arrogance. The phrase he had once used against her echoed in her head again, but in a different context. Griff wanted to help find their daughter. She had come here because she was desperate to contact someone who could. Even more easily than Jordan or Hawk, Griff would be able to do that. And he would have more reason to, of course.

"If you're wrong... If they don't call..." She took a deep breath and, setting aside her anger over the lie he had lived, she asked, "Will you find her for me? Will you find Gardner?"

Will you help me find your daughter? Will you return to me your child? The child you gave me. The child who was my only comfort in the long empty darkness of your death.

"Yes," he said.

No equivocation. A simple statement. A promise and a vow. And without questioning whether he could really do what he had just said he would, Claire found herself, as always, believing him.

WHEN GRIFF HAD ELICITED every detail, every piece of minutiae Claire knew—which were too damn few, he acknowledged—he had sent her home to wait for the contact from the kidnappers he'd promised. That would come eventually, he believed. And when it did, he wanted to be ready to move.

And if it didn't... Then he would call on those same people who had answered every call he had made on their strength and courage and intelligence during the past ten years. There were more than a dozen men who had worked on the special operations team known as External Security. And he knew that any of them would respond to his plea for help.

Each of them had, however, very specialized skills, and he wasn't sure yet which of those he would need. That depended on the conditions the kidnappers demanded for the exchange. That was always the trickiest part, of course. And although it wasn't their usual mission, the team had handled a few of those kinds of negotiations in the past.

Once they had been sent to recover an operative whose cover had been blown. Once it had been to achieve the release of an MIA, by whatever means. Those situations had been too politically sensitive to be made public, but they'd been successful. So Griff had no doubt they could arrange this exchange.

Maybe Claire felt that the man she was involved with, the baby's father, wasn't equipped for this. Not many people were, which was why Griff had offered her his help. One of the reasons, he acknowledged.

He sat down behind his desk, propping the cane against the edge. It had been a long day and a longer night, and he could feel every minute of it aching along the damaged nerves and muscles of his leg.

He debated whether or not to try to contact Jake again, or whether to grab a few hours of sleep, whatever was left of the night. That was something they had all learned to do—sleep when they had the opportunity. When things weren't happening.

He glanced at his watch. It was almost 2:00 a.m. They needed to formulate a plan for what they would do if, worse case scenario, the kidnappers didn't contact Claire. For that he would need a clear head. And given the strains of this day, he knew he didn't have one.

He had already, during his first call, asked Jake to check for anything that looked suspicious in Claire Heywood's world. That reminded him that he needed to tell Jake about the malfunctioning security alarms. Griff had chosen the company that had installed Claire's system, and they were the best in the business. Whoever had rigged it to short-circuit last night had to be pretty sophisticated. That expertise might give them a starting point.

He glanced down at the keyboard of the computer, thinking about sending Jake an e-mail at home. It wouldn't be encrypted, but that shouldn't matter in this situation. After all, this wasn't agency business.

It took a second for his brain to register what he was seeing. A single piece of paper, folded once, lay on top of the keys. His name had been typed in all caps across it— GRIFFON CABOT—and he knew it hadn't been there earlier tonight when he had called Jake. Or when he had made the arrangements for the chopper. He would have seen it. Which meant...

Which meant that someone had put it there while he'd been gone. He had given his housekeeper the holiday weekend off, so it couldn't have been her. Maybe Carl had come back for some reason and, finding him gone, had left a message. After all, Steiner was one of the very few people who knew the man who lived in this house by that name.

Griff found a silver letter opener in the desk drawer and carefully inserted its point between the edges of the opening formed by the two sides of the folded sheet. He lifted the top half and read what was written there.

It was a message that changed everything he thought he

knew about the kidnapping. Everything about his relationship with Claire Heywood. And if what was written on this piece of paper were true, then everything about his own life, as well.

Chapter Five

Poor dear, Rose Connor thought, listening to the sounds the baby she held was making. *Poor little darling.*

She pushed the rocking chair back and forth, her broad, bare toes barely making contact with the wooden floor. The soft creak of the chair was relaxing, and her eyelids drifted downward. When she realized what was happening, she jerked them up again, fighting the urge to sleep.

Only a little longer, she told herself, patting the small bottom held securely in the crook of her arm. The baby had gradually relaxed, the screams that had awakened Rose turning into soft sobs and then finally into small, hiccuping breaths. Now even those were fading, as the little girl's dark head rooted in the soft flesh of Rose's shoulder.

Almost asleep, Rose thought, her toes pushing rhythmically against the floor. *Almost…creak…asleep…creak…* The same steady rhythm of the human heart. Never forgotten.

And as soothing to her as to the dear ones she cared for. She smoothed thick, spatulate fingers over the tiny back, cherishing its regular lift and fall. Savoring this incredible moment of triumph. Of success.

She had always loved this feeling. She had begun caring for her brothers and sisters when she was just a wee bit of a thing herself. Her mother had so much to do to tend to them all during the day, and too little sleep at night.

So when the baby cried, Rose would slip out of bed, and moving through the darkness of the cottage on bare feet, she would hurry to the crib to comfort the newest addition to the family. Holding the infant against her narrow chest, she would croon the same wordless lullabies her mother had sung to her.

Just the two of them in the quiet world of night. She and a babe who needed her. Who responded to her touch. Who loved her. As near to heaven as Rose Connor expected to get here on earth.

Soon, she knew, she'd be able to put this one back into her crib. Then maybe the blessed sweetheart would be able to sleep out the rest of the night. And if she couldn't, poor little mite, then old Rose would come again and hold her.

Chase away the shadows. Soothe the nightmares and frighten away the bogeyman. Stand in for that sad little mother who must be missing the quiet joy and satisfaction of this closeness.

Poor little thing, Rose thought again, her toes pushing and then relaxing against the floor. And this time, it wasn't the baby that her warm heart pitied.

CLAIRE THOUGHT she had probably slept less than three hours. And those had been spent in a half-waking consciousness that something was very wrong. Listening with dread— for the phone, for a knock on the door or for any of the sounds she should have heard last night and had not.

When the doorbell did ring, a little before six, she was in the kitchen making coffee. It was something to do besides worry. And if the technicians and investigators who had passed in and out of the house yesterday came back today, she thought she should at least be able to offer them a cup of hot coffee.

She realized that whoever was at the door was in all probability simply the first in the long line of people who would ask her questions or take pictures or dust one more object in the nursery for nonexistent fingerprints. However, the adrenaline had kicked in so strongly with the sound of the bell that her hand was shaking as she hurried to turn off the alarms and open the front door, leaving its security chain in place.

Griff Cabot was standing on her doorstep. An obviously furious Griff Cabot. "I saw your light," he said, the words bitten off. "We need to talk."

"Something's happened to her," Claire said, her sudden fear as paralyzing as when she had first discovered Gardner was missing. "Oh, my God, Griff, something's happened to Gardner."

Eyes wide, she watched his face change, the anger fading, or at least controlled, with his recognition of her terror.

"No," he said quickly. "No, Claire, I promise you that isn't what this is about."

That isn't what this is about. The words made no sense, since there was nothing else between them now. But she could see the truth of what he said in his eyes. And the same compassion that she always remembered from the dream. The compassion that had been there the night he had opened *his* door and found her outside.

"Do you swear that's the truth, Griff?" she demanded, but she already knew it was, and her racing pulse began to slow.

"As far as I know, Gardner is safe. I swear to you."

As far as I know. That's really all she could ask him for. So she nodded, and then slid the knob of the chain out of the slot and opened the door.

"I made coffee," she said. "We can talk in the kitchen."

He hesitated, lips compressed, before he stepped inside. She noticed for the first time that he held a cane in his right hand. And then, as he limped past her, she realized why.

She let him lead the way. He knew the house, of course, but that wasn't the reason. He seemed totally in charge, in command. That was Griff's personality, but today that quality was even more pronounced. And, of course, that was exactly what she had asked him to do, she acknowledged.

To take charge of whatever was going on. To get Gardner back.

When they reached the kitchen, the smell of freshly brewed coffee permeated the room. It was a comfortable aroma, familiar, making things seem almost normal. Even between the two of them.

"Sit down," she suggested. "I'll bring your coffee to the table."

She knew at once her unthinking offer had been a mistake. She would probably have said the same thing to any other guest, but she had never waited on Griff. She had never treated him as a guest in her home because he had been so much more.

And she knew by his face how he had interpreted what she'd said. Even she couldn't be certain that she *hadn't* made that offer, at least in part, because of the limp and the cane.

She would have felt free to ask about those had they still been the same two people they had been before. Had their relationship been the same. But it wasn't. So, despite what was in his eyes, she said nothing.

The awkward silence lasted only a few seconds before Griff obeyed, shrugging out of his overcoat and throwing it over one of the kitchen chairs before he eased down into another, leaning the cane carefully against the edge of the table. She watched his movements, and when she realized she was, she turned to the cabinet above the sink and took down two mugs, filling them with the fragrant Jamaican blend Griff had introduced her to. Something she still unthinkingly bought because he had liked it.

She put one of the steaming cups in front of him and then sat down across the table, preparing to hear whatever had brought him out here so early this morning. Whatever had made him angry. She held her mug with cold fingers, savoring the warmth as she watched him lift his to take the first sip.

His eyes met hers over the rim of his cup, and the almost

physical connection that had always been between them flared within her, igniting memory. And the slow-burning fuse of desire. Nothing had changed, she realized, in how she felt about Griff Cabot. The same way she had always felt. Since the very first time she had seen him, standing with her grandfather at some crowded Washington party.

She had thought he was the most attractive man in the room. Remarkably, nothing had changed about that initial assessment, even after she'd arranged to be introduced. It had never changed. To her, Griff Cabot would still be the most attractive man in any room.

Watching him complete the interrupted motion of his cup, which hid whatever had been in his eyes, she was forced to acknowledge, however, that he was different from the man he had been then. Some changes, like the limp, were terribly obvious. Others were more subtle. And she guessed there were some no one would ever be allowed to see.

The physical ones were the easiest to trace, of course. The coal-black hair threaded with gray. The deepened lines around the corners of the sensitive mouth she had known so well. Etched by pain? Or by the frustrations she knew he would feel over the limitations a damaged leg would impose on the man he was?

Remembering the limping journey down the hall, she realized for the first time that he had really been seriously injured in the attack at CIA headquarters. Last night, she had assumed the agency had used that act of terrorism as an excuse to further their own ends in some way. Now she recognized that the terrorist's bullets might actually have been the cause of the story they'd put out—that Griff was dead. And she remembered what he had said about being in no condition to stop them.

Of course, none of that explained why he hadn't contacted her later. When he was once more in control of his own destiny. Their destiny, she amended bitterly.

He was watching her, she realized, when she looked up

from her coffee. The dark eyes were unreadable now. Lips unsmiling.

"I know what they want," he said.

It took a moment for the import of that to sink in.

"You know what the *kidnappers* want?"

"I received a ransom note last night," he said, his voice as hard as it had been when she'd opened the door.

That even made some kind of sense, she supposed. Their contacting Griff. After all, he was much better off financially than she was.

"How much?" she asked.

"You're not surprised the ransom demand was sent to me?" he asked instead. His eyes were cold. And so dark they were almost black.

"I don't..." She hesitated, again sensing, and yet not understanding, his anger. As soon as her words faltered, he spoke, filling the silence.

"*I* was," he said. "But then, I didn't know, of course."

"Didn't know what?" she asked, trying to understand what was wrong. This was what they had been waiting for, and yet Griff was acting as if... As if it wasn't good news that the kidnappers had contacted them.

His eyes held hers. Held them long enough that the blood began to pound in her temples.

"The truth," he said finally, his voice flat. "Something you apparently saw no reason to tell me," he accused softly. "Not last night. And not before."

"The *truth?*" she repeated. And hearing the tone of accusation, she thought of the long lie he had lived this past year. Whatever he meant, Griff didn't have much room to chide her about truth. "The truth about what?" she asked, truly bewildered.

Again the silence stretched, but angry now herself, she didn't allow her eyes to fall, and finally he spoke again.

"About why they think I'd be willing to do whatever they want in order to get *your* daughter back?"

His voice was soft. And reasonable. But she didn't like

what she heard there, underlying those surface qualities. And she didn't understand the emphasis on the pronoun.

"What do they want you to do?" she asked.

"She's mine, isn't she, Claire?" he asked, ignoring her question. "Gardner is my daughter, and that's why these people are so certain they can call the tune, and I'll have to dance to it. She's my daughter. And you never told me."

Then, of course, it all fell into place. His anger. The tone of accusation. But if he hadn't known, then who the hell *did* he think had fathered Gardner? And how was she supposed to let him know about the baby when the agency had lied to her, telling her he was dead?

"My God, Griff, I thought you were dead. Or have you forgotten that?" she asked bitterly. "I don't do seances. Or maybe I was supposed to whisper that I was pregnant to your tombstone."

"And last night?" he asked.

"I thought you knew," she said truthfully. "I thought that's why you called. Why you offered to help."

He said nothing for a moment, but the coldness didn't leave his eyes. "I did the math," he said. "If she's six months old, as this morning's paper said, then you had to have known you were pregnant. *Before* Langley."

Before Langley. A pleasant euphemism for what had happened to him. For the lie the CIA had told her. But he was right. She had known. Not long, but long enough to have picked up the phone and told Griff.

And she hadn't. The unexpected pregnancy had complicated everything. And it had all been too complicated to begin with. By their conflicting ideologies. Their matching stubbornness.

And by her stupidity, she admitted, remembering the sleepless nights of regret after his death. Regret that she hadn't told him about the baby. But of course, Griff was dead, and eventually she had forced herself to acknowledge that it was too late to change anything she had done.

"It happened that night?" he asked. He already knew the

answer, of course. Since he said he had done the math, it was the only answer.

That night. The night she had come to him. Because she couldn't stay away any longer. The night she had dreamed about over and over again.

She hadn't intended to go to him, of course. Not even when she had left this house. But driving aimlessly through the fall darkness, she had found she couldn't resist any longer what she had wanted for the last three months. She couldn't deny herself another minute. Because she loved him. And she wanted him. Wanted to be with him.

"Yes," she admitted.

"I thought you were protected," he said.

After she had broken off their relationship, there had been no need for protection. She hadn't been involved with anyone else, and she had known she wouldn't be. When her prescription had run out, she hadn't even bothered to renew it.

And when he had taken her hand that night and drawn her across the threshold, the fact that she hadn't never crossed her mind. Maybe, she admitted, because she didn't want it to. She had always heard there was no such thing as an unwanted pregnancy.

"I wasn't. Not…then," she admitted.

"You got pregnant that night," he said. "And you didn't tell me."

"There wasn't time," she said quickly. That was the same excuse she had offered herself after his death. There hadn't been time. "I intended to. But…"

She hesitated, knowing some part of that was a lie. There *had* been time. Only a few short weeks, but time nonetheless. She had still been trying to decide what to do when they'd informed her, through her grandfather, that Griff Cabot was dead.

There were some admissions, however, that were too painful to make. And ultimately, of course, she had made all the right decisions. The only one she had ever regretted was not to tell Griff as soon as she knew she was pregnant.

"I know what they want in exchange for the baby," Griff said, not even waiting to hear what excuse she might offer for what she'd done. "*If* you're interested."

"If I'm interested?" she repeated disbelievingly. "Of course I'm *interested*, Griff. This is my daughter."

"And mine. I might have been prepared for this if I'd known."

She wasn't sure if he meant prepared for the kidnapping or for whatever the kidnappers wanted him to do in exchange for Gardner's return. She knew from what he had already said that it wasn't money, but something they wanted Griff to *do*.

Give them information? Something classified? With that thought, her heart squeezed painfully because she wasn't sure Griff would ever commit treason. Not even to save the life of his child.

"Will you do what they want?" she asked.

It was a far more important question than those he had been asking. She waited for his answer, afraid the code of honor he had lived by so long would keep him from getting Gardner back.

"First, I think I need to hear you say it, Claire. I think your telling me is long overdue. Why should I do what they want?"

She didn't know why he thought this was necessary. A form of punishment, maybe? Or simply a need to hear her say it, as he'd claimed? But whatever his motives, she could think of no reason not to comply. Not when it was so important.

"Because Gardner is your daughter," she said, her voice low.

He nodded, holding her eyes.

"What do they want?" she asked again.

His lips moved into a semblance of his familiar smile. Unlike any other smile she had ever seen on Griff Cabot's face. Not in all the time she had known him. It was totally without humor. Without amusement. As cold and as empty as the nursery had been yesterday morning.

"They want me to kill someone," he said softly.

"*Kill* someone?" she repeated, after a stunned second or two of thinking that she couldn't have heard that right. She could hear her horror at the thought echoing through her question.

"An assassination. After all, I've arranged those before. Given the orders for them to be carried out. That's all they're asking, Claire. They just want me to arrange another assassination."

Bile surged into her throat as she realized he was serious. *Assassination*. This was part of what had driven them apart. There had been other things about his job that bothered her, of course, but this…

That had been the one thing she could never condone. Never forgive. Or accept. Not from the man she loved.

"As soon as it's done, they'll give Gardner back."

There was a silence, so deep she could hear her blood rushing through the veins in her ears.

"I assume," Griff added softly, "that you won't object to me paying their price."

The silence grew and expanded, and his eyes held hers, waiting for her response.

"Who?" Claire whispered instead, still fighting the sickness climbing into her throat.

This was a growing nightmare she couldn't escape. Instead, with each minute that had passed since she'd found that open window, it had grown worse, more frightening, more horrifying.

"The less you know about that the better," Griff said.

"I have a right to know."

She supposed she did. That didn't mean, however, that she really wanted to. Griff was right. The less she had to think about all this…

"And when you do?" Griff asked quietly.

She knew what he was really asking. Would she refuse to let him do what they demanded? Was she prepared to sacrifice her daughter's life for a principle? And she didn't have an answer for him.

"I have a right to know," she repeated stubbornly.

Griff took a breath, his lips flattening, his eyes still on hers, and then he said, "His name wouldn't mean anything to you."

"But it *does* mean something to you?"

"I know who he is."

"And you know why someone wants him dead?" she asked, knowing from his tone that he did.

"A lot of people probably want him dead," Griff said.

That was almost comforting, until she realized she was falling into the same trap she had almost fallen into before. Long ago when they had argued—intellectually then—about this. It was a trap of logic that said it was all right to take someone's life if he were engaged in actions that were reprehensible. Threatening to others. Or inhumane.

"Are you going to do it?" she asked, because she believed she had read that in his eyes as well. And then she waited, bracing herself for the questions he had only implied before.

Do you want me to? Do you want your daughter back badly enough to tell me to do what they've asked? Even if doing it is something you have always condemned, no matter the justification.

Moral arrogance. Did she want Griff to get Gardner back like this? At this cost? Yesterday she would have said she would do anything to get her baby back. And she would have thought she was speaking the truth.

"Let me handle it, Claire," he said, his eyes almost as soft now as his voice. "I'll stay in touch."

Dear God, she wanted to let him handle it. How could she weigh her daughter's life against everything she had ever believed? Against everything she had been taught?

Her daughter's life. And all the precious images of Gardner's short existence ran through her head. Suddenly, Claire wanted to tell Griff how much his daughter looked like him. How her minute chin could tilt at exactly the same angle his sometimes did. If he were being challenged. In the heat of argument. And how Gardner's eyes, as dark and beautiful as Griff's, would sometimes study Claire's face as intently as his were now.

She wanted to say all those things to him. She wanted to tell him about their daughter, so that he would love her as much as she did. So that *he* would make this decision. So that he would do what they had told him to do, no matter what she said. No matter what she had once argued. No matter what she said she believed was morally right.

But instead, the confusion of too many conflicting emotions made her strike out at Griff instead. Just exactly, she would realize later, as she had always done.

"I *should* leave it to you," she said bitterly. "After all, this is your fault. You're the one who brought these people here. Into Gardner's life. Into mine. This is *your* filth, Griff. This whole nightmare is the result of how you chose to live your life. I damn well hope you're satisfied with the results."

She saw his eyes change. There had been compassion in them when he'd told her to let him handle it. That was replaced slowly by pain, an agony so unbearable it was visible. And then his entire face hardened, accepting that unforgivable blow.

He didn't say another word. He pushed up from the table, picking up his coat and the cane. Then he turned, limping back down the hallway to the front door.

She listened, unmoving, as the uneven footsteps faded. It was not until she heard the slam of the front door that she remembered to breathe. And then, using the heels of her hands, to wipe away the tears.

She had no right to blame Griff for what had happened to Gardner. This was simply the inevitable intrusion of the world he had warned her about. A world that lay in wait just beyond the confines of the safe and protected one in which she had grown up. The one she had arranged for her daughter.

Maybe what had happened to Gardner *had* originated in his world, but she knew Griff had done everything in his power to protect her from it. She had once thought he was too obsessive about keeping their relationship private. Too secretive.

This was, of course, what he'd feared. That she would be used against him in this way. A victim of the violence he knew so well. Instead of threatening her, they had used his daughter. A daughter he had never known and couldn't possibly love as much as she did.

So in her fear, she had struck out at Griff, just as she had done before. And struck out at him because she knew in her heart she wanted him to do anything to get Gardner back. God help her, *anything*. Even this.

Chapter Six

"His name is Jake Holt. And I *know* he's still working for the agency," she said to her grandfather. "I need to ask him only one question. And I promise I won't make you contact the director again."

It had taken her two days to reach this point. Two endless days during which nothing had happened. She had talked to Minger, of course. Several times. And to the FBI. During those interviews, however, her mind had been only half-engaged, because she had known that it didn't matter what they asked or what she told them.

The police weren't going to find Gardner. Nor was the FBI. No one was going to contact her and demand ransom. That demand had already been made. Not to her, but to the person at whom this kidnapping had been directed.

And whoever had known enough about Griff and his team to pull this off was not going to be discovered by the local police. So whatever they were doing was pointless, and she knew it. This playing field was not on their level. Even the bureau was probably not capable of influencing events in this arena.

She couldn't tell the authorities that. She hadn't even told her parents or Mandy and Charles what was going on. Only her grandfather knew what had happened the night she had driven to Griff's house in Maryland. And the morning he had come here.

She had slept last night on the floor of Gardner's room, an exercise in trying to recapture the serenity their life had once held. To reconnect with her daughter. But Gardner was both too near and too far away in that room.

And Claire had acknowledged that Gardner might never be there in reality again if Griff didn't do what they'd asked him to do. And given the unforgivable things she had said to him, she could no longer be certain of anything he was doing.

So she had driven out to the Maryland house again today, searching for him, and had found it empty. There had been no sign that anyone had been there in months. No sign of her meeting with Griff. As if she had dreamed the entire episode.

I'll stay in touch, Griff had promised. But that had been before she'd lashed out at him, accusing him of being responsible for what had happened to Gardner. She had heard nothing from him during these two endless days. And she knew she couldn't live through another one without knowing what was going on.

"Cabot told you to let him handle it," her grandfather said. "That sounds like excellent advice, Claire."

"Actually," she said, finding a smile for him, because she understood he was trying to comfort her, "it sounds like blatant male chauvinism, but we'll ignore that for the moment."

"I don't know what you believe this Holt can tell you."

"Where they are," she said simply.

"They?" Her grandfather's voice reflected both his frustration with her and his puzzlement.

"Griff. Jordan Cross. A man called Hawk. And maybe Jake Holt as well. But...I think he would stay at headquarters. I think he's their contact there. And he would probably need the agency's computers."

She was thinking out loud, of course. Articulating all the things she believed she had figured out in the last two days about what Griff might do.

"You think they're really going to do this," the old man said. "You think Cabot intends to do what the kidnappers demanded. And you want to try to stop them."

"No," she said. "I don't want to stop them. God forgive me, I want to help."

"I HAVE NO RIGHT to ask you," Griff Cabot said, his eyes touching on the face of each man in turn, "but I would like to have you with me," he said softly.

"I've got vacation coming," Jake Holt said, his voice laced with amusement, a contrast to the quiet solemnity of Griff's. "After all, *I'm* the only one who's still working for a living. Since you're paying all the expenses for this little excursion and since I think Florida's a really nice area to visit this time of year, you can count me in."

Griff nodded, not really surprised by Jake's acceptance, or by the cheerful nonchalance with which he'd made it. Jake wasn't a field agent, of course, but he had grown up around the area where they were going, so his knowledge of it would be invaluable. And Jake was a bachelor.

The other two men he had called had new lives, an existence outside the agency. And they had families. The fact that they had answered his summons spoke of the depth of their friendship, but Griff knew he had no right to ask them to lay their lives on the line for a mission that was purely personal.

"Quid pro quo," Jordan Cross said. "I owe Claire Heywood a couple of favors. And more than a few to you," he said, smiling at Griff. "I'm in."

Griff nodded, his gaze lingering unconsciously on Jordan's altered face. It was disconcerting, although he had known what to expect. And it was a little eerie when Jordan spoke to find his deep voice totally unchanged.

"Are you waiting for me to agree?" Hawk asked, and Griff's eyes swung to his face, its harsh contours reassuringly the same.

"I need to hear you say it," he said.

Just as he had needed to hear Claire tell him Gardner was his child, needed to hear her say the words, although there had really been no doubt after he'd received that ransom note. And he needed to know that each of these men knew going in exactly what they would be up against.

"Then I'm in," Hawk said.

Three words, but Hawk's ice-blue eyes, locked on his face, said all the other things Griff knew he would never hear from Lucas Hawkins. No words about bonds of friendship. Or old debts. Those would remain unspoken, because, between the two of them, they didn't need to be expressed. They never had.

"Then I'll let Jake tell you what he's found out," Griff said, fighting unwanted emotions, especially gratitude for a brotherhood that had been forged on missions just like this one would be. Dangerous. Precisely planned. And dependent on each other for its success.

"We'd never get him at home," Jake said, "not without losses. Security's too tight. Location's too isolated. Griff doesn't want to take that chance, and there's no need."

"So where?" Hawk asked.

"He has a meeting set up with his major distributors in three days," Jake said. "In the States. We need to do it here. But he'll fly out of Miami on the fifth or the sixth, so that's our window of opportunity."

"Not a lot of time," Griff interjected, "but doable. We've planned missions in less. Jake will fly down in the morning and make arrangements for the equipment we'll need. The three of us follow on different flights."

"I don't understand how they could have known you're alive," Jordan said. "Or how they could know about the baby when you didn't."

The fact that he hadn't been aware of Gardner's existence was something Griff had rather not go into. They had the right to ask questions, however, considering what they had just agreed to do, motivated by nothing more than friendship.

"People in the agency knew I was alive," he said. "They probably knew about the baby as well."

"You think they could be behind this? Steiner and that crowd?" Hawk asked.

There was no love lost between Hawk and the man who had taken Griff's place, but as much as he had thought about the possibility that this was someone within the agency, Griff couldn't fathom a motive. Not for the assassination or for wanting him involved in something like this. The agency had more to lose with the possibility of his involvement becoming public than anyone else.

"Someone was in the system during the last couple of months," Jake said softly. "I could feel them. Someone who had to be operating from inside."

"*I* was in the system," Griff said, remembering Steiner's frustration over how he had known what was going on with his team. "I kept expecting you to backtrack to me."

Jake laughed, sounding a little relieved. "Guess I taught you pretty good."

"You really didn't know?" Griff asked.

"Not that it was you," Jake said. "But that still doesn't explain how these people could know what they seem to know."

"If I could get in, Jake, so could someone else," Griff said. "Someone from the outside."

"When pigs fly," Jake said softly, but obviously challenging that conclusion.

"Then figuring out *how* they knew is your job," Griff suggested. "*While you're at it,* figure out how they sabotaged Claire's alarms."

"What about the exchange?" Jordan asked when Jake nodded.

Griff looked up and found Jordan's gray eyes on his face. At least they were still familiar.

"Down there," he said. "I've already arranged that with them. They're demanding proof. And that's going to be the tricky part, given how security conscious the subject is."

"But you've already figured out how we're going to do it," Hawk said, amusement threading the quiet comment.

Griff's mouth moved slightly in response before his eyes again found Lucas Hawkins's face. "I've figured out how *you're* going to do it," he said. "All I'm going to do is take a plane ride and work on my tan."

"Sounds like business as usual," Jordan said. "We take the chances, and you and Jake get a vacation."

Hawk laughed. For the first time in months, Griff heard the sound of his own laughter, joining that of the others. And despite the grim purpose that had brought these few members of his team together, he knew that Carl Steiner had been right. He had missed this. And he had missed them.

DESPITE HER GRANDFATHER'S efforts within the agency, Claire hadn't been able to get in touch with Jake Holt. Maybe she had been wrong in thinking he would remain at headquarters. Maybe he didn't need their computers to do whatever it was he did.

And that thought had led her to undertake tonight's journey—a drive to the old summer home on the coast of Virginia that the Cabots had owned for generations and that Griff had utilized before for the activities of his team. A place where both Jordan and Hawk had sought refuge. A place where there was a lot of computer equipment that Griff had used for agency business.

And a place that now seemed as dark and devoid of human life as a tomb, she acknowledged, looking up to where the towers of the Victorian house loomed above her on the top of the seaside cliff. If Griff and his team were working here, they were being damned low-key about it.

Wild-goose chase, she thought, beginning the climb up the flights of wooden steps that snaked along the side of the cliff. She had managed more than half of them when she remembered Griff's cane and realized again how foolish this visit was.

Pausing to catch her breath, she looked up at the structure, so dark and forbidding and obviously unoccupied. She almost turned around and left, but since she was already here, she decided that she might as well make sure.

WILD-GOOSE CHASE, she thought again, as she directed the beam of her flashlight about the dark, empty rooms. She had been a little surprised that the codes for the security locks hadn't been changed. It seemed, however, that nothing had changed, she acknowledged, letting the light probe the perimeters of Griff's study.

She had already turned away, heading back to the hall and the front door, when a small flash attracted her attention. It had come from something on the desk, so she allowed the flashlight to play again over its surface. What she had caught out of the corner of her eye, she realized, was a reflection of her light off the glass of a photograph.

She stepped back into the room and walked over to the desk to pick it up. A snaggle-toothed, towheaded tomboy laughed out at her from the silver frame. A moment from her own childhood. A single moment that had been captured in time, almost as Griff's face had been that night in the garden. Frozen. Unchanging.

Griff's study. And her photograph. The only one he had ever asked her for. A picture no one could associate with the woman she was now. And that caution had been for security reasons, to prevent the very thing that had happened to Gardner.

Claire put the picture down where she had found it, but she didn't go back to the door. She stood there instead, remembering the times they had spent in this house. They hadn't been able to get away often, given their conflicting and equally crowded schedules, but the weekends they had stolen had been very special to them both. And rare. Far too rare in their relationship.

A relationship she had destroyed, she acknowledged, just

as Griff had said. Destroyed deliberately and after careful thought. Over principle.

Her lips tightened, but resolutely she turned away from the desk and retraced her steps across the room. She had almost reached the door when she heard a noise. She stopped, quickly pressing the off button on the flashlight with her thumb. Then, holding her breath, she listened.

It had taken only a second to place the first sound. And then those she was hearing now. Someone had closed a door and was coming down the hallway, his steps echoing slightly in the long empty space.

Griff? she wondered, but instinctively she shrank against the wall beside the door. Not Griff. She had realized that by the even rhythm of the footsteps. She closed her eyes, putting her head back against the wall. Maybe there was a caretaker living nearby. Maybe he had seen her light and had come to investigate.

Whoever this was, she realized, he was apparently doing exactly what she had done, stopping in each doorway and examining each of the rooms that led off of it. But he was working from the back of the house.

She opened her eyes and turned her head toward the door. She could see the light he carried moving sporadically. Sometimes it seemed brighter—directed down the hall toward the room where she was hiding—and then it would fade as it was turned in another direction.

It was clear, however, that whoever held the flashlight was coming this way. She began edging to her right, toward the door that led from the study and out onto the gallery that ran around the back of the house. The footsteps were getting louder, and moving on tiptoe, she hurriedly closed the distance between herself and that outside door. She had her hand on its knob before she remembered the alarms.

She looked for the security pad, but couldn't find it in the darkness. And then, suddenly, it wasn't dark anymore. She whirled, and the beam of a flashlight focused on her face.

Just as Griff had done that night, she put her hand up to block the intensity of the light, and it went out at once.

"Sorry, Ms. Heywood. I wasn't sure who was up here."

She lowered her hand, but her eyes were momentarily blinded. Gradually they adjusted to the return of darkness, and the figure standing in the doorway swam into focus.

"Jake said you'd been looking for us," Lucas Hawkins said.

She had met the man called Hawk only once, during the abortive meeting she had arranged for him with his superiors at the CIA. A meeting where he had traded his freedom for Tyler Stewart's life.

She had seen Hawk, however, before that meeting. At the time, she hadn't known who he was. She had realized when she'd met him later that he, too, had been visiting Griff's grave. And she wondered how *he* felt about the lie Griff had told them. Or had he had known all along Griff wasn't dead?

"And how did Jake know that?" she asked.

Since all her efforts to find Holt had ended in the same denials her previous inquiries about Hawk and Jordan had provoked, she was really curious.

"Jake knows everything," Hawk said easily. "Or didn't Griff tell you that?"

"You know he's alive," she said.

"I didn't. Not until this."

Not until this. Not until Griff had gotten the demand from the people who had taken Gardner and had called on his friends for help. She had been right about that, at least.

"And it doesn't bother you that they lied to us?"

Hawk had killed the man who'd ordered that terrorist attack at Langley. He had killed him because Griff Cabot had been one of the victims of that massacre. And since they now knew that he was not, she was curious as to how Hawk felt about the deception.

"I'm just glad he's alive."

"You *killed* a man because they told you Griff was dead."

Even to her, it sounded like an accusation. She didn't think she had meant to accuse him. Perhaps she just wanted to be reassured that Hawk felt as betrayed as she did by what Griff had let the CIA do. Or as angry, perhaps.

After all, Hawk's life had been as disrupted as hers by that lie. Perhaps more so. Only her intervention, and Jordan Cross's, had saved Hawk's life. And he had lost his profession as a result of the revenge he had taken for Griff's death.

"The man I killed had a lot of blood on his hands. A lot of murders through the years had been laid at his door. The five who *did* die at Langley were only his latest victims. And I'll save you the trouble of asking again. It doesn't bother me."

"And this?" she said, her voice very low. "Does…this bother you?"

"The assassination the kidnappers have demanded?" Hawk asked, putting the reality she had skirted into concrete terms.

She nodded and then was unsure he could see her clearly enough to detect the motion. "Yes," she whispered.

"I don't make those decisions, Ms. Heywood. I take orders. But I take them from a man I trust. And I always will. As long as he wants to give them to me."

The simplicity of Hawk's answer left her with nothing to say. *A man I trust.* That was the kind of loyalty Griff evoked in those who worked with him. Only she, apparently, had not been able to give him that unquestioning trust.

"If you want to talk to Griff," Hawk offered, "I'll take you to him."

She hesitated only a second before she stepped out of the shadows beside the gallery door and moved across the room to where the man called Hawk was waiting.

"WHAT ARE YOU DOING HERE, Claire?" Griff asked.

He glanced up when Hawk opened the door, but only

long enough to see who was with him. Then he redirected his attention to the display on the monitor he had been studying, leaning over the shoulder of the man who was seated in front of the computer.

Jake Holt? she wondered. If so, apparently she had been wrong about what he needed. There didn't seem to be any more computer equipment in front of him than she had at home.

Finally, when she didn't answer his question, Griff straightened away from whatever he had been concentrating on and really looked at her. His eyes were shadowed, but even across the room, she could feel their impact. A physical impact.

Unexpectedly, a slow, roiling wave of heat moved through her body. The same hunger, the same need, that had driven her to come to him that night more than a year ago. The night Gardner had been conceived.

"I need to talk to you," she said.

He didn't say anything for a moment, but his mouth tightened, the grooves she had noticed beside it deepening with the pressure he was exerting.

"I think you know everyone here except Jake," he said. "Hello, Claire."

Jordan Cross's deep voice, touched with that unmistakable Southern accent, came from across the room. Across the basement, she amended, her eyes lifting to find a man leaning against the original bricks of the cellar wall.

Jordan, she realized, although he looked very different from the man she had met at the Lincoln Memorial that day. The new face, courtesy of the CIA's surgeons, was almost as attractive as the old.

"It's good to see you again," Jordan added.

At least his tone seemed friendly, Claire thought. Uncondemning. But of course, Hawk's had been, too, even when he had made that pronouncement about trust. She had time to wonder what Griff had told them before the man at the computer turned, looking directly at her for the first time.

She was too far away to be able to tell anything about the color of his eyes. In the light from the computer, his hair appeared to be lighter than Griff's. A dark chestnut, perhaps.

Then he stood up and crossed the room toward her, putting out his hand. Automatically Claire took it, and found that his handshake was as warm and friendly as his smile. And his eyes were amber, she realized. Far too golden to be called brown.

"So you're the head hotshot's woman," Jake said. "Nice of you to drop by. I wondered what you'd be like. We all did. Nobody but me will ever tell you that, by the way."

The head hotshot, she thought. She couldn't imagine anyone using that phrase to describe Griff. Especially not in front of him. Her lips tilted, despite the seriousness of the task that had brought her here.

"Don't mind Jake," Jordan said from across the room. "He likes to rattle cages. Sometimes he forgets what's inside."

"Hotshot number two," Jake said, almost under his breath.

"You're not…a hotshot?" she asked, smiling openly at him, a little of the stress of the last three days easing with his friendliness.

"I'm the geek. No field trips for me. I just tell them where to go and keep them safe."

She nodded, not quite sure how to respond to that. "You do that with the computers," she said finally.

"I see someone's been taking my name in vain," Jake said.

"Griff said that's what you do."

"I find things," he said.

"Have you found my daughter?" she asked softly.

The teasing light faded from his eyes. "No, ma'am," he replied, all amusement gone from the pleasant voice as well. "I wish I had, Ms. Heywood, but I haven't found out much that tells us anything useful about where your baby is right now.''

''Then what is that?'' she asked, gesturing with her head toward the screen they had been so focused on when she entered.

Jake held her eyes a moment before he turned to face Griff. ''You want to tell her or do you want me to?'' he asked.

''I think that depends on why she's here,'' Griff said.

Her eyes moved to Griff's. In their dark depths was a challenge. And clearly, there was bitterness as well. And she couldn't really blame him, not after what she'd said.

''I'm here because I want to know what you're going to do.''

''Whatever it takes to get her back,'' he said simply.

His tone was as cold as his eyes. Cold because she had unfairly blamed him for what had happened to Gardner. And Griff was, she knew, the only hope for getting her daughter back.

Because of that, they would have to find some way to deal with their past. With their conflicts. Some way to put them into perspective and concentrate on what was important. She knew it was up to her to make the first move.

''I'd like to talk to you about that,'' she said. ''Alone,'' she added softly, her eyes still locked on his.

''Upstairs,'' he said finally, and when he led the way, again she followed.

''HIS NAME IS RAMON DIAZ. He's one of the most powerful of the new below-the-border drug lords.''

''Drugs?'' she asked, feeling some small portion of her guilt over being here ease.

Griff had told her that a lot of people would want this man dead, but she hadn't known exactly what the implications of that might be. And frankly, understanding now what he had meant by that, she was relieved.

''A couple of years ago he was a middleman for the Colombians," Griff said. "Now he's a major supplier to the States. Mostly heroin."

"So...who would want to assassinate him?"

She was thinking that this might be someone official. Some government agency. Perhaps even the CIA themselves. Or the DEA. But surely the government wouldn't have used Gardner as a means to accomplish that.

"Someone who wants control of the network he's built. Someone who wants to run his show," Griff suggested. "Or maybe someone out for revenge. Who knows?"

"And their reasons don't really matter to you?" she asked.

Suddenly, she wished she hadn't. That sounded too much like the things she had said to him before. The arguments she had made. Too much like an accusation.

"Not in this situation," he said, his voice almost as cold as it had been upstairs.

"Why would they want *you?*" she asked. "How would they even know about you? About the team?"

"They want us because we can do it. Given the security Diaz surrounds himself with, there aren't many people who could. Apparently they were smart enough to realize that. And as to how they know about the team..." He shrugged. "We're in the process right now of trying to figure that out. But we're still trying to figure out a lot of things. And we don't have much time to do it in."

Claire didn't like the sound of that. Not when she thought about Gardner.

"What does that mean? The not-much-time part?" she asked.

"Diaz is coming to the States for a meeting with his major buyers. As soon as it's over, he goes back to his stronghold in the mountains of central Mexico. Once he's there, it becomes much harder to get to him."

"But...you could?" she asked, fighting the fear that even they might not be able to pull this off.

"Maybe," Griff said. "But it would be more dangerous.

Dangerous for those involved, so we'd rather hit him here. *Before* he leaves.''

''When will that be?''

''Two or three days,'' Griff said.

Gardner had already been gone for three, and they had seemed endless. And endlessly painful. The thought that Griff might be able to bring this off and get her back in two or three more seemed overwhelming.

''And then…when you've done that, they'll give Gardner back?'' she asked, hoping this was what they had promised him.

''As soon as they have verification of the hit.''

Those words were like a foreign language in her safe, narrow world. A language she had never wanted to learn. Things she had never been able to think about without feeling sick. At least not in conjunction with her own life. Not in conjunction with the man she loved.

Now her daughter's life depended on the skills Griff Cabot and those hard men in the room downstairs had honed by doing the very acts for which she had once rejected him. The same things for which she had told him she never wanted to see him again. His past, on which she had blamed Gardner's kidnapping.

''I want to be with you,'' she said. ''While you do this.''

''Why?'' Griff asked.

It was, she supposed, a simple enough question, but there wasn't a simple answer. Not that she had been able to come up with. Not one that would make sense to anyone else.

''Because if I go along with this… If I allow you to do this for Gardner,'' she amended, ''then I should be part of it. Otherwise…'' She hesitated again, but he kept his eyes steady on her face, waiting to hear whatever conclusion she had come to. And after two days of thinking about it, this was the decision she had made. ''Otherwise, I'm a moral coward.''

She wondered if he would even remember what he had said. He had accused her of moral arrogance. She certainly had none now. She wanted her baby back, and if the price was the death of a drug lord, then she would be able to face that. If Griff, who didn't even know his daughter, could deal with that guilt, then surely she could. *If* it was the price of her daughter's life.

"You don't have to prove anything, Claire," he said. "Not to me. Not even to the others. This isn't about morality. There's nothing moral about what they're demanding. Nothing honorable. You don't have to be involved."

"You'll ask Jordan or Hawk or Jake to help you. But not me."

"They all had a choice. You didn't. The people who took Gardner didn't give you any."

"And she's not their child," she said softly. "She doesn't belong to Hawk. Jordan didn't struggle to give her birth. None of them, including you, have held her when she cried all night. Or saw her first smile. None of you. So I don't need to hear about choices. Or about right and wrong. In case you've forgotten, I'm the one who made all those arguments before."

She hesitated again, and then she went on with what she had come here to tell him. "But right or wrong, I can't make them now. Not when Gardner's life is at stake. And if I'm not willing to tell you no, don't do this, then…" She hesitated, still holding his eyes, before she made her demand. "I have a right to be here, Griff. To be involved in this. I have more of a right to that than any of the rest of you."

She waited for him to deny her reasoning. She waited for him to turn the old arguments against her. Or to remind her of what she had once said. And of what she had done. Of what she'd accused him of. But of course, being Griff, he didn't do any of those things.

"Jake will show you what you can do to help," he said.

Without another word, he turned and limped back toward the hallway. She stood in the darkness watching until he disappeared. Then, after she had heard the door to the basement stairs close behind him and she was again alone in the dark, upstairs emptiness of the house, she walked over to the desk and picked up the photograph in the silver frame. Her photograph.

Given the coldness in Griff's voice when she'd arrived, she needed the hope this provided. Maybe the fact that he still had her picture on his desk didn't mean a thing. Maybe it had simply been forgotten in the turmoil of what had happened to him. After all, this house had been closed for more than a year, the same year during which she had thought Griff was dead.

But despite the fact that, several months before the attack at Langley, she had told him she never wanted to see him again, her picture was still on Griff Cabot's desk. And despite the terrible accusation she had made that morning in her kitchen, he hadn't made her leave.

Chapter Seven

Beyond the blue-green expanse of Biscayne Bay and in front of a backdrop of violet sky, the lights of Miami shimmered into life through the deepening twilight. The cruiser swayed gently on the swells, and except for the soft slap of water against the hull, it was surprisingly quiet. Surprisingly peaceful.

The unmoving figure at the rail added to the serenity. Claire had stood behind Griff for several minutes now, studying the broad shoulders and muscled back, both clearly delineated by the black cotton knit shirt. It was obvious, too, that under the tightly stretched material of the faded jeans he wore, his waist and hips were as narrow as before he'd been hurt.

It had been hard for her during the last two days to remember what had happened to Griff, especially when he was standing, unmoving, as he was now. At moments like this, he seemed unchanged. He hadn't used the cane at all during the two days they'd been on the boat. Claire assumed that was because they had traded the cold, wet climate of the D.C. area for the heat of the tropics.

In the two days she had been with the team, she hadn't sought Griff out. They had been together, of course, but always in the company of the others. Never alone. And they hadn't talked. Not about anything.

She wondered why he was up here, looking at the city.

Was he thinking about what would happen tomorrow? Worrying about it, just as she had been all day?

"Do you really believe this will work?" she asked.

As she spoke, she moved up to stand beside him at the rail, her soft-soled shoes making no sound on the gleaming mahogany of the deck. Seeming to become aware of her presence for the first time, Griff turned his head, looking down into her eyes.

The bridge of his nose was sunburned from the long days they had spent on the boat. Even the high cheekbones were touched with color, despite the darkness of his skin. His blue-black hair, its natural curl enhanced by the humidity, moved slightly in the breeze.

In this forgiving light, the changes the past year had wrought in his face were less obvious. Right now, he looked exactly like the Griff she remembered. So much like that Griff.

Her breathing faltered with that realization, and she felt her pulse rate increase. A whisper of need brushed through her lower body, triggered by the memories of his lovemaking. Memories she couldn't afford to indulge in right now.

"If I *didn't* believe it would work," Griff said simply, "we wouldn't be out here." He turned his eyes back to the lights across the water, to the city where Hawk and Jordan had already begun to carry out the plan he had devised.

His hands were resting on the rail, and her eyes examined them now instead of his face. And found that contemplation no better for her peace of mind. Almost worse, in fact, because she could remember exactly how they had felt moving over her skin. Tantalizing and then satisfying.

Griff had almost been able to anticipate her needs. And certainly to read her responses. He had known everything about her. Things no one else had ever guessed. And, of course, there had never before been anyone who could evoke the feelings he had.

Before she met Griff Cabot, Claire had never considered herself to be sensual. Or sensuous. When she was with him, however, she was both. And she relished that. It was an incredible freedom, which he had first created within her mind and body and had then invited her to explore.

She pulled her eyes away from the temptation of remembering those long, dark fingers against her skin and looked out instead, as he was doing, across the panorama of sky and water. The lights of the city, glittering in the darkness like diamonds, rimmed the edge where the two met. She lifted her chin, closing her eyes and letting the breeze bathe her face. Enjoying its touch. Savoring the smell of the sea it brought with it.

"Don't worry," Griff said.

Surprised by the quiet command, she opened her eyes and turned to face him. He was looking at her again. Looking at her, and not through her, almost for the first time since she'd come to the summer house to find him.

"Nothing's going to go wrong," he said, his deep voice softer than it had been before. More intimate.

"Is that a promise?" she asked, smiling at him.

The question had been almost idly asked. Something to say besides "Do you remember...?"

"At least, nothing we can control will go wrong," he amended. "Nothing the team is responsible for will be left undone. Or left to chance. I *can* promise you that, Claire."

He had never broken a promise to her. He hadn't been the one who had broken the vow she had forced him to make. She had done that. Her arrival at his door that night had certainly been something out of his control. And just as much out of hers.

She nodded, turning back to the darkening sky. She knew the bare bones of the plan, although she hadn't really been in on its conception. Jordan and Hawk had left early today to carry out their part of it. And by this time tomorrow, it would all be over. *Nothing we can control will go wrong.* But there were, of course, so many things that couldn't be controlled.

She drew another breath, deep and slow. She supposed

she was only borrowing trouble, and she had more than enough of that already, but today, as she had watched Hawk and Jordan's departure, she had felt a prickle of apprehension.

A premonition, perhaps, that there were elements about all this that none of them understood. Things that moved beneath the surface of what was happening, as unseen and unknown as whatever swam below them in the depths of the tranquil waters on which the yacht bobbed and dipped.

She looked down at the waves lapping against the hull. There was nothing there but the gentle rise and swell of the ocean. Nothing was visible under the surface of the water, which she knew teemed with life. Despite the humid warmth of the surrounding night, so thick it was almost palpable, she shivered.

"I told you not to worry," Griff said again.

She looked up, away from the hypnotizing rise and fall of the ocean, and straight into his eyes. They were as dark as the shadows behind the lights of Miami, and yet tonight they seemed to have lost the bitterness she had put there.

She wondered if he had forgiven her for the accusation she'd made. And she wondered if she had completely forgiven him for involving her daughter in the violence of his world.

But if there was any lesson she had learned from losing Griff, it was that there was never a guarantee of tomorrow. There might not *be* a second chance to make things right. And regret was something she had lived with a long time.

Despite the fact that Griff wouldn't be physically involved in what would happen tomorrow, and shouldn't be in the kind of danger that Hawk and Jordan seemed so willing to face, there were still things she needed to say to him.

"Griff," she said softly.

Suddenly, she shivered again, feeling the same chill of foreboding that had touched her before glide again along her spine. When she spoke his name, he turned to face her, propping his elbow on the railing and leaning against it.

"I should have told you," she whispered. "As soon as I knew about the baby, I should have called you."

She waited for some response, but his face was unchanging. No longer cold, but...something. Some emotion was reflected there that made her afraid again.

"You should have told me," he said finally.

Simple agreement. But in his tone was much more, a regret that almost matched that which had crushed her spirit during those months when she had guarded his child beneath her broken heart. Hearing it, she grieved anew that he had never known his daughter. Had not even known of her existence. And that loss had been Claire's choice. Something that had been within her control.

It had taken her these last two days to realize that if she had told him about Gardner at the beginning, everything might have been different. Griff would never have let her believe he was dead if he had known she was carrying his child. He would never have left her alone with that responsibility.

And he would never have left his daughter unprotected— *if* he had only known about her existence. And he hadn't, because Claire had chosen not to tell him. So if anyone was to blame for what had happened to Gardner...

"I'm so sorry," she whispered. "Sorry for not telling you I was pregnant. And...sorry for what I said. It's not your fault these people exist. I shouldn't have blamed you for what happened to Gardner."

I'm sorry. The words seemed pitifully inadequate, but they were all she had. All anyone ever had.

His left hand lifted, and he touched her bare shoulder, exposed by the sleeveless tank top she was wearing. Offering comfort? she wondered. Or forgiveness.

He ran his thumb slowly down and back up, caressing the sensitive skin on the inside of her arm. And the unhurried movement was seductive.

What was in his eyes was just as evocative, reminding her of all they had once been to each other. Almost unconsciously, reacting to the touch of his hand and to what was in his eyes, she moved closer, drawn to him as she had been in the dream. Suddenly, his fingers closed hard around the soft flesh of her upper arms, pulling her to him. Her left hand found his cheek, cupping the pleasantly rough texture of his skin with her palm. And that, too, was a sensation she remembered.

His mouth lowered, opening slightly, aligning itself to fit over hers. She watched his eyes close, the thick fan of lashes dropping to hide their darkness. Then her own fell, surrendering to her need as a relieved and exhausted child finally gives in to the sleep it has mindlessly fought.

This was part of why she had demanded he let her come. Not only because she knew he was the only one who could rescue Gardner, but for this. For Griff. For his touch. His kiss. For all they had once shared. And could share again.

His mouth fastened over hers, moving with the same unquestioning surety. The same possession. And briefly, before her consciousness was overwhelmed by sensation, she remembered the hesitant movement of John Amerson's lips. This was why that kiss had been meaningless. Why anything else was unimportant. Anyone else. And why anyone else always would be.

Her hand found the back of Griff's head, and her fingers slipped into his hair, longer than it had been before, but warm and alive, as fine as silk. She pulled his head down, straining on tiptoe, pressing her breasts against the hard wall of his chest.

Trying to deepen the kiss. To prolong. To tell him again, this time without words, that she had been wrong. And that she knew and regretted her mistake. It had been such a long, aching emptiness of regret.

His hands found her shoulders instead. Gripping them, he pushed her away from him. The contact of the kiss was broken, of course, but his fingers still held her prisoner, and he was looking down again into her eyes.

Slowly, too lost in the sensations he had created to react

immediately, she closed her mouth, still hungry for his. His eyes followed the movement and came back to hers.

"Whatever happens…" he began, and hesitated. His lips tightened, denying whatever he had intended to tell her. Thinking better of it, perhaps?

"Whatever happens?" she questioned. "Tomorrow?"

Had Griff, too, felt that cold undercurrent of fear that had run through her veins all day? A dread of the unknown? Terror of something they couldn't control?

"We'll get her back," he said.

"I know," she whispered. "I know you will."

For some reason their roles had reversed. She was comforting him. And she had never known Griff Cabot to be afraid before. Or in need of comfort. In need of anything.

His hands released her shoulders as suddenly as he had broken the kiss. Then he turned and, without looking back, limped across the deck to the stairwell and disappeared through it into the darkness below.

She listened a moment to the sound the waves made, and then she looked across the bay toward the lights. Griff's words echoed in her head. And in her heart. *"Whatever happens…"*

Warning? Premonition? Or was it possible that Griff had reacted as strongly to their kiss as she? Had he been as shaken as she had been by the reality that nothing had really changed between them? Nothing except Gardner's existence?

Somewhere in the darkness beyond those distant lights, two men were working to get a baby back. And somewhere below, the man who had devised the plan and had told them how to carry it out seemed as worried about what was about to happen as she was.

Worried about a daughter he had never known. And at this point, Claire wasn't certain if that genuine though unspoken concern was something she should be glad about.

IT WAS MUCH LATER that she heard the sound of the inflatable returning. Its motor woke her, and then she listened to its cushioned side bumping against the hull of the yacht as the two vessels rocked together in the current. It seemed that either Hawk or Jordan had returned. To report? Or for further instructions?

Either way, the meeting was one where she knew she wouldn't be welcome. So she lay in her bed and listened until she heard the inflatable's engine kick into life again and then roar away, gradually fading into the deep, night-time silence of the sea.

She lay awake even after it was gone, thinking about the kaleidoscope of events of the last four days. The images were fragmented, wheeling in her head exactly like those bits of colored glass, but refusing to make a pattern she could read. And underlying them all was the cold sense of dread that she had felt since she'd watched Hawk and Jordan leave the boat that morning.

She was asleep, however, when the cruiser itself began to move, its powerful engines making little noise as it cut a path of foaming whiteness through the obsidian waters. Heading for a rendezvous that Claire had been told nothing about.

AT LEAST HE HAD TOLD HER the truth about one thing, Griff thought. Nothing they could control would go wrong. That had been a palliative, of course, intended to relieve some of her anxiety. He had been in this business too long to think there was much that could really be controlled. Meticulously planned for, yes. Anticipated. But never really controlled.

So far, however, the sequence had played out exactly the way it had been planned. As always, Jordan's and Hawk's execution had been flawless. By the time Diaz and his body-guards had arrived at Opa-Locka Airport, the private jet that awaited them had been secured. The cameras, which would faithfully record Diaz boarding the doomed plane, had been set up. And the explosives that would destroy it were in place.

"Nothing we can control will go wrong," he had promised Claire, and nothing had. Everything about this had gone according to plan. It had almost been too easy, Griff thought. Too pat. But he was too much a professional to argue with success. He knew he should be celebrating instead of worrying.

Still, he acknowledged, the uneasiness that had been in the pit of his stomach for the last two days wouldn't go away, despite the fact that the operation, the dicey part of it at any rate, was almost over. Almost done.

Only his job remained, he acknowledged, as he put his hand on the throttle lever and eased it forward. The jet responded like a well-trained thoroughbred feeling the whip. It rocketed down the runway through the heavy tropical darkness.

He watched the needle on the air speed indicator climb, and when it reached the takeoff point, he gently pulled back on the yoke. The nose of the Citation came up, and the jet lifted away from the ground. Then he rotated it toward the ocean, which stretched dark and wide under the star-sprinkled sky.

Now it was all up to him. Up to him to keep the promise he had made. Another promise to Claire. And to a daughter he had never known.

WHEN SHE WAS JERKED out of sleep, there was no doubt in Claire's mind what had awakened her. The only question was whether the explosion had been real or a dream. The noise had been distant, but the echoing boom had been strong enough to bring her out of the restless, nightmare-filled sleep she had finally fallen into.

An explosion, just like the one that was supposed to destroy Diaz's plane. Tomorrow, she thought. That was tomorrow, and not…

Her gaze found the porthole and verified that it was almost light. Almost light. Almost tomorrow. *"Whatever happens…"* Griff had said. *"Whatever happens…"*

She threw the sheet off her body, the foreboding that had haunted her now so strong it was thick and vile, clogging her throat like a sickness. She opened the door to her cabin and hurried through the dark, silent salon, across the narrow galley and up the steps that led to the bridge. She could hear the soft, mindless noises of the instruments.

When she reached the top of the stairwell, she realized that Jake was at the helm, totally focused on the equipment in front of him, exactly as he had been during most of the last twenty-four hours. She wondered if he had even slept.

In the darkness the faint glow of the dials and screens that stretched before him was eerie. It gave the tense figure hunched forward in the command chair an otherworldliness—strange, supernatural, almost demonic.

"Jake," she said softly.

He jumped visibly, startled by the sound of a human voice in his familiar world of machines.

"God, Claire, you scared the bejesus out of me," he said, turning to look at her over his shoulder.

"Sorry," she said. She walked across to stand behind him as she had seen Griff do a hundred times in the last two days. Depending on him. "I heard a noise."

Before she reached him, Jake leaned forward and moved a couple of dials or switches. The pattern on the screen he had been studying changed. A radar screen, she realized, the sweep of the line around its circumference and its beeps making its function obvious.

"What are you doing up?" she asked, her eyes moving across the expensive array of gadgets.

Then, almost without her conscious volition, her gaze lifted above them to the dark gray world that stretched beyond the windows. An expanse of black sea meeting a slowly lightening sky, a void unbroken except for a distant glow.

Fire, she realized. Something was burning on the surface of the ocean. It was far enough away that it was only a smudge of light, flickering over the dark water, but near enough that there was no mistaking it for anything else.

"What's that?" she asked, raising her hand and pointing. "Could that be what I heard?"

She turned to look down at Jake, and found that rather than following the direction of her gesture, his eyes had remained locked on her face. And suddenly she knew why.

"That's the plane." She barely breathed the words, soft and shocked. "That's Diaz's plane."

This had been part of the plan, of course. They were planning to put explosives on Diaz's plane. A device that would be triggered by a certain altitude, one that wouldn't be reached until the jet was out over the ocean, well away from the city and the pleasure boats that dotted the bay. No danger to anyone on the ground and leaving no possible doubt in the minds of the kidnappers that the ransom they were demanding had been paid.

Paid in full, she thought, looking back at the fire. Now that she knew what it was, it was as ghostly as the other had been, as eerie as the light that had been bathing Jake's figure when she entered the bridge.

Out of the corner of her eye, she caught the movement of Jake's head. His attention had gone back to the screen he'd been watching when she came up. The long sweep of the needle and the soft automatic beep was monotonous. Unchanging. Finding nothing in the vast emptiness of the ocean that surrounded them.

Finding nothing. Her eyes tracked another slow circle. Still finding nothing. "Where's Griff?" she asked.

She knew Griff Cabot too well to believe he wouldn't be up here watching his plan unfold. Studying what was going on with the same intensity Jake had been when she'd interrupted him. Griff should have been standing at Jake's shoulder, just as he had during most of the last forty-eight hours.

The silence between her question and Jake's answer was too long. Long enough for her pulse to quicken and for the cold sense of dread that had been in her stomach all day to increase sickeningly. Long enough to know something was wrong.

"I don't know," Jake said finally. His voice was flat, emotionless. "I wish to hell I did."

"You don't *know?*" Claire repeated. "What does that mean?"

There was another pause, again prolonged and full of something she couldn't read. Reluctance to answer, certainly, but something else as well. Jake was keeping things from her, and if that were true... If that were true, then it meant Griff had been keeping them from her as well.

Son of a bitch, she thought, feeling anger surge through her body, almost strong enough to replace the ice of her fear. They had been keeping things from her. Griff's precious team. And apparently everyone had been in on the conspiracy.

"Where is he, Jake?" she asked again, her voice tight. "What the hell is going on? I have a stake in this, remember. A bigger stake than the rest of you. I deserve to know what's happening, damn it."

He didn't answer, but deliberately his eyes lifted from the screen, away from its meaningless, monotonous sweep to the vast ocean that lay beyond the window. Maybe even as far as the fading glow of the fire that was burning on top of the water.

THE WATER HAD BEEN much colder than Griff expected. Despite the fact that it was January, this was the tropics, and the water temperature should have been in the seventies. It certainly hadn't felt that warm when he had plunged into it.

Now he couldn't seem to feel his legs, dangling beneath the black-ink surface of the ocean. They seemed detached from the rest of his body, especially the right one, the leg that a burst of bullets from the terrorist's Uzi had shattered. But considering its usual protest of any kind of physical demand he might make on it, he supposed he should be grateful for the numbing cold.

"Like taking a bath," Hawk had said when they were planning this. Neither he nor Jordan had tried to talk Griff out of the role he had assigned himself. And neither had questioned that he would be able to carry it off. For that unspoken confidence, he had been infinitely grateful.

Griff was the only one of them who had flown a small jet before. They could have hired a pilot, but he had known he could do this. All he had to do was take the plane out over the ocean, set the automatic pilot to continue its climb, trip the time-delay on the explosives Hawk had rigged, and jump. His leg shouldn't be a hindrance in any of that, not even the drop into the ocean.

It hadn't been. Everything had gone as smoothly as he had anticipated. He had landed and gotten free of the chute in time to watch the plane's disintegration. It had blown apart in a firestorm of debris that rained down, far ahead of him, for seemingly endless minutes after the echo of the boom had faded away.

Now all he had to do was wait for Jake's equipment to pick up the radio signal from the ELT that was attached to his life vest. So in the darkness Griff floated on the surface of the water, waiting for the deep throb of the yacht's engine and thinking about Claire.

Chapter Eight

"You're telling me the transmitter Griff's wearing isn't working, and the chances of our picking him up on radar are somewhere between nil and zero."

Jake hadn't put it that bluntly, of course. Claire had had to pry every piece of information out of him. Like the fact that Griff had decided to take the plane up himself and trigger the explosives manually, to make sure it was far enough out when it blew. When he had, he'd bailed out, depending on an emergency transmitter to pinpoint his location.

"It's a damn big ocean," Jake said, his eyes on the unchanging sweep of the needle. "And the chances of the radar picking up a body—"

Obviously realizing the frightening connotations of that phrase, he broke off abruptly, and in the light from the screen, she watched his mouth tighten.

"Why isn't the thing transmitting?" Claire asked, her eyes drawn back to the dying smear of the distant fire.

"I don't know," Jake said. "It just...isn't. I checked it. Griff checked it. Hawk checked it right before he left. It was working then. It damn well should be working now."

She could hear the frustration in Jake's voice. And perhaps a thread of anger as well. In reaction to something in her tone? She wasn't accusing Jake of incompetence, even if her question had sounded that way. But he was the equipment man. It was his job to prevent something like this from happening. Suddenly, Griff's words echoed in her head. *Nothing we can control...*

How could a man's life depend on something this insignificant? Of course, if that radio signal was the only way Griff could be tracked in the vastness of the ocean that lay beyond the windows of the yacht, then the emergency transmitter really hadn't been an insignificant part of the plan at all.

And she still didn't understand why it was Griff out there. Someone else should have been flying that plane. Anyone else. Just not Griff. Not now.

"Why isn't there some kind of backup?" she asked.

"Because..." Jake hesitated, and then he turned in his chair to face her. "Look," he said, "we've used these things a hundred times. They're practically fail-safe. And we checked this one out, damn it. All of us did."

The anger she thought she had heard before was certainly there now. It was obvious Jake was blaming himself, and there was no use belaboring the point that there should have been some provision made in case this happened. But no one, not even Griff, as meticulous as he was, could control everything. He had told her that himself.

"What do we do?" she asked instead.

"We start at the debris field, while we can still find it, and we move out from it in widening circles."

He had probably already been thinking about that. And Jake was in charge, of course. She couldn't see any flaw in his plan, especially since she didn't have another one to offer.

"Okay," she said.

"Your job will be lookout."

It would have to be, given the necessity of Jake's keeping a watch on the instruments and directing the search. Her job would be to spot the small, living speck that was Griff Cabot in the vast blackness of the ocean that surrounded them.

THE DAY WAS WARMER than yesterday had been, Claire thought, wiping the sweat off her forehead with the back of

her arm. And she wasn't sure whether that was good or bad.
The water temperature wouldn't rise that much, and even
the winter sun here was strong enough to burn. More than
strong enough to lead to dehydration, which was the real
danger.

Her eyes ached from the hours she had spent focusing
them beyond the gray-green roil of water that foamed at the
prow. She had swept the binoculars across the surface of
the ocean, moving them slowly from horizon to horizon, too
many times to count.

The cruiser was far enough out that they hadn't encountered much traffic. A Coast Guard cutter had passed them
early this morning, undoubtedly heading out to check on the
plane that had disappeared off Opa-Locka's screens. They
had paid the yacht no attention, obviously in a hurry to reach
the scene of the crash before there was nothing left to mark
the spot. Claire suspected Jake had been relieved not to have
to answer their questions.

She closed her burning eyes, wondering even as she did
if she could afford that small luxury. At first, her heart had
thudded wildly with each piece of flotsam that drifted in
front of the boat. She had followed its movement with the
binoculars, eyes wide and straining, until it was close
enough to identify. And none of them had been Griff.

"You need to come in and get something to drink," Jake
shouted from inside the bridge, gesturing broadly at her
through the glass to make sure she understood.

Reluctantly she obeyed, wondering again if they should
go back to Miami and report Griff missing. But Jake
claimed that was the last thing Griff would want. His being
in the water in this area would be highly suspicious. Griff
wouldn't want any of them connected with that exploding
plane, Jake had argued. And besides, in her naïveté, Claire
had been sure they would find Griff before now.

As she entered the bridge, she glanced at her watch. No
wonder her eyes hurt, she thought. She had been at this now

for almost eight hours. Jake had been, as well, and at least she had gotten some sleep the first part of last night.

"You okay?" she asked, taking the bottled water he held out.

"Am *I* okay?" he responded, his voice quizzical.

"How long has it been since you've slept?"

"I'll sleep when this is over."

She didn't ask when he thought that might be. Or if he still believed they could find Griff. By now, even she had realized the odds of that. Claire wasn't willing to give up, of course, and she suspected that Jake, like Hawk and Jordan, would endure whatever was necessary until they had located Griff—alive or dead.

"I don't understand why we haven't found him," she said. "You said his chute would have come down somewhere between the wreckage and where we were anchored last night. We've already covered most of that."

She took another long drink from the bottle as she waited for his answer. She hadn't realized how thirsty she was until the first sweet, cold draught bathed the dryness of her mouth and throat. She poured a little of the water over her face and then her neck, letting its coolness trickle into the scooped neckline of the cotton shell she was wearing.

"You see that?" Jake asked.

He pointed at an object bobbing gently in the water. It was a large, rectangular piece of metal that she had watched through the binoculars until it had become something more than a distant blur. Until she knew it wasn't the man they were looking for.

"Maybe part of the plane," she suggested, her eyes automatically following its motion away from the yacht.

"Maybe," Jake said. "That's not really what I meant, though. Whatever it is, it's moving."

"On the current," she agreed, pulling her gaze away from the object and back to his. He wasn't looking at her, so she raised the water again to her lips.

"We're running out of time, Claire," Jake said softly.

She lowered the bottle slowly, eyes widened. "What does that mean? The water's warm. The sun's...bearable," she said, glancing up toward the afternoon dazzle of clear, blue sky and then, eyes narrowed, quickly away.

"That's the Gulf Stream. Probably the most powerful current in the world. If Griff is caught in that..."

Her eyes lifted again to the floating object. Even in the short time they had been talking, it seemed to have grown noticeably smaller. Of course, that was probably the power of suggestion, but it frightened her, just the same.

"Then we'll follow the current," she said, feeling a tinge of excitement at that thought. A resurgence of the hope that had begun to falter. "We can plot it. You know where we were last night. Where the plane went down. We ought to be able to figure out how far out the current would have carried him. Surely there are charts with the information we'd need to do that on board."

"Except we're supposed to be making contact with the kidnappers in a few hours," Jake stated, interrupting that more hopeful line of thought.

"Do it from here," she suggested. "We know Diaz is dead. Tell them that."

"Griff's the one they're expecting. He's the one who's talked to them. And the arrangements were very specific. And pretty sophisticated," Jake admitted. "They seem as security conscious as we would be in this situation. Calls from shipboard are too easily monitored, so the call Griff is supposed to make has to be placed to a particular Miami number from a specific pay phone there. They don't want any mistake about who they're dealing with."

"What happens if he doesn't make that call?" she asked, watching Jake's eyes, trying to read the truth of what he would tell her. And when he spoke, she thought she could.

"The crash will have been mentioned on the news. Word that it was Diaz's plane will probably get out to those involved. I'm not sure, however, if it will be enough to satisfy them that we've done our part. Or to satisfy them that, despite the delay, we'll be in touch. And they were pretty adamant about proof.''

"What kind of proof?" Claire asked, trying not to think about Gardner. Trying not to picture her daughter in the hands of people growing increasingly angry about not receiving the message they were waiting for.

"Video of Diaz boarding the plane. The takeoff. Hawk and Jordan have that. We're supposed to rendezvous with them on one of the smaller keys and pick them and the video up. Then Griff makes the phone call in Miami and offers the package to the kidnappers. They tell us where to go from there. At least that's the way it was supposed to work.''

"Surely they'll wait," she said. "If they know that Diaz's plane went down.''

"*If* Diaz was what these people are really after," Jake said.

"I don't understand," Claire said, shaking her head. What else was this all about, if not that? "Griff thought this might be a rival who wanted to take over Diaz's operation.''

"Maybe," Jake said.

"*You* don't think that's what it is?" she asked carefully.

"Drug cartels don't have access to information about the internal operations of the CIA," he suggested. "At least not about something as sensitive as what this team does. Or about how it operates. And how did they even know about Gardner? Or know that Griff was the only one who could set this up?''

"Maybe they got the information through the computers," she said, remembering what Griff had told her, about how much information was stored within them. And remembering what he had said Jake could do with them. But she also remembered that Griff had told her that these questions, the same ones Jake was asking, were things the team had already been trying to figure out.

Jake's mouth tightened again, as if he were thinking about what she'd suggested. "Maybe," he conceded. "I don't think so, but... I mean, I guess it's possible, but in my opinion someone like that breaching our system would be highly unlikely.''

"So...who else would have that kind of information?" she asked. "Outside the agency, I mean."

Jake's lips pursed a little, and then he looked past her to the sea. An empty sea. And he didn't answer her question.

GRIFF CAME AWAKE with a start. He had no idea how long he had been asleep, but at least the sun was setting. It had beaten down mercilessly throughout the day. Despite the natural darkness of his skin, he knew his face and scalp were burned.

Of course, he thought, lifting his eyes to the shifting horizon that composed his limited view of the world, that was the least of his problems. His cracked lips lifted a little at the corners, despite the seriousness of his situation.

After all, he'd been in worse spots through the years. And the best thing he had going for him was the fact that they would be looking for him. The team. At least Jake. And Claire.

Obviously, the damn transmitter he was wearing wasn't working. Which meant, he supposed... He closed his sun-and-salt-burned eyes, trying not to think about all the things it might mean. And of course, those were the very things that continued to circle in his brain.

That maybe he wouldn't ever have a chance to say to Claire what he should have told her on deck last night. She had wanted him to kiss her. Had invited it. He knew Claire too well to have had any doubt about that.

Instead, he had pushed her away. And right now he couldn't quite remember why. Guilt, maybe? There had been a lot of that circling in his head as well throughout this endless day.

Guilt because he knew Claire had been right. The kidnapping had been his fault. Guilt because he hadn't told her the truth about what was going to happen. And because for a year he had let her believe the agency's lie. And Griff was honest enough to admit the things she had said to him when she had ended their relationship had played a role in that decision.

But he hadn't known about the baby. His daughter. His child, whom he had never even seen. And with everything else that had been going on, he realized he hadn't even asked Claire what she was like.

He had always considered himself to be a rational man. Logical. That had been the guiding principle in most of his relationships. Except with Claire Heywood, he acknowledged, his cracked lips moving again into a painful parody of a smile.

Except with Claire.

He turned his head to the left, resting his chin on the cushion of the life vest, and watched the sun begin to sink beneath the slow rolls and swells of water that lay between his line of sight and the bands of gold and red disappearing slowly into the sea. His eyelids began to drift downward, the urge to sleep almost too powerful to resist.

He pulled them up by sheer force of will. He scooped up a handful of water and splashed it on his face. The salt in it burned the sun-damaged skin, but its chill was refreshing. Stimulating. Helping him to think more clearly.

He dipped his cupped hand in the water again and raised it, a small silver stream overflowing each side of his palm. Almost unconsciously he began to carry it to his lips, painfully dry with heat and dehydration. He even knew how the water's soothing coolness would feel on them. And on his tongue.

He opened his mouth, burned skin cracking further with the movement. He couldn't gather enough saliva to swallow. All this water, all around him, and his mouth was too damn dry to spit.

His hand journeyed closer to his lips until it bumped against the forgotten bulge of the vest, spilling most of the water it held. Only with that bump did his brain kick in. Seawater. Saltwater. No matter how thirsty he was, that would only make things worse. He turned his hand, releasing the small, remaining puddle of water from his palm and letting his arm fall.

Claire and Jake would find him. Somebody would find him, he told himself. All he had to do was endure. Just hold on. Stay awake so he could wave if he spotted them. Or another boat. All he had to do was just stay awake. And not do anything stupid.

THE SEARCHLIGHT PLAYED slowly over the dark water. Claire wasn't sure anymore that even if her eyes found anything bobbing on the surface, the discovery would register on her tired brain. Too tired. Too many hours. Too many empty miles of ocean. And she felt as if she had examined them all.

She turned and looked over her shoulder toward the dim light coming from the bridge. She couldn't see Jake, but she knew he was there. The last time she'd gone inside, he had looked almost worse than she felt. If the two of them, who had access to water and shade during the course of the day, were like this...

She turned her head to look back over the sweep of ocean. It was dark enough that the point where the sky met the sea had been lost, but at least the moon was rising. Her eyes lifted to find it, floating silently, low in the sky.

Except she wasn't supposed to be looking at the sky. She followed the path the moonlight threw across the swells. Like a road. Yellow brick road. No, not brick. Water. A silver moon path lying across the black water, and in the middle of it...

She didn't dare breathe, watching the object rising and gently falling with the movement of the waves. Slowly, almost with a sense of dread that she might be mistaken, she raised the binoculars. It took a moment to find through them the path of moonlight. A moment to follow it.

And then to focus on the patch of color it illuminated.

Yellow. Not the pale gilt of the moon path, but the bright yellow of a life jacket.

And then the glasses moved minutely upward to focus on the dark head that lolled lifelessly between the inflated sides of that yellow vest. She watched it, still not breathing. Without lowering the glasses, she closed her eyes, squeezing them together to make sure that they were moist. And when she opened them again, the object was still there. Still the same. A man.

Her hands began to shake because, she realized, she had really given up hope. Whatever had kept her out here looking for Griff hadn't been belief that they would find him. Stubbornness instead. Endurance. And not having sense enough to know when to give up.

"Jake," she screamed. "I see him! Oh, my God, Jake, we've found him!"

GRIFF WAS CONSCIOUS when she reached him, but he seemed to drift in and out as they worked to get him on board. Claire had been the one who had gone down into the water because she couldn't wait to make sure Griff was all right. Now she had managed to maneuver him near the ladder. Jake was waiting at the top, ready to pull Griff over the rail, something which Claire, with less upper body strength, wouldn't have been able to do.

Jake was directing the small, portable spotlight down on them. From the surface of the sea, the side of the yacht stretched a seemingly impossible distance above them.

"Griff," she shouted, taking his chin in her hand and turning his head to face her.

His eyelids opened, moving in slow motion. In the glare of the light, she could see that his skin was burned. Beneath the surface red, however, it had a gray tinge, especially around the sunken eyes. His long, dark lashes were beaded with water, and the eyes they framed were rimmed with red, the whites bloodshot. His lips were cracked and almost blue. And yet, in the depths of his eyes, fastened now on her face, was the same intelligence and force of will that had always been there.

"You have to help me," she said, making each word a command, clear and distinct, her voice raised to reach him above the noise of the water and the idling engine. "You have to climb that ladder, Griff. Far enough up so that Jake can pull you over."

She gripped the rung that was just above the swell of the waves. The fingers of her other hand were fastened in the straps of Griff's life vest, and as a result his body floated nearer.

"Put your hand on the ladder," she ordered.

She was almost afraid to try to help him do that. Afraid that they'd move away from the yacht if she released the ladder and afraid that if she let go of Griff, he would somehow drift away and disappear again into the darkness. And she wasn't sure, if either of those things happened, whether she would have the strength to do this all again.

Sluggishly, Griff lifted his right hand, bringing a string of phosphorescent drops up with it. They shimmered in the glare of the spotlight. Although he reached out, his hand didn't connect with the rung of the ladder, but fell into the sea by his side. She could even hear the small splash it made when it struck the surface, distinct from the slap of the waves against the side of the boat.

"You have to hold on," she said.

In desperation, she released the ladder and fished under the water for his hand. By the time she found it, gripping his wrist and bringing it up to the surface, they were too far away from the boat for her to put his fingers over the flat, wooden rung. She took a few awkward strokes with her free arm, again bringing them against the hull.

"Put your hand on the ladder and hold on," she shouted.

"I'll get a rope," Jake yelled down, his voice seeming to come from a great distance above them. She glanced up, but couldn't see anything except the spotlight. She closed her eyes immediately, but was still almost blind when she opened them again.

Slowly Griff's face swam out of the darkness. If anything, he looked worse than he had a few minutes ago. Grayer. Less focused. Less capable of doing what she was asking him to do.

Which was probably, for a man in his condition, little short of impossible, she realized. Of course, finding him in this black wilderness of water had been little short of impossible. And she and Jake had done that.

Surely they could do this. They had to. They had come too close to give up. And, as Jake had reminded her more times than she wanted to think about, time was running out. Time to contact the kidnappers. Time to get to Gardner.

"We have to get back to Miami," she said to Griff. "We've already missed the deadline."

She was no longer shouting at him. She was so close her mouth was against his face. Close enough that she could occasionally feel the brush of his whiskers against her cheek as a wave lifted and then released them. Her lips were right beside his ear, and her tone had changed. She had stayed out here, looking for him, while those bastards had Gardner, and now...

"If we don't get back, they may kill her," she warned.

She didn't know that. But it was the thought she had fought since Jake had told her about the deadline, and finally giving utterance to it made it more real. Infinitely terrifying.

It had been five days since they had taken her baby, and Claire couldn't even remember how it felt to hold her. And if Griff didn't help her, didn't make this effort, then she might never hold her again.

"She's your daughter, Griff," she said. "Your daughter, damn it, and you promised me you'd get her back. And if you don't help me get you up that ladder right now, then we won't reach her in time."

A wave, stronger than the others, pushed them apart, the

water slapping against the plastic of his life jacket. She ducked her head to keep the resulting spray out of her eyes.

When she looked up, she realized that Griff was looking at her, the dark eyes more focused. More coherent than they had been since her trembling fingers had first touched his cold cheek. She had been afraid that he was dead, and then, with a rush of gratitude so overpowering it made her weak, she had watched his eyes open and fasten on her face.

Almost the way they were fastened there now. Holding on her eyes. Full of recognition. And understanding.

His hand lifted again, and the parched, cracked lips closed into a taut line. This was a look she had seen on Griff Cabot's face a hundred times, and seeing it there now, her heart lifted.

His hand reached out and gripped the wooden rung of the yacht's ladder. This time the long, dark fingers held. And then he carefully fitted his foot into one of the rungs that hung beneath the surface. And then his body began to lift away from her. Moving upward.

Chapter Nine

"Just a little more," Claire said, fitting the rim of the bottle against Griff's lips again.

She was sitting on the bed in the largest stateroom, the one where she'd been sleeping. Her back was against the headboard and she was sitting behind Griff, her arms around his bare chest. Despite her concern for him, she was finding this physical proximity as evocative as watching his hands had been last night.

Griff was still shivering occasionally, but once she had gotten the wet clothing off and covered him with a blanket from the compartment above the bed, those involuntary tremors had gradually lessened. His lips were also regaining their color.

Just as he had obeyed all the other demands she had made, he obeyed this one, drinking from the bottle she offered. Jake had suggested she get the ginger ale from the galley while he helped Griff down the stairs. Because of its sugar content, he claimed the ginger ale would be better than plain water to fight shock.

Claire had no idea if that were true, but it made sense. And Griff certainly wasn't protesting. She suspected he would have just as readily drunk anything she gave him. Trustingly. Obediently.

After all, since his hand had first locked around the rung of the ladder, he had done everything she'd told him to do.

Even to putting his arm across their shoulders once she and Jake had finally managed to get him on board.

Getting Griff down the steps to the living quarters had been the worst. That had been the only time in that nightmare journey Griff had made a sound. Because the passage was so narrow, she'd had to step back and let Jake support his weight alone.

Until then, Griff hadn't revealed how painful his leg was. His groan of agony had obviously been torn from him against his will. And she knew something about the nature of Griff Cabot's will.

But he was safe, she told herself. At least he was safe, and the yacht, under Jake's tired but steady hand, was racing belatedly to the rendezvous with Hawk and Jordan that they had missed while they searched. And as for their being late for the other, for the call Griff was supposed to make from Miami...

Claire had refused to think about that. About the kidnappers' reactions. There was nothing she could do about those things. And there was a lot she could do for Griff.

It had been surprising—and a little frightening, knowing Griff—how much he had let her do. Supporting him across the deck. Undressing him. And now this.

Never before had she taken care of Griff Cabot. Not as long as she had known him. Of course, he had never before been in a position to need her care. She suspected that Griff had never really *needed* anyone. Right now, however, no matter how much he might hate this dependence, he did.

"Enough," he whispered, turning his head.

A drop of the liquid fell on her arm, still wrapped around his chest. She took the ginger ale away, leaning forward enough that she could see the side of his face. With her thumb, she wiped off the small trickle that had escaped the corner of his parched lips. Beneath her fingers, she could feel the growth of a two-day beard, rough and somehow very pleasant. Thankfully, the skin under it was beginning to warm.

"Better?" she asked softly.

She waited for his answer, but his eyes were closed, as was his mouth—a little too tightly closed. After a moment, she set the bottle on the table beside the bunk and leaned back against the pillows she'd stacked behind her. He didn't have to talk. She was content to hold him, to feel again the strong, steady rhythm of his heartbeat, lying just above hers.

"Why didn't you go back?" he asked. "Jake should have tried to make the call. Tried to do something."

"Go back without finding you?" she questioned.

"Of course," he said.

"It didn't seem like a good idea at the time," she answered, allowing a hint of gentle mockery to color her denial.

She didn't confess that she hadn't known it would be as hard as it had been to locate him. Then, once they had stayed long enough to know they would miss the deadline for the call, it didn't seem to make much sense to head back without finding him.

And they *had* found him. Eventually. Now Griff was safe. And maybe, while they had been looking, Hawk and Jordan had done what he was suggesting she and Jake should have tried. To make the call. To try to exchange the video for Gardner.

It had not been a conscious decision on her part to choose to look for Griff rather than make that call on time. They had been in the midst of the search when Jake first told her about it. And Jake had thought the kidnappers would deal only with Griff. He surely knew more about those things than she could.

But she had known that to leave Griff out there would have been a desertion. And a decision that would almost certainly have condemned him to death. She hadn't been capable of making such a decision, and she was glad Jake hadn't suggested it.

She resisted the urge to put her lips against Griff's still-damp, darkly gleaming hair. She would only need to lower her face an inch or two to press a kiss against its softness.

Griff might not even be aware that she had. He might not feel the tenderness of the gesture she longed to make. And after the kiss she had invited, the one which he had deliberately broken off, she had no idea how Griff would react to her touch. No idea how he felt about her. About the unforgivable things she had said to him. All of them.

"What about Hawk and Jordan?" he asked into the silence.

"Jake's trying to reach them by radio."

"Trying?"

"The last I heard, he hadn't gotten an answer."

There was another silence, this one even longer.

"Why was it you in that plane?" she asked, remembering the fire flickering over the surface of the dark water. And the frightening hours she had spent scanning the empty expanse of ocean that stretched in front of the prow of the boat. "Why the hell did it have to be *you* who took that plane up?"

She waited through the silence, listening to the soft thrum of the cruiser's engine.

"Griff?" she said, finally leaning forward again to see his face. Trying to determine if he had fallen asleep.

But his eyes were open, focused on the opposite wall, or on the black, featureless porthole that looked out on the sea and the night.

"Why you?" she asked again, and watched a muscle at the corner of his mouth tighten and then slowly release.

"A macho bull-crap exercise in self-aggrandizement," he said softly.

She wondered for a second if he could be drifting into incoherence. Dehydration could do that. As could shock. And then, although she didn't really understand what the phrase meant, she laughed at the sheer absurdity of it.

Her breasts moved against the hard muscles in his back, and a wave of desire seared her lower body. She was breathless with the force of the memories it brought. Griff's hands. Her body moving against his. Under his. Things she couldn't afford to think about. Especially not here. Not now.

"What does that mean?" she asked instead.

"I wanted to prove I could still do it," he said.

"Still fly?"

"Still do this. Plan an operation. See it carried out."

She thought about why that might be so important to him. Important enough to risk his life for. And then she realized she had never once considered what his disassociation from the CIA might mean to Griff. His disassociation from the team, she amended.

That was a much more important disruption. A break in the bond of brotherhood these hard men had formed through the years. A bond that had, for most of them, taken the place of family. The place of love.

Once that bond had been broken by Griff's death, it seemed that for the first time some of them had become aware of the lack of those other things. Hawk had uncharacteristically rescued Tyler Stewart and then married her. Jordan had taken care of Rob Sorrel's small, vulnerable family and eventually made it his own. And Griff…

For the first time, she wondered what Griff had done during the long months she had existed without him. Apparently, none of his friends had known he was alive. His parents were both dead, and he had been their only child.

She had had Gardner to love and to care for during those months. But Griff, she realized, had had no one. In that terrorist attack he had lost his profession—a job he valued and was very good at. He had lost his friends. And even before that, he had lost what he and Claire had once had together. *She* had taken that from him. Her choice. Something within her control.

And Claire thought about what that particular loss might have meant to him. Wondered how he had handled it. Wondered, for the first time, if someone had taken her place in those long months of their separation.

Although Griff had not been her first lover, he had taught her more about her own sexuality than anyone else. And she had known, of course, that his sure, unthinking expertise came from experience. She had never wanted to think about that. About the time *before* she had known him. Before he had known her.

And she didn't really want to think about the possibility that there was someone in his life now. Was that why his initial approach to her had simply been an offer to help? Why he had made no attempt, other than the aborted kiss, which she had blatantly invited, to rekindle any of the physical connections that had existed between them. Was it because there was someone else in his life?

There had been for her an endless deprivation between the last time he'd made love to her and now. But maybe…~~maybe that~~ had not been the case for Griff.

"I guess now I know the answer to that," he said softly.

Her concentration had gone so far afield that she had to think about what he had said before. Dredge it up out of a mind that had been totally focused on something much more important. Griff had been wondering if he could still plan and carry out an operation. And this one…

"It's going to work," she reassured him softly, no matter her own doubts. "That may be why Jake can't reach Jordan and Hawk. They may have gone ahead and made contact with the kidnappers. They may have already made the exchange."

She couldn't know that, not given what Jake had told her about the arrangements, but there didn't seem to be any point in letting Griff punish himself for what had gone wrong. The things that had happened had been out of his control. And that was all he had promised her.

He didn't respond to her attempt at reassurance. She knew he didn't need to deal with this right now. He needed to build back the strength those long hours he had spent in the ocean, deprived of fluid, had stolen. He needed to sleep rather than to talk about what had gone wrong in this operation. Things he couldn't change now.

And she needed to check on poor Jake. He had had as little sleep as she in the last twenty-four hours. Maybe they could keep one another awake until they reached the rendezvous point where they were supposed to meet the others.

Griff didn't protest as she slipped out from behind him, carefully easing his upper body down onto the pillows she'd pushed against the headboard. When she was standing beside the bed, she realized that his eyes were closed again, the black lashes lying unmoving against the smudges of fatigue under them.

His eyes were a little less sunken than when she'd found him. At least they seemed to be, so the liquids she had given him must have had some positive effect.

"I need to check on Jake," she explained, not certain if Griff was asleep.

There was no response. She bent and pulled the blanket up over his chest. Her fingers made unintentional contact with his bare skin, but there was no reaction. She had already begun to turn away when he spoke.

"What's she like?" he asked. His voice was low, and he still hadn't opened his eyes. He wasn't looking at her. Maybe deliberately.

Gardner, she realized. He was asking about Gardner. And that had been another regret, one she had thought a lot about as she and Jake searched. She had thought of all the things she wished she'd told Griff when she'd had the chance.

"Like you," she said, her throat tightening with the realization of how true that was. Being with Griff again had reinforced what she had already known. "She's really...a lot like you."

His eyes opened. In the dimness they were so dark they were black. Without color. Deep and fathomless.

"Like me?" he asked, his gaze touching briefly on her hair, which she knew had been lightened even more by its brief exposure to the tropical sun. Then his eyes settled on hers, which were nothing like Gardner's either, of course.

"Black hair. Your eyes. She's even got your chin," Claire said, remembering, in spite of how much it hurt, that small, determined tilt. Fighting the pull of emotion, she said, "You'd have a hard time denying she's your flesh and blood."

Until the words were spoken, echoing painfully in the quietness, she didn't realize how inappropriate they were. How out of place between the two of them. Griff had never attempted to deny Gardner. He couldn't have, because he had never known anything about her. And that was a result of something Claire had done. Her choice. Something within her control.

He held her eyes a long time, but he didn't say any of the hurtful things he might have said. None of the accusations she probably deserved.

Claire didn't move, waiting to hear whatever he wanted to say to her. Knowing that eventually it would all have to be said. She had denied him his daughter. And twice she had come very close to never having a chance to make that right.

Finally Griff turned his face toward the wall, closing his eyes. A signal that the conversation was over, she supposed, but she waited a few seconds longer. Then she turned again and went out of the cabin, leaving him alone.

"DAMN IT TO HELL," Jake said under his breath.

Startled, Claire looked up. She had almost been asleep, she realized. And she was supposed to be keeping Jake company. Keeping him awake. Except it seemed she was the one who was more in danger of succumbing to exhaustion.

"What is it?" she asked, her eyes moving around the small cove the boat was entering.

"They're not here," Jake said, expertly easing the cruiser into the shallow waters.

Claire glanced at her watch, but since it was dawn, she

really didn't need to. They were hours late, and apparently Hawk and Jordan had given up waiting.

"Maybe they've taken the film and arranged the exchange on their own."

Jake didn't bother to answer. His eyes searched the tangled undergrowth that lined the narrow beach against which the aquamarine water became slow-breaking, cream-white rollers.

"The inflatable's not here," he said.

It wasn't until he said it that she understood what he'd been looking for. If the boat wasn't here, then neither were Hawk and Jordan. They wouldn't attempt walking out through that nearly impenetrable tangle.

"What do we do now?" Claire asked, glancing at Jake's set face. It was a question she had had to ask too often in the last few days. Now she was simply looking for something positive to hang on to. Some comfort. Reassurance.

"We contact the kidnappers," Griff said, his voice coming from behind her.

He had come up the steps while their attention had been focused on the cove. Neither she nor Jake had heard him. That might be explained by the fact that Griff was barefoot. He was wearing nothing but the same faded pair of Levi's he'd worn the night they'd stood together by the rail and watched the distant lights of Miami.

"Without the film?" Jake asked. "What do we tell them if they ask for proof?"

"We bluff," Griff said, moving carefully onto the bridge, his hand against the wall, using its support. "We pretend we have proof. And we set up a meeting to make the exchange."

Jake held his eyes a long heartbeat, and then, obeying Griff Cabot, just as he always had, he put the engine in reverse and began to back slowly out of the cove.

"You need to rest," Claire said.

Griff looked over his shoulder and found her behind him.

He had thought she and Jake were both still asleep, but it was obvious she'd been up long enough to take a shower. She had changed into fresh clothing, a pair of white shorts and a navy tank top, but she was barefoot.

Her hair was damp, and he could smell the soap or the shampoo she had used, its fragrance stronger than the hint of brine the morning breeze carried. He fought the images it evoked. They had showered together a few times. Washing one another's bodies. Slowly. Erotically. An act of love.

Without speaking, he turned back toward the front of the boat, the remembrance of Claire's naked body too strong in his head. He looked out through the bridge windows instead, fighting memory. He had thought about Claire Heywood almost every day of the last eighteen months. Every day since she'd told him she never wanted to see him again.

And he had thought about her, and his daughter, almost constantly throughout these last few days. Days when he and Claire had finally been together again. And during those long, lonely hours he'd spent in the ocean, he'd had far too much time to think. About everything that had happened between them.

One conclusion he'd come to, sometime during the course of that ordeal, was that despite the argument he'd made about their agreement being no different than letting Claire believe he was dead, he knew better.

He had known she would have been devastated by his "death." He had known it, and yet he still hadn't contacted her to tell her it was a lie. Not until he'd sent her that single bloodred rose. A message that obviously hadn't meant to her what he had thought it would.

And as he had floated in that dark, cold water, finally forced to face what he had done, Griff had also come to the realization that there was only one explanation for why he hadn't. Somewhere inside, in a cold, bitter place in his soul, he had wanted to hurt Claire as much as she had hurt him.

When she had broken off their relationship, she had rejected who and what he was. And she had made some pretty damning accusations. Eventually he had retaliated, in the cruelest way imaginable. But he hadn't known about the baby, which would, of course, have changed everything.

"Where's Jake?" she asked.

"Still sleeping."

"He needs it," she said.

She was standing beside him, but Griff resisted the urge to look at her. Now wasn't the time or the place to try to make amends. He had a job to do first. A job that had been badly botched. And he could only hope that in spite of all that had gone wrong, he could somehow manage to get her daughter back. *Their* daughter.

When they had docked again this morning in Miami, he had gone ashore to contact the kidnappers, leaving Jake to see to getting the yacht ready to go out again, and leaving Claire asleep. Surprisingly, despite the missed call, whoever had answered at the number he'd been given agreed to a new rendezvous, giving him precise navigational directions. Which was where they were headed now.

He had bluffed his way through their questions about the delay by fabricating a mechanical problem. And he had lied about having the proof he'd promised them, just as he'd suggested to Jake they should do.

It had all been easier than he could have hoped for, probably because Diaz's name had already been released to the media. And that should also tip the odds of success a little more in their favor, despite the fact they didn't have the film he'd promised.

He was increasingly worried about Hawk and Jordan, however. According to Jake, they hadn't been heard from since the Citation left the airport two nights ago. They hadn't been at the prearranged rendezvous. And it seemed obvious from his phone conversation that they hadn't tried to contact the kidnappers on their own.

"When we get there…" Claire began, and then hesitated.

"We play it by ear," Griff said.

"Will they accept that Diaz is dead?"

"Would you?" he asked. It wasn't a trick. It was the same question he had been asking himself.

"I don't know. I guess it would depend on how trusting I was," she said finally.

He laughed, the sound low. Unamused. "I don't think these people are very trusting. But the plane crash has been widely reported, and they've released Diaz's name."

"What about Jordan and Hawk? What do you think's happened?"

Griff didn't like the images those words conveyed. He hoped to hell nothing had "happened" to them. They hadn't hesitated when he had asked for their help, but everything was different now than when they had been members of his team. This wasn't their job. And they had responsibilities they hadn't had then. People to protect. And to care for.

"I don't know," he said truthfully, wondering how he would tell those who were waiting for their return if Hawk and Jordan didn't make it back. What would he say to their wives, and in Jordan's case to Kathleen Sorrel's children, if something had gone wrong?

Keeping his men safe was something he had always managed to do before, no matter how dangerous the situation. No matter the odds against their survival.

"They seem capable of looking after themselves," Claire said softly, probably reading his anxiety.

And they were, of course. No one knew that better than Griff, but he was worried. There seemed no reason to respond to her comment, however, and again the silence stretched, tense and uncomfortable. Which he found sad, because, although they had been many things when they were together, they had never before been uncomfortable. Not even the first night.

"Well," she said hesitantly. "I just came up to check on you and Jake. I guess...I guess you'd rather be alone."

She turned, moving silently across the deck.

"No," he said. His voice was so low he wasn't sure she would hear. And he didn't understand why he had made that admission. Other than the fact it was the truth. He didn't want to be alone.

He was pushing the cruiser through the coastal waters as fast as he dared. Probably faster than was safe, but that wasn't why he wanted company. After all, he hadn't wanted Jake up here.

But Griff didn't want Claire to leave. He wanted her with him. Of course, he acknowledged, again remembering, he had always wanted that.

"Thank you," she said softly.

He looked up. She was standing at his side once more. He reached out and took her hand. The bones were fine and delicate, and they felt as fragile as porcelain under his fingers. He pulled her forward a little, directing her without speaking to the pilot's chair beside the one he was occupying.

She obeyed, but when she was seated, he didn't release her hand. Her eyes, focused on his, were questioning, and the smooth oval of her face was as beautiful to him as the first time he'd seen her.

She had borne his child, and he hadn't even been there. And she had mourned his death. Hawk, his controlled voice more emotional than Griff could ever remember it, had told him about Claire's visit to his grave. About the solitary rose she had left there. As much a message as Griff had intended the one he had sent her to be. A symbol of what had once been between them. And, in a way, what still was between them. Embodied in their child.

"I'd like to hear about her," he said.

He ran his thumb slowly over the fine-textured skin on the back of her hand, the gesture unthinking, provoked by the familiarity of her fingers resting, relaxed and unmoving, in his. Again. In spite of everything.

"I'd like to tell you," she said.

And so, her voice low and unhurried, and very intimate, she talked to him about Gardner until they reached their destination.

Chapter Ten

The path that disappeared into the low-growing vegetation on the tiny key had been visible even from the cruiser. And from there it had looked a lot less rugged than it was proving to be, Griff acknowledged, as they fought their way through the dense undergrowth of saw palmetto and salt-wort.

He and Claire had waded through the shallows and climbed around the exposed mangrove roots. Then they had hit this. His damaged leg probably made progress over the terrain even more difficult for him than for Claire, which was particularly frustrating.

According to the instructions Griff had been given during the phone call he'd made in Miami, their meeting with the kidnappers was supposed to take place in the small gray house he could see beyond the overgrown palmetto and scrub palm.

Jake had stayed on board by the radio, hoping to hear something from Jordan and Hawk. Griff had intended for that to be Claire's job, but she had been adamant about going with him. She was going to be there when they gave Gardner back, she had said, her eyes challenging, just as they used to.

Jake had shrugged his agreement. His expression warned that he thought Claire had probably reached the breaking point. So Griff had given in, which, he acknowledged, was turning out to have been a smart move. This undergrowth would have made it difficult for him to carry a six-month-old. And neither he nor Jake, he had to admit, knew a whole hell of a lot about babies.

"Almost there," Claire said, as she turned to wait for him. He had let her lead the way after they'd gotten over the mangroves, preferring that to having her walking behind him, watching his progress.

Right now, her gaze was focused on his face—rather obviously focused there, he decided bitterly. And then, looking at her more closely, he realized that the thick vegetation and tangled roots had probably demanded an equally strenuous physical exertion on her part.

Her face was covered with a film of perspiration. A strand of hair clung to the moisture there after escaping the confinement of the long single braid, which lay over her left shoulder. As he watched, she pushed the tendril off her temple with the back of her fingers.

The gesture was so familiar, almost exactly like the one he had seen her make on television. Obviously feminine, it was enormously provocative as well. Griff lowered his eyes, fighting memory, fighting need, forcing himself to concentrate again on the uneven ground.

When he reached the place where Claire was waiting, he didn't look at her, but focused instead on the house that stood behind her. It was located in a ragged clearing, surrounded by more of the same vegetation they had just fought their way through.

It was apparent that the cleared area around the house had at one time been much larger. Given the climate, however, the creeping undergrowth had reclaimed almost everything that had originally been hacked away.

Weathered, squat and close to the ground, the house had probably withstood its share of tropical storms. It certainly looked as if it had been designed for that purpose.

Griff wondered briefly why anyone would want to live in this place. Maybe someone's idea of paradise, but its isolation, the unremitting heat and humidity, and the prospect of what might be hiding in the surrounding scrub meant it wasn't his.

"Do we just knock on the front door?" Claire asked.

Her question had a thin edge of sarcasm, probably injected to hide her anxiety. She was now facing the house as well, standing at his left shoulder.

"If they're in there, they know we're here."

"*If?*" Claire repeated.

"There was no boat in the cove. No sign of activity there or around the house."

"But Jake *is* sure that this is—"

"This is where they told him," Griff confirmed before she could finish the question. "Jake knows these keys like the back of his hand. Come on," he ordered.

Without waiting for her to obey, he started across the clearing. In the heavy stillness, there wasn't a bird cry. Not even a whisper of wind rustling through the dry spikes of the palmettos. The silence around them might simply be the result of their presence in a place that didn't get many visitors, but it was strange that there seemed to be no sound here at all, other than their own labored breathing.

When he reached the front door, Claire trailing closely behind him, Griff hesitated, again listening. The quietness of the clearing was unbroken, and despite it, Griff could hear no sound from inside the house. No conversation. No radio. Nothing. It felt as if he and Claire might be the only two people on the planet. Certainly the only two on this island.

As he thought that, Claire reached past him and fastened her hand around the knob of the door. She didn't turn it immediately, hesitating long enough to give him time to protest. But despite his misgivings, and a growing sense that something was very wrong here, he knew they had to go in.

When Claire's hand began to move, the knob turning slowly beneath the same fingers that had rested in his while she had told him about his daughter, he didn't stop her. She pushed the door open, revealing a sheltered dimness that seemed almost inviting after the outside glare.

There was still no sound. Nothing emanated from the dark interior but a miasma of late afternoon heat, mildew and rot, all ubiquitous in the tropics.

Griff moved past her and into the entrance hall, pausing just across the threshold to give his eyes time to adjust. He heard Claire follow, the soles of her running shoes making a faint noise on the old-fashioned terrazzo floor.

He fought the urge to call out to the people who were supposed to meet them. Whoever had set this up had to know they were here. They should have been watching ever since he and Claire climbed down the ladder of the yacht and waded into the shallows.

Claire, who was now beside him again, touched his arm, questioning his hesitation with arched brows. He tilted his head down the hall and then stepped forward, making no effort to mask the sound of his steps.

The hallway, when they reached the end of it, opened into a spacious room, obviously the main living area of the house. The ceiling seemed very high, especially compared to the low entryway they'd just left. On one side was a wall of glass, fogged by years of buffeting by the sea wind.

At one time the vegetation, which could still be discerned through the salt-hazed windows, must have been kept cut back, revealing a view of the ocean. All that could be seen of the water now was a blear of turquoise beyond the palmetto spikes and moss-draped dwarf cypresses.

Part of the musty odor that pervaded the house came from the furniture. Sun-faded cushions covered a matching set of chairs and couch that hadn't been in style for more than forty years. Now, especially along the seams of the pillows, black mold almost obscured the once-bright colors of the fabric.

There was no one waiting to meet them. And still no sound except an indistinct buzzing. Insects, Griff decided, dismissing the low, distant hum from his evaluation of the situation.

His gaze slowly circled the long room. There was a kitchen on one end, separated from the living area by panels of white latticework. On the other end was an opening that led into another hall, this one even darker than the entryway had been.

"Stay here," he ordered, starting across the expanse of terrazzo to explore it.

His uneven footsteps echoed off the stone floor. But he had already decided it didn't matter how much noise they made. The house was empty. It *felt* empty, devoid of life, and obviously it had been for a long time.

He didn't know what game the people who had taken Gardner were playing, but the frustration he had fought throughout the last year was again boiling up inside. A sick disappointment about failing at something this important. And almost as powerful as those, his dread of having to justify his failure. To Claire, and perhaps even more importantly, to himself.

When he entered the hallway, he discovered there was a windowless bathroom on his right. A few steps farther down on the left was the open door of what he assumed would be the bedroom. The hum he had vaguely been aware of since they'd entered was louder back here.

A broken window? he wondered, walking toward the doorway. It seemed strange he hadn't heard the insects outside. He'd been aware of that hum only after they had come inside. Only after they'd reached—

The sick sweetness of the smell should have warned him, but he didn't put it all together until he stepped into the room. Then he didn't need any of the clues he had missed.

Whoever had done this had opened all the windows in the bedroom before they'd left, very probably to ensure that what was going on would happen. The open windows had made the smell less obvious in the rest of the house. And of course, the body had to have been here less than forty-eight hours.

Griff closed his eyes, blocking out the image of what was on the bed. He fought a surge of nausea so strong he literally swallowed against it, trying desperately to push the bile out of his throat. And he forced himself to stand in the fetid dimness, trying to make his mind work. Trying to make this an intellectual exercise. Trying to figure out exactly what message he was supposed to receive from this obscenity.

Because there was no doubt in his mind this *was* a message. And that it was what they had been sent here to find.

"Dear God," Claire said, her anguished whisper coming from behind him.

Griff opened his eyes. They felt as burned as they had yesterday, unprotected from the blaze of the sun reflecting off the water. Listening to the sounds of Claire's retching behind him, he made himself take another look at the thing on the bed.

His lips flattened with disgust, but he realized he hadn't been mistaken. The second look left no doubt. Despite the condition of the body, he hadn't been wrong about his identification.

He turned around, moving a few steps out into the hallway before he took a breath. He hadn't even realized that he had been avoiding breathing while he was in the bedroom, an action automatic and unthinking.

Claire was standing at the end of the hall, her head bent forward, her right hand resting high on the wall beside her, as if for support, her left clamped over her mouth. The diffuse light from the salt-glazed wall of windows limned the back of her body and touched the long blond braid with silver.

He walked up behind her and put his hand on her shoulder. Immediately she turned, leaning into him, laying her head against his chest. His left arm enfolded her. He could feel her trembling, her slim body vibrating as strongly as his had when they'd pulled him out of the water last night.

"It's all right," he whispered. "We're all right. Whoever did that is gone, Claire. Long gone."

Without thinking, he lowered his head, setting his chin on the top of her head, feeling the sun-warmed softness of her hair under it. He closed his eyes, remembering other times he'd held her. The good times.

The fragrance of the shampoo he had noticed before had been released by the heat and exertion of their trek. He took a deep breath, welcoming the sweet normality of its scent. It cut through the sickness that was thick in his throat. Purifying it. And him.

"Who *is* that?" Claire whispered, her face still buried against the front of his shirt.

He thought about lying to her, but he had done enough of that. There had been more than enough tricks. On both sides. More than enough cleverness to go around. Griff's mouth tightened briefly before he opened it, but he told her the truth.

"Ramon Diaz," he said.

It took a few seconds for the name to register, as he had guessed it might, and he waited through them. It might take a few more for all the implications of what he had just said to sink in, but Claire Heywood was very bright.

Her head lifted suddenly, and she took a step back, moving away from him. Breaking whatever bond had been between them.

Her eyes seemed very blue now, as blue as the water in the lagoon they had crossed to get here. And despite yesterday's ordeal, the whites were clear. The dark pupils had widened, however, as they focused on his face. Trying to read it despite the dimness. Trying, he knew, to understand.

"Diaz?" she whispered.

Her voice sounded puzzled, but the knowledge of what this meant was already in her eyes. Her intellect was fighting against accepting it, he supposed. Just as his had done when he'd identified the body.

"He's...he's supposed to be dead," she said finally.

"He is," Griff said bitterly. "Spectacularly dead."

They had cut his throat, the wound deep and running from ear to ear. There was a lot of blood, but most of it seemed to be on his clothing rather than on the bed, which argued that Diaz hadn't been killed here. This was strictly for show. A message intended for Griff.

Claire shook her head, the movement contained, and her eyes didn't release his, still questioning. "Dead and in the ocean," she clarified. "That plane *exploded*."

She said the last word as if there was no doubt. As if that phrase answered everything. Diaz's plane had exploded over the ocean. She had seen it or heard it, and had seen burned and broken evidence of the crash in the water. Therefore, Diaz shouldn't be on the bed in this house with his throat cut.

"But he wasn't *on* the plane," Claire said softly, coming to the obvious conclusion. "He was *never* on that plane."

The last was accusatory. And Griff deserved it. Whatever she wanted to say, he knew he deserved to have to listen to it. And to have to explain.

"Briefly," he admitted.

"Just so the cameras you'd set up could film him boarding."

When he nodded, she went on, piecing together what they had done. What they had done and not told her about. That was the one part of this, he suspected, she would find unforgivable.

"Then you got them off the plane somehow...." She paused, thinking about it. "Hawk and Jordan got them off, out of camera range—Diaz and his bodyguards—and you took the plane up alone. You exploded an empty plane over the ocean, so..." Again she faltered. "So the kidnappers would *think* Diaz was dead."

Maybe this was better, letting her work it all out in her head. Without him having to tell her all the reasons he had chosen to do it that way.

"But you never intended to kill him," she whispered, her

voice shocked and then accusing. "Not from the first. But you didn't tell *me* that."

"What we do... What the team did," Griff amended, "was never like what they wanted. We never killed for personal reasons. I would never ask my people to do that, Claire. Not even in this situation."

As far as he was concerned, killing Diaz had never been an option. What the team had done instead was to arrange a performance. A trick to make the kidnappers think they had done what they been asked to do. And he hadn't told Claire what was going on.

"You wanted me to think I had agreed to Diaz's death," she said accusingly.

"I thought if you didn't know we were planning to do it that way, you wouldn't worry as much about something going wrong. About the kidnappers finding out. We've always operated on a need-to-know basis. If you don't have a role in the operation, then you aren't briefed about it."

"Oh, I'm sure that's true," she said softly, her voice bitter. "But that isn't why you didn't tell me, Griff. You didn't tell me because you wanted me to agree. You wanted to *hear* me give permission for Diaz to die."

Griff hadn't demanded that. He could have, and to his shame he had even thought about it. What he *had* done, however, had been almost as despicable. *"Unless you tell me no,"* he had told her. And she hadn't. Because her baby's life was at stake.

"You wanted me to understand that the decisions you had to make were always hard," she said. "Maybe as hard as that one."

Perhaps he had, he admitted, remembering their arguments. Remembering how many times he had explained the difficult choices involved in what the team did. Remembering how many times he had tried to make her see that sometimes a madman has to be destroyed to protect the innocent. But he had never succeeded in convincing her that taking someone's life was ever justified. Not under any circumstances.

"You wanted me to *know* what making that decision feels like," she said, her eyes cold.

He had been right before. Claire Heywood was very smart. Because that *was* what he had done, of course. He had destroyed the validity of those old arguments by showing her that she, too, would come to that same decision. No matter what they felt about the sanctity of human life, about the sin of destroying it, almost everyone would make such a decision in order to safeguard those they loved.

"You never intended to kill Diaz," she said. "You never intended to keep your part of the bargain with the kidnappers, did you, Griff? And Diaz wasn't dead when you left him with Hawk and Jordan."

He hadn't been. They had all been alive—Diaz and his bodyguards. But like everything else... Just like everything else, this had gone wrong. And it shouldn't have, Griff thought, going over all the meticulous details of the plan in his mind.

Hawk and Jordan had gotten everyone off the plane, using the refueling truck as cover. All they'd had to do then was to take Diaz and his men to the rendezvous and hold them there. After Griff blew up the plane, he and Jake would pick up the video of Diaz boarding the plane and exchange it for the baby. Then they would turn Diaz over to the DEA, and hope he'd cut a deal with them, talk his head off in exchange for protection.

That's what was supposed to happen. But they hadn't made that initial rendezvous because the emergency transmitter had failed. And when they'd finally arrived, Hawk and Jordan hadn't been there. Now Diaz was dead, his body miles from where it was supposed to be. And Griff had no idea who had killed him and brought him here. No idea where Jordan and Hawk were.

"What do we do about Gardner?" Claire asked softly, her voice full of fear as she realized the rest of it. As she came to the conclusion he'd already reached. "If the kidnappers *know* this was a double cross, and they must, since they put Diaz's body here, then…" Her voice faded, her eyes almost pleading. "Then how are we going to get Gardner back?"

And that was the question, of course, Griff had already asked himself. A question for which he had no answer.

"SOMEHOW THEY KNEW you hadn't killed Diaz," Jake said, "that you didn't plan on killing him, so they did it for you."

They were headed back to Miami, the cruiser cutting through the water like a knife, leaving behind them the island where Ramon Diaz's body rested in a dark bedroom. Exactly where they had been sent to find it.

Claire waited for Griff's response to Jake's comment. His features were hard, as if set in stone, his eyes as bleak as she had ever seen them. Bleaker even than they had been the night she had made him promise he would never try to see her again.

"How could they know?" Griff asked quietly. "How the hell could the kidnappers have known we didn't intend to kill him?"

That wasn't the primary question Claire wanted an explanation for, but it was a good one. She had assumed it was rhetorical, but surprisingly, Jake answered it. Whether what he said was *the* answer, she had no way of knowing, but when Griff heard it, the grooves around his mouth deepened, his lips compressing into a thinner line.

"They knew because somebody told them," Jake said.

He looked braced for a scathing denunciation, but Griff said nothing for a long time, his silence indicating that he was at least considering the idea.

"Only four of us knew," he said finally. "Are you suggesting that someone on this team—"

"I'm *suggesting* there have been a hell of a lot of things going on in the last six months I didn't understand. Like the situation with Jordan…"

Jake hesitated, glancing at Claire, as if reluctant to discuss business in front of an outsider. And to them that's exactly what she was, she realized. She had been forced to acknowledge just how much an outsider when she learned that not only had Griff double-crossed the kidnappers by faking Diaz's death, he had double-crossed her as well.

"Go on," Griff ordered, without following Jake's gaze to its focus on Claire's face. "What *about* the situation with Jordan?"

"There were too many things about what happened to Cross that never made sense to me. Things nobody should have known about then, either. But they did."

"Like what?"

"How did Helms know where to find Jordan and Kathleen Sorrel? How did he get past the security system in your summer house?"

"Jordan says they tracked him through the e-mail he sent you," Griff said.

"An encrypted e-mail, Griff. And nobody's gotten into one of those. Not yet. And while Jordan was on the run, somebody got into the agency's system. I told you that. I couldn't backtrack them, but I knew they'd been there. They could have been reading files. Reading everything I was doing to help Jordan. Tracking his movements, just as I was."

"I told you *I* was in the system, Jake."

"Did *you* betray Jordan?" Jake asked softly.

The logic was irrefutable. Griff Cabot would be the last person who might be suspected of doing that.

"And if you didn't," Jake continued, "then who did? And how the hell did they do it if *not* like I said?"

Griff remained silent for a moment, his eyes considering Jake's face. "There's not a system built that can keep a talented hacker out," he said finally.

"Not even mine?" Jake asked mockingly.

His was an arrogance that, given what everyone said about him, was probably deserved, Claire thought.

"The agency's got the best security system in the world," Jake added. "We both know that."

"Helms was FBI. He used the bureau to get information about Jordan's movements."

"And the kidnappers? Who you think are some rival drug cartel? Are they using the bureau, too?" Jake asked.

Griff's eyes didn't leave Jake's, but he didn't answer.

"How else can you explain how they could have known—" Claire began, only to have her question overridden by Griff's.

"You really think this is someone operating from inside the agency, Jake?" Griff interrupted. "Is that what you're suggesting?"

Jake's mouth pursed, and then he nodded. "Realistically, who else could know about this team and what it does?"

"How would they find out what we intended for Diaz?"

"I don't know. But…Jordan was at the summer house when Helms found him."

"You said the house was clean. No listening devices."

"Maybe I was wrong," Jake said.

"Why would the agency set this up?" Griff asked softly. "What would they have to gain?"

The silence grew and expanded. Finally Jake broke it, his voice low, expressing the fatigue and disappointment they all felt at what they hadn't found on that island.

"I don't know. Just like I don't know what's happened to Hawk and Jordan. Or why we were sent to find Diaz's body. Or who killed him. But if *you've* got some other logical solution for all that's happened on this operation, believe me, Griff, I'd be more than happy to listen to it." He stopped, his eyes holding Griff's, seeming to ask for a denial.

Griff said nothing. Finally, he turned and limped across the control room toward the stairs that led to the cabins below. Claire listened as the sounds of his footsteps faded, and then she turned back to Jake.

"What do we do now?" she asked, the words producing a sick sense of déjà vu.

"Damned if I know," Jake said softly, his gaze on the dark stairwell where Griff had disappeared. "Damned if I have any idea at all of where we go from here."

Chapter Eleven

"Jake's just trying to make sense of what happened," Claire said, the tone of her voice comforting. "I think I need help doing that as well."

She was standing in the door of his stateroom. Griff wished he'd remembered to close it, but he wondered if even that would have kept her out. He had hoped for more time to come to grips with what had happened, but this confrontation was inevitable.

He wished to hell, however, that Claire didn't feel the need to comfort him, he thought savagely. What he heard in her voice now was almost as difficult for him to accept as her help had been last night.

He had expected to have to deal with her anger over his deception about Diaz. He had been prepared for that. Hearing concern in her voice instead was pretty damned disheartening. Too much had changed between them. Their roles had shifted, somehow. Moved out of the familiar and comfortable dimensions they had once assumed. Or maybe, he acknowledged, those had only been comfortable for him.

Claire had the right to know the truth, no matter how unpalatable that might be. And figuring out that truth was exactly what he had been trying to do since he'd left the bridge.

"Jake's probably right about some of what he said,"

Griff admitted, looking up at her, eyes lifting from their pretended contemplation of his joined fingers.

When Claire appeared in the doorway, she had caught him with his elbows on his knees, forehead resting in his hands. Which went a long way toward explaining what he had heard in her voice. As soon as he realized she was there, he had lifted his head, obviously too late to prevent her from reading the despair his posture implied. A despair he was actually feeling.

"Right about which parts?" she asked.

As if taking his response for permission to enter, she stepped into the room and walked over to sit down on the other end of the bed. Griff's eyes didn't follow her movement; he was looking down again at his hands instead. Which was safer, of course. And he didn't look up even as he answered.

"Whatever's going on here—and probably most of the problems the members of the team have experienced during the last few months—haven't been coincidental. Nor have they originated with someone from outside the agency. There are too many things that indicate events are being...manipulated," he said carefully. "Too many things that point to insider knowledge."

"Events are being manipulated by someone on the team?" she asked. "Is that what you're saying?"

"From someone within the agency," he clarified.

"Why?" Claire asked.

That was the pertinent question, of course—one he thought he had answered a couple of weeks ago. An answer that had prompted his message to the director. And the timing of that and Gardner's kidnapping seemed obvious now. He wondered why it hadn't before. Because he had allowed himself to be thrown off track by Steiner's visit, he acknowledged. And by Carl's dismissal of his suspicions.

"Are you drumming up a conspiracy because you miss it?" Steiner had asked. *Because you miss the team? The*

excitement? The thrill of the chase?'' And Griff had thought that maybe, just maybe, Carl was right. But now...

"They're trying to destroy the team," he said softly.

He had suspected all along that was what the agency was up to. He had known it in his gut, and he had let Carl's ridicule push those well-honed instincts aside. Because he liked Carl. And because he trusted him.

"I thought..." Claire hesitated. "I thought they had already done that."

"I don't mean disband it," Griff said, thinking about the reality of the phrase he had used. "They're out to destroy us. To get rid of *us*. I think that's what has been going on from the beginning."

To Claire that would probably sound like a lunatic-fringe theory, Griff supposed. Paranoia, maybe. Or maybe it would simply sound like an excuse to explain his own ineptitude. A cop-out for his responsibility in the fiasco this had become.

Carl had said they'd retired him because, given the extent of his injuries, they were afraid he could no longer do the job. Maybe they had been right.

"Destroy you because the existence of the team is potentially an embarrassment to this government?" Claire asked.

He looked at her then, turning his head and focusing on her face. He could still remember the things she had said in that last brutal argument. About him. About what the team did. And suddenly he remembered Steiner's remark. *"There are a lot of people who think that about all of us in the agency."*

Griff Cabot had heard all the variations on that theme through the years. All the accusations and insinuations about what the CIA did. He had learned to ignore most of the comments, even those about the immorality of the so-called black operations in which he had played such a major role.

He had been able to play that role because he truly believed what the team did was essential to the survival of democracy. And because he saw their missions as necessary to defeat the evil that too often threatened the world. Claire, however, had seen the team as something as reprehensible as what they were fighting against. Which meant Carl Steiner was probably right about public opinion. In any case, the new leadership was determined to distance themselves from the kinds of activities the External Security Team had once been involved in.

And apparently to distance themselves from the men who had once carried out those sanctioned missions. *Permanently* distance themselves, he thought. And who would be left then to defeat the next madman with a hunger for world domination and a few nuclear weapons at his disposal?

To preserve and protect. To stand guard over this country. And those they loved. *Standing guard.* He had repeated that phrase to his team like a litany. Because that had been what he truly believed they were doing. But now the worldwide arena where he had once operated was no longer where that war was being waged. His fight was here. His battle. And at stake this time was the life of a little girl. A baby.

His baby, he amended, for the first time allowing himself to view this not as an assignment, about which he could be coldly detached and intellectual, but as a personal crusade to find and rescue his daughter. A daughter whom he had never even seen.

"If what we did ever becomes public knowledge," he said, "there will be a hue and cry from certain aspects of our society. And a demand for heads to roll," he added.

Claire laughed. Surprised, he looked up. Although he hadn't intended that comment to be a joke, he supposed in a way it was. Ironic, at least. They were the ones being targeted for destruction because they had once done the exact same thing.

The current government didn't have the stomach to admit what they knew and had even condoned in the past. That violence is sometimes necessary to preserve democracy. Necessary to insure peace—the fragile, uneasy peace that was all the world had at the moment. A peace that would end in an instant with the detonation of just one of those nuclear weapons so readily available on the terrorist black market.

"Why do they think it might?" Claire asked. "Become public, I mean? Why, all of a sudden, are they so afraid of that?"

"They made the decision to dissolve the team and then belatedly realized that the connections between the members were far stronger than they had believed. Our loyalties had become more...personal than professional."

Carl had even told him that, but Griff hadn't realized then how much they feared it. The CIA valued loyalty to the agency above almost anything else, because it insured that the code of silence would be maintained. Once they began to suspect that another loyalty might supersede that one, then they would suspect disloyalty where none had existed. Their own brand of paranoia.

"That's why they were afraid of Hawk," Claire said. "Because he threatened to go public with what he knew. Because he disobeyed *their* orders in order to get the man who had killed *you*. The man he thought had killed you," she corrected.

"Maybe," Griff acknowledged.

"So they tried to insure that even if he went public, he would never be able to make anyone believe him. They destroyed all record of Hawk's existence so he could never tell what he knew," she said.

And suddenly, as Claire remembered the cold hatred that had been in Hawk's eyes that day, a hatred of Steiner and everything he represented, the explanation for everything that had gone wrong with what they were trying to do shifted into place like a piece of a puzzle slipping smoothly between two others. Completing the pattern.

"Hawk," she said softly.

Griff's eyes, which were once more focused on his hands, lifted to her face. She could only imagine what it must reveal.

Griff believed that the CIA was out to destroy the team. And maybe he was right. They had been furious because Hawk had disobeyed their orders. Maybe they had targeted Jordan because he had helped Hawk rescue Tyler Stewart at the airport that day and had then protected Hawk by taking the blame. Claire could go along with all that, but maybe…

The more she thought about it, the more it made sense. There was something else going on here as well. Something that would explain how the supposed kidnappers could have learned that it had never been part of Griff's plan to kill Ramon Diaz. Something that would explain how Diaz's body had shown up miles from where it was supposed to be. And would explain why Hawk and Jordan had disappeared.

"Hawk?" Griff questioned, his voice puzzled.

"Hawk's behind this," Claire said, all at once absolutely certain of the validity of her reasoning.

She understood, even as she said the words, how difficult that would be for Griff to accept. It was, however, the only thing that could explain why everything from the beginning of this operation had gone wrong. Griff had said it himself—insider information.

"*Whatever* is going on," Griff said, "I can promise you Hawk has nothing to do with it."

Claire's eyes remained on his, but she didn't answer the denial she had been expecting. Not for several long heartbeats. Instead she reviewed everything she knew, her mind searching for flaws in her logic. And she could find none. Because it all made sense.

"The CIA destroyed Hawk," she said. "They did it deliberately. Mockingly. I was there, Griff. I saw how Steiner treated him. And then, after Hawk had done everything they demanded of him, Steiner almost let Tyler Stewart get killed."

"So Hawk betrays the rest of us?" Griff said, his voice almost amused—or pretending to be.

"He doesn't see this as a betrayal," she said. "None of you have been hurt. Not that we can verify, anyway," she amended, wondering about Jordan. What would Hawk have done with Jordan?

Or… The thought was as sudden as the first had been, but it, too, made sense. Was it possible Jordan could be in on all this as well?

If he believed, as Griff and Jake now seemed to, that what had happened to him had been set up by the agency, if Hawk had convinced him of that, then maybe Jordan would be more than willing to go along with whatever Hawk had planned.

"Hawk would never—" Griff began.

She interrupted, her tone uncompromising. She didn't understand it all, but some of this just made too much sense not to be true.

"The CIA cut him off, destroyed him, without even the pension he was entitled to. Hawk's smart enough to know there are a lot of ways to make money. Especially with the skills he's acquired. Maybe he saw the contract some rival put out on Diaz as a way of bankrolling the retirement they'd forced on him. Or maybe he just figured somebody owes him something."

"You think Hawk is bitter enough about what Steiner did to pull something like this? Something that would put friends in danger? Something that would endanger a *baby?* And do all it for money?"

Hearing the anger underlying the mockery in the deep voice she knew so well, Claire said nothing, but again she held Griff's eyes, letting his questions hang unanswered between them. Giving him time to work out the answers for himself.

"I asked you a question, Claire," Griff demanded. "Are you suggesting Hawk set this up? That *Hawk* took Gardner?"

Was she? she wondered. Could the man they called Hawk be angry enough to design this kind of elaborate hoax? It would almost be comforting to believe that. To believe that someone she knew had taken her baby.

"I...I don't know," she admitted.

"Look," Griff said, moderating the fury that had been in his voice, maybe because of that faltering admission. "If Hawk *had* arranged all this, what would be the purpose? Even if he wanted money, even if someone was offering money for killing Diaz, Hawk could have done that by himself. That's exactly the kind of job he did for the team. So what purpose could it serve to take Gardner?"

"Because it involved you," Claire said.

Again Griff held her eyes a long time before he answered her. "Hawk's the one who went to Baghdad," he said.

For Griff. To avenge his death. That was probably the strongest argument Griff could make against what she had just suggested. Out of all the members of his team, Hawk had been the one who had sought vengeance for his death.

But maybe he didn't realize that particular act didn't argue against what she had suggested. If anything, it seemed to prove her case. Hawk *was* the kind of man who would never let something go. He would always be the one who would seek revenge.

"You're right," she said. "He *is* the one. He put his life on the line for yours. And doing that cost him his career."

"So he's angry at the agency for retiring him. Angry at Steiner for destroying his identity. For putting Tyler in danger. I agree, but I don't see how any of that would lead you to the conclusion that he took Gardner to involve *me* in this."

"Think about how all of that started," she said softly.

It had started with Griff's death. Which had not, of course, been a death at all. Only another forced retirement. The destruction of a member of a black ops team the CIA had decided no longer had a role in today's world.

"You think Hawk's angry at *me* for letting the agency put out the story that I had been killed?" Griff asked incredulously. "You think he blames *me* for setting him off on that hunt?"

"A hunt that eventually led to everything else that happened," Claire said. "To his situation. Tyler's danger. Even Jordan's. If Hawk *hadn't* gone to Baghdad to get revenge for your death, then the agency wouldn't have made him a target. And none of those other things would ever have happened."

"So in revenge he kidnaps a baby?" Griff suggested, his voice sardonic, ridiculing the whole idea.

"*Your* baby," Claire corrected, and saw the impact of that in his eyes.

She could imagine how difficult this would be for Griff to believe. But it had a twisted kind of logic if he would only think about it. A man like Hawk wouldn't like being manipulated or lied to. It was obvious he felt the agency had done both. And that they had betrayed him after his years of service. Those feelings had been very clear during the meeting with Steiner—clear to her, at least.

"How could Hawk know Gardner is mine?" Griff asked.

"I can accept Hawk knowing Gardner is your child more easily than I can accept that some Mexican drug dealer knew it," she said. "Besides, Hawk also knows exactly how this team works. They couldn't. He could *do* this, Griff. Nobody else could."

There was another long silence. Which meant he was thinking about it, she supposed. He was at least considering what she had said. And the longer she'd talked, the more convinced she was that she was on the right track.

"Why?" Griff asked again.

"I don't know. Not...exactly. Maybe to prove to Steiner that he was smarter than they gave him credit for? Or because you let their lie stand? You were his friend. Hawk was more than willing to put his neck in a noose for you in Baghdad. Willing to take the official flak for that hit. But then he found out somehow it was all a lie. One you'd gone along with."

She remembered how that felt—to realize Griff had let her believe he was dead. Hawk had denied that finding out the truth of that had affected him, but she hadn't believed him. She *couldn't,* because she knew how she had felt.

Griff's eyes, still fastened on her face, were very dark, almost empty. After all, she was asking him to believe the worst of a man he considered a friend. And she could be wrong, of course. At least wrong about Hawk trying to get revenge on Griff. But she knew she wasn't wrong about the other. It made too much sense.

"Maybe he did it to get back at the CIA. At Steiner," she said, trying not to go too far. No further than she could really defend. "And at the same time he sets himself up very nicely financially."

"How does this get back at Steiner?" Griff asked. "Or at the agency?"

"Because Hawk created a situation where he believed you'd be forced to kill someone. He thought you'd have no compunction about targeting Diaz because of what he was. Hawk wouldn't have. He also knew you'd call for help from the team. And he knew he'd be included in this mission."

That bond between the two of them had been obvious, even in the short time she'd been around them. And as Griff had reminded her, Hawk had been the one who had gone to Baghdad.

"Then, when it's done, when Diaz is dead, Hawk goes public. He takes this assassination, along with the history of the External Security Team, to the media. And *this* time, Griff, they'll believe him. After all," she added softly, "this time he has the film to prove what you did."

She could see it happening in his eyes. She watched the anger fade as his intellect began to push aside the emotional barriers that had prevented him from accepting how much sense this made. How much it explained. And despite the fact that he hadn't told her about Diaz, she ached for his betrayal.

"Griff," she said softly, sorry that she had had to be the

one to do this, but she wondered, given how he felt about Hawk, if Griff would ever have figured it out on his own. She had always imagined him to be so rational. Almost unemotional. But looking into his eyes now, she knew how wrong she had been.

She put her hand on his arm. The feel of it must have broken the spell of horror her words—or rather his acceptance of them—had created. He turned his head away, no longer willing to look at her.

She could see only his profile. She watched the muscle in his jaw slowly tighten, his gaze focused on the dark, empty doorway. After a moment, his lips compressed. Then, as if willing himself to move, he turned back to face her.

"He wouldn't hurt her," he said.

In the midst of dealing with this treachery, she realized, he was trying to reassure her about Gardner. She nodded, her throat tight. She had once believed Hawk and Jordan would be more than willing to help her find her daughter because she had helped them. And now, it seemed…

The threat of tears bleared her vision. Fighting them, she focused on her fingers resting against Griff's forearm. She didn't really believe Hawk would hurt Gardner. Or allow her to be hurt. For all his hardness, Hawk had never struck her as cruel, and Griff knew him much better than she. But of course, this entire episode had been the ultimate cruelty. To take someone's baby. No matter what your motives.

Griff shifted his body, turning toward her. He lifted his hand to her cheek. His thumb moved under her chin, applying an upward pressure, and she obeyed it, raising her eyes to his.

"I told you I'll get her back," he said.

"I know," she whispered.

"I will. I promise you, Claire. No matter what else is going on here, I *will* get Gardner back."

She nodded. Seeing the moisture in her eyes, Griff smiled at her. The smile was intended for reassurance, she supposed, but without thinking, she returned it. He ran his thumb across her lips, a small, intimate caress.

She had invited his kiss on deck that night. Less than forty-eight hours ago, she realized. It seemed longer, because so much had happened in the meantime. She had wondered then if there were someone else in Griff's life. And if so...

His head began to lower. His dark eyes held hers a long moment, and then they closed. Even as she watched, his head tilted so that his mouth would fit over hers, a natural and familiar alignment. And she wanted his mouth there. No matter what else was going on, she wanted Griff to touch her again. To kiss her. To keep the senseless terrors of the world they inhabited at bay. Only Griff had ever been strong enough to do that. For her. And for Gardner.

Claire had always known that, but for some reason, she had fought against it, using intellectual arguments rather than acknowledging the truth of what he believed. That the world was evil. A terrifyingly dangerous place. And that there must be someone willing to stand against its depravity. She had just never wanted that someone to have to be Griff. She didn't now.

She closed her eyes, lifting her chin until she felt the warmth of his breath on her lips. Her mouth opened, welcoming the heat and movement of his tongue, which immediately pushed inside. Seeking. Demanding a response. And finding it.

Whatever anger she had felt or whatever foolish arguments she had once made against the possibility of their being together disappeared. Any remaining trace of doubt about the rightness of this melted away in the promise of his kiss.

She put her hands lightly on either side of his face, the rough, masculine texture of his skin familiar, branded on her senses and never forgotten. *Never* forgotten.

With only the force of the kiss, mouth against mouth, he pushed her down onto the bunk. Once she was on her back, he placed his hands flat on the mattress, one on either side of her shoulders. She put her feet up on the bed, and he moved his right knee to the other side of hers.

Then, bending his elbows, he lowered himself until he was lying on top of her. Her breasts crushed by the weight of his chest. His hips aligned on top of hers, the strength of his hard erection blatant. Exciting.

She had tried to maintain contact with his lips, but their movements down onto the mattress had resulted instead in a series of touches and releases between their open mouths. When she felt his arousal pressing into her hips, she caught his bottom lip in her teeth, biting it teasingly.

She heard his gasp of reaction, and then his tongue invaded, once more hard and demanding, almost punishing. Controlling. The same control that had once taught her so much about making love. Enough that when he was gone, she had dreamed of this. Of him. And she had awakened trembling with need and regret.

He pushed his hips into hers again, rocking them against her pelvis. The movement was small, very deliberate. And so tantalizing, especially with the barrier of their clothing between them. The soft gasp of breath this time was hers.

His right hand moved, sliding under her top. His palm was rough against her bare skin, more callused than she remembered. Its feel was incredibly masculine. As it slid over her stomach, the abrasiveness was also exciting, provoking a rush of desire, heat and moisture spreading like smoke, thick and rich, through her lower body.

She wanted the roughness of his palms against her breasts. Imagined the sensation. Envisioned it. The softness of her breast enclosed in the masculine strength of his dark fingers.

It had been too long since Griff had touched her. An endless loneliness. That had been at first through her own choice. And then because of the cold despair of his death. And finally, again, they had come to this.

She eased her own hand under her shell, placing it over

the back of his and urging it upward. He obeyed, cupping his fingers under the fullness of her breast.

She had only recently stopped nursing Gardner. Neither of them had been ready for it, but because of the demands of resuming her profession, because of its long, uncertain hours, the process had become increasingly frustrating for them both.

Her breasts were, therefore, much fuller than they had ever been before. Much more sensitive. A thousand nerve endings were demanding Griff's attention. Aching with need.

His lips had drifted away from her mouth to find her throat. They slid, opened, hot and wet, over the small pulse that had begun to race under the thin, delicate skin beneath her ear. Her fingers slipped into his hair, holding his head against her body as his mouth moved downward, trailing moisture against her neck. And then lower.

The anticipation with which her aching, milk-filled breasts had once welcomed the touch of Gardner's mouth surged through her belly. Perhaps there was something strange, Claire acknowledged, in the juxtaposition of those two images—Griff's mouth and her daughter's fastened over the nipple of her breast. Something she should push from her head. But she didn't. She wanted to feel Griff's lips there as much as she had wanted Gardner's. Both were natural. And right. Her right.

Desire for the fulfillment of that right was so powerful she tried to tell him, but the sound she made was inarticulate. Husky with need, it originated too low in her throat to be verbal communication.

It must have delivered its message, however, for Griff moved his hand, slipping it out from under her top. It lifted, his thumb hooking around the straps of her shell and her bra to pull both off her shoulder. Then he reached into the scooped neckline of the garment and cupped the globe of her breast, lifting it free.

She waited for the descent of his lips, her breathing ragged. Griff had gone very still. The hands that had been caressing her body were now unmoving.

Slowly, she opened her eyes. His face was just above hers. His eyes were dark and hooded, screened by his lashes. She could see enough to know, however, that they were focused on her exposed breast. It was only with the intensity of his gaze that she realized why the seductive movement of his hand had stopped. He had known her body so well, and he was now becoming aware of all the changes that had occurred during the last fifteen months.

Changes in her breasts. Not just in size, but in shape as well. In the subtly increased darkness of their nipples. And in the tracery of small, silvered lines. All the telltale evidence left by her pregnancy and by nursing his daughter.

Griff had never seen any of those before. Because the last time they had made love, of course… The last time they had made love… Thought suspended, she waited, almost frightened by his stillness.

His eyes lifted to hers. They seemed unfocused. Then they traveled over her face as if they had never really looked at her features before. Examined them one by one. And still she waited, wondering what he was thinking. What he was feeling.

She knew there were other subtle differences in her body. Things he had not yet seen. Or felt. And now, suddenly, she was unsure of what she was doing. Of what they were doing together. Unsure for the first time that the sheer physical passion that had always, instantly, arced between them would be the same.

His eyes moved down to her breast, and then, so slowly her throat went dry and her bones melted, he lowered his lips to the dark, slightly distended nipple. She watched his tongue touch it. Circle. Lave with such incredible deliberation that she held her breath. Waiting. Waiting. The heat and wetness between her legs building in anticipation.

And then his mouth began to lower again, descending a fraction of a millimeter at a time. Her eyes closed, an involuntary response because she truly wanted to watch what he was doing, and she couldn't. She could do nothing but anticipate what he would do next. She was powerless to resist him. Without will. Without control.

His lips finally settled around the areola, exactly as Gardner's had often done, and then he, too, began to suckle. With the first pressure, her lower body exploded, arching upward again and again into the hardness of his.

She was mindless with want. With need. And when his teeth delicately touched on either side of the sensitive nipple, nibbling erotically, she lifted her legs, locking them around his hips.

An effort to increase their closeness. To become one with him. Again and again she arched into his arousal as waves of sensation roared through her body. The roughness of his jeans rubbing against the skin of her inside thighs was as erotic as his callused palm had been. As erotic as his mouth moving over her breast.

But she wanted more. She wanted the heat of his sweat-dampened skin sliding against hers. His moisture jetting to join the torrent of hers. His body moving inside hers, driving away the pain and loneliness and need of the months she had been forced to exist without him.

Despite everything that now lay between them, all the hurt and lies and betrayals, nothing about this had changed. And she could no more deny what she felt for Griff than she had been able to deny herself the night she had come out of the fog to place her trembling hand in his. The night Gardner had been conceived.

Her fingers found the fabric of his shirt, tearing at it, desperate to pull it free of his jeans. She wanted to spread her fingers against the dark, hair-roughened chest. To move them slowly over the flat, ridged stomach. To slip the tips of them inside the low waistband of his jeans. To unfasten the metal buttons one by one until flesh met flesh.

"Claire," Griff whispered.

His mouth was no longer against her breast. The moisture

it had left there was caressed by the breath released with her name, and she shivered with the subtle eroticism of that sensation.

"I need you so much," Griff said, his voice hoarse, the soft Virginia accent she had loved more pronounced.

A need she understood. And echoed.

"Tell me yes," he begged softly.

The words were almost shocking. Interrupting what had been happening. They seemed…out of place. Certainly out of place between the two of them.

She had *never* told him no. Not even the first time. And Griff had never before verbally asked her permission. He hadn't needed to, of course, and she wondered why he would believe he should now.

It confused her. And then it made her wonder. In all the years she had known him, Griff Cabot had never begged her for anything. Why would he now?

The frantic movements of her hands had stopped, her once-desperate fingers locked unmoving in the material of his shirt. *"I need you so much,"* he had whispered. A need based on his love for her? Or on something else? Something that had never before had any place in their relationship.

She had seen his despair when she had stood hesitantly at the door watching him. And had seen his pain when she had tried to convince him of Hawk's betrayal. Had Griff turned to her for comfort? Using her body for solace for failure and betrayal?

But whatever happened here, whatever happened between them, shouldn't be about comfort or loneliness. Not even about her fears for Gardner. If she and Griff made love again, it should only be about them. About how much they loved one another. Just as it had always been. And maybe…maybe this wasn't what tonight was about.

With her continued stillness, Griff pushed himself up, lifting his upper body away from hers to look down into her eyes. His were again cold. Dark and unreadable.

"Tell me yes," he had said. And she hadn't.

And still she didn't. No matter how much she wanted to make love to Griff, she knew it wasn't the time for this. It wouldn't solve any of the unresolved issues that lay between them. It would simply be another complication. And there were already enough of those in what was happening. More than enough complications.

"Claire?" Griff said softly. A question.

"No," she whispered.

No explanation. She couldn't have made one. Even she didn't fully understand why she hadn't said yes. Why she hadn't agreed to what they both wanted.

Griff nodded, his lips thinned, cruelly compressed. The same lips that had drifted so knowingly over her breast. Then he pushed away from her, the movement abrupt. Removing his body from all contact with hers.

The positions involved in making love are always slightly awkward, but there was something inherently more embarrassing about assuming them and then having to retreat from their intimacy. When she looked up, Griff was standing beside the bed, looking down on her. She realized that she was lying exactly where he had placed her, unmoving, her breast exposed, still damp with the moisture of his mouth.

Slowly, she pulled the straps of her bra and shell up over her shoulder again, her own movements clumsy now. An awkwardness between two people for which intimacy had never before been awkward. Or uncomfortable.

"I'm sorry," she whispered.

She rolled to her side and put her feet on the floor, sitting up on the edge of the bed. She realized that she was shaking. She wanted to stay here a moment, maybe put her head in her hands, as Griff had done.

But this was his room. His retreat. So she put her palms against the edge of the mattress and pushed up. Tiredly. Moving like an old woman. She expected him to try to stop her, but he didn't. He didn't move. He didn't say another word to her.

"Tell me yes," he had begged.

She hadn't.

And right now, at least, she supposed there were no other questions between them that really mattered.

Chapter Twelve

The cruiser was no longer moving. Perhaps that was what had awakened her, Claire thought, lying in the stifling darkness of her stateroom, listening to the silence. There was no lulling vibration of the powerful engines. She had been far too aware of their sound as she tossed and turned in this lonely bed after leaving Griff's cabin last night. Now there was no engine noise thrumming like a heartbeat through the hull. Which meant, she supposed, they were back in Miami.

That's where Griff had ordered Jake to take them last night. Back to where this misadventure had all begun. And, after too few hours of restless, nightmare-interrupted sleep, she was back again to wondering what happened next. And to the realization that she had no control over any of it.

Claire Heywood wasn't accustomed to feeling helpless. She had always had control. Of her career. Of her life. Always. Until someone opened a second story window on New Year's Eve and took her daughter. She closed her eyes, trying not to think about the images that had seethed in her brain last night.

Images of Gardner. Wondering if someone would make sure she was warm and hold her when she fretted. Wondering how they would know to sing the same lullabies to her as Claire had. Wondering if her baby were alone and frightened instead, somewhere in a darkness that matched this one.

Images of Hawk. Remembering her impressions of him, formed in the few times she had met him. Wondering if she were right to suspect him. Right to tell Griff what she believed. Wondering if Lucas Hawkins could really be cruel enough, vindictive enough, to have been the guiding hand behind Gardner's kidnapping and everything that had happened since.

And images of Griff... Those had been the hardest to deny. It was so hard to push all thought of him from her consciousness. Almost impossible because he was here. And because she knew that all she had to do to change what had happened between them was to go back to his cabin.

To open the door to that dark room where he was sleeping and let him make her forget. Forget the pain of this. At least for an hour or two. To have that respite from thinking about things she could do nothing about, all she had to do, she thought again, as she had thought so many times last night, was to go to him.

Instead, she closed her eyes, squeezing them tight against the burn of tears. She pushed her legs out from under the weight of the sheet. It was too hot, heavy against her bare skin and damp with the ever-present south Florida humidity.

She opened her eyes, turning her head toward the porthole, wondering if it were too early to get up. There was the faintest hint of gray in the blackness of the sky. It was not yet dawn. Which meant Jake was probably still asleep in the narrow crew cabin that had been built into the side of the pilothouse. As Griff almost certainly would be in his stateroom next door.

Next door, she thought. Next door. But of course, considering what had happened last night, he might as well be as far away from her as he had been before this all started.

She sat up on the edge of the bed, wondering about the oppressive heat. Maybe the air-conditioning didn't work if the engines weren't running. Or maybe Jake, sleeping topside, hadn't realized how hot it would be down here without it.

There would be a breeze on deck. At least there would be a breath of fresh air that wasn't contaminated by regret and worry, which seemed to have permanently thickened the atmosphere of this room. And it would do her good to watch the sun come up.

The promise of another day that, please, dear God, *had* to be better than the one that had just passed. Claire had always found a sense of renewal in watching the streaks of gold edge upward from beneath the rim of the ocean and push into a dark sky. Despite everything, she knew she would feel better watching that eternal phenomenon.

She stood up, not bothering to look for the robe she had bought to go with the thin cotton nightgown. There would be no one else on deck, and besides, part of the purpose of going up was to escape the heat and humidity. Putting on more clothes wouldn't accomplish that.

On bare feet, she crossed the floor to the door. Once there, she hesitated, unconsciously listening. There was nothing. No sound. Only a silence that seemed as deep as the unnatural stillness on the island had yesterday.

Pushing away the image of what she and Griff had found there, she opened her door and walked down the short, deserted companionway to the stairs, resisting the urge to look toward the door of Griff's room. As she climbed, the air around her seemed to freshen as well as brighten. She took a deep breath, savoring it.

Daylight was a little nearer than she had thought. Near enough that objects were almost discernible. As she watched, eyes adjusting, shapes began to form out of the surrounding darkness. The ghostly white hulls of the other cruisers in their moorings nearby. The outlines of the marina.

She walked over to the rail, her bare feet making no sound on the varnished deck. Or if they did, it was soft enough to be hidden by the low splash of the waves. No one was stirring on the nearby boats.

They would be soon, she decided, leaning against the rail.

Pleasure boats or working boats, for most of them the day started at dawn and ended when the sun set. The water lapped seductively against the side of the yacht, a larger wave occasionally hitting the bottom rung of the ladder with a sharper, distinctive slap.

The monotony of sound was relaxing. She lifted her face, trying to let the salt-tanged breeze blow away the miasma of disappointment and worry that had oppressed her since there had been no kidnappers to meet them on the key. Griff had promised, she told herself. Promised her that no matter what, he'd get Gardner back. And she still believed that if anyone could—

There was a sound behind her. It was dark enough that she reacted just as she would have in the city, looking over her shoulder, eyes searching for whoever or whatever had made the noise. She expected to see Jake walking across the deck to join her. Or Griff, appearing at the top of the stairs, unshaven, the stubble of yesterday's beard on his lean cheeks, his eyes as tired as they had been last night.

There was no one. She turned all the way around to be sure. Her eyes moved across the cruiser, sweeping slowly from stern to bow. Everything looked eerie in the strange half-light of dawn, but it seemed there was nothing—and no one else—on deck.

Maybe the noise, whatever she had heard, had come from the yacht on the far side. She took a step in that direction, craning her neck to see if someone had come out on deck. Her bare toes bumped against something.

The object was small and light enough to go skittering across the polished deck as if she had deliberately kicked it. Curious, she bent, eyes searching in the near dawn dimness to find it. The defective transmitter, she realized. She picked it up, holding it up to the light. It must have fallen off when she and Jake had been struggling to get Griff on board.

A reminder of all that had gone wrong, she thought. A reminder she didn't need. She turned, intending to toss it over the side. She had raised her arm, poised to throw, when she realized there was no reason to add this to the other garbage polluting the ocean. She had seen more than enough flotsam during the hours she'd searched for Griff to understand how much was already out there.

Instead, she closed her fingers around the transmitter. She'd dispose of it later. Or give it to Jake. Maybe it could be fixed, although she wouldn't want to trust anyone's life to it again. She glanced toward the helm in response to the thought of handing the transmitter over to Jake.

Hawk was standing by the rail on the opposite side of the yacht. He was watching her, blue eyes luminescent in the darkness, his strong features set, composed and unsmiling. He must have just come over the side, she realized. That had been the noise she heard.

He was wearing jeans and nothing else. And he was barefoot. As hers had been, his footsteps would be silent crossing the deck. By intent, she realized. Silent by intent. Her eyes lifted slowly from his feet. When they reached waist level, they stopped again, no longer focused on Hawk or on what he was wearing, but on what he held in his hand.

It was a knife, as broad and long as a bowie knife. The blade turned slightly as he adjusted the grip of his hand on the haft. The moving blade caught a shaft of light from the rising sun, reflecting it onto the varnished planks.

Her heart jumped, literally skipping beats in its normal rhythm. Other than that fluttering pulsation, nothing about her body seemed capable of movement. Her terror, invoked by that subtle flicker of light off the edge of his knife, was paralyzing.

She had always hated the thought of blades. The thought of being cut. Some people feared being trapped in a fire. Or drowning. Some were terrified of airplanes. But her own personal phobia had always been a fear of being attacked in some dark alley. Of feeling a razor-edge blade slice into her skin.

Still unbreathing, she watched Hawk take a step toward

her. He turned his head, looking toward the helm. She couldn't make her eyes follow his. Not even to see if Jake were there. Then Hawk looked toward the stern, blue eyes searching the length of the yacht, just as hers had done only seconds before.

When his gaze came back to her, his brows lifted, their meaning obvious. A question. Despite her fear, she certainly recognized the expression. She wasn't sure, however, exactly what he was asking. Where the others were? Did he really expect her to tell him that?

Slowly, she shook her head. He was Griff's friend, she told herself. Even the scenario she had described to Griff to explain what Hawk had done didn't mean she believed he would be angry enough, or crazy enough, to want to hurt the people who were on this cruiser. Jake was his friend. She had helped Hawk set up the meeting he wanted with Steiner. And Hawk had once been willing to die for Griff—or to kill for him. Surely now...

As he took another step away from the railing, his eyes again scanning his surroundings, he reminded her of some sleek predator. Totally alert. Looking for danger.

Looking for danger. For some reason the phrase echoed in her head. That was exactly what Hawk appeared to be doing, she realized. But why would he expect danger here?

Because he thought Jake or Griff would by now have figured out what he had done? After all, she had, and she wasn't nearly as skilled at this game as the two of them.

Was Jake still asleep? she wondered. And why not? So far there had been no sound. The cruiser, the whole marina, was as quiet as the island had been yesterday. Suddenly the unwanted image of Diaz's body was in her head. His throat cut from ear to ear. With the knife Hawk was holding?

With that thought, she took an involuntary step backward, pressing again the rail. Hawk's fair head tilted again. Listening to something? Or questioning her movement? Using the knife, he pointed at the stairs that led belowdecks.

Where Griff was sleeping. Was he looking for Griff? My

God, could he be insane enough to want to do to Griff what he had done to Ramon Diaz? What someone had done, she amended, trying to think rationally, despite her terror.

This time she made no response to his question, not even the small negative movement of her head she had made before. He pointed again with the knife, stabbing it toward the companionway. Demanding information?

It was almost daylight, she realized. The sun was creeping up over the horizon behind her, illuminating the marina with its thin, pale light. Surely someone on one of the other boats would come up on deck soon and realize what was going on.

Or maybe, disturbed by the rising sun, Jake would stir, come out of the crew cabin and see Hawk. See the knife he held and understand what was happening. Jake never seemed to sleep. Surely—

"That's far enough," Jake said.

His voice was low, but commanding. Maybe Jake wasn't one of the hotshots, as he had called Jordan and the others, but still, right now he seemed an answer to prayer. It was almost as if she had conjured him up with the force of her fear.

Somehow Claire managed to pull her eyes away from their terrified fascination with the knife and look to her left. To where Jake's voice had come from. He had come around the bridge, and she wondered how long he had been hiding there. Since before the first sound she had heard, of course. The narrow cabin where he slept was on that side of the cruiser, so Jake would have had more warning of Hawk's arrival than she.

Jake was on the same side of the yacht as she was, looking across the expanse of its deck at Hawk. And he was holding a gun. A big gun, which he held as if he knew what he was doing.

"Jake?" Hawk said, his tone questioning.

Surprised? Or trying to sound as if he were? Or trying to sound…innocent? Claire wondered.

"Are you all right?" Hawk asked. "We were worried that—"

"Put the knife down," Jake ordered, his words louder and more forceful than that first quiet command had been. The muzzle of the gun lifted a little, pointing at the center of Hawk's chest. "Bend your knees, arms out to your side, and lay the knife down on the deck. *Then* we can talk."

The cold blue eyes of the man they called Hawk held on Jake's face. He seemed to be considering the demand, but he didn't obey. For endless seconds nobody moved.

"Do it now," Jake said. "Don't *make* me have to shoot you, old buddy. I sure don't want to have to do that."

Despite that seemingly reassuring avowal, Jake's voice had hardened. Sharpened with certainty. And suddenly there was no doubt in Claire's mind that he would do exactly what he had threatened.

Hotshot or not, Jake Holt was a CIA agent. No one got to that position without the kind of training it would take to pull that trigger. The kind of courage necessary to put a bullet into the heart of a man he had once considered to be his friend. A man that he had evidently decided, as she had last night, might be an enemy instead.

Apparently Lucas Hawkins heard in Jake's voice the same quality Claire had heard. His arms moved slowly upward, lifting carefully away from his body. His eyes remained on Holt's face as they did. His knees began to bend, however, the powerful muscles in his thighs stretching the faded material of his jeans.

When Hawk had stooped as low as he could, his right arm began to lower, that movement as smooth and unhurried as the other had been. He laid the knife on the deck.

"Push it toward me," Jake directed, while Hawk's fingers were still touching the hilt. "Hard enough for it to get here."

There was a half second of hesitation before Hawk sent the knife sliding along the slick surface. It came to rest about two feet from Jake's right foot. Jake's eyes had never left their contemplation of the man who was still squatting, balancing on his bare toes, across the cruiser from him.

"Good job," Jake said softly.

His lips tilted a little as he made the compliment. The smile didn't have a warming effect on Hawk, whose lips were thinned and set, his eyes even colder.

Moving slowly, he began to reverse the process that had brought the knife close enough to the deck for him to leave it there. Arms again lifted slightly away from his sides, he pushed up out of the low squat until he was standing once more.

"What's going on?" he asked.

"You tell me, man," Jake countered softly. "You tell me what the hell's going on."

Hawk's eyes held their focus on Jake's face for a few seconds more before he nodded and began to talk. "When we got to the rendezvous, we were ambushed. They took Diaz and his bodyguards and left us tied up."

"Must have been a hell of an ambush," Jake said, sounding amused. Sarcastic. "Your reputations obviously hadn't preceded you."

He didn't believe Hawk's story, Claire realized. Jake had worked with these men for years, and of course, considering all she had heard about them, it would be pretty difficult for her to believe that someone could catch Hawk and Jordan unaware.

She had just seen a demonstration of the kind of caution Hawk would bring to an operation. No wonder Jake had his doubts about the scenario Hawk had described.

"We were expecting to meet Griff," Hawk said. "We weren't expecting a trap."

"Neither were we," Jake said.

"You had trouble?"

"You could say that," Jake said.

"Where's Griff?" Hawk asked.

For the first time, his eyes left Jake and moved back to the stairs that led below. Then they rose, finding Claire's.

"Griff downstairs?" he asked.

There was no doubt the question was directed at her. She just wasn't sure what Jake would want her to say. It was an obvious attempt to get information, but she wasn't sure why Hawk needed that particular piece. Just to place everyone? More of that habitual caution? Or because he was really concerned about Griff, which was what his tone implied?

In any case, she opted for saying nothing, waiting for Jake to step into the breach and tell Hawk whatever he wanted him to know. And after a second or two, he did.

"Griff's asleep. He had a pretty rough couple of days."

Hawk's eyes had remained on Claire, even after Jake answered the question he'd posed. And then, moving with what appeared to be a deliberate redirection, they went back to Jake's face. He had never once looked at the gun, which was still pointed, steady and unmoving, at his heart.

"What does that mean?" Hawk asked softly. "A rough two days?"

"Spending more than twelve hours in the sea for one thing," Jake said. "The transmitter didn't work. You got any explanation for that, Hawk?" Again there was an edge in Jake's voice. Mockery. Or a challenge.

"It worked when I checked it," Hawk said. "There wasn't a damn thing wrong with the transmitter when we left."

"Well, it didn't work when it needed to. And that's a real big ocean out there. Too frigging big to be lost in. If it hadn't been for Claire..." Jake shrugged.

Hawk's eyes came back to her face, quickly this time.

"That's why you weren't at the rendezvous," Hawk suggested, his own voice without inflection.

"We had a choice. We leave Griff out there or we miss picking you up," Claire said, wondering how long Hawk was going to pretend that he hadn't known any of this.

"And the kidnappers?" Hawk asked.

You tell me, she thought. That's exactly what she wanted

to demand of him. *Tell me where my baby is, you bastard. Tell me how to get her back.*

She opened her mouth, and Griff's voice interrupted.

"What's going on?" he asked.

From where she was standing, she couldn't see him. Obviously, he was in the stairwell that led down to the companionway. Hawk was far enough away from the other rail that he probably *could* see Griff.

"He climbed over the side," Jake said. "Carrying a knife."

"We thought something must have gone wrong," Hawk said. "That something had happened to you. You didn't make the rendezvous, and we got ambushed when we did."

"Ambushed?" Griff repeated.

"Somebody sneaked up on Jordan and Hawk and tied them up," Jake said.

His voice was no longer sarcastic. Or amused, but somehow he still made it obvious he didn't believe Hawk's story. And obvious he didn't expect Griff to, either.

"Where's Jordan?" Griff asked, instead of commenting on the ambush.

"Trying to contact the kidnappers," Hawk said. "Trying to find the baby."

"And you came here to rescue us?" Griff asked.

Unlike Jake's, his voice was totally devoid of inflection. Even Claire, who knew him so well, couldn't read the emotion behind those words.

Hawk shrugged. "We thought you'd run into trouble, too. We thought the same kind of thing might have happened to you that had happened to us. I've been waiting to see if the yacht showed up back here."

"How did you get back to Miami?" Griff asked.

There was a fraction of a second's hesitation. Hawk's eyes went back to Jake before he answered, and when he did, Claire knew why.

"They left the skiff behind," he said.

"Whoever tied you up left the inflatable?" Jake asked,

his tone openly disbelieving now. "How very considerate of them," he said, smiling. "That was just real convenient, old buddy. Wouldn't you say?"

It *was* a little ingenuous, Claire thought, but maybe it was the best Hawk could come up with. Maybe he hadn't ever intended to have to answer questions.

"What *I'd* say is that's exactly the way they planned it," Hawk said quietly, his voice controlled, not responding to Jake's obvious incredulity. "Just exactly what they intended."

"Why?" Griff asked.

Hawk looked at him again. Griff was standing now at the top of the stairs. That air of being in charge, of being the one who had the right to ask the questions, emanated from him. Despite the fact that he was, as she had envisioned earlier, unshaven, and his eyes were as tired as she'd remembered them being last night.

"Setup," Hawk suggested, blue eyes focused on Griff's face, his voice still unemotional. "And I think I know who's behind it. Jordan and I have figured out who's been behind everything that's happened to all of us. And more importantly, Griff, we think we know why," he added.

Chapter Thirteen

Whether or not he had been right yesterday about the agency's intentions, Griff thought, watching Jake hold the semiautomatic on Hawk, the result of what they had done had been exactly what he'd feared. The destruction of the External Security Team had become a reality.

And that it was happening in this way seemed far more painful than the other would have been. All the bonds they had formed during the last ten years were being irreparably broken by the distrust that spread like a virus between them.

"Unless you're not interested in who's behind this," Hawk said softly.

Griff realized that Hawk had been waiting through his silence. Waiting for a response. For some indication that Griff wanted to hear whatever theory he and Jordan had devised. But Griff kept thinking instead about the one Claire had suggested last night. And, despite his feelings about Hawk, despite their friendship, about how much sense it had made.

"I'm interested," he said aloud.

Hawk nodded, the acknowledgment small, totally controlled, as was every action Lucas Hawkins ever took.

"This has to be Steiner," Hawk said.

Griff realized that after he'd appeared, some of Hawk's tension had eased. Of course, one would have to know Hawk very well—and few people did, certainly not as well as

Griff—to even recognize that he had been tense. Or to recognize that he'd relaxed as a result of Griff's appearance.

Griff wasn't entirely sure why that had happened. Because Hawk believed he would never allow Jake to pull that trigger? Or because he and Hawk had always been so close, closer perhaps than anyone else on the team? Griff knew the reason for that, although he had always recognized the dangers inherent in that closeness. In the jealousies it might foster. Hawk, however, had never had anyone else. Nothing besides the team. The next mission. And Griff's friendship. At one time those had comprised the whole of Lucas Hawkins's world.

They didn't anymore, of course. Hawk had found a woman who loved him, without any questions about who he was or what he had done. Like the rest of them, however, Jake Holt excluded, Hawk no longer had a profession. Or the missions. The friendships.

"Why do you think it's Steiner?" Griff asked, watching Hawk's face, a face he would have said only a week ago he could read like an open book. Somehow, that no longer seemed so easy.

"If they could get us to do this," Hawk said, "if they could make it appear we'd done it—that's all the excuse they'd need."

"Excuse for what?" Jake asked. "What the hell makes you think the bureaucrats ever need an *excuse* for what they do?"

"Because there are people who understand the value of what we did," Hawk said. "People who know *you*, Griff. And who aren't going to be so easily convinced that doing away with the External Security Team is the best thing for this country."

Jake's snort of laughter expressed his ridicule. It was loud enough to be distracting, and Hawk's eyes briefly left their concentration on Griff to track back to Jake's face. His thin lips tightened before he went on.

"The oversight committees have read the reports. I think

Steiner will have a hard time convincing them that there won't be a need for our kind of missions in the future.''

More words than he'd ever heard Hawk put together before, Griff thought, resisting the urge to smile. Because he recognized that most of them were words he'd learned from Griff. *Standing guard.*

"Why now?'' Griff asked.

After all, the decision to disband the unit had probably been made not long after the terrorist attack in which he'd been injured. A year ago.

"Somebody in a position to do something about it finally got wind of what they were planning,'' Hawk suggested.

"How?'' Jake asked, the sarcasm that had been in his voice no longer there. It had been replaced by interest.

"Because they haven't been particularly discreet about their intentions for standing down the team,'' Hawk suggested. "Ms. Heywood's grandfather may have figured out what they were doing. You asked for his help in setting up that meeting with Steiner,'' Hawk said.

His eyes had shifted again from Griff's face, this time to focus on Claire's. Griff found his own gaze following Hawk's, and then he wished it hadn't. Deliberately, he hadn't looked at her since he'd come up from below, but he had known exactly where she was standing. He had been totally and completely aware of her position. Just as he had always been when they were in the same room. Completely and totally aware of everything about her.

She was on the other side of the deck from Hawk, with the rising sun behind her. The thin white cotton of her nightgown was made transparent by its light, the outline of her slender body clearly revealed.

And despite the seriousness of what was happening here, Griff's thoughts went back to last night. When she had lain on his bed and allowed him to touch her. Allowed him to see the changes the last year and a half had made in her body. Changes that had come as a result of the birth of a child they had conceived together. A baby who was now a pawn in a game that seemed to grow more complicated as each layer of motivation and corruption was peeled away.

"I asked for his help," Claire agreed, "but…I never told him what that was all about. And he never asked me," she said.

"Maybe because he had his own sources," Hawk suggested. "He knew Griff. With his connections, your grandfather had to be aware of exactly what Griff did for the agency. He probably knew that Steiner had taken Griff's place. Your request could have been enough to make him start asking questions. And questions from a former DCI about what they were doing with External Security would make a lot of people nervous. Your grandfather has been a player in Washington politics for half a century."

"Nobody has better connections than an old spook," Claire said softly.

That was a truism often repeated in the capital, maybe because it *was* so damn true, Griff thought.

"But even if that's what happened," he said, "even if Claire's grandfather asked questions they didn't want to answer, how does kidnapping Gardner fit into that?"

"Taking your daughter—Ms. Heywood's daughter," Hawk amended, "was guaranteed to get you involved. Guaranteed to make you take the bait. To force you to kill Diaz. They know they have to discredit *you* in order to discredit the team."

Hawk's voice was softer than it had been before. But the conviction in it seemed just as sincere. His eyes had been on Griff as he made that argument. And then he glanced again at Claire before he went on.

"And it might also have been intended as…a reminder to your grandfather. A warning that no matter how much influence he has, he can't protect his own family. He can't protect anybody. Not if they really want to get to them." The silence that fell after those words was broken when Hawk added quietly, "And maybe it was even a warning to you."

"To me?" Claire said. "A warning to *me?*"

"You threatened Steiner with going public about what they were doing to me."

Griff hadn't known that, but he wasn't surprised. That was exactly the kind of courage Claire had always had. The same courage it had taken to constantly challenge him. To make him argue the right and the wrong of what he did. If she really had threatened Steiner—

"And then you helped Jordan gather the media when he needed them to turn over the money Sorrel took," Hawk added. "Maybe Steiner just figured he ought to remind you of the nature of the league you'd chosen to play in."

A tough, dirty league, Griff acknowledged. Tougher and dirtier than anything Claire Heywood had ever faced in her entire life. And the agency was certainly capable of issuing that kind of warning. In this case, however, Griff didn't believe anything they had done had been intended as a threat to Claire. Or to her grandfather, although he didn't doubt that the old man was capable of digging deeper than they would be comfortable with.

Griff believed this had all been arranged with him as the target. Because he had dared to question their intentions for his men. And because they were people who didn't like being questioned. Griff had known that all along. He just hadn't dreamed they would retaliate against his family. Even as the word formed in his mind, he recognized that he had no right to use it. He and Claire weren't a family, despite the fact that they had conceived a child. A child who, even now…

"Put it away, Jake," he ordered quietly, remembering the mission. But Jake's gaze didn't falter from the man he was targeting. And the muzzle of the Glock didn't lower.

"Griff," Claire protested.

"Hawk had nothing to do with this," Griff said to her. "He thinks he's the cause of it, but he isn't even right about that. And if you couldn't hear what was in his voice when he talked about your standing up to Steiner on his behalf, then you're not nearly as intuitive—or as intelligent—as you used to be."

He had allowed a thread of amusement into that explanation, intending it to reassure her, just as listening to Hawk had reassured him. Hawk had nothing to do with Gardner's kidnapping. Griff would stake his life on that. It was obvious the others thought he was.

"He had a knife," Jake said, the focus of his gun unchanged. And unchanging. "He came up over the side, Griff, barefoot and carrying a knife."

"He thought we'd been victims of the same people who attacked him and Jordan. This was a rescue, Jake, not an assassination."

Assassination seemed to reverberate through the sun-touched air that shimmered between them. Griff wished he had been more careful in his choice of words. Because that was exactly what Hawk did, of course. Assassinations. That had been his job in the years he'd been with the team. He had assassinated a few madmen—including the one with the suitcase nukes.

It was what he had done in Baghdad. That time to revenge the death of those senselessly killed at Langley. To avenge Griff's death. Which had not, of course, been a death at all.

"Claire thinks I owe you an explanation for the CIA's version of my retirement," he said.

"You don't owe me anything, Griff," Hawk said softly. "You never have."

There was far more unspoken in that quiet statement. A lot of memories hidden in that soft, deep voice. Memories of a mission that had gone wrong. Of a long, unpleasant recuperation in Virginia, which Hawk had silently endured. As he had endured Griff's inept nursing. And maybe a long delayed acknowledgment of friendship that had been offered to a bitter loner long before there was any sign that it might be reciprocated. Acknowledgment of things they had never before seen any need to express because they both understood them so well.

"Put the gun down, Jake," Griff ordered again, his voice even lower than it had been before.

This time, however, his words had an effect. Slowly Jake lowered the weapon he held. Then he turned and walked over to the rail near where Claire stood, every motion an indication that was an order he had unwillingly obeyed.

"What if you're wrong?" Claire asked.

Griff looked at her, pulling his gaze from Hawk's face, more than satisfied by what he had seen there.

"I'm not," he said simply. And then he smiled at her. "But you're more than welcome to argue the point."

His sudden surety about Hawk was like a weight lifted from his spirits. Maybe things had gone wrong. Maybe he had made mistakes. But not about this. And the people he would have staked his life on when this started were, thank God, unchanged.

"You have to know that *someone*—"

"Not Hawk," he denied, breaking into her disclaimer, despite the invitation he had just issued. This wasn't the time or the place for the debate he'd invited.

"This is my daughter's *life*," Claire argued.

"My daughter as well," Griff said. "I haven't forgotten."

Perhaps because she knew him so well, well enough to recognize the implacable quality of his voice, she didn't try to plead the case she had made last night. Instead, she walked across the deck toward Hawk. She stopped just before she reached him, looking up into his harsh features.

Although Claire was tall for a woman, Hawk topped her by at least six inches. He met her eyes, unflinching before their assessment. She studied his face for a long, silent minute.

Finally, she shook her head, moving it from side to side only once or twice. Not so much, Griff believed, a denial of what he had said as an indication of her own uncertainty. She had turned away, starting toward the stairs that led belowdecks, when she hesitated, turning back to face Hawk again.

"Here," she said.

She held out her hand, fingers cupped downward over what

it held. Automatically, Hawk held his out, palm up. Claire placed the transmitter on his outstretched hand.

"A souvenir," she said softly, her tone bitter.

Without waiting for a response, she turned again and walked across the deck to the stairwell. Griff moved out of her way, but she didn't even meet his eyes as she went by.

Hawk was still looking at the object that rested in his palm. Then he closed his fingers over it and raised his eyes to Griff's.

"Is Jordan where you can reach him?" Griff asked.

"I can try," Hawk said after a small delay, after seeming to think about it.

"Can you do it from here?"

Hawk nodded, walking toward the helm. Griff glanced to his left, where Jake was still standing at the rail, his back to them, shoulders stiff. With anger? he wondered. Or with resentment over having his judgment questioned?

When Hawk got to the helm, he reached toward the bank of instruments and turned a dial. Immediately there was a small steady beep, the sound soft, but very clear in the dawn stillness. Hawk's brows lifted slightly, blue eyes finding Griff's again. His mouth moved, one corner lifting.

"Your locator seems to be working," he said.

"Damn cold comfort," Griff said. "And just a little late."

"That's what I heard," Claire said, her voice coming from behind him. "That night," she said. "I came up here after the explosion, and as I was coming up the stairs I heard that sound."

The three of them listened to the small steady message the beacon was sending out. The same message it had apparently been sending the night Griff had exploded Diaz's private jet and parachuted out of it into the emptiness of that cold, dark sea.

"I heard it," she whispered. "And then Jake reached out and touched something and…the sound stopped."

He should have reacted sooner, Griff thought, when his eyes swung to find Jake. Because Jake certainly had. But then

Jake had probably known exactly what was going to happen as soon as he heard the first beep of the beacon's transmission.

By the time he and Hawk had figured out what Claire's words implied, it was too late to do much about it. Nothing beyond staring at the dark eye of the weapon Jake was once again holding, competently directed this time at the two of them.

"Join them, Ms. Heywood," Jake ordered, "or I'll put a bullet in his kneecap. The good one," he added softly.

Considering all that had already happened, including Diaz's brutal murder, no one could afford to doubt Jake would do exactly what he had threatened. Griff didn't. And his stomach tightened, guts clenching in sick anticipation.

Apparently, Claire didn't doubt Jake's threat, either. She walked across the deck, putting herself in Jake's sight. And in the line of fire.

"Thank you," Jake said softly when she had joined them. "Now if we only had Jordan here..." he suggested, the thin edge of sarcasm back in his voice, touched now with triumph as well.

Because he had bested the hotshots? Griff wondered. Had that familiar raillery, which they had all dismissed as Jake's way of putting them in their place, played any part in this? *Jake's way,* Griff thought, fighting the same sense of failure Claire's accusations of Hawk had caused last night. It had been Jake all along. One of his team.

The problems associated with this particular mission had been Jake's doing. And perhaps he had been involved with what had happened to Jordan, as well. Maybe even with what they'd done to Hawk. Jake had certainly been in a position to affect the outcome of those events.

Suddenly, he remembered Carl Steiner telling him that it had been Jake who had confirmed that Sheik al-Ahmad's assassination was an extremist plot. Which was the reason Steiner had released Tyler Stewart from protection and almost gotten her killed.

"Why, Jake?" Griff asked. Why would he endanger people he had worked with for more than ten years?

"Because I got tired of the bureaucratic BS," Jake said, his voice seeming too calm to reflect enough anger or resentment to enable him to do what it was obvious now that he had done.

"We're not the bureaucrats," Griff said.

"This had nothing to do with you, Griff."

"Nothing to do with me?" Griff asked, his voice incredulous. "It's my *daughter* they took, Jake. Or are you saying you weren't in on that?"

He thought about that possibility, but if Jake had used the transmitter to keep them from making the rendezvous with Hawk and Jordan, obviously to give his fellow conspirators a chance to get to Diaz, then he had to have been in on this from the beginning.

"Nothing's happened to the baby," Jake said. "Harming her was never part of the plan."

"Then what exactly *was* the plan? What the hell has been going on here?"

"You don't have a clue, do you, Griff? But then I shouldn't be surprised. You never had a clue about what it's like for the rest of us. They screw you over, they destroy you, and you retire and live out your life in luxury. They screw us, and we stay screwed. I didn't like that."

"So you target the rest of *us*?"

"There's nothing personal about this," Jake said. "None of you were ever the targets of what I did."

"And now?" Griff asked quietly, allowing his eyes to fall to the Glock. "Aren't we the targets now?"

Jake didn't answer, and in the waiting silence, they could hear subtle sounds beginning to emanate from the boats moored around them. Their occupants were starting to stir. Maybe even to come out on deck. And soon, someone would notice what was going on here.

"It wasn't supposed to be this way," Jake said finally. His

voice had lowered, perhaps in recognition of what was taking place on the boats around them.

"How *was* it supposed to be?"

"I had something coming to me. But I watched what those bastards were doing to the others, and I knew that unless I did something, it wasn't going to happen for me. Not unless I made it happen. But nobody on the team has been hurt by what I did. Not Jordan. Not you."

"And Tyler Stewart?" Griff asked. "You're the one who told Steiner to release her. You had to know what would happen to her when you did."

Beside him, he felt Hawk move. A start of reaction, small enough that it would have been indiscernible to the others.

"I thought if Steiner believed it was just regional politics, he'd see that he didn't have any legitimate reason to hold Hawk. As soon as I realized that idiot had released her, I called Jordan. What happened at the airport..." Jake shrugged. "You can't hold me responsible for Ahmad's insanity."

"And what happened to Jordan?" Griff asked. "Or can't you be held responsible for that, either?"

Jake's denial of his responsibility for Jordan's situation was several seconds longer in coming than it should have been.

"You son of a bitch," Hawk said softly as the silence stretched. "You set Jordan up. That whole deal was a setup."

Hawk didn't move, however, despite the fury in his quiet voice. Griff thanked Hawk's habitual control for that—a control that had been acquired the hard way.

"Nothing happened to Jordan," Jake said, seeming to be trying to make his case to Hawk now. "I saw to that."

"You *saw* to it?" Hawk repeated unbelievingly. "You were controlling things? You were up there playing God with people's lives?"

People's lives, Griff thought. Jordan's life. And the lives of the Sorrel family, which included a couple of small children. And apparently—

"Jordan rescued Sorrel's wife and kids," Jake asserted. "He got them out of a situation they'd been living in for three years. Nobody else could have done that. And nobody was hurt."

"Except an FBI agent named Helms," Griff said.

"Helms was willing to take his chances."

For a sixteen-million-dollar payoff. A lot of people would have been willing to take their chances. Including Jake Holt.

"You and Helms were in on that together," Hawk suggested.

They had to have been, Griff realized. And that's how Helms had found Jordan and the Sorrel family at the Virginia mansion. Not through an outside invasion of Jake's computers, as Jordan had thought, but through Jake.

"You did it all for the money, Jake?" Griff said unbelievingly.

For the Mafia's sixteen million dollars. Money that everyone else was looking for. Except Jake Holt had the inside track. Insider information. And he had had Jordan's friendship and trust, as well.

It had taken him too long to put this all together, Griff conceded. It had taken all of them too long. Distracted by what he had known were the agency's intentions for his people, he hadn't been aware of the traitor in their midst. A traitor who had tried to use the skills of the team Griff had built to provide for his own retirement, something Jake obviously believed was impending. Except, of course, his situation was different from the rest of them. Because Jake wasn't one of the hotshots.

"You could have written your own ticket, Jake," Griff said. "Whatever the agency did with the rest of us, they weren't going to let you go. You're too valuable to them."

Jake laughed, the sound short and bitter. "Like I said. It's okay for you to work all your life for the company rate and a miserable little pension when it's over. The rest of us weren't born with any silver spoons in our mouths. And I don't intend to analyze satellite data in a hole in the wall at Langley for the rest of my life."

For *money,* Griff thought again. He really had done it all for money. But of course, Jake was right about a part of that. Griff had never needed the salary the agency paid him. Just as he hadn't needed the generous pension they had given him when they had put him out to pasture.

And as soon as they had, they had begun dissolving his team and retiring his men. The beginnings of this hadn't been Jake, of course, although the agency's own disloyalty seemed to have set him off.

"Where's my daughter?" Claire asked, breaking into his useless self-recrimination.

Jake's eyes focused briefly on her face before they came back to concentrate on the men, whom he wisely saw as the greater threat. "Somewhere safe," he said.

"Did you do what Hawk said?" Claire asked. "Did you try to use Gardner to discredit the team? To embarrass the agency?"

"His motives weren't quite that noble, Ms. Heywood," Hawk said. "How much was the contract on Diaz, Jake? How much did you stand to make on this?"

"What do you care?" Jake asked. "You didn't do the hit. Nobody owes you."

"And when you found out that Griff wasn't willing to kill Diaz, you told whoever had put out the contract where to find us. And you gave them Diaz, bound and gagged, so they could do it themselves."

"Actually, they kind of liked it that way," Jake said. "A little bad blood between the parties involved. And nobody got hurt," he added.

"Nobody but Diaz," Hawk reminded him softly.

"You know, old buddy, I find concern for Diaz pretty funny coming from you," Jake said. "Diaz deserved to die every bit as much as those bastards you lined up in your sights and blew away."

"That was never my decision," Hawk said.

"No, it was always Griff's decision. Based on information *I* supplied. Situations *I* analyzed. Based on *my* assessment of the threat they presented. And there was nothing different about this one. So let's don't pretend to be sentimental over some scumbag drug runner, Hawk. Morality doesn't become you, good buddy. It doesn't really become any of us. Not after the things we've been a part of through the years."

"If you felt that way—" Griff began, only to be cut off.

"None of your sermons, Griff. I've had a bellyful of those, too. Sanctimonious defenses of just exactly what I did to Diaz. I made my choices. And you made yours. Who's to say one was better than the other? They're all still dead. There aren't going to be any resurrections."

Griff said nothing, his eyes on a man he had known for ten years and had realized only now he hadn't known at all. Maybe he hadn't really known any of them.

Hawk's hands were clenched at his sides. But after his small, involuntary reaction to the knowledge that Jake had been responsible for what almost happened to Tyler, he hadn't moved.

"Now what?" Claire asked softly.

Not the ideal question in this situation, Griff thought, but she couldn't know that. He just didn't want Jake pressured into making any sudden choices. They might not be the right ones.

"We get the hell out of here," Jake said. "Before somebody gets curious."

"What about Jordan?" Griff asked.

"I'll deal with Jordan later," Jake promised. "Take her out, Griff," he ordered. "We're going back out to sea. And once we're there..." He hesitated, thinking about his narrowing options. "Once we're there, *I'll* decide what we do next."

Chapter Fourteen

"I'm afraid it isn't going to be quite that easy, Jake."

Only Jake didn't react to the quiet voice they all recognized. The eyes of the other three lifted to find Jordan Cross standing on the flybridge of the cruiser in the next bay. He held a rifle, sighted carefully at the back of Jake Holt's head.

Griff supposed he should have been expecting Jordan to show up. If they suspected something had gone wrong on the cruiser, Hawk and Jordan wouldn't have split forces. They would have done exactly what it appeared they had. They would have come at the situation from two angles, prepared to back each other up.

Griff didn't know how long Jordan had been up there. Since the beginning? Since Hawk had come over the side? Or maybe the sounds he had heard seconds earlier had been Jordan climbing to his perch.

With Claire on deck, he had never allowed his concentration to waver from Jake and the gun he held, always prepared to put his body between hers and a bullet. Whenever Jordan had arrived, however, it was obvious that he had been up there long enough to figure out what was going on.

And Jordan, of course, had been as much affected by Jake's treachery as he and Claire had been. Maybe more so, Griff acknowledged, remembering what had happened at the summer house. Jordan had taken a bullet from Helms in order to protect the Sorrel children.

"Put the gun down, Jake," Jordan ordered softly. "This is over. Even you have to realize that. You can't kill us all."

"I can take one of them out before you can squeeze that trigger," Jake said, his voice still calm, seemingly unaffected by the threat Jordan represented. "I'd even be willing to let you choose which one it's going to be."

That offer was sheer bravado, designed to make Jordan think about the reality that one of them would be dead, no matter how fast he got off his shot. Jake would have already selected his primary target—long before Jordan's challenge.

And of course, Jordan should have killed Holt outright instead of talking to him. That's how it *should* have been done. How any professional would have handled this. Jordan, of course, realized the dangers inherent in trying to do it this way. In trying to make Jake see he couldn't win. And that there could be no going back to how it had once been.

Somehow, however, Griff found he couldn't fault Jordan for choosing not to shoot Jake in the back. He, too, would have had a hard time putting a bullet into the back of any one of them. And Jake and Jordan had been friends for a long time, a friendship that was maybe as close as his and Hawk's.

Which was why Jake had been able to get away with what he had done when he'd sent Jordan to find the Mafia's sixteen million dollars. Of them all, Jordan was the best equipped for that job. Jake had known that. He had used Jordan's skills then just as he'd intended to use the skills of the team to kill Diaz and collect on the contract. And his plans had worked in both cases because they had trusted him.

Holt's gun didn't waver as he waited for Jordan's response. From where Jordan stood, Griff knew it would have been hard to say which of the three Jake was targeting. It was even hard for him to be sure.

Not Claire, Griff thought, the unspoken words almost a prayer. It would be him or Hawk. There had been enough underlying bitterness in the things Jake had said to see either of them the focus of his resentment. And his target.

Griff, because he had been born with everything Jake had plotted and schemed and betrayed to acquire. And Hawk? Maybe because he was what Jake had never been. One of the hotshots. Jake had undertaken only one mission, which had come down, finally, to this moment.

"You can kill one of them," Jordan agreed. "I'm not Hawk, but I'm still good enough that I won't miss, Jake. Not from this distance. You said you never intended to hurt any member of the team. That you had tried to take care of us. If that's true, why kill one of us now?"

Jake didn't respond, but the muzzle of the gun he held didn't shift a millimeter. Neither did Jordan's.

"It's over, Jake," Jordan said. "Nothing you've done so far is a capital offense. Even in Diaz's death you're probably only an accessory. But if you do this—"

Jake laughed, the sound as harshly derisive as that he had made earlier. "Wrong threat, old buddy," he said. "Wrong argument."

And then the gun he held began to move.

It wasn't Jordan who reacted. It was Griff who started across the deck, but of course, he never had a chance of reaching Jake in time to prevent what was about to happen. Even though Jake's hand seemed to be moving in slow motion as Griff ran toward him, his uneven gait making the desperate sprint awkward, he knew he'd never get there in time. The muzzle continued to lift inexorably toward its target.

"Jake!" Griff shouted.

The protest was too late, of course, sounding almost on top of the gun's report. Even in the open air the noise of the shot was shocking.

Not as shocking as the sight of Jake, his mouth closed around the barrel of the Glock, slumping onto the mahogany deck. His fingers, instructed by some dying reflex of nerves and muscles sent from his shattered brain, seemed unable to release their hold on the weapon, not even in death.

At the shot, Griff had stopped so suddenly he skidded on the polished boards. He knew that this image would linger forever in his head. Etched on his memory by his sense of failure, which was as strong now as the acid of Jake's betrayal.

"Jake," he said softly, regretfully. The whispered name had no more effect than his shout had had. And then he closed his eyes, at least physically blocking the sight. Because, just as Jordan had said, it really was all over.

THEY HAD HAD TO DEAL with the authorities, of course. Jake's death had been too public an event to avoid that. The gunshot had shattered the peaceful south Florida morning as effectively as it had blown out the top of Jake's skull.

And it had been sheer, blind luck that they had been able to avoid a media circus as well. The only reason they had was that the cops arrived before the cameras. Although it was obvious Jake's death had been a suicide, after the gunshot enough people had seen Jordan on the flybridge of the next boat, rifle pointing downward, to cause the authorities to take them all in.

None of them was carrying any official identification. If it hadn't been for Carl Steiner's long-distance intervention with the locals, Claire thought, they would probably still be answering questions back in Miami.

"Tell them as much of the truth as you can," Griff had advised before the police arrived. And that's exactly what she had done. Told them the truth. That Jake had been involved in the kidnapping of her daughter. That they had been in south Florida to pay the ransom the kidnappers had demanded.

Exactly what that ransom demand had been was something she knew Griff and his men would never disclose. If they did, it might lead back to the team. And eventually to the agency. In their loyalty to the CIA, they would see that as a betrayal. And so, for some reason, Claire hadn't told the cops what they had been asked to do in order to get her daughter back, either.

Not because she had any loyalty to the CIA. But Ramon Diaz was dead. So was Jake, who wouldn't, of course, now benefit from Diaz's death. And she had never known who'd put the contract out on Diaz's life. Or where they had taken Gardner.

That was a secret Jake Holt would take to his grave. Just as Jordan had said, it was all over. And they still didn't have any idea where Gardner was.

Claire closed her eyes, turning her head toward the dark window of the plane, so that if she couldn't conquer the almost constant urge to cry, at least no one would see her. She wasn't sure why that mattered anymore.

She had acknowledged, to herself at least, that her courage was broken, her hope that they would find her baby almost too faint to allow her to go on. For some reason, however, she was determined that those hard men who were flying back to the capital with her wouldn't be allowed to see her cry.

Griff's fingers closed around hers, lifting her hand from where it had lain throughout the flight, cold and unmoving, in her lap. She didn't resist the gesture, but she didn't respond to it, either.

Illogically, she had again been blaming Griff. He should have known, she thought. Jake Holt was his man, a member of his precious team. And Griff should have known what was going on.

"We have more to work with than we did before," Griff said softly. "That house on the key, for one thing. We'll run the ownership records. It should give us somewhere to start. When we figure out who would benefit the most from Diaz's death, we'll have an idea about who put out the contract Jake accepted. The DEA is already working on that."

She turned her head to look at him. Maybe to tell him

that it wasn't enough. Or that all this was his fault. His fault for knowing the Jake Holts of the world. For associating with them. For trusting them.

When she looked into Griff's eyes, she realized that whatever she was feeling, whatever pain and anger choked her heart, making her chest too tight to take the next breath, she couldn't say any of those things to Griff. Not now.

His eyes were as haunted as hers. She had caught a glimpse of herself in the mirror of the police station rest room, and startled by the stranger who appeared there, she had turned back to examine her reflection, too clearly illuminated by the garish fluorescent lighting.

Someone else's face stared back at her. Eyes that had seen too much horror and were imagining more. Skin that beneath its superficial tan was as gray with fatigue, as lined with worry, as Griff's was.

And so she nodded, clamping her lips over the bitter, accusing words she wanted to throw at him. Intellectually, she knew this wasn't Griff's fault. This was simply the world he had always warned her about. And she had denied what he said, never believing that its evil could touch her life. Or her daughter's.

"Claire," he said softly.

"Don't," she whispered, too angry and disillusioned to deal with this rationally. To deal with him. "Just…don't."

Don't make me any promises. Or tell me any more lies. Just get my baby back. And then… Maybe then…

She was unsure what the "then" that had formed in her head would be. Or even what it *could* be. So she turned her eyes back to the window and the night sky and tried very hard not to think. Not to think about anything. Especially not about Gardner.

"WE GO PUBLIC," Claire's grandfather suggested. "We flood the media with pictures of Jake Holt, together with pictures of Gardner. And we ask anybody who's seen either one of them, but especially anyone who has seen them together, to call.''

They were sitting around the kitchen table of Claire's house in Georgetown three days after their return from Florida. Its familiarity should have been comforting, she thought, but nothing had felt familiar since she'd been home.

Her world no longer existed—the one she had once occupied. The one where babies slept safely in their cribs. Where the worst thing she had to worry about was whether the house was warm enough or whether she'd get home in time to spend an hour or two with Gardner before the nanny put her down for the night.

Now the image of Jake's body, the back of his skull blown away, was her world instead. The reality of a trusted friend's betrayal. The mutilated corpse of Ramon Diaz was there as well. Diaz, who might have been killed by the same people who had taken Gardner. And if that were true…

"I'm not sure that will do any good," Jordan said.

"Has anything else done any good?" Claire asked.

She regretted the bitterness in her voice. She knew Griff would believe she was still blaming him. She was past that now. Her sense of fair play, or her logic maybe, had reasserted itself. It wasn't Griff's fault that he had trusted Jake Holt.

After all, that was what she had railed at him for so often in the past. For *not* trusting. For believing people were capable of the things his team was supposed to guard against. But if one of his vaunted team could do these despicable things, then what hope was there for the rest of the world?

Of course, that was an old argument. One she had made to him during their last quarrel—that Griff and his team were no better than the people they were fighting against.

"What could it hurt?" Hawk asked, his deep voice considering. "Besides sending Steiner and the agency ballistic.''

"For one thing, it will bring out the crackpots to muddy

the waters with a lot of false information—all of which would have to be investigated," Griff said. "It might be better to concentrate on the legitimate leads we have."

"Which have led exactly nowhere," Claire said, her bitterness more open this time. She was sorry about that when Griff's eyes lifted quickly to her face.

The FBI had discovered that the house where they found Diaz's body had once belonged to Jake's family. Jake had lived there when he was a child. But as far as they'd been able to ascertain, he had never returned to the island where he'd grown up. Not until he'd put this plan into action.

And as for tracing the people who had put out the contract on Diaz, the DEA was still working on that. There were a dozen emerging potential rivals for Diaz, all of whom would probably like to get in on what he had put together. And all of whom had enough money to make them suspects. So it seemed to her that she and the others were right back where they'd started.

"Doing what your grandfather suggests would also mean a further loss of privacy for you and the baby," Griff said.

For you and the baby. No mention of his role in their future. Her eyes searched his face, but she could read nothing there. Nothing but professional detachment.

"You're afraid this would make them...more vulnerable," Hawk suggested. "Afraid someone else might try the same thing. Maybe not for the same reasons," he added.

"Up until this happened, Claire had kept the baby out of the spotlight," her grandfather said. "Virtually no one knew of her existence. No one but family and close friends. It didn't seem to make much difference."

No one knew of her existence. No one except Jake Holt, Claire thought. She remembered Jordan's words: *Jake knows everything.* He had known Griff was alive, maybe from backtracking Griff's invasion of the CIA's computer system, although he'd denied that. Or maybe from the message Griff had sent to the director just before this had all begun. And he had known about Gardner, the second piece of information he had needed to bring this off. Then he'd just used his computers to interrupt Claire's security system and he was on his way.

"With all due respect, sir," Griff said quietly, "I don't think anything Claire could have done would have made a difference in what happened."

"Because Holt was really targeting you?" Monty Gardner suggested, his eyes piercing, the intelligence behind them still obvious and demanding, despite his age.

"I'm not even sure that's true. At least not the whole truth. Jake Holt was brilliant, but…there were a lot of things going on under the surface that none of us suspected. But…maybe it wasn't about any of us. Maybe it was just what he said it was. Just about the money."

"But *you* don't believe that," Claire's grandfather suggested.

No one said anything for a long time, and then Griff said, "Ultimately…I'm not sure I do."

The old man nodded, and then he turned to look at Claire. "It seems to me we've got nothing else to lose, my dear," he said. "And everything to gain. Cabot's right, however, about the loss of privacy. About future threats. And especially about the crackpots. They'll come out of the woodwork. So…I think it must be your decision."

Nothing to lose. And everything to gain, she thought. First she had lost Griff. And then Gardner. Her grandfather was right. She really had nothing else to lose.

She knew that if they didn't succeed in getting Gardner back, then nothing could ever be the same between her and Griff. Not because she wouldn't want it to be, but because she understood Griff Cabot well enough to know that he would never be able to forgive himself for that failure.

Most marriages didn't survive the loss of a child. And she and Griff didn't even have a legal connection that would have to be dissolved. Griff would just disappear. He would go out of her world. Disappear from her life. Again.

She knew now that wasn't what she wanted. What she

really wanted was to go back to how things had been before. Such a simple phrase for all it encompassed. Back to what she and Griff had once had. Back to being Gardner's mother. Back to the idealism about the world that had seemed so easy and so noble.

Maybe she could never go back to the last, but it still seemed that she had to pursue every avenue available to get Gardner back. And then Griff. *Nothing else to lose. And everything to gain.*

"Do it," she said softly. "Put Gardner's picture on the front of every newspaper and on every TV station that beams a signal out tonight," she said, looking around the table. "A description of what she was wearing. A description of anything about her that might make someone realize…"

Her throat closed suddenly over the rest of it. *That might make someone realize they have my baby.*

"And I want Jake Holt's picture right beside hers," she added, controlling that first surge of emotion with her anger over what Holt had done to them all.

Her grandfather nodded approval. Neither Jordan or Hawk said anything. She could imagine what the CIA would feel about making Jake's identity and his role in the kidnapping public. They would be afraid, of course, that somehow the media would trace Holt back to them. Maybe even back to the unit known as the External Security Team.

But she didn't care how Carl Steiner would feel. And by the time he had a chance to do anything about it, this could already be accomplished. That would be up to Griff.

"Can you do that?" she asked him. "Can you give them Jake's picture? And tell them his name?"

His eyes held hers, the concern in their dark depths obvious. He probably knew how fragile her control was. After all, he knew her so well. He knew, and understood, everything about her.

"I can do it," he said softly.

And he would. She was certain Griff would do what he'd

promised. He'd do exactly what she'd asked, no matter what Steiner or anybody else in the CIA thought about it.

"THE CLOTHES ARE different," Detective Minger said, "but that doesn't mean anything. They probably bought everything they gave this woman new. Just in case."

"But you really think this is Gardner?" Claire said softly, her voice strained.

Griff understood her caution, of course. They had almost been afraid to hope. Although, with Claire's connections, the media outlets had given the news release a lot of play, the pictures of Jake Holt had been out there less than six hours when they got Minger's call.

"Let's just say we haven't discovered anything to make us think she might *not* be. She seems to be just what she claims. She even gave us references from people whose children she'd cared for in the past," he said, his voice touched with amusement. "There's nothing in the computers about her. She doesn't seem like a crazy, and believe me, I've got radar where those are concerned. We all do around here. We think she's the real thing, Ms. Heywood, although I should warn you we're still checking out her story. And of course, we can't be sure about any of the rest of it until you ID the baby," he added softly.

The crux of the matter, Griff realized. And why they had been sent for. Claire's identification would end this entire episode as far as the cops were concerned. Minger had already been told what had happened in Florida. Not all of it, but as much as the Miami police knew.

"Of course," Claire said.

Her eyes left Minger's and found Griff's. In them he read all that he was feeling. Hope, of course. And the fear that this wouldn't be what they were hoping for. That in spite of what Minger said, in spite of his reaction to the woman who had called, this might not be what they had been praying for.

"She's naturally concerned that she'll be in trouble,"

Minger said. "But as far as we can tell, she really is innocent. Totally unaware of what was going on. And we've had a doctor check out the baby, Ms. Heywood. If this *is* your daughter, she's none the worse for her experience. And if she is your baby, I think you'll have to thank this woman for that."

"If this is Gardner," Claire said quietly, "I assure you I intend to."

"Do you think we can see her now?" Griff asked.

Minger had explained enough. It was time to do this before Claire reached her breaking point, something he had been anticipating since Jake's death. Griff wasn't sure how much more she could take. With the question, Minger's eyes shifted to his face, probably wondering who the hell he was and why he was here.

"You want to see the woman?" he asked.

"We want to see the baby," Griff corrected.

There would be time enough for expressing gratitude. *If* Minger was right. But right now...

"Of course," Minger said. "I'll have them get her."

He picked up the phone on his desk and punched one of the buttons. "Bring the kid up," he said.

"Alone," Claire suggested softly. "May we see her alone?"

Minger looked up at her as he put the receiver into its cradle. His lips pursed, and then he shrugged. He took his suit coat off the back of his chair and held it, the loop at the neck hung over one beefy finger as they waited.

So far tonight they had managed to escape the media's attention. The news crews had been stationed in front of the precinct house, lights and cameras set up behind the barricades the cops had erected to keep them away from the front entrance.

They had come in one of the back doors, arriving in Claire's grandfather's car. Hawk had backed Claire's out of the garage of the Georgetown house ten minutes before they themselves had left, drawing most of the media who had been waiting in the cold darkness outside it away with him.

And Jordan, who had volunteered to drive them here, had somehow managed to lose most of the others. The small success had generated more satisfaction than it probably deserved, Griff thought. Something that had finally gone right. As he hoped releasing the pictures to the media had.

This was the moment of truth, he supposed. He wasn't sure Claire could stand it if this woman turned out to be one of the crackpots he had warned her about. But Jake had said that the baby hadn't been harmed. That hurting her had never been part of his plan. If this were on the up-and-up, then at least Jake hadn't lied about that.

The door opened, and a young, black female cop came in. She was holding a bundle wrapped in a pink blanket. The covering had been drawn around the baby's head, probably because of the damp January chill that pervaded the police station.

It had been long after dark when they'd gotten the call. Long after the evening news broadcasts where the story had run. But the wheels of the bureaucracy turned slowly. Even in situations like this.

The woman's eyes touched on Claire's face and then on Griff's before they settled questioningly on Minger's. The detective tilted his head toward Claire, and the cop walked over and held out the baby.

Claire hesitated a few seconds. Griff saw the ratcheting breath she took before she reached out and took the child from the officer's arms, the transfer as smooth as if they had done it a hundred times.

Then, after another quick, inquiring glance at Minger for direction, the officer stepped back, removing herself from whatever would happen next. Claire's hand was trembling enough for the movement to be visible as it slowly lifted.

She touched the edge of the blanket, and then, without looking at any of them, she turned it back, revealing the face of the sleeping child.

After that, she remained completely still, looking down at the baby's features a long time. Almost as long, Griff thought, as it had taken Jake Holt's gun to reach its destination. An eternity of waiting.

Finally, her eyes lifted. To meet his rather than Minger's, as he'd expected. Griff realized that their blue shimmered with tears, one of which had already escaped, making its slow way down her cheek, which was totally devoid of color.

He couldn't read what was in them, however. It was neither the triumph he had been hoping for nor the despair he had feared. It was almost as if she were looking through him. As if she didn't see him at all, and his thundering heartbeat faltered.

Then she broke the connection between them to look at Minger. She nodded, a small up-and-down motion of her head, quickly made, before her eyes returned once more to the face of the sleeping baby she held.

Chapter Fifteen

"Holy Mother of God, I said to myself when I seen the news. Not blasphemy, you understand," Rose Connor said earnestly, her eyes moving from Claire's face to Griff's. "But I was that surprised, I can tell you. He seemed such a *nice* man."

She paused, her eyes again searching each face. There could be no agreement for that assessment, of course. Neither he nor Claire would ever feel that Jake Holt was "such a nice man," Griff thought. Not now.

"And yet here was this darling he'd brought me. Which must be, I knew, the baby they was looking for."

Without asking permission, Rose Connor leaned closer to Claire, smoothing a proprietary hand over Gardner's head. The baby was awake now, disturbed by the noises of the squad room they'd passed through on the way to the office where Rose Connor was waiting to meet them. Claire held the little girl upright, securely against her shoulder, but the baby seemed enthralled by her surroundings, dark eyes trying to take in everything.

"I don't know how to thank you for looking after her," Claire said.

Griff was aware that she had to force herself not to turn her body and move the baby away from this woman, who was, despite everything, a stranger. That tendency to over-protectiveness would take awhile to disappear, he supposed.

If it ever did. And he certainly couldn't blame Claire for feeling it.

"That's my job," Rose Connor said proudly. "And my joy. Looking after the little ones. I looked after my brothers and sisters when I was only a bit of a girl myself. So I've been doing it all my life, you might say. I don't suppose…" The pleasant lilt faltered, Rose Connor seeming shy for the first time. "I don't suppose you need someone," she said finally, raising her eyes hopefully from Gardner's face to Claire's. "To look after her, I mean."

The broad, winter-reddened fingers dipped under the baby's double chin for a tickle. Despite the strangeness of her surroundings and the lateness of the hour, Gardner grinned, new teeth prominently displayed, and then she ducked her head as if embarrassed to respond to such blatant cajolery.

"I have a nanny," Claire said softly, her eyes meeting Griff's above Rose's shoulder. "But…we want to do something to compensate you for your trouble, of course."

"Oh, no trouble," Rose said, smiling back at the little girl, whose eyes were again fastened on her face. "He paid me. Give me the money up front, he did. For two weeks. And it hasn't been quite that, now has it?"

Not quite two weeks, Griff thought, and yet everything about his life had changed. Both their lives—his and Claire's.

"Not quite," Claire said, her eyes still on his.

He nodded to let her know that he'd do something very generous for Rose Connor. "We'll stay in touch, Mrs. Connor," he said. "To let you know about Gardner. About how she's doing."

"I'd appreciate that. You get attached to them so fast. But it's just Rose," she corrected. "Never was a Mrs. Too old to hope for that now," she added, laughing.

Then she stepped back, moving away from the baby. She plucked her coat, a serviceable gray wool tweed, off the coat rack. And when, with Griff's help, her ample girth had been stuffed into it, she retrieved the knitting she'd been working on from the table and put it into a tapestry sewing bag. Finally, almost reluctantly, she removed the strap of a well-worn vinyl purse from where she had hung it over the back of her chair.

"You keep that darling good and warm on the way home," she said. "It's a bitter night for having a baby out."

"We will," Claire promised. "Detective Minger has your address?"

"All the particulars," Rose assured her with a smile. "I thought I was in trouble for sure. All them questions."

"You're not in trouble," Griff said. "And we *will* be in touch."

"Well, I'll be looking forward to hearing about the darling, no mistake about that. No matter how long or how little they're with me, they're mine, you know. For the moment. And I don't ever forget them."

Her eyes fell again to Gardner, who was chewing her fist. She had been following Rose's movements with big brown eyes.

"She looks like you," Rose said, her gaze moving consideringly from the baby's face to Griff's. "You'd think for a girl, she'll take some after her mother, but I'm guessing from the looks of her she's going to be all you when she grows up."

Griff studied his daughter's face. He was unable to see any reflection of himself, other than the obvious one of shared coloring, in the baby's delicate features. Claire had said the same thing, however, so there must be something of him in the softly rounded cheeks and doll-like mouth. His daughter, he thought again, almost in wonder. His daughter, and he realized this was the first time he had seen her face.

"You take care of her," Rose Connor ordered. The pleasant voice had softened. "You take good care of the both of them."

Griff's eyes lifted to Claire's, seeking permission perhaps

to do just that. She had been watching him, but whatever emotion he had surprised in her eyes was hidden by the quick fall of her lashes. Then she lowered her face, cupping her hand on the side of Gardner's head and pulling it gently toward her. She pressed a kiss on the silken down of her daughter's hair before her eyes rose again to meet his.

And whatever he thought he had seen in them before was gone.

WHEN THEY GOT BACK to the house in Georgetown, there was no one there. Hawk had picked Jordan up at the police station. They had left the keys to Claire's grandfather's car with the desk sergeant. It seemed the old man had gone as well, maybe taking a taxi back to his daughter's house or to Maddy and Charles's.

However the arrangements for emptying the big, dark house had come about, they found themselves alone. Together and alone for the first time since that night on the cruiser when Claire had made it clear she wasn't willing to resume their relationship. At least not the same relationship they had once had.

And maybe, despite the daughter they had conceived together, she never would be, Griff acknowledged, looking out into the winter darkness. Claire had taken the baby upstairs to put her down in her crib. She hadn't invited him to accompany them.

He had retreated to the kitchen, where only this morning, sitting at the round oak table, they had finally planned the strategy that had been successful in securing Gardner's return. Unlike the one Jake had planned for them, he thought bitterly. Unlike the operation Jake had controlled from the beginning.

With the others around during the last four days, there had been less tension between him and Claire, just as there had been in the Keys. There had been too many distractions to be able to dwell on all the unresolved issues that lay between them. The CIA's lie about his death. The fact that he hadn't told Claire they didn't intend to kill Diaz. Her long-ago decision not to tell him she was pregnant. And of course, underlying those was still the central question that had driven them apart.

If he and Claire and Gardner were ever to become a family, all of those, he supposed, would have to be discussed. If Claire were willing to discuss them. And he wasn't sure at this point she would be. He knew, however, that she would come back downstairs tonight, to double-check the locks if nothing else. Claire Heywood had never run from anything in her life. Nothing except who and what he was, he reminded himself.

And it was always possible, of course, that she would choose to do that again. Maybe leaving him alone down here, purposely excluded from her joy in Gardner's homecoming, was her way of telling him that. He took a deep breath, wondering if she would ever forgive him for exposing their daughter to the world he had inhabited for so long. A world that, despite his retirement, Griff knew he could never completely escape.

It was his past. His life. His world. And its echoes and images had probably been too clearly demonstrated to Claire during the last few days for her to ever be able to forget that.

"I could make some coffee," she said.

He turned and found her standing in the kitchen doorway, watching him. She was still wearing the dark slacks and white sweater she had put on this morning. There were smudges of exhaustion under her eyes, and her mouth was tight again, almost as if it had forgotten how to relax.

"No," he said. "Thank you, Claire, but...no."

The silence drifted between them, as wide as the stretch of shining white kitchen floor that separated them. Wider even, because it was full of regret. Too many mistakes. And all the baggage of the past. Of their divergent views of the world. Of their roles in it.

"You must be tired," he said. "You probably want to get to bed."

Despite his offer, he didn't move away from the sink where he had been standing when she had come into the room. Looking out at the night through the windows above it. There was nothing out there, of course. Nothing threatening. Nothing dangerous. There was only the safe, pleasant quietness of the exclusive neighborhood where his daughter would grow up. Maybe without him.

Claire nodded, her eyes on his face. She seemed to be waiting, but there was nothing else he could say. Nothing that could erase the nightmare he had brought into their lives. Nothing that would change the possibility that no matter what precautions they took, his past might again touch them. Contaminate them with the violence he had lived with so long it hadn't seemed so terrible to him anymore. Not until it had threatened those he loved.

He didn't even have the right to do for them what he had once believed he was good at. The one thing in this insane world that had always made sense to him. The commitment his entire professional life had been built around. *Standing guard over those we love.*

Claire took a step forward and then another. The leather flats she wore echoed slightly on the ceramic tile. Just before she reached him, she stopped, her eyes again searching his face. Almost as if she had never seen it before. Or as if she were trying to imprint it on her memory. With that thought, his heart began to pound, just as it had at the station.

She had done this once before. Sent him away. Told him to get out of her life. And in his pride, he had refused to beg. Refused to change who he was because he knew he was not what she thought him to be. But this time...

This time, he admitted, he would beg if he had to. His mind briefly visited the nursery upstairs, a room he had never seen, but a room where someone had opened a window one cold dark night and stolen a baby. His baby.

Claire was crying, he realized suddenly. The slowly well-ing tears emphasized the blue of her eyes, their color as intense as that of the shallows around the island where Jake had taken them.

Slowly she raised her hand. And he forgot to breathe. Forgot to hope. He only knew that whatever she demanded this time, he couldn't agree to. He couldn't leave the two of them alone again.

Standing guard. It was all he had that was worth offering. His life, willingly given, for either of theirs.

Her hand flattened. Palm up, she held it out before him. Several long heartbeats passed before he accepted that this was an invitation. Exactly like one he had once made. The night she had shown up at his door.

He had demanded no explanation for why she had come, despite the bitter things she had said to him. He hadn't needed an explanation of why she was there. It was enough that she was. Enough that when he held out his hand, she had laid her cold, trembling fingers into it and let him draw her inside.

Unquestioning now, as he had not questioned that night, Griff put his hand into hers and felt her fingers close around it. Warm and strong, they didn't tremble tonight. Not even when they led him on the same journey they had taken together once before.

CLAIRE HAD LEFT the bedside lamp on when she came downstairs to find him, and its soft light was welcoming. And familiar. He had often spent the night here. More often than she had come to his house in Maryland.

And tonight, given all that lay between them, that familiarity was soothing. The door to the adjoining room was not completely closed. He assumed that what had once been Claire's upstairs office had been transformed into a nursery for Gardner.

Knowing their daughter was sleeping next door had been inhibiting, at least in the beginning. But of course, any anxiety either of them had felt when they entered this room quickly faded.

After all, for him there could be no doubt Claire wanted him here. No doubt about the message she had intended when she'd offered him her hand. That night, the last night they had spent together, was too clear in their memories for either of them to doubt the significance of her gesture.

And so, when he had finally pulled her to him, slipping his hands under the soft wool of her sweater and tracing, through the silk of her skin, the outline of each rib as his fingers moved upward, his mouth sought hers, certain of her response. He had not been disappointed.

That night on the yacht all the things that had come between them had seemed insurmountable. Here, tonight, they seemed unimportant. And that was because of Claire's generosity. In issuing her invitation, she had demanded nothing. Asked for no explanations. Either for who he was or for what he had done. Or for what he had allowed to happen to their daughter.

"Make love to me," she whispered, her lips moving against his temple as his mouth caressed the delicate skin of her throat. "Make love to me, Griff."

It was permission that he hadn't needed. Not after the other, but hearing her whisper those words drove the hot blood through his body in a demanding wave of need and desire.

He had always desired Claire. And always loved her. But after what they had been through, it was more important than ever to show her. To prove to her again how he felt.

And through the course of the night, he had done that in every way he could conceive. With his hands, drifting against the well-known and beloved places he had slowly discovered, one by one, during their previous lovemaking. With his lips, brushing with tantalizing tenderness over the most erogenous areas of her sensitized body. With his teeth, teasing nerve endings that had never before seemed so responsive to his touch.

He had once known Claire's body better than he knew his own. Yet in the course of this night, he learned things he had never imagined about her ability to respond. And found places newly awakened to his touch and to his tongue's caress.

He had left nothing unexplored, delighting in inventing ways to make her gasp his name, in hearing it float away into the darkness, or in feeling the breath of its single syllable sighing against his own skin, as his lips trailed wet heat over hers.

There had been nothing one-sided about their lovemaking. One by one, Claire had examined each of the scars he had acquired since they had been together. And she had traced with her tongue and her fingertips the uneven ridges left by the surgeries.

He had been surprised to feel the hot fall of tears, but somehow they had served to burn away his guilt. Guilt that she hadn't been allowed to be with him. Guilt that they hadn't even told her he'd been hurt, as desperately as she would have wanted to know. As desperately as he would have wanted her beside him.

Maybe if he had been able to express that desire, they would have sent for her. Then the long, dark coldness that had come between them wouldn't have existed. But he hadn't, and by the time he had been capable of making his own decisions again, that tragic one had already been made for him.

He could have defied the agency, of course, but in his new bitterness over the changes the terrorist's bullets had made in his life and his body, he had included the old bitterness over Claire's rejection, as well. She had told him she never wanted to see him again, and for months he had savagely, angrily, complied with that demand, fighting other battles, physical ones, while he struggled to conquer his never-ending need for her.

He had been such a fool, he thought, his mouth lingering over the hardening nipple of her breast. So much time wasted. So many things missed. So many things. He raised his head, looking down on the smooth, milk-white skin around the dark areola of her breast, marked with a thin tracery of blue veins and faint, silvered lines.

"You breast-fed her?" he said, his eyes lifting to hers.

There was a moment's hesitation before she answered, and he wondered if that had sounded like a criticism. And then she smiled, the corners of her mouth, relaxed as they had not been throughout the ordeal of these long days, tilting in amusement.

At least she could still read him well enough to know that his question was simply the result of his fascination with a subject he knew nothing about. A process he had missed having any share in. Another regret. Another loss.

"I thought about that the night on the boat," she said. "About your mouth—and Gardner's. Both of them on my breasts."

The image produced by those words, which had been so soft he had to strain to hear them, was surprisingly erotic. His hard erection suddenly strengthened. And Claire was certainly aware of that, given the intimacy of their positions.

"Very different sensations, I would think," he said, lowering his lips to fasten around the nipple again, the idle suggestion made just before his teeth nibbled at its peak.

"No," she whispered.

He raised his head so he could see her face.

"Not so different. Not the feel," she said. "Not the way it made *me* feel. Not at the beginning."

He nodded, watching the memories move in her eyes.

"A little like the first time with you," she said. "Making love the first time. Nervous. Unsure, I guess, but... anticipating so much what it would be like."

"You don't do that anymore?" he asked.

"Anticipate making love to you?" she teased.

"Feed her."

"You like talking about this," she said, a hint of surprise about that discovery in her voice.

And he realized that he did. He wished he had seen them, Gardner's small dark head against Claire's breast, a contrast to the almost alabaster skin of her body.

"You think that's strange?" he asked. "That I like to think about you feeding her? About seeing you like that?"

"I used to look down at her while she nursed. At her hair. The shape of her head. And I'd remember *your head* there. So, no…I don't think it's strange that you would like to think about that," she said. "She's a part of us. Both of us. A part we created. Just…like this."

"Is that a warning?" he asked, smiling at her.

"Maybe," she said softly. "If you want to be warned."

He thought about the possibility of another baby. He didn't even know the one they had. He had already missed so much. So much of watching her learn and grow and develop. Of being around to take an active role in that.

"I don't think I do," he said, lowering his mouth to reclaim her nipple. "Want to be warned, I mean," he whispered, just before his lips closed around it, beginning to mimic the image that had been in his head.

"Yes," she whispered. And then again, after a long time, as his hands moved against her body, "Oh, yes."

That was what he had asked her to say on the cruiser, he remembered. A word he had thought he needed to hear. And now, tonight, it hadn't seemed important anymore. Because between them it was just as it had always been. And would always be.

"I THINK SHE'S HUNGRY," Griff said.

Claire struggled to open her eyes, squinting against the sun that was pouring into the room through the windows whose draperies she had forgotten to pull. Griff was standing beside the bed, wearing nothing but his slacks, wrinkled because he had dropped them on the floor early on last night.

His belt was through the loops, but he hadn't taken time to buckle it. The waistband gaped a little at the closure, revealing the trail of fine, dark hair that ran down the center of his flat stomach and crossed his navel to disappear into the opening.

"Feed her," Claire suggested, closing her eyes against the temptation that sight offered. She pulled the pillow over her head, trying to block out the painful sunlight and the endless allure of Griff's body.

She must have had at least a couple of hours sleep last night, but she couldn't be sure. After all, she and Griff had had a lot of lost time to make up for. A lot of cold, empty nights to forget. And forgive.

Despite the pillow, she could still hear the baby. Gardner was always talkative in the mornings. An incomprehensible string of syllables, gradually growing in volume, always accompanied the sound of her rattle being drawn back and forth against the bars of her crib, exactly like a prisoner's protest to the warden.

Claire must have missed the rattle signal this morning. *If* Griff had left Gardner in her crib long enough for that second stage of waking to begin. But the baby was certainly well into the talking phase.

Claire lay there, head under the pillow, listening to those familiar sounds and knowing that for the first time in a long while things really were right in her world. Gardner was safe, and Griff… Griff was back.

Unable to resist, she furtively inched the edge of the pillowcase aside with her fingers until she could see them. Griff's size dwarfed Gardner's. It was obvious that he was holding her very carefully—and a little awkwardly—ready for any unexpected move. Amused, Claire wondered if Griff Cabot had ever before held a baby in his entire life. If not, it seemed to her that the experience was long overdue.

A lot of things had been overdue, she acknowledged, but she refused to let regrets spoil today. Or spoil the sight of Gardner's small fingers now gingerly touching the dark mat of hair that covered Griff's broad bare chest. That would certainly be a new texture for her to explore, Claire thought in amusement.

Griff was looking down on those tiny fingers, so that she could see only the top of his head. There was more gray intermingled with the raven's wing blackness of his hair than she had realized before. The morning light highlighted the contrast, but it also emphasized how very much alike were those two dark heads, together for the first time.

"You want to give me some instructions here, Claire?" Griff said impatiently, raising his head and focusing his attention on the pillow under which she was hiding.

At the sound of his deep voice, Gardner leaned back in surprise, and then, quickly overcoming that reaction, she poked her fingers toward his mouth. Griff automatically avoided them by raising his head, ending up with a couple of chubby fingers grazing his chin. Gardner reached out to touch him again, apparently deciding that she liked the feel of whiskers almost as much as the texture of chest hair.

"Cereal," Claire said, her voice muffled. "There's some in pantry. It says cereal on the jar. She isn't picky."

"Just spoon it in?"

"Straight from the jar," Claire agreed.

That breakfast menu would be the easiest for him to handle. And based on the fact that he'd bravely rescued the crib prisoner without waking Claire, Griff certainly deserved a chance to succeed with his first foray into baby feeding.

Especially deserving after last night, she decided, her reminiscent smile hidden by the pillow.

"THAT COLOR'S GOOD ON YOU," she said, watching them from the doorway. Left alone upstairs, she'd finally decided she'd better check on them.

Griff hadn't opted for the state-of-the-art high chair against the wall. He was doing it the old-fashioned way— baby held securely in his lap, left arm around her middle, spoon in his right hand and a goodly portion of cereal on them both. Gardner had reached the stage where her hunger had been satisfied enough to allow her to be creative.

"It's called rice and bananas," Griff said, looking up.

Gardner's mouth made a couple of futile attempts to capture the elusive bite on the spoon he was holding. Griff's attention was rather flatteringly directed on the length of leg exposed under the short silk robe Claire was wearing, however, instead of on what he was doing. After another open-mouthed lunge toward the spoon, Gardner finally gave up and batted at it with her hand, sending more cereal to join the splatters on the table and on her father.

"Did you taste it?" Claire asked, watching him guiltily stuff what remained on the spoon into Gardner's mouth.

"Was I supposed to?" he asked, looking up again.

"I can't ever resist. It's all pretty yucky, if you ask me."

"I've always preferred my bananas flambéd in brandy," he said. And then he smiled at her.

Griff Cabot's smile had always made her knees weak. Right now, coming at her from over their daughter's head, with an endearing splotch of rice cereal on his dark, be-whiskered cheek, she thought it was the most sexually devastating thing she had ever seen.

"Will you marry us?" she said softly.

The silence that followed her question was too long, broken only by Gardner's monosyllabic chant and the slap of her palms against the oak table.

"Nothing's changed about who I am, Claire," Griff said, the smile gone, replaced by the same sternness of expression with which he had dealt with all the setbacks of the last two weeks. "Or about what I've done. And, as much as I wish I could, I can't guarantee it won't ever touch your lives again."

She thought about the truth of what he said. About Gardner. But somehow, seeing them together, seeing Griff hold the baby she knew he would give his life to protect, she knew how right this was. And therefore, she also knew how wrong she had been before.

"I know," she whispered. "But...*I've* changed, Griff. At least in thinking the world is black-and-white. Thinking that I'm right about it all, and that you're wrong. Nothing is ever that simple. And there are no guarantees for anyone that evil won't touch their lives."

She hesitated, thinking how to phrase the hard lessons she had learned this last year. And then she decided that what was in her heart was best said exactly as she felt it.

"I just know that if it ever threatens her again, I want you here. Protecting us."

Standing guard over those we love, Griff thought.

That had been the standard under which his team had operated. Something that the world would perhaps never understand about what they did. Something Claire had never believed. But never before had the meaning of those simple words been so real to him. Or so personal. And so damn right.

"If you're sure, Claire, that this is what you want," he said. "If you're sure, then yes."

She smiled, the strain that had grown around her lips as she waited easing. Her eyes touched briefly on Gardner's face and then came back up to his.

"I don't think I've ever been as sure about anything in my entire life," she said softly. "Except maybe a political position or two," she added, her tone teasing, her smile widening as he reciprocated it. "But we can discuss those later."

"Or agree to disagree about them," he said, his tone lightened to match hers.

Her eyes were again on their daughter. "Especially since we've got all the important stuff sorted out."

Griff nodded, feeling his throat tighten unexpectedly. Just as he had seen Claire do last night, he cupped his big hand around Gardner's head and pulled it near enough to kiss the top, pressing his lips for the first time against the shining softness of his daughter's hair.

Standing guard. Today and for the rest of my life, he promised silently. *Always, standing guard.*

Epilogue

"I need the practice," Tyler Stewart Hawkins said. She reached to take a squirming Gardner from Kathleen Cross's capable arms and settled the baby on her hip, one chubby leg resting atop the small bulge of her pregnancy.

"Well, *I* certainly don't," Kathleen said, laughing. She smoothed her hand over the baby's head, and then looked up to smile at Hawk's wife, whom she had met for the first time today.

The party that celebrated Griff Cabot and Claire Heywood's wedding had been small and intimate, but there had been no doubting the joy the guests had taken in this union. The living room of the Maryland house had been transformed by hundreds of roses, the scent of which filled the room.

Claire had been radiant when she had entered on her father's arm. Her eyes hadn't left Griff's face as he waited by the windows that looked out on the sleeping garden, except once, to touch briefly, smilingly, on Monty Gardner, who was serving as Griff's best man. Perhaps either of the other two men in attendance might have had a better claim to that role, but neither had objected to Griff's choice of the old man.

The bonds of their friendship, forged in danger and commitment—to each other and to the missions they had undertaken—were too strong to need any such outward confirmation. Despite the fact that the team they'd once belonged to no longer existed, the ties that bound them surely did.

"I wonder what they're talking about," Tyler asked, her famous violet eyes focused on the three men, who were visible through the open door of Griff's study.

"The good old days, I hope," Kathleen suggested lightly as her gaze followed Tyler's.

Then, almost unconsciously, it was redirected to her children, who were being entertained by the story Rose Connor was telling. Her broad face was beaming, her hands gesturing enthusiastically, and Meg and Jamie were listening with the rapt attention they usually reserved for when Jordan read to them.

Safe, Kathleen thought. The need to know that they were, no matter the situation, would always be in the back of her mind. She couldn't imagine how Claire Heywood had endured having her baby stolen.

With that thought, her eyes sought and found the bride, elegant in a winter-white wool suit. Claire seemed so beautifully serene as she saw to the needs of her guests, as much at home in this huge house as Griff himself. And just a little intimidating, Kathleen thought in amusement. She had felt that same sense of awe when Jordan introduced her to Griff.

Of course, considering the respect Jordan had for his former boss, Cabot had already achieved near-legendary status in her mind, long before she'd met him. Her gaze returned to the room where the three men were talking. At least Hawk and Jordan, standing before a huge desk, were talking. Griff, seated behind it, seemed to be merely listening. He was, however, giving whatever they were saying the same serious attention he had devoted to Jamie's meandering narrative about his new puppy.

Finding that Griff was warm and down to earth enough to listen to an excited two-year-old's disjointed story had been a pleasant surprise. But then this entire day had been surprising, Kathleen thought. She had expected the ghost of

Jake Holt's betrayal to overshadow the joy of this wedding, but it hadn't. Probably because everyone was determined it wouldn't.

"It looks as if they might be up to no good."

Surprised, Kathleen turned to find Claire Cross standing at her elbow, her eyes, like Kathleen's and Tyler's, focused on the meeting in Griff's study.

"What do you think it means?" Tyler asked, shifting Gardner into a more comfortable position on her slender hip.

"Why don't we ask them?" Claire suggested, including Gardner in the smile she directed at Tyler. "After all, I think the three of us have a vested interest. Don't you?"

"You lead the way," Kathleen suggested, smiling. "After all, you're the one who's married to the boss."

Belatedly, she wondered if Claire might be offended by that teasing comment. When Claire laughed instead, Kathleen decided that she just might like this woman, whose face she had seen dozen of times on her television screen, as much as she liked Tyler, whose face was, she realized, equally famous.

"That position as the boss's wife is still a little new for me to feel totally confident of my reception, but somehow..." she paused, her eyes finding Griff again "...somehow I don't think he'll throw me out. At least, maybe not today." And still smiling, she lead the way to the room where the men they loved were talking.

Griff spotted them first, his smile at Claire probably warning Hawk and Jordan that their conclave was about to be invaded. Not that she believed he would really mind this very feminine invasion.

Especially when Gardner reached for him, almost lunging out of Tyler's arms as soon as she spotted him.

"Obviously a daddy's girl," Kathleen said, smiling at Griff as he took his daughter. Then her eyes shifted to Jordan's face, and she added, "I have one of those."

Jordan returned her smile, holding her eyes, the unspoken

communication obvious. And seeing it might have been what prompted Hawk to put his arm around Tyler's spreading waistline, pulling her firmly against his side.

"We were wondering what you three were up to," Claire said.

The silence that followed her comment lasted too long, and it was Jordan who answered it.

"Hawk and I were offering Griff an employment opportunity," he said, his tone amused, because they all knew Cabot's financial resources.

"An employment opportunity?" Claire repeated carefully.

"We're offering Griff a job," Hawk said. "Since we've found out that he's not really dead. Just unemployed."

"Like us," Jordan added.

"A job doing what?" Claire asked.

"Standing guard," Hawk said softly, his tone free of amusement. "It's what we're good at."

"You don't mean…" Claire hesitated, trying to imagine exactly what he did mean.

"Going private," Jordan said, clarifying what they'd been thinking. "Providing protection for people who have problems like the three of us have had recently. We think there may be others from the team who might be interested in something like this as well."

"After all," Griff said softly, his eyes on Claire's face, "we have the skills."

It was what he had told her before. And he had offered to use those skills on her behalf even before he had known the truth about Gardner's birth.

To find and retrieve what was lost or stolen. To guard and protect the innocent. Like their daughter. Like Jamie and Meg Sorrel. Like Kathleen, and Tyler Stewart.

The skills these men possessed had been acquired on a very different battlefield. They had proven, however, that what they had learned in that war could be adapted to the kinds of missions the three of them had undertaken during the last six months. Protecting lives rather than destroying.

"We'd like to use them for other battles," Griff said, echoing her own thoughts. "To fight other wars."

"There isn't any other war," Claire said softly, and saw by the sudden pain in his eyes that he hadn't understood. And so she clarified it. After all, this was one of the things she still needed to say to him.

"It's all the same war," she said, her eyes leaving his to touch on the faces of the men and women who had gathered today to celebrate their union. "A war against evil—the same evil you've always fought. And if people like you don't choose to fight that war...then eventually evil will win."

The silence in the small circle of friends was profound and complete. No one knew better than these six people about the reality of that evil. It had touched each of their lives.

"And it must not," Claire said softly, her eyes coming back to Griff's. "It must never be allowed to win. Not even one small battle. Not if any one of you can prevent it."

"I take it then I have your permission," Griff said after a moment, smiling at her.

She wondered if she could really bear to let him face the dangers this kind of enterprise would involve. Then Gardner's hand touched Griff's mouth, and smiling, he put his lips against her fingers, a father's kiss.

"*And* my blessing," she said softly, letting him go to be again what he had always been. A good, strong man fighting evil. And it had taken her too long to realize that.

"And mine," Kathleen said, watching the same interplay between father and daughter. "I know what it's like to live in fear. If the three of you can do for someone else what Jordan did for me and for my children—our children," she corrected, smiling again into Jordan's eyes, "then you must."

Tyler's fingers were unconsciously spread, almost protec-

CIA operative Shackley, 'the Blond Ghost,' dies

THE ASSOCIATED PRESS

BETHESDA, Md. — Theodore Shackley, who ran the CIA's Miami operation during the height of U.S. tensions with Cuba in the 1960s, has died of prostate cancer. He was 75.

Shackley died Monday at his home in Bethesda, according to Joseph Gawler and Sons funeral home.

As Miami station chief, Shackley directed about 400 agents and operatives during the Cuban missile crisis of October 1962 and Operation Mongoose, a U.S. effort to topple Cuban leader Fidel Castro.

He later served as the CIA's associate deputy director for clandestine operations from May 1976 to December 1977.

"Shackley was an emblematic figure of the Cold War — the epitome of the clandestine bureaucrat who had been involved in the key chapters, many of them dark, of the CIA's history," said David Corn, Washington editor of The Nation and author of "Blond Ghost: Ted Shackley and the CIA's Crusades."

Nicknamed "The Blond Ghost" because he hated to be photographed, Shackley has been described by those who knew him as an exacting, intense, elusive covert operator.

He was "a brilliant mind, a tremendous tactician and strategist," said Miami attorney Thomas Spencer, a friend of Shackley's for three decades. "He was able to pick up the phone and talk to virtually every world leader that existed in the last 20 years."

Shackley held several high-profile posts during a 28-year career with the CIA, including work as a senior CIA officer in Berlin, Saigon and Laos.

He retired from the CIA in 1979 and set up a Washington-area consulting firm that offered security strategy to corporate executives. He also wrote a book on counterinsurgency in 1981 called "The Third Option."

tively, over the baby she carried, and her eyes had found Hawk's face. She studied the rugged features and then drew a deep breath.

"In all honesty..." she began and, wide violet eyes still focused on her husband, she hesitated, as if reluctant to say aloud what she felt.

And they were all waiting, Claire realized. Silently waiting, breathing suspended.

"In all honesty, Hawk's not too handy around the house. I've been a little disappointed in that," she said apologetically, speaking to Hawk before she turned back to face the others. "But I can tell you from personal experience," she continued, the corners of her beautiful mouth tilting, "he's hell on wheels at protecting people."

Hawk was the first to laugh, the sound of his laughter unexpected, rich and free. The others joined in as soon as they understood that Tyler had given her permission, as well.

"To the future," Claire said, her eyes on Gardner's face. Then she lifted them to her husband. "And to your new team."

"Something new, rising from the ashes of the old," Griff said softly.

He was right, Claire thought. They had all risen from the ashes of their pasts. Hawk, who according to the CIA no longer even existed. Jordan, who had been transformed into someone else. And Griff... Griff, who had literally come back from the dead.

"Like the mythical phoenix," she said, "born from the fire that destroys it."

"The Phoenix Brotherhood," Griff said.

And they knew, just as he had, that it was exactly right.

HARLEQUIN®
INTRIGUE®

What do a sexy Texas cowboy, a brooding Chicago lawyer and a mysterious Arabian sheikh have in common?

CHICAGO
CONFIDENTIAL

By day, these agents pursue lives of city professionals; by night they are specialized government operatives. Men bound by love, loyalty and the law—they've vowed to keep their missions and identities confidential....

You loved the Texas and Montana series. Now head to Chicago where the assignments are top secret, the city nights, dangerous and the passion is just heating up!

NOT ON HIS WATCH
by CASSIE MILES
July 2002

LAYING DOWN THE LAW
by ANN VOSS PETERSON
August 2002

PRINCE UNDER COVER
by ADRIANNE LEE
September 2002

Available at your favorite retail outlet.

HARLEQUIN®
Makes any time special®

HICC

If you enjoyed what you just read,
then we've got an offer you can't resist!

Take 2
bestselling novels FREE!
Plus get a FREE surprise gift!

Clip this page and mail it to The Best of the Best™

IN U.S.A.	IN CANADA
3010 Walden Ave.	P.O. Box 609
P.O. Box 1867	Fort Erie, Ontario
Buffalo, N.Y. 14240-1867	L2A 5X3

YES! Please send me 2 free Best of the Best™ novels and my free surprise gift. After receiving them, if I don't wish to receive anymore, I can return the shipping statement marked cancel. If I don't cancel, I will receive 4 brand-new novels every month, before they're available in stores! In the U.S.A., bill me at the bargain price of $4.74 plus 25¢ shipping and handling per book and applicable sales tax, if any*. In Canada, bill me at the bargain price of $5.24 plus 25¢ shipping and handling per book and applicable taxes**. That's the complete price and a savings of over 20% off the cover prices—what a great deal! I understand that accepting the 2 free books and gift places me under no obligation ever to buy any books. I can always return a shipment and cancel at any time. Even if I never buy another The Best of the Best™ book, the 2 free books and gift are mine to keep forever.

185 MDN DNWF
385 MDN DNWG

Name	(PLEASE PRINT)	
Address	Apt.#	
City	State/Prov.	Zip/Postal Code